A Well Regulated Militia...

John J. Carpenter

PublishAmerica
Baltimore

First printing

ISBN: 1-4137-8889-0
PUBLISHED BY PUBLISHAMERICA, LLLP
www.publishamerica.com
Baltimore

Printed in the United States of America

Acknowledgments

The writing of this book has proven to be a great learning experience. I've been blessed to have a circle of friends and acquaintances who've willingly shared their time, expertise, and vast knowledge to provide color and realism to this story. I would like to publicly thank all of them for their invaluable contributions. But before any of them, I'd like to thank both my Father in Heaven and Savior Jesus Christ for the eternal endowment of freedom that all men possess. Our inalienable rights of life, liberty, and the pursuit of happiness are derived from our Creator and can not be usurped by any man, government, or global organization. I am also grateful to the founding fathers of the United States who, first and foremost, both understood and honored this eternal truth before they set forth to establish this nation. I openly acknowledge the hand of the Lord in inspiring these wise and blessed men and pray that their work will never be erased from the face of the world and may those who desire to destroy what they created be forever damned.

I proclaim my deepest and most sincere thanks to the following people: My mother and father who raised me in righteousness and taught me through love and example. My sister who watched over me spiritually and pulled me back from the edge. My beloved wife who continually blesses me with her love, devotion and wisdom. My son who so recently came into my life; you have softened my heart and each day lead me, by the hand, down the road towards heavenly love. I am grateful to the "Golden Tone" who told me to save my tears for big things, because big things were coming. My mother and father in law who have passed on a great legacy to my son. I am grateful to my friend Karl who has been around in both the good times and the bad.

I'd like to acknowledge all the Patriots who, each day, stand in the breech to defend liberty: Wes L., Kandi B., Richard S., Craig B., Naish, Gabe S., Rush L., Shaun H., Oliver N., RAWHIDE, Joseph S., GBH, ETB, Abby the PK, Randy A., Gaston G., Joel S., Ken R., GSP, Randal R., Uncle Ted, Mark J., Ryan V., AEN, Cope R., James F., Thomas J., Val G., Dr. Valerie H. and the Soldiers, Sailors, Airmen, Guardsmen and Marines who stand between evil men and my family. Thank you for your service and sacrifices. There are a host of others who, although unmentioned, are no less important. Special thanks go out to the real men who inspired the characters in my story and all the active Patriots who honor the tile of Militiaman. This story is dedicated to you for keeping the faith in spite of relentless and ignorant attacks. To all my friends I say: be bold in your defense of righteousness; you will inspire those who sustain you and give pause to your enemies.

Casa de Alma
May, 2005

"Dad, say you're skydiving and both your main and reserve chutes fail to open at 10,000 feet, what would you do?"
"I'd grab on to the nearest cloud, and if that didn't stop me, I'd keep trying until I succeeded."

Chapter 1

The saddest epitaph, which can be carved in memory of a vanished liberty, is that it was lost because its possessors failed to stretch forth a saving hand while yet there was time.
— Justice George Sutherland (1938)

Outside of Florence, Arizona

Gringo led his squad slowly up a dusty arroyo, using the scattered scrub brush to hide their movement. The route provided a perfect approach to their objective. Not only did the arroyo provide concealment, it also shielded them from the soft moonlight that lit up the rocky desert landscape. Mike West, a.k.a. Gringo, led a five-man patrol consisting of Taylor "Arrow" Johnson, Mark "Thor" Miller, John "AK" Soto, and Richard "Hot Dog" Franks. After four months of training, the men had developed into a cohesive, well-tuned team.

Seeing a sharp bend up ahead, Gringo raised his hand signaling his team to stop and take a knee. The squad slowly blended into the scattered foliage while continuing to cover their predetermined fire zones. Gringo knew that moving his team around the bend before first taking a quick look could expose them to an ambush, and that was a mistake he wasn't going to make. Gringo rolled back the wrist of his sage green nomex glove and checked his watch. *Twenty-two fourty-five, we're making pretty good progress. Better to take a couple extra minutes than to screw up and blow this patrol.* Gringo reasoned.

After kneeling motionless for a minute and listening to his surroundings, Gringo signaled the next man in the column, "Arrow" Johnson. Arrow tapped Thor on the shoulder and signaled that he was going forward. Once Arrow arrived Gringo leaned in close until his lips were nearly touching Arrow's ear and quietly whispered his intentions. "I'm going to crawl up towards the bend and recon what's on the other side. You stay back with the team, but keep an eye on me. I'll signal you with my microlight." The microlight is a small LED light that was a standard piece of kit carried by all team members. It was perfect for night operations because it would neither illuminate the team nor destroy the user's night vision. The standard operating procedure (SOP) called for the signaler to hold the light steady as a safe signal or to wave the light back and forth to signal danger.

Arrow firmly gripped Gringo's shoulder to acknowledge the instructions, and then signaled back to the rest of the team to stay alert. This procedure had become almost second nature. Whenever the patrol approached a "danger zone," they took similar actions to assure the protection the team. As each man scanned his sector, they all knew that time was ticking away, but they also knew it only took one foul up for time not to matter anymore. As instructions were passed, man to man, individuals slowly and quietly adjusted their gear to find whatever momentary comfort was possible.

Nearly two-and-a-half hours had passed since the patrol had started, and their uniforms were already soaked with perspiration. From his position as "Tail-End Charlie," Hot Dog, the youngest member of the team, felt a drop of sweat, mixed with camo paint, slowly roll down his cheek while he meticulously lifted the hose of his water bladder to his lips and drew a mouthful of warm, but quenching, water. Even though it was still early May, it was already starting to heat up in anticipation of another scorching Arizona summer. Nonetheless, this was where Hot Dog wanted to be, and the thrill of operating in the bush with his teammates was reward in and of itself.

Gringo scanned ahead and identified a boulder that would provide cover while he reconned ahead. As he slowly crawled forward every motion was exact and precise as he concentrated on smooth, uniform movement. The human eye is particularly attuned to motion, especially unnatural motion. *Nature has its own rhythm and keeps beat unless something alien interferes,* Gringo reminded himself. *The trick is to allow the surrounding elements and ambient sound to mask your presence. Easier said than done*, he thought to himself. Wearing his homemade Ghillie hat and sporting a camouflaged face, he thought alien might be an appropriate term, as he certainly didn't look natural. Gringo approached the boulder slowly, working hard to stay as low as possible, pushing his body forward with his toes and elbows. Once he reached the large rock he stopped and again listened for anything out of the ordinary. *This is always the hardest part,* he reminded himself. *My mind tends to make up noises that seem out of place*. After a minute or so, Gringo rolled to the side of the boulder and scanned ahead. The moonlight cast a soft, pale light on the terrain and created grey/blue shadows that exaggerated the depth of every object. His eyes took in as much as possible as they scanned left to right. Whenever his gaze fell upon an object large enough to conceal a human he'd stop, and think, *Does that look right? Is there anything out of the ordinary?*

Everything looked the way it should, and Gringo felt his muscles begin to relax. As he started to inch back from the edge of the rock, an unnatural noise seized his attention. *Whoa, what the heck was that?* The sound was metallic, definitely man made. But was it someone or just trash blown around by the breeze? All his senses heightened to a point where it seemed every nerve ending was raw and exposed. Gringo's heart pounded in his chest, and his breathing slowed. *Okay, let's go over this again,* he thought. This time he remembered to focus his attention just off to the side of each object. The human eye is made up of rods and cones. The rods form a parameter around the outside of the eye and are more sensitive to light. By looking to the side of an object your night vision is slightly improved, and this is what Gringo was hoping to take advantage of.

One-by-one each shape checked out. But as his gaze passed a distant bush he noticed the dim outline of a canteen being eased into its carrier. "Gotcha, dirtbag," he whispered to himself. Obviously, this guy hadn't seen Gringo, or he wouldn't have been worrying about taking a drink. Slowly, even slower than before, Gringo moved back from the rock. He reached into his chest pocket and drew out a small LED light. Like all his gear, it had a dummy cord attached to it, which he unwrapped.

Gringo aimed the light in the direction of his teammates and pressed the activator button allowing its soft glow to pierce the darkness. As per SOP he moved the light side-to-side.

Arrow remained focused in the direction that his buddy had gone, and after seeing the signal, he returned it silently with his own light. Then he looked back at Thor; pointed two fingers at his eyes and made a slashing motion across his throat as he pointed ahead. Thor acknowledged the silent message and passed the signal back to the others. While this was happening, Gringo carefully inched back toward the group. Once he arrived, he whispered the news into Arrow's ear. Arrow's reply was delivered the same as before, by a squeeze to the shoulder.

Gringo wanted to move the team away from the ambush zone, then up and out of the arroyo. His plan was to box around the immediate area to ensure all was clear, flank the enemy, and set up a counter ambush. He waited for his order to filter down the line of silent men. Then in unison, the team silently rose from their positions like ghosts ascending out of the grave.

This reversed the patrol order, placing Hog Dog on point, a position he was never really comfortable with. Being the youngest member of the team he felt an added pressure not to screw up. As he moved forward he made sure to point to loose rocks or overhanging foliage, so the others wouldn't trip or make undue sounds. Like a mantra, Hog Dog continually repeated, *Left, up, over, down*, in his mind. This helped prevent tunnel vision and forced his mind to remain alert to his surroundings.

As the column arrived at a point where they could exit the arroyo, Hot Dog raised his hand and stopped the team. After a moment, he felt rather than heard Gringo creep up beside him.

"Dog," Gringo whispered, "take point. When you get to the top of the ravine recon it and signal if it's clear."

Hot Dog nodded and moved toward the arroyo wall, concentrating on silence. He slowly ascended the slanted wall, careful to avoid scraping his equipment or dislodge any rocks. As his eyes cleared the depression he froze with most of his body still below the rim so as not to silhouette himself in the moonlight. Conscious of how very alone he was, Hot Dog scanned the flat plain. *"Slowly,"* he thought. *"Take your time. They're out there somewhere."* The okay signal was again sent and returned. Hot Dog scanned once more, then jumped out of the arroyo and ran towards the concealment of a large bush. As he ran his mag dump pouch flopped against his left leg, "*I'd better cinch that up when I have time*," he thought. Each member took turns exiting the arroyo and finding what little concealment the sparse desert foliage afforded. Now, Gringo resumed point. As usual, the team remained still for a minute allowing their surroundings to settle down, before stealthily moving forward. Gringo paced the distance off and just short of the objective, he passed the signal to fan out and get into position.

Looking forward and slightly down into the widest part of the arroyo, Gringo saw four men arranged in a modified L-shaped ambush. From this angle, it was much easier to see the men as their cover was to their front. Surveying the scene before him he thought, *If that dork hadn't been messing with his canteen, I'd never have seen him. Oh well, too bad for you.*

One last time, hand signals were passed to assure everyone was set. Everyone knew the SOP: initiate the ambush on the team leader's actions, empty two magazines, and then cease-fire unless the enemy was still resisting. *Okay, we're ready.* Gringo identified his target and sighted in. *Bam, Bam, Bam, Bam*! The night erupted with noise as the team members yelled out, each counting off his rounds. The targeted men jerked around and realized they'd just been whacked.

"Cease-fire, cease-fire.... You losers are dead!" Gringo hollered.

"Where the heck did you guys come from?" barked Tom "Cowboy" South.

"From behind you, buttface!" jeered AK revealing himself from behind a spindly cactus.

"All right, good exercise, everyone. Let's gather around for a quick after action report (AAR) before returning to camp." All eight men joined in a circle, and the team leaders took turns describing their group's movements and observations.

Cowboy began by defending why he'd positioned his team in the arroyo. "I decided that if I had to cross this ground, I'd use this arroyo for cover." Cowboy explained. "Once we found that bend, it only seemed natural to set up there. It provided good cover and an ample kill zone."

"Yeah, that was the right move. Matter-of-fact, we would've walked right into it if it wasn't for Wildcat taking a drink." Gringo pointed out. "I heard a snap and then watched as he replaced his canteen."

"Hey, is this enough reason for you to buy a fricken bladder?"

"Kiss my butt, Slim." Wildcat fired back. "Not everyone can afford to be a Gear Queer like you."

"All right, settle down. We all know Slim is the biggest gear head around, chided Cowboy.

"Yeah, Slim can't stand to show up for an FTX without new kit," Ghost added with a chuckle.

"Hey, I'm always improving my gear. I can't help it. I'm a Stitch Bitch."

Gringo silently smiled to himself as he enjoyed the good-hearted banter and camaraderie. This was the way it was every time the group got together.

It was all very natural, and everyone understood that the jiving and ribbing was done out of respect. Being in the bush at night, on patrol, was something that everyone enjoyed. The group tried to get together once a month to train and learn new skills. Each individual had joined the group at a different time and contributed unique talents. One thing that united the men was their devotion to freedom and the Constitution. They were a citizen's militia

The Patriot movement had experienced ups and downs over the last decade and suffered unfair attacks in the media for longer still. But, the abuses of the government and its continuing slouch towards socialism seemed to ignite a flame in those who treasured their legacy of freedom and cherished the republic established by the founding fathers.

After being driven underground, following the OKC bombing and relentless attacks by overzealous government agencies, Patriots found a new home in cyberspace. Individuals created websites allowing Patriots to unite and discuss the future of the movement. Little-by-little, these sites began linking together. Soon people all over the country had the opportunity to share and explore what the Patriot/Militia movement was all about.

San Diego, California: Eighteen Months Earlier

When Mike first began logging onto Patriot sites he lurked around trying to get a feel for what it was all about. All through school he'd listened to professors' pontificate about how the movement was a sanctuary for racists and angry, uneducated white men. But after reading the posts and interacting with several members, he soon realized the stereotypes were unwarranted. As was often the case, the media and Washington elitists simply slandered the groups they feared. Mike realized the feelings he'd cherished for so many years weren't misguided at all. He wasn't alone.

This revelation struck Mike like a lighting bolt. Not only were his intense patriotic feelings normal, they were shared. Ever since his childhood he'd felt a powerful affinity for freedom and duty. Standing up during the pledge of allegiance was as natural for him as running through the sprinklers on a hot summer day. Something deep inside reaffirmed that he had a duty to his country, not just to obey laws and be a good citizen, but to defend the blessings that had been purchased at the cost of so much suffering and sacrifice.

Whereas his contemporaries seemed perplexed with the writings of Thomas Paine, James Madison, Patrick Henry, and Thomas Jefferson, their words and ideas seemed so logical and natural as to achieve an almost scripture-like status. Additionally, Mike instinctively felt the call of the warrior spirit burning within his soul.

Instead of a confused cacophony of anger and destruction that most people associated with militarism, Mike's mind was calmed by the knowledge that he wasn't exempt from the demands of freedom. His blood might be unique, but it wasn't sacrosanct.

Indeed he felt an affinity with those who'd fought freedom's enemies and understood that regardless of his station in society, he, too, needed to defend those eternal blessings that God had endowed to His children. Mike didn't harbor delusions of grandeur or a reckless disregard for life. He simply accepted the importance of learning the skills needed to defend himself and his freedoms.

Mike grew up in a military family. His father was from Nevada, and his mother was a second generation Mexican-American from New Mexico. His maternal grandparents had immigrated to the United States to escape the corruption and nepotism that fed on the dreams of millions in Mexico. His grandparents understood they wouldn't fully enjoy the blessings of America, not at their age and not without a formal education. But their children could. To this end they encouraged their children to learn English and study hard.

They embraced America and its grand promise, while still honoring their Mexican roots, which included their native language. Spanish was spoken in the home, and each child cultivated a love for its beautiful and highly descriptive prose. This dedication to excellence was passed down to Mike from both his Grandparents and his mother. That's where his nickname, Gringo, began. In high school Mike always seemed to contrast with those around him. His complexion was fair, and he acted like any other American boy, but he embraced his Mexican heritage. One area where this diversity proved to be an asset was with the girls; they just loved it when Mike recited Spanish poetry, especially when it was punctuated with soft kisses.

Mike's father was less of a romantic and more of a pragmatist. From his father Mike learned a love for the outdoors. His father was way ahead of the curve when it came to no-trace camping. Not out of some devotion to Mother Nature and tree hugging, but because, as he was quick to say, "A true outdoorsman knows how to blend with the terrain." Regardless, being sloppy in the bush was a good way to lose valuable gear. Each time Mike reminisced on those early excursions, his father's voice pierced the span of years with a mantra worthy of a Tibetan monk. "Take care of your gear son, and it'll take care of you." Another one of his favorites was, "Be sure to clean and stow away that gear; it worked harder than you did this week." Later, Mike learned these anal-retentive rants reflected hard-learned lessons in Vietnam. Mike's father served two tours there and then rounded out his career with twenty additional years before retiring as an Army Sergeant Major.

Growing up Mike always intended to serve in the military and looked forward to experiences that would translate into stories he could tell his children. Unfortunately, a car accident when he was a teen ended that dream. Although not crippling, Mike suffered a back injury that prevented him from joining the military.

Learning to deal with this reality was difficult, but quickly Mike determined that if he wasn't able to join the military, he'd learn as much as possible about it and experience as many aspects of it as he could. At least in this small way he'd be able to share in his father's experiences. So while pursuing a business management degree at the University of Arizona, Mike learned to skydive, SCUBA dive, climb, and shoot.

Mike received his first gun on his eighth birthday and had enjoyed shooting ever since. Now he embraced combat shooting. It wasn't enough to shoot from a static position; the real challenge came with movement, being able to negotiate a course while engaging targets and performing tactical reloads. This wasn't simple shooting; it was a thinking man's sport. Knowing how to move, which target to engage, when to utilize cover, and how to efficiently switch between your primary and secondary weapon was all part of the challenge. All this took place while working against a clock, another shooter, and ignoring the close-in report of gunfire ringing in your ears. Now, that got the heart pumping!

Mike felt comfortable, almost intimate, with his weapons. He'd worked with them so frequently that they weren't simply pieces of steel, but extensions of his body. He'd held, touched and manipulated his guns so often that he believed he'd developed a sixth sense; like people do when they are blinded. When he handled his weapons it was as if his fingers transmitted more than feelings; they transmitted sight.

Gunsite Academy: Paulden, Arizona

Gunsite Academy is regarded as one of the premier firearms training schools in the United States. Col. Jeff Cooper, whom many revere as the finest combat instructor in the world, built Gunsite on sixteen hundred acres of land that includes twenty-seven ranges, six outdoor simulators, and a four-hundred-yard rifle range.

Gunsite was Mike's favorite place on earth. On this occasion he'd returned to attend a tactical carbine course. During the first live-fire exercise he noticed another student who really moved well. Hell, this guy didn't move, he glided. Better still, he didn't miss a target. Watching this guy attack a course was like watching Fred Astaire dance; only in this case Ginger was an M-4. Moving effortlessly from one target to another, his hands performed reloads and handled malfunctions like a veteran pickpocket. There was no doubt who the best shooter in this class was...forget the class, this guy was the best shooter Mike had ever seen. He had to meet this guy. After the morning session ended Mike approached his classmate and introduced himself. "Hi, my name is Mike West."

The shooter looked up pleasantly from the bench where he had stripped his carbine for cleaning. "Good to meet you Mike, my name is Taylor Johnson. I was hoping to speak with you." Taylor extended his hand and added, "You're pretty good."

"Look, man, I appreciate the compliment, especially from a shooter like you, but frankly I've never seen anyone move as smoothly and shoot as accurately as you do. Brother, you're a machine. Where'd you learn to shoot like that?" Mike enthusiastically asked.

"Thanks for the kind words," Taylor answered. "I'd like to say I'm a high-speed, low-drag special ops guy." Taylor said with a shrug."But the fact is I've just always been comfortable with a gun. I guess it comes naturally."

"Well, whatever the reason, you're definitely the man to beat." Mike chuckled. "And since I don't think I'm going to beat you, I'd better befriend you. How about some lunch? We have a couple hours before the next session begins, and I know a great restaurant in Prescott...by the way, my friends call me Gringo."

"Gringo, huh? I'm sure there's a story behind that. I've never had a nickname," Taylor said.

"Well, the way you engage a target I'm going to start calling you Arrow."

"Arrow...yeah that sounds pretty good. I think I can live with that," answered Taylor, "Thanks, Gringo."

During lunch and over the next three days, Mike and Arrow discussed different shooting techniques and rehearsed movements in preparation for the final competition that rounded off the course. The two shooters shared complementary styles and worked well together. A bond of mutual respect, trust, and healthy competition developed between them, and they graduated the course first and second. Arrow took first, but that was all right with Mike; he knew he'd found a true friend, which was nearly as good as the top gun trophy.

As the two men were preparing before leaving for home, Mike handed Arrow a business card. "Hey, Arrow, this is my card. If you're ever in my area, give me a call."

Arrow looked at the card:

Mr. Mike West
Senior Consultant
International Business Consultants Inc.
1300 N. Camino del Suelo, San Diego, CA 92129

"Are you kidding?" asked Taylor. "You live in San Diego?"

"Yeah, why?" answered Gringo.

"Well, that'll make it easy for us to get together. I live in Oceanside."

"You've got to be joking." Gringo replied in disbelief. "How is it we've never met at IDPA matches?"

Shaking his head Arrow answered, "I have no idea, man, but I bet we will in the future."

Pacific Beach, California

Mike leased a three-bedroom house off Garnet Avenue about five blocks from the Pacific Beach Pier. Luckily for him, the owner was an old friend of the family, so the rent was far more affordable than the going rate for this area. You couldn't ask for better weather than San Diego. The average yearly temperature was seventy-two degrees, which made for ample viewing pleasures along the beach. It was just the kind of place that a bachelor hoped for.

Los Coronados Islands, Baja Mexico

Mike had actively dated a number of girls over the years, but never quite found one that he'd consider a lifelong companion. Nevertheless, the pursuit had its own pleasures, and San Diego was a target-rich environment. UCSD and SDSU provided a steady stream of eligible young ladies who took full advantage of the near-perfect weather to enjoy the outdoors. Lately, Mike had been dating a beautiful redhead named Rachel O'Conner. Rachel was finishing her graduate degree in bioengineering at UCSD. They'd met on a dive trip to the Coronados Islands. The Coronados consisted of two main islands about forty minutes south of Mission Bay, off the coast of Baja, Mexico. The islands offered the best diving in the area with visibility reaching upwards of seventy feet on a good day. Mike often purchased half-day trips out to the islands through a local dive shop. These trips included two dives at the islands and a third in the Point Loma kelp beds.

While on one of these trips, Mike asked Rachel if she'd like to be his dive buddy for the day. They were both solo, so it was only natural. Mike was impressed with his new dive partner right away. As Rachel suited up for the first dive, he took time to inspect her equipment; after all they were dive buddies, and safety was the reason for pairing up. At least that was the line he'd use if she took offense at his gawking. Rachel stood about 5'11" and wore a black, one-piece wetsuit. Due to its design it wasn't the typically bulky mass of neoprene most commonly associated with dive suits. Its cut allowed it to fit her body...very nicely.

Standing in her suit, with a dive knife strapped to the inside of her calf, and the sunshine illuminating highlights in her French-braided red hair, Gringo thought, *This girl looks like Laura Croft from Tomb Raider.* He hadn't seen the movie, but all of a sudden, a trip to Blockbuster seemed like a good idea.

On their second dive Mike found a large lobster peeking out from under a rocky ledge. Unfortunately, Gringo's first attempt to grab it was too slow, and his prey darted deeper into the protection of its small cave. As the eight-legged crustacean looked back, its antennae waved up and down in an almost mocking fashion. Mike knew he couldn't take lobster in Mexican waters, but he sure wasn't going to allow this "bug" to get the best of him. After surveying the situation, Mike decided he'd be able to reach the lobster if he could only wiggle under the ledge a foot further. Unfortunately, the tank valve and first stage wouldn't fit under the rock, and each time he tried to reach the lobster, his efforts were rewarded with a sudden, grinding stop.

This isn't working, Mike thought in frustration. *Fine, I'll simply eliminate the problem. If I take off my BCD and replace my primary regulator with my secondary that should allow me to reach the stupid lobster.*

Mike owned a Zeagle® Buoyancy Control Device (BCD), and as the core of his SCUBA rig, it held his tank, on which was attached a first-stage regulator. For safety, he carried a secondary regulator just in case the primary malfunctioned. This regulator was attached to a much longer hose so it could be shared with another diver in an emergency.

Mike figured his plan was sound, but unfortunately, in his blinding desire not to be bested by a "bug," he forgot that this BCD also housed twenty-eight pounds of lead shot as counter buoyancy for his wetsuit. So as soon as Mike slipped out of his BCD his body instantly became positively buoyant. Before he realized what had happened he found himself hanging above the ocean floor, tethered to his gear, literally, by his teeth. The danger of shooting to the surface and suffering a lung embolism quickly realigned Mike's priorities. He struggled back to his BCD and slipped it on. After making sure that everything was in the right place, he searched for Rachel. He found her about ten feet away, lying on the sea floor, bent over in what could only be described as uncontrollable laughter. It was all she could do to hold the regulator in her mouth so it wouldn't fall out as she enjoyed the best laugh she'd had in a very long time.

Once on the surface Rachel pulled her mask down around her neck, and while laughing remarked, "That was the funniest thing I've ever seen. Dangling above your rig you looked like a kite. I even think the lobster was laughing."

Great. I really know how to impress the ladies. Mike thought. *She'll get lots of mileage out of this one.*

"Well, I have to admit, I didn't think that little stunt through very well. I bet I looked pretty stupid," Mike responded with an awkward chuckle.

"Well, at least you're not afraid to laugh at yourself," said Rachel, "I can appreciate that."

The two decided they'd had enough fun for this dive, so they kicked over to the boat and waited for the deck crew to take their fins and help them aboard. After organizing their gear, they each grabbed a sandwich and a Coke and walked out to the bow. Rachel twisted her torso out of her wetsuit with moves that would make a belly dancer jealous, allowing the top half of the suit to hang down around her waist. Instead of a bathing suit she wore a thin, Lycra suit that cleaved tightly to her wet, well-endowed, athletic body. *This just gets better and better.* Mike thought as he continued to stare at her.

The longer they talked; it seemed Mike's underwater "stupid pet trick" wasn't going to be held against him. The beautiful redhead entranced Mike. Everything about her electrified him, especially her laugh. Mike concluded that Rachel's father was either a dentist, or deeply in debt to one; her teeth were perfect and glistened in the sunlight.

But the best part about her laugh was the way she tilted her head back exposing her delicate neck, and then finished by coquettishly staring back at him with a mystifying gaze. Rachel was more than good-looking; she was intelligent and possessed a sharp wit. Gringo could tell she wasn't the typical co-ed you'd see in those *Girls Gone Wild* videos. She knew she was attractive but didn't flaunt it. Instead, she sent out a wholesome vibe that was captivating. No, she wasn't some boy toy, bar princess; she was different, and Mike knew he needed to treat her accordingly.

Pacific Beach, California

Over the past several months Mike and Arrow had partnered up at several shooting matches around San Diego County and built a solid friendship. This afternoon Arrow was bringing a couple of friends down to Mike's house for a barbecue. They arrived around 5:00 p.m.

"Welcome to Casa de Gringo," Mike proclaimed as he welcomed his guests.

After shaking hands, Arrow introduced his friends. "Gringo, I'd like you to meet Tom South; we call him 'Cowboy.' And this is Ethan Biggs. His handle is 'Ghost.'"

"Good to meet you guys; come on in and make yourselves comfortable. The barbecue is heating up, and we've got steaks marinating in the fridge and drinks on the porch."

The four men walked out to the backyard, selected drinks, and sat in some assorted chairs Gringo had picked up at a local garage sale.

Cowboy looked like a poster boy for a Marine Corps recruiting drive. He stood about 6' 2" and probably wore a 46" jacket and 34" waist pants.

Even a passing glace told you this guy was tough. His face was chiseled at right angles, and veins intersected his face and neck, and judging from his deeply tanned face, Cowboy spent a lot of time in the field. But what was most striking about his appearance was the predator look that resided in his eyes; this man had "been there and done that," no doubt about it.

Cowboy had a firm handshake without the intimidating crush of a less confident man. "Taylor speaks highly of you and says you're pretty dangerous with a weapon."

"That's nice to hear," responded Mike as he shot a glance towards Arrow. "But if you guys have ever seen Arrow shoot, you know who the dangerous one is."

"I can see you're in the Corps; what do you do?" Mike asked.

"I'm a Gunnery Sergeant with 2nd Force Recon Company at Camp Pendleton. I recently finished a deployment to the Persian Gulf with 4th platoon/ 13th MEU. That'll be my last deployment, though. My enlistment is up next week, and I've decided to pursue other opportunities."

"I know a guy that served on the USS *Port Royal*." Mike said. "Wasn't it attached to the 13th MEU?"

"Yeah, it was. It was nice having one of those Aegis-class cruisers protecting our butts while we were floating around on the *Peleliu*. Once we're feet dry we can take care of ourselves, but out at sea we're a big target."

"What about you, Ghost? What's your story?" Mike asked.

"Well, I met Cowboy and Taylor at some shooting competitions held at the Oceanside Shooting Academy a year ago. I work for a computer research group in Sorrento Valley...you know, over by Qualcom."

"Yeah, I know the area well. I use to have an office on Nancy Ridge Drive, just above that executive golf course. So what kind of computer work do you do?" Mike inquired.

"Mostly software development. It's not as sexy as Cowboy's line of work, but it pays well, and I enjoy the challenge. I guess that's why I started attending matches at the academy; I needed something a bit more aggressive to feed the monster inside."

"So, how did you get the nickname Ghost?"

"From friends at school. We used to hack into the university's mainframe to gather information and mess with people we didn't like. You'd be surprised how much trouble you can cause by making a few minor adjustments to official records.

"I became pretty good at covering my trail and was never caught; I guess you can say I was a 'black hat;' anyway that's when they started calling me Ghost and the name just stuck."

"That, my friend, could earn you both a lot of friends and a lot of enemies," Mike remarked. "But, you're definitely the kind of guy to have handy."

Ghost was in his early thirties and didn't fit the computer geek stereotype. His physique was more like that of a tri-athlete. He was obviously intelligent, and it was clear that his fortes weren't limited to one field. He had a confident air about him that was somehow reassuring. Mike could tell he was probably the "go to" guy in his office.

"Well, gentlemen, the menu says the main course for this afternoon is Ribeye steak. How do you like them cooked?" Mike asked.

A burst of flame engulfed the steaks as they were placed on the grill. Mike liked to sear the steaks for a couple minutes on each side and then move them off to the edge for a couple more. Any longer and they'd cook too much, and overcooking an USDA Prime Ribeye just seemed wrong. Luckily, the others agreed. After the men finished, Arrow conferred briefly with Cowboy and Ghost before looking over at Mike.

"Mike, we have a proposition for you. We've been looking for the right guy for a project that's been in development for the past year, and we'd like to let you in on it. Why don't we top off our drinks, go into the living room, and we'll lay out the details?"

Mexico City, Mexico

Muhammad Mahdi Al-Salih was tired and dirty. He'd just landed at Mexico City's Benito Juarez International Airport after a twenty-two hour flight. After passing through customs with a counterfeit Jordanian passport, he blended into the throng of arriving passengers and walked to the baggage claim area. There he retrieved a single, black, hard sided suitcase and headed for final inspection and the exit. Slowly, a Mexican approached and with a light tap on the shoulder said, "*Disculpme Señor*, will you need a taxi tonight? I offer excellent rates both within and outside the DF."

"Possibly," Muhammad replied, "Do you charge by the hour or the mile?"

"That's entirely up to you, *Señor*."

What had transpired was a classic sign and countersign established to ensure that the right assets met and recognized one another. This procedure had been worked out prior to Muhammad's leaving Damascus, and now he knew who his contact was, at least for this portion of his trip. The Mexican took Muhammad's suitcase and led him towards the underground parking lot. As soon as they reached the exit the automatic doors parted and the Syrian was assaulted by a wave of sounds and smells emanating from the world's largest city.

The Mexican put Muhammad's suitcase down, making sure to straddle it between his legs for security, and waved to a small Fiat waiting about one hundred meters away. The driver acknowledged this signal with a flick of his headlights and pulled up in front of the two men.

"*Señor*, this is our car. We'll take you to a safe house, where you can rest."

"*Pedro, ayuda el Señor con su equipaje.*" Please, *Señor*, get inside the car. The driver will take care of your luggage.

As Muhammad entered the car he whispered a short prayer under his breath. "*Subhanalla-thee sakh-khara-lana haatha wa-ma kun-na lahoo muqrineena wa inna ila Rabbina la-mun-qali-boon.*" This was a customary prayer that all devout Muslims recited before entering a vehicle. Translated it meant, "Glory to Him who has subjected these to our [use], for we could never have accomplished this [by ourselves]. And to our Lord, surely must we turn back!"

The small car pulled away from the curb and merged into the twenty-four-hour-a-day traffic of Mexico City. After such a long flight Muhammad didn't care too much for watching the city pass by. All he knew was he'd met his contact and was heading to a place where he'd be able to shower and rest. Intercontinental travel wasn't new to Muhammad, but flying coach was. His flight had left Damascus and flew to Athens where he had changed planes and passports, flew to Frankfurt, then switched planes again to connect to Mexico City. Now, he found himself in a small, dirty car weaving its way through oppressive traffic towards what was sure to be an even less impressive house. Muhammad drew an open hand over his face and hair and deeply sighed.

I'll feel better after I clean up and get some rest; tomorrow will be another long and dreadful day, he thought to himself, *but I'll survive this ordeal just as I have all the others, Insha'Allah.*

Just then he gazed out the window and noticed a tall column in the middle of a turn about, topped by a golden angel holding a wreath in its outstretched hand. As it passed by he thought, *Do these infidels actually believe the angels are watching over them? Not likely.*

Pacific Beach, California

Gringo was caught off guard by Arrow's announcement. He'd believed this evening's get together was going to be nothing more than a good, old fashioned BS session between guys. Nonetheless, Gringo had developed a level of trust with Arrow, so he was intrigued by this unexpected announcement. He stared at Arrow and without saying a word, examined his demeanor and searched his eyes for any sign of reluctance. None was found.

Arrow started off, "First, let me thank you for having us over and for the great steaks. Since we met at Gunsite I've sensed something about you that was familiar and admirable."

"Whoa, big guy, you know I have a girlfriend. I don't swing that way." Gringo proclaimed with a laugh that broke the tension in the room.

"Okay, that didn't sound right. Let me simply say that I've always considered myself a good judge of character, and right from the beginning I sensed you were a trustworthy and honorable guy." Arrow backpedaled. "We've spent a lot of time talking about our mutual commitment and dedication to the founding principles of this republic and the vital nature of freedom. I feel comfortable saying that we're on the same page; wouldn't you agree?"

"Absolutely." Gringo adamantly replied.

"Well, these two guys are right there with us. I've known them a little longer than I've known you, and I can attest to their passion in this regard. Furthermore, I can vouch for their character."

"That's fine, Arrow, but I don't see where this is heading." Mike said.

"All right, let me speak plainly. You know California is a political disaster. Sacramento is a nest of Communists and Socialists who've long since stopped serving the people...instead they rule us. Taxes are out of control, the treasury is broke, and the politicians have the courts in their back pockets. Whenever the people pass a proposition the aristocracy doesn't like, they get one of their judges to proclaim it unconstitutional. Just like when the people voted to prohibit illegal aliens from getting certain taxpayer-funded benefits. You and I have bitched about unconstitutional gun laws and how we risk going to prison for owning AR-15s. For goodness sake, we have to creep around like criminals just to shoot them."

"And what have we done to deserve this stigma? Nothing. You and I, and thousands like us, are the backbone of this state. We work hard, pay taxes, and contribute to our communities. But, we're the ones forced to live secret lives. Mike, this state is screwed, and it won't get better anytime soon. So we're leaving. We've been making plans to start our own business in Arizona."

Arrow was clearly building up to something big, and Gringo wished he'd get on with it. "Okay," he said. "But what does this have to do with me?"

"We plan to build a full-service shooting academy outside of Phoenix, similar to Gunsite, and we'd like you to join us. We need someone who understands business and can help us make it a success. What do you think?"

"Wow! Mike exclaimed, shaking his head. "I have to admit I didn't see this coming."

"You know I agree with everything you said regarding California. Lord knows we've had that discussion a thousand times." Mike answered. "Who's going to bankroll this project?"

"As you know I'm an asset manager. Gratefully, I've been pretty successful. I've obtained funds from several venture capitalists and liquidated some personal investments. So we have all the capital we need. We've already purchased the land and started the permit process. What we need to do now is start filling key positions, and that's why we're here tonight. We're offering you the position of Director of Business Operations. Cowboy will be our Director of Training, and Ghost will fill the role of Director of IT. What do you think?"

"This sure sounds good. Why don't you keep talking and fill me in on the other details?" Mike suggested.

Over the next couple hours the four men discussed the whole project. They were going to do something that had never been done before. As the cliché goes, "They were taking it to a new level." This facility would have air conditioned classrooms, outdoor ranges from fifty yards for pistols to over a thousand yards for .50-caliber rifles, multi-level kill houses for CQC, open areas for patrolling, and field craft, gunsmiths, and retail space. They were even talking about bringing in a guy who would manufacture tactical gear on-site.

The facility would be huge, and the low cost of undeveloped land in Arizona would make it financially feasible. They'd purchased the land in Pinal County, in the Southeast part of the valley, an area called Queen Creek. Not only was this undeveloped land with extremely low taxes, it was also close to one of the fastest growing metropolitan centers in the US. Due to its rapid growth, Arizona was funding major infrastructure projects all over the valley. A brand new freeway was under construction that would connect the east part of the valley with a network of freeways that had been constructed over the last decade.

Better still, Arizona had some of the best gun laws in the country, so they'd be able to operate in the open without having to worry about bureaucrats trying to shut them down at the drop of a hat. There was no doubt this plan was well thought out, but then again Mike didn't expect anything less from his friend. Arrow approached business the same way he shot: smooth, methodical and aggressive.

But there was one big problem. Mike didn't want to leave Rachel. She was like no other woman he'd ever known. She was ever present in his mind.

Everything he did, even the smallest thing, seemed to be weighed against what she'd think. It wasn't that she demanded it—far from it. Mike wanted to please her or at least not to detract from the incredible feeling he enjoyed whenever they were together.

The more he entertained the thought that he might be falling in love with her, the more he tried to resist it. It was a losing battle. He loved her and couldn't deny it.

"I have to admit, I'm impressed." He said at last. "You guys have done a first rate job in researching and designing this project." Mike admitted. "I appreciate this opportunity, but I can't give you an answer tonight."

"I completely understand. We didn't expect you to drop everything and leap into our arms," Cowboy said with a comforting smile. "But, I want you to know I believe you're the man for the job. So it's yours if you want it."

"Let me take a few days to think it over." Mike proposed. "Can we meet again...say a week from tonight?"

"No problem. Tell you what; next time I'll buy the steaks." Arrow offered.

"Sounds like a deal."

The four men stood up, shook hands, and walked to the door. After the others left Mike glanced at his watch. It was 9:15 p.m., not too late. *I'd better call Rachel. We have a lot to talk about.*

Mexico City, Mexico

The small Fiat exited the congested traffic of downtown and drove towards a suburb called *Naucalpan de Juárez*, a nondescript, middle-class neighborhood with mostly single-level homes built in traditional Mexican style. Ten minutes later they arrived at a two-level villa. The house was situated close to a highway on-ramp and had good visibility both up and down the street. A pair of large ornamental iron gates guarded the entryway into a large courtyard on the east side of the property. The driver honked his horn three times and the gates crept open allowing the car to enter. Inside, a familiar face was waiting to greet Muhammad.

"As salumu alaykum wa Rahmatullahi wa Barakatuh." Welcome to Mexico City, *Ra'id*. The man was Sayf Al-Din Al-Mashhadani. He'd arrived in Mexico six months earlier to establish a base of operations and prepare for Muhammad's arrival. Sayf addressed his superior by rank calling him *Ra'id*, Arabic for Major. Both Muhammad and Sayf were members of the Syrian Army and worked as liaison officers with *Hezbollah*.

The major exited the car with his left foot and embraced Sayf. While lightly kissing him on both cheeks he said, *"Alayka wa alay-his salaamu wa Rahatullahi wa Barakatuh, Mulazim."* Muhammad returned his Lieutenant's greeting. "Sayf, it is good to see you. Is everything in order?"

"Yes, Major. All is as it should be. Please, allow me to take your luggage. We have prepared a room for you upstairs where you can wash and rest."

"Excellent. What time will we leave in the morning?" The major asked.

"Our car will be here just after morning prayer," replied Sayf. "It's a little over a thousand kilometers to Torreón; the trip should take about fifteen hours. We'll meet an important contact with the *Aztlán* movement there before heading to Hermosillo."

Another fifteen-hour day. Although the major did not look forward to the trip, security demanded a low profile. Two Arabs flying direct to the US/Mexican border following the Iraqi war, and while September 11 was still in the minds of Americans, might draw unwanted attention. In his line of work, it was far better to do things slow and careful than to risk failure. As the *Qur'an* teaches, "Haste is of the Devil, but slowness is of Allah."

Yes, Allah will surely bless us. He reflected.

Sayf led the major to an upstairs room that had been prepared for him.

"*Ra'id*, I hope you'll find these accommodations to your liking." Pointing across the room he added, "That door leads to your bathroom, and I have placed an *Azan* clock next to your bed. It is programmed for Mexico City."

An *Azan* clock calculates local time relative to *Fajr* time, which is the time all Muslims are required to pray. By using this clock Muhammad could coordinate his morning prayer with the rest of the *Umma* (Worldwide Islamic community).

"May Allah bless you for your dedication. This will be sufficient. Oh, one last thing...what is the local *Qibla*?" the major added.

"The *Qibla* is calculated by the clock, I believe it is thirty-six degrees east. Do you require an appropriate compass?" Sayf answered.

"No, I have my own. Thank you."

In addition to praying at the appropriate time, it is also important for all Muslims to pray facing the most direct bearing to Mecca. By using spherical trigonometry it's possible to calculate the most direct bearing from one point to another, taking into consideration the curvature of the earth. But to be as exact as possible, all calculations must be made using as many of the same variables as possible. Since most compasses point to magnetic north and not true north, it is important to have a compass that compensates for this variation.

For some western Muslims the strict demands of Islam had become cumbersome and annoying, but Muhammad found assurance and order in the rites. He took comfort in the knowledge that all true believers prayed the same words, at the same time, and in the same direction. There was no point where he ended and Islam began; they were inseparably one, making him a *Mujahedin* (a warrior of jihad). After showering, Muhammad sat on the edge of the bed and contemplated his mission. This operation was conceived soon after the fall of Baghdad. Watching the American *infidels* destroy the Iraqi army and occupy Baghdad was a humiliation suffered by all Arabs and a dreadful warning for Damascus. Suddenly, Syria found 150,000 Americans solidly entrenched along their Eastern border and themselves in the cross hairs of "The Global War on Terrorism."

The American President had proven he was not to be taken lightly. After a rapid victory in Afghanistan followed by a powerful campaign in Iraq, Damascus worried about the possibility of a combined Israeli/American attack that would force Syria to fight on two fronts. As Syria looked around, it found itself isolated. Turkey, although a Muslim nation, had grown far too casual in its approach to true Islam and far too dependent upon the Western *kafirs*. Between Turkey's disputes with Syria over the Hatay Province, Syria's support of the Kurdistan Workers Party, and the fact that Ankara had actually joined the infidels' NATO pact; Turkey was virtually an infidel regime itself. The Turks might file a diplomatic grievance with Washington or the UN, but they'd never fight against another NATO partner.

Jordan couldn't be relied upon either. Their military was too small, and King Abdullah politically undependable due to his affections for the West. After all, he studied in the United States, and his mother, Queen Noor, was an British by birth. That left Saudi Arabia, which had been occupied by the Americans since 1991.

The house of Saud was corrupt and unreliable, but worst they'd surrendered their military role in the region after the 1967 war with Israel. No, Syria was isolated and vulnerable. The pressure the Americans were placing upon Damascus was intolerable. Since Syria's options were limited at home, it needed to find solutions elsewhere. Sun Tzu wrote:

The nature of water is that it avoids heights and hastens to the lowlands. When a dam is broken, the water cascades with irresistible force. Now the shape of an army resembles water. Take advantage of the enemy's unpreparedness, attack him when he does not expect it; avoid his strength and strike his emptiness, and like water, none can oppose you.

Muhammad's mission was to exploit the imperialist *infidels* where they were weakest, on their Southern border. For years the Syrian intelligence agency watched, with great interest, the progress of the *Aztlán* movement. *Aztlán* is the name Chicanos gave to the land that was ceded to the United States after the Mexican-America War of 1846. Today, this land comprises the majority of the American Southwest. Leaders of this movement had adopted an anti-Israeli and pro-Palestinian position, and Damascus wanted to exploit perceived commonalities.

Muhammad's task was to convince the *Aztlán* leadership that Islam considered the Chicanos the Palestinians of the West. He was also to extend an offer that Islam wanted to support their efforts to reclaim their ancestral homeland. By doing this, Syria hoped to create such anarchy along the border that America would have to withdrawal its forces from Iraq and redeploy them to their western states. It was also hoped this action would strengthen the Democrats in Washington who opposed the president's foreign policy and would eventually lead to his demise.

The enemy of my enemy is my friend. Muhammad reflected. This was the motto the Americans had embraced throughout the Cold War. Wasn't it ironic that now that same maxim would be used against them, this time on their own soil? Yes, we will flatter these Mexicans and offer platitudes of unity for their cause. We'll equate their struggle with that of our Palestinian brothers, and they will gladly serve as our pawns. In the end the Americans will defeat them and crush their pitiful movement. Nevertheless, their sacrifice will help minimize the American threat to Syria. Once America pulls its forces out of Iraq, it will be ten times harder to send them back. Only Allah could inspire such a plan where two *infidels* are weakened while His followers find relief. *Allah u Akbar*."

Chapter 2

> Whenever the legislators endeavor to take away and destroy the property of the people, or to reduce them to slavery under arbitrary power, they put themselves into a state of war with the people, who are thereupon absolved from any further obedience....
> —John Locke 1690

Pacific Beach, California

After closing the door behind Arrow, Cowboy, and Ghost, Mike walked back to the kitchen, poured himself a Coke, and sat down in his favorite leather chair. The offer to move to Arizona and be part of a first-rate shooting academy was tempting. It would be good to leave California. True, there weren't many places where you could SCUBA dive in the morning and snow ski in the afternoon. But California had become an uncomfortable place to live for anyone who was concerned with freedom. The California of his childhood had long since faded away, and what remained was a pitiful reflection of what he'd loved. Mike constantly recoiled from one abuse or another coming out of Sacramento, and things weren't going to change. Because of this realization, he had adopted an attitude of quiet rebellion, especially with regard to concealed carry laws.

Mike was tired of tyrannical politicians imposing their insecurities on the people and expecting him to remain defenseless in the face of clear threats. So for the past year, he'd carried a concealed pistol in spite of the immoral law. Yes, he was ready to leave *Kalifornistan*.

The idea of building a high quality-shooting academy in Phoenix made a lot of business sense. He'd already begun thinking up marketing ideas, from concealed carry permit classes, to law enforcement and advanced tactical training. But still, if he accepted the offer he'd have to leave Rachel behind.

Damn it. How did I allow myself to get into this position? He frowned. No, that wasn't right. *Get into what? Rachel isn't a consequence of a bad decision. She's the most wonderful woman I've ever met.* Then he remembered something an old preacher once told him. "Sacrifice is giving up something good, for something that will prove better." The more he pondered the saying, the stronger the impulse to call Rachel grew. He glanced at the clock. It was nearly 10:00 p.m.; if he was going to call her it better be now, before she went to bed. Mike picked up the phone and dialed Rachel's number.

"Hello?" Rachel answered.

"Hey, Babe, its Mike; how did your study group go?"

"Hi, Mike, I was just thinking about you," she replied in a soft, caring voice. "The group went well. We're working on a new protocol for testing the biocompatibility of polymers. It's a new group, so we're still trying to identify who should do what. How was your guys-only night?"

"It was great. Arrow brought a couple of friends down with him and we had a good time." He paused. What should he tell her? Blurt it out over the phone? Ask if he could come over? No—when in doubt, procrastinate. "Hey, I was wondering if we're still on for tomorrow night?"

"Sure, I've been planning our picnic for a couple weeks now. Why, is there a problem?"

"No, everything's still on. I just wanted to make sure everything was still a go. I, uh…just want to see you."

"Are you sure everything's all right?" Mike noticed the sudden change in Rachel's voice. "You sound a little distant."

"Yeah, I promise everything's fine, babe. It's just that you've been on my mind, and I miss you." Mike replied.

"That's sweet. You know, my roommate is doing her psychology rotation at the hospital; I think she'd be impressed that a tough guy like you would be willing to admit such a thing. Maybe you're finally getting in touch with your feminine side," Rachel teased.

Go for the joke, he thought. "Yeah, I'm thinking about touching a feminine side all right, but it's not mine."

"You're such a bad boy." Rachel's tone said yes, though her voice invariably said no.

"I may be a bad boy...but I'm a *real* good man!" Mike said with a chuckle. The Tim McGraw song was always a good line.

"You're going to get me in trouble, Mr. West." Rachel shot back in a devilish tone. "I think it's time for me to go to bed and for you to take a cold shower."

"All right, babe, I'll pick you up about 5:30 p.m. tomorrow. Sleep well, I..."

"I what?" Rachel asked in an inquisitive tone.

"I..." Mike hesitated, "I...I guess I'll see you then."

"I guess I'll see you then, too. Goodbye."

Even after the line went dead, Mike still held the phone to his ear. He'd almost said I love you. That had never happened before. He was a little shocked, but then again, it seemed so natural. Mike was startled back to the present by a sharp tone in his ear, and put down the phone. Sitting around and thinking about this whole thing would drive him crazy, so even though it was late, he decided to go outside and wash his car. It was irrational, but therapeutic. Besides, the car was dirty and needed to be cleaned. As he walked outside, the thought occurred to him that in his present state his car might end up with a tune-up and oil change before he got to bed.

La Jolla, California

Mike arrived early to pick-up Rachel. "Goodness, Mike," she said staring at Mike's truck in amazement, "I've never seen your car looking so good. Did you have it detailed, just for me?"

"Uh...well, not exactly. I couldn't sleep last night. I got into a cleaning mood." He said trying to ignore her perplexed stare.

Rachel had been planning this picnic for almost a month, and from the size of the cardboard box Mike loaded into the back of his 4-Runner, she must have been preparing food about that long. He helped her into the passenger seat and closed her door while she buckled herself in. Then he drove to his favorite picnic spot, a big park overlooking La Jolla Cove. As usual, the weather was perfect. A slight breeze blew in from the ocean, and a cloudless dusk quickly turned into a moonlit night.

Rachel began spreading out the meal, and Mike began to feel a little self-conscious at the obvious amount of work she had put into its preparation.

"Rachel, you really outdid yourself. Everything looks great! With all your school projects I'm surprised you found time to prepare all this."

"Actually, my roommates helped quite a bit," she said as she poured mineral water into fluted glasses. "They say you're good for me and wanted to make sure you were impressed."

"Well, tell 'em thanks. But I've been impressed with you for a while now."

For an hour and a half, they ate and talked about small things, while the big thing hung over them like a bank vault on a rope. Finally, Rachel packed the plates, flatware, and other accessories into the simple cardboard box she had assembled the meal in, and they walked back to Mike's car.

"It's still early." Mike said checking his watch. "How about going for a walk?"

"Great idea; let me grab my sweater," Rachel replied, "It's getting cool."

Mike laid a light yellow cardigan over Rachel's shoulders and buried his face into her silky, auburn hair, then lightly kissed her right ear. "Thanks for a wonderful dinner, babe."

"You're *very* welcome." She said rolling her head back onto Mike's chest.

The two walked along the breakwater that protected the manmade cove called the Children's Pool, leaned against the railing, and watched the waves roll in from the vast Pacific. Now was as good a time as any other. While looking out over the ocean, Mike started to speak.

"Last night Arrow let me in on a business deal he's been planning for nearly a year," he said. "He's going to build a world-class shooting academy in Phoenix. He already owns the land and has investors lined up to cover the cost of construction and start-up. He and his partners offered me the position of Director of Business Operations." Mike turned to look at Rachel, but she remained fixated on the horizon.

"I have to be honest with you, Rachel. This sounds like a wonderful opportunity, but I believe I'm going to decline the offer."

This news turned Rachel's head. "*Decline*? I thought you'd jump at a chance like that."

"Yeah, so did I," Mike took a deep breath. *Spit it out*, he thought. "But that was before I realized how much I care about you and how empty I'd be if I left." Mike turned back towards Rachel, softly placed his left hand along her right check and drew the fingers of his right hand through her hair. "Babe, I'm crossing new ground here, so I'm asking for some patience. What I'm trying to say is I love you. The thought of losing you makes me feel sick inside. Right now, I can't think of anything that would change that."

For a moment Rachel didn't say a word. Then she looked up into Mike's eyes, as if she was searching for something deep in his soul, leaned in and kissed him. After a moment Mike tried to pull away, but Rachel shifted her hand to the back of his head and forbade his withdraw. After a second or two more, their lips parted.

"Mike, you're the most wonderful guy I've ever known. I love you, too. Listen, I don't want to end this moment with a bunch of talk, so trust me when I tell you I have options, and I'm going to make some calls on Monday."

"What options?" Mike asked before Rachel cut him off.

"No more words. Just kiss me."

Torreón, Mexico

Due to road construction on Route 49 between San Luis Potosi and Zacatecas, the drive to Torreón took longer than expected. Mexican roads were far longer than those in Palestine, but their condition was almost as poor. During the long drive Sayf continually obsessed over the major's comfort. He often, probably too often, asked the major if he was thirsty or if he required a stop. But more often than not, Sayf was perplexed by the major's calmness and apparent serenity. The major sat quietly in the backseat, meditating and sliding a string of prayer beads through his fingers. There was no doubt he was a pious and devout follower of Islam. Everything from his prayers to the simple wooden beads he used testified of his strict and unwavering devotion. But Sayf also knew how quickly the major's demeanor could change in the face of incompetence or disrespect. Once, the major had a soldier severely beaten for misinterpreting an intercepted Israeli communiqué. The punishment was so severe that the soldier lost the use of his right arm, making him a pariah in Islamic society. That knowledge was what drove Sayf to attend to the major's needs so earnestly.

"Excuse me, Señor." The driver asked. "I'm confused and was hoping you could answer a question?"

"That depends." Sayf replied as he continued staring out the window.

"Señor, I know you are both Muslims...so why does your superior pray the Rosary?"

Sayf's initial reaction was a spark of anger that he quickly extinguished. *Praise Allah that the question was posed to him and not directly to the major*. Sayf thought. "That is *not* a rosary, it is a *Masbaha*. They are similar to your Catholic rosary beads, in that they are used to keep count of one's daily *Zikr*. That is to say, 'prayers.'"

Although the major seemed in an apparent trance, he was acutely aware of everything around him including the subdued conversation in the front seat. He spoke up unexpectedly. "Hazhrat Ibn Abbas said, 'Paradise has eight gates, one of which is reserved exclusively for those who are engaged in Zikr.'" He proclaimed in a firm, confident voice, before falling silent again with only an indistinguishable movement of his lips to bear witness to his silent prayers.

They arrived in Torreón a little before midnight. Sayf had reserved rooms at a hotel that was close to the airport, on a street called *Paseo de la Rosita*. After checking in under the name Sanchez, he took the elevator to the third floor and made sure the major's room was appropriate. Then returned to the front desk to confirm the conference room he had reserved for tomorrow's meeting also met his expectations. Once he was assured all was well he retired to his own room for the night.

Muhammad entered the small, sparsely furnished room, closed the door behind him, and ensured it was locked. From his suitcase he unpacked a few items, including a handheld satellite phone. There was an eight-hour time difference between Mexico and Damascus. His superiors would be in the office by now and expecting a report. The phone Muhammad held was specifically modified to send and receive messages using a combination of asymmetric 1,024-bit and symmetric 128-bit encryption for high-level security. The system was very user-friendly and only required that both parties have the same type of phone. Muhammad thought about sitting down, but reconsidered and paced instead. From memory he dialed, 011-963-11-775-6482, which connected with a matching phone held by Brigadier General Taha Al-Din Maruf, then pushed a button labeled "crypto." The line rang several times before being answered.

"*As salumu alaykum wa Rahmatullahi wa Barakatuh 'Amid Maruf.*"

"*Alayka wa alay-his salaamu wa Rahatullahi wa Barakatuh Ra'id Al-Salih*. What is your report?"

"*'Amid*, we have arrived at point Blue and will meet our contacts tomorrow as scheduled. So far everything is proceeding according to plan. Appropriate security measures are in place, and I expect our meeting will be successful, *Insha'Allah*."

"Very well, *Ra'id*. I do not have to stress to you the importance of this mission. The council is depending upon you to maintain the timetable we've discussed. Our allies are preparing their actions as we speak; if you are not successful the coalition will fall apart. I expect a full briefing tomorrow."

"Yes, sir. Goodbye."

Whitaker Institute for Biomedical Engineering: UCSD

After returning home from her date, Rachel's mind continued reeling over what had transpired. She was overwhelmed with happiness by Mike's declaration of love for her. She had quickly fallen for him and had come to the realization that she was in love several weeks prior; nonetheless, she remained silent out of fear of scaring him off. She was attracted to Mike's strength and confidence, not to mention the way he treated her. Rachel had found it difficult to find guys to date, at least the kind of guy she was attracted to. The Bioengineering department isn't usually the first place girls think of when they're looking for good-looking men. Most of the guys she'd met were more focused on research or being published in JAMA than they were in her. Then there was the other group who just couldn't deal with dating another engineer, or for that matter any girl with an IQ higher than 150. But Mike was different. He wasn't intimidated by her strength or her intelligence; on the contrary, he seemed attracted to it.

In Mike, she believed she'd found an equal. Sure there were differences between them, but they were complementary, kind of a *Yin and Yang* type of balance. Most of all, whenever they were together she felt an overwhelming sense of security, as if he could protect her against all of life's storms. It had been a long time since she'd felt this way. When he began telling her about the project in Arizona, a sick emptiness began to grow in the pit of her stomach. She was sure it was a prelude to the classic break-up, but when he said he was willing to decline the offer in order to stay with her, she could hardly believe her ears.

No one had ever been willing to do that for her. It was always, "This opportunity is too great to pass up" or "I've been working for this all my life." She'd heard it all, either personally or through a girlfriend's grief. No, this was for real...he was for real. At that moment she knew that he was "the one." It was as though Mike had uttered some magical incantation. She remembered the discussions she'd had with girlfriends in high school, when they'd ask questions like, "How will you know when you've found the right guy?" No one ever had an answer. But now she knew.

Rachel approached an office door that read Dr. Wei Lie-Yuan. The door was part way open, so she peeked inside. "Professor Yuan, may I come in?"

The small woman inside swiveled her chair. "Of course, please have a seat. How may I help you?"

"Dr. Yuan, I don't know if you remember me; my name is Rachel..."

"O'Conner, right?" The professor said pointing her pencil at Rachel.

Oh good—she did remember. Maybe she had a shot, "Yes, that's right. I took your Fluid Mechanics class last semester."

"I remember...you sat in the first row."

"I was hoping to speak with you about BioPharm in Tempe, Arizona. If I remember correctly, you know someone on the board of directors, and mentioned they offered research internships."

"That's correct. The person I referred to is my brother Xue. He's in charge of research personnel. Are you interested in applying?"

"Yes, very much." She said with an eager tone. "Can you tell me if they have any openings and when they normally accept applications?"

"I don't know off the top of my head, but I could call tonight and find out for you. Why don't you give me your e-mail address, and I'll forward you the information along with an application."

"That would be fantastic. I really appreciate your help," Rachel said as she tore a piece of paper from a folder and wrote down her E-mail address, then stood up, shook the Professor's hand, and thanked her once more as she left.

Torreón, Mexico

Francisco Estrada sat in the front passenger seat of a white Ford Taurus parked down the street from the *Hotel Torreón.* Also in the car were two bodyguards and another leader of the *Partido por la Liberacíon de Aztlán* (PLA). The four men had flown to Torreón the day before from Hermosillo to observe the area and ensure that the meeting was not a set-up. They had been watching the hotel the previous evening when the Syrians arrived and continued their surveillance until 0300 when Francisco and his operations leader, Carlos Ochoa, returned to their hotel to get a few hours rest and prepare for this mornings' meeting. Now, they were making one last recon of the area before their 0800 meeting.

"Has anyone suspicious arrived within the last few hours?" Carlos questioned his driver.

"No. Just a deliveryman from a local store," the driver continued. "I sent Manuel to follow him and confirm that he made other deliveries and returned to the store. Other than that, everything has been normal."

"What about scanner traffic?" Francisco asked.

"We've been monitoring the police bands all night, and nothing out-of-the-ordinary has been broadcast." Pedro answered.

"All right, let's go meet our Arab friends." Francisco confidently said.

The driver started the car, pulled away from the curb, and drove around the block so they'd approach the hotel from a different direction. As they pulled up in front of the hotel, a valet approached and asked if they were checking in. "No." The driver sternly replied. "We're here for a business meeting with one of your guests."

"Very good, Señor; I will gladly park your car for you."

Francisco's driver politely refused the valet's offer. "I'll stay with the car, if you don't mind."

"Very well, you can park just forward of that white zone." Then turning back to Francisco he added, "You can ask for your party at the front desk. It's inside the lobby and to the right."

The driver pulled forward while Francisco, Carlos, and a bodyguard walked towards the entrance. As they climbed the steps that led to double glass doors, the bodyguard adjusted something in the back of his waistband.

Sayf watched the men with a pair of small binoculars from a window in the major's room. "They've arrived. There are three of them…Estrada, Ochoa and a bodyguard, looks like the bodyguard is carrying a weapon in the small of his back."

"That's to be expected. Are they carrying anything else?"

"Nothing. They're in the lobby now."

"Well, *Mulazim*, we should receive the call any minute now." The major said nonchalantly. "Let's get ready."

Normally, Muhammad would never have met with a contact at the same hotel where he slept; it simply wasn't a secure practice. Standard operating procedure would be to keep the location of the meeting secret so a possible enemy wouldn't be able to set up an ambush or place electronic monitoring devices at the meeting place. Typically, the opposition would be informed of the location thirty to forty minutes before the meeting. Fortunately, Sayf had been meeting with the PLA for months and was able to assure the major that bending the rules wouldn't place him in any danger. That aside, the major needed to show the PLA a demonstration of good faith and openness to reassure his new allies that *Hezbollah* was trustworthy.

The smiling desk manager met the arrivals at the counter. "*Buenos días, Señores.* Welcome to the Hotel Torreón. How may I serve you?"

"My name is Señor Santámaria," Francisco courteously answered. "I am here to meet with a Señor Sanchez. I believe he checked in late last night."

"Ah, yes. I will ring his room and inform him that you have arrived. We have reserved a conference salon for your meeting. It is down the hall to your left. I'll let Señor Sanchez know that you'll be waiting for him there."

Francisco thanked the manager, and the three men walked towards the conference room. When they arrived they found an assortment of fruit laid out on the large conference table along with a punchbowl filled with ice. Arranged in the ice were bottles of water and an assortment of Mexican soft drinks. Francisco and Carlos selected chairs facing the entrance while their bodyguard assumed a sentry position against the wall behind them. As they were preparing to sit down Muhammad and Sayf entered.

"Gentlemen," said Sayf with a large, disarming smile, "it is so good to see you again." He walked over to Francisco and extended his hand. "I'd like to present Major Muhammad Al-Salih." He turned to Muhammad. "Major, please meet Señor Francisco Estrada, leader of the *Partido por la Liberacíon de Aztlán."* He gestured toward Carlos, "Major, I'd like to also present Señor Carlos Ochoa, the Operations Leader for the PLA."

Muhammad gave them a broad, warm smile, and added with an eager tone to his voice. "I am very happy to meet you gentlemen and am honored to have the opportunity to initiate, what I hope will be a historic partnership between our two organizations."

The major gestured toward the chairs. "Please be seated. I'm sure you have many questions, and we have so much to discuss." Muhammad selected a seat next to Francisco so he'd be able to watch his expressions and notice any change in his demeanor. The major had been trained by the *Idarat al-Amn al-'Amm* (Syrian Internal Security Directorate) on how to read the physical manifestations that take place when someone is lying or hiding information. Sitting close to Francisco would allow him to notice the slight pupil dilation and facial color variation that often signaled deception.

"I'd like to express my great appreciation for this opportunity to meet with you, Major Al-Salih," Francisco said. "I know you have traveled all the way from Syria, and I want to assure you that your trip will not be in vain. When Lieutenant Al-Mashhadani approached us six months ago, I was pleased to hear that our sufferings had been recognized, and our cause had the opportunity to gain such an experienced ally." Francisco continued, "I'm sure your lieutenant has briefed you concerning the PLA, but I would like to hear, from you, why you are willing to create this alliance."

The major nodded. "Señor Estrada, we are both professionals who serve our countrymen. We are true patriots who have struggled against a common enemy that is responsible for killing, oppressing, and denying our brothers their basic human rights. Although our individual battles have taken place half a world apart, our enemies are the same, America and Israel. Why it has taken this long for our forces to unite and support one another is a question for another time. But, anyone can see that the plight of your people and that of the Palestinians is the same."

"As you know," he continued. "I work directly with *Hezbollah* and have done so for close to fifteen years. In that time we have been the only organization that has defeated Israel and expelled them from an Arab country. When Israel invaded Lebanon in 1982 their justification was to destroy the PLO. But, instead they occupied Lebanon in an attempt to expand their Zionist control over the region. While the PLO quickly fled to Cyprus, it was *Hezbollah* that took up the fight and defeated the IDF. After the Israelis capitulated in Lebanon we continued the struggle against them, this time on behalf of the Palestinians. Because of our willingness to bleed the enemy in their own streets and attack the foundations of their society, the Palestinians are closer today, than ever before, to regaining their homeland."

He smiled. "Don't be confused by the news reports that claim the PLO is the driving force behind the successes of late. The PLO has long since become political "window dressing" that is used for diplomatic maneuvering. The real force that has driven the Zionists to negotiate has been *Hezbollah*." Muhammad shifted in his chair so he could better face Francisco. "Señor Estrada, your people have suffered for over a hundred years under the oppression of the Americans. They stole your sacred lands, denied your people their culture, and they demean their humanity. The Americans use the people of Aztlán as their slaves to advance their own imperialistic designs and enrich themselves by your blood and sweat."

"The Americans pompously speak of freedom and beat their collective chests as they proclaim how they ended the evil practice of slavery, but the truth is that they simply stopped importing slaves from Africa and shifted their malevolent ambitions to Mexico. The truth is hidden in plain view. In the 1800s Africans harvested the fields; today it's the people of Aztlán. The similarities don't stop there. Just as the Israeli Zionists build settlements in the homeland of our Arab brothers you face exactly the same problem with the Americans. The only difference is your oppressors exacerbate their insults by treacherously deceiving your people into actually building and beautifying these illegal settlements."

"Yes." said Francisco. "Everything you say is true. I can see that you indeed appreciate our struggle and the challenges we face. But...may I be frank?"

The major controlled his anger; it did not show on his face. In the Arab world negotiation is a subtle art where one shows respect for the other by taking time and delicately presenting his position. The major was a professional and understood that Westerners lacked a certain sophistication. Probably, this uncultured savage meant no disrespect. "Of course," he said without hesitation. "That is why we are here."

"What does *Hezbollah* expect to gain by this alliance?"

"I appreciate your directness," the major lied. "I will answer your question with equal directness. We wish to make the Americans suffer for their sins. They sit back in their opulent homes, fattening themselves as others starve and suffer. Their arrogance is unmatched, and it offends the whole world.

"They haughtily speak of their strength and derive sadistic pleasure from watching smart bombs destroy 'lesser' peoples. Then they celebrate how brave they are with self-serving speeches that extol their superiority. This is their hubris. When *Al-Qaeda* martyrs destroyed the World Trade Center towers the oppressed people of the world watched and cheered while the weak and pathetic Americans ran, screaming and crying. The Americans hid in their homes and clutched their children just as hundreds of thousands of their victims have done for decades. You see, the Americans are weakest when they are directly attacked. Why? Because for them, war and suffering is something that happens in faraway lands or on TV screens.

"When it appears in their front yards or outside their office buildings it throws them off balance and forces them to make decisions they've never had to make; it forces them to choose personal security over their unadulterated worship of hedonism."

By now all the people in the room were fixated on the major, as if his words had hypnotized them. The major knew the hook had been set. Now it was time to reel them in. "My brothers, we stand at a critical point in our struggle against our oppressors. America is off balance; they have overextended themselves militarily. They are committed on too many fronts, not only in Iraq and Afghanistan but also in the Philippines, Africa, Korea, and a dozen other places."

"They're chasing shadows and rumor. Like a child in a tantrum, they lash out in every direction exhausting their finite energy. Now is the time to strike where they least expect it...in their soft underbelly."

"How do you propose we do this and with what weapons?" Carlos asked. "And furthermore, how do we do it without having smart bombs rain down on us?"

"Are you familiar with Judo, Señor Ochoa?"Asked the major.

"Of course."

"I'm sure you are. Tell me, in Judo what is the best way to throw an opponent?"

"By using his weight and momentum against him and maximizing leverage to your advantage," answered Carlos.

"Exactly. I'm sure you are an impressive fighter, Señor Ochoa."

The major rose from his chair and faced the Chicanos. "Gentlemen, consider what you have already accomplished. You have infiltrated literally millions of potential combatants into enemy territory. This is an achievement that even the Soviets, were unable to accomplish. Frankly, it is even more than my brother Arabs have done. I have read estimates that there could be upwards of eleven million undocumented Mexicans living in the United States.

"Furthermore, through your efforts you have convinced legislators, mayors and governors all over America to enact laws that protect your people from prosecution and deportation. Never before in history has an opportunity so great been afforded to a potential adversary. All that is needed now is funding and direction. That is where we come in, and when I say we, I speak on behalf of the entire Islamic community. Together we can strike a blow against America from which the whore will never recover.

"As far as smart bombs are concerned, you need not worry about that. I assure you as soon as the international community saw US smart bombs destroying Mexico, the outcry would be overwhelming. No, they might destroy faraway lands and people, but they won't do that on their own border."

The major scanned the room and saw that his message had struck a chord in his audience. He could tell they believed what he said and were overwhelmed with the possibilities it offered.

Francisco leaned towards Muhammad, extended his hand and said, "Major, on behalf of the Chicano nation of Aztlán I welcome your alliance. Now, let us further discus details; I have a number of questions, and we have many things to work out."

Pacific Beach, California

Three days had passed since Mike and Rachel's picnic, during which Rachel had been in contact with Dr. Yuan at BioPharm and received information regarding openings in the research department. A position that seemed tailor-made for her started in two months. Her application had been accompanied by very strong recommendations from several of her professors, including Dr. Yuan's sister. She knew she shouldn't make assumptions, and she still needed to fly to Tempe for a face-to-face interview, but she was very confident. Rachel decided that even though all the strings weren't neatly tied, enough was in place for a celebration. Although it was mid-week, she made reservations at a small restaurant in Mission Beach where she would deliver the news to Mike.

Mike didn't quite know what to make of her unexpected invitation. Normally weekday dates were taboo due to Rachel's workload at school, but she reassured him that everything was fine, and one night wouldn't put her back too much. They decided he'd pick her up at 7:00 p.m.

Mike rushed home so he'd have time to press a shirt and get ready in time for their date. He knew Rachel was working on something important, but didn't know what. Of course, he still had to tell Arrow that he'd have to decline his offer. Mike wasn't looking forward to that. But, he was confident he'd made the right decision to stay with Rachel. After all, he already had an excellent job. Though he was increasingly dissatisfied with the way things were in California, he'd be able to continue skirting around the more onerous laws until something changed.

Mike selected a pair of pleated khakis and a white, button-down, long-sleeved shirt for tonight's rendezvous. He slipped an inside-the-waistband holster in his pants, into which he inserted a Glock 27. The model 27 was a sub-compact chambered in .40S&W. Mike preferred the smaller pistol for concealed carry because it was more comfortable. To completely hide the pistol he added a lightweight sweater vest that hung loosely below his waist, completely masking the outline of the pistol.

California is a "May-Issue" state when it comes to concealed carry permits, leaving the decision entirely to the prerogative of the County Sheriff or Chief of Police whether or not to approve an application. In most cases this means that unless you're a politician, celebrity, major campaign donator, or close personal friend of a powerful politician, you'll be summarily denied a carry permit.

Mike didn't fall into any of those categories, so he was forced to make the decision to carry illegally. No matter, he reasoned, the law was both immoral and unconstitutional, and he had long since decided not to observe a law that was either against the will of God or the Constitution. As Chief Justice John Marshall opined in 1803, "A law repugnant to the Constitution is void."

Not long after he began dating Rachel he made a point of letting her know he carried. At first she was a bit skeptical, but the more she got to know Mike the more comfortable she became with the idea. After all, he was better trained than the majority of police officers in the city.

Mike arrived at Rachel's apartment a couple minutes early. Rachel's equally attractive roommate, Laura, answered the door.

"Come on in," she said with a West Texas drawl. "Rachel is just about ready."

"Thanks. You wouldn't happen to know what Rachel has planned...do you?" Mike asked.

"No. But I do know she's pretty excited about it. I'm sure she'll tell me all the details in the morning. Laura responded with a hint of anticipation.

Rachel walked into the room with her purse in hand, and Mike stood up to greet her. "Hiya, Babe, you look great." Mike gave her a kiss. "So where are we going?"

"I made reservations at that new seafood restaurant in Mission Beach, *Breakers*."

"Excellent. I've been craving seafood all week. We'd better get going. Traffic was kind of heavy on the way over, and I don't want to lose our reservation." On the way out the door he said good-bye to Laura and escorted Rachel to his car. During the drive they mostly spoke about her classes and his work projects, both avoiding what they knew would be the real topic of the evening.

When they arrived at their destination they found the small parking lot full, so they reluctantly drove around the block until they found a space off a side street. Just as Mike had feared, they'd got caught in traffic and were late, so they ran to the restaurant.

"Hi, we have a reservation for 7:45 p.m., the name is O'Conner." Rachel announced to the hostess.

"O'Conner..." The hostess repeated under her breath as she drew her finger down the ledger. "Yes, here it is. I believe your table is ready. Please follow Monica, and she'll seat you."

Breakers was a fairly new restaurant that had received excellent reviews in the *San Diego Tribune*. Two chefs who'd worked together for several years in La Jolla opened the restaurant, and it had quickly grown into one of the most talked about spots in the city. After ordering Rachel decided she couldn't wait any longer to tell Mike about BioPharm.

"Mike, I know you're wondering why we're here. Before I explain I want you to know how much I love you. The other night, at the beach, was magical, and I couldn't be happier. I want us to be together, and I want our relationship to rise to the next level."

"I feel the same way, Babe."

"I know how badly you wanted to accept that position in Arizona. Remember when I told you I had options?"

"Yeah...what are you getting at?"

"Well, I know a professor whose brother works for a company in Tempe called BioPharm, and I've applied for a position in their research department. I've already had a phone interview, and I'm flying to Phoenix next Friday for a face-to-face meeting."

Mike felt his heart begin to race. "This is fantastic! But what about school?"

"Well, the position is a paid internship, not a full-time staff position. It would start after I finished this semester, after which I'd only have my Master's thesis to finish, and then I'll be done. I can easily write my thesis while I work. Best of all, you can accept Arrow's offer, and we can be together."

"This is unbelievable. How sure are you that you'll get the position?"

"Nothing's written in stone, but the phone interview was great, and the doctor in charge of the program sounded extremely positive. I feel very confident about this; if I didn't I wouldn't be telling you. Mike, I believe this is going to work."

For Mike, it was like hearing he'd won the lottery. In fact, he was so overwhelmed that it was all he could do not to stand up and embrace Rachel in the middle of the restaurant. Instead he reached across the table, took her hands, and kissed them. Once again he stared deeply into her eyes and considered himself the luckiest man in the world.

"Thank you for doing this," he said softly. "I hope this works out, but I want you to know, regardless of the outcome, I appreciate what you've done. I love you very much, Rachel."

They continued to talk about the BioPharm opportunity through dinner and about what each one of them would have to do before leaving San Diego. If Mike accepted Arrow's offer, he'd have to leave a month or so before Rachel, but that would give him time to get things started with the academy and allow time to find a place to live. Even though it would be hard being away from Rachel, Mike thought, she'd need that uninterrupted time for her finals. Dinner was outstanding. After a light desert, Mike asked for and paid the bill.

Leaving the restaurant Mike and Rachel slipped past a small line of people waiting to get inside. As they approached his car, Mike noticed something move in the space between two parked cars up ahead. At first he thought it might be a stray dog, but as he got closer he realized it was larger. Mike slowed his pace and scanned the surroundings. To his left, cars were parked along the street, in front of him the sidewalk led down a poorly lit street. Mike wondered why he hadn't noticed the lighting when they arrived, but then remembered they'd been in a hurry to get into the restaurant. A little in front and to the right an alley passed behind a row of buildings.

"...then Laura told me to..." Rachel stopped in mid-sentence as she felt Mike's arm wrap around her stomach and push her back.

Rachel looked at Mike and immediately realized something was wrong. His eyes were focused and darting back and forth. As he continued to push her behind him, she could feel the muscles in his arm tighten into iron. Smoothly, Mike's left hand crossed over his abdomen and clutched the bottom of his sweater vest, and began pulling it straight up. A man emerged out of the darkness directly in front of them. He wore dirty jeans and a dark, sleeveless t-shirt. His greasy hair was pulled back in a braid that hung down the back of his head, and in his right hand he held a large threatening knife. Just as the man started to raise the knife, Mike's right hand reached up to his waistband, clutched the handle of his pistol and in one fluid motion pulled it straightout of the holster before punching it straight out, aiming it directly at the man's chest.

"Drop the knife! Now!" Mike shouted in a powerful, commanding voice. "Drop the knife, or I will kill you!"

The attacker silently froze for what seemed an eternity. He'd been caught completely off guard. When the mugger saw Mike and Rachel walking down the street he'd assumed they would be an easy mark. After all, the normal thing people do when confronted with a weapon is to comply and plead for mercy. He wasn't even able to voice a demand before he was looking down the barrel of a pistol. The gun was bad enough, but the look of determination and fury on Mike's face sent a wave of nausea into the pit of his stomach .

This guy isn't joking; he's going to kill me.

In an instant, the mugger's countenance switched from shock to horror; he dropped the knife and with open hands raised in front of him pleaded, "Hey man, its cool. Don't shoot me!"

"Kick the knife into the street!" Mike commanded.

The man instantly complied with Mike's order.

"Don't fucking shoot me. Please!" the mugger begged.

Mike paused as he considered whether or not to pull the trigger, and then decided it wouldn't be worth the potential legal troubles. Mike's trigger finger relaxed, releasing its grip on the criminals' life

"Run!"

The man took a few hesitant steps backwards before turning and disappearing into the darkness.

Immediately Mike scanned from one side to another before turning completely around, searching for other possible threats. Satisfied there were none, he lowered his pistol to the low-ready position, looked back, and grabbed Rachel by the wrist.

"We've got to go right now. Get in the car." With his gun held in a guarded *sul* position he escorted her to the car, all the while scanning for targets. When they arrived at the car, he reached into his pocket, pulled out his keys, and pressed a button on the key fob that unlocked the doors.

"Get in and get low." Mike's words were short and direct. Rachel was in shock, but his directions cut through the confusion and disbelief that clouded her mind like a thick fog.

Once in the passenger seat she bent over and wrapped her arms around her knees, burying her face in her lap. Mike moved to the rear of the car, checked the space between his car and the one behind, then swiftly moved and cleared the drivers' side. He climbed into the driver's seat, placed the pistol between his thighs, started the car and screeched out of the parking place. Mike raced down the street, turned right onto a main avenue and blended into traffic.

"It's over. You can relax. Are you all right?" Mike asked in a much less threatening voice.

"Yeah, just really scared. Are you okay?" Rachel asked in a shaky voice as she began to cry.

"Everything's fine, Babe. You're safe, and no one's going to hurt you," Mike assured her. He reached his right hand over and began stroking her soft, red hair. "Don't worry, everything's okay, now."

The rest of the way home neither one spoke very much. Rachel continued to cry. By the time they arrived at her apartment, she'd composed herself. Mike parked the car in the front row of the lot. He turned off the engine, set the parking brake, then took the pistol from between his thighs and slid it back into its holster.

"Are you ready to go inside, or would you like to stay here and talk about what happened?" He asked.

"I'm feeling better now. Let's go inside. I think I'd feel better there."

The two exited the car, and Mike walked Rachel to her apartment, and she unlocked the door.

"Go on in and have a seat on the couch. I'm going to put my purse away, and I'll be right in."

When Rachel returned, the two faced each other on the couch.

"I didn't even see the guy until he was right in front of us with that knife," she said. "By then you already had your gun out. How did you know he was there?"

"I saw some movement as we started down the street and realized it was probably a man. I got an uneasy feeling seeing someone sneaking around in the dark. It didn't seem right.

"At Gunsite they teach a course on the mentality of survival. When we're in a completely safe environment, like we are now, we can operate on a white threat level. That means we relax and don't worry about danger."

He shifted on the couch. "Anywhere else, especially on the street at night, we need to step up our threat level to yellow and sometimes orange. In this stage we take in information and analyze our surroundings for possible threats. When we're confronted by a threat, like when I saw the guy coming at us, we're taught to elevate ourselves to red, draw our weapon, and confront the danger. In other words, we prepare to use deadly force to protect ourselves. The last stage is condition black. That's when you start shooting."

"So how close were you to condition black tonight?"

"Let me put it to you this way...I had all the slack out of the trigger and that guy was three and a half pounds of pressure away from dying."

Her eyes focused on her lap. "Don't take this the wrong way," she said. "But when I saw you tonight with your pistol, there was something different about you, something primitive. It was as if you were an animal. When you yelled at that guy to drop his knife, you growled more than spoke. You were going to kill him...weren't you?"

"Absolutely. Why, does that bother you?" Mike's answer was unwavering and direct, while still tender and concerned.

"That depends. Why were you willing to kill him? Did you want to?"

"That's an honest question," he said. "I'll try to answer it as honestly as possible. This is the first time I've ever been this close to killing someone."

"You mean shooting, don't you?" Rachel interjected.

"No, I mean killing. If I am forced to shoot, it's because my life or someone else's is in grave danger. In that situation my duty is to stop the threat immediately. It's not like the movies where the hero shoots the bad guy in the arm or leg. When I train, I shoot two rounds to the center of the chest, and if the threat doesn't stop, I follow it up with one to the head.

"That means the bad guy dies before he hits the ground. So in response to your question, I was willing to kill him because he was willing to use a deadly weapon against us."

Mike took a deep breath before continuing. "And as to whether I 'wanted' to kill him, well, that decision isn't up to me. He makes that decision; I simply provide the consequence. Do you understand?"

"Yeah, that makes sense. Thank you." Rachel stood up and started towards the kitchen then stopped and slowly turned around. In a methodical voice she said, "For what it's worth...I wanted you to kill him."

Fallbrook, California

Gringo made an appointment with Arrow. He'd explained, on the phone, that Rachel had an interview in Phoenix the following week, and if she got the position then he would accept Arrow's offer. He also explained that things looked very good, and if possible, he'd like to begin moving forward. Arrow agreed and asked if Gringo could drive up to Oceanside and sit in on an interview he had with a guy named Josh Eckman. Josh owned and operated a small tactical nylon shop called *Grunt Gear*, just east of Oceanside bordering Camp Pendleton.

He got started in the business working for another company called *Tactical Operations Equipment,* constructing designs and repairing personal gear brought in by Marines and local police. After a few years Josh began designing unique pieces for himself and friends and was encouraged to break out on his own. He'd been running *Grunt Gear* for nearly two years and had begun to make a real name for himself as a master of custom design. Arrow first met Josh when he was looking for someone to make a few improvements on his personal equipment. After seeing the results of Josh's work, Arrow knew he wanted him to operate *Grunt Gear* out of his new shooting academy.

Grunt Gear was an unassuming store anchored in a strip mall, flanked by a dry cleaners and a pizza parlor. Inside, the walls were covered with displays and bins containing dozens of different styles of tactical gear, everything from traditional load-bearing equipment (LBE) to newer MOLLE designs and custom load bearing vests (LBVs). The store was organized into four sections: first-, second-, and third-line gear, and custom projects.

On the wall above his custom area he'd painted a replica of the Skunk Works symbol used by the Lockheed design bureau of the same name. As Arrow and Gringo walked towards the back of the store they found Josh on the phone taking an order from the local police SWAT team.

"All right, let me read this order back to you:

Two Drop leg tactical holsters cut for Glock 19s

Four pair of Nomex gloves

Riggers belt, size large

Dual pistol magazine pouches

Six pair of goggles

Did that sound right? And you'll need all these in black, right? Great, you should get these in two or three days, Thanks. Bye."

Josh looked up. "Taylor, how's it going?"

"I'm doing well. Sounds like you're keeping busy," Arrow added as the two men shook hands.

"Yeah, the local SWAT team calls an order in every couple weeks or so. The department orders are usually small, but I've done custom work for nearly every member on the team, and that usually makes up the difference. Who's your friend?"

"Josh, I'd like to introduce you to a good friend of mine, Mike West."

"It's a pleasure to meet you, Mike," Josh said as the two men shook hands. "Why don't you two look around the store; I need to lock up. Then we can sit down and talk."

"I feel like a kid in a candy store," Mike told Arrow with a giddy smile. "I know several guys who use *Grunt Gear*, but I've never visited the store before."

"As I mentioned on the drive over here, I've been impressed with Josh's work for a while. He's got a real talent for coming up with innovative designs. Did you notice he's doing stuff in second-generation MARPAT?" Arrow pointed to a display in the custom work area.

"I didn't know that material was available to the public," Mike remarked.

"It's not," Josh interrupted as he returned from locking the store up, "at least not to everyone. I was asked by the Force Recon guys at Pendleton to do some special work for them, and they arranged for me to order material direct from their supplier. That stuff is for display purposes only. Let's go in the back. I have some chairs back there where we can relax."

The three men walked behind the counter and entered into what could only be described as chaos. The front of Josh's store was spacious and well merchandised. But the back room, where his creative juices flowed, had dozens of packs, vests, pouches and other items in various stages of completion strewn in virtually every corner.

On one wall hung bolts of Cordura in a number of colors and camouflage patterns. Next to them were spools of cordage and webbing in various diameters and widths. The opposite wall contained dozens of drawers and bins that held hardware of every kind, shape, and size. In the middle of the room sat three large industrial sewing machines with great cones of heavy-duty nylon thread intricately woven into the equipment.

Hanging from the rafters above were works in progress and completed orders ready to ship. Next to the back door was a small, rickety table that functioned as an all-purpose shipping department. Under the table were dozens of collapsed boxes of various sizes, rolls of tape, UPS and FedEx forms and a scale. Above the table was a chute and hopper from which Styrofoam pellets could be poured into boxes. Gringo estimated the entire manufacturing area was less than 800 square feet.

"Welcome to Frankenstein's laboratory," Josh said as he spun around with open arms. "I know it's a bit unorganized, but that's the way I like to work."

As Mike looked around the workshop he saw a number of items he'd have loved to get a hold of. "Hey Josh, I might need a towel to wipe up the drool. There's a lot of great stuff in here. What's that bin full of stuff over there?"

"That's the bone pile, designs that didn't pass muster. Instead of taking the time to disassemble them I toss them in that bin until I need something. When I do, I dig around until I find what I need and cannibalize it.

"Your rejects look like other company's production models." Mike added.

"Yeah, in addition to my rejects you'll find some gear in there from Black Raven, London Tower, Special Forces, and Golden Eagle. I take a lot of trade-ins from my custom customers, which I use for R&D. Let's be honest, there aren't too many different ways to recreate the wheel. What I do is tweak it a little here and there to make it spin a little faster and smoother."

"Well, if Mike will stop fondling the gear, we can get started." Arrow stated with a chuckle. "Josh, several months ago you mentioned you were looking to expand your business and move into a larger space."

"That's right. My lease is up in two months, and the landlord is going to raise the rent. I figured if I could move into a larger space I'd be able to bring on a couple guys to help with the front of the store, which would allow me to focus more on the creative side of the business. I'd also like to improve my Internet presence.

Currently, an outside company is hosting my website and bandwidth. I figure instead of paying higher rent for the same space, it makes more sense to invest the money into the business and make those improvements."

"I agree. I believe *Grunt Gear* is ready to explode. You've really made a name for yourself in the industry. I believe that with a little additional investment and space to grow, you'll really take off."

Arrow sat down. "That's the reason we're here tonight. I have a project in the works, and I'd like you to play a part in it." Arrow began explaining the details of his project in Arizona. "We've planned a full-service training facility that would include *Grunt Gear* as an integrated business unit. You would maintain full control of your brand and designs and be able to market your products as you do today. The only difference is you'd be based out of the academy, which would own the facilities. *Grunt Gear,* Inc., would pay rent to the corporation. The great part is you'd be on the board of directors,, so basically you'd be paying yourself.

"In return, the academy would have full use of your brand for advertising and promotion. You'd create a proprietary line of gear, under our label, that would be exclusively sold on location or via the academy's website. Of course, that line of gear would have to be unique enough so as to not directly compete with what you're doing now."

"What about Internet hosting?" Josh asked.

"We've hired an experienced guy to be our director of IT. He's designing an in house IT department that will allow us to operate all our computer needs, including websites and Internet commerce.

"His department will also provide organic web design services, which will save us the costs associated with outsourcing. As with the rent, *Grunt Gear* will pay the corporation for the use of bandwidth, but that'll end up being reinvested in the business."

Josh had several other questions, each of which was answered in turn. He was very impressed with the deal and realized it would offer him an opportunity that would be very difficult to duplicate on his own.

"Well, it sounds like a great deal," Josh said. "Why don't you have your lawyer call my lawyer? If they're satisfied, it looks like we'll be doing business." Josh said.

"Outstanding. I'm pleased to hear you say that." Arrow remarked."I have one last issue before we leave."

"What's that?"

"Once we begin working together, will you offer us any discounts?"

The three men enjoyed a good laugh, shook hands again, and Josh escorted them to the door. On the drive back to Oceanside, Gringo and Arrow stopped at a Mexican restaurant to grab something to eat. Partnering up with an established and respected name brand right from the start would provide a halo effect to the academy and give them access a mature database of potential customers. They'd use the list to seed their grand opening promotions and get some testimonials.

"We've been talking about this deal for a couple weeks now, but I haven't heard what it'll be called. Do you have a name picked out?" Mike asked.

"Interestingly enough, that's been one of the most difficult issues to decide on. I've considered a variety of names, and one seems to hang on...Direct Action Academy. What do you think?"

"Yeah, I like it." Mike raised his drink to a toast. "Here's to Direct Action Academy."

Hermosillo, Mexico

Muhammad spent an entire day in Torreón discussing details with Francisco and Carlos before accompanying them to their headquarters in Hermosillo. There they'd prepared a house for the major. It was a comfortable two-level home with rooms for both the major and his lieutenant. As instructed they'd employed both a cook who was familiar with Islamic dietary codes and a woman to clean the house. From this location he would coordinate operations.

Hermosillo is far enough from the US border to provide a buffer zone against any US attacks. In addition, Hermosillo is the capital of the state of Sonora, which guaranteed access to banks, technology, and a major airport. Finally, here he was close enough to the Gulf of California for him to monitor shipments and to escape by sea if needed.

He'd successfully brokered a partnership between the PLA and *Hezbollah* and worked out the financial details needed to establish funds transfers to the front organizations used by the PLA. A variety of organizations would diversify and minimize risk to the group. The primary account belonged to a local charity that supported underprivileged individuals with handicaps. To protect against unwanted attention, every few months the charity would invite a sympathetic member of the press to interview a recipient of their assistance.

If the PLA was to be convinced that *Hezbollah* was serious, the major reasoned, the first installment of support had to be impressive. After receiving authorization from Damascus, Muhammad presented a package that included $350,000 in cash and another $150,000 in equipment, mostly small arms and ammunition. This represented seed money needed to begin operations. At the beginning of the second stage, an additional $400,000 in cash and $100,000 in supplies would follow, totaling one million dollars. Muhammad assured his new partners that *Hezbollah* would continue to support their cause with whatever they needed.

In the grand scheme, one million dollars was inconsequential, especially considering the majority of *Hezbollah's* support came from Iranian petrodollars. But in this situation one million dollars would go along way.

Muhammad had to admit the PLA's successes were impressive. With patience and using the tactic of incrementalism, they'd wormed their way into the hearts and minds of their supporters on both sides of the border. By exploiting the misguided sympathies of the Americans they not only operated openly, but also received support from the same local and state governments they targeted.

Americans were such an enigma. Having no common foundation to provide stability, they were easily manipulated. They allowed themselves to be deluded by so many ideas that the soil on which they stood quickly turned to quicksand, which slowly engulfed them. How had they ever grown so strong?

Muhammad gloried in the wisdom of the Prophet and His teachings. As Islam spread from one corner of the earth to the next, it laid down a common foundation of laws that all respected and obeyed. It didn't matter if one follower was Syrian and another Indonesian. What mattered was that both were Muslim, which superseded nationality, local culture, and politics.

America boasted of its freedom of religion, and went out of its way to accommodate every manner of blasphemy, which in turn only polluted their collective soul. Ironically, the American president even made a point to publicly proclaim the virtues of Islam, as though he could possibly comprehend or appreciate the teachings of the Qur'an. Watching the president praise Islam was like watching a rat trying to befriend a snake. Didn't he know a *fatwâ* had been issued ordering the destruction of America and its people? It was inconceivable to Muhammad that a leader could ignore the reality of such a direct threat. *Would a man freely allow a cobra into his home without concern for the safety of his family? Only a man blinded by arrogance would permit such a thing. So it is with America,* he thought. Muhammad planned to exploit that flaw to the fullest possible extent. During meetings with his new partners he described America as a great battle tank. It rolled across the battlefield firing its cannon with impunity, trusting its impregnable armor for protection against incoming barrages. To attack it head on was suicidal, but if it was attacked in its soft underbelly it could easily be destroyed.

The first phase of their plan was to organize the assets already in place: the Atzlán movement and the vast number of Mexicans who lived the United States illegally. These assets would be enlisted to attack cities, infrastructure, and unsuspecting Americans.

Another important role would be played by a group called the *Organización Juventud Chicano de Aztlán* (OJChA), the Aztlán Chicano Youth Organization. OJChA was established to organize the Aztlán movement in the schools and universities of the US. It openly indoctrinated students in the revolutionary cause and prepared them to liberate their people and reestablish Aztlán. The symbol of OJChA was a hawk with outstretched wings bearing a *mecauittle* in one claw and a bomb in the other. Below the hawk was the phrase, "*El Triunfo Por La Fuerza*" (Victory by Force).

Muhammad asked Carlos what a *mecauittle* was and was told it was an ancient, wooden, Aztec broadsword edged with razor-sharp obsidian. The symbol made it clear that OJChA was willing to use whatever means necessary to achieve its goals. As these students graduated they took professional positions throughout the American Southwest to proliferate their agenda. And the Americans...did nothing. Muhammad shook his head. He sometimes worried that there was something in all this he did not yet see. Such madness should long ago have collapsed under its own weight

Like a retrovirus, these activists manipulated the opinions and views of those around them until enough people accepted their viewpoint that policies and then laws could be enacted to protect and bestow civil rights on the Mexicans nationals living in the United States. Many cities had gone as far as to unilaterally declare themselves as sanctuaries for illegal aliens. In these cities the police were impotent to enforce immigration laws. Additionally, many cities deliberately enrolled thousands of illegals in their public assistance programs. Millions of dollars were tied up in medical, educational, and family assistance.

Often these policies resulted in major deficits in city budgets, that in turn, forced cuts in police and fire departments, and forced the closure of emergency rooms and hospitals.

Currently, efforts were under way to oppose safeguards that prevented non-citizens from voting in state and federal elections. If voting rights could be achieved for illegals, OJChA and the PLA could organize millions of Mexicans to vote for Aztlán-friendly candidates and establish a shadow government in the disputed territories. Once the revolution succeeded, these politicians would assume control of the new Chicano nation. Although these strategies had already paid substantial dividends, they'd also taken years to achieve. The Chicanos were growing impatient. They were tired of waiting for their oppressors to give a little here and a little there. They were impatient to take back what they felt was rightfully theirs, and *Hezbollah* was ready to lead the way. The major planned to use many of the same tactics deployed in Israel. Although the Israelis had adopted counter tactics to defend against them, the Americans didn't have the will to do the same.

The Jews in Israel were not like the Americans. Their iron will was forged in conflict and the threat of total destruction. There were still Jews in Israel who bore the tattoos of Nazi concentration camps. They knew what appeasement in the face of a determined enemy produced. Every Israeli citizen was required to serve in the military; every Israeli home had suffered the loss of a loved one in conflicts and wars, and therefore, had a vested interest in victory. As much as Muhammad loathed the Jews, he was a professional soldier and would not permit his hatred to underestimate his enemy.

But, the Americans were different. Weak and undisciplined; they wouldn't have the stomach to do what was necessary. Instead they'd whine and complain about their precious rights. Americans didn't fight back; they organized rallies and concerts, flew cheap plastic flags from their expensive automobiles, and called 911 when they were threatened. Long gone were the days when Americans formed posses to hunt down the criminals that attacked their homes. Instead, today they strip-searched old women and cripples at airports least they offend one group or the other with "racial profiling."

As Muhammad contemplated his enemy, a devious smile spread across his face. Eagerness swelled within him to kill Americans and begin stockpiling the blessings of *Jihad.*

"Pardon me, Major." Muhammad was jolted back to the present by his lieutenant's respectful voice. "Francisco and Carlos have arrived with the regional OJChA representatives. They are waiting in the garden."

The major lifted his head. "Thank you, Sayf. Please remind me of their names again."

"Of course. Their names are Marco Valdez and Maria Cortez. They represent OJChA chapters in Southern California and Arizona. Most of these are located at major universities, including those in San Diego, and Los Angeles, California, and Phoenix, and Tucson, Arizona. This is the most powerful and militant region in the organization. They report directly to the National OJChA Coordinating Council (NOCC) that oversees the entire organization." Sayf had learned over the years to provide the major with succinct reports just prior to his meetings.

"Excellent, Sayf. Thank you for that summarization. Let's not keep our young friends waiting." The major stood up, and the two men walked out towards the garden.

"Ah, Francisco, how are you this morning?" The major said as he warmly greeted his new partner.

"Major, may I present Señorita Maria Cortez and Señor Marco Valdez, Regional Representatives from the National OJChA Coordinating Council.

They flew in this morning from Phoenix, Arizona. Señorita Cortez, Señor Valdez, may I introduce you to Major Muhammad Mahdi Al-Salih, who represents *Hezbollah*."

"Thank you for accepting our invitation to meet. Please, let us sit down. I'm sure you have many questions, and I am eager to get to know you better."

The first to speak was Marco Valdez. He was an engineering student at San Diego State University, and had been a member of OJChA for three years. Even before entering SDSU, Marco was involved in the Chicano struggle. He grew up in Tijuana, Mexico until he was fourteen, and then crossed the border into San Diego to live with his uncle who had illegally entered the United States ten years prior. During the last amnesty program his uncle obtained his green card and then became a US citizen. Nonetheless, he made sure to teach Marco all about the history of Aztlán. On many weekends, Marco rode the bus to Chicano Park, located under the on-ramps of the Coronado Bay Bridge, where community rallies were held. Surrounded by Chicano murals that were painted on the bridge's supporting columns, Marco listened to leaders from the barrio tell stories about the Aztecs and the great civilization they'd built. They also told of how the Europeans came to Mexico and pillaged the riches of his homeland, how they introduced smallpox and other diseases into the Aztec cities that destroyed hundreds of thousands of his ancestors.

Marco learned how the foreigner *gabacho* stole the sacred lands of Aztlán. He knew his destiny lay in helping his people reclaim their lands and rebuild the greatness Mexico once enjoyed. "Major Al-Salih," he said. "We have been briefed by Señor Estrada regarding the impending operation. I want to assure you that OJChA is dedicated to victory and welcomes your assistance. We have been and continue to be supporters of your efforts against Israel. We recognize the Palestinians as our brothers and would very much like for you to convey our sincere prayers for their victory."

The major nodded politely. "I appreciate your sentiments and will indeed convey your thoughts to our Palestinian brothers."

Maria listened in silence. Likewise, she was willing to do whatever was necessary in order to obtain victory. She had grown up in a strongly nationalistic family that instilled in her a fiery pride for her people. She was a Chicana by blood and an American by birth. Both of her parents had come to America legally and became naturalized citizens, but she saw the racism they suffered. Even though they followed the Gringo's rules, they were never accepted. Her father worked all his life in a small, neighborhood grocery store and her mother in a beauty shop. As long as they served the Gringo, they were allowed to enjoy the basics, but nothing more.

Maria was first exposed to OJChA during a rally held in her hometown of Guadalupe. It was then her eyes were opened to the opportunity to establish her own homeland. On that day she had decided that she would be one of its leaders.

"Excuse me, Major," Maria asked. "Once Aztlán is liberated, what will *Hezbollah* expect for its support during the revolution?

"This is an excellent question. If our nations are to survive in this age, people with common values must support one another. We share the common goal of freedom from oppression, and our efforts are mutually beneficial. We look forward to strong trade and political ties with the nation of Aztlán. Once your homeland is free it will immediately become one of the wealthiest nations on earth, and the whole Islamic world will wish to establish a strong relationship with you. We believe that relationship will prove valuable enough."

"Very well; I have one other question," said Maria. "Francisco and Carlos have outlined the role the PLA will play, but I'd like for you to explain your vision for OJChA."

"As history has shown, the way to defeat the United States is on two fronts: military and political. This is the way the North Vietnamese triumphed, and this is also the way we will win."

"But Major," Marco interrupted. "The North Vietnamese suffered over a million causalities in their war. We can't possibly sustain such losses."

"Señor Valdez, I assure you that your concerns are unmerited. The US reaction to our attacks will be nothing like the way they have responded in the past. Let's not forget that these battles will be fought in their own cities and among their own people. When Americans are offended by a dusty third-world nation most cannot even find on a map, Washington is quick to send in the B-52s. But can you actually imagine them carpet bombing Los Angeles?" He chuckled. "No, indeed. The Americans reserve these 'tools of democracy' for others, not for themselves.

"This time they'll find that none of their weapons of mass destruction and terror are useful. As I was saying, our victory lies in the strategy of asymmetrical warfare."

"We'll use their weakness against them and keep them off balance. This is the role that OJChA will play, and it very well could be the most important tactic towards victory."

Major Al-Salih explained that OJChA would accelerate its protests and political activities to create cover for the PLA's attacks. "When people speak out against guerrilla raids," he said. "OJChA will immediately protest and claim racism. The American media loves to see students marching in protest against their government. Perhaps it reminds them of their youth in the 1960s. Who knows? Whatever the reason, it has always proved a powerful image."

"Hezbollah learned these lesson years ago and made sure to organize 'spontaneous' student protests in Palestine whenever they needed to create pressure on Israel. OJChA will use its political contacts to hamstring local police and federal agencies, interfering with their ability to stop the PLA."

"Finally, OJChA will need to broaden their coalition with allies of convenience such as the ACLU, La Raza, and militant eco-terrorist organizations like the Earth Liberation Front (ELF), Animal Liberation Front (ALF) and PETA. OJChA needs to befriend these groups, while keeping them in the dark to the overall plan. By encouraging them to carry out their own attacks, the limited police and federal resources will be brought to the brink of collapse. All the while, the PLA will execute coordinated assaults against vital points of interest and infrastructure. For this to work," the major concluded, "we all must play our parts and remain dedicated to the plan. If you follow through, I promise you that Aztlán will rise and you will be victorious."

Francisco looked around the table, then sprung to his feet, "This is the chance we've been waiting for all our lives. This is the opportunity our fathers and grandfathers sacrificed for. We can achieve what millions of our ancestors only dreamed about. All that is needed is our dedication and willingness to serve to the end.

"If we fuse our resolve we'll go down in history alongside Símon Bolivar and the other great liberators. As the major has said, we all play a crucial role in this operation. If our alliance breaks then we will all be destroyed." Francisco drew a knife from his pocket and slit his forearm, allowing his blood to run down to his wrist. "Here, by my blood, I swear that I will be victorious or die." He passed the knife to Carlos, who followed Francisco's example repeating the same oath.

Then the knife was passed to Maria and Marco and they also entered into the oath in the same fashion. Then the four militants joined hands and watched as their blood flowed together creating a small pool on the table below them.

"We are warriors of Aztlán. Just as our Aztec forefathers entered into blood oaths before battle, so have we. Now that our blood has spilt, let our enemy's blood flow until the streets turn red. *Viva la Raza! Viva Aztlán!*

Chapter 3

A long habit of not thinking a thing wrong, gives it a superficial appearance of being right.
—Thomas Paine

San Diego, California

Mike breathed a sigh of relief. He had seen Rachel off at the airport for her flight to Phoenix and her interview with BioPharm. He'd accompanied her to Nordstrom the night before, witnessing the tortuous process women endured to buy clothes. As far as Mike could tell, helping a woman shop was about as productive as training a cat to fetch. The whole process seemed to be a punishment worthy of one of Dante's rings of hell. *Why do women put themselves through this ordeal?* Mike pondered. *It's so much easier being a guy; all you need is a new shirt and tie and you're done.* If he didn't love spending time with Rachel, no matter where they were, the entire process would have been intolerable. As Rachel searched through dozens of racks full of dresses, she continually muttered to herself, cursing the lighting, the designs, and the misogynist who sized women's clothes.

Every once in a while she'd ask an impossible question like, "Does this color make my hair look too red?" Or the all-time worst question, "This makes me look fat...doesn't it?"

There was no way Mike was going to even think about answering that one. The one enjoyable part of the evening was having dinner after the torment was over. The most unbelievable thing was that Rachel commented on how much fun she'd had and how much she enjoyed shopping. Mike decided to file the experience under the dual categories of "sacrifices made for future bargaining" and "things guys will never, *ever* understand about women."

****

That afternoon Mike waited in the teeming terminal for Rachel. Once he would have been able to greet her at the gate, sparing her the lonely walk down the terminal. But ever since 9/11 those days were gone. On his way to the airport he stopped at a florist shop to get some flowers for Rachel. If the interview went well, the flowers would be a bonus. On the other hand, if she arrived disappointed, a bouquet would go a long way towards helping her feel better.

While waiting, he watched a few newly graduated Marines mill around the airport before their flights. He couldn't help but notice how well they comported themselves. While other eighteen-year-old kids acted like a bunch of delinquents, twelve weeks of boot camp had instilled these new Marines with a level of discipline and self-confidence that permeated the air around them.

Mike understood this would wear off as the new privates readjusted to the world outside of MCRD, but for now, the voices of their drill instructors still echoed in their ears making them walk straighter and sit taller than everyone else around them. Because Mike had lost his chance to serve, he went out of his way to always congratulate the Marines he met in the airport and thank them for their service. Often, the privates were caught off guard by the compliment and wouldn't know what to say. Mike simply shook their hands and congratulated them on graduating boot camp, then walked off. For most of these guys, finishing boot camp was the greatest accomplishment of their young lives, and Mike wanted them to know that others both recognized and appreciated their achievement.

As Mike continued to search the arriving passengers, Rachel came into view, and he immediately knew the interview had gone well. Rachel's beaming smile set her apart from the others around her, and she nearly skipped as she waived to Mike. Mike greeted her with an embrace and kiss.

"Well, it looks like you have good news," Mike said as he gave her the flowers. "I'm assuming the interview was a success?"

"Oh, thank you. They're beautiful." Rachel said as she inhaled the sweet aroma of the flowers. "Yes, everything went great. Dr. Yuan was very kind, and we hit it off right away. He's going to hold a spot for me on his research team, and he even spoke about the possibility of a full-time position as soon as I graduate."

"Fantastic! I knew you'd do great. What did you think about BioPharm?"

"I loved it. It's a first-class facility and they're doing some very advanced work. If you don't own BioPharm stock, you might want to think about it. I saw some projects they're working on that are really cutting edge."

Rachel didn't bring luggage on her short trip, so they walked straight to the car. After leaving Lindbergh Field, Mike drove south down Harbor Drive along San Diego Bay. It was just turning to dusk, and the lights of the city cast a colorful reflection off the placid water. Mike loved the Embarcadero area, especially being able to look across the bay and see which aircraft carriers were docked at North Island. Mike made a left and merged into traffic going north on I-5, towards Rachel's apartment.

With the success of the BioPharm interview, Mike could now set plans in action, starting with giving his notice at work and letting his landlord know he'd be moving out of the house. As soon as he started asking friends if they had any interest in picking up his lease, he realized finding someone to pick up his lease wouldn't be a problem.

After dropping Rachel off Mike called Arrow and told him the good news. Now he was one hundred percent and eager to get the ball rolling. Arrow explained that he wanted the group, which included Cowboy, Ghost, Ethan, and himself to fly over to Phoenix the first part of next week.

Arrow had arranged a meeting at the building site with the contractor and wanted to tour the site with the management team. Mike agreed, and they decided to meet Sunday evening.

La Jolla, California

On his way to meet Rachel for lunch at UCSD, Mike heard the low, rhythmic thud of a drumbeat and what had to be a chant broadcast over a bullhorn. No doubt it was a rally about something. Protesting had become part of the modern university experience. Though Mike suspected that the subject of a campus protest was often irrelevant to the experience for the participants, he was interested to find out what the cause *du jour* was. Not that he cared, but he had to admit, sometimes these groups were pretty creative, just as long as it wasn't those idiotic PETA knuckleheads. He didn't have much sympathy for them. As he thought about it he remembered a bumper sticker he'd once seen: *Vegetarian: an ancient Indian word for lousy hunter.* Every time he thought of that sticker, it brought a smile to his face.

As Mike entered the main quad he saw the gathered protestors and began listening to the speaker.

"...We do not acknowledge unreliable frontiers on the bronze continent. Brotherhood unities us, and love for our brothers makes us a people whose time has come and whose struggles against the foreigner *gabacho* who exploits our resources and destroys our culture. With our heart in our hands and our hands in the soil, we declare the independence of our *Chicano* nation.

"We are a bronze people with a bronze culture. Before the world, before all of North America, before all our brothers in the bronze continent, we are a nation; we are a union of free pueblos, and we are *Aztlán*!"

The assembled protesters roared in approval, raising their fists in defiance while chanting *Aztlán, Aztlán, Aztlán*! The speaker joined in, using his bullhorn to ensure everyone on campus would hear, and began to speak once more.

"Listen to me, my Chicano brothers and sisters. We have lived too long under the tyranny and racism of the Gringos. They stole our beloved land, and they endeavor to destroy our culture. What they are doing is no different from what the Serbs tried to do to the Bosnians. But, will anyone come to our aid and help us prevent cultural genocide? No! Therefore we must rise up and take back all that has been stolen from us. Now, is our time; we are strong and grow stronger every day. The time is fast approaching when Chicanos will drive the exploiters out of our communities, our pueblos, and our lands. We will fight for and defend the lands that are rightfully ours. For the young there will no longer be acts of juvenile frustration, but revolution!"

Mike continued to walk towards the library while listening to the speaker, paying half attention to what was being said and half to where he was walking. As he moved past the assembled crowd he accidentally rear-end a girl who was chanting, "*La Raza, La Raza*!" As they collided the girl snapped around and glared at Mike with a look of unqualified contempt.

"Watch where you're walking *pendejo*!" shouted the girl.

"Take it easy, it was an accident." Mike apologized as he continued to weave through the crowd.

Mike was surprised by the co-ed's seething rebuke. It wasn't so much what she said; *pendejo* was basically the equivalent of "stupid." It was the absolute revulsion in her voice. Mike was especially bewildered that another Mexican-American would confront him in that manner. As he continued to pass by the crowd, he noticed Rachel leaning up against a large decorative planter. He waved and called out her name. Once she'd recognized him, she closed her book and walked over. Rachel wore a light-colored, cotton sundress and sandals. Instead of the ubiquitous daypack that most undergrads carried, Rachel had adopted a more refined bag that was a combination of a satchel and a soft-sided briefcase. Evidently, this was the fashionable carryall for grad students.

"Good to see you, Babe. You've got quite the protest going on here. I always though UCSD was more sophisticated, and SDSU was the home of the extremists." Mike commented.

"Tell me about it. OJChA is in charge of this rally, I don't recall the exact name of the organization, but its some kind of Chicano group that believes the US stole California. They've been gaining strength over the past couple years, and they tend to coordinate with other local chapters to really make an impression. What's your take on all this Chicano Nationalism?"

"I'm aware of OJChA, and frankly, I've never understood their position. Growing up I never questioned being an American or the blessings this country offers. Although my Mexican heritage has always been a point of pride for me, the idea that the Southwest was stolen and is occupied by the United States has always seemed bizarre. I've never been able to understand how they expect the United States to simply hand over the Southwest and say, 'Sorry, can't we all just get along?'"

Rachel and Mike ate a quick lunch before Mike needed to return to his office. Even though he had submitted his two-week's notice, he was still involved with a crucial project, and it required his full attention. On the drive back, Mike continued to reflect on the OJChA rally and particularly on the militant nature of the speaker. Although he had heard rumblings about Chicano nationalism over the years, they seemed more like folklore in nature and never so revolutionary. Organizations like *La Raza* had been extremely vocal, and in some cases, persuasive in getting laws enacted protecting illegal aliens in California.

One of their recent campaigns was to dissuade the use of the term "*illegal alien*" in public discourse. They claimed the term disparaged Mexican immigrants and encouraged racism.

As far as Mike was concerned this was nothing more than Orwellian "newspeak," and he wasn't going to try to appease the radicals by adopting it. Furthermore, the whole idea personally offended him. The illegals were just that, *illegal*. They didn't immigrate to this country the way his grandparents did. They broke the law and entered without documentation. To characterize them as immigrants simply dishonored the sacrifices made by those that came to this country legally.

There was no ignoring the fact that Mexico was a disaster, and America was a tempting alternative. But, there were procedures in place to allow immigration and ensure those who did come to this country would be afforded every opportunity available. In Mike's opinion, the whole contention that the US should have open borders was hypocritical. He'd been to Mexico several times and knew that the Mexican government was very protective of its border with Guatemala. So the idea that it was fine for Mexico to protect its southern border, while it was racist for the US to do the same, was hypocritical at best.

But this wasn't simply an issue about immigration. These people wanted to forcibly take back five states, including California. Regardless of his current opinion of California, it was still one of the largest states in the Union and had the seventh-largest economy in the world. There was no way the United States would allow that to happen. At least he hoped not.

Fox News Channel

"This is a Fox News Alert. Fox News has learned that Iran's Revolutionary Governing Council has announced it has built several nuclear weapons and intends to deploy them on *Shehab-4* intermediate range ballistic missiles, and is, in their own words, '...taking its rightful place among the nuclear armed nations of the world.'

"Defense sources tell Fox News that the *Shehab-4* is a modified *Taep'o-dong-1*, three-stage missile manufactured in North Korea with a range capable of reaching Israel to the west and Afghanistan to the east.

"Global response has been both strong and diverse. In the Islamic world, Iran is being cheered and venerated for its willingness to stand up to the United States and Israel. Until this recent announcement, Pakistan was the only Islamic nation that openly possessed nuclear weapons. But due to its close ties to the United States, Pakistan has been largely marginalized by other Islamic nations.

"Iran's announcement was met with somber warnings from Washington and Jerusalem. Sources report that back-channel diplomatic messages have been sent to Tehran warning against nuclear proliferation and saber rattling. Sources in Jerusalem indicate Israel may deploy two Dolphin class diesel-electric submarines to stations within striking distance of Iran. These German-built submarines are extremely quiet and are suspected of carrying what defense department officials call the 'Popeye Turbo' Sea Launched Cruise Missile (SLCM) capable of carrying a two hundred kiloton nuclear warhead.

"In May of 2000, Israel successfully carried out test launches of these weapons off the coast of Sri Lanka, hitting their targets at a range of 1,500km (930 statue miles). Pentagon sources confirm the USS *Kittyhawk* (CV-63) battle group, based in Yokosuka, Japan, is en route to the North Arabian Sea. Sources tell Fox News the battle group has a heavy anti-submarine warfare (ASW) component and will probably be stationed near the Straits of Hormuz in an attempt to dissuade unilateral action by Israel. We'll keep you up-to-date on news as it breaks. This has been a Fox News alert."

Queen Creek, Arizona

Mike, Arrow, Cowboy, Ghost, and Josh had reservations on a 7:00 a.m. Southwest flight to Phoenix. Although dealing with the security measures at the airport was a major hassle, the fact that the flight was only an hour and cost about the same as driving, made it worthwhile.

Once the team landed in Phoenix, they rented a car and took Interstate 10 towards Tucson, then exited on Riggs Road and continued east to Power Road which took them straight to the construction site.

The team had a meeting scheduled for 10:00 a.m. with the architect and contractor in charge of the project. As they arrived Arrow was pleased to see work had already begun.

"Good morning, Mr. Johnson. Welcome to Phoenix. I'm Robert Gaulden of Gaulden & Associates, and this is Jim Kellerman from Wabash Construction."

Arrow greeted the two men, and then introduced the rest of the team. After everyone was introduced, the group followed Jim to a trailer that served as a temporary office during construction. Inside, blueprints for the project were laid out for the presentation. On the walls were complicated charts that indicated when each part of the project began and which subcontractor would be involved.

"Why don't y'all gather around the table, and I'll go over the plans with you." Robert suggested. "Afterwards we'll go outside and walk the site so you can get a better perspective."

Pointing to the blueprints, the architect started his presentation. "This is where you drove onto the site. What we've planned for the entrance is a driveway separated by a landscaped island leading to a security point here." He pointed at a spot about 1/8 of a mile onto the property. "This whole entryway will be lit by street lamps and provide a very professional and welcoming approach to the academy. The main building will be located here. As we've discussed, it will be built in a modified ranch style and will include administrative, classroom, retail, and computer space." The architect continued to point out all the different areas of the project, including the CQC houses and ranges. After the presentation was finished the group donned hardhats and followed Jim outside. Everyone was impressed with the overall size of the site and how natural and manmade terrain features were incorporated into the landscaping to separate the areas, allowing separate groups to use the facilities without interfering with each other. There would be two CQC houses constructed, a single and a four story. A unique design feature allowed the interior walls to be modular. The staff would be able to easily change the layout of the rooms to replicate offices, warehouses, apartments, or whatever the training scenario required.

Additionally, cameras in armored housings would be installed in the walls so student movements could be recorded on video for post-action critique. Finally, the group drove out to where the one-thousand-yard range would be constructed.

In addition to precision rifle training, this range would be the new home for the local .50-caliber shooting club and hopefully the future site of regional .50-caliber championships. California had recently banned all .50-caliber rifles, so competitions were forced to hold their events outside the state on BLM land. Direction Action Academy would be one of the only operations in the West to have a dedicated range for the purpose.

By mid morning the tour was completed, and the weather was already starting to get uncomfortably hot, so the group went in search of a local restaurant. Currently, there were very few stores or restaurants close to the site, but as they drove towards town the contractor pointed out farmland that had been purchased and re-zoned for a variety of strip malls, hotels, and other commercial sites. Soon the group arrived at a Mexican restaurant where they got a table and ordered.

"So, what do you guys think?" asked Arrow.

"I'm very impressed," Cowboy replied. "I had a general idea of what the facility would look like, based on our conversations, but now I have a much clearer image of how it'll come together. I'm excited. I've got to tell you, Arrow—I've trained at a lot of military schools around the country, and what I see here exceeds anything I expected." He leaned back in his chair. "Guys, I honestly believe this is going to become the premiere training facility in the country. It'll draw both civilian and police groups."

"That's the plan." Arrow assured his team. "You'll also notice there's enough land for future expansion. For instance, I'd like to add a rappelling tower between the main building and the long range."

Mike looked over at Jim Kellerman. "How long do you expect construction to last?"

"We're planning on five months before you're able to move-in," said Kellerman. "With most of the venues being ranges and open area, it'll really cut down on the amount of construction. Plus, here in Arizona we don't have many work delays, such as rain, so construction moves fast. Since the grading is already done we'll go vertical, meaning you'll see walls in place, by next week."

After lunch Jim and Robert headed back to the site, and the team drove over to city hall for meetings with the chief of police and a city council member. One of the first projects Mike had on his list was to convince the local police departments to use the academy for training and qualification. Currently, the local departments used the sheriff's facilities on the other side of the valley. They could shoot there, but no advanced courses were offered.

Chief Dan Meadows was a black man whose large build testified of his bodybuilding past. He'd been a police officer in Phoenix for fifteen years before transferring to Mesa's department for another ten years. As Queen Creek grew from a small farming town into a popular suburb of Phoenix it established its own police department, with Meadows as its first chief of police.

Working in Phoenix so long, allowed Dan to developed excellent contacts with both local and federal agencies, which brought a wide range of experience and connections to the fledgling force.

After listening to Mike's brief presentation, the chief committed his support, but cautioned that the change in training venues would need to be approved by the city council. Nevertheless, he believed the council members would understand the advantages offered by the academy and be impressed with the program. The east valley was growing at an exponential rate. Mesa had recently surpassed Philadelphia in population, and the surrounding cities were receiving thousands of new residents every month. Most were refugees from California, escaping the high taxes and governmental regulations. With the increase in population the east valley police departments wanted to improve training and establish special operations teams to meet the demands the growth demanded.

He also committed to coordinating meetings with his counterparts in Mesa, Chandler, Gilbert, and Apache Junction, all of whom trained at the sheriff's facility. As the team left the meeting, Mike felt confident Chief Meadows would prove to be a valuable resource and an excellent client.

"Our next appointment is with Councilwoman Alejandra Gutierrez," Arrow remarked checking his PDA. "What we want to do is simply introduce ourselves and make sure she feels in the loop. Chief Meadows will need her support with the council vote."

The team took the stairs up to the second floor and followed the hallway down to office #245. On the door was painted: "Councilwoman Alejandra Gutierrez (D)." Arrow entered the office and approached the receptionist. "Good afternoon, my name is Taylor Johnson. My associates and I have a 2:00 p.m. meeting with the councilwoman."

The young woman checked her agenda and then made a quick note next to the appointment. "Yes, Mr. Johnson. Please have a seat and I'll let the councilwoman know that you've arrived."

The councilwoman's office was comfortably decorated with an overstuffed couch along one wall and several chairs surrounding a coffee table. Mike selected a chair and shuffled though a stack of magazines on the table. He was surprised to see the official journal of *La Raza* and *Mestizo* among the publications. *Those are some pretty radical magazines for an elected official to have in her office,* Mike thought to himself. He picked up the copy of *Mestizo* and read the titles of the featured articles: "Palestinian Holocaust in Israel," "Trouble in Gringolandia," and "France Accuses the US of Endangering the World."

"What are you looking at, Mike?" Arrow asked.

"Are you familiar with these magazines?" Mike said as he passed the periodical to Arrow.

"No. I've never seen it before. Why?"

Just as Mike began answering Arrow's question the receptionist approached the group and announced the councilwoman was ready to receive them. "We'll talk about it later," Mike said as he replaced the magazine and stood up.

The men were escorted past the reception desk and down a short hallway. The young lady lightly knocked on a door and then opened it. "Councilwoman Gutierrez, may I present Mr. Taylor Johnson and his associates."

The councilwoman approached Taylor and shook his hand. "Mr. Johnson, I'm pleased to meet you. Please come in and have a seat."

"Councilwoman Gutierrez, I'd like to introduce my associates: Tom South, Ethan Biggs, Josh Eckman, and Mike West." The councilwoman shook hands with each man before returning to her desk and sitting down.

"Gentleman, I understand that you're building a shooting range off Power Road."

"Actually, it'll be a firearms academy. The difference is it will incorporate instruction on a variety of shooting techniques and disciplines. The facility will be opened to the general public as well as local police." Taylor remarked.

"I see. How may I assist you?" asked Gutierrez.

"We just finished a meeting with Chief Meadows where we presented a proposal that would allow the police department to use our academy for training and certification. Currently, they train at the sheriff's range on the other side of town, which is a two-hour drive and does not offer the advanced instruction we'll provide. We were told that in order for the department to accept our offer, the council would have to approve the deal. We're hoping for your support."

"When you refer to advanced instruction; what exactly would that include?" asked the councilwoman.

"I'll let Mr. South, my director of training, answer that question." Arrow replied.

"That's an excellent question, Councilwoman. As you are aware the East Valley is growing rapidly. The majority of your new residents are arriving from outside the state, which poses unique challenges that'll need to be met by the police. Direct Action Academy will provide instruction for SWAT teams and urban conflict. We're constructing close-quarters combat houses that will allow your police to learn proper techniques that will help them successfully deal with hostage and barricade situations."

"Close-quarters combat? That sounds pretty aggressive," the councilwoman remarked in an unpleasant tone. "I don't know how comfortable I am with the idea of police acting like a military force."

"Please excuse my choice of words. I've spent the last twelve years in the Marine Corps, and that's the term we used. As you are aware, sometimes events require the police to enter a building to rescue a hostage or confront a threat. The methods we teach allow them to accomplish this with greater safety, less damage to property, and better security for the public. These techniques require a high degree of coordination, teamwork, and training in specially constructed buildings. Currently, this level of instruction isn't offered at the sheriff's range, so your department is forced to send officers out of town. As you know, this is both expensive and time consuming. We'll be able to fulfill these needs at a savings and ensure your police remain in the community where they're most needed." Cowboy explained.

"I see. I assume you have information you can leave with me."

"Of course," Arrow handed a folder to the councilwoman. "This portfolio outlines the services the academy will offer and includes biographies of our principle directors."

As the conversation continued, Mike discreetly scanned the councilwoman's office and noticed that the US, Arizona, and Mexico flags were prominently displayed behind her desk. She also had a wall of pictures and certificates celebrating her political connections and professional achievements. Mike noticed one picture featuring her with former President Clinton, another with House Minority Leader Paula Alberti, and others featuring her with influential Mexican politicians. But most striking was a map of Mexico that included the US Southwest labeled Aztlán.

"I see you've noticed my picture with Presidente Baranca," Gutierrez said, startling Mike and grabbing his attention.

"Oh, excuse me, Councilwoman. I apologize. Your collection is very impressive. I see you are acquainted with many Mexican politicians."

"Yes, I am. Do you follow Mexican politics?"

"A little; my maternal grandparents were from Sonora, so I've always taken interest in Mexico."

"So, you're part Mexican. Do you speak Spanish?"

"*Si, hablo Español*," Mike replied

"Well, Mr. West, I'm sure we have a lot in common. I work closely with the immigrant community in the valley, assisting them and ensuring they receive the support they're entitled to from our local agencies. You know, I sponsored the city's guest-worker program. Maybe we can arrange to have your contractor hire some immigrants to work on your academy."

"I wouldn't feel comfortable speaking on behalf of Wabash Construction. I'm not familiar with Arizona labor laws, but I'm sure they'd be open to all options," Mike responded.

"Very good, gentlemen, thank you for your time. I'll look over this information and hopefully will be able to work together. If I have any questions I'll have my assistant contact you."

"We appreciate your time, Councilwoman. Please feel fee to contact me." Arrow rose out of his chair and shook hands with the councilwoman. Gutierrez escorted the men to the door and presented her hand to Mike. "*Adios, Señor West, fue un placer conocerle.*"

"It was a pleasure to meet you as well." Mike politely answered.

The group walked down the stairs and then out to their car. The day had gone by quickly, and they needed to start heading back to the airport for their return flight. As they drove towards Interstate 60 the conversation revolved around how the meetings had gone and individual questions relating to the construction schedule.

"So Mike, what was your impression of Councilwoman Gutierrez?" Arrow asked.

"I'm glad you asked. Remember those magazines I pointed out to you in her office?"

"Yeah, what about them?"

"One of them was an official publication from *La Raza,* and the other was *Mestizo*. Both groups are militant Mexican organizations that support the return of the southwest to Mexico. For years these groups have been working to bring illegal aliens across the border in an attempt to reoccupy lands they claim were stolen from Mexico."

"I know illegal immigration is a major problem," Ethan remarked. "Heck, I see them hanging out in front of the Home Depot every morning. But, I've never heard of plans to retake California and Arizona."

"Listen, guys; this movement has been in existence for decades and has recently gathered a lot of momentum. Now that Hispanics are the largest minority in the United States and have achieved majority status in California, they're wielding a lot of political power. You've all seen the news reports detailing how all the political parties are looking for ways to get the Hispanic vote. Sacramento wants to allow illegals to have driver's licenses. If that happens they'll be able to vote in both state and federal elections. Imagine the difference millions of aliens would make at the ballot box. Don't misunderstand what I'm saying; as you all know I'm half Mexican, and I love that part of my heritage, but this is an attempt at subverting US sovereignty."

"Do you really think illegal aliens can take control of the entire Southwest?" Cowboy asked in a dubious tone. "That seems a little far-fetched to me. After all, this country fought a civil war to prevent the south from seceding in the 1800s. Washington would never allow that."

"Do I think the Mexican army will march across the border and raise their flag above the Capital in Sacramento? Of course not. But, these groups have gained a lot of political power over the last decade, and they're organized.

"Did you notice the map Gutierrez had in her office? It showed the southwestern US as a part of Mexico. It was labeled Aztlán, the name these groups claim the southwest was called before it was ceded to the US. Gutierrez is a believer, and she's using her position to help promote the agenda.

"What's more, it seems she is well connected with Mexican politicians. I don't know of any official support these groups get from Mexico City, but I do know Mexico has never openly come out against them.

"I liken illegal immigration to a pressure valve. There's no way Mexico could deal with ten to twelve million additional jobless citizens on their streets. They can barely deal with the problems they have now. If we sealed our southern border and deported every illegal back to Mexico, that country would explode, and we'd have anarchy on over a thousand miles of southern border.

"No, Mexico wants as many of their people in this country as possible, and they want them to come as fast as possible, which means illegally. Here's another reason why it's in their best interest to flood illegals across the border. Mexicans who work in the US send billions of dollars back to Mexico every year. Matter-of-fact, that revenue stream is second only to Mexico's petroleum profits."

"I had no idea Mexico was making that much money from aliens." Ethan remarked in near disbelief. "You know, it shouldn't surprise me that the media won't report the facts; they're so liberal they won't even say illegal alien anymore. I believe the term they use is "*undocumented immigrant.*"

"I don't know if you noticed, but the councilwoman used the newest phrase they're trying to mainstream, *guest worker*. It's a much warmer term, but in the end it's simply another euphemism," Mike added.

"If these groups are so radical and openly threaten to take over the US, how does an elected official get away with overtly supporting them?" Arrow asked.

"Actually, it's pretty simple. America has been so conditioned by multiculturalism and political correctness that no one will question a minority about her cultural extremism. If people do, they're immediately labeled racists and openly attacked. I'm the first to admit that someone's ethnic history is an important part of their life, but even though I'm half Mexican, I'm one-hundred-percent American, and nothing will ever make me turn against my country."

Hermosillo, Mexico

Carlos had spent the last few weeks preparing for operations against targets in California and Arizona. According to the new chain of command, his task was to select targets, assign operatives, and then coordinate with Lieutenant Sayf, who would approve the resources needed to run the mission. The strategy they developed would be executed in two phases. The first component was a series of operations designed to strain police and firefighters until they were besieged and unable to meet the demands placed on them. The second would be direct attacks against economic objectives.

The goal of the strategy was to destroy the public's confidence in their government, leading to civil unrest and a general breakdown of society. Then Aztlán sympathizers, already in local leadership positions, would step in and wrest control of state and local governments, declare independence, and invite the Mexican army into their states as peacekeepers.

Marco and Maria returned home and presented the National OJChA Coordinating Council (NCOC) with an outline of what was now called *Operation Macahuittle.* At first the NOCC was hesitant. But when they saw proof that the money Hamas had promised was real, the council recognized the unique opportunity and approved the measure. OJChA would support the PLA in the preliminary phase, and then take a leading role in the secondary. Before leaving Hermosillo, a communications protocol was established between the PLA and OJChA.

In all communications, PLA headquarters would be called *El Zocalo*, which was the name of the main square in Mexico City. Francisco's codename would be known as Siren; Carlos would be referred to as Knife.

The major would be called Bi-plane, and Sayf, Bicycle. Marcos chose the codename Flag, and Maria's codename was Rabbit.

All communications would be conducted via a 2,048-bit encrypted e-mail program developed for Syria by a renegade Russian crypto-analyst who sold his talents after the break-up of the Soviet Union. To ensure the analyst wouldn't sell the same software to other clients, Syrian Internal Security agents executed him when his task was complete.

Although it would have been easier to simply issue satellite phones similar to the one the major used to communicate with Damascus, there was no need to risk sensitive equipment being discovered by the authorities. While, students with encrypted satellite phones might raise questions, it was perfectly natural for students to use the Internet. The encryption program invisibly embedded itself in the computer's word processing program. A series of random keystrokes activated the program allowing the user to easily send and receive messages anywhere. As a measure of last resort, the program also included a self-destruct command that could completely destroy all data on the hard drive within thirty seconds.

As Carlos continued to work on the details of a contingency plan, he was startled by a knock at his door. Carlos raised he head and noticed Sayf walking in.

"Señor Ochoa," said the lieutenant, "may I come in?"

"Yes. Of course, have a seat."

Sayf dropped into a chair. "I met with the major this morning," he said, "and he approved Operation *Aztec Wind*. The equipment has been ordered and should arrive in a week. The funds you requested have been transferred into your account. You can begin executing the plan at your convenience."

Carlos felt his heart swell. After so many years of empty rhetoric and wishful plans, it was all moving so quickly! Moslems or not, these newcomers were a gift from God.

He refrained from leaping to his feet and grabbing the reticent Arab's hand. "Thank you, Lieutenant Sayf! This is such good news. We will continue without delay."

Sayf rose and moved toward the door. Then looked over his shoulder and added, "I have several errands to attend to, so I cannot stay to chat. I just wanted you to hear the news as quickly as possible. You and your people have done excellent work."

Carlos followed him to the door. "I am very glad that you and the major are pleased. I will keep you both fully briefed as the mission unfolds."

"I am sure you will."

Carlos returned to his desk and pumped his fist in a subdued celebration. *Operation Aztec Wind*, he thought, *would be a wind that would blow the Norte Americanos out of Aztlán forever*.

Operation Aztec Wind targeted housing tracts in California and Arizona. The explosion of new homes was a chief aggravation to the PLA. To them, the similarities between Israeli settlements in the West Bank and new housing tracts across Alta California and Aztlán were unmistakable.

These houses were for wealthy *Norte Americanos*, not Chicanos, and were part of an obvious strategy to displace more Hispanics from their homeland. Even more troublesome was that huge tracts of rich farmland were being destroyed to build these homes, farmland that had been planted and harvested by Chicanos for generations, land that provided jobs and stability to the people of Aztlán, as it had for centuries. There was a spiritual connection between the people and the land that couldn't be underestimated. The ability to enjoy the fruits of your labors year after year, generation after generation, was what the Aztlán culture was founded upon.

Of course, Hispanics were employed in the construction industry, but this was temporary and empty labor. Once the houses were completed and the gringos moved in, the workers who labored to build these *bourgeois* dwellings would be ostracized unless they were invited back for additional backbreaking work such as landscaping.

The PLA operation called for coordinated probing attacks on several housing developments in San Diego and rural Phoenix. These two areas were selected because they both had booming housing markets and were large media markets, so the impact of the raids would be broadcast across the entire Southwest region. PLA operatives in both cities would carry out the attacks using time-delayed incendiary devices provided by the Syrians. The devices were US military AN M14 TH3 thermite grenades with modified fuses that would allow forty-five minutes before ignition. The grenades had been captured on battlefields across the Middle East and sanitized of any markings that would identify them as US issue. Multiple targets would be attacked in each area of operation to create maximum damage and to strain the local fire departments' ability to react. The saboteurs would work in teams of three and withdraw to Mexico after the devices were planted. Due to the cell structure of the PLA, no cell had direct connection with another. The groups in California had no idea that similar actions were being taken in Arizona and *vice a versa*, and none of them could lead investigators to upper leadership.

Each cell leader monitored the classified section of the local Hispanic newspapers for an innocuously coded message that prompted them to send an e-mail to a specific address. The return message was routed through several international hubs before reaching its recipient.

In a worst-case scenario where authorities intercepted the e-mail, the message would be traced back to an invalid address, and the trail would dead end. Now that *Aztec Wind* had been green lighted, Carlos needed to start writing warning orders for his regional commanders. The orders instructed the commanders to contact the cells selected for the missions and begin training evolutions. Once the incendiary devices arrived in Hermosillo, they'd be transported via PLA networks to Tijuana and Nogales where they'd be distributed via the local command structure to the cells involved in the operations.

Queen Creek, Arizona

It was just before 6:00 a.m., and Tim Sanders was opening up the work site. Today would be busy; the schedule called for pouring foundations for the main building and several other locations around the academy. All the plumbing and power conduit leads were in place and the rebar tied off in preparation for today's work. From now on, the appearance of the site would change rapidly. This was the part of the job Tim always looked forward to. Tim had worked in the construction business for almost twelve years, and this was the biggest project on which he had been the foreman.

He'd learned everything he knew from his father, who had worked construction most of his life. His father began his career in the Navy as a Sea Bee, where he was taught not only the science of construction, but also the art of finishing projects under pressure. After leaving the Navy he continued to work in construction until his death five years ago from a heart attack. Tim admired the way his father could juggle different subs at the same time to get work done and meet deadlines. A good foreman had to be familiar with every discipline used on a project, whether it was framing, wiring, plumbing, laying tile, roofing, or concrete. He had to understand the building codes and ensure everything was done properly. If he didn't, a disreputable sub might try to cut a corner to save a little money. But, the most important skill a successful foreman had to master was how to properly manage the workers who had a well-deserved reputation of being hard to handle. As his father always said,

"There's a fine line between being a good guy and a tough guy. Knowing when to cross the line makes all the difference."

As Tim was unlocking the on-site generators a truck drove onto the site loaded with men. Tim was expecting workers to begin showing up, so he didn't pay too much attention to the group as they dismounted the truck and began to mill around. As he was finishing, a man walked up and began unfolding a piece of paper.

"Excuse me, I'm looking for Tim Sanders, is that you?"

"Yeah, that's me. Are you from Roadrunner cement?"

"No. My name is Juan Moreno. I'm from the East Valley guest worker project. I have twelve day laborers I was told to deliver to this site."

Tim lifted his hard hat and scratched his head. "I didn't order any workers. Who sent you?"

Juan handed the foreman the sheet of paper, "This work order says Councilwoman Gutierrez requested twelve men be delivered here, this morning."

Tim looked over the work order and saw that indeed the order had originated from the councilwoman's office, but he didn't know anything about twelve additional men, and nothing had been cleared with him. "I don't know anything about this, Mr. Moreno."

Moreno looked unhappy and stubborn. Tim grimaced; it was too early in the day for this sort of thing.

"Tell you what," he said. "I need to call the general contractor and find out what's going on. Why don't you wait here with your guys, and I'll make a call and work this out."

As Juan began walking back towards his truck, Tim took a closer look at the men that had arrived and noticed they were all speaking Spanish and didn't have the normal tools most construction workers brought with them from one work site to another. Tim pulled his cell phone out of its pouch and keyed in Jim Kellerman's number. The line rang a couple times and then was answered.

"This is Jim."

"Good morning, Jim, this is Tim at the academy work site. I have a question for you."

"What's up, Tim?"

"Well, a truckload of men from the East Valley Guest Worker Project just showed up with a work order for this site signed by a Councilwoman

Alejandra Gutierrez. I wasn't told about it, and I didn't approve any additional labor. Do you know what's going on?"

"I'm just as much in the dark about this as you are. This is the first I've heard about it, and I certainly didn't approve it," Jim explained with a tone of disbelief in his voice.

"I don't know if you're aware of this guest worker project, but it's a organization that helps mostly illegal aliens find jobs around the valley." Tim said. "As you know, this is a union project, and I can't allow non-union labor to just show up, not to mention the legality issues. If you don't object, I'm sending these guys back where they came from."

"I don't have any problem with that. Just explain that there must have been a mistake, and you can't accept the men. By the way, can you fax me a copy of that work order?"

"No problem. I'll shoot it over to you as soon as I break the news to these guys." As Tim began walking back towards the assembled men he thought about the trouble the local union would make for him and Wabash Construction if he allowed a bunch of non-union guys on the site. Their agreement with the union made it very clear whom they could use and the penalties associated with non-compliance.

Tim approached Moreno, who was standing beside his truck. "Mr. Moreno, I just spoke with the General Contractor, and he didn't request these men. This is a union project, and I can't allow non-union workers on site. I'm afraid you're going to have to return these men to your office. I'm sorry you had to come all the way out here, but that's the way it'll have to be."

To Tim's surprise, Moreno made no argument. "I understand. You'll need to sign this form indicating that you rejected the men." Juan pointed out the area on the form and handed Tim a pen.

Tim signed the form and returned the pen. Moreno shouted out some instructions to the gathered men, and they began climbing back into the truck. As the truck began to turn around, another arrived. This one had a sign on the door that read Roadrunner Concrete. Tim was happy to see the right guys had shown up and hoped the rest of the day would go as planned.

Oceanside, California

Arrow and a representative from the moving company in charge of his move to Arizona were meeting. As they were working out final details Arrow's cell phone rang. Arrow picked up his phone and read the caller I.D.; it read Wabash Construction.

"Excuse me; I'll need to take this call," he told the sales rep as he opened his phone.

"Hello."

"Mr. Johnson, this is Jim Kellerman in Phoenix. Do you have a minute?"

"I'm in a meeting but I can spare a minute. What's up?"

"Unfortunately, I've got some bad news concerning the project."

"Oh? Hold on a second." Arrow looked over at the salesman and explained he'd need to take this call and asked if they were done. The salesman replied everything was in order, and if there were any additional questions he'd call. After walking the man to the door Arrow returned to Jim's call.

"Okay, Jim. You've got my undivided attention. What's going on?

"I was just notified that, pending a public hearing, one of our building permits has been temporarily revoked. Unfortunately, we'll have to stop construction until it's reissued."

"What? How did this happen?" Arrow tried to keep anger out of his voice. "I thought we had all the permits we needed."

"We're still putting the pieces together. Before I tell you what I think is going on, let me ask you a quick question. After our meeting last week, did you meet with a Councilwoman Gutierrez?"

"Yes. We met with Chief Meadows and then spent a few minutes with the councilwoman. Why?"

"During your meeting, did you grant her permission to send workers to the site?"

"No. She talked about a guest worker project and asked if we'd be interested in helping out. But I didn't give her permission. Matter of fact, when she asked us, Mike made it clear that we couldn't speak on your behalf. Why, what happened?"

"Well, it turns out she sent about a dozen men over to the site a couple days ago. Since we're using union labor we can't have non-union workers on site, so we sent them back. Evidently, the word got back to Gutierrez, and now she's pulled one of the permits. She's challenging the environmental impact study, questioning the impact of lead on the land."

"Lead?"

"Yeah, you know, lead bullets?"

"*Aw, shit.* Jim you've got to be kidding me. A top-rated environmental engineering firm did that impact study. All we need to do is have them present the analysis data, and it'll show there's no threat to the environment. It sounds to me like she's just ticked-off that we're not supporting her 'guest worker' program, and she's decided to piss in our cereal bowl."

"I agree. I've already contacted the engineering firm and informed them they'll need to send a representative to the next council meeting to present the study data."

"I've also notified our attorney. He told me he'd call the councilwoman's office, but in his opinion, she's acting within her power. The next council meeting is in ten days; that's when we can appeal this. But until then the site is closed. Sorry, there's nothing I can do."

"Where is this council meeting? I'd like to be there." Arrow said.

"Actually, I asked the attorney about your being there, and he suggests that you not show up. He's afraid that your being there might turn this into a personal affair. He believes it's best if he handles this alone. Apparently, he's dealt with this type of thing before and thinks he can get the permits reissued without having to go through the public hearing. He asked me to tell you he had a court date this morning, but would call you later this afternoon."

Arrow had been in business a long time. All lawyer jokes aside, sometimes trusting your attorney was as important as trusting your doctor. The councilwoman's temper tantrum pissed him off, but he couldn't let his anger get in the way.

Arrow knew he'd received all the information Jim had, so he thanked him for taking care of business and hung up. *Gutierrez is just sending a message. If Direct Action Academy wants her support, there'll be a quid pro quo.* He thought to himself. *If that's what she expects...she's got the wrong idea.*

Tijuana, Baja, Mexico

Javier Muños had been a member of the PLA for seven years and was recently given command of his own cell. He'd grown up in Tijuana and dealt each day with the tantalizing view of San Diego. As a child he hadn't paid much attention to his conditions. Like most children, he didn't worry about what he didn't have; the world's worries could be erased by a good game of fútbol. But as he grew older he began noticing the great disparities between his country and the oasis lying just beyond the steel fences and invisible lines in the back country.

On his fourteenth birthday, Javier started working at an uncle's store in downtown Tijuana, a stereotypical souvenir shop on Avenida de la Revolución a few doors down from a pharmacy. Javier's uncle was the success story of the family. He'd begun working in the shop around the same age as Javier, cleaning and stocking shelves. After finishing high school he was promoted to a sales position that paid a slight commission. Each week he saved some of his pay, and after many years was able to purchase the store. Javier's uncle made a good living and was able to buy a nice home and marry a beautiful woman from a fairly wealthy family. Even though Javier's mother and father encouraged him to follow his uncle's example, as the years past he found himself resenting everything about the business.

One morning Javier surveyed the small, narrow shop, and all he saw was cheaply made, colorful, trash that was supposed to represent his culture. The idea that Mexico's great civilization could be represented by plaster figurines of donkeys and lazy drunks in oversized sombreros or by black velvet paintings of banditos with bandoliers crossed over their chest infuriated Javier. His country had a great history and a culture that reached back thousands of years. The Aztecs built magnificent cities and mastered complicated astronomy while Europeans were still crawling out of the dark ages. Instead of examples of Mexico's greatness, this store and every one like it sold contemptible sarapes, knives, bongs, and a hundred other worthless trinkets that degraded his cherished legacy. The worst part was that Mexicans perpetrated this cultural insult on themselves. Like whores they sold their collective souls, allowing the gringos to further devalue them by haggling over prices in a distasteful and insolent manner.

One day Javier reached his limit. An overweight American couple waddled into the store and began sorting through the souvenirs. As they scrutinized each object they'd comment on how tacky one thing was or how shoddy another appeared. After a few minutes the lady selected an ironwood figurine of a dolphin. As she began walking towards the cashier, her husband, without even attempting to be discreet, said, "Be sure to bargain with them, they expect that. If not you'll get swindled."

As Javier watched the grotesquely obese woman waddle towards him holding the statuette in her chunky fingers, he thought to himself, *Yeah, like this gorda had ever been denied anything in her privileged, sheltered life.* When she approached the counter she asked, *How...Much...For...This*?

Like so many other *pendejo gabachos* she spoke in a loud, slow voice, as if doing so would help the poor, illiterate Mexican better understand. As he stared at the loathsome symbol of ignorance and overindulgence, Javier felt his blood begin to seethe. All he wanted to do was lash out at the woman and her boorish husband; instead he leaned in towards the woman and in a soft, yet piercing tone replied, "The fucking price is on the tag, you stupid, fat bitch!" Then he turned and walked out of the store.

The rest of the day Javier wandered around town trying to calm down and sort out his thoughts. As the hours passed he found himself surrounded by evidence of the crimes the Americans committed against his country. Afternoon turned into evening, and Javier watched as hordes of gringos in their late teens and twenties assembled in the bars along *Avenida de la Revolución* to drink and party. They came down every night to get drunk and chase prostitutes. The local police looked the other way as the drunken gangs moved from one bar to the next. The gringos were allowed to do almost anything they wanted. As long as they could pull dollars out of their pockets, everyone was happy. Javier wasn't opposed to partying, but this went beyond simple revelry; it was pure debauchery, and it was saved for Mexico.

These people would never abuse their own city in such a way. To them Tijuana was a dirty little town where they could trash bars, openly urinate on the street ,and were protected by their powerful dollars. This image summed up Javier's impression of Americans; they pissed on his country with impunity because they could. It was this epiphany that ultimately led him into the arms of PLA.

As a cell leader, one of Javier's jobs was to monitor the local newspaper for communications from PLA commanders. Each week he got an anonymous e-mail, disguised as spam, containing a code phrase he'd look for in the classified section of his paper. Sometimes the e-mail instructed him to monitor the sporting goods section, and other times it was the auto section. This week, he was supposed to check the tools column. Each week he studied the assigned section, and each week he was disappointed.

The ad he was searching for advertised a 127mm socket wrench used in shipbuilding. To his surprise, he found the ad about a quarter of the way down the page. The ad repeated the word shipbuilding, which identified it as the codeword. Javier closed the newspaper and walked down the street to an Internet café where he ordered a coffee and purchased an access card for one of the computers. Javier logged on and then opened the e-mail program where he entered the address shipbuilding@mutemail.com. Then he wrote the following message: Interested in the 127mm socket set. Please send details.

Later that afternoon Javier returned to the Internet café and checked his e-mail account. He had one message. Its subject line read: 127mm socket set. Javier opened the e-mail, which gave the name of a book and a page number. Javier wrote down the information, deleted the e-mail, and walked out of the café toward the bus stop. He took a city bus to the downtown library where he located the book in the stacks.

Javier selected the book, then walked down the row and selected two more before finding a cubical where he could sit down in private. The cell leader then spent ten minutes reading through the other books and making sure no one was paying undue attention to him, before opening the book mentioned in the e-mail to page 266 where he found an action order activating his cell for an operation called *Aztec Wind.*

Chapter 4

To compel a man to subsidize with his taxes the propagation of ideas which he disbelieves and abhors is sinful and tyrannical.
—Thomas Jefferson

Phoenix, Arizona

Kevin Stevens had been stuck at the State Court House for the better part of the morning. A community group was trying to prevent one of his clients from expanding into their neighborhood, and he'd met with the judge to fight the injunction. It seemed half his time was spent fighting against NIMBYs. It wasn't like his client wanted to build a toxic waste dump; they just wanted to build a large-box super center that would add value to the area and make everyone's life easier. But people are strange when it comes to change, and it's easy to raise concerns about traffic and monopolies. Now that this wildfire seemed to be under control, he'd be able to shift his attention to the roadblock Councilwoman Gutierrez had thrown up against the Direct Action Academy.

This wasn't the first time Kevin had crossed swords with the councilwoman. She'd earned a reputation for this type of tactic. It was her signature way of pressuring local business to support immigrant labor. The last time one of his clients faced this situation, the client was forced to hire a group of day labors to re-landscape their already-landscaped property just to get Gutierrez out of their way. As far as Kevin was concerned this was nothing short of a shakedown. Kevin, and for that matter, most people, didn't have issues with immigrants trying to start new lives in the US, But when elected officials abused their power just to win some points with the immigrants, the private sector rebelled, which resulted in compassion fatigue. Unfortunately, either Gutierrez wasn't able to or didn't care to see that although she might make some short-term gains for immigrants, she was causing long-term problems for them. But, politicians rarely look at the long-term results of anything. Usually their terms last only a few years, so they need to score as many small victories for their voting base as possible to get re-elected.

Kevin referred to this phenomenon as "Happy Meal" legislation. The way he explained it was, politicians are like a parent driving a carload of irritable children around town. After a while the children begin yelling and screaming because they're bored, so in an attempt to pacify them, the parent drives to McDonald's and buys each kid a "Happy Meal." The Happy Meal is nothing but empty calories, sugar, and a cheap toy. In reality, there's very little redeeming value in it at all, but the parent looks like a hero, and it temporarily appeases the children. Most of the ludicrous laws passed by politicians seemed to be the same.

On his way back to his Tempe office, Kevin called his assistant to confirm his appointment with the councilwoman for the next morning. He knew the environmental study was irrefutable, so Gutierrez' tactic was nothing more than harassment. Kevin was confident this "problem" would be resolved by tomorrow afternoon and then construction could resume.

La Mesa, California

Marcos awoke early to go to the gym before his chemistry class. Before getting in the shower he opened his laptop to check e-mail. While it was connecting, he poured a cup of strong coffee and opened the *Union Tribune* to the Sports section. Although the Padres jealously protected their perennial right to last place in the NL West, he held out hope they'd crawl out of the cellar. As he looked over the results from last night's game, he determined it was going to be a bad week. The Dodgers had just taken two out of three games from the Padres, and the Giants were coming to town for another three game series.

Marcos pushed the paper aside and double clicked his inbox. As usual, about three quarters of the messages were spam, everything from the ubiquitous porn sites to chain letters. As he scanned the entries he noticed a message from Knife. Marcos saved the e-mail, then picked up his laptop and returned to his room where he entered the appropriate keystrokes to launch the encryption program. When prompted, Marcos entered the alphanumeric, case-sensitive pass phrase that decrypted the message.

To: Flag
From: Knife
Re: Operation Aztec Wind
ACTION ORDER

Prepare for operations in your AO within the next 24 to 36 hours. You are required to monitor local media response and gather after action intelligence regarding ability of local services to respond to strikes. You are directed to send daily intelligence briefs to Knife.

Be prepared to organize political protests upon further directions.

End
ACTION ORDER

Marcos reread the message to make sure he understood his orders, then obliterated it using a deleting program that overwrote the file nine times, making it completely unrecoverable. Looking at his watch he thought, *That could be tomorrow; I didn't realize things would start so quickly.*

The message was clear; he wouldn't be required to perform in a direct role, with the exception of monitoring the media response. The best thing he could do was go about his day as if everything was normal, but inside Marcos knew the wheels had begun turning, and the revolution had started. He felt an odd mixture of trepidation and excitement as he thought of the events that would surely unfold in the next several months. Inside he hoped he would be able to play a more substantial role in the Aztlán war of independence.

Queen Creek, Arizona

"Hello. My name is Kevin Stevens from Webster, Lowe and Stevens," Kevin said as he presented his business card to the attractive Hispanic receptionist. "I have an appointment with the councilwoman."

"Yes, Mr. Stevens, the councilwoman has been expecting you." The young woman spoke into her telephone. "Councilwoman Gutierrez, Mr. Stevens has arrived; should I send him back? I see...I'll let him know." She looked up and smiled thinly and remarked, "Mr. Stevens, the councilwoman asks that you take a seat. She'll be ready for you in just a moment."

Kevin sat down and double-checked his cell phone to make sure it was on vibrate. The councilwoman had made him wait the last time he'd met with her. It was her way of demonstrating she was in control. Evidently, this was a tactic she reserved for all attorneys. Some people just had an innate urge to prove who the Alpha dog was. *Fine.*" Kevin thought. *It won't change the fact that I'm holding all the cards in this game.*

After a few minutes the phone rang, and after answering it, the receptionist informed Kevin the councilwoman was ready to receive him. Kevin picked up his briefcase and followed her down the hallway to the councilwoman's office. When they entered the office Gutierrez was firmly seated behind her desk. After hesitating briefly, she rose and greeted Kevin.

"Mr. Stevens, thank you for coming. Would you like some coffee?"

"No thank you, Councilwoman." Kevin selected a seat and waited for the receptionist to leave. "Councilwoman, as you know my firm represents the Direct Action Academy, and we'd like to come to an agreement regarding the environmental impact study that you've rescinded."

"Well, you get right to the point, don't you?" The councilwoman's voice had a slight edge to it.

Blowing off the snide comment Kevin continued, "Councilwoman Gutierrez, I have a copy of the impact study that was done by our environmental engineering firm. I assure you it is complete and meets every local, state, and federal requirement. If you have any questions or doubts about its contents I've been assured that an engineer will be happy to meet with you and explain any part of it to your satisfaction."

Gutierrez crossed her hands on her polished desk. "Mr. Stevens, it's my responsibility to ensure the safety of my constituents, and I take the protection of our environment very seriously. I pulled that study because I had doubts regarding the ecological impact of hundreds of thousands of lead bullets being introduced into the soil. I will act whenever I believe there might be a danger in my district."

Kevin neither smiled nor frowned. Both players knew that these opening remarks were meaningless; the game had not yet begun. "I appreciate your dedication to your constituency, Councilwoman." He said. "But I'd like to remind you that my clients have invested a significant amount of money into your district, and the academy is expected to generate even more revenue in the form of jobs, sales, and property taxes. My clients are eager to play a part in the development of the Queen Creek area, but none of this can happen unless the facility is constructed. We'd like to resolve this issue so further loss of time and resources can be avoided."

As much as the councilwoman tried to keep her composure, she shifted in her chair, betraying the fact that she was losing her cool. Kevin recognized she understood the weakness of her position and more importantly, knew she wasn't going to get a concession out of him.

"I have no doubt the study was performed properly, but I'd simply feel better if I had the opportunity to review the sections dealing with the lead impact so I could address any potential questions that might arise. I'm sure you understand." She shifted in her chair. "Of course, Mr. Kellerman, you must not imagine that I am acting out of any malice toward your clients in particular. As a public servant, I must remain open to all opportunities and seek a balance. It may be possible to offset a negative impact in one area with a positive impact in another."

Here it comes, Kevin thought, and he thought he knew just what it would be. He decided to present a large, soft target. "And what sort of positive impact would you have in mind, Councilwoman?"

She leaned back in her chair. "If your clients were to relax their unwarranted hostility toward the East Valley guest worker project, and help provide needed employment among the area's migrant families...well, that might go a long way toward offsetting the negative impact of their Academy on the surrounding environment."

Kevin still did not smile. So that really *was* all she had. Very well.

"You are aware, of course, Councilwoman," he said quietly, "that to do that would violate the contractor's agreement with the building union. The union representatives would take a dim view of the contractor for doing any such thing, and of anyone who pressured him to do so."

As much as the councilwoman tried to keep her composure, she continued shifting in her chair. "Union" was a conjuring word for any politician of Gutierrez' ilk. However much personal power a politician might wield, offending local unions would turn off the money flow that kept her winning elections. Kevin recognized she understood the weakness of her position, and more importantly, she knew she wasn't going to get a concession out of him.

"Of course," Kevin went on, "You have every right to demand a further study of the environmental impact report. But I must inform you that we intend to exercise our right, under the law, to sue your office for all costs related to our inability to work while you educate yourself, that is, unless you can find a legitimate omission that would violate the environmental statute. Kevin looked down at his papers and located a memo. "We estimate these losses to be $12,000 a day." Kevin pulled the memo out of its folder and presented it to the councilwoman. "We've itemized the charges in this memo for your convenience." Kevin could tell, by the look on Gutierrez's face, that he had struck the *coup de gras*.

The councilwoman took the memo and superficially gazed at it, before flicking it onto the desk. Then she folded her hands in her lap and stared towards a wall containing many pictures of her and other politicians.

Without looking back at her adversary, she said, "I see the study was completed by a qualified company, and from what I've read, I'm satisfied that everything falls within current environmental guidelines. You can notify your client that I will call the construction commission and withdrawal my opposition. I'm sure they'll be able to resume work by this afternoon."

Kevin could hear the oozing dissatisfaction in her voice. She had grown accustomed to winning, and didn't like to capitulate to anyone. But, she also knew that she'd been outgunned, and it was time to retreat.

"Thank you, Councilwoman. I'll pass that information along. I'm sure my client will be relieved. I'll follow up with the construction committee this afternoon to ensure your retraction is received. Thank you for seeing me this morning. It was a pleasure...as always." Kevin returned the folder to the briefcase, stood up, and presented his hand to the councilwoman, who weakly shook it. On his way out of the building he speed dialed Wabash Construction to let them know they'd be able to reopen the site that afternoon. Then he called Arrow and gave him the good news.

"...Taylor, my advice to you is to give this councilwoman a wide birth. I doubt she's going to let us have the last word in this matter. We won a battle, but may have made an enemy for life. I suggest you befriend some of the other members of the council to counterbalance her."

"I agree. Thanks for taking care of this so quickly, Kevin. We'll be in touch."

Chula Vista, California

For the last three days Javier's cell had planned their mission. The first step was to recon potential targets for accessibility, security, impact value, and egress. Two locations were selected. The first was a large, master-planned community called *Mesa Verde,* under construction on a hilltop overlooking Interstate 5. The second was a military housing development being renovated in Imperial Beach. Both targets were situated near major transportation arteries that flowed south to the Mexican border, and both would garner a lot of media attention. A preliminary recon of the target showed the housing tract was scarcely populated, with only a few models and spec homes having been completed, so collateral risks were low. A security company had been contracted to provide roving patrols, but didn't have enough personnel to adequately cover the site. Furthermore, they patrolled in golf carts that didn't have searchlights, and none of the guards was armed.

To gather intelligence Javier selected two couples out of his group to pose as potential home buyers. They brought digital cameras and notepads with them to better capture vital information. One set of operatives arrived at the *Mesa Verde* sales office and selected informational brochures about the area from a rack of data sheets. From these flyers they learned that the closest fire station was located four and a half miles away, and the closest police sub-station was about seventeen miles to the west. Currently, the only entrance into the subdivision was the two-lane road used to drive up the hill to the sales office. Other access roads were currently under construction and scheduled to open next month, but until then there was only one, which was more than enough to handle the construction and home buyer traffic. After a brief discussion with the sales agent, the team left the office to tour the model homes.

The couple walked around the corner and past several houses that had recently been framed out. They stopped and took pictures of the lots, making sure to note the locations of hydrants and areas where flammable materials were stored. They identified several spots where four adjacent houses were being built. These would be prime targets, since one device could potentially ignite all four houses. They also noted large cranes and front loaders that could be targeted for greater collateral damage. Finally, they searched for a way into the site other than the main entrance. They found a canyon trail that meandered down the hill to a dirt road where a car could be positioned for a quick escape. The recon lasted about an hour, and the team left with more than enough information. More importantly, nobody had paid any attention to them.

A second team reconnoitered the military housing. This location was not on a base, so security wasn't an issue. Part of the project was still inhabited and waiting remodeling, so traffic continued to move in and around the construction site. The contractor erected fences to keep people out of the work zones, but there were several areas where the fence line sagged and where soil erosion created holes under the chain link. This team surveyed the site in simple construction disguises that consisted of orange and yellow reflective vests, blue jeans, and hard hats. With cameras and clipboards they undertook a similar target assessment as the *Mesa Verde* team. The major difference was that since this was a government project on government land, the construction crews left far more materials and equipment lying around. A closer examination revealed several containers labeled flammable. These would create excellent secondary fires that would add to the overall effectiveness of the raid. The biggest problem the team encountered was the number of people in the area who could compromise their mission. As far as inserting and extracting was concerned, there were several ways into and out of the area. Although this would offer greater options for the raiders, it could prove difficult for denying access to emergency vehicles. Of course, there was the most direct route, which would be the obvious choice, but that didn't guarantee the others wouldn't be used. Other than that, the target was soft, and the team felt confident they'd be successful.

The day of the mission Javier picked up a large crate at the downtown bus depot. It was labeled "Auto Parts" and addressed to a fictitious body shop. Inside were four-dozen modified, US-made AN M14 TH3 thermite grenades and twelve Chinese-style chest harnesses with four pouches on each. Two boxes contained hundreds of multi-pronged road stars. The stars were simple but effective devices made from two u-shaped pieces of metal with sharpened ends, welded together so regardless of how they landed, three ends acted as legs and the fourth pointed straight up like a mini petard. Before dividing the equipment each of the assembled cell members pulled on gloves to prevent fingerprints being transferred to the equipment. Each operative donned a harness, adjusted the straps to fit, and inserted a grenade into each pouch.

The AN M14 TH3 thermite grenade is 5.7 inches tall, cylindrical, and weighs thirty-two ounces. It's slightly larger and heavier than a can of soda, making it easy to carry. Initially manufactured for the US military, over the years these particular grenades ended up in the Middle East where they were purchased and modified by Syria. Once ignited each grenade would burn for forty seconds at a temperature of 4000° Fahrenheit (2200° Celsius), long and hot enough to burn through ½ inch of steel with a burn radius of twenty-five meters. In the process, the device would essentially transform into a molten blob, making identification virtually impossible. By generating such an enormous amount of heat the devices would incinerate construction equipment.

Javier had seen to it that maps were drawn of each target. The teams rehearsed where they'd insert, which targets would be hit, and how they would extract. Each squad had six members paired up into three buddy teams. The squads would insert together then separate to place their devices. As one deposited a grenade, the other would provide over watch; this arrangement would continue until all the devices were set or the team was compromised.

Although they weren't expecting trouble, each buddy team carried a .22-caliber, seven-shot revolver to be used as a last resort. There were sexier guns in the PLA arsenal, but the .22 revolver was ideal for this application. The .22 LR was adequate for silencing dogs or for close range headshots. The round they selected was called a Quick-Shok™; the 32-grain bullet was factory pre-stressed so it broke into three pieces upon impact, making ballistic identification virtually impossible. One advantage often over looked with a revolver was that spent casings are not ejected, as with an auto loader, eliminating evidence. Each member knew the guns were underpowered, and with no reloads they wouldn't be able to fight off anyone, especially police.

Once the actions were completed, the teams would reunite and extract together, driving to several locations where sanitized cars were positioned. Each person wore overalls over street clothes so they could quickly change. These overalls would be bagged and deposited in various thrift store donation bins around town by friends of the movement. Then the raiders would return to Mexico and split up. Their orders were to lay low and not reunite for two weeks. Total time on target was expected to last twenty minutes, and complete mission time was set at one hour and ten minutes.

In preparation for the mission, each operative checked the overalls of his or her buddy to ensure the pockets were empty and no identifying items were present. Each person received a pair of new Converse All-Stars, not for any fashion statement, but to ensure footprints left behind would all be uniform and none of the prints would have any distinguishing marks. The shoes would be discarded along with the overalls. Finally, they loaded handfuls of road stars into fanny packs and strapped them on. Everything was ready, and the teams loaded into cars by1:45 a.m. The attack would begin at 2:30 a.m.

Alpha team drove off the street and onto the dirt road that lead behind the *Mesa Verde* site. The driver slowed and eased towards the insertion spot. Once they arrived, he turned the car around using a three-point turn and shut off the ignition. The team sat silently in the dark for ten minutes before leaving the car and assembling for one last equipment check. The canyon was quiet except for the rhythmic sound of crickets. They'd already ensured that the interior lights of the vehicle had been disabled so they would not come on when the doors were opened. Alpha team paired off and headed up the canyon towards the buildings on its rim. Once the team reached the top they began spreading out towards their targets. The first pair stealthily moved across several streets towards the main road that led up the hill towards the sales office. Their first objective was to stop emergency vehicles that would respond to the fires.

The buddy team distributed about eighty of the tire puncturing road stars across both lanes of the main approach, and then returned to place their grenades. Another pair was tasked with placing charges on each of the hydrants. They used bailing wire to affix the grenades directly to the large valves used to turn the hydrants on and off. Although the thermite would quickly burn through the wire, it would hold long enough for the heat to weld the valves shut, making the hydrant completely inoperable. As this was happening, other teams moved from building to building setting charges in the rear corners of each identified structure. As they placed each grenade, they activated digital timers starting a 45-minute delay on the fuse. The last team located the heavy construction machinery, including the cranes and front loaders, and placed charges either in the engine compartments or on the transaxles. As each of the teams finished their work they made sure to disperse road stars in the street behind them. The operation went off without a hitch, and all the charges had been set within the expected twenty minutes. As Alpha team joined up at the extraction point they made a quick head count, then everyone loaded into the car for the drive to the escape vehicles.

Across town, Bravo team was finishing at the military housing. Like Alpha they also placed charges in machinery, but also around flammable materials. They used larger volumes of road stars to properly cover the many streets leading into the target area, the difference being that since the area was inhabited, only streets inside the immediate area were littered with stars.

Once completed, Bravo reassembled and extracted as planned. The initial phase of the operation was completed and successful.

While the two teams drove towards the pre-positioned cars, grenades began igniting at the target sites. As each device burned, the immediate area lit up as though small suns had risen. Sparks danced and fire crept up the supporting beams of the buildings. Forty seconds later fires engulfed the structures and spread from lot to lot. At the same time the cranes and front loaders also smoldered and caught fire. In less than a minute several blocks had ignited, and conflagrations lit the early morning sky.

****

Fred Williams was sipping his fourth cup of coffee and listening to Coast-to-Coast with George Noory on the radio. Fred was the overnight watchman in charge of the *Mesa Verde* site and worked from 9:00 p.m. till 5:00 a.m. Like many rent-a-cops, Fred was retired and used the job to pick up extra cash. The radio host was interviewing a scientist who was explaining the existence of human alien hybrids and what their mission was on earth. Fred didn't believe in the whole alien thing, but Coast-to-Coast was the only program on at this time of the morning and was better than listening to rookie disk jockeys cut their teeth on music stations. Fred got up from his chair and started walking towards the toilet when he noticed bright, flickering light rising into the sky. He stopped and gazed out the window of his trailer and saw a huge and spreading fire erupting two blocks down.

"*Oh my goodness*!" Immediately Fred grabbed the phone and dialed 911.

"911...Do you have an emergency to report?"

"Yes. There's a huge fire raging at the *Mesa Verde* subdivision at 7861 East Colinas Drive. Please notify the fire department."

"I understand. I'm notifying the fire department right now. Please stay on the line and reconfirm your address." The operator's voice was smooth and calming.

"I'm at the *Mesa Verde* subdivision at 7861 East Colinas Drive in Chula Vista. I'm the night watchman; my name is Fred Williams."

"Okay, Mr. Williams, the fire department has been notified and should be on their way. Are any of the houses occupied?"

"No. We haven't opened yet; we're still under construction. Oh my goodness, the whole place is on fire. I can't believe this."

Fred continued talking with the operator until he heard the sirens of the approaching fire trucks.

"I hear the fire trucks; I think they've arrived." Fred told the operator. As he continued listening the sound of the sirens seemed to stop getting closer. "It sounds like the engines have stopped. Did you give them the right address?"

"Yes, Mr. Williams. Hold on please. Mr. Williams, are you aware of any road blocks leading to your location?"

"No. There's just one road leading into the site, and it's wide open. Why?"

"I'm hearing a radio message from the engine company saying they've hit something and lost all their tires. Evidently, they're stuck and can't move."

KGTV Channel 10 Morning Show

"Good morning and thank you for joining us. I'm Ted Galland, and the top story this hour is two massive fires that began around three o'clock this morning completely consuming a Chula Vista subdivision and a large section of naval housing under construction in Imperial Beach. First we go live at the scene in Chula Vista with KGTV reporter, Jody Adair."

"Good morning, Ted. I'm at the *Mesa Verde* development in Chula Vista, where we're told fire destroyed over fifty homes in various stages of construction early this morning. Arson investigators are on site, and we're hearing that this was no accident. What I'm holding in my hand is a road spike. These were purposely scattered all over the access road leading into the construction site. When the fire department arrived all their tires were shredded, preventing the crews from reaching the burning structures."

"Additionally, we're receiving reports that once fire crews entered the fire zone, they found that every fire hydrant had been sabotaged, rendering them completely unusable. Because of these premeditated acts, the fire crews were forced to fight a battle of containment, sacrificing the consumed structures. Fortunately, no one was injured, but damage estimates are projected to be close to three-hundred-million dollars."

"Jody, I understand that investigators are still gathering clues. Have you heard anybody speak about terrorism?"

"Ted, investigators tell us this fire and the one in Imperial Beach were part of a coordinated attack. Reports are that the two fires were of the same design, and both included sabotage of hydrants and emergency vehicles. The prevailing theory is that these attacks follow similar strikes committed by the radical Earth Liberation Front, the ELF. As you recall, they've used arson in the past to protest construction projects. But investigators want to make it clear that this is only a theory being bandied about. 10 News has received no official declaration, nor has the ELF admitted responsibility. This is Jody Adair reporting from Chula Vista for 10 News. Back to you, Ted."

"Thank you, Jody, for that report. Now, we're taking you to the scene of the other fire in Imperial Beach. On site is Barry Franklin, who has been collecting information all morning. Barry, what can you add?"

"Ted, I began this morning by flying over the site in the Sky 10 news helicopter. I can tell you from that perspective it was easy to appreciate the severity of the situation. Several blocks have been completely burned out, and the firefighters did a heroic job in preventing the fire from spreading to the populated homes. As Jody pointed out in her report, the arsonists spread dozens of these tire spikes all over the area. Firefighters told us the first engine to arrive lost all its tires; fortunately, this housing complex has other entrances that were not sabotaged, so follow up engines were able to avoid the same hazard. In addition to the destroyed homes, expensive equipment was also ruined. We're told initial estimates place losses at close to twenty-five-million dollars. This is Barry Franklin reporting for 10 News. Back to you, Ted."

"Ten News is now receiving reports that similar attacks were carried out in two Phoenix, Arizona, suburbs. Evidently, the attacks mirror those in the South Bay and were extensive in scope. As we continue to receive information we'll keep you updated. In other stories…"

La Mesa, California

So this is how our war of independence has started, Marcos thought to himself as he watched the news reports. The images flashed before his eyes, and a feeling of exhilaration grew within his soul. For so many years it seemed as though liberation was only a fable passed down by old men and armchair revolutionaries. But now it was actually happening, and he was involved.

Marcos taped the news coverage on several stations and cut articles out of the newspaper to include in the analysis that he'd transmit to Bicycle. Later, he'd ask students on campus, including other OJChA members, for their feelings about the attacks. As he watched the news he began to feel a sense of jealously overwhelming his heart. Of course, making sure accurate reports made their way back to the PLA was important, but he felt impotent as he watched the first shots of the revolution from the comfort of his couch. Marcos wanted to play an active role; he wanted to fight against his oppressors and be able to tell exciting stories of how he helped establish the new Aztlán. He didn't want to tell his children that during the revolution he cut articles out of the newspaper and taped television programs. Surely he'd been placed at this critical point in history to do more than that. There was no doubt that he'd be active in future operations, but for now he wanted to get the word out that the rebellion had begun.

Hermosillo, Mexico

Major Al-Salih and Francisco gathered their teams together to review the results of *Operation Aztec Wind* and determine what successes and failures occurred. They'd pulled down satellite feeds from the San Diego and Phoenix news stations and had received newspapers from the same cities. This information was supplemented by after-action reports from the regional commanders involved in the operation. All reports indicated the attacks were executed without problems. The teams were able to easily infiltrate their targets without any compromises. The damage carried out exceeded mission expectations, especially the destruction of high value equipment and the immobilization of first responders. All teams reported back, and all equipment was accounted for. Overall, it was an excellent operation. The major was man enough to admit it; he was impressed with the training and competence of the PLA cell units. They had far exceeded his expectations.

Carlos was finishing up his report to the assembly. "As you all know," he said, "this operation was an aggressive probe to determine the overall readiness of our enemy and to gather intelligence on the response of fire and police assets. All indications are that in spite of security measures adopted after September 11, Americans had reverted to their natural condition of indolence. The attacks are predominately being blamed on environmental groups, as we had hoped, and there has been no indication of backlash on the Mexican community. Lastly, although the primary purpose of this mission wasn't asset destruction, reports are that *Aztec Wind* caused close to $750 million in damage."

Francisco thanked Carlos for his report and then read two messages from vital assets in the governments of Arizona and California, codenamed *Obispo* and *Puente*. The report stated that even though the attacks had received considerable attention in the media, no one was indicating terrorism. In fact, American officials everywhere were clearly trying to avoid the "T-word" for fear that people's reactions might damage the weak economic recovery. Additional police attention had been focused on environmental groups, but the authorities were proceeding with extreme caution so as not to appear unsympathetic to the environmental lobby.

Overall *Obispo* and *Puente* believed the mission proved that PLA operatives could function with relative ease and expand their assaults without unreasonable risk. The major stood up and looked around the room, making eye contact with each person. "Gentlemen, I want to congratulate you on an outstanding operation. As you know, I have served in my country's military for most of my adult life and have worked with *Hezbollah* since the late 1970s. I have rarely seen such a professionally executed operation as *Aztec Wind.* There is a famous saying in the military, 'Most plans never survive first contact.' You have proven another widely accepted adage, 'The better you train in peace, the less you bleed in war.' Although this was only the beginning, and we have a long road ahead of us, I can honestly say that I have a renewed respect for you and your fighters. Well done."

In reality the major *was* impressed with the success of the mission. Even though he still had his reservations, the fact that several teams were able to enter the United States, infiltrate their targets, complete the mission, and withdraw without any losses was impressive by any standard.

This revelation encouraged Muhammad, not only because of the accomplishment, but because he now anticipated more aggressive attacks that would bring even greater suffering to the Americans. Once again he marveled at Allah's infinite wisdom and silently gave thanks for this opportunity to ravage the great Satan. Now that the PLA had been proven it was time to test the political wing and see how successful they could be in organizing Mexicans within the US to assist in the cause.

"Francisco, contact Flag and Rabbit and instruct them to initiate recruiting efforts among Mexican nationals in their areas of operations. Also, we must organize a system of safe houses for upcoming missions. Carlos, instruct your people to identify secure routes across the border. We'll need information on where the Border Patrol is currently operating and their rotational schedules. From this point forward the key to success will be sustained asymmetrical attacks focused on breaking the American people's confidence in their government and destroying their economy."

Francisco and Carlos nodded in agreement and exited the room to fulfill their new orders. After the two PLA leaders had left, the major signaled to Sayf to join him in private. Sayf followed the major into another office and closed the door behind him.

"Yes, *Ra'id*, what are your orders?"

"Sayf, I wanted to inform you that earlier this morning I spoke with Brigadier General Maruf. He notified me that North Korea is ready to begin operations against the South."

"*Allahu Akbar*. This is excellent news."

Almost eighteen months ago Syria, Iran, and a select group of Saudi wahabists had negotiated a pact with North Korean leader Kim Jong-il in an attempt to persuade the enigmatic leader that they would support his ambitions to reunify Korea. Pyongyang had long considered China its closest ally, and often relied upon the might of the People Liberation Army to assist them in the event of another war on the peninsula. But, since the end of the Korean War relations between the two Communist states had vacillated. Beginning in the 1990s, Beijing purposely sought to distance itself from their Mutual Cooperation Treaty with Pyongyang. In 1995 The Chinese Ministry of Foreign Affairs published its most blatant betrayal of Korea to date, when it announced, "China does not believe the friendship treaty between Beijing and Pyongyang is a treaty requiring the dispatch of military forces."

This declaration was followed in 1997 by then Vice Foreign Minister Tang Jiaxuan (who later rose to Foreign Minister) when he assured South Korean officials and press that China was not willing to automatically intervene if North Korea were to start a war. Tang went on to characterize the treaty between his nation and the DPRK as a "*dead document.*" Later that same year, Chinese Premier Li Peng called North Korea, "only a neighbor, not an ally."

It became increasingly clear to leaders in Pyongyang that in order to realize Kim Jong-il's personal philosophy of *Juche* (self-reliance), which had been the guiding light for North Korea's development, they'd needed new allies. The cash-strapped state found itself increasingly isolated and sought new sources of revenue to support its massive conventional and nuclear arms build-up.

It was in this atmosphere that the Arab coalition approached Pyongyang with an offer of financial support for their fledgling nuclear program. The wahabists offered to buy North Korean missile technology at grossly inflated prices and provide discounted oil shipments if the North committed to attacking the South within a predetermined timetable. Furthermore, Iran went so far as to promise to create a regional crisis that would draw troops away from any US response to the Korean conflict. Now, at last, Pyongyang was prepared to keep its part of the bargain and strike at the South. The timing could not have been better, for now the major's mission looked as if it would have a much better chance at success.

Cochise County, Arizona

J.R. Miller drove down a dirt road in his battered Ford pick up heading towards the southern boundary of his ranch. This place, straddling the Mexican US border to the south and the Coronado National Forest on the West, had been J.R.'s home since the day he was born. J.R.'s great-grandparents moved to Cochise County, Arizona in 1877 as part of the silver rush that centered in the Tombstone hills. His great-grandfather was one of the successful ones. He owned a lucrative mine and had the foresight to know that the silver wouldn't last. By the time the hills were mined out, he had used his profits to amass nearly fifty thousand acres of land adjacent to the Huachuca Mountains.

Over the last 126 years his family had lived on the land and established a cattle ranch they'd named the Double C. J.R. attended Montana State University at Bozeman, where he earned a B.S. in Animal Science before returning to the Double C. Unlike the Phoenix valley, his ranch was at a higher elevation and nestled against the mile-high Montezuma Peak. Because of this topography the location was perfect for ranching, and the family had built a successful business raising cattle and sheep.

Today, J.R. was out checking fence lines. Lately, he'd needed to repair a number of sections that had been cut by illegal aliens crossing his land on their way north to a new life. Regrettably, this seemed to be an increasingly popular route for illegals heading to Tucson and Phoenix. Probably, J.R. figured, increased Border Patrol activity near Nogales was pushing the illegals further east.

Unfortunately, an increasing number of illegals died in their attempt to circumvent these patrols by crossing between the Patagonia Mountains and the Canelo Hills. This region was very dangerous for people who were not properly prepared for the natural features, and many illegals either fell to their deaths or died from exposure. As word of these deaths got back to Mexico, prospective immigrants decided to move further east past the

Huachuca Mountains into the Miracle Valley area, which was where the Double C was located.

Inspecting fence lines was a major irritant, not only because of the time needed to make repairs, but because cattle often found the holes first. Then J.R. and his few ranch hands had to round up the wayward cows before they entered the San Pedro Riparian National Conservation Area. If the cattle wandered into the conservation area, J.R. had to get federal permission to enter and retrieve his stock. As J.R. drove on he found another hole in the fence. He pulled over and examined the area around the gap, noticing several sets of tracks; he estimated that upwards of twenty people had crossed at this point. J.R. decided to follow the tracks as they meandered deeper onto his land.

Following the tracks for about a quarter mile, he saw what appeared to be, a rest area sheltered by large mesquite trees. He'd found these "rest stops" before, and they all looked alike. The area was trampled down and strewn with food wrappers, water bottles, and assorted clothing. As far as he could tell, the coyotes herded their human cargo across the border at a fairly brisk pace, probably warning them to keep moving to avoid Border Patrol agents. This pace was probably maintained for a couple of hours until they stopped at places like this. Once they arrived they must have been dehydrated and worn out, which explained why so many articles of clothing along with other goods were found among the dozens of empty water bottles. Then the powerful stench of human waste assaulted his nose. Just beyond his position was an area where the group had collectively relieved themselves. Feces and toilet paper covered the ground, and the foul smell polluted the air. Years of working with animals had taught him how to read feces, and what he saw told him that many of these people were sick and undernourished.

After a short break the coyotes would get the people back on their feet and start moving them towards Route 92 where they'd have a truck waiting to transport them north to Tucson and Phoenix. For years Phoenix had been a major distribution point for illegals.

Usually the aliens would be dropped off at a safe house, where they'd await airline tickets or ground transportation to cities across the US. At least that's what happened to the fortunate ones. Often, coyotes would load these small houses with thirty, sometimes forty aliens, and then hold them prisoner until they came up with additional money. Those who couldn't pay were often forced into indentured servitude, which is a nice euphemism for slavery, until they "worked off" their supplementary payment.

As J.R. gathered up the trash, he found himself examining different items that revealed bits and pieces about their previous owners. Whether the items were intentionally discarded to lighten someone's load, or they'd accidentally fallen out of a pack or pocket in the darkness of night, many of them were probably treasures—small books, pictures, knitted curios and other items that told a story about where the person had come from and the people they'd left behind.

Looking at the arrayed odds and ends evoked a confusion of emotions within J.R. He could appreciate the human yearning to start a better life and escape the hopelessness of Mexico's underclass, but at the same time he recognized the dangers posed by this incremental invasion of his country.

Then there was the anger he felt towards the coyotes who preyed upon their own people like cannibals. That people, in this day and age, would still enrich themselves by enslaving the vulnerable was abhorrent to him. But worst was the knowledge that US politicians facilitated it by eagerly providing welfare, medical care, access to schools, and a hundred other social entitlements that enticed these people north towards an irresistible mirage that for many was just a lie.

J.R. finished cleaning the area and loaded the garbage bags in the back of his pick-up, then returned to mend the fence. It was approaching four o'clock, and he needed to get back to the house to clean up before his wife had dinner on the table. She was always a stickler on the family sitting down together for dinner, and he knew better than to be late.

Tempe, Arizona

Samuel and Julia led the OJChA chapter at Arizona State University. They'd recently received a message from the regional council informing them of a very important event scheduled for the following weekend in Phoenix. Unlike previous gatherings, where only OJChA members attended, this time Samuel and Julia were instructed to gather as many Chicanos as possible from the community, with special attention given to undocumented workers. Since the meeting was scheduled for a Saturday morning, OJChA would provide *menudo* for everyone attending.

Menudo is a traditional Mexican soup made with cow stomach and feet. It is usually eaten on Saturday mornings due to its alleged ability to cure hangovers. Additionally, OJChA had provided pre-paid phone cards to give away as an added incentive for people to attend. The phone cards were very popular among undocumented workers since it allowed them to make local and long distance calls without having an established account with the phone company. Usually these cards were printed with logos of Mexican companies or popular futbol teams.

The ASU chapter worked to design and copy five hundred flyers advertising the meeting and instructing the participants where to meet for transportation. Of course, there was a healthy dose of curiosity about the topic of the meeting, but the regional council promised the chapter members that everything would be explained at the meeting. In a separate message, not to be shared with the general membership, the council asked Samuel and Julia to submit the names of those members they considered the most dedicated to the cause and who had shown leadership within the organization over the last couple years. They decided on six names to submit, including themselves, three guys and a girl. Julia unrolled a map of Phoenix and divided it into sections, assigning teams of two to each. The teams would cover their assigned sectors and distribute the flyers to workers on the street, construction sites and small taquerías where local Chicanos gathered.

One of Julia's aunts operated a small taquería called *La Luna* that had served as a local meeting place for the Aztlán movement for years. Although small, it did brisk business beginning early in the morning providing breakfast for the many workers who'd come in to eat before waiting on the corners for day jobs, and throughout the day serving burritos, tacos, and caldos. Julia's aunt had moved from New Mexico to Arizona nearly 15 years ago and purchased the restaurant several years later.

Originally, she'd entered the US illegally, but since had gained citizenship. But, she remained true to her culture and believed it was her obligation to support other Mexican immigrants with her business. To this end she only hired Mexicans, not caring whether they were illegal or not. That support extended to her suppliers. There were several national and local wholesale companies that sold food and equipment to restaurants, but she vowed never to use them. Instead, she sought out small companies owned by Mexicans who employed Chicanos. Sometimes these policies led to occasional deficiencies and problems, but she was determined to support *La Raza*, as it had supported her.

Maricopa County Fair Grounds

The Great Western Gun Show was the largest event of its kind in the west, traveling between locations in several states, normally featuring more than two hundred exhibitors. The show stopped in Phoenix every other month and regularly drew people from across Arizona, California, New Mexico and southern Utah, making it one of the best-attended shows in the western United States. One of the reasons Phoenix drew such large crowds was Arizona's gun laws.

The politicians who established Arizona's constitution ensured that the right of the people to keep and bear arms followed the original intent of the founding fathers, which was to guarantee that all those who desired to bear arms and were not felons, would be able to exercise that right freely and with as little government interference as possible. Samuel Adams best summed up this idea when he stated: "*The Constitution shall never be construed to authorize Congress to prevent the people of the United States, who are peaceable citizens, from keeping their own arms.*"

For this reason Arizona has no "assault weapons" ban, and does not prohibit the possession or sale of full-auto weapons, as long as the owner fully complies with federal laws. Furthermore, there are no restrictions on the open carrying of firearms in public, although a license is required for concealed carry. Arizona is a "shall issue" state, making it easy to obtain a permit, as is the case in most states in the country. Because of these reasons the Great Western Shows were always popular venues where firearm enthusiasts could gather and be able to examine and purchase all types of arms and accessories. Mike decided this show would afford him an excellent opportunity to promote the academy to a large group of potential customers.

He purchased a 12-by-12-foot area and erected a multi-paneled display he'd ordered from a corporate display company in Los Angeles. On a side table he placed a scale model of the academy showing the different ranges and CQC houses. Josh had sent over a variety of load-bearing vests and other tactical gear from the *Grunt Gear* collection, as well as a few prototypes he'd made especially for the academy line. Finally, Mike set up a table with full-color brochures that outlined the different courses and provided short descriptions of the instruction. As an added touch he also had t-shirts printed with the Direct Action Academy logo that he intended to sell or give as gifts to those who signed up in advance for classes.

Mike was putting the finishing touches on his booth when the show opened and people began filing into the large exhibition hall. As if instructed, the crowd began forming a serpentine-like line that wove its way up and down the aisles, filing past a gauntlet of vendors selling everything from guns to beef jerky. Mike watched as the people began filing past and couldn't help but make mental notes about individuals and their mannerisms. Mike mentally began sorting the people into different categories; there were the cowboys who wore white straw Stetsons, boot-cut jeans, and the roper-style short boots; military guys with their high and tight hair cuts and military-themed T-shirts; and the *wanabes*, who wore the gear but didn't have the look that real operators developed in their eyes.

Personally, Mike didn't care what a man did or what he was capable of, just as long as he was honest. There was a place for everyone. Over the years he'd learned that most people who enjoyed shooting were good people. As hard as he tried, he was unable to remember a single incident when anyone had posed a problem at a range or in a shooting class. Sure, there were always those who acted up, but the community was self-regulating, and those people were quickly separated and ostracized.

There was a saying that Robert Heinlein coined in his book *Beyond This Horizon*: "An armed society is a polite society." The truthfulness of this phrase had been proven time and time again in his dealings with other enthusiasts. Whenever people got together to shoot, each person knew the other was capable of defending him, so there were no lions and sheep, just co-equals. So it was with the crowds of people filing past his stand, each one moving so others could pass by or excusing himself as they reached for literature. As the hall began to fill, people started congregating in Mike's booth and asking questions about the academy and the classes that were advertised.

Mike shook hands with several people and answered as many questions as possible; his only regret was that he didn't bring Arrow or Cowboy along to help out. Response to the academy was terrific, and many expressed their eagerness to take classes and visit the facility.

Around noon a couple of young guys arrived at the booth and began looking the scale-model over. Both were clean cut and appeared to be in their mid- to late-twenties. The two were physical opposites. One was tall with a medium frame, and the other was average height but had the build of a competitive wrestler in the 230-lb. weight class. Mike could see they were impressed, so he decided to walk over and describe some of the features of the academy.

"That's a mock-up of the facility we're building in the East Valley. What you're looking at there, is our one-thousand-yard range where we'll teach long distance shooting skills and host local .50-caliber competitions."

The powerfully built man spoke up with excitement in his voice. "This is fantastic." He said. "You say this facility is under construction in the East Valley? Where?"

"It's being built in Queen Creek, off Power Road. Our grand opening is scheduled in six weeks. By the way...my name is Mike West. I'm the Director of Operations."

"Good to meet you. I'm Mark Miller, and this is my buddy Rich Franks. I've been shooting .50s for a little over a year. I really enjoy the sport, but I've had to drive way out to BLM land or up to Nevada in order to shoot. Having a range in the valley will be great!"

"So you shoot .50s. What type of rifle do you have?"

"I have a Barrett M95 with a 10-power scope and quarter-inch mil dots." Mark answered.

"Wow, that's quite a rifle. How long have you had that?"

"Well, it took me a while before I could afford it, but it's been worth every penny. I've had it for about a year. I wish I could have purchased the semi-auto version, but I can work the bolt nearly as fast, and I believe the accuracy is better."

"How much does the M95 weigh?"

"It's not too bad. The whole rifle, including the integrated bi-pod weights twenty-two pounds, slightly more with the scope and a fully loaded magazine. The thing I really like about it is it's easier to handle and a bit shorter than the semi-auto model due to its bullpup design." Mark looked past Mike and saw the *Grunt Gear* vest on display. "Are you going to be distributing *Grunt Gear*? That's the best stuff on the market."

"Matter-of-Fact, the owner of *Grunt Gear* is one of our partners, and he'll be manufacturing his products at the academy. Additionally, he's designing a line especially for DAA, which will only be available at our retail shop or website." Mike explained.

"Fantastic. You know, I've tried gear from a lot of manufactures, and his is by far the best. I've been meaning to have a custom vest made that will allow me to carry several of the M95 magazines. Having him local will make that a lot easier."

Mike could tell this guy really enjoyed shooting the big gun. He'd had the opportunity to fire a .50-caliber and it was truly motivating. The .50 BMG is the largest round you can buy over-the-counter, and it's a beast. Normally a .50-caliber round is built around a 647-grain full metal jacket (FMJ) bullet; compare that to a standard 5.56mm round, used in an AR-15, weighting only 62-grains, and you quickly begin to appreciate its power.

The round's size demanded respect, even without its being fired. Standing nearly 5 ½ inches tall, it was the goliath of bullets. In the past the round was only used in heavy machine guns like the Browning M2, but about ten years ago technological advances in metallurgy and machining allowed rifles and muzzle brakes to be manufactured, allowing a person to comfortably shoot the heavy round with no more felt recoil than a 12-guage shotgun. Although several companies manufactured the rifles, they were still expensive, costing in excess of $5,000 a piece.

There were two kinds of people who shot the .50, the ones that did it for the thrill, and the ones that enjoyed the science. Mark seemed to fall into the latter category. Mark's buddy, Rich Franks, wasn't a .50-cal enthusiast, but he definitely enjoyed shooting, especially tactical courses.

Rich ran a Bushmaster AR-15 and had recently purchased a four-power ACOG sight. Behind him he pulled a cart stacked with three ammo cans, each containing one thousand rounds of .223. Rich moved with a bit of a swagger, the type borne of confidence and a slight touch of cockiness, and Mike could tell right off he had a great sense of humor.

As the three men continued to talk Mike sensed these guys were intelligent and disciplined, just the kind of guys he could use at the academy. Reaching into his pocket, Mike pulled out two cards and began writing down his number.

"Tell you what guys...this is my business card and this is my cell number. I'd like to speak with you some more regarding a couple opportunities we might have at the academy. Why don't you call me next week, and we can meet again, possibly at the academy site. How does that sound?"

Mark and Rich gratefully accepted the cards and assured Mike they'd call him on Tuesday. In addition to promoting the academy, Mike also needed to find a few people he could use to build classes with. He hoped Rich and Mark would be good choices, but only time would tell. The rest of the day the booth stayed busy, and by the end of the weekend Mike was exhausted.

But he'd sold out most of the classes for the first month and had developed leads that would fill even more after that. It looked like everything was falling into place, and DAA was off to a great start.

Since moving to Phoenix, Mike had purposely stayed busy. There were a lot of things to do before the academy opened, and his laundry list of action items never seemed to end. Mike had decided to take advantage of the low cost of housing and buy a house. To help defray the cost, Ethan agreed to rent a room from him. Mike was scheduled to close on the house on Wednesday, so he and Ethan would be able to move-in the following day. Mike was grateful for all the work, because it kept him from missing Rachel too much. But at the moment, the only real concern Mike had was loading the display cases into his truck and getting back to the hotel where he could relax and organize the class schedules he'd sold.

For the grand opening he'd decided to open the ranges to the public and offer child gun-safety classes for free. As a public service the academy would provide classes for local Boy Scout troops interested in earning any of the firearms merit badges. Once a week would be ladies night at the range. One of the fastest growing segments of the firearms industry was women who were getting into the sport for the first time. Mike needed to take advantage of this important trend and wanted to hire female instructors specifically for those classes. Studies had shown that women responded better when other women taught the classes.

The problem of where to find qualified female instructors got him to thinking about the whole subject of women and armed self defense. Unfortunately, society had indoctrinated many women into thinking they shouldn't be aggressive when it came to protecting themselves. This mentality had to be a fairly recent phenomenon, and it was no-doubt a learned behavior, because it certainly wasn't natural and didn't reflect the history of the American woman. Everyone knew the worst place you could find yourself was between a sow bear and her cub; likewise, it was the female lions that were the hunters in the pride.

Of course, Mike reflected, animals are not the same as humans, but even a cursory study of America history proved the strength and courage of women, especially in the West.

The "so-called" women's movement completely ignored self-defense issues for their constituents. Not one group advocated the right of women to carry weapons. On the contrary, they supported anti-gun groups and myopic organizations like the Million Mom March, while at the same time openly declaring that twenty-five percent of American women were at risk of being raped or sexually molested. What was their answer to that grisly statistic? Disarm more women and comfort the violated by ensuring they'd have easy access to abortions. That type of self-serving, useless response was being rejected by hundreds of thousands of women. They understood that the first and best way to take charge of their bodies wasn't to vote pro-choice...but pro-gun.

Agua Prieta, Mexico

Abel Puente received orders to join a group of immigrants, cross the border into Arizona, and identify possible routes that PLA operatives could use for future missions. This reconnaissance was especially important because the US Border Patrol had quintupled in size over the last five years, making it harder to cross the border. There were still open routes north, but the PLA needed current intelligence on which ones were safe. For this mission he was supposed to act like any other immigrant. Abel traveled to the border town of Agua Prieta and began asking for information regarding coyotes. Nicknamed coyotes for their skills at evading the law, smugglers enjoyed a reputation among Mexicans as a modern-day Underground Railroad, bringing the impoverished to jobs and the persecuted to freedom. He soon located a taxi driver who said he knew a coyote who was very skilled and reliable, and for twenty dollars he'd make a phone call and arrange a meeting. Able agreed and thanked the man who, after pocketing the fee, called and made an appointment. The driver informed Abel that the guide was preparing a trip the following evening and agreed to meet Abel that afternoon. The driver dropped Able off at a cantina where he was told to wait inside for a man named Jesus.

After about forty minutes, a man approached Abel and asked if he was waiting for someone. Able answered that he was expecting a friend named Jesus, and then the stranger identified himself as a representative of the guide. The two men shook hands and then selected a table in the back of the cantina, where they ordered a couple shots of Mezcal as Jesus explained the terms. The price would be $800 to cross the border, $1100 to travel to Tucson and $1700 to go to Phoenix.

"We are part of a network that operates inside America," said Jesus. "We can get you over the border, no problem. For just a little more money we can get you a job and deliver you safely anywhere in the country."

"Thank you," Able replied. "But I only need to get across the border into Arizona. I have relatives in Douglas who can help me from there."

"Well," said the smuggler, "That's all right, too. Lots of people already have family in America." He sipped his drink. "I'll tell you what; you look honest and strong. I can arrange a little discount for you, if you'll do a favor for us while you cross over."

"What sort of favor?"

"If you'll carry a duffel bag with you when you cross, I can see that you get across for $100 less."

Able had heard about this sort of thing. It was not part of his mission to help drug-running parasites. "What would be in this duffel bag?" he asked.

The smuggler shook his head. "That's not your concern," he said. "All you have to do is carry it until you arrive at your destination."

"I appreciate the offer," said Able. "It would be nice to save another hundred dollars, but I think I'll pass. I can pay you what you ask."

He gave the man a $400 down payment. The other $400 would be due once they crossed the border. Able was told to meet his group at the local bus station the following evening at the benches next to the south entrance. The two men stood up, and once again shook hands, then separated.

Able left the cantina and walked several blocks before hailing a cab, which drove him to a small park. Able walked around the park ,making sure he wasn't being followed, and then took another cab back to his hotel. Once he was back in his room, he began organizing the gear he'd bring on the trip. The PLA had supplied a small GPS receiver that was sewn into a pocket on his jacket. The on/off and waypoint buttons were positioned so he could easily activate the unit and input data along the way. The receiver could log up to one hundred waypoints that would track his progress so it could be used by the PLA if the route was determined to be safe. In a small rucksack he had several candy bars, two one-liter water bottles, and some additional clothes. Just in case the *La Migra* captured him he carried counterfeit identification papers identifying him as a resident of Chiapas, Mexico.

Finally, Able carried a compact 9mm pistol for protection against the possibility that his coyote was a bandit. If the *La Migra* caught him, he would have to find a way to get rid of it. But he trusted his luck with them more than with *banditos*. After ensuring that everything was in order Able made a phone call to a local cell member and reported that he'd found a group and would leave the following evening.

La Luna Taquería

La Luna was a small Mexican restaurant located in the older district of Chandler. When it was first built it was in the center of town, but over the years new construction had moved most business north. Now, this area was primarily populated by Hispanics and had taken on the appearance of a traditional barrio with *carnecerías* and thrift stores. *La Luna* had become a *de facto* gathering point for immigrant workers to eat before heading off to the corners to await contractors looking for day labor. To better serve the alien immigrant community, Rosita cashed paychecks and sold money orders, wire transfers, and phone cards. Julia introduced Samuel to her aunt Rosita and explained they were going to handout flyers for the OJChA meeting. Rosita was more than happy to help out and volunteered to bring food for the meeting.

Identifying immigrants wasn't difficult for the two students. Like most groups the immigrants subconsciously conformed to an unofficial dress code: Jeans, long sleeved collared shirts and either a white straw cowboy hat or a baseball cap. But what seemed to identify an immigrant the most were his shoes. There was something about Mexican-made shoes that seemed to stand out from those most Americans wore. It was hard to put it in words, but for some reason the shoes always gave them away.

Samuel worked one side of the street and Julia the other. They approached each group and warmly greeted the men, explaining that there was a meeting and everyone was invited, which included their wives or girlfriends. They made sure to mention the gifts and free food, and then moved on. Soon contractors began arriving, and the men climbed in the trucks to be driven off to the various worksites. Julia and Samuel passed out about fifty flyers, which they considered a good quantity.

They speculated that of the fifty they distributed, and the fifty they'd left at *La Luna*, maybe half would be returned at the meeting, which could translate into a couple hundred attendees citywide, if the other teams averaged the same.

US/Mexican Border

Able entered the bus station and casually walked towards the meeting place designated by Jesus. As he approached the benches he surveyed his fellow travelers gathered together, wearing jackets and carrying a variety of bags and backpacks. They looked as though they'd been traveling for several weeks, and Able thought they probably had. Many of the hopeful immigrants who risked the trip across the border were from the state of Oaxaca and Chiapas in southern Mexico. The economies in those regions were in near collapse, especially Chiapas, where a small civil war had raged for several years.

As Able approached, most of the people turned and looked at him. In their eyes Able read volumes about their lives and their dreams. These were good people who worked hard and yearned for a chance to live a better life. They knew it wouldn't be easy, and they understood that many sacrifices lie ahead of them. The mere fact that they were gathered here in this station was a testament to that. Able had already paid $400 and committed to pay an additional $400 upon arrival. Each of these people paid at least that much, not to mention the cost of traveling to Agua Prieta. Able received his money from the PLA, but these people weren't so lucky. Their money was the sum of hard work, painful saving, and generous gifts from family and friends. Looking at these people renewed his dedication to the *reconquista de Aztlán*.

These were his brothers and sisters, and through his efforts they would see the dawning of a new day of freedom and prosperity. Able approached the assembled immigrants and politely greeted them, then set his rucksack down and leaned up against a kiosk that had been locked up for the night. He began adjusting the straps on his bag when a small girl approached. Her shiny black hair was braided and tied with colorful ribbons, and her eyes sparkled with the excitement that children get when they're ready to embark on a new adventure.

"Hola, niña. Que bonito pelo tienes."

"Gracias, Señor. Se va con nosotros?"

"Si linda." Able responded with a tender smile.

At that moment Jesus appeared and waved the group towards the exit. They gathered their belongings and began walking towards the door and a waiting van. The van had all its back seats removed, which allowed everyone to fit inside, but made the trip out of town uncomfortable. As the van passed the outskirts of town, Able noticed they were heading west instead of north, towards the border.

"Why are we heading west?" Abel asked the driver. "I thought we were going to cross at Douglas?"

"Change of plans. La Migra intercepted the last two groups that tried to cross at Douglas. We're going to try a different route to the west. Don't worry; it'll be safer."

Since the Border Patrol began Operation Gatekeeper several years ago, arrests near San Diego, Nogales, and El Paso had skyrocketed, making the routes unprofitable for the coyotes. So naturally, the coyotes shifted to Douglas. At first the Border Patrol only had a couple dozen agents in Douglas, but over the last year that number had grown to over two hundred. Now the Douglas route was too dangerous. But the guide had been successful in getting a group across last week by a new route west of Douglas, and believed the route would still be open. This particular route crossed private land, which was not patrolled by the Border agents, so there was a far less chance of being caught.

The detour added hours to the trip. The van arrived at its departure location around 10:00 p.m. so the crossing time would correspond with the local Boarder Patrol shift change. When the van stopped, the guides opened the doors, and had everyone assemble for some final instructions.

"Okay, this is where we're going to cross." The coyote turned north and pointed into the darkness. "The border is a little more than a kilometer from here. Once we start we'll need to keep moving until we're across. As we're traveling I don't want anyone to talk. We need to remain as quiet as possible. As you can tell, it's dark, and you won't be able to see very far, so stay together and don't get separated. I crossed a group last week on this same route and everything was fine.

"But if we're intercepted by *La Migra* don't run. Those of you who are carrying duffels should throw them as far away as possible. The Gringo's won't hurt you, they'll only ask for your names and where you're from. If this happens, they'll ask you who the guide is...don't tell them. Our story will be that the guide abandoned us, and we just kept going. If anyone turns me in, I'll make sure you never get another guide in the future. Does everyone understand?" Everyone nodded in agreement.

Able relaxed a bit. Apparently this coyote was a good man who only wanted to make money and had no intention to hurt or lead the group into an ambush. Able had no patience whatsoever for the scum that preyed on the downtrodden. Everyone heard stories about criminals who'd led immigrants into ambushes where they were robbed, beaten and abandoned in the desert to die. For this reason most people who crossed the border looked for coyotes who'd been recommended by friends and other family members who'd successfully made the trip north. The coyote waved to Jesus, and the van drove off. Then the group began its brisk walk into the darkness. Abel reached into his pocket and pushed the waypoint button on his GPS receiver, fixing the coordinates of the start-off location into memory. He decided to enter a waypoint every few minutes, which would create an accurate map of the route that he could send back to his superiors. Although this was supposed to be a newer route, it followed a narrow path through the scrub brush and up dry creek beds that had obviously been used by many others.

The rocks and briars that lined the path like a gauntlet didn't bother Able because he was wearing sturdy work boots, but some of the women, and especially the little girl had problems negotiating the obstacles with their dress shoes and sandals.

As the coyote guided the group into another arroyo, the little girl tripped. She was a tough kid and didn't cry, but Able knew she'd probably cut her legs on the sharp rocks that were scattered on the ground. As he made his way over to the young girl, her mother reached out to her and encouraged her to keep moving. Able placed his hand lightly on the mother's shoulder.

"It is late," he said quietly. "Let me carry her until we get to flat ground."

The woman smiled at Able and thanked him for his kindness. She bent down and whispered some words into the girl's ear. The little girl turned towards Able, smiled and raised her spindly arms high in the air. Able reached down and lifted the girl unto his shoulders and clutched her ankles to steady her, and then they hurried forward to catch up with the rest of the immigrants that were already disappearing into the inky darkness.

Fox News Channel

"This is a Fox News Alert. Pentagon sources are reporting that heavy North Korean activity has been monitored just north of the DMZ. We're told that Democratic People's Republic of Korea (DPRK) military forces are assembling in heavy concentrations at what are being referred to as "primary avenues of approach" leading into South Korea at locations identified as the Kaesong-Munsan approach and the Chorwon Valley approach. It is reported that elements of the DPRK I, II, IV and V Corps are taking up what officials refer to as 'war footings.' Additionally, heightened supply activity has been monitored around the nearly five hundred artillery emplacements that are within range of the South Korean capital of Seoul.

"Approximately forty percent of the South Korean population lives within forty miles of the capital. Military leaders have long believed that any invasion of the South would begin with a massive artillery bombardment of Seoul. If that happened, estimates upwards of 40,000 casualties are expected.

"The 2d Infantry Division (2ID) of the US army, based at Camp Casey, is the primary American ground combat asset in Korea. These recent actions have led US and ROK forces to raise alert levels to Watchcon 1 and Defcon 1, which are reserved for eminent wartime action.

"In response to this threat, the Secretary of Defense has issued deployment orders for the 3d Marine Expeditionary Force stationed in Okinawa, Japan. Military experts tell Fox News that the 3d MEF is a division-scale unit comprising the 3d Marine Division, 3d Force Service Group, 1st Marine Air Wing, 3d Marine Expeditionary Brigade, and the 31st Marine Expeditionary Unit, all totaling 17,000 officers and enlisted personnel.

"Also, the 49th Fighter Wing based at Holloman AFB, New Mexico, and the 7th Bomb Wing out of Dyess AFB in Texas, have received deployment orders to Korea. The 49th FW commands two squadrons of F-117A "Stealth Fighters," and the 7th BW operates three squadrons of B-1B bombers.

Finally, the Navy has deployed two additional carrier battle groups to the Western Pacific. These include the USS *Nimitz* (CNV-68) and the newest carrier in the US inventory, the USS *Ronald Reagan* (CVN-76), both based in San Diego. These two carrier groups will join the USS *Carl Vinson* (CVN-70) that is already on station off the Korean coast.

"Pentagon officials' stress that the United States is dedicated to the defense of the Republic of Korea and resolute in its commitment to peace on the Korean peninsula and throughout the region.

"The House and Senate minority leaders gave a joint press conference today where they placed the blame for the current Korean crisis squarely on the administration. Senate Minority Leader Charles Snow (D-MA) remarked, 'This president has no concept whatsoever of international relations. His myopic view of global politics is limited to what he can see through the sights of a gun. The current crisis with North Korea has festered for the better part of his presidency, and when Senate and Congressional leaders have urged, in the strongest possible fashion, for him to engage Pyongyang in constructive and respectful dialogue, his response has been willful neglect and dismissal.'

"House minority leader, Paula Alberti (D-WA) added, 'With the current round of deployments announced today, the military is spread so thin that it is at a breaking point. This president has seemed to forget that we have a State Department whose job it is to interact with our international neighbors on a diplomatic level.

"'Past administrations have been able to accomplish remarkable achievements by sitting down and discussing complex issues. This coupled with his dismissal of the UN's authority leads me to believe the president suffers from a Napoleon complex, and is using the Pentagon as his personal tool for world domination. As opposition leaders, Senator Snow and I are committed to putting the brakes on the runaway and reckless ambitions of this administration before he leads our country into another world war.' This has been a Fox News Alert."

Miracle Valley, Arizona

The train of immigrants had been traveling north for close to two hours when their coyote passed word back that they'd crossed *la frontera* and would soon make a rest stop. Able was in good physical condition, but even he was happy for the break. Many of the immigrants were long overdue for a rest. The terrain the group was crossing was fairly open, with little cover, so he understood the need to keep moving. It would do no one any good to sit out in the open where the Americans could easily find them with their night vision devices.

The route they were on had gradually risen in altitude for the past half hour. The grade wasn't steep, but he noticed larger brush and small trees growing along the way, which confirmed they had climbed off the desert floor and closer towards the mountains. The little girl, having fallen asleep on his shoulders, was slumped over on his head. Able smiled. He always marveled at the way little children were able to fall asleep in the most awkward positions. Able had a little brother who'd been the same way. It didn't matter where they were or what was going on, his brother somehow managed to fall asleep, and once he was out nothing bothered him. Unfortunately, his little brother died several years ago after contracting hepatitis and suffering liver failure. After his skin began turning yellow his parents brought him to the hospital, but by that time his liver was ravaged, and the hospital just didn't have the resources to save him.

Able closed his eyes at the memory. Losing his brother was very hard on him. Perhaps it was that trauma which had pushed him towards the more militant wing of the PLA. Every time he'd see one of the American TV shows about hospitals, like *ER*, he became angry. The Gringos had so much and were able to help so many, but no one offered to help his brother. Not the rich movie stars or the fancy charities that like to boast of their largess while surrounded by poor, third-world children, not even the elegant hospitals with their sophisticated technology. No, all of that was reserved for the bourgeoisie imperialists and their pampered children. Sure, every once in a while some child would receive a free operation to correct a cleft palate, or maybe some conjoined twins would be given a multi-million dollar operation to separate them, but this was a transparent effort to convince the world that the Americans were concerned for others. For the price of just one of those fancy operations, Abel's brother, and a dozen like him could have been saved.

Once the revolution succeeded, resources would be equally distributed to the people. Neo-aristocrats would either humble themselves or reap the fruits of their selfishness and overindulgence.

The column of people approached a wire fence. Abel lifted the girl off his shoulders, passing her to the waiting arms of her mother. Abel walked to the front of the column and helped the coyote spread the wire open so each person could slip through. After everyone had passed under the fence, the guide encouraged them all to rest. The group assembled behind a large stand of bushes that provided concealment. Able could tell others had used this spot for the same purpose; probably the group the coyote had guided the pervious week. Evidently, the fence marked private land, which prevented the border agents from patrolling here.

Abel made sure to enter the location on his GPS and then opened his rucksack. He pulled out a bottle of water and drank it slowly. The guide told everyone they'd rest for another twenty minutes and then head towards the highway, which lay only a few miles away. There, a van would take them to the outskirts of Douglas and onto Tucson and Phoenix. As Able rested and drank his water, he reviewed the route in his mind. He was encouraged that they'd not once had to hide from a border agent, truck or helicopter. Evidently, this coyote had found a route that wasn't patrolled and should prove beneficial to the PLA.

Tempe, Arizona

Trucks and vans delivered men, women, and in some cases whole families to the gathering sponsored by OJChA. As the immigrants entered the discothèque, Tejano music and the aroma of menudo greeted their senses. Young Chicanos were on hand to welcome each person individually. The discothèque was a perfect location for the meeting. It was well known in the local Hispanic community, had an excellent sound system, could accommodate the numbers of people that were expected, and offered ample parking, not to mention the fact that it was provided free of charge.

The owner was an OJChA alumni, and this was one way he continued to support the movement. While the guests were waiting in line for their food, Julia briefed her team leaders on how the meeting would proceed. The purpose of this event was to enlist people for upcoming protests and work stoppages that OJChA planned for the whole region. The protests would be coordinated with chapters all over the Southwest to focus attention on immigrant rights. Their job was to gather information on people in the crowd who'd commit to participating. While Julia was speaking with her team, Samuel was addressing a smaller group with a different mission.

Their job would be to watch the crowd during the speeches and identify individuals who responded aggressively and displayed militant reactions. Once identified, these people would be pulled aside and approached regarding special duties. After everyone received his or her menudo and found a seat, Julia approached the microphone and welcomed everyone.

She explained they had important information to share about upcoming events in support of immigrant rights and hoped they would be willing to assist. They had a couple different speakers who would explain the news, and afterwards everyone would receive a ten-dollar calling card as a thank you for attending the meeting.

Both speakers presented fiery messages that were replete with a combination of ardent nationalism and victimization. It wasn't long before the crowd was passionately caught up in a steady stream of rhetoric, defiantly thrusting fists in the air and chanting slogans as led by the speakers. As this was occurring Samuel and his team were circulating through the crowd looking for those who demonstrated the fervor that they needed.

As the saying goes, "The eyes are the windows to the soul." It is truly amazing what can be learned about a person by closely examining the eyes. Whether we recognize it or not, when we first meet someone we intuitively look at the persons eyes to gauge that person's attitude. As Samuel walked through the crowd he searched each person and saw a whole spectrum of emotions. Some were excited, others were uncomfortable, and still others displayed simple happiness. But as he walked towards the edge of the assembly, he spotted a man who in all respects seemed at ease, and in his element.

Most of the others were agitated, but this man looked calm, except for an intensity that burned in his eyes. Samuel stopped and watched the man as he listened to the speaker. While most reacted to the speakers as though they'd never heard ideas expressed in quite that bold a fashion, this man listened as though the speaker was simply repeating ideas he'd held for years.

What he was hearing wasn't new to him...it was familiar, so much so that instead of the words boiling his emotions to the surface they simply warmed him, like a welcomed friend. It was obvious this man had harbored these feelings in the protected recesses of his soul for years and pondered them so often that they'd long since become a part of his reality.

His eyes betrayed his outward appearance of serenity. Instead of squandering his rage into the cauldron of mob emotion he allowed it to distill into a potent toxin that could become a weapon against his enemies. This was exactly the kind of man Samuel was searching for...a committed and dangerous man.

Chapter 5

> Before a standing army can rule, the people must be disarmed; as they are in almost every kingdom of Europe. The supreme power in America cannot enforce unjust laws by the sword; because the whole body of the people are armed, and constitute a force superior to any bands of regular troops that can be, on any pretense, raised in the United States.
> —Noah Webster

Direct Action Academy

Mike slipped through the crowd that had gathered for the grand opening of the academy. Evidently one of the local news stations had arrived, and he'd received a call on his cell phone to meet Arrow and Josh at the administration building for an interview. Mike had promoted the grand opening for several weeks on local radio stations, at the Great Western Gun Show, and at firearms dealers throughout the valley. As advertised, the ranges were open to the public, free of charge, and one of the classrooms had been reserved for firearms-safety classes. A country and western station provided a remote broadcast, and academy employees were busy grilling hot dogs in the parking lot for hungry visitors. Everything was coming together, and Mike was glad to see the facility finally open.

The senior staff members were taking turns providing tours of the facility to local residents, police, and a couple members of the city council. Tours were scheduled throughout the day, so as many people as possible could see the facility and understand what DAA was all about. Mike learned long ago that people fear what they don't understand. By giving tours of the academy he hoped to dispel fears and concerns about what they'd be doing. One thing that couldn't be underestimated was the fact that people were still dealing with the national trauma inflicted by September 11, and anything to do with guns still gave people pause. Why this was the case, Mike wasn't sure; after all, the terrorists that flew the airliners into the World Trade Towers didn't even have guns. They'd used box cutters to hijack the planes. Yet no one became traumatized whenever a stock boy opened a box of peaches at the local grocery. Nevertheless, Mike understood how guns had been demonized, and he wanted everyone to feel comfortable with the safety, security, and professionalism of the academy and its staff.

As Mike entered the main lobby of the administration building he noticed the news crewman busily setting up their lights and camera, while another politely clipped lapel microphones to Arrow and Josh.

"Look at you guys; you look pretty official. When are they going to send you to make-up?" Mike teased his buddies.

"Don't get smart; you're next." Josh answered.

An attractive Asian woman approached Mike and introduced herself. "Hi, I'm Cindy Kwan with Channel 5 News. You must be Mr. West."

"Good to meet you, Ms. Kwan. How do you want to do this?"

"What I had in mind was a short interview with a couple questions. It's all very routine; let me clip this mike on your shirt, and we should be ready to go." The reporter finished adjusting the mike and then looked back at the cameraman who flashed her the thumbs-up. "Okay looks like we're ready to go." The reporter took her position along side the partners and readied herself.

The cameraman peered into his viewfinder and calmly stated, "Stand-by, we're rolling...in three, two, one..."

"We're at the grand opening of Direction Action Academy in Queen Creek. With me are Taylor Johnson, Mike West, and Josh Eckman, who are in charge of this high-tech facility. Gentlemen, could you tell us a little about the academy and exactly what it'll offer the community?"

Taylor leaned forward and addressed the camera. "Direct Action Academy is a full-service, world-class teaching and shooting facility, where individuals can come and enjoy the shooting sports. We've assembled an excellent staff of instructors who will offer courses in everything from hunting safety to advanced personal protection and tactical program for law enforcement."

"How is this facility different from others in the valley?" The reporter asked as she turned to face Mike.

"Well, as my associate said, DAA is open to all valley residents. We offer facilities where students can learn proper tactical techniques under the highest supervision. This ensures the safest environment possible for everyone, whether they're a local police department practicing hostage rescue scenarios or a housewife taking a concealed carry course."

"Mr. Eckman, I understand you are the owner of a very popular business and teamed up with these gentlemen to add a unique dimension to Direction Action Academy. Would you explain?"

"Thank you, yes, I own a company that manufactures tactical equipment for police, military, and private shooters, it's called *Grunt Gear*. I relocated my business from Southern California and teamed up with this operation because I believe it will quickly become the premier facility of its kind in the United States. I have a retail store in this building as well as an e-commerce site where I'll be offering my regular line of equipment, as well as an exclusive line for DAA."

"So you believe the success of this academy will bring business to the area from around the country?"

"That's our belief. We're expecting to draw students primarily from the surrounding states, but eventually, we believe our reputation will spread, and we'll see students arriving from all over the US" Taylor interjected.

"Thank you for your time, gentlemen, and good luck. This is Cindy Kwan reporting from the Direct Action Academy in Queen Creek."

"Well, that was painless." Mike remarked to his partners as the camera lights dimmed. Usually Mike didn't give the media the time of day, but since this was free advertisement for the academy, he relented. "So how'd we do, boss?" Mike asked Arrow.

"I think it went well; there's not much you can say in a minute, but we hit the 'hot button' words: professional, safety, etc., so I'm sure it'll be fine. At least she wasn't doing one of those investigative reports where you have to worry about them editing your words to meet their agenda."

The production assistant walked over and began taking the mikes off the partners as the cameraman disassembled the tripod and packed up his gear.

Mike checked his watch and noticed that his 1:00 p.m. tour was about to begin, so he excused himself and walked outside towards the flagpole where the tours began. As he approached he noticed the previous tour had just ended and was starting to disperse. Among the group was a familiar face, Councilwoman Gutierrez.

Great, I wonder what this black cloud will bring, Mike thought to himself. *Hopefully she hasn't seen me, and I won't have to talk with her.* After the councilwoman's little maneuver with the environmental impact study, she'd received the honor of joining Mike's *special* short list. Mike took the long route around the group so he could purposely avoid any contact with the councilwoman. Arriving at the flagpole he noticed several people milling around and warmly greeted them.

"Welcome to Direct Action Academy, my name is Mike West and I'm the Director of Operations. I assume you're here for the tour?"

****

Councilwoman Gutierrez, like most politicians, possessed a sixth sense that helped her find cameras, and so it was with the news crew that was leaving the academy. She spotted Cindy Kwan and her crew walking across the parking lot and decided she needed to get their attention. Turning towards no one in particular, the councilwoman called out, "I'll be sure to bring it up at the next city council meeting." For a reporter the words "city council" was like a pheromone.

Cindy immediately spun around and recognized the councilwoman as she waved to some anonymous person. Cindy had been reporting in the valley for nearly six years and had followed Gutierrez's rise to power; furthermore, she knew the councilwoman's reputation for controversial sound bites. In all honesty she was a bit disappointed with the interview she'd taped with the owners of the academy. She'd hoped they'd say some off-hand remark or possibly show up in camouflage. Instead they were professional, well-dressed, articulate businessmen who didn't fit the popular media image of gun fanatics. Catching the councilwoman and getting a few choice remarks on tape, may justify the long drive she'd endured to get to the academy. Cindy grabbed her cameraman's shoulder and gestured towards the councilwoman. "Alex, get your camera ready and let's see if we can get a few words with the councilwoman."

"Councilwoman Gutierrez, do you have a minute?" Cindy hollered as she fast walked across the parking lot.

The councilwoman feigned her best expression of surprise as she looked towards the news crew. "I'm sorry, you seem to have the advantage...who are you?"

"I'm Cindy Kwan from Channel 5 News. I'd like to ask you a couple questions, if you have time."

"Well, I don't have much; I'm due back at the office for an important meeting with the city commissioner. But, I'm sure I can spare a few minutes," the councilwoman graciously replied to the reporter as she adjusted her blouse and primped her well-styled hair.

Cindy established the shot, and the cameraman set the white balance on his camera. "This looks good Cindy," the cameraman said as he handed Cindy the stick mike and adjusted the camera focus. "Stand-by, were rolling in three, two, one."

"We're here with Queen Creek City Councilwoman Alejandra Gutierrez. Councilwoman, could you tell us why you attended the grand opening of the Direct Action Academy?"

"Of course, Cindy. As you know the academy is in my district, and I make it a point to visit as many businesses as I can to meet my constituents and make sure I'm accessible to as many of them as possible."

"What were your impressions of the facility?" The reporter questioned.

"Well, I'm glad you asked. The facility is very nice, but I have to admit that I'm a little troubled with the courses being offered. I have always supported the second amendment, and I know Arizona has many hunters, but this facility is offering classes in close-quarters combat, tactical shooting, and sniper techniques. To me these seem like paramilitary skills, not the kind of things common citizens should be allowed to learn.

"I was shown a one-thousand-yard range where rifles as large as .50-caliber will be used. I'm no expert, but I doubt anyone needs that kind of training or that size gun to hunt ducks."

"What it sounded like to me was a type of 'Camp Al-Qaeda,' and with the threat of terrorism in this country, I'm not sure I'm comfortable with providing that kind of instruction to just anybody."

"What are you planning to do about these concerns?" the reporter inquired.

"I'm still trying to decide, but I feel it's my duty to the people of this community to ensure their safety is protected. I'll be meeting with my staff in the following days, and we'll come up with an appropriate course of action."

"Well, thank you for your time and for your sincere comments." Cindy looked back into the camera and presented her closing line. "This is Cindy Kwan reporting from Queen Creek for Channel 5 News."

The reporter and Councilwoman shook hands and thanked each other. Both women were satisfied. They'd gotten what they wanted. The reporter had her controversial sound bite and the councilwoman had the opportunity to make a veiled attack against the academy while appearing to be concerned with the safety of her constituents. The brief interaction had been truly symbiotic as each party left with contented smiles.

****

Mike gathered his tour group around the entrance of the single story CQC house and began to explain the purpose of the building and how it was used in training.

"This is our single-story, close-quarters combat house. It is the most sophisticated structure of its kind for public use in the state. We constructed this house for advanced training in room clearing and hostage rescue. Its primary use will be to instruct police and sheriff departments on how to enter a hostile building in order to eliminate a barricaded threat and secure hostages."

A lady in the front of the group was intently listening to Mike as he explained the purpose of the CQC house, and when he paused for questions, meekly raised her hand. "Excuse me, I have a question about what you just said," the lady asked in a sheepish tone. "I understand why police and other law enforcement personnel would need to train for these scenarios, but, why would you teach these skills to the general public?"

Mike could tell the lady was uncomfortable with the idea and frankly a little embarrassed asking the question. "That's an excellent question. Thank you for asking it. We believe people are safest when they're self-sufficient; I believe that's what the Boy Scouts teach, isn't that right, sir?" Mike asked a scout leader in the back of the group.

"Yes, sir," the man answered. "Our motto is 'be prepared.'"

Once again addressing the lady who'd just posed the question, Mike continued. "Let's say you live in a rural area, and one night you're awakened by a crashing sound in your home. You and your husband hear voices in your living room and call 911."

"Since you live far from the city the police tell you it'll take twenty minutes to get an officer to your address. By training in this facility you can learn how to safely negotiate blind corners and doorways so you can gather your children and protect your family from threats. I'm a big fan of the police, and I appreciate all they do, but in most cases they're little more than uniformed historians. They arrive after the crime and record what happened. The simple fact is no one will protect your children with the same zeal as you, and if the worst happens, people deserve to know the techniques necessary to safely protect their homes and families. Does that answer your question?"

The lady nodded her head in agreement. "I've always worried about that situation. I've heard things before and have gotten up to search the house and was terrified as I walked around corners. Do you think I could learn those skills?"

"Absolutely. We plan on offering classes for couples and single mothers. I just hired an outstanding instructor named Susan who'll teach our ladies' courses; if you'd like I'd be more than happy to introduce you to her when we finish the tour."

"I'd like that. Thank you," the lady remarked with renewed determination in her eyes.

"Great. If there're no other questions, why don't we walk inside, and I'll show you how the interior can be modified to simulate different types of buildings." Mike began to turn towards the door when another employee approached him.

"Excuse me, Mr. West. Mr. Johnson asked me to tell you to return to the front office. I'll finish your tour."

"Is there a problem?" Mike asked with obvious concern.

"I don't know, but he seemed pretty anxious. You'd better hurry."

Mike thanked the messenger and politely excused himself from the group before hurrying off towards the administration building. *The whole idea of senior staff running the tours was Arrow's idea; whatever it is must be important*, Mike thought to himself. As he approached the glass doors leading into the front office, he noticed Arrow and Ethan standing around someone. Mike's first thought was he hoped no one had been hurt. "Taylor, did you need me?"

"Yeah, a VIP just showed up, and I need you to take her on a special tour." Arrow replied as he moved aside. Standing next to him was Rachel. Mike was completely caught off guard and stood stunned for a second, then quickly crossed the distance between them and wrapped his arms around the beautiful redhead.

"What a great surprise! I didn't know you were coming," Mike whispered into Rachel's ear as he embraced her.

"I know; I decided to surprise you and come over for the weekend, and the guys thought it'd be fun to play along."

"I told you to take this special lady on a personal tour of the facility. I suggest you get started." Arrow said in a commanding voice.

"If you can't handle it, I'd be happy to take the job," Cowboy added.

"No thanks. I think this assignment falls under my job description. I'll escort this precious cargo personally. Thanks again, guys, I really appreciate this."

Even though they'd only been apart a few weeks, Mike was surprised how much difference it made to see and hold Rachel. Mike had never felt this way about a woman. In the past he'd enjoyed the company of the girls he'd dated, and of course, he'd had feelings for them, but he'd never felt such a dependency on someone else. This realization was both troubling and comforting for him. Mike wondered how he might feel if something happened to her or if events were to pull him away from her, but at the same time he was grateful he'd finally found someone whom he could truly love and share his life with. As he walked Rachel around the academy, pointing out the various ranges and other training locations, he caught himself gazing at her as the Arizona sunlight danced off her silky sundress and unblemished complexion. He wondered how he'd ever found such a beautiful woman, and once again he confessed to himself he was deeply in love with her. As they arrived at a secluded spot Mike pulled Rachel around the side of a building, then carefully pushed her against the wall and kissed her passionately. At first he was surprised by how his desire had overtaken him, but Rachel's response confirmed she felt the same way. She held him tightly, digging her fingernails into his hair while she wrapped her right leg around his thigh; the rest of the tour would have to wait.

Channel 5 Evening News

"A new shooting academy opened today in Queen Creek, and our reporter Cindy Kwan is here to give us a report on the event…Cindy?"

"Thank you, Wayne. I visited the Direct Action Academy and interviewed three of its founders to find out more about their business." The video of the interview began rolling which featured the partners answering questions posed to them by the reporter.

As audio of the interview continued, footage showing the facility and the people who'd gathered for the grand opening appeared on screen. Then the video ended and the image returned to Cindy Kwan in the studio.

"Although the owners of the academy painted an attractive picture of the new facility, not everyone who attended the opening felt comfortable with the curriculum offered at Direct Action Academy. Councilwoman Alejandra Gutierrez, in whose district the academy was built, attended today's grand opening and shared some insightful comments with News 5."

The video of the councilwoman's remarks was played with creative editing that focused on children and mother s holding babies. As the segment finished the camera returned to Cindy Kwan who was wearing a concerned expression. The anchor looked towards Cindy and remarked, "That is troubling."

"I agree. The idea of professionals providing sniper and combat training to *just anyone* is indeed disturbing. We'll make sure to follow-up on this and whatever the councilwoman does and keep you informed."

"Thank you Cindy."

Arrow, Mike, Rachel, Josh and Ethan had gathered for a celebratory barbecue and were watching the interview on television. As the segment ended there was a moment of silence that punctuated their collective disbelief in the biased report on the academy.

"What a bunch of crap!" exclaimed Ethan, breaking the awkwardness of the moment. "She made us sound like some kind of terrorist-training camp."

"I knew I shouldn't have allowed that left wing propagandist to interview us. I'm calling the station manager and demand they retract the report or offer us the opportunity to offer a rebuttal." Arrow added.

"Who's this Gutierrez woman, and why does she have it in for you guys?" Rachel asked.

"She's the one who pulled our environmental impact study because we wouldn't allow illegal aliens to work on the project. I guess she decided this would be a good way to get a little revenge." Mike answered. "I'll tell you, unless Sean Hannity, G. Gordon Liddy or Roger Hedgecock asks for an interview...I say no more reporters." He added in an angry tone. Mike had never trusted the media, and this was proof his distrust was well justified. "At least she should have shown enough professionalism to call and tell us what Gutierrez said, so we could counter her bias. But I guess that would be asking too much."

"That's exactly what I'm going to tell the station manager. This was a complete hatchet job, and I'm not going to allow this to go without raising some hell." Arrow responded.

Mike looked over at Rachel and took her by the hand. "Hey, babe, it's a nice evening. Why don't we go for a walk?"

Rachel agreed, and the two excused themselves and walked outside. As they left the house, Rachel looked down at Mike's pistol and remarked, "It's strange seeing you wear your gun in the open."

"Does it bother you?"

"No, not at all. It's just different. I know you always carried in California, but it was concealed. I guess out of sight, out of mind, you know what I mean?"

"Yeah, at first it was weird walking around town openly armed, but I figure it's my civic responsibility to remind people it is legal and to emphasize that not everyone with a gun is evil. You know it's just like that idiot councilwoman, she wants everyone to believe that guns are bad and people with guns are worse. But she doesn't understand, or worse, she knows and purposely deceives the people she's sworn to serve. The fact is many people are willing to take care of themselves, and unfortunately, in the world we live in that often requires being armed. The truth is, elitists like Gutierrez don't want self-reliant people, because then *they're* not empowered."

"There's a difference between politicians and public servants. Public servants work towards improving their community, state, or nation. Politicians work solely to enhance their own personal power, and the more people they can make dependent upon them, the more powerful they become. I'm no anarchist. I believe in government, but this country was founded upon the idea of limited government, not the Orwellian, cradle-to-grave leviathan that has metastasized into what we have now. So, let the sheep feel the uncomfortable twist in their stomachs when they see me carrying."

"Maybe it will shock them out of their apathetic comas long enough to remember they share a responsibility to protect and defend freedom, and maybe one day a child will look at its father and ask, 'Daddy, why don't *you* carry a gun?' Then what will the man say? Will he admit to his child that he's surrendered his duty as a citizen and a father to protect and defend the most important things in his life, or will he have the courage to search his soul and accept that his freedom and family are personal endowments from God, and no hireling will suffice as sentinel?

Rachel had learned that when Mike spoke in this fashion it wasn't for approval, it was a way of getting in touch with the feelings that defined his character. It was as though a spirit whispered an unknown language to his soul, and by voicing the words he came to understand the message. Rachel sensed a power in Mike's words. Maybe it was the confidence behind them. Perhaps it was the knowledge that he was a man with vision, a man who understood that there was something greater than himself, something worth fighting for. Rachel was tired of the narcissists at school with their omnipotent attitudes. Sure, these guys were intelligent, some were even geniuses, but they allowed that single trait to define their personality to the detriment of every other facet of their character. They believed they were the best and brightest, and as such, society should orbit them, and their intellect would expunge all the woes in the world.

In fact they were nothing more than one-dimensional children clinging to the one gift in their lives that had never forsaken them, unwilling to take a chance because failure was too great a price to pay.

As Rachel slid her arm tightly around Mike's waist she understood that what made him a great man wasn't his intellect or strength; it was his unconquerable spirit and willingness to risk everything in the face of uncertainty, not for wealth, power, or fame, but because honor demanded it. As they continued to stroll in the warm desert night she secretly smiled to herself, jealously storing her thoughts where only she could enjoy them. She'd share most of her thoughts with friends and loved ones, but this one was just for her…as it should be.

Hermosillo, Mexico

Over the past month PLA headquarters stayed busy processing intelligence reports from cell units across the border region and inside the US. They'd analyzed the after-action reports from *Operation Aztec Wind* and developed a clear picture of response times, assets, and vulnerabilities of the police and fire departments. Additionally, the information provided a clear picture of how the media could be manipulated to their benefit.

Major Al-Salih was impressed with the way the organization came together, and processed the information. The PLA was disciplined and dedicated to their mission, but the major was most impressed with OJChA.

He expected a military wing to be disciplined, but he'd underestimated the degree of commitment displayed by students and politicians. He admitted to himself that in this regard they were better structured than parallel organizations in the Middle East. The success of *Aztec Wind,* and the impressive work that had followed led the major to immediately request additional funds from Damascus in order to carry out larger operations.

Since arriving in Hermosillo he'd became intimately familiar with the extent of OJChA's political contacts within state governments and the groundwork they'd already established. The more he learned about the laws these operatives had been fundamental in passing, the more astonished he was that America still remained intact. Across the United States cities had declared themselves immigrant sanctuaries where illegals would not have to worry about prosecution or deportation. Furthermore, they were guaranteed public support in the form of finances, heath care, education, and housing. It was no wonder so many of these cities were in financial ruin. Nevertheless, additional progress was being made, including allowing illegals to have driver's licenses. On the surface this seemed innocuous, after all they needed licenses in order to drive to work and contribute to the economy. But since most states accepted a state-issued driver's license as proof of identification, this allowed Mexican nationals to register and vote in local, state, and federal elections.

It was no wonder they'd been able to accomplish so much in such a relatively short time. The major simply couldn't believe the naïveté of the Americans; they were so preoccupied with not being labeled a racist, that they were willing to forfeit their entire country. A nation so weak and delusional shouldn't be allowed to survive; it just wasn't the way an omnipotent God worked. *Aztec Wind* was a test. Now a steady stream of attacks would begin, each one focused on destroying the economy of the Southwest and bringing the Americans to their political knees. The economy was the Achilles' heel of America. It was the centerpiece of every election and the one issue that influenced all others. As long as the Americans could freely worship at the altar of hedonism, nothing else mattered. But once their idolatries were interrupted they quickly eroded to a state of social cannibalism, devouring their own leaders and morals for the mere hope of a return to their lives of luxury.

The US stock market was experiencing the first sustained recovery following three years of recession. Consumers were beginning to feel more confident about their financial security, and this confidence translated into an increase in consumer spending. After many months of struggling, stores were beginning to see sales increases, and manufacturing was ramping up to meet renewed demand for products. With this rise in spending, new jobs were being created, and once again employees began to receive long-forgotten bonuses and increases in their 401(k)s and stock portfolios. The consumer sector had kept the economy afloat during the recession, but just barely. Now with Washington pursuing worldwide wars of imperialism and throwing its military might against Islam, defense contractors began rehiring laid-off workers to build new equipment in order to meet orders for more weapons and war machines.

The latest economic recession was a natural result of a change in the mode of production. With the rapid adoption of the Internet, companies raced to find new ways of doing business in cyberspace, and the " dot com" economy was thrust on an ill-prepared business world. Every major American corporation got caught up in the frenzy to stake their claim on "The Net." The problem was, few understood the new technology or had the slightest idea how to exploit it. Thus, corporations blindly spent billions of dollars in a panic to hire anyone who even remotely promised them access to the wealth of the Internet; it was like a corporate quest for the mythical *El Dorado*.

One of the few positive outcomes of the entire dot com experiment was the success of parcel delivery services, like FedEx and UPS. Even while dot com companies were struggling to become profitable, these companies were busy transporting hundreds of millions of packages each day, becoming as essential to internet business as the stacks of high-tech servers that dominated IT departments. The fact is that all the technology of e-commerce comes down to the product showing up intact and in a timely fashion at the customer's front door. Because of this phenomenon the parcel delivery truck became as ubiquitous in American society as McDonald's golden arches. The difference is that McDonald's makes an effort to be visible in order to attract business, whereas UPS is its virtual antithesis.

Its brown, utilitarian trucks and equally understated employee uniforms make parcel deliverymen the quintessential ghost in American society, able to go almost anywhere unchecked and become almost invisible, even though people constantly surround him. UPS is the paradigm of this theory, so it was decided to use their trucks as platforms for truck bombs that would devastate targets in Los Angeles and Phoenix.

The problem is that UPS trucks are custom made by a company in Indiana, and once they reach the end of their service cycle they are scrapped under the supervision of company inspectors. Thus, getting a hold of the numbered vehicles is extremely difficult. On the other hand, obtaining copies of the blueprints used to manufacture the uniquely-shaped trucks was just a matter of paying off the right disgruntled employee.

Union City Body Company, Indiana

Fred Wilcox had worked in the design department of Union City Body Company for nearly five years. Union City Body is the exclusive manufacturer of UPS trucks. He'd been a loyal employee and worked hard in order to position himself for advancement and greater responsibility. Through the difficult times he made sacrifices for the company and even forfeited vacations in order to prove his dedication to his department management staff. Now, he learned that he'd lost yet another promotion to someone with less time on the job. The kid that would now be supervising his group was chosen because he had a master's degree, and the company believed he'd prove to be a long-time asset. Fred felt betrayed. So what if he didn't have a fancy degree? What he had instead was years of experience and loyal service, but he figured that didn't matter anymore. Upper management was nothing but a fraternity where a secret handshake and some Greek letters tattooed on your ass opened doors and made all the difference.

While brooding at the local bar over his latest defeat, a man approached Fred and struck up a conversation. Before long the two guys had begun a new friendship built on common experience, dirty jokes, and a bottle of Jack Daniels. Over the next few days the friends met and further solidified their relationship. Then one day Fred's buddy told him about a guy who'd pay $10,000 for a copy of blueprints used to manufacture trucks for UPS. Fred was told the man was starting a parcel delivery service in Brazil and wanted to design a truck similar to, but not exactly like, the ones that proved so successful for UPS. At first Fred rejected the proposal, but the more he contemplated the offer the more he liked the idea of sticking it to the company. Better still, he reflected, if it were ever learned that someone had gotten a copy of the plans, his new supervisor would probably take the heat and be fired. Anyway, Brazil was a long way away from Indiana, so the chance of anyone finding out had to be pretty remote. In the meantime $10,000 would buy him an excellent bass boat. After a couple more beers, Fred agreed to deliver the plans.

Direct Action Academy

Mike escorted Chief Meadows down a hallway towards the monitoring room that was christened "The Nintendo Room." The two men approached a door that had been painted with a brightly-colored cartoon depicting a crazed teenager with wild hair and bloodshot eyes playing a video game in the dark.

"Nice depiction! How'd you get my son to sit still long enough to paint it?" joked the chief.

"This is the monitoring room where we'll be able to watch your SWAT guys do their room entry drills." Mike opened the door, revealing a room set up theater style with three tiers of tables and chairs.

Against the opposite wall were three banks of giant, color LCD screens. These monitors displayed the live video that was fed by the closed circuit cameras positioned in the CQC houses. The video feed ran straight to Ethan's IT room where it was stored on disk, much like the digital video recorders that attach to your TV for recording programs without tape. The video stream was then transferred to a control station in the corner of the room where the data could be manipulated, allowing stop and slow action, rewinds, or real-time. Each SWAT member wore a small transmitter that sent an alphanumeric signal to the computer so his number would be superimposed on his image allowing the viewer to distinguish who was doing what. The entire exercise was recorded and could be downloaded onto VHS tape or DVD for future review.

"This is a fantastic setup. I've seen this technology on the Discovery Channel, but it was at a military base somewhere back East." The chief commented.

"Yeah, it used to be only the military could afford it, but over the past several years it has become more affordable. It's a perfect example of Moore's law."

What Mike was referring to was a theory created by Gordon Moore, the co-founder of Intel. He hypothesized that computer power doubles every eighteen months. Thus, technology that was cutting edge two years ago will have been surpassed, making that technology both more obtainable and affordable. The chief had scheduled his SWAT team for room entry and clearing training. They'd be using the single-story house, and Cowboy was instructing them. They'd done this type of training before, but dynamic entry skills were easily lost if not continually practiced; there were just too many variables involved, and the more practice a team could accomplish, the better they'd respond in a real situation. Cowboy had done a lot of CQC training in Force Recon, so his instructions were clear, and each one was backed up with real life experience.

Ethan brought the team up on the center screen. They were stacking up outside the main door in preparation for entry. Today they were rehearsing an entry known as a "buttonhook." On the hinge side of the door one officer acted as the breecher and another as an assistant breecher. Normally the breecher would either place an explosive charge on fortified doors, or use a battering ram to knock the door down, creating an entry and diversion for the assault team. In today's exercise, a battering ram would be used. Although the battering ram only weighted thirty-five pounds, it created nearly 19,000 pounds of kinetic force, more than enough to take most doors off their hinges. The assistant was in charge of throwing in a flash bang grenade. Members of the entry chalk held their weapons, which in this case were H&K MP-5s, with the stocks up against their right shoulder and right hands firmly clutching the grips. Their left hands were placed on the shoulder of the man in front of them. While the lead officer focused his attention on the door, the second man turned his head and said something to the man behind him who passed the message down the line.

Each man then gripped the shoulder of the teammate in front of him until the number one man knew everyone was ready. He signaled to the breecher, who stepped in front of the door, and with one powerful swing of his ram, the door blew open. The assistant breecher then tossed a flash bang into the room.

The second screen presented a split view, one side focused on the entry from inside the room, and the other presented a view that was 90 degrees from the door. A flash bang grenade is loaded with a mixture of finely powdered aluminum and potassium, which when ignited, burns extremely fast, producing a spectacular flash equaling 40,000,000 candlepower and creates a momentary pressure wave of three thousand pounds per square inch. This combination temporarily incapacitates the senses of anyone in the room, allowing the entry team about five seconds to enter and engage their targets. The instant the grenade detonated, the team leader stepped into the doorway and immediately stopped to engage a target directly in front of him. This momentary pause forced the rest of the team to slam into one another in sequence, throwing off their momentum. After shooting the target, the leader peeled off to his right and engaged another target in his primary point of domination before taking a position in the right-hand corner covering the one to two o'clock sector.

The number two man then cleared the doorway and immediately turned left to cover the nine- to eleven-o'clock area, and the third man cleared the center portion of the room with an overlapping field of fire covering eleven to one o'clock. The last man in the room moved up behind the number three man, who then moved into a back-up position behind the team leader. "Clear right...Clear left...Clear center!" each officer yelled out, before stacking up again in preparation for entering an adjoining room. As soon as the team was set for their next entry, a flashing red strobe light went off in the room signaling a stop in action. Since the trainees wore ear protection, Cowboy insisted on installing the light as a visual signal to cease fire and safe weapons in preparation for instruction.

"All right, guys, I want magazines out and all actions opened on the range." Cowboy announced over the speaker system in an authoritative Marine Corps bark. Once all shooters had cleared their weapons, Cowboy entered the room.

"That was pretty smooth, but there were some problems...did anyone catch 'em?" The SWAT members looked at each other but didn't say anything.

"We got all the targets, right?" asked one of the men.

"Yes, you did, but the ends didn't justify the means. When you entered the room..." Cowboy said pointing to the team leader. "...you engaged a target in the middle of the kill zone. That's not your sector. Whose is it?"

"Number three has the middle sector," the officers said. "But, I had a clear shot."

"Yes, you did, but by taking the time to engage that target you forced your team to pile up in the funnel. In the fraction of a second it took you to shoot, the rest of your team was piled up in the doorway. If this were for real you all would have ended up becoming bullet sponges. Another problem was that you left your right flank unguarded. You guys are a team and have to work as one. You have to trust the guy behind you to engage that target as you move to your point of domination. Remember, if you're stacked up correctly, you'll be nuts to butt and he should be looking directly towards his field of fire. That target is his, just like the one on the right is yours. Does everyone understand?"

As Mike and the chief sat watching the replay in the "Nintendo" room they noticed that the target on the right side of the room was beside a cabinet, upon seeing this, the chief remarked, "That guy had cover and could have used it to protect himself from the effects of the grenade. If that happened, he might not have been incapacitated to the same degree as the others, allowing him to react quicker and giving him a chance to shoot. Your man's right. If the leader was shot he would have gone down in the doorway, blocking the rest of the team and compromising the whole entry."

"You're absolutely correct. That doorway is called the 'fatal funnel,' so we instruct our students to clear it as quickly as possible. If you're going to take a casualty, chances are it'll be in the funnel. Wait until they reset for the next entry. Cowboy will probably move a piece of furniture in front of the door creating an obstacle. I've watched whole teams end up in a heap because they run right into something. It's funny on tape, but it'd be a catastrophe in a real operation."

"Being able to watch things from this perspective is fantastic. This will improve our training by leaps and bounds." the chief remarked.

The SWAT team moved out of the house and began regrouping for their next entry while Cowboy reset the room. During the short break Mike decided to ask a few questions of the chief.

"Dan, do you mind if I ask you a few questions regarding those fires that destroyed the housing tracts last month?"

"No, what would you like to know?"

"I was wondering if you were able to find out who was responsible and why they did it. After all, it seemed like a well-coordinated operation, and no one has claimed responsibility. That struck me as strange." Mike took political violence and terrorism courses at school, and knew that attacks like those in question were done to gather media attention, and were always proudly claimed, especially the successful ones.

"The local departments were almost immediately removed from the investigation as soon as the attacks were linked to the fires in San Diego, making it a federal jurisdiction. But, since I have federal contacts from my days in Phoenix, I've been able to follow the investigation and learned the BATFE gathered samples of the ignition substance and had them analyzed back in Washington."

"They learned that thermite grenades were used to start the fires. Evidently, the chemical composition of thermite varies worldwide; further analysis proved the thermite was of US origin. The strange part is they were able to track the composition back to where it was produced and even which batch it belonged to. My sources tell me that that particular batch was sold to the Israelis in the late 1990s."

"Israel? So how did it get from Israel to the Southwestern United States?" Mike questioned.

"Actually, the question is, how did they get from the Middle East to the United States? The IDF is involved in operations all over the region, so those grenades could have ended up almost anywhere. They could have been captured or simply lost by a careless Izzy in half a dozen countries." the chief remarked.

"So, why haven't I heard anything about this on the news? I mean if there's a possible Middle East connection I'd think the media would be all over this." Mike was amazed by the information; he'd thought it was just another radical environmental group trying to make an issue over urban sprawl.

"First, no one has proof pointing to any Middle Eastern connection. Those grenades could have circled the globe being bought and sold by one arms dealer after another. After all, they're simple devices. It's not like we're talking about howitzers. But I'll tell you this much, the government is extremely careful with the 'T-word' these days. Nothing takes the wind out of the economic sails like the word *terrorism*...especially when it's the Middle Eastern type. I know this'll sound crazy, but domestic terrorist are nearly welcome versus Islamic terrorist. The animal rights whack jobs and the granola crunchers like the ELF might spray paint SUVs, burn down houses, or raid laboratories, but they don't fly airliners into buildings full of people. At least that's Washington's mentality. To me they're all the same and should be treated as such. But then again, I'm just a small-town police chief in Arizona."

Mike was surprised by the chief's forthrightness. He agreed that terrorist were terrorists, regardless of where they were from or what their agenda was. If not, then why bother calling them terrorists? Just call them criminals; after all there was a difference. But he had to admit the Animal Liberation Front and the Environmental Liberation Front seemed to get a pass from the feds.

It was just like when the anarchists rioted in Seattle during the WTO conference. When the press interviewed President Clinton, he smiled and with a nostalgic glimmer in his eyes simply said that political protest was the hallmark of a free society. Political protest has nothing to do with looting stores, breaking windows, and burning cars. Those were riots, and they cost the city of Seattle millions of dollars.

It seemed like whenever left wing socialists destroyed property or disrupted society, federal officials gave them a slap on the wrist. On the other hand, have a group of gun owners who support the Constitution gather together, and the BATFE and FBI deploy tactical teams in order to save the country from the militia. Over the years the ALF had broken into laboratories and freed lab animals carrying all manner of diseases. These animals were allowed to roam free where they might have spread these diseases among the population. As far as Mike was concerned this was biological warfare, but were these groups demonized in the media? No. Tens of millions of dollars in property have been destroyed by these groups, but had they been hunted down and eliminated? Once again the answer was a resounding no. Yet, patriot groups were under constant attack and scrutiny. To Mike it simply didn't make sense.

The SWAT team was ready to make another entry into the CQC house. Just as Mike had expected, this time Cowboy had rearranged the furniture so a couch blocked the doorway. "This ought to throw a wrench in their routine." Mike told the chief.

As before the breaching officer knocked the door open, then the assistant breecher tossed in the flash bang. The screen momentary went white from the powerful explosion of light. As soon as the image returned, the first man entered the door and saw the couch obstructing the funnel. With his right hand still controlling his submachine gun he smoothly reached down with his left hand, grabbed the corner of the couch and flung it out of the way, then proceeded to the right where he put a three round burst into a target and took up a covering position. The rest of the men followed in an orderly and smooth manner. Their upper bodies remained erect, virtually motionless, while their legs glided them forward. The second man through the door nearly ran into a target that was just slightly to the left of the doorway. Immediately he put a round squarely into the forehead of the target, then used his left forearm to chop the target to the ground. On his back the third man cleared the funnel and engaged two targets in the center of the room, each with three-round bursts that tore fist-sized holes into the centers of the targets. Before the echo from the flash bang device had faded, the whole team was in the room and each man was hollering out, "clear!"

As the rest of the team maintained their defensive positions, two officers moved from one target to another where one simulated "eye-thumps" and flex cuffing, and the other provided cover. An eye-thump is performed by flicking a person in the eye with your finger. This is to ensure that the bad guy isn't playing possum; if he is it'll produce an involuntary flinch that'll alert the officers.

The red light began to flash and once again Cowboy called to clear weapons. After everyone's weapon was safe, Cowboy reentered the room.

"That's the way a room is cleared! You guys were a machine." Speaking to the team leader Cowboy said, "You must have been pretty pumped up, because you threw that couch half away across the room."

"Yeah, this training is pretty motivating. Nothing like explosions and gunfire to get the pucker factor up." The leader breathlessly answered.

"Well it looked picture perfect to me. Let's go watch it on tape and see if we can find any problems."

Montebello, California

Montebello is located between East L.A. and the San Gabriel Valley. Hector Guzman had grown up in this traditionally Mexican part of L.A. and now operated a body shop where he'd gained a reputation for creating award-winning Low Riders. He was especially fond of OG-style cars, but occasionally built Euros and Hoppers. Although he was an excellent mechanic his forte was the artwork he painted on the hoods of the cars. He paid tribute to his Chicano heritage by painting beautiful murals depicting traditional icons like the Virgin of Guadalupe and of course sensual Chicanas. His talent was at a premium, and custom jobs cost as much as $10,000 just for the artwork.

Hector's talent came naturally, and his only schooling was obtained at car shows and from other artist in the community. He'd learned mechanics and bodywork from his father, who'd started the garage after returning from Vietnam. While in the Army his father worked in the motor pool repairing trucks and anything else with wheels and an engine. Maybe it was an act of rebellion against all the olive drab paint and no-frills features of Army vehicles that drove his father into the world of low riders. Whatever it was, he took to it with a vengeance and became one of the top designers in the Valley. Growing up around the garage Hector learned from his father and uncles and later introduced a new generation of technology to the family business, like hydraulics that would allow the car to raise and lower at all four corners. The

Guzman family adopted the low rider motto of "Low and Slow, Mean and Lean" and took it to a new level.

Although Hector never attended college, his cousin Marcelo did, and while at San Gabriel Community College he joined OJChA. Every month the chapter would have a low-rider gathering, and Marcelo would bring Hector along with one of his cars. The two were always the center of attention, and his cars acted as a magnet for *las chicas*.

It was at one of these meetings that Marcelo met his wife, Carmen. Carmen was a beautiful, raven-haired Latina with strong features and a passion for her culture; she was primarily responsible for introducing a militant attitude about Aztlán into the family. For a wedding gift Hector painted an incredible mural of Carmen wearing a revealing leather Aztec warrior outfit and holding a *Macahuittle* high above her head on Marcelo's Monte Carlo. It was one of his favorite pieces and won him his first grand prize at the annual L.A. Low Rider Show.

Today Hector was meeting a new client who'd been recommended by Marcelo and Carmen. Evidently this potential client had an important job for Hector that would make a difference not only for him, but also for *La Raza*. Around ten o'clock in the morning, Marcelo and Carmen arrived at Hector's garage and introduced Jaime Salazar, who they said was a liaison for the *Partido por la Liberacíon de Aztlán*.

"*Bienvenido, Señor Salazar,* it's good to meet you. Please come in and have a seat." Hector said as he welcomed the man into his office.

Jamie, Marcelo, and Carmen took seats around a small table with various drawings spread on it. Hector closed the door and then joined the trio at the table.

"Hector, I've seen your work at various shows and in Lowrider Magazine; I'm a big fan." Jamie said.

"Thank you, Señor. That's very kind of you. My *primo* tells me you're with the PLA. What can I do for *la raza*?" Hector asked his new acquaintance.

"Señor Guzman, as you know the PLA is dedicated to reclaiming the historical land of Aztlán from the Anglos that stole it from our forefathers. We know that you and your family are faithful Chicanos who share this goal. The time has come for Aztlán to rise again and take its place among the powers of the world, and your people have an important role for you to play. Because of security concerns I do not have all the information you may wish to receive, but what I do know I will gladly share with you. First, I must ask you to take a leap of faith and accept the mission I've come to offer. I'm asking that you accept this job in the name of the Chicano people and the glory of our cause. If you refuse, no harm will come to you, but this meeting will end, and you will never be approached by the PLA again. Do you understand what I've said?"

Hector was caught off guard by the weighty nature of the man's announcement. He had expected to be offered a job designing a special car or artwork for OJChA to be used as a publicity tool. Suddenly, he was being asked to play a role in the reestablishment of the Chicano homeland. He looked across at his cousins; both wore resolute expressions on their faces that silently conferred confidence and approval of what had been presented by the PLA representative. Over the years Hector had learned to trust Marcelo and Carmen's advice, since they both had degrees and were successful professionals.

Hector reasoned that if they were comfortable with this issue then he should be as well. Hector straightened his posture, looked directly at Jamie and replied by quoting the motto of OJChA, "*La raza es todo.* "(For the race is everything.)

Hector's declaration replaced the tension of the moment with an electric sense of excitement. Jamie reached across the table and shook Hector's hand, thanking him for his willingness to serve in this historic cause. Jamie reached down and picked up his briefcase, placed it on the table, and withdrew a thin stack of diagrams. He spread the blueprints out and proceeded to explain what Hector's job would be.

"We'd like you to build six trucks according to these plans. You'll need to build them from scratch using materials gathered from various sources. You are to construct the trucks as close to these plans as possible. Most important is the final vehicles must be able to carry a payload of at least two-tons."

Hector examined the plans and immediately recognized what they were. "You want me to build UPS trucks?"

"Yes. Don't ask me why, because I don't know. But, I do know you'll need to have all six completed within ninety days. Furthermore, this project must be accomplished under the strictest security. We're going to ask you to close your shop to all further business and focus entirely on this project. We understand this will affect your business, but we're prepared to compensate you generously for your work as well as cover all expenses."

"May I ask what your definition of generous compensation is?" Hector cautiously asked.

"We are prepared to offer you $50,000: $10,000 now, another $15,000 after the first three trucks are completed, and the remaining $25,000 when all six are finished. Furthermore, if you finish early, you'll receive an additional $10,000 bonus. Are you comfortable with those terms?"

Hector was caught off guard by the size of the offer, but the idea of over fifty thousand dollars excited him like a charged wire. Before Hector could answer, Jamie once again reached into his briefcase and produced an envelope, which he passed across the table. Hector opened the unassuming envelope and ran his finger across the edges of a hundred, one hundred dollar bills. *This is for real.* Hector thought to himself.

"That sounds fine. I have a couple jobs currently in progress, but they're small and my crew ought to be able to finish them by the end of the week. Speaking of my crew, do you have any problems with them working on this job?"

"Actually, we've been watching your employees and gathering information on them over the past couple weeks. We believe all of them, with the exception of Luis, should be fine. You'll have to let him go. But, we've found another job for him at a garage across town. We suggest you offer him an appropriate severance check so he leaves without conflict or negative feelings. If you need a replacement for him, we'll recommend one. After your team is set, I'll return, and the two of us will brief the group and further discuss security measures."

"That sounds good. When will we meet again?"

"I'll call you at the end of the week to get an update on how your remaining jobs are coming. We'll set up another appointment then."

Hector closed the envelope and slid it into his waistband, then reached across the table and shook Jamie's hand once more. "I have a lot of work to do before the end of the week...I better get started."

Fox News Channel

"The Middle East topped the list of issues debated today in the House of Representatives. Democratic leaders continued their assault on the president's Middle East plan, calling it ill conceived, irresponsible, and grossly over budget. Democratic House Minority Leader Paula Alberti demanded that the administration begin to withdraw troops in accordance with the ninety-day limit granted by the War Powers Act of 1973. Republican leadership quickly pointed out that due to concurrent resolutions the president's authority has been constitutionally extended.

"Senate Democrats presented a letter to the White House today calling for the president to recall recent troop deployments to Korea and commit to new UN-sponsored talks aimed at addressing the Korean and Iranian nuclear crises. Sources tell Fox News that if this proposal is rejected, Democrats plan on initiating steps leading towards impeachment.

"In other news Mexican-American groups staged mass protests in Los Angeles, San Diego, and Phoenix. Protestors demanded greater workers' rights for Mexican immigrants, including state-funded workers' compensation and Social Security benefits for undocumented workers. Organizers pointed out that thousands of Mexicans are working around dangerous machinery and chemicals every day, and they suffer appalling injuries that should be covered by medical insurance, and they should have paid time off for physical recovery, just like other workers. They are demanding an end to the double standard they believe is because of racial bias against Mexicans. In an interview, Raul de Soto, spokesman for Workers International, remarked, 'Why is it in the twenty-first century, we continue to allow men and women to work in dangerous conditions without the protection of government? The answer is that immigrant workers from Mexico are used by business like African slaves were in the nineteenth century.'

"The protest shut down large sections of downtown San Diego by blocking major intersections and streets. Police were called in to break up the protesters and reopen streets to vital business traffic.

"Now let's find out how stocks did on Wall Street..."

Buenos Aires, Argentina

Buenos Aires once enjoyed the reputation as the Paris of Latin America. In the 1950s it was considered one of the most beautiful cities in South America; its European-influenced architecture and cosmopolitan flair made it a destination for tourists from every corner of the globe. One of its most recognizable features, the grand avenue, *9 de Julio,* is the widest street in the world and has been called the *Champs Elysees* of the Americas. But all that is in the past. Today Buenos Aries is a shadow of what it once was. The beautiful buildings that once massed along well-groomed streets are now dirty and in need of repair, and the European boutiques that drew socialites have long since closed.

Today Argentina is an economic basket case with runaway unemployment and a currency that has lost nearly eighty percent of its value in the last three years. International businesses that once made Argentina their South American headquarters have fled the economic and political quagmire. In 2002 Argentina had five different presidents in a span of two weeks, each one resigning after realizing they couldn't succeed given the massive corruption and economic malaise they'd inherited. Once-proud Argentines now desperately search for whatever work they can find. Across the city scientists and engineers now walk dogs in the city parks or drive taxis for a fraction of what they once earned.

Instead of saving money in banks, merchants stock large warehouses with as many products as possible, knowing that merchandise holds its value better than the fiat currency of the republic.

Diego Salinas was one of the fortunate who had maintained a steady job and had been able to preserve a semblance of normality during the turbulent years. Diego earned his doctorate from the University of Buenos Aires in chemistry and had worked for the last eight years at the Buenos Aires Department of Agriculture, heading a team tasked with preventing diseases in livestock. Argentina had a long tradition of cattle ranches run by gauchos. The romantic image of Argentine gauchos with their bolos is as important as that of Western cowboys with six-shooters in the United States. Protecting this vital cultural and economic resource is a national priority. The primary pathogens that concerned the department were Bovine spongiform encephalopathy (BSE) a.k.a., mad cow disease and hoof-and-mouth disease. BSE is a disease that attacks the central nervous system, manifesting itself in loss of coordination, stumbling, and decreased milk production. One of the most difficult challenges faced by scientists is that BSE has an incubation period of 6-8 years, making identification and containment exceedingly difficult. Given the extremely long incubation period, upon the onset of clinical signs, death occurs in 100% of affected animals within two weeks to six months.

Luckily for Argentina and the rest of the world, ninety-five percent of reported cases have manifested in Great Britain and Europe. Since no cure has been found for BSE, the only recourse is to destroy all cattle in the affected region. In addition to the dangers posed by this disease to cattle, BSE is classified as transmittable spongiform encephalopathies (TSE), which means it can also be transmitted to humans, attacking brain tissue, causing similar damage. Affected brain tissue dies, creating holes and giving the brain the appearance of a sponge.

The other major pathogen of concern was hoof-and-mouth disease (HMD), known in Latin America as *fiebre aftosa*. Although HMD has an extremely low fatality rate in animals, it is regarded as one of the most virulent animal diseases in the world. It is highly contagious and can be transmitted in aerosol form. Studies have estimated that a quantity sufficient to cause an outbreak can be carried on the wind as far as two hundred and forty-one kilometers, making containment nearly impossible. It affects all cloven-hoofed animals, including sheep, goats, and pigs, and can also be transmitted to humans. Although it isn't fatal in humans it will cause fever, headaches, rapid heartbeat, and extreme loss of appetite for up to two-weeks.

Due to the ultra-high risk of cross contamination, the primary strategy of containment is to destroy all affected animals, including those in proximity to the outbreak. While this action may seem extreme, it is the only recognized way to suppress further infection.

When HMD spread through farms in Great Britain in 2001, nearly four million animals were slaughtered, costing an estimated $20 billion in lost jobs and tourism. Unfortunately, most countries have suffered from HMD outbreaks, including Argentina.

The only countries thus spared have been the United States, Canada, and Australia, which is due to their exceptionally stringent restrictions of imported agriculture products from countries reporting HMD, as well as customs enforcement of items brought in by travelers from affected regions. Like most agencies that work with dangerous pathogens, the Argentine Department of Agriculture maintains samples of these and other diseases for experimentation in hopes of finding a vaccine.

It had been an exceptionally difficult day of meetings, and Diego was glad to leave the office. He enjoyed his work and co-workers, but detested the never-ending battles he fought in order to preserve even the most basic funds necessary to run his department. It seemed to him that every week another small, but essential item was removed from his budget in order to cut costs. This ongoing process was like a death by a thousand cuts; no single cut was enough to kill by itself, but together they would soon prove fatal. He was approaching a point of diminishing returns where he spent more time justifying costs than doing actual research. It seemed he'd ceased being a scientist, and had crossed a despicable line that forced him to become an accountant; instead of finding solutions to potential threats, his daily pursuit was now justifying basic equipment and supplies. Diego found the entire ordeal repugnant and yearned for the opportunity to leave it all behind, but he was a realist and understood that having an income, regardless of how insulting, was better than nothing at all. Now in his late forties, Diego felt as though he was a failure.

When he'd received his Ph.D., it seemed as though his future was secure, and he'd be able to enjoy the respect and benefits of success for the rest of his life. Now, all of that was gone, not because of anything he'd done, but because of incompetent and corrupt politicians who destroyed his beloved republic and drove millions of his countrymen into an economic quagmire. Diego cursed the government thieves each time he thought about his situation.

Lately the one oasis in Diego's turbulent life was his mistress Esma. He'd met Esma two months earlier at a bar he frequented after work. She was a beautiful, slender, and delightfully fresh woman who possessed a glow that had long since abandoned most *Porteños*.

Esma approached Diego one afternoon asking for directions. During their conversation he learned that she'd recently been transferred to the Mexican embassy in Buenos Aries. It was her first international posting, and although she was enjoying the adventure of working abroad, she was also suffering from a bout of loneliness. Diego was surprised that such a lovely woman would have any problem finding friends, but then again, he knew, men were hesitant to approach attractive women, thinking they were untouchable. After a couple drinks, Diego decided to take a risk and offered to give Esma a personal tour of the city and point out various places of interest. To his surprise she warmly accepted the proposition, and they spent the next several hours driving around the capital.

Even though Diego had been married for twelve years, having a mistress was a man's privilege, or so was the custom. A man needed two women in his life, a wife to raise his children, and meet his social and religious obligations, and a mistress to fulfill his sensual needs. As far as the church was concerned, its unofficial position was, as long as the man didn't allow his extramarital affairs to interfere with his obligations to his family or his community, the sins could be dealt with in the confessional. After all, it just wasn't right to indulge your erotic fantasies with the woman you married before God and who mothered your children.

Normally they'd meet at her apartment or one of the many cafés in the Palermo district, where they'd have a drink and talk. Lately, Diego had been helping Esma learn how to tango; after all, if you were going to live in Argentina you needed to know how to tango. The tango was more than a dance it was the embodiment of the Argentine character. Unlike many other styles of dance that were, for the most part, a free-for-all, the tango had specific rules and styles. Diego and Esma attended a tango salon called *Milongas*. This was a play on the term, since the word *milongas* signified a social dance party. They'd arrive early in order to take advantage of *practica*, which was a time reserved for people to rehearse dance steps and learn new styles. Practica was important, because custom forbade such interruptions once the band began playing its sets, or as they're called, *tandas*. Unlike most dance clubs that pride themselves on their unique dance mix, in a tango salon the band plays long sets of music that follow a particular style or artist. During these sets, it is considered a social *faux pas* to leave your dance partner.

Esma found herself intrigued by all the nuances, and more than once expressed her appreciation that Diego was so knowledgeable. As the two danced during a tanda featuring Angel D'Agostino, Diego realized he was truly happy for the first time in many months. Being able to display his talent to a beautiful and grateful woman gave him renewed confidence in himself. He knew it was vanity, but having a younger woman on your arm told all who saw you that you were more than the average man; you had something special and desirable.

As Diego guided Esma counter-clockwise around the dance floor he held her body firmly against his and manipulated her in a dominant fashion. Each time he'd pull her in closely he'd watch her sharply inhale and then smile as if to affirm her acceptance of his strength. As the band transitioned into a *Cortina*, Diego escorted his trophy back to their table.

"You're making excellent progress; I can tell you're a fast learner. You know, not everyone learns so quickly." Diego told his partner.

"Well, I'm sure it has a lot to do with my teacher. I've always loved to dance. Before coming to Argentina I danced a lot of salsa. Like the tango, it is very passionate and demands a lot of stamina." Esma coquettishly replied.

The band began to transition into another tanda, this time featuring Diego's favorite artist, Osvaldo Pugliese.

"I know it's getting late, but we must dance this tanda. It features the music of the greatest composer of tango ever. I couldn't imagine missing an opportunity to enjoy my favorite tango artist with such a beautiful lady," Diego pleaded with his lover.

"Of course, who am I to deny you such a pleasure?"

As the couple danced they didn't say a word; they only looked into each other's eyes and allowed their movements to speak on their behalf. As the Cortina ended, both were relieved, and quickly exited the salon to return to Esma's apartment, where they began another style of dance that Esma was well acquainted with.

Direct Action Academy: Queen Creek, Arizona

In general, most people misunderstand shooting. Maybe Hollywood was to blame for perpetuating the idea that guns have the magical ability to hit whatever the shooter looks at, but the fact is, hitting a target requires a combination of science, skill, and discipline. This is especially true when the target is a thousand yards away. The academy offered beginning, intermediate, and expert courses in long-range marksmanship. Today was the second day of the intermediate class which required students to operate in teams, one shooter and one spotter. Mark and Rich pre-registered for the course at the gun show and were one of five teams zeroing in on targets on the range.

As Rich peered down range through his spotting scope he processed information on more than just the position of the target; he took notice of how trees, foliage, and heat mirages moved, which allowed him to gauge wind speed. The students were taught to observe these objects halfway to the target, since that was where the wind would affect the bullet most. Rich divided his field of view into four sections that allowed him to communicate what he was seeing more easily to the shooter.

For instance he might make reference to a tree in sector three, which would be the lower left quadrant. Immediately the shooter would know which tree was being referenced. After making a few mental notes on wind direction and speed, Rich announced his targeting solution to Mark.

"You have a quarter-value wind crossing from right to left at five miles an hour. Come right four clicks and down two."

What he was telling Mark was that a five-mile-an-hour wind was moving diagonally from behind him, right to left. The four clicks right would compensate for the wind, and since the wind was coming from behind the shooter, it would slightly push the round down range, so he wouldn't have to aim quite as high. Once Mark adjusted his aim he squeezed off a shot.

The concussion of the large round slammed into their faces. The power of the .50-caliber round created an overpressure that immediately increased the ambient pressure of air spaces in the immediate area; this was most dramatically felt in the sinuses. Sometimes shooters who weren't lined up correctly behind the big gun were known to get bloody noses from the concussion. Rich kept his eye focused on the half-way point down range and actually tracked the round to the target by following the condensation trail it left in its wake.

Once the round hit the target, Rich called out the sight adjustment by announcing its target placement: up, down, left, or right. By doing this, the team was able to walk the rounds into the center of the target. Once they were placing rounds on target Mark would lock his scope. Rich was responsible for recording all this information into a log that detailed what round was used, under what conditions, and at what distance. In practice, if given the same variables, the same round and solution should produce similar results. This was a detailed process but it helped the two men work as a team and improve their shooting more than if they acted alone. Although Rich took turns shooting, it was obvious that Mark was the better triggerman and Rich the better spotter. Mark decided to switch to a black-tipped, armor-piercing round.

"Hey, Rich, let's give those AP rounds a try. They're the black-tipped bullets in the green box." Rich grabbed the AP rounds and loaded five into a fresh magazine and then passed it over to Mark. Mark inserted the magazine into the rifle and methodically slid the bolt forward, then with equal delicacy slightly retracted the bolt, and using his right index finger performed a chamber check to ensure a round had been properly stripped from the magazine and chambered. After making a slight adjustment for elevation he aimed down range and fired.

The round exploded out of the muzzle and ripped down range at over 3,000 feet per second impacting the target just below and to the right of center. Rich watched the round hit, and immediately called out the sight adjustment, "Up and left."

Mark adjusted his elevation and windage then fired off another shot. This round was right on target. "Dead center!" exclaimed Rich.

For the next hour the teams continued to practice in preparation for the competition that would determine which team would be named Long Gun Champs. Mark and Rich went head-to-head with another team but in the end beat them out and walked away with top honors. At the awards presentation

Arrow and Mike congratulated all the participants and handed out certificates and awards to the students. After the ceremony they invited the two champions out for dinner where they continued to talk about the class and their victory.

During the ensuing conversation they developed a mutual friendship and offered Mark and Rich positions as part-time assistant instructors at the academy. They'd help out as line coaches with the long-range marksman course.

The academy was gaining greater notoriety, and with it, the classes were growing, so adding additional instructors had become a priority. After a trial period, the academy would pay for NRA instructor certification courses for Mark and Rich, and they'd become full instructors. During their conversation they learned that Mark's family had been in Arizona since the 1800s and his uncle owned a huge ranch that straddled the Mexican border.

Evidently, Mark had learned his shooting skills on the ranch picking off coyotes and other predators from long ranges. Unfortunately, the problem facing his uncle now were illegal aliens crossing his land, destroying fences, and lately, killing his cattle. Mark and Rich had traveled down to the ranch just the other week and helped his uncle repair fence lines that had been cut. Evidently, it was getting pretty bad, and he was thinking of allowing one of the local citizens' border patrol groups to operate on his land in hopes of stemming the flow and damage. The Border Patrol didn't have authority to operate on private land, so the illegals naturally crossed where they knew the authorities wouldn't or couldn't go.

Unless his uncle wanted to allow federal agents full rein on his property, his only recourse was a citizen group. Although these groups had received mostly negative coverage in the media, they were made up of locals who'd become fed up with the government's reluctance to enforce immigration laws and secure the southern border. So they accepted their duty as Americans and began to organize.

"I've heard of those groups. Apparently, they've been patrolling private property and have intercepted aliens and drug smugglers. I read a story about one group that stopped a bunch of aliens near El Paso and recovered nearly five hundred pounds of marijuana," Arrow remarked.

"Yeah, a lot of the citizens groups have been operating in Texas and have been able to shut down the incursions on ranches over there. We're hoping to organize some local groups to do the same in Arizona. Maybe you guys could help get the word out at the academy?" Mark asked.

"That's not a bad idea," Arrow answered. "We should start organizing and training a team that could help out. We ought to talk to Cowboy and see if he'd be interested in training us in small unit skills and interdiction tactics. Why don't we start asking some of the staff and the regulars if they'd have any interest?" Arrow added. "Mike, you're half Mexican, what are your feelings about this?"

"You know how I feel about it. I consider it an invasion. America needs to secure its borders and protect the homeland against terrorism, especially after September 11. As I've mentioned before, my family immigrated to this country legally, and we were raised to love America. All that aside, I'd be interested in helping out because of all the atrocities committed against poor Mexicans by border robbers and modern-day slave runners; there's a real humanitarian side to this as well. Tell you what; I'll teach the team basic Spanish so we'll be able to have some rudimentary communication skills."

"Also, I think we should offer some refresher courses in basic first aid in case we need to assist some of the people we might come across."

Rich glanced at Mark and then the others. "We have a couple friends who would probably be interested in helping. One guy is named John Soto; I believe he's part Chilean. He speaks Spanish, is a decent shooter, and he's a pilot, he flies tourists up to the Grand Canyon on sight-seeing trips. The other guy is named Joe Young. He served two-years in the Army as a medic and is now attending nursing school at the U of A. I'm sure our group would benefit from an additional Spanish speaker and a medic."

"Yeah, we could definitely use their talents," Arrow said. "They sound like good guys; how well do you know them?" "Well, Mark and I have known John for several years; we went to high school with him. After we graduated his church sent him back to Chile for a couple years to work as a missionary; he's Mormon. After he returned we hooked up again at ASU, then he transferred to Embry Riddle Aeronautical University in Prescott, where he graduated."

"He's about as safe and straight-laced as anyone I know. I'd have no problem having him watch my back."

Mike looked over to Mark and asked, "What about this Joe guy?"

"Rich and I ran into Joe a couple years ago at a shooting competition in Nevada. He's also a marksman, shooting in the .30-caliber class. The guy is a real threat with an M1A and has several trophies to prove it. From what I understand he almost joined the Army's shooting team, but decided to get out and pursue his nursing degree. Joe is one of those extreme sports enthusiasts who likes to basejump and run around with his hair on fire. That's probably why he got into medicine. He's broken nearly every bone in his body, but he's not reckless. I know that sounds like a contradiction; he's the kind of guy who takes every safety measure into consideration, but occasionally pushes the envelope a little too far and then pays the price. One thing I can say about him is he's fearless."

The group continued to talk about organizing a group until the restaurant was ready to close. They decided to have another meeting the following week when they'd try and get Ethan, Cowboy, and Josh together as well as Mark, Rich, and their friends. If everyone was on board with the idea, they'd begin some low-intensity training exercises to see how well they performed as a team. Once they became comfortable with each other they'd get in touch with Mark's uncle and volunteer to patrol his ranch.

PLA Headquarters: Hermosillo, Mexico

Activity at headquarters had been running at a rapid pace. Sayf had proven to be an excellent adjutant to the major; he possessed outstanding organizational and management skills. If he weren't in the military then he'd probably be a project planner or crisis-management director at a multi-national corporation.

Francisco worked closely with Sayf as they organized several different operations, making sure funds were transferred into accounts, and communications were securely transmitted to the various assets operating on more than three continents. The PLA had never functioned at this level before, and Francisco found himself thrilled by the challenge.

For years it seemed they were chained to a leash that kept them from moving outside a small circle, but now they were free to prowl and were able to operate without restrictions. It wasn't that he resented the previous years; after all, it was during that time they'd been able to establish their organization and ensure the authorities wouldn't bother them. But, now it seemed the sky was the limit. Morale was at a high, and an urgent sense of purpose radiated from every level. Everyone knew that history was being made, and soon their efforts would bring to pass the long-sought-after homeland of Aztlán.

Francisco checked his e-mail and noticed a message from one of his covert operators codenamed Piñata. After opening the encrypted message heprinted it out and walked it over to Sayf's office. After knocking on the door, Francisco entered and passed the message across the desk.

"It seems Piñata has been successful in establishing a relationship with her target. She believes she'll be able to get a hold of the material within the next couple weeks." Francisco reported to the Lieutenant

"Excellent. Tell Piñata we'll contact our shipping assets in Paraguay and direct them to prepare for transport. Give her permission to proceed with the mission."

"How's the work proceeding on Operation *Prestamista*?" Sayf asked.

"Everything is running according to the timetable. Our asset has confirmed three of the vehicles are completed, and work is ahead of schedule on the remaining three."

"That's good. Our explosives expert should arrive in four days; then we'll need to get him across the border in order for him to construct the devices."

The PLA didn't have a bomb maker who was familiar with the intricate nature of constructing car bombs, especially ones on the scale planned for Operation *Prestamista*, so the major received permission from Damascus to bring one of Hezbollah's top explosives technicians to Mexico in order to head up the final stage of the operation.

Ibrahim Al-Sadi was a brilliant man who possessed a keen intellect for understanding complex theories. As a child he was regularly in trouble because he was continuously bored with school. His parents didn't appreciate his genius and believed he lacked discipline, so they enrolled him in a *Madrasa* run by fundamentalists, where he was taught a combination of religion and nationalistic politics.

The teachers, also known as *motawa*, were extremely strict and often beat the students with sticks if they didn't pay attention to their studies; they referred to these beatings as medicine and informed the students it would cure their inabilities to learn. Most of the curriculum consisted of studying the Koran and memorizing its passages with exactitude. Memorizing the words was not enough; the holy verses had to be pronounced properly and recited with exactly timed pauses. If a student failed to perform correctly, he was subject to beatings and ridicule by his motawa and often chained to the floor until he learned his lesson properly. Because of Ibrahim's intellect, he was able to memorize the Holy Koran in less than a year, an accomplishment that took most students around two years to complete.

This achievement is called *Khitmat Al Koran* or *Tawmeena* and is so widely respected in Islam that it elevates the individual to a higher social status. It can even get a prisoner's crimes pardoned. In Ibrahim's case he received a full scholarship to Al-Azhar University in Cairo, Egypt, where he earned a degree in Electrical Engineering and a master's in chemistry. While in school he joined the Ba'th party, and after graduation moved to Damascus, where he worked within the Security Directorate training Hezbollah guerrillas in explosives theory and construction.

His designs for large explosive devices revolutionized the tactics of car bombs from anti-personnel devices to mechanisms capable of destroying large buildings, as was done in the 1983 bombing of the Marine barracks in Beirut.

Once he arrived in Mexico the plan was to infiltrate Ibrahim into the United States by using one of the routes scouted out by PLA cells along the border. Several routes had been located that were not regularly patrolled by US agents. A PLA member would act as a coyote, and Ibrahim would be disguised as a common Mexican immigrant in order to blend into the group of other crossers. With the right clothes and haircut it would be virtually impossible for anyone to tell the difference between an Arab and a Mexican. Once in the US Ibrahim would be transported to a secret location where he'd construct the bombs for the UPS trucks that would begin the destruction of the economy in the Southwest.

Chapter 6

> It is not the function of the government to keep the citizen from falling into error; it is the function of the citizen to keep the government from falling into error.
> —US Supreme Court Justice Robert H. Parker, Chief Prosecutor for the United States of America at the Nuremberg Trials

Montebello, California: Three Weeks Later

Hector's group had worked like slaves on their special project for more than a month, and was now finishing the last truck. The process became streamlined on the latter trucks, and work progressed at a faster pace then it had on the first group. Since Hector's team specialized in custom work, where unique detailing was required, each man took special pride in fabricating one-of-a-kind parts and allowed his creative skills to run free. But this job required Hector's men to work together in a kind of assembly line to produce vehicles that were as close to identical as possible. This was diametrically opposed to the way they normally worked, and was difficult to get use to at first. As the work progressed there were jokes about adding hydraulic lifts, tricked-out wheels, and maybe even a small, chrome chain steering wheel on one of the trucks. There were also occasional questions as to why the PLA wanted delivery trucks. Nobody, including Hector, knew the answer to that. The consensus was that the trucks would be used to smuggle Mexican immigrants or possibly even drug shipments. Either way the crew didn't care; all they knew was the money was good, and if they finished ahead of schedule it would get even better.

Once the crew was satisfied they disguised each truck. Additional pieces of sheet metal created a façade to hide its lines before it was moved to storage where it would await the others. As soon as all the trucks were completed the façades would be removed, and the bodies prepared for painting.

Once the last vehicle passed inspection, the crew moved it into the painting booth. As a team sprayed on the dreary brown paint that was the trademark of UPS, Hector used his design skills to perfectly replicate the company logo. Every detail had to be as exact as possible to ensure that no one would notice anything was wrong. The crew even went so far as to open and close the doors dozens of times to create slight wear marks and scratches on the rolling back and side sliding doors. After the last truck was painted, and Hector was satisfied with the results, he called Señor Salazar and informed him they were ready for delivery.

Jamie received the call on his disposable cell phone, thanked Hector for his hard work, and ensured him he'd earned the $10,000 bonus for completing the work ahead of schedule. He arranged to meet Hector at the garage in two days to take delivery of the trucks and make final payment.

After ending his conversation, Jamie made some additional calls and then carefully destroyed the phone. He sealed the broken parts into several cans that he disposed of in different garbage bins in the backs of nearby restaurants. There was no way this phone would be traced back to him.

Buenos Aires, Argentina

Reclining on a couch in Esma's apartment, Diego and his mistress shared a bottle of wine. As Diego stared at his beautiful Mexican lover he felt an overwhelming sensation of confidence and happiness, a feeling that had been missing in his life for a very long time. *This is the way things should be*, he thought to himself. After all, he was a successful, highly educated professional. For too long he'd allowed the plight of his country and the monotony of his life to affect his attitude. Each morning as he looked in the mirror he was greeted by a depressing expression common to most of his countrymen, and that look more often than not set the tone for the day. Now that had changed. Since meeting Esma his life seemed to have renewed meaning. Instead of a middle-aged man mired in a bureaucratic nightmare, his reflection showed a man who was appreciated for his knowledge, admired for his experience, and self-assured in his ability to succeed. More than that he saw a man desired by a young and vibrant woman, and to a Latin that was indispensable.

"You know, my love," Esma said in a soft compassionate voice. "I worry about you. You work so hard and your efforts go unappreciated by your department. You've told me a hundred times about the rules and regulations you have to deal with and how difficult it makes your research. If you lived in another country you'd make ten times as much as you do now.... You deserve better."

"Esma, you are the shining jewel in my life," Diego whispered as he kissed her right hand. "As long as I have you I can deal with the other disappointments."

"Yes, but what we have isn't permanent. You're married, and I am here on a temporary assignment. Who's to say when this could all end?"

Diego stopped kissing Esma and stared at her with an anxious expression. "What are you saying?"

"I'm only saying that we need to be sensible and accept that we're adrift on a beautiful river, pushed downstream by forces beyond our control. What will happen when my government recalls me or if your wife learns about our relationship?"

"I don't want to think of those things." Diego said with an alarmed expression. "It would destroy me if I lost you."

"But if you were financially secure, you'd be able to leave Argentina and come to Mexico with me, where we could be together. Then you could afford to divorce your wife and provide for you children, and most importantly, you could get a job in Mexico that would pay you what you're worth. Like I said, you deserve so much more."

Diego frowned. "I agree with everything you've said, but it's all a daydream. My savings were destroyed after the convertibility law was dissolved in 2001. Even the dollars I have in the bank are frozen by the government for another six months, and after that they'll be converted into Argentine pesos and devaluated thirty percent."

"What if I knew of a way for you to make enough money to leave this all behind and start a new life with me in Mexico," Esma cautiously said, as she lightly stroked Diego's thigh. "Would you be interested?"

Diego looked at her and paused. *Is she serious*? he wondered.

Esma's eyes met his, then she leaned in and softly kissed his lips, "Well, would you?"

"Of course. But what would I have to do, and how much money are we talking about?"

"There are men in my government that are interested in obtaining a quantity of *fiebre aftosa* and would pay handsomely for it."

Diego chuckled. The silly woman was dreaming. "Why? Most laboratories around the world commonly held the hoof-and-mouth virus. If they are so anxious to obtain a sample they can get one from almost any major university. You must have misunderstood them."

"No, I'm pretty sure that's what they said. Something about needing *Fiebre Aftosa* in aerosol form and paying generously for it." Esma spoke in a seductive tone as she unzipped Diego's pants and slid her hand into the opening. "But, I don't want to talk about this any longer...I have other things on my mind."

Gilbert, Arizona

The last several weeks had been a blur. In addition to the normal work schedule at the academy, Mike had also driven to San Diego to help Rachel move to the valley. It was the end of a difficult separation for the two, so when Rachel told Mike she could handle the move alone, and it really wasn't necessary for him to take time off work to help her...well, he wouldn't hear of it. Having six hours of uninterrupted time alone with Rachel, while driving back to Phoenix, was something he'd been looking forward to for a long time. Rachel had arranged to share an apartment with two other girls who also worked at BioPharm. This worked out great since she hadn't had time to search for an apartment, and now she'd be able to carpool to work with one of her roommates.

Mike was astonished at how much difference it made to have Rachel close by. It was hard to put his feelings into words, but when she was nearby he felt calm and peaceful, as though he'd taken a soothing drug. While pondering this enigma he was reminded of the saying, "Music calms the savage beast." Well, if that was true, Rachel was a symphony.

Mike and Arrow had discussed the idea of assembling a tactical team ever since their conversation with Mark and Rich. The following day they'd shared the idea with Ethan and Josh, and they were just as excited about the proposal. The hard part was getting everyone together, especially the two new guys, John and Joe. After a little phone tag they were able to set a date that was mutually agreeable. Tonight's barbecue would be a type of introduction for everyone and a chance to flesh out ideas relating to the project. Everyone gathered at Arrow's house because he had a beautifully landscaped backyard with a built-in grill and a large pool. Since everyone except John and Joe knew each other, the introductions went pretty fast. After dinner the group gathered beside the pool and began discussing the team. Since Arrow was the host, he took the lead in the discussion.

"I hope everyone had enough to eat; if you're still hungry there are a couple more steaks in the kitchen. I'd advise anyone, other than Cowboy, to seize the opportunity before he gets his second wind. It amazes me how much a Marine can eat."

After a short laugh he continued. "As you all know, you've been invited here because we'd like to organize a tactical team. This idea was developed for a couple of reasons. First, we all enjoy shooting, and putting together a team will allow us to train in tactics that we just can't perform alone. Second, Mark has informed us of opportunities to patrol private property down south along the Mexican border. We're all aware of the problems illegals are causing, and we all know the government is unwilling to stop the continuous flood of aliens crossing into the US.

Unfortunately there's nothing we can do to eliminate the whole problem, but there's an opportunity for us to help in a limited fashion by volunteering to patrol on privately owned ranches and land. The Border Patrol can only operate on government and public land, which is why so many ranchers are seeing an increase in traffic across their land."

John raised his hand and asked, "So what exactly would we do on these ranches, and what powers would we have to stop any illegals we ran across?"

"That's an excellent question," Arrow replied, "I've been in touch with several organizations based in Texas who have been doing this exact thing, and they've shared their standard operating procedures. Basically, they respond to the solicitations of the landowners and operate under their authority.

"If a rancher wants a team to patrol his land, he dictates what restrictions and permissions he wants to extend to the team; some ranchers only want a human presence with radio communication. Others allow a more aggressive approach allowing the team to wear full field gear and carry long arms.

"With regard to intercepting illegals, under the authority of the landowner, we can stop trespassers, place them under a citizen's arrest, and hold them until we could safely turn them over to immigration agents for processing and deportation. A couple of the groups I've spoken with in Texas have told me they've intercepted drug smugglers intermixed with the illegals and recovered hundreds of pounds of marijuana and other drugs."

Mark stood up and added some additional information. "My uncle has experienced a major increase in traffic across his land over the last several months." He said. "It is costing him a lot of money in repairs and lost livestock. Rich and I have spent several weekends on the ranch helping him repair cut fence lines and clean up the trash and waste the illegals leave behind. The most serious problem is when the aliens cut the fences to enter his property; the gaps left behind allow cattle and sheep to leave the ranch. They're often lost or killed on the highways around the area." My uncle estimates his losses at upwards of $20,000.

"My uncle understands the plight of these people, and he's sympathetic to those who only want to better their lives. But imagine if people continually damaged your property and dumped garbage and human waste in your yard. Then imagine losing thousands of dollars worth of stock because of the vandalism they caused. I'm pretty sure we'd all act the same way...we'd call the police. Unfortunately, in this case the authorities are unwilling to assist, so he's forced to find another solution. That's where we come in."

"Mike," Ethan said. "You're part Mexican, you probably have a unique perspective on this. What are your thoughts?"

"Yes, I'm half Mexican," said Mike. "And yes, that does give me a unique perspective. First I want to make it clear that I am all for this and eager to participate. It's not just because I believe it's important to do something about the illegal problem, but also because thousands of Mexicans are robbed, raped, and kidnaped every year by border bandits, and hundreds more die in the desert because they're abandoned by their coyotes or attempt to cross without guides and proper equipment. If I can help prevent some of those tragedies, then I feel obligated."

Cowboy stood up and addressed the group. "The last point I'd like to bring up is possibly the most critical. As you are all well aware, we are at war with terrorists who have vowed to destroy this country, and as many Americans as they can in the process. I've spent the last twelve years serving our country, and lately fighting terrorists overseas. I can tell you the enemies we face are dedicated, creative, and are masters at guerrilla warfare. There's no doubt in my mind they are aware of how porous our southern border is.

"Let me make this as clear as I can. If our southern border isn't a modern-day Ho Chi Min trail by now, it will be soon. Just like in Vietnam, the enemy knows we can't defend the whole length of it. Frankly, they know our politicians don't have the desire to defend it. During the Vietnam War we knew thousands of NVA were entering the south; we saw them from above, and we even had photos showing columns of troops, but the politicians wouldn't act because they didn't want to expand the war.

"The same thing exists today. Aliens are entering the US by the thousands, but the government doesn't want to upset Mexico or the bleeding-heart liberals, so we do a half-assed job of protecting the border.

"If I were a terrorist looking for a way into the US, I wouldn't try to fly into a major airport. I'd just fly to Mexico and then cross the border with a group of illegals.

"You know, when I joined the corps twelve years ago I took an oath to protect and defend the Constitution of the United States against *all enemies* both foreign and domestic. When I got out earlier this year, I wasn't relieved of that oath. I believe individual citizens play a vital role in the security of this country. Our founding fathers understood the danger of letting the government have the sole responsibility of defending the country. They knew that would lead to a police state where individual freedoms were sacrificed for an appearance of security. So, they guaranteed the right of individuals to keep and bear arms, not just for recreation or hunting, but because they knew that the best defense against tyranny, from abroad or within, was armed citizens.

"Now, oddly enough, we've got a situation where we *want* the government to take action, and it won't. We're the last line of defense, as it should be. In my opinion we are obligated as citizens of this country to step up and fulfill our duty as Americans."

"So are you proposing we organize a militia?" Joe inquired.

"I'm aware of the negative image the media has branded the militia with," Cowboy said, "but in reality the militia is an established element of the constitution. Matter-of-fact, each of us is already a member of the unorganized militia. Let me read you a couple of quotes..." he pulled a folded piece of paper from the hip pocket of his jeans.

"'Militias, when properly formed, are in fact the people themselves...and include all men capable of bearing arms.' Henry Lee, 1788

"'The right of the people to keep and bear...arms shall not be infringed. A well-regulated militia, composed of the people, trained to arms, is the best and most natural defense of a free country.' James Madison, June 8, 1789

"I'm not saying we have to call ourselves a militia. That's not important. But I am saying we shouldn't run from it either. As far as I'm concerned, we're just a group of like-minded individuals who are willing to serve our fellow citizens and protect ourselves."

Mike interrupted. "I'd like to add a little information on this topic. As many of you know, I've been active in the Patriot community for years, and I can tell you that there are a number of citizens' militias all around the country. I've gotten to know a lot of these guys, and I'll tell you the great majority of them are just like us."

"They aren't interested in overthrowing the government, and they're not a bunch of lunatics with guns. They're everyday people who are concerned with their rights and their communities, just like we've been talking about tonight. The web sites that I monitor are full of great information that we can learn a lot from."

"It doesn't matter what we call it. I suppose we can steer clear of the 'M-word' if we have to, but like Cowboy said, we needn't run from it. I'm with him; considering everything that's going on, organizing a group would be in our best interest."

Joe nodded. "Well, I want to hear the details," he said, "but at least provisionally, I'm in."

The group continued to discuss the idea and voice opinions for the next half hour. The main issue they faced was how they'd train and what type of tactics they'd employ. The advantage they had over most was they already had a world-class training facility and instructors with real-world experience in the classes they taught. As at the academy, Cowboy would take charge of the training, but others accepted roles as instructors as well. Ethan was the obvious choice for communications, Joe handled medical training, Mike and John would teach basic Spanish, and Josh offered his skills to make sure everyone had good equipment.

"I suggest we all choose handles we can use in radio transmissions and while we're operating; it will make communication easier and more efficient," Ethan said." I've always had the nickname Ghost, so that'll be mine, and we all know Arrow and Cowboy. Mike, do you want to keep Gringo?"

"Yeah."

"Mark, what about you?"

"Actually, I haven't thought about it. Any suggestions?"

"Well, considering that big .50-caliber you shoot...what about Thor?" Arrow suggested.

"Yeah, I like that. My .50 is definitely a War Hammer." Mark remarked. "Thor, it is!"

"Well, if taking your handle from your weapon is allowed, how about my handle being AK?" asked John.

"That'll work fine." Cowboy said. "But sometimes you don't get to choose your handle; sometimes it's given to you. So as head instructor I will take it upon myself to name our good friend Rich." Cowboy walked over to Rich who was sitting on an ottoman, and with an imaginary sword Cowboy knighted him. "I hereby dub thee Richard 'Hot Dog' Franks."

The group erupted in laughter, and Rich protested to no avail. The name was perfect, and everyone knew it. Even if Rich continued to object it wouldn't make any difference.

That left Joe and Josh without proper handles. After seeing what happened when you didn't choose your own handle the two quickly announced their preferences. Josh chose his childhood nickname of "Slim," and Joe adopted the name of his school's mascot, "Wildcat."

The team would field an eclectic but balanced array of weapons, including four AR-15s, three AKs an M1-A and a .50-caliber. Of course the .50 would be used in a standoff sniping role, and it packed enough punch to even take out bunkers and lightly armored vehicles. Wildcat's M1-A fired a .308 round that also provided a lot of reach and power. It would be used as a back-up sniping rifle. The ARs and AKs both lacked the range of the other rifles, so they'd handle the majority of the maneuver fire. As a team they ought to be able to control a decent-sized area and lay down a severe amount of fire. Team members would be encouraged to carry a sidearm, but since they'd only be used as secondary weapons, it really didn't matter what was carried. After discussing this it was found that there would be an almost three-way division between .45s, .40s and 9mm.

Slim asked that each member make an appointment with him so he could look over their gear and make recommendations on what they should be using. Gear was intensely personal; what you used and how it was carried depended on several factors including: your weapon, dexterity, preference, mission profile, specialty, and area of operations, just to name a few. So even though Slim was a professional gear manufacturer, he wanted each team member to design his own set-up, then he'd offer suggestions, options, and make modifications to bring it all together.

Another consideration was communications. Although Ghost was able to get all kinds of high-tech equipment for the types of missions they'd be undertaking, simplicity seemed to rule the day. He suggested using commonly available FRS radios transmitting on General Mobile Radio Service (GMRS) frequencies that would give them a range up to five miles depending upon terrain. In addition to being widely available, they were also relatively cheap, lightweight, and simple to operate. These radios would be used for tactical communications, but he would carry a more powerful Yaesu VX-5r HT radio, which operated on three different bands: 6 meters, 2 meters and 440 MHZ.

This would give him the flexibility to communicate with the team, while at the same time be able to transmit on bands that the Border Patrol and other authorities monitored. These radios all used AA batteries that were common in most civilian electronics including GPS receivers, night vision, lasers, and range finders. Being able to use the same batteries for everything made logistics much simpler.

Wildcat would put his medical training to good use by teaching field trauma techniques and by organizing a medical kit that would allow him to stabilize a variety of medical conditions in the field. He began writing down first-aid skills he needed each team member to master before they began operations.

Most of these techniques were taught to every soldier in the army, mainly how to stop bleeding, perform CPR and administer IVs. Part of the training would include each man assembling his own field first-aid kit that would be carried on his gear. In addition he'd cover potential problems they might encounter in the desert, such as how to recognize heat ailments and treat them effectively.

After several hours the group completed the basic organization of their fledgling team and decided to adopt the national Field Force/Battalion system that had been established by the Patriot community; they'd be known as the 13th Battalion of the 48th Field Force "D" Corps. The way the system was organized, each state was recognized as a Field Force. The number designator corresponded to its admission to the Union. For example, Delaware was the first state, so it was designated as the 1st Field Force. Hawaii was the 50th. Next, the states were broken down by county, and each was given a battalion number. In this case, Maricopa County was the 13th

Battalion. Depending on the size of the county and the number of units therein, some counties were further broken out by platoons, which used alphabetic identifiers such as, "Alpha" Platoon. Finally, the various regions of the country were grouped together into corps. Arizona, New Mexico, Oklahoma and Texas were combined to create "D" corps. Thus a national standard was created to assist militia units in training, organization, and communication. In addition, a set of national training and rank standards were also recognized, so a cohesive regiment of skills and knowledge would be shared between all militias.

It was getting late, so the group decided to call it a night. As Mike drove Rachel back to her apartment the two continued to talk about the idea of organizing patrols on the border. About halfway home, Mike noticed he was doing most of the talking and sensed Rachel was holding something back. He pulled his truck into a parking lot alongside a park and set the parking break. "Hey, babe, I'm getting the feeling that you're holding something back. Are you okay with this?"

Rachel shifted in her seat and paused as she searched for the right words. "I have to admit I'm a bit thrown by the idea of you guys loading up for war and heading down to an international border. I understand that something has to be done, and I appreciate the importance of securing the border, but I don't want to see you arrested or worse...dead. I guess the thought that's running through my mind is, why you? Certainly someone else can do this.

"Look," she said. "I just got here, and we're together again, and frankly I want it to stay that way. In all honesty, I don't want anything to mess up what we have...or better yet, what we could have."

Mike reached over and took her by the hand, intertwining his fingers with hers. "I understand what you're saying, and I'd be lying if I said those exact thoughts hadn't crossed my mind. But really, it's just something we've got to do. It's not *right* to sit still and do nothing."

"Mike, I understand that. I respect the people in the military and for that matter the police. But, you're not in the army or the police. Why does it have to be you?"

"Just because I'm not paid to do a job, doesn't mean I don't have a duty as an American. Are only mercenaries allowed to act? I believe it's a fundamental obligation of every citizen to come to the aid of their country."

"I agree. But it's not just about whether or not you're paid, it's about having the proper authority. You can't pull someone over for speeding...can you?"

"Of course not, but that's not what we're talking about. Speeding is an infraction of a law. Even police don't cite everybody who drives over the speed limit. What we're talking about is life and death. As a citizen I have the responsibility to intervene when someone's life is in danger. Rachel, what's happening on the border is a foreign invasion. The only difference is that the tens of thousands of foreigners coming across our border aren't wearing uniforms or carrying guns. They're still damaging our infrastructure and wrecking our economy."

"Besides, we don't pose any threat to these people. We just want to stop them, give them whatever aid they require, and then turn them over to the authorities. My concern is for those Mexicans who might be in danger from bandits or who might die in the desert. Remember, we're looking to operate on private property and that's all. Honesty, there's a good chance we won't even run across a soul."

"Mike I hear what you're saying, and I trust you, Arrow, and the others. I just don't want anything bad to happen." Rachel squeezed Mike's hand then leaned over and kissed him. "Thanks for talking with me. I just need time to get used to the idea."

Sonoran Desert: Southern Arizona

A crowd of parishioners and news reporters gathered together in the middle of the desert to celebrate the installation of the first of ten planned water stations that would provide emergency relief to Mexicans who were crossing this part of the desert on their way into the United States. Reverend Emmanuel Robertson was the spiritual leader of the *Bridge of Light Ministries* in Louis Springs, located just east of the Fort Huachuca Army Base.

The water station consisted of a bright yellow and blue striped pole that stood ten feet high. The pole was topped with a bright red nylon flag and a battery-powered strobe light that turned on at dusk and off at dawn via a photoelectric sensor. On the pole the group had welded chain links that had been cut in half, and acted as attachment points for heavy-duty, Cordura bags. Inside the containers were emergency supplies consisting of sealed Mylar bags of water, vacuumed packed energy bars, sunscreen, and a variety of first-aid items. The pouches also included a rescue radio tuned to an emergency frequency monitored by the Border Patrol and a laminated card with the GPS position of the station printed in easy-to-read, bold characters.

Reverend Robertson raised his arms to let everyone know he was ready to begin. The reporters in the crowd pulled out their notepads and tape recorders to make sure they documented the event properly. "Brothers and Sisters, I want to thank each one of you for being here this morning to help us dedicate this oasis of hope. This water station is the realization of hard work, sacrifice, and prayers on behalf of our Mexican brethren who risk everything for their dream of a better life.

"Last year we began searching for a way to serve our neighbors. After learning of the senseless deaths of more than one hundred and thirty immigrant workers, we determined to do something to help." The Reverend reached into his pocket and retrieved a brass plate, which he held high above his head, "On this plate is inscribed our inspiration: *Verily I say unto you, Insomuch as ye have done it unto one of the least of these my brethren, ye have done it unto me. (Matthew 25:40)* This will be permanently attached to the water station so anyone who encounters it will know that Christian men and women are looking out for those in need. The immigrants who cross this forbidding desert in search of a better life are often looked down upon in our society, not unlike the Samaritans were by the Jews. But let us remember the story of one Samaritan that came across a Jewish man who'd been beaten, robbed, and lay near death along the side of the road. This Samaritan looked beyond cultural differences and the biases of his day and bound up the wounds of the Jew. But that wasn't all...he brought the helpless man to an inn where he paid the innkeeper to care for the man."

"Brothers and Sisters, let us remember the lesson of the Good Samaritan and take care of our Mexican brothers, regardless of social stigmas." The preacher took the inscribed plate, and with a pair of pliers affixed it to the brightly colored pole, then he said, "In this spirit, I dedicate this water station...Samaritan One." Once the plate was securely attached the reverend called for the crowd to join him in prayer.

MSNBC News

"This is Sandra Newman reporting from the Southwestern/Mexican Summit in Mexico City, where Gov. Ernesto Buenamonte (D-CA) and Gov. Barbara Slater (D-AZ) are finishing unprecedented talks with Mexican President Baranca.

"News from sources inside the conference have confirmed that the leaders have agreed on a variety of issues relating to Mexican immigration and worker status that will grant rights and entitlements to all Mexican nationals currently in the United States. These include state-funded worker's compensation, free access to state schools and universities for themselves and their families, and the ability to participate in local and statewide elections. Raul de Soto, spokesman for Workers International, a workers' rights group based in Calexico, California, explained that since immigrant workers are actively participating in the economies of the Western states with labor and taxes, there's no reason they shouldn't have access to the social and political benefits their efforts and tax dollars support.

"When asked about allowing non-citizens to vote in elections, Mr. De Soto remarked, 'Not allowing immigrant workers the opportunity to choose the leaders that make laws affecting where they work and live amounts to taxation without representation, in fundamental opposition of American political orthodoxy.'

"In return for these concessions, Presidente Baranca has agreed to introduce new measures aimed at improving opportunities for Mexicans at home and allowing greater access to domestic jobs via increased spending on education and job training. It is hoped this will encourage more Mexicans to stay in Mexico and reduce the volume of undocumented workers in the US. From Mexico City, this is Sandra Newman for MSNBC."

Buenos Aires, Argentina

Diego sat impatiently at an upscale restaurant located inside the Marriott Plaza Hotel. It had been two weeks since he'd last seen Esma, but it seemed like a year. She was ordered to return to Mexico for a trade conference and decided to take an extra week to visit family and friends before returning to Argentina. When he'd first learned of the trip, he didn't think it'd be too difficult. After all he had a lot of work at the office and two weeks wasn't that long. But, after just a few days he felt as though his heart had been torn out, and frankly, he missed having sex with his nubile Chicana. To establish a proper alibi, he'd asked his wife to drop him off at the train station under the pretense that he had a meeting in Rosario. Instead he rode the train downtown to the Retiro station and walked the remaining four blocks to the Marriott.

Diego reserved a room at the posh hotel that overlooked San Martin Square, for a night he was sure would be memorable. Before arriving he stopped at a florist and purchased three-dozen red roses that the waiter had placed in a fine crystal vase and set on the table. Diego nervously checked his watch for the third time in ten minutes and wondered if he'd left the correct time on Esma's voice mail.

For goodness sake, I'm acting like a schoolboy waiting on his date, he thought to himself as he took another drink of water. The fact was, over the last two weeks he'd made a decision that would affect the rest of his life, and once he'd crossed that mental Rubicon he couldn't think of anything else but starting the journey. Before Esma left they'd spoken about selling a quantity of *fiebre aftosa* to some individuals in the Mexican government. At first it seemed like a ridiculous proposition. After all, they probably had their own samples. But Esma's short absence was harder to deal with than Diego expected. All he knew was if somebody wanted to pay him for something they could get elsewhere, fine. He'd take their money, and with it he would build a new life with Esma, away from the misery of Argentina. The idea of losing her was more than he could stand. Perhaps someday conditions in Argentina would improve and they could return. As he sat contemplating his decision Diego felt a sense of relief; now he only needed to follow through. As he took yet another look at his watch, he saw Esma enter the restaurant. Diego stood up and watched her as she sauntered towards the table.

She wore a short skirt and high heels that accentuated her long, smooth legs and a beautiful, low-cut silk blouse that glided over her breasts as she walked.

"*Hola mi amor.*" Diego said as he took her into his arms and kissed her full, red lips. "I've missed you more than you will ever know."

Her laugh was as silky as her blouse. "But it's only been two short weeks."

"For me it has been an eternity. Seeing you is like having sunlight back in my life." Diego kissed her again and then retrieved the vase of roses that sat on the table. "These are for you, my love."

"They're beautiful; thank you."

As the two sat down Diego reached across the table and took Esma by the hand and gazed into her eyes. He felt as though his heart had just begun to beat again, and the world around him narrowed to include only her.

"Querida mia, I've planned a wonderful evening for us. First we'll have an intimate meal, and then I've reserved a suite overlooking the plaza. Nothing is out of limits tonight."

Esma and Diego enjoyed a four-course meal and two bottles of Salentein Mendoza Cabernet Sauvignon before retiring to their room. When they entered the suite Esma discovered a trail of rose petals covering the floor leading towards the bedroom.

The bellman had brought their luggage up while they ate and hung their clothing in the closet, with the exception of a revealing black negligee that was draped across the bed. Esma looked at Diego with a smile and kissed him passionately. After an hour of sexual release the two sat in bed and sipped champagne.

Diego cleared his throat. "Before you left, you mentioned some men were eager to buy a sample of *fiebre aftosa*. If they're still interested, I am willing to work with them. How much are they willing to pay?"

"Yes, they're still interested. I believe they want several aerosol canisters of the virus, and they've offered to pay $50,000. I can speak with them tomorrow and get specific details. Do you mind my asking why you've change your mind about this?"

"It's simple, my love, because I can't stand the idea of being without you, and if this is what it takes…then so be it."

Diego placed his champagne flute on the nightstand, turned back towards Esma, and kissed her again. The sweet taste of the champagne balanced the salty residue of sweat on her lips, which renewed his excitement as the two resumed their sensual pursuit.

Montebello, California

Ibrahim Al-Sadi arrived in Montebello after an extremely long journey that seemed to have taken months. In reality it was a little more than a week, but considering everything he'd been through his fatigue was understandable.

After arriving in Hermosillo he had met with Major Al-Salih, Lieutenant Al-Mashhadani and the PLA leadership. They briefed him again on Operation Prestamista and the vital role he'd play in its success. He was shown copies of the diagrams used to construct the delivery trucks they'd use in the strikes and reviewed the plans for the bombs he'd construct once he arrived in Los Angeles. This wasn't the first time he'd seen the stolen blueprints, copies had been sent to Damascus where he'd evaluated them before selecting the materials he'd selected to construct the devices. Even so, the repetition did not annoy him. He had learned, sometimes over the rapidly disappearing bodies of confederates, that no amount of preparation was *too* much.

Indeed, it was not until he arrived in Los Angeles and could evaluate the targets and the trucks that he even decided upon the type of bomb to use. The majority of what he needed could easily be purchased in Los Angeles, but the primarily ingredient, RDX, was a different story. The RDX would be obtained from supplies transferred from the Iraqi ammo dump at *Al Qaqaa* to Syria during the first days of the American invasion. He had arranged to have it smuggled on a container ship out of Singapore into the Port of Long Beach.

RDX is a synthetic explosive developed in the 1920s in England, thus it gained its acronym, which stands for Royal Demolition Explosive. It is considered the most powerful military explosive currently used, and is the foundation for the majority of ordnance currently deployed by militaries worldwide. The chemist side of Ibrahim knew RDX by its rather lengthy name, Cyclotrimethylenetrinitramine or 1,3,5-trintro-1,3,5-triazine. To avoid this rather difficult description chemists started calling it Cyclonite or Hexogen, and finally the name devolved into RDX.

Although he understood the need to simplify complex names, there was a part of him that resented the oversimplifications science made on behalf of the uneducated. Regardless of what you called it, RDX was an impressive explosive that detonated at a rate of 8,639 meters per second (28,343 feet), which is more than five miles per second, making it the most brisant substance available. Considering its enormous power, it is remarkably stable. You could even light it with a match and it wouldn't explode, but if you made the mistake of stomping on it... well, stability has its limits.

The US had increased inspections at their ports of entry, but that was not a serious concern. The Americans' appetite for material goods was insatiable, and immense quantities of imports entered the country daily. Even with the increased inspections, only about two percent of incoming containers could be screened.

Since Singapore isn't a targeted port of departure by the Department of Homeland Security, shipments from that country are not scrutinized to the same degree as those from countries such as Indonesia and Pakistan. The RDX was hidden inside the shells of dozens of televisions, mixed in with a large shipment from a Japanese electronic company. Once the container ship docked in Long Beach, PLA dockworkers removed the forty-foot container and trucked it off to an East Los Angeles warehouse where they secured the explosives until Ibrahim's men claimed them.

Bombmaking is an unforgiving art; if a process is not followed to exactness the creator is usually consumed by his creation. Because of this fact, explosives experts are extremely regimented in the materials they use and the way they assemble their devices. This pattern of assembly is known as a "signature" and can be as unique as a fingerprint. Ibrahim was no exception to this rule, and in this regard his strict Islamic discipline served him well.

Ibrahim was knowledgeable with many types of explosives and maintained a mental recipe book of each design, which he followed every time he assembled a bomb. For this mission he chose the same bomb that was used in Lebanon to destroy the Marine Barracks, a RDX propane-enhanced bomb. In addition to being exceedingly powerful, he knew that once the FBI and ATF experts analyzed its composition it would send a shockwave through the very heart of Washington. Now that both Ibrahim and the RDX had been smuggled into Los Angeles, he began organizing the rest of the materials needed to manufacture the devices.

Like most types of plastic explosives, RDX was detonated by a shocking charge. The detonation sequence for Ibrahim's bomb would require three explosive charges. A smaller primary explosion would ignite an intermediate charge, which would create a pressure wave that ignited the bursting charge. For the primary and intermediate charges Ibrahim would use blasting cord and gel, respectively. Both were readily used in construction and mining, so they'd be easy to obtain and shouldn't draw unwanted attention.

In fact, they were the same primary and intermediate charges Timothy McVeigh had been instructed to use by the Hezbollah operative who had designed the truck bomb used in the Oklahoma City bombing. John Doe #2, as the media referred to the operative, was spirited out of the US the morning of the bombing and returned to the Middle East where he now worked on behalf of the Palestinian Authority.

PLA agents across several states were collecting the various materials so their purchases would be harder to trace. This left the final element, the propane, which was by far the easiest item to obtain and could be purchased from a dozen different home improvement stores. Ibrahim's design called for the main charges to be positioned down the centerline of the cargo space with stacked propane tanks surrounding them. The combination would create a massive explosion that would be able to destroy semi-hard targets as well as shower anyone within fifty meters with deadly shrapnel. The one difference between these truck bombs and others that Ibrahim had constructed was that these devices required remote detonators.

Islam teaches the glory of martyrdom in the cause of jihad, and if a Muslim were driving the trucks he'd be expected to detonate the bombs while still inside. But these Chicanos were Christians and didn't embrace suicide, so they demanded the ability to detonate the explosives from outside the kill zone. Plans were for the remotes to be placed inside the type of clipboards that most parcel deliverymen carried. After parking in front of the target the driver would jump out and walk away from the truck just as anyone would expect a UPS driver to do. Once he was clear of the blast radius the driver would press the remote and detonate the explosives, then exit the area during the ensuing chaos.

Now it was time for Ibrahim to begin his work.

Fresno State University, California

Raul sat on the elevated platform that had been erected for this afternoon's address to the Chicano Student Union. He'd grown accustomed to speaking at these meetings. In fact, this was his fifth speech in the last two weeks before Chicano groups at universities in California.

As he waited for the organizers to finish their introductory remarks he looked out over the assembled students and tried to gauge the spirit of this particular crowd. Every group was different, and Raul always endeavored to tailor his remarks to the people he addressed. Fresno State had a reputation of being a hotbed for the Chicano movement, and the local OJChA chapter was one of the most active in California. Located in the eastern portion of the fertile San Joaquin Valley, nestled between the Sierra Nevadas to the east and the Coastal Ranges to the west, this area had a long history as a hub of California agriculture. Chicanos and immigrant Mexican workers were the literal backbone of this industry, providing the stoop labor needed to harvest the bounty of the region.

Now the children of those original pioneers were attending universities, like this one, and preparing to seize the power that had for too long been denied them. As he scanned the congregated students he could see the fire in their eyes, and he felt their unconquerable spirit, which seemed to flow into his soul and invigorate him.

"*Hermanos y Hermanas*," announced the Dean of the Chicano Studies Department, "I'd like to introduce our guest speaker Señor Raul de Soto, who is the California Co-Chairman and International Spokesman for Workers International. WI has been at the vanguard of the Chicano struggle to protect our people and regain the rights stolen from us by our Anglo oppressors. Recently, Señor De Soto led the effort that resulted in the governors of Alta California, Arizona, New Mexico, and Nevada granting immigrant workers rights to state-funded worker's compensation, free access to community colleges and universities, and the right to vote in local and statewide elections."The students roared in approval and waved black and red United Farm Workers posters and OJChA signs. "Without further delay, I present to you Señor Raul de Soto."

Raul stood up and waved to the cheering students as he walked towards the lectern. While the crowd continued to cheer, a drumbeat began somewhere in the back of the multitude giving tempo to a chant of *Aztlán, Aztlán, Aztlán*.

Raul took his place behind the microphone and sanctimoniously gazed out over the chanting throng, and after a moment, gestured for the students to finish. Once it was quiet and all attention was focused on him, Raul threw his fist to the sky and shouted, "*Por la raza*!" This action reignited the crowd, renewing the chanting and waving of signs and flags. Raul enticed the multitude to join him in raising their fists in a massive display of revolutionary defiance. The crowd's response fueled Raul's raw zeal and focused his words.

"*Hermanos y Hermanas* of the bronze race, thank you for that powerful and generous welcome. It's great to be back at Fresno State University and to look out upon so many courageous future leaders of the sacred nation of Aztlán. We live in momentous times when the dreams of past generations are beginning to come to fruition. Today we are witnessing the reunification of our Chicano homeland with the *Madre Patria* of Mexico. As the Dean mentioned during my introduction, Workers International has fought an unending battle against not only our Anglo oppressors, but also the criminal corporations that have exploited our mothers, fathers, uncles, and aunts as indentured servants for generations. We've been successful in uniting workers and forcing the bourgeois corporations to acknowledge our rights as human beings. With the recent signing of the Southwestern/Mexican Accords our people have the opportunity to seize control of political power and take back what was stolen from us so long ago." Once again the crowd erupted in militant chants that echoed across the school's campus.

"Our fathers laid down a foundation of sweat, blood, and tears that fertilized this valley so this dawn would break, and we, their progeny, could achieve what they knew they could not...a Chicano homeland! This is our time and our struggle. We have been prepared for this glorious cause and have the tools needed to win. Will you accept the challenge and join the battle?" The ensuing explosion of emotion bore witness of the student's enthusiasm and of Raul's almost-hypnotic power over them.

"The time is at hand when a clarion call will be sent out, and you will be required to act. Aztlán is rising, and the slave owners who once controlled are waning. The imperialists in Washington are exhausting their power and bankrupting the treasury to support their Zionist masters in Israel. Even now hundreds of thousands of troops are engaged in an unlawful occupation of Afghanistan and Iraq that is depriving our people of critical programs and social support. The billions being wasted on protecting the Zionists could be funding healthcare for our children and housing for the migrant workers who are despicably used to feed the bourgeoisie capitalists. The people ask why billions of dollars are being spent to build homes, schools, and roads in Afghanistan and Iraq and not here...the answer is simple: oil. The administration is laying a gilded trap to ensnare the peace-loving Islamic people of those countries into believing America and its imperialistic cohorts care about them. What they don't know is the only thing they care about is stealing the oil which God gave them as an endowment.

"The Zionists only know one tactic: deception and thievery. The Anglos stole Aztlán from us, the Jews stole their land from our brothers the Palestinians, and now they are united in stealing oil from the Arabs. Will we apathetically stand-by and watch as yet another great culture is raped by these criminals?" A resounding, "*No!*" burst out of the crowd in unison.

"Since 1948 the United States and its Jew bankers have given nearly $1.3 trillion to Israel, while at the same time encumbering ever-increasing financial debt upon the backs of nations like Argentina, Brazil, Colombia, Mexico, and Peru. We call on Washington to end its support for Israel and forgive the debts of all Hispanic nations.

"Brothers and Sisters, I believe in dreams and the power of making dreams come true. But I am also a realist. Because of that I know our dreams and expectations of justice will not be given to us. Nothing of value is ever freely given...it must be taken. Chairman Mao taught us, 'Freedom comes from the barrel of a gun.' He taught that true freedom cannot be given to a people, it must be purchased, and the price of freedom has always been blood. Unless we are willing to fight for self-determination, we will continue to beg for the scraps that fall from the oppressor's table. Anyone who doubts this need only look at our Palestinian brothers. When I call the Palestinians our brothers, some are confused. But let me make this very clear. We may not share the same blood, but we suffer the same debasement at the hands of the same enemy. Their land was stolen...our land was stolen. Their culture is under attack...ours is as well. Their enemies build settlements on their sacred land...so do ours. They are a people of faith and peace who were forced to defend themselves against racism, and so are we."

"Currently, there is a specter of racist anti-migrant vigilantism spreading along the Texas/Mexican border with the sole purpose of hunting down poor, defenseless Mexican immigrants. These camouflage-wearing storm troopers are heavily armed and focused on establishing their hatred by any means necessary. What will it take before the government recognizes these hate groups for what they are...dead Mexicans tied to cactus?

"What these groups represent are the last death throes of desperate Anglos who know that soon they'll be the minority and will have to prostrate themselves before those whom they've victimized for generations and beg forgiveness.

"Nonetheless, we cannot minimize the threat posed by these so-called 'citizens militias.' If a border war is their aim, then we must ensure the millions of Mexican/Americans and Chicanos in this country will rise up and destroy these terrorists!"

By this point the students had been worked into a near frenzy by Raul's words. They pressed against the stage and violently shook their fists at an imaginary foe. Their shouts had morphed into blood-curdling screams. Even the organizers who sat on the podium were astonished by the fierce transformation that had taken place and showed their uneasiness by shifting in their seats and whispering to one another.

The electric aura that engulfed the assembly teetered on the verge of spawning a mob mentality that threatened to explode into a riot and engulf the campus in an orgy of vandalism. One of the professors sponsoring the speech decided this had to end before things got out of hand. The professor carefully stood up, walked over to Raul and whispered in his ear, "Señor De Soto, I think you need to end your address and dismiss the students, and please, try to calm them down before you end."

Raul looked at the professor with a gaze that conveyed his annoyance that someone would interfere with the captivating moment he'd produced. But then turned to the microphone, "I see that your hearts are true to the cause and you will indeed accept your duty as Chicanos. I encourage you to preserve your passion deep inside and allow it to churn and grow until the time comes to release it in righteous fury. This is not the time...but it is fast approaching.

Until then I encourage you to persist in your preparations and continue to spread the word... *Viva Aztlán!*"

Near Casa Grande, Arizona

Dawn would be breaking in two hours, and Slim was sitting in a fighting position on the parameter of the team's bivouac. He was nearing the end of his three-hour watch, and knew he needed to alert the others so they'd be able to man their designated positions before sun up. SOP called for all team members to man their positions one-hour before dawn and dusk. Slim looked down to ensure his radio mike was properly positioned, then spoke into the mike that was plugged into the VOX port of his FRS radio.

"Come in, AK, this is Slim."

"AK, over."

"It's ninety minutes till dawn; I'm going to wake the team. Keep your ears and eyes open. Slim out."

As Slim began to shift his weight his muscles reminded him of the workout Cowboy had put everyone through the day before. This was the third FTX the team had been on, and each time the training got a harder and more intense. After arriving at the training area, located near the Picacho Mountains, the team geared up for a seventy-two-hour patrol. Two fire teams were formed and designated Alpha and Bravo. Arrow led Alpha, and Gringo was in charge of Bravo.

Team leadership changed during training to allow each member to gain experience. The best way to learn squad tactics was to lead and learn from your successes and failures. While patrolling Cowboy occasionally halted the teams to offer quick instruction on terrain recognition or to point out natural formations that could be used as choke and rendezvous points. These skills were ingrained into him during his years in Force Recon. As the name implies, the primary mission of a Marine Force Recon group is reconnaissance and surveillance, but they are also skilled in limited-scale raids, security operations, demolition, signal intelligence, and non-combat evacuation operations.

Although all these abilities fall within their skill set, their day-to-day training consists mainly of deep reconnaissance and direct action missions. These were the two areas that Cowboy believed best served their team. At times being able to move stealthily and efficiently seemed to be contradictory, as it always seemed gear would rattle or loose ground would betray your every movement. But little-by-little each man overcame the problems as he learned how to walk and allow ambient noise to cover his movement. In the beginning the guys were so focused on trying to move correctly that they shut out what was happening around them. This was illustrated one day when Mike was leading a squad along a compass heading, and they nearly walked headlong into a stray cow. That incident quickly earned a spot in team legend. How anyone could miss a five-hundred-pound cow became a question for the ages. But now as individual skills improved each man began "growing antennas," as Cowboy would say.

Mike likened the training to fine tuning the focus on a camera lens. At first almost any improvement seemed immense, but the tighter the focus became the more critical you became, until even the smallest deficiency was intolerable. At this stage the guys began examining everything they wore in the field, looking for ways to improve sound discipline and effectiveness. This included rearranging the position of pockets and modifying the collars on their shirts, to not washing their BDUs unless they were filthy, and when they did, it was in water alone or detergents without brighteners and fragrance.

Then, one day Cowboy introduced them to the magic of spray paint, and from that point forward nothing escaped a misting, including their weapons. In a short time the team looked and acted like a true military unit, but more importantly, they began trusting one another and learning each man's nuances so they didn't simply work together...they operated.

Slim made his way over to Mike, who was asleep in his sleeping bag, and nudged him awake. "Gringo, it's almost dawn," he whispered. "Time to man your fighting position." Mike lazily opened his eyes and looked up at Slim. "Gringo, what did I just tell you?"

"It's dawn and time to man our fighting positions." Mike repeated in a groggy whisper.

"All right, now get out of the sack and help me wake up the others."

As Slim silently moved off into the pre-dawn darkness, Mike unzipped his bag and slid out of its warm and welcoming interior. As educational and even enjoyable as each FTX could be, he really hated this part. Even in the desert, temperatures can drop down to an uncomfortable level at night, so a lightweight sleeping bag can make a big difference. Some chose not to carry one and instead opted for wrapping themselves in a poncho liner. Mike had tried this on their first FTX and quickly learned to appreciate the saying, "Travel light and freeze at night." After that he invested in a lightweight and highly compact bag. It helped him sleep, which helped him when he was awake. But crawling out the bag took a lot of will power.

Mike reached down into the foot of the bag, retrieved his boots, and quickly laced them up. He donned his web gear and boonie hat, grabbed his rifle, and crept over to wake up Hot Dog. It only took a few minutes for the entire team to man their fighting positions. Once in place Cowboy asked for a roll call on the radio.

"Gringo ready."

"Arrow ready."

"Thor ready."

"Wildcat ready."

"Slim ready."

"Ghost ready."

"Hot Dog ready."

"AK ready."

The men silently manned their positions as the sun rose in the eastern sky. There were several reasons why the entire team needed to be in position at sunrise and sunset, most importantly was to protect against enemy attacks. Once the sunrise watch was complete each buddy team took turns getting something to eat and preparing their gear to leave.

"Gringo, why don't you eat and get your gear organized? I'll stand guard," Slim offered. Since he'd manned the last watch, his gear was already packed, and he'd munched on some snacks during the night to stay awake. Mike gratefully accepted the offer and crawled back to his bivouac site to pack up his sleeping bag, making sure nothing was left behind. After all his sleeping gear was stowed in his patrol pack, he crawled back to his fighting position. Mike reached into one of the pockets attached to the back of his pack and pulled out an MRE.

Since he'd removed the small bag from its chipboard box before leaving home, he didn't know what entrée he was holding, but that really didn't matter. Mike used his knife to slit open the green pouch along its long side revealing what looked like red beans and rice. *Well, it's not bacon and eggs, but it'll do,* Mike thought as he spooned a hearty portion in his mouth. After finishing his "breakfast," he made sure to pack away the trash so no sign would be left behind.

Arrow's voice sounded in Mike's earpiece. "Gringo, this is Arrow, we need you for a Patrol Leaders briefing in ten minutes."

"Roger, Gringo out."

Mike crept back to Slim's side and told him about the briefing, then made sure he'd be ready to leave upon his return. The morning light was becoming brighter, illuminating Slim's features. His face was covered with layers of camouflage paint and dirt outlining two beet-red eyes. "Hey man, your eyes are blood red. Are you all right?"

"Yeah, I started falling asleep on my watch so I used the Tabasco sauce that came with my MRE as eye drops. Hurt like hell, but it kept me awake."

Mike gave Slim an astonished look and shook his head, "After this is over, I suggest buying some No-doze. Try not to hurt yourself while I'm gone. I'll be right back."

At the briefing Cowboy laid out the training schedule for the day. They'd practice a direct action drill against a six-man command post/ observation post (CP/OP). In his briefing he pointed out that the most difficult thing to do in combat is close with the enemy.

Once bullets begin to fly the natural reaction is to dig a hole and crawl into it. But to survive you must move, shoot, and communicate. Terrain and maneuver are weapons that will either be used by you or the enemy. If you allow your fear to paralyze you then you'll be outmaneuvered and killed. To prevent this, men must train themselves to react in predetermined ways, based upon the dangers they encounter.

As Cowboy continued with his briefing, Mike remembered a psychology class he'd taken in school. The professor described how different regions of the brain functioned; the frontal lobes of the brain are dedicated to rational thought; this is where humans differ from the lower primates. The central region of the brain operates the basic day-to-day functions we take for granted and have learned through repetition a.k.a. psychomotor skills. For example, after finishing a phone call while driving, you arrive at your destination safely, but most likely you can't remember details about the streets you've taken or the intersections you've passed. Through repetition you've trained yourself to drive so well that the complexities of the action can be handled in the center of the brain, while the less familiar phone conversation is handled in the frontal lobes.

This is the goal of military training, to train the soldier so thoroughly that when he encounters danger, his mid-brain reacts instinctively overriding the analytical thoughts that might urge him to run and preserve himself. That's not to say soldiers are mindless robots, but by relieving the frontal lobes from the basic skills of combat, the soldier retains the ability to think critically and better react to changes on the battlefield. This explains why soldiers, and other first responders, tell how their training kicked in and they simply reacted, as they were trained.

Today's training would include reaction to direct and indirect fire as well as ambushes. Cowboy finished his briefing, and the leaders returned to their squads where they repeated the briefing and prepared to move out.

Mike led Bravo team, consisting of Slim, AK, and Ghost. Arrow was in charge of Alpha team including Hot Dog, Wildcat, and Thor. Because of the nature of the training, Thor replaced his .50-caliber Barrett with a FAL, which relieved him of nearly twenty-five pounds. He was grateful for the lighter load, but being a big guy the extra weight he'd grown accustomed to carrying didn't affect him much, and being able to bring the power of the .50 into a situation more than made up for the added burden. This was the last day of the FTX, so they'd patrol back towards the cars and train en route. Staying off the trails the two teams followed parallel compass headings towards a rounded hill in the distance. Mike placed AK at point, followed by Slim, and then himself and Ghost, who operated as his radioman. AK moved off into the brush to scout ahead. Normally he'd stay about fifteen meters ahead of the team, or as far ahead as terrain and foliage would allow maintaining visual contact with the second man in the team.

Mike looked over at Ghost and told him to let Alpha know they were starting off. Ghost leaned his head towards his left shoulder, keyed his microphone, and sent the message,

"Alpha, this is Bravo. Be advised we're stepping off on heading Zero One One. Over."

"Bravo, this is Alpha. Roger on heading Zero One One," Hot Dog's voice replied.

The two teams had been skillfully moving along their parallel courses for about thirty minutes, each man carefully taking in as much information as he could about the environment. Although it was only 0845 the temperature had already climbed into the mid-nineties, and Mike felt sweat gathering in the middle of his back where it was covered by his LBE. Before the two teams started their patrol, Cowboy had left camp to set up training targets along their route. The man-sized targets were attached to rebar that he'd hammered into the ground and positioned to simulate ambushes and accidental contact. The first groups of targets were positioned just beyond a clearing on the opposite side of a dry wash with about fifty meters of open ground between where Alpha and Bravo were expected to emerge from the concealment of the brush line.

As Mike's team continued on their heading he saw AK signal a halt and then pointed his weapon forward indicating enemies in sight.

Mike passed the appropriate hand signals back to the rest of the team and then motioned that he was going forward to speak with AK. The rest of the team silently assumed firing positions covering their flanks. Mike crept forward until he reached AK and asked for a report.

"There's a clearing up ahead with enemy forces in sight. I count six with light weapons. They're not very active, and by the look of their gear they're probably regular forces. They're positioned on the opposite side of a wash with light cover." AK reported in a whisper only Mike could hear.

Mike gave AK the thumbs up and signaled him to stay put while he notified the rest of the team. After crawling back to the team he motioned for everyone to gather on his position before giving a quick report about what lay ahead. The team formed a tight 360 and Mike radioed Arrow.

"Alpha one, this is Bravo one. Over."

"Bravo one, go ahead."

"Alpha one, my point has identified six enemy, lightly armed in light cover ahead of our position about seventy meters. Can your pointman confirm? Over."

"Bravo one, Wildcat is on point and confirms the situation. It looks like that dry wash moves around their right flank; if Bravo can engage and hold them in position, Alpha will move up the wash and flank them."

"Roger, Alpha one. Let me know when you're in position. Bravo one, out."

By this time Mike had returned to AK's position. AK pointed forward and whispered the position of the enemy in Mike's ear. Mike nodded to AK, then pulled his binoculars out and scanned the enemy position. After a quick assessment of the terrain, Mike decided to form an assault line twenty meters to his left in an attempt to draw the enemy's attention away from the right flank, where Arrow's team would attack.

Once both teams were in position, Bravo would open fire, and each man would expend one full magazine. Then the teams operating in pairs would run forward while the others laid down covering fire. Then the second team would follow suit in a leapfrog maneuver until all members of Bravo reached the protective cover of the wash. Once in position, Mike again radioed Arrow.

"Alpha, this is Bravo. We're in position. Over."

"Bravo, this is Alpha. In position and ready to go. We'll start our assault as soon as you begin to fire. Keep an eye open and don't kill us, okay?"

"Roger that, Arrow."

Mike knew Cowboy was still out there, probably watching and evaluating how the teams would handle the exercise he'd set up. Since this was a live-fire evolution, he wanted to make sure the range was safe, so he radioed Cowboy to ensure he was clear. Mike looked down his line and gave a thumbs-up to his team, who returned it man for man. After sighting in his target, he opened fire. As soon as he initiated the rest of the team opened up. The distinctive report of the 5.56mm rounds of the ARs and the heavier 7.62mm rounds of the AKs ripped the morning tranquility. Using well-aimed two- and three-shot bursts, Mike quickly emptied his magazine.

"Stoppage!" Mike yelled as he pulled the empty magazine out of the rifle and jammed it into the dump pouch that hung off his left hip. Then he drew a fresh magazine from its carrier and smoothly inserted it into the empty mag well and slapped the bolt release. "Ghost, you're with me. Let's go!"

Ghost had just finished his own reload as the two men rose from concealment and ran towards a point about half way to the wash. As soon as Ghost and Mike hit the ground they rolled to their right and re-engaged the targets. Slim and AK finished their magazine changes and began their dash forward.

As AK approached Mike's position he yelled out, "Coming through!"

Once they were a couple meters in front, they flopped down and began providing covering fire. Mike reloaded again then pushed himself up and moved forward. "Coming through!" Mike yelled as he passed AK, who was pouring fire into the targets.

By the time Mike jumped into the shallow wash, his legs and lungs were burning from lack of oxygen, and he was breathing so heavily that he had to limit his shots to single fire to maintain accuracy. Suddenly AK tumbled into the wash beside him adding his contribution to the rain of bullets saturating the enemy position and ejecting hot, spent shells onto Mike's head. One of the shells found a gap in his collar and slid down his neck, scorching his skin.

Although it burned, Mike worked hard to focus his attention on what was going on. He knew Arrow's team should be flanking by now and wanted to stay alert.

As soon as Bravo team opened fire, Arrow moved his team out of the brush towards the wash. As Arrow ran forward, the volume of fire from the four members of Bravo surprised him. Although he knew they only had semi-auto rifles, it sounded as though someone had set up a machine gun.

"Move forward!" Arrow shouted out to his men as they ran towards the wash. Once Alpha team was in position, they opened up on the enemy location, which was quickly obscured by a cloud of dust created by the impact of hundreds of rounds of ammunition.

"Cease fire, cease fire!" Cowboy announced over the radio.

Immediately the instruction was repeated down the firing lines as the men pulled out magazines and emptied chambers. Mike stood up and waved over towards Arrow's group, then exited the wash and walked forward. Both teams converged on the targets and witnessed the results of their maelstrom. The targets were shredded with dozens of holes. In some cases the targets displayed long gashes that tore across the front, caused by the crossfire inflicted by Alpha team.

Cowboy slapped a few guys on their backs as he walked into the group. "Bravo's assault was executed with maximum violence and extreme prejudice, which allowed Alpha's flanking maneuver to succeed. I have to say I was impressed."

Cowboy's admiration didn't come easily, so they knew they'd performed in a highly professional manner. As was the group's custom they gathered, and beginning with the team leaders, each gave their impressions of the exercise. This informal AAR allowed each member to understand what transpired and gain a micro view of the action. After policing their brass and storing the targets and rebar, the teams split up again and returned to their original route, back to the cars.

The teams arrived at the cars around 1400 and had one last briefing before splitting up to return to their individual homes. Arrow stood up and thanked everyone for their hard work and professionalism, noting that whenever you complete a live-fire FTX without anyone getting shot...it's a success. Then he turned to Mark, "Thor, I think we're ready for our first deployment. Why don't you call your uncle and ask him when we can come down."

"Sounds like a plan. I'll call him tonight and get back to you on Monday with the details. He's pretty open to us coming down whenever we can. Last time I spoke with him he told me that traffic across his ranch had really picked up over the last month."

"Wildcat, make sure your trauma kit is stocked up and be sure to add a few more IV bags. I want to be ready to assist anyone we find in distress. It's really starting to get hot out here, and I want to be ready for heat casualties." Mike added.

"I'll get in contact with the Border Patrol in that area and make sure I have the correct radio frequencies for their station." Ghost said.

The team passed around a package of moist towelettes to clean the layers of camouflage paint and grime from their faces, and changed into street clothes. They didn't want to "freak" anyone out along the way home. Everyone was excited that they'd finally have a chance to do some real patrolling. They looked forward to heading down to Double C.

PLA Headquarters: Hermosillo, Mexico

Francisco read the latest message from Piñata. Evidently, she had suffered a set back in obtaining the *fiebre aftosa* virus. It turns out her mark was enjoying her feminine pleasures a little too much and had begun taking them for granted. So she faked a trip back to Mexico and gave him two weeks of celibacy to gain a better appreciation for her erotic delights. Now, it seemed, he was ready to do whatever it took to keep her near. Francisco considered how similar sex and drugs were. After all, they both stimulated the pleasure center of the brain releasing dopamine that created the euphoric feeling so common with all intensely enjoyable actions. What Piñata, and for that matter women all over the world did, was get their mark hooked on an incredibly powerful drug, then take it away allowing him to feel the effects of severe withdrawal. Now, that he was humbled and desperately in need of a "fix," she was willing to give him ready access to the drug his body craved...but this time, at a price. In its most simplistic form, she wasn't much different from a crack dealer on a street corner who allowed new customers a free taste of a drug, the better to addict them. But then, Francisco thought, addiction might be a fair price to pay for the drug Piñata offered. She was a beautiful woman, not supermodel beautiful, but what she lacked in physical attributes she more than made up for in erotic aptitude. She approached sex like a surgeon; it was more than a pastime...it was her profession.

Piñata reported she expected to receive the virus at their next meeting. Transportation had already been arranged via a Hezbollah cell that operated a training camp in the tri-border region of Paraguay.

This area, where Argentina, Brazil, and Paraguay meet, had become the Becca Valley of the Western hemisphere and had earned the nickname "The Muslim Triangle" by South American intelligence agencies. To supplement their training, al-Qaida, Hezbollah, Islamic Jihad, and Hamas cells had established a lucrative drug and weapons smuggling program out of this lawless region, so all Piñata needed to do was deliver the package to Hezbollah operatives in Buenos Aires and it'd be on its way to PLA headquarters. Piñata's last question dealt with how she should handle her mark after delivery. Francisco left that up to her, encouraging Piñata to leave Buenos Aires as soon as possible and return to Mexico.

The major forwarded another message of importance to him. It was from Trinity, the codename Ibrahim Al-Sadi selected for this mission. He enjoyed irony so he chose the codename given to the site in New Mexico where the first atomic bomb was tested. However much he might indulge his humorous impulses, Trinity's work continued to show its almost legendary precision and efficiency. He reported the RDX had arrived without incident and that work on the truck bombs was progressing on schedule. He estimated two weeks before operation Prestamista could commence.

Timing was everything. The strikes had to be executed simultaneously. Once *Prestamista* was unleashed the Department of Homeland Security would raise the threat level to red, making further infiltrations virtually impossible. But more importantly, both strikes were required to create the economic shock needed to bring the Western States to their collective knees. *Obispo*, *Puente,* and the other PLA governmental agents needed wide scale panic and chaos to justify declaring a state of emergency and seizing power.

One unexpected, but minor issue that continued to cause problems was the increasing presence of armed citizen militias operating in Texas. These militias were blocking off vital routes into the US used by the PLA and had begun to spread into neighboring states. *Obispo* received information that similar groups were forming in Arizona. She said she had a plan to prevent the militias from getting a local foothold. But the major was confident her plan would lack the strength to properly address the problem. *Obispo* was dedicated to the movement, in her own way, no doubt. But she was still an elected official and had limited ability to act without consideration of consequences. Regardless of how careful politicians were, they always left trails that led back to them. On the other hand, the major didn't officially exist, and therefore, was able to act without the same constraints. That's not to say he was untouchable. He was aware of the tightrope he needed to walk with his Mexican allies. If they had any hint of what he was now planning, the results could be disastrous. But he'd been operating covertly much longer than anyone in the PLA, so he was comfortable carrying out black operations.

There's an old Arab adage that states, "The greatest aid is often given in the dark of night." Therefore, the major decided to provide *Obispo* with the help she'd need to destroy these troublesome militias. In the end it wouldn't matter how it was done...simply that it happened.

El Rio de la Plata, Argentina

Esma insisted on planning a special occasion to repay Diego for the romantic night they'd spent at the Marriott. So she arranged a private evening dinner cruise on the Rio de la Plata. She explained the yacht they'd be using was owned by a wealthy Mexican, now living in Buenos Aries, who made it available to embassy staff for diplomatic, cultural, and trade events. The boat was moored at Puerto Nuevo, a marina just north of the Costanera Sur Ecological Park located on the city's east side. Esma and Diego arrived around 7:00 p.m., and the yacht promptly pulled away from its dock and motored into the middle of the river. The Rio de la Plata is a large, navigable waterway that serves as a natural border separating Argentina and Uruguay, emptying into the Atlantic Ocean.

During the summer it is a major attraction for both Argentines and Uruguayans, but in the fall and winter months, as it was now, mostly commercial traffic sailed its length. Esma and Diego sat in the forward lounge enjoying a glass of wine before dinner was served. Diego raised his glass and offered a toast. "Tonight is the beginning of a new life for both of us. Let's drink to love and fortune in Mexico."

Esma raised her glass, smiled, and sipped the dark red nectar, then seductively drew the tip of her tongue across her full, glistening lips.

"So, you have the canisters containing the virus?"

"Yes. It took some delicate maneuvering to reproduce and convert the virus into an aerosol and load them into canisters, but I was able to complete the job this week. I have them in the cooler I brought aboard. When are we going to meet your friends and make the trade?"

"They'll be waiting for us at the dock. I figured it would be awkward having them on-board during our special dinner and...afterwards." Esma gave a schoolgirl giggle as she teasingly played with Diego's ear. Esma leaned into Diego, allowing her breasts to push against his chest, and whispered in his ear, "I don't know if it's the wine or maybe the lights of the city, but I'm feeling especially hot tonight. Maybe you can help cool me off in the shower before we eat?" Esma punctuated her proposition by licking Diego's ear and biting his earlobe. Diego was instantly aroused.

"I believe that could be arranged, *Preciosa*," Diego added as he set their wine glasses on a nearby table.

Esma stood up and led Diego down a circular staircase towards the forward master bedroom. The owner of the yacht had spared no expense in its décor. The room was spacious. Centered on the far wall was a king-sized bed that had been turned down, revealing satin sheets. To the right was a doorway that led into a marble-tiled bathroom and shower large enough to comfortably accommodate two people. Esma dimmed the lights then turned her back to Diego and asked him to unzip her dress.

Diego willingly submitted to her request. As he slowly lowered the zipper, Esma coyly looked over her shoulder and slipped the thread-like straps off her shoulders. The silken dress fell to the ground revealing her slender, firm, naked body. Diego reached around her and caressed her velvet body while softly kissing the side of her neck.

"You are the very breath that keeps me alive, the very thought that allows me to rise each morning. I willfully give my soul and complete devotion to you...*Reiña mia*."

Esma turned around and stroked the side of Diego's face. "Why don't you undress and start the shower. I'll put on some music and be right in."

Diego nodded and walked towards the bathroom. Esma turned the opposite direction, walked toward the entertainment center, inserted a CD and adjusted the volume. Then she retrieved a handbag that sat on a chair. After unzipping the bag she withdrew a small Beretta model 85 and screwed a silencer on the end of the barrel. Esma firmly held the grip and eased back the slide to ensure a round was chambered. The water began flowing in the shower as Diego called out, "I like that music. But I'd like it more if you were with me."

"I'm coming, Diego. You're going to love what I have planned for you." Esma answered as she leisurely walked towards the bathroom. Billowing steam filled the bathroom as Esma's erotic form appeared like an apparition through the mist. Her eyes were focused on Diego who held his head under the cascading water, eyes closed while he drew his hands over his thinning hair.

Esma slowly opened the decorative shower door. Feeling the cold draft, Diego turned and looked straight down the barrel of the pistol in Esma's hand. Without hesitation she squeezed the trigger, firing a .380 caliber hollow point bullet that punched a perfectly round hole in the center of Diego's forehead. His body involuntarily jerked backward and collapsed on the floor of the shower as a small geyser of blood pumped from the lethal wound. Esma looked down on the human pile without expression, and fired two more superfluous rounds into his chest. The shots sounded like puffs of air; in fact the spent casings that danced across the tiled floor were louder. Esma watched as the shower washed Diego's blood and gore down the drain.

Squatting down to retrieve the spent shell casings, the nude assassin looked into Diego's lifeless face. His eyes and mouth were wide open in a macabre expression of surprise. She reached her hand into the shower, stroked his leg and with a sympathetic voice said, "Oh Diego, it seems I've ruined you for all other women."

Esma returned to the bedroom where she redressed, then picked up the phone and called another room. "He's ready for you. Get in here and clean this mess up." Five men entered the room wearing surgical smocks and gloves, carrying cleaning supplies and a plastic body bag. The crew inserted Diego's limp body into the bag and zipped it closed.

Then they washed down the entire bathroom and cleaned every surface with a bleach mixture. The drain cover in the shower floor was removed and carefully scrubbed out and sterilized. Once the bathroom was completely cleaned, the men carried the body bag up to the deck and loaded it with rocks and metal debris. They cut holes in the bag to ensure it would sink and to allow access to bottom feeding fish that would devour Diego's remains. By this time the captain had reached an especially deep section of the river, where they intended to dump the body. The men slid the body bag over the railing, and it splashed into the cold, inky water where it floated feet down for a moment before gliding silently to its final resting place.

Direct Action Academy: Queen Creek, Arizona

Mike looked on as Rachel's concealed carry class performed their shooting test. Arrow sat on the bleachers to his right and Slim to his left.

"She looks pretty good." Arrow remarked. "Her presentation is smooth, and she's got a solid group on her target. She's a fast learner."

"Yeah, she's doing great." Mike answered.

"Is she using your G23?" Slim asked.

"Yes. It fits her hand better, and she likes the larger capacity."

"So you've seduced her to the dark side...way to go, Darth," Slim added in an accusing tone. Slim was a 1911 man. A fierce rivalry raged between traditionalists who were devoted to John Browning's timeless design and those who embraced the more modern Glock.

Mike chuckled at Slim's jibe. "Well, you're going to love this," he shot back as he pulled out a black, plastic box, "I bought her one as a graduation present."

"Mike...you're a romantic!" Arrow remarked. "Forget about flowers and diamond rings. Nothing says I love you like a new blaster."

"Damn straight," Mike replied. Actually, he was a little concerned how Rachel would respond to it. As fine as a gift of a customized Model 23 might be, it wasn't exactly a traditional gift. What if she didn't like it? After all, women were capable of weird reactions.

Susan Franklin, who'd been hired specifically to teach ladies-only classes, was in charge of Rachel's course. Market research showed that some women felt intimidated by male instructors and wanted someone they could better relate to. Susan had served eight years in the Marine Corps where she became an instructor in hand-to-hand combat and was a highly decorated member of the USMC pistol team. After leaving the Marines she joined an international company that provided executive protection training for governments and multi-national corporations. Susan didn't look the part of a gunfighter. She stood 5' 6'', with sunny blonde hair that she wore in a loose ponytail that hung out the back of her instructor's cap, and like all the staff, she wore a riggers belt supporting her holster, a double magazine carrier, a pouch containing a small first aid kit, and a Surefire tactical light. Unlike her fellow instructors, she also carried a Strider DB backup knife tucked diagonally behind her waistband, just to the side of the buckle. This was a carry over from her close quarters combat days. If she ever found herself grappling with an attacker, she could quickly pull out the knife and use it to stab, tear, and rip at her assailant to prevent him from accessing her gun. Susan was a devotee of Paxton Quigley and taught her students that *real* feminists believed pro-choice meant choosing between a .45 APC and a .40 S&W.

Susan called a cease-fire, and the women cleared and holstered their guns. Rachel turned around and noticing the guys, flashed a thumbs up accompanied by a wide, beaming smile.

"She looks like she's really enjoying herself," Slim said.

"No doubt about it. The more she shoots, the better she likes it. If I'm not careful I'm afraid she'll start taking my AR out on dates without me...actually," Mike paused in thought, "the mental image of her with my AR is kind of erotic; maybe that's not a bad idea after all," he remarked in a devilish way.

"All right, that's enough!" Slim protested while flinging his arms in the air in mock surrender. "I don't need these thoughts polluting my mind. I've got orders to fill, and you," he added pointing an incriminating finger at Mike, "you need to get some religion."

"Amen, Pastor!" Arrow and Mike sang out imitating devoted parishioners. "See you later."

Rachel walked over to the bleachers with her target in hand. "Hi guys! Take a look at the groups I shot. Controlled pairs to the chest followed by head shots."

Mike wrapped his arm around Rachel giving her a big hug. "I love it when you sweet talk like that." Rachel rolled her eyes as she shoved him away.

"You'd better be careful; I'm a dangerous woman now."

"What do you mean...*now*?"

"All right, enough," Arrow pleaded. "I can't take anymore. You two are ruining my testosterone high with all this sexual tension crap. Why don't you give your sweetheart her gift?"

"*Gift*...did I hear the G-word?" Rachel asked as her eyes lit up with a Christmas-morning sparkle.

Mike reached down and handed a black plastic box to her.

"Oh Mike, I love the wrapping job," Rachel chided in a sarcastic tone. "It's right out of *Martha Stewart Living*."

"Yeah, yeah, yeah. I didn't have time to get it wrapped. Consider it a belated graduation gift and congratulations for finishing your CCW course."

Rachel opened the Tupperware-like box and pulled out the pistol. She gripped it in her hand pointing it down range checking the sight alignment.

"Cowboy installed a three and a half pound trigger connector and extended magazine and slide releases." Mike said. "He also replaced the regular sights with tritium models for night use." Mike hesitated. "Do you like it?"

"It's...great, I'm just kind of stymied on what to say. I've never had a guy give me a gun before. You know, it's not the kind of thing mothers prepare their daughters for." She paused for a moment...then turned her smiling face towards Mike and said, "*Gotcha!* I love it, thanks!"

Montebello, California

The construction of the bombs progressed on schedule. The additional materials needed were gathered from a variety of sources throughout California, Nevada, and Arizona. Ibrahim was amazed that even after the attacks of September 11 security remained so easy to circumvent in the United States. The problem with Americans, he thought, is they suffered from mass schizophrenia. One moment they'd cry out for greater security, but before they were able to institute the appropriate measures needed for that security, they'd sacrifice them to gratify their deranged craving for universal approval. In this case, all that was needed to purchase the Tovex and Primadet required for the primary and secondary charges, was a state-issued drivers license.

Fortunately, California, Nevada, and Arizona had passed laws allowing Mexican nationals, regardless of their legal status, to obtain licenses with nothing more than a Matrícula Consular card issued by a local Mexican consulate. The appropriate bribe to the right official at the consulate would ensure these identification cards were issued without background checks and in virtually any name desired. The irony was that the very government Americans depended on for safety was the same institution that made it so easy for their enemies to kill them. Ibrahim shook his head as he contemplated the satire. It was like a Greek comedy. How could leaders perpetrate such blatant deception on a supposedly free people? Either the people had to be ignorant, or the leaders were simply traitorous. Nevertheless, Allah in His greatness had mercifully opened the door, and Ibrahim was going to use it to further jihad against the Great Satan.

A PLA technician led six men into the factory and approached Ibrahim. "Excuse me for interrupting you, sir. These are the six men who were selected to drive the trucks." The men were recruited at OJChA-sponsored events in Arizona and California. They were selected for their extreme militant attitudes and desire to strike a blow against America.

All were in the US illegally, and all were guaranteed $20,000 and protection upon completion their mission. Among them was the man selected by Samuel in Arizona; his name was Antonio Lopez.

Ibrahim inspected the men, then spoke to the technician. "Very good. These men need haircuts and need to have all their facial hair removed. Once they're done at the barbers make sure they're measured for their uniforms, then have them report to the classroom where they begin instruction on the remote detonating devices."

The technician nodded and led the group out an adjoining doorway. The men needed to look like UPS drivers, so they had to reflect the grooming standards people had become accustomed to seeing, which included short, trimmed hair, no beards or mustaches, and a neatly pressed uniform. They also needed to learn how to properly arm and detonate the explosives that were now being installed into the trucks.

Each driver would be part of a team that included an extraction unit whose job it was to get the driver out of the area after the explosion. The actions of these teams needed to be coordinated to ensure success. Most importantly, they needed to understand how far away from the explosion they needed to be before detonation or they'd be killed.

Double C Ranch: Cochise County, Arizona

The team made the five-hour drive down to the Miller ranch in three cars and a supply van. Along with each man's personal gear, they'd brought extra food, water, and medical supplies they'd hoped they wouldn't need. Cowboy had also insisted on buying a couple of digital video recorders to document any interceptions they made. Not for some kind of trophy video, but as evidence against possible accusations of abuse. Not to be outdone, Arrow donated two ITT PVS-14 third generation night vision scopes (NVG) for the team leaders to use during night patrols and in Listening Posts/Observation Posts (LP/OPs).

J.R. met the team at the ranch's east gate to guide them to the main house. After lunch J.R. and the team sat down with a large topographical map and identified the areas where he'd noticed considerable activity over the past several months. Each location, along with ranch boundaries, possible rally points and other points of interest, was marked on individual maps. Additionally, each location was marked with its GPS coordinates to ensure no one would get lost if they were separated in the darkness. Ghost gave a communications briefing so everyone would understand and follow proper radio discipline. Then the group suited up for a final equipment check and patrol orders.

Tonight's mission would be broken into two patrols: Alpha led by Arrow, and Bravo by Cowboy. Alpha would man two semi-covert LP/OPs, along a known insertion route about 1.5 kilometers inside the southeast border of the ranch. These two posts would have the simple designations of Alpha One and Alpha Two. Bravo Team would act as the interdiction team if Alpha identified any intruders.

SOP for the operation was to intercept any illegals crossing the area of operations (AO), render aid if needed, and turn them over to Border Patrol agents as soon as a pick-up could be arranged. Unfortunately, the local Border Patrol Commander wasn't very excited about the guys being on the border and provided a stern warning that they'd be arrested if they were found outside of private property.

After the final briefing the guys loaded up in pick-ups and were driven to their insertion point about two kilometers from where they'd decided to establish their LP/OPs. After dismounting the trucks the team gathered in a 360° defensive parameter and patiently waited for their night vision and senses to adjust to the surroundings. They waited about ten minutes then split into patrols and began to move towards their objectives. A slight breeze blew into their faces, but it offered little relief since the temperature was still in the high nineties after a daytime high of 110 degrees. They patrolled across a minor plateau covered by mesquite trees and scrub brush. As the teams continued on their compass heading, crickets and cicada bugs seemed to compete in an attempt to drown one another out with buzzes and rhythmic chatter.

After half an hour most of the guys were covered with sweat. Wildcat knew the heat would quickly take its toll so, he'd insisted each man drink a complete canteen of water before they left the ranch house. Not only was their load-bearing vests (LBV), ALICE gear, patrol packs and other equipment heavy, but it also restricted air circulation, making it difficult for their bodies to cool off. Wildcat instituted a strict hydration policy and made sure everyone adhered to it religiously.

Arrow halted his patrol, and the men instinctively gathered in another tight 360. He then whispered, "GPS says were at the coordinates designated for our LP/OPs." He slipped the receiver back into its pouch and pulled his NVG out of another. Lifting the monocular to his right eye he scanned the terrain around him.

The NVG painted the desert in bright hues of green by amplifying the ambient light provided by the moon and stars. Being a GEN 3 scope, it provided sharp detail and illuminated even the slightest contours of the terrain. Immediately he could make out the well-traveled path the Mexicans had been using to cross this section of the ranch. Arrow identified two locations where he instructed his team to begin setting up their LP/OPs. These locations would provide them with a clear view, not only of the path, but also of its flanks. Mike and Hot Dog buddied up in one LP/OP, and Ghost joined Arrow in the other. Before releasing Bravo for their first patrol, Ghost conducted a radio check to make sure everyone was on the correct frequency and understood communications protocol.

Everything checked out, and Bravo slowly vanished into the darkness. Everyone accepted the chances of actually intercepting a group of illegals was slim; in fact, the prevailing thought was they'd simply enjoy yet another FTX. Alpha made their first radio check an hour into their patrol and then each hour after that. Now they were on the way back, and the teams would switch roles allowing Alpha to man the LP/OPs and rest. As planned, each team would complete two patrols before they returned to the insertion. Arrow heard what he thought was an animal and lifted his NVG to make an identification. Moving the scope to the left and slightly down the trail he saw a young man crawling up the middle of the path.

"Contact," Arrow announced into his radio. Immediately everyone in Alpha team sprang to attention. "I see a man crawling about 20 meters down the path."

"Alpha one, repeat. Did you say you had a visual contact?" Mike asked over the radio.

"Affirmative, Gringo. I can see a man, and it looks like he's hurt."

By now, Cowboy heard the announcement and radioed in. "Alpha one, this is Bravo one. I copy your transmission; we're half a klick southwest of your position moving north. Over."

Arrow continued to observe the man through his scope as he crawled on his hands and knees. Suddenly he stopped, began vomiting, then collapsed.

"Bravo one, this guy's in trouble. He's throwing up and just collapsed. I believe we have a medical emergency. Get your men up here as fast as you can, we can't move until you're in position to provide cover."

"Roger, Alpha One. We're on our way. Out."

Mike and Hot Dog left the cover of their position and carefully hiked through the brush alongside the trail. As they moved, Arrow kept a close watch on the situation with his scope and radioed directions to them since they couldn't see far in the obscure darkness. Soon they closed in on the man and saw his outline lying on the path.

"Alpha one, we have the contact in sight."

Mike called out to the man in Spanish, "¡*Manos arriba*!" The man didn't react. "*Necesitas ayuda*?" Still no response.

"Alpha one, I think this guy's hurt. We're going to check him out."

"Roger, Gringo, approach with care." Arrow said in a cautionary tone. "Bravo team is on their way, and I'm watching you on night vision."

Mike and Hot Dog emerged from the concealment of the brush and approached the man who was lying beside a pool of vomit. Hot Dog stood back in a guarding position while Mike slung his rifle across his back. Mike leaned down and saw the man was barely conscious. "*Hablas inglès*?" Mike asked.

In a weak voice the man replied, "Yes...a little."

Mike began a quick examination of the man, checking for weapons, drugs, or anything else out of the ordinary. The man was wearing several layers of clothing and carrying a bundle slung across his shoulders. His clothing was soaked in sweat, but his skin was dry and hot to the touch. Immediately, Mike recognized the symptoms of possible heat stoke.

"Dog, help me out. We've got to get his clothes off and cool this guy down before he dies." They began pulling the clothing off the man, but soon found it to be too much trouble. Mike slid his patrol pack off, unfastened the pouch containing his first-aid kit and pulled out a pair of rescue scissors, and began cutting the layers of clothing off the injured man.

"Why is this idiot wearing so many clothes in the desert?" Hot Dog asked in a clearly annoyed tone.

"The coyotes limit people to just one bag, to keep them moving fast. By wearing several layers of clothes he must have thought he'd be able to bring more with him." Mike answered. "The problem is most of these people either don't have any idea how much desert they'll have to cross, or the coyotes lie to them. So they underestimate the conditions they'll encounter."

While they continued to free the man from the suffocating layers, Mike radioed to Wildcat. "Wildcat, this is Gringo. Over"

"Gringo, I hear you. Go ahead. Over."

"Wildcat, I've got a male in his late twenties, who appears to be suffering from heat stroke. He's semi-conscious, his skin is hot and dry, he's vomited and isn't sweating. We're cutting his clothes off to help cool him down. What else should we do? Over."

"Gringo, get him cooled off as quickly as possible. Begin pouring water over his torso. If he's able to drink without choking, get some water in him. I'm moving towards your position. Over."

Mike told Wildcat to hurry as he continued to work on the victim. After they'd cut the last layers of clothes off, Hot Dog reached back and pulled out a canteen and started pouring its contents over the man's chest and abdomen. At the same time Mike reached into his pack and extracted three chemical ice packs. The packs were designed to activate when an inner pouch was crushed, combining two agents that produced an icy slurry. Mike passed one of the packs to Dog, "Here, put this on his genitals."

Mike took the other two and placed one under each armpit. By placing the cold packs on the man's genitals and under each arm he hoped to rapidly cool down the man's body by exposing his brachial and femoral arteries to the cold.

"*Mi…mi…hermana*, help…please help *mi…hermana*,"the Mexican said in weak, broken English.

"Where's your sister…is she hurt?" Mike asked.

"Coyotes *mi hermana*…took."

"Where did they take her?"

"I…*no se*…coyotes bad. She need help."

Mike radioed to Cowboy, "Bravo one, this is Gringo…come in."

"Go ahead, Gringo."

"Cowboy, our victim says his sister was taken by coyotes and is in danger. He doesn't know where they took her. What's your location? Over."

"Gringo we're about two hundred and fifty meters south of your location. If they were on the trail, chances are they took her into the brush. We'll begin a search. Wildcat should be approaching your position soon. Over."

"Roger, Bravo One, Gringo, out."

****

Bravo team moved forward in a wedge formation; spaced so that each man could just make out the other. Everyone monitored the conversation between Cowboy and Gringo, so now they knew what they were looking for. Suddenly, an interesting exercise had become the real thing. Everyone knew that coyotes often carried weapons and were dangerous. These guys had probably kidnapped the girl.

Cowboy signaled a halt, and the team slowly kneeled down. Cowboy lifted his night-vision scope and scanned the area in a wide arc. Silently, he scrutinized the flat terrain looking for anything out of the ordinary. Off to the right about twenty meters stood a clump of mesquite trees. There was movement behind them.

"Bravo team, I have a possible contact about twenty meters to our right. We're going to check it out. Stay low and maintain trigger discipline." Cowboy slid the night scope back into its pocket. Bravo team crept towards the outcropping of trees with their weapons up and at the ready. As they got closer they heard the distinct voices of two men speaking Spanish and the whimpering of a girl's voice.

Cowboy signaled the team out of its wedge formation and into a semi-circle surrounding the enemy position. As soon as they were in position, AK commanded the men, in Spanish, to freeze and raise their hands. The coyotes stood up and frantically searched the darkness for the disembodied voice.

Cowboy was watching the coyotes in his night scope, making sure they were unarmed. "Bravo team, they don't have guns Thor and AK, move-in. Keep your weapons up but your fingers indexed. Slim and I will provide security"

Thor and AK rose from their positions with their rifles covering the coyotes and began quickly moving towards the two startled men. As they moved forward the team continued to yell instructions, "*Manos arriba, manos arriba*!"

The coyotes continued searching in every direction for the people they knew were there, but were hidden in the darkness. Then shapes began to appear all around them, dark, sinister shapes that were human size, but had irregular dark outlines. One coyote fixed on one of the emerging figures with an expression of utter curiosity; suddenly; he recognized a black face and the business end of a rifle pointing at him.

Thor moved towards the man yelling for him to get down. In the excitement of the moment he'd forgotten the Spanish phrases Gringo taught the team, which probably explained the strange, confused look on the Mexican's face. As he reached the man he decided all his yelling wasn't making a difference and slammed the barrel of his FAL into the unsuspecting man's sternum, dropping him like a sack of potatoes.

The two coyotes were on the ground and being covered by the team as Thor and AK slung their rifles and used plastic zip cuffs to secure their hands. The man AK was cuffing had his pants down around his ankles. While this was happening Cowboy and the others moved in. After securing the area, Cowboy pulled out his red-filtered Surefire® flashlight and searched the surrounding vicinity.

Against the trees he saw a young girl, no older than sixteen, curled up in the fetal position. Her dress was ripped open exposing her naked body. She'd obviously been viciously gang raped by the two coyotes. AK finished searching his man, before moving to the girl and began comforting her in Spanish. "You're safe now. It's all right." As he spoke to her he gently examined her for any wounds. In the red illumination provided by Cowboy's light, he couldn't see much but could tell she'd been beaten and savagely violated.

"Those two bastards gang raped her!" AK yelled out as he covered her with the tattered remains of her clothing.

****

"Gringo, this is Cowboy. Over."

"Go ahead, Cowboy."

"We've found the girl and apprehended two coyotes. How's your victim?"

"Wildcat is here and he's started an IV. How's the girl?"

"This isn't good. You and Arrow need to get down here. Bravo out."

Arrow and Ghost arrived just before Wildcat and helped stabilize the victim. Following Cowboy's request, Ghost, Hot Dog, and Wildcat stayed and continued to care for the injured man while Arrow and Mike left to meet up with Bravo team. When they arrived at Bravo's location they found Cowboy's men surrounding the coyotes who were kneeling with their hands tied behind their backs. Cowboy walked over to Arrow and Mike.

"How's the girl?" Mike asked.

"AK examined her. Physically she'll recover...but she's been traumatized and isn't talking much." Cowboy answered. "The coyotes told us the brother kept falling behind and finally passed out. They thought he'd died from the heat, so they stole his money and took the girl. I guess they decided to rape her since they were alone. These assholes have probably done this before. I say we shoot the bastards and dump them on the other side of the border."

Mike looked at the girl who was still curled up against a tree and appeared to be catatonic. His first thought was to agree and kill the dirtbags, but he knew it wasn't right. If they'd had guns, it would have been perfectly acceptable to waste them...but they were unarmed. Still, they destroyed a young girl's life. So what was the difference?

"You're right," he said, "These assholes should die for what they did. But we can't shoot them. It would have been different if they'd had guns, but they didn't. I wish to hell they had...it'd make this whole conversation unnecessary. But we can't ignore the law. If we do, then everything we've said about the rule of law and the constitution doesn't amount to a pile of shit."

Even in the dark and through the camo paint, Mike could see Cowboy's face darken. "You want to see a pile of shit?" Cowboy yelled. "Look at the two bastards that raped and sodomized that little girl. They're rabid animals and should be destroyed. To hell with the law!"

"If we turn them over to the Border Patrol they'll either jail them at taxpayers' expense or deport them back to Mexico so they can repeat this and destroy another girl's life. Instead, we shoot them and dump their asses across the border as a sign to other criminals."

"Cowboy!" Arrow hollered stepping between the two men and grabbing Cowboy by his vest. "Stand down, now. You know damn well we can't shoot them. If we do the word is going to get out and we'll all be arrested." Arrow added, "Listen, we all feel the same way about this. Those pieces of shit should die for what they've done, but if we kill them chances are we'll all get arrested, and that won't help anyone."

Cowboy stared at Mike and Arrow with a look of frustration that was palpable.

"Cowboy," Arrow said, "I feel the same way. But you know what we're saying is right. In a different time and under different conditions we'd all waste these animals without a moment's hesitation. But this isn't right...not now." Arrow placed his hand on Cowboy's shoulder.

Cowboy took a deep breath and relaxed a bit. "Fine, then what do you want to do with them?"

"We need to turn them over to the Border Patrol. But first we need to document the crime scene with the video recorders. I'll try and get the girl to tell what happened to her. A video-taped testimony is acceptable in Arizona. We'll get her brother to do the same." Mike added.

"The three leaders walked back to the rest of the team, who were guarding the coyotes, and explained what they had decided. Although most felt the rapists should be killed, they accepted the reality of the situation. After recording the crime scene and the girl's testimony they prepared to return to the LP/OP where they'd reunite with Wildcat, Ghost and Hot Dog and then extract back to the ranch. Just as they began to leave, Thor spoke up.

"Listen guys, I understand why we can't waste these guys, but I'd like your opinions. I happen to know that since a felony was committed, the Border Patrol will turn these guys over to the local Sheriff, who'll throw them in jail to await a hearing. I also know that other inmates consider child molesters the lowest scum on earth. They have a way of getting beaten, raped, and sometimes even killed. I say we make sure everyone knows what these bastards did, and let their fellow criminals handle them."

Thor looked around at the others and waited for a response. "Well, what do you think?"

"How exactly do you propose we do this?" AK asked.

Thor walked over to the first coyote and tore his shirt off. Then he extracted a permanent black marker from a pocket on his web gear and began writing something on the man's back. After finishing, he looked up and asked Mike, "How would you write: "I rape children," in Spanish?"

Mike stared at Thor for a second, then looked around the group. He walked over, grabbed the marker and wrote the phrase in large letters on the man's back. The bilingual notice was also printed on his chest and then repeated it on the second man. As a failsafe measure the notice was written down the backs of their legs.

Cochise County Jail

Border Patrol agents picked up the two coyotes at the Miller ranch; J.R. turned over the videotape and filled out the paperwork needed for the arrest. The brother and sister we're taken to the county hospital and the rapists to jail. When the agents turned the coyotes over to the Deputies they made sure to tell them about how they'd brutally raped and sodomized the young girl.

After fingerprinting and photographs, the head deputy, seeing the condition of their clothing remarked: "You know we'll have to get these prisoners some new clothes."

"Yeah, you're right," said his partner. "But first they'll need to get cleaned up. Let's put them in line with the next group going into the showers." Later that night other inmates beat both of the coyotes to death. An investigation into the murders is currently underway.

Samaritan One Water Station: Sonoran Desert

It was nearing 2:00 a.m., and the temperature had finally dropped below one hundred degrees. The three men and two women had walked for nearly eighteen hours since being separated from their coyotes. None of them had any idea which way they needed to walk, and this confusion forced them to meander aimlessly through the desert hoping to find some kind of sign that would lead them towards a town. They all knew the dangers associated with hiring coyotes, but since none of them had crossed the border before, they had no experience and were at the mercy of the guides. Unfortunately, their worst fears materialized when an hour into the trip the coyotes stopped them in the middle of the desert and at gunpoint tried to rob them of everything they had. Fortunately, they were able to escape in the darkness and confusion. But now they found themselves exhausted, dehydrated, hungry, and helplessly lost in the middle of what seemed an endless desert.

In an attempt to conserve energy, the group decided to rest for a few minutes before moving on. The breaks were becoming more and more frequent as their bodies weakened from thirst and fatigue. One of the women had been stung by something, and her leg was now swollen to nearly twice its normal size. One of the men reassured her that it wasn't life threatening, but as he examined the wound, he could only imagine how painful it must be to walk on. He patted her shoulder to encourage her before moving towards a rock where he intended to relax and rest his feet. Just then, his attention was drawn towards a flashing light in the distance. His first thought was that *La Migra* was searching for them, but the light seemed to stand still. The young man watched the beacon for a few minutes and realized that it was probably a strobe. In their current situation, even if the light turned out to be a trap or a border agent, at least they'd get the help they desperately needed.

"Hey," he said pointing towards the horizon. "There's a light out there. We'll probably find someone there who can help us."

"Where?" Asked one of the women.

"Out there, in the direction of that hill."

The women and the other two men rose to their feet and looked off into the night sky. Suddenly the flash ignited the darkness, quickly illuminating its surroundings.

"That doesn't look too far away. We can easily reach it. Let's go." Remarked the other man.

The five migrants rose to their feet and staggered toward this beacon of hope. It didn't take long before the water station began to take shape in the distance. As they approached the tower, no one knew exactly what they'd found, but they quickly located the large nylon bags containing water and food and abandoned their apprehension. The five Mexicans tore into the Mylar water pouches like ravenous beasts and poured the life-giving liquid down their parched throats. Although the water was hot, it was welcome. It was as if they'd stumbled upon a magical oasis, and they all frantically partook of the water as though it was fine champagne.

"There's food in here, too." One of the women called out as she withdrew several energy bars.

"I wonder who left all this out here?"

"Hold on, here's a sign. It says it was left by a Christian church and they named it Samaritan One."

"*Gracias a Dios!*" another woman cried out as she continued to drink and eat.

The five migrants began to laugh and smile for the first time since they were nearly robbed. Hope flashed in their eyes, and a renew sense of happiness glowed in their faces. This was surely a miracle; God had guided their footsteps towards this place where they could be saved. Like manna that fell from heaven to feed the Israelites, this aid station had been placed here by God to save them from certain death.

"We have been blessed by God, and we need to give thanks for the Christians who placed this here. Come and gather around and we'll say a prayer of thanksgiving." Remarked the woman whose leg was swollen.

The five Mexicans gathered together and bowed their heads as the woman started praying, *"Nuestro Padre, te damos gracias por su amor y por la bendiciones hemos recibido esta noche. Padre..."*

Before the woman could finish her prayer, a cacophony of shots ripped the stillness of the night. The five Mexicans began to violently contort as they were struck by dozens of bullets. In less than ten seconds the shooting ceased, and the last shots echoed across the desert like thieves fleeing a crime scene. Two dark figures emerged from the concealment of their ambush and walked towards the five motionless shapes. Both held smoking rifles at the ready as they approached the grisly setting. As they drew near their victims they fired well-aimed shots into the head of each person, spreading grey matter across the desert landscape. No words were exchanged between the assassins as they completed their macabre act, but as they turned to leave one of them carefully placed a card in the hand of one of the dead men. The card read, "Mexicans go home or die—US Border Militia."

Chapter 7

> Oh, my countrymen! What will our children say, when they read the history of these times? Should they find we tamely gave away without one noble struggle, the most invaluable of earthly blessings? As they drag the galling chain, will they not execrate us? If we have any respect for things sacred; any regard to the dearest treasures on earth; if we have one tender sentiment for posterity; if we would not be despised by the whole world—let us in the most open, solemn manner, and with determined fortitude, swear we will die, if we cannot live free men!
> —Josiah Quincy, Jr., 1788 published in the *Boston Gazette*

Selma, California

Umberto casually walked up a dirt road towards a large corporate feedlot. It was nearly midnight, and the moonlight lit up the surrounding area with a soft glow that made it easy to see the road ahead. This part of the valley was filled with dairies and feed lots where hundreds of thousands of cows helped produce the dairy products that made California the leading dairy-producing state in the country. Since 1993 California had surpassed Wisconsin in every dairy production category except cheese. Overall, more than 20% of all dairy products in the US were produced in California, and annual sales estimates were close to $4.6 billion.

As far as Umberto was concerned he only cared about making an easy hundred dollars. All he needed to do was toss what looked like a bug fogger into one of the large holding areas where the cows were kept. When he was approached with the offer he was a bit curious as to what was in the can. The man making the offer assured him it wasn't lethal and insisted he needed to either accept or reject the one-time offer on the spot, which made the decision easy.

Umberto approached a large, smelly lot full of mature, black-and-white Holsteins. After taking a quick look around to ensure he was alone, he reached into a paper bag and pulled out an aerosol can. Then making sure to point the spray nozzle away from him, he activated the valve. Immediately it began spraying a fine, odorless mist into the midnight air. Umberto threw the can into the middle of the cows and walked off.

Across California and Arizona similar events were taking place. Compared to the apocalyptic images of biological warfare the US had been prepared for, this attack was anticlimactic. But in three to five days things would be very different.

Phoenix, Arizona

Carlos left Montebello at 1:00 a.m. on his way to his target in downtown Phoenix. Now it was 6:00 a.m., and he was approaching the outskirts of the city. Driving at night along Interstate 10 he didn't see many other drivers, and those who did pass him never gave his UPS truck a second glance. At this hour the roads were full of people driving their sedans and SUVs to work. Most were focused on the traffic, while others carried on animated conversations on their cell phones. Carlos began feeling edgy as he contemplated the destruction he would inflict on the city around him. He had no doubts about the justice of his mission and was struck by the gravity of the moment in which he found himself. He was on the brink of making history, a history that would be remembered by Mexicans for a dozen generations. His only concern was that he'd be successful. Traffic slowed as the skyline of the city began to appear over the horizon, so he lightly touched the brakes and merged into the center lane. Soon traffic stopped all together, giving Carlos an uneasy feeling. *Maybe there's a police roadblock ahead...what if the police know what's happening?*

Looking over his shoulder, Carlos could just make out the stacked propane bottles surrounding the white barrels that housed the powerful bomb. Brightly colored rope-like explosives weaved around the device leading to a simple electrical box with green and red lights installed on its face. Carlos quickly returned his attention to the road ahead; the last thing he needed was to crash into the back of another car. Over the cars in front of him, he could see the flashing red and blue lights of a police motorcycle. His stomach began to twist, making him feel nauseous as he scanned forward to see if there were more police in the area. Beside him his cell phone began to ring.

"What's going on? Why are there police up ahead?" he asked another operative driving a 4-door sedan that would act as an escape car.

"Don't worry," said the other man. "There's an accident about a quarter mile ahead, and everyone has slowed down to look. Everything is on schedule."

Carlos could just make out the escape car, up ahead in the traffic. "You need to start moving through traffic and get behind me," said his accomplice. " We're approaching the tunnel."

"Okay, I'll be coming up on the left side." Carlos responded.

Carlos checked over his left shoulder before merging into the next lane, and saw another UPS truck just behind him jockeying for position as it navigated the stream of cars. Seeing a break in traffic Carlos accelerated into the gap and then switched back to the center lane directly behind a non-descript tan car . As he nestled into position the other UPS truck pull up next to him, now both trucks were in position behind their escape vehicles.

Up ahead he could make out the entrance to the tunnel that passed under downtown Phoenix. The tunnel allowed traffic on Interstate 10 to flow uninterrupted through the heart of the city. Above the tunnel was a federal courthouse surrounded by a pedestrian area that included the usual array of coffee and sandwich shops that were crowded with people this time of morning. The park-like surroundings provided a perfect location for lawyers and office workers to sit and drink their morning lattés before heading into their offices to escape the oppressive heat of day.

"Okay, we're approaching the tunnel; it's time to arm your device," the voice on the cell phone instructed. Carlos reached forward and pushed a red button installed on his dashboard, which lit up.

"The device is armed," he reported.

The two UPS trucks drove side-by-side as they entered the tunnel. The escape cars began to gradually slow down allowing traffic in front of them to pull away creating a clear opening. Carlos's heart began to thunder in his chest; he knew yet another UPS truck on the west-bound side of the tunnel was getting into position just as his truck and the one next to him was. Carlos unfastened his seatbelt and moved it out of the way, then placed a clipboard containing the remote detonator on his lap. Up ahead the escape car switched on its hazard lights, indicating they were approaching the detonation point, then the brake lights flashed and the car stopped. Carlos halted his van, set the parking brake, turned off the engine and broke the key off in the ignition. He jumped out of the truck, taking care to lock the sliding door behind him, and ran towards the escape car. His ears were immediately assaulted by a cacophony of car horns as commuters displayed their frustration at yet another traffic jam. Carlos climbed into the sedan that began pulling away even before he closed the door.

"Go, go, go!" Carlos yelled. "Let's get the hell out of here!"

Los Angeles, California

Three hundred and sixty-nine miles away, Antonio maneuvered his UPS truck through the morning traffic of Los Angeles as he worked hard to stay on schedule. He needed to arrive in the underground parking lot of the Grand Hollywood Hotel by 6:30 a.m. The hotel was booked solid following a charity event held in the main ballroom the night before.

The more he thought about the dozens of pathetic, rich fools who'd die in the explosion, the more eager he became. The plan called for him to park his truck next to the main elevator bank, ride up to the lobby and walk out the front doors to a car waiting across the street to spirit him away to a safe house.

Antonio exited I-10 at La Cienaga and drove north past Pico Blvd. Just past Beverly Center he saw the entrance to the hotel parking lot on his right. At the entrance, a parking attendant apathetically manned his booth. When Antonio pulled up the attendant paused long enough to see the UPS logo and opened the gate to let him in. Driving slowly down the ramp and into the parking lot, Antonio located the elevator banks and carefully parked his truck in the loading zone. He armed the bomb and locked the driver's side door before taking the elevator to the lobby. As he ascended, Antonio marveled at the lavish interior the elevator. Evidently the rich couldn't stand to be away from opulence even for the few moments it took to change floors. As soon as the doors slid open, he causally exited the elevator and walked across the granite-floored lobby towards the main entrance. There were about a dozen people in the lobby, mostly checking out at the front desk. As Antonio walked past them it was as though he was invisible. A few people looked his way as he passed, but the vacant look in their eyes attested to their disinterest.

His smooth progress through the lobby faltered slightly when he caught sight of several Chicana maids cleaning, dusting, and replacing flower arrangements. It had not occurred to him, until that moment, that not everyone in the hotel was idle rich, or even Anglo. But a moment's reflection assured him there was nothing he could do, and he kept walking. The Chicano hotel employees would be remembered as martyrs of the revolution.

As he approached the main entrance the huge glass doors automatically opened, and Antonio exited into the Southern California sunshine towards a car waiting across the street.

Selma, California

Jack Franklin walked around his truck, making a quick inspection before leaving the feedlot with his cargo of cattle. He'd been driving trucks for nearly fifteen years, and during that time he'd moved everything from toilet paper to caskets. Lately, he'd been hauling cattle cross-country from feedlots in California to slaughterhouses in Georgia and Florida. The ranch hands had just completed loading the steers into his 53-foot, double-level trailer and were securing the ramps and doors. The cattle were still moving around a bit, but they'd settle down quickly, and then he'd be off on his cross-country trip. In two days he'd drop off this load and pick up another heading back west.

Tempe, Arizona

Rachel had overslept and was now scurrying around her apartment gathering things before leaving for work. She sorted through several bills looking for the ones that needed to be mailed and then grabbed a banana and a yogurt to eat in the car. As she lifted her purse to her shoulder she realized it was too light, which meant she'd forgotten her pistol. For a second she hesitated and considered not taking it, but then let out a sigh of frustration and walked back to her room to get it. *I went through the trouble of getting my carry permit…I might as well make the effort of having the gun with me.*

Rachel hurried down the stairs that lead to the underground parking garage. The complex had an elevator, but Rachel always took the stairs as a way of getting a little extra exercise. She unlocked her car and juggled her purse, banana and yogurt to free up a couple fingers needed to open the door.

After starting the car and backing up she made sure the radio was tuned to the local talk radio station, then zoomed out of the garage. She was fifteen minutes behind schedule and knew the ramp to the 101 would start backing up soon if she didn't hurry.

Gilbert, Arizona

At the same time Mike was just getting out of bed. It had been a late night of cleaning gear and talking with the guys after returning from the Miller ranch. The mission had been a success, not only because they captured the rapists, but they also saved a young girl and her brother. Most importantly, everyone was eager to make another trip to the Double C as soon as possible.

Mike tuned the radio to the local morning talk program and then stepped into the shower. Mike was a news junky and constantly monitored radio and TV news programs for information. As the water ran over his head and body, he soaped up and was amazed that even after a couple long showers he was still finding dirt and grime left over from the patrol. After washing and rinsing his hair he turned off the shower, grabbed a towel and dried off, then walked over to the mirror to continue getting ready.

Downtown Phoenix, Arizona

Officer Williamson finished filling out the on-scene accident report for the fender bender on the east bound I-10 and walked back to his motorcycle. While mounting his motor he noticed that traffic had come to a stop just short of the tunnel entrance. He started his bike and cursed as he thought about how this was going to be long morning commute. *If stupid people would just hang up their cell phones and drive, things would be a lot better.*

Williamson weaved his motorcycle between the stopped cars as he accelerated towards the tunnel. "Dispatch...Tom 582."

"Tom 582...Dispatch, go ahead."

"Dispatch, show me Code 34 inside the I-10 Eastbound tunnel." Up ahead he saw what looked like two UPS trucks stalled side-by-side. *Well, I've never seen this before.*

The officer stopped his bike and walked over to one of the trucks. Stepping up on the running board he looked in the driver's side window and noticed the cab was empty. "*Maybe the driver is in the back.*" He thought as he began pounding on the door in an attempt to get the driver's attention. "This is the police, is everything all..."

****

Three quarters of a mile away, still accelerating away from the tunnel, Carlos looked over his shoulder as he counted down on the phone with the other truck drivers. "3...2...1...Now!" The three men simultaneously pressed the detonation buttons on their remotes. Behind them a bright light bloomed like millions of flash bulbs going off at once. A fraction of a second later an enormous explosion ripped through the morning commute creating a shock wave that radiated outwards at over 28,000 feet per second, hurling nearby cars off the highway and into each other like bowling pins. The reinforced cement walls of the tunnel were shattered by the shock wave as though struck by a giant sledgehammer. A fraction of a second later the weakened walls blew apart, creating massive boulders that flew through the air like meteors and crashed into nearby buildings, ripping vast fiery holes as they tore through gas mains and electrical wiring.

As the pressure wave expelled the surrounding air from the epicenter of the blast, and the expanding fireball from the explosion fed on what was left of the oxygen a vacuum was created which began to draw air into the void. As air rushed back into the center of the explosion at near-hurricane speed, it sucked dirt and debris into the updraft created by the tremendous heat of the burning explosives. This chain of events produced a boiling mushroom cloud that steadily rose over the Phoenix skyline.

Los Angeles, California

Antonio focused on walking as normally as possible so as to not draw attention to himself. But at any moment, he imagined, someone would wonder why a UPS driver was walking away from the hotel, with no big brown truck in sight. His heart was pounding with excitement as his sweaty palms tightly gripped the remote detonator. He walked down the stairs towards the circular driveway of the hotel that was lined with taxis waiting to attend to guests. Weaving his way past an obstacle course of car doors, luggage, and people, he briefly looked over his shoulder at a pretty young girl exiting a cab. At that very moment a valet pushed a baggage cart around the back of a shuttle van colliding with the bomber. The cart was loaded with nearly a dozen suitcases, so even though it wasn't moving fast, it knocked Antonio off his feet. As he crashed to the ground he fell on top of the detonating button.

The truck bomb was positioned beside the bank of elevators that were integrated into the central supporting structure of the hotel. The two-thousand-five-hundred-pound bomb demolished the reinforced concrete supporting structures that were closest to it and pulverized the concrete in the surrounding ones, leaving only bent rebar to fight against the enormous weight of the structure above. The initial force of the explosion blew the doors off the elevators, allowing fireballs to race up the shafts. As the conflagrations climbed upwards, the overpressure blew elevator doors off at each floor, spreading fire and destruction throughout the structure. In a fraction of a second the hotel began to implode as upper floors collapsed into the underground parking lot. Without the support of the center load bearing columns, the grand hotel split in two.

Antonio fought to get to his feet, but the shock of the explosion knocked him back down. His only thought was to get up and run towards the car that was waiting to drive him to safety. Once again, he struggled to get his feet under him, but before he was able to begin running the large glass front doors of the hotel exploded and slammed him to the ground, rendering him unconscious.

Hundreds of people were trapped in the crumbling structure and crushed by heavy furnishings and decorations. Water pipes burst, flooding air spaces and preventing the sprinkler system from putting out the spreading fires. The once-grand hotel quickly became a huge jumbled tomb.

KPAZ Radio: Phoenix, Arizona

"We interrupt our morning show with an emergency alert. A massive explosion has taken place in downtown Phoenix. Early reports say the entire I-10 tunnel and the Federal Courthouse on top of it have collapsed. We're receiving reports of a huge mushroom cloud rising over the city. We want to caution everyone that we do not know whether this was a nuclear attack or not. Initial indications point to a conventional bomb, since we haven't experienced any disruption in our signal. Emergency response teams are being dispatched, but since the explosion took place during rush hour causalities are expected to be very high. We'll continue to cover this event without interruption, and will report the details to you as we receive them.

Needless to say, we're urging people to stay away from the downtown area and the I-10 tunnel."

Gilbert, Arizona

Mike stood motionless in front of the radio. *No...this isn't good.* He had always believed that another terrorist attack would happen; the odds were simply stacked against the US. To prevent another major attack the government would have to be right one hundred percent of the time, but the terrorist only needed to succeed once. Mike had driven through that tunnel dozens of times and knew it would take a huge bomb to destroy it. He was also aware of the volume of traffic that would be there this time of day.

Suddenly, he thought about Rachel. BioPharm was in Tempe, not Phoenix. But he didn't want her running around town when bombs were exploding. Still wearing only a towel, Mike grabbed his cell phone and called Rachel. The phone rang a few times before she answered.

"Hello?"

"Rachel, this is Mike. Are you listening to the radio?"

"Actually, I turned it off because I had to call the office to tell them I was running late. Why?"

"There's been a major terrorist attack downtown. Evidently a huge bomb exploded in the I-10 tunnel and the whole thing has been completely destroyed. I want you to get back here as fast as possible."

"Hold on, I'm turning the radio on now...when did this happen?"

"Evidently about five minutes ago. I want you off the streets as fast as possible."

"I have to go to work, Mike. I can't just *not* show up."

"Listen, this isn't a normal day. Your safety is more important. Believe me, your boss will understand."

KPAZ Radio: Phoenix, Arizona

"Reports out of our sister station in Los Angeles are beginning to come into our news offices. They're reporting that several devastating bombings have taken place around downtown L.A. One has collapsed the Grand Hollywood Hotel. Another severely damaged the primary interchange for the I-5 and I-10 highways, and a third exploded at an oil refinery in the City of Industry. Initial reports claim the refinery is completely engulfed in fire.

"The Department of Homeland Defense has raised the National Terror Threat Level to Red, the highest possible alert. This is the first time the threat level has reached this level. Officials are reporting that these were coordinated attacks that seem to mirror Al-Qaeda operations."

"We now have Tom Martin reporting live at the scene of the bombing in downtown Phoenix. Tom what can you tell us?"

"Jerry, emergency officials are now confirming that this was *not* a nuclear explosion, and there is no radiation threat. That's not to say the devastation isn't overwhelming. The entire I-10 tunnel is completely destroyed, as is the Federal Courthouse that was constructed over it. There's a pile of rubble that looks to be at least six stories high with dark black plumes of smoke rising out of it.

"We're told by firefighters this smoke is coming from dozens of burning cars that were in the tunnel at the time of the explosion. Rescue efforts have begun, but given the amount of traffic that was in the tunnel and the number of people in the Federal Building...I'd hate to speculate on the number dead and injured. This is Tom Martin, reporting live from Downtown."

Gilbert, Arizona

Every news station on TV and the radio dedicated wall-to-wall coverage to the bombings. At the time of the attack, Wall Street had just begun its trading day. Upon hearing the reports out of Arizona and California, a panic sell-off began that dropped the market nearly eight hundred points before automatic trading curbs kicked in. As the news shot across the globe, overseas investors began dumping US Dollars and buying Euros as fast as possible. In a matter of hours the dollar fell to an all-time low of $.38 to one Euro, and gold skyrocketed to $1,200 an ounce.

Locally, gasoline stations shut down in the wake of panic buying, preferring to hold onto supplies that were bound to double in price in the coming days. Grocery stores were inundated with hordes of shoppers who began cleaning the shelves of water, canned goods, batteries, plastic sheeting and duct tape.

Around 10:00 a.m. the mayors of Phoenix and Los Angeles declared states of emergency which gave them the power to impose curfews and bypass standard union regulations governing the number of hours police and firefighters could be forced to work. The mayors also asked their state governors to call up National Guard units to enforce curfews and assist with rescue efforts. But to their dismay, the governors of both states refused to call up any units outside of Los Angeles and Phoenix. Their reasoning was that too many federalized guardsmen were still in Afghanistan and Iraq. And those who had been rotated back home, the governors' spokespeople said, had been away from vital jobs too long. Those units that were called up were not allowed to deploy with ammunition. In a press conference, the governor of Arizona stated, "I'm not going to allow National Guardsmen to create a police state and threaten their fellow citizens with lethal force. We have laws prohibiting this type of behavior. We need to come together as a community, and soldiers running around with machine guns aren't going to help."

Military bases in Arizona and California were immediately locked down to protect against future attacks. As it had following the 9/11 attacks, the Pentagon ordered a 24-hour combat air patrol (CAP) to be flown over both L.A. and Phoenix.

Mike knew he needed to gather as much information as possible and keep the rest of the Patriot community informed. He logged onto the two leading militia web pages and immediately began to write a situation report (SITREP) outlining what was happening in Phoenix and the surrounding areas. As he'd expected, there were already a lot of posts out of Southern California. Most of the groups had already raised their alert level and were in the process of notifying their members of contingency plans. Since 9/11 various procedures had been established to alert members of potential crisis.

Since militia units were sometimes scattered across large cities and counties, a system of beepers, e-mails and cell phones were used to notify everyone. Each unit had its own set of procedures based upon the unique skill sets of its members and anticipated threats to their AO.

In this case, units in and around Los Angeles and Phoenix were going on full alert as a precaution against further attacks and societal breakdown. Groups in the nearby regions were placing their people on alert for possible deployment to assist the groups closest to the attacks. Mike posted all the information he'd gathered from news reports as well as from his contacts within city government and the police. He also let the other groups know that currently there was no need for outside assistance.

Lost in the momentous news of the day was a short story about five Mexican nationals found shot to death at an aid station located in the Arizonan desert. The news report mentioned that citizens' militias were suspected of the murders. The governor of Arizona had asked legislators to draft an emergency bill expanding the government's power to crack down on militias.

PLA Headquarters: Hermosillo, Mexico

As reports of the bombings began flooding into PLA headquarters a mixture of elation and foreboding quickly spread from person-to-person. The PLA had never been able organize such an attack before, and seeing the massive damage and destruction caused by the bombs gave them pause. After all they'd just executed the largest attack on American soil since September 11, and some worried about inevitable retaliation.

Four of the six drivers were in safe houses waiting to be spirited back to Mexico. The other two had apparently died in the attacks. The driver who targeted the oil refinery had martyred himself to detonate his truck as close to the gasoline storage tanks as possible. The other missing driver was reportedly killed in a premature detonation at the Hollywood Hotel.

Reports estimated that upwards of three thousand people were dead and scores injured. The oil refinery was one of the largest in Southern California and responsible for nearly half the gasoline used in Los Angeles and San Diego. The initial blast detonated two of the eight colossal, above-ground storage tanks, each containing over one million gallons of gasoline.

The secondary explosions ignited two other tanks and spread down the connecting pipelines into the refinery and then to the off-loading facility located offshore. If the fires could not be controlled soon, firefighters believed the whole complex would be lost. If that happened L.A. and San Diego would be starved for gasoline, and immediate rationing would go into effect.

The I-10/I-5 interchange was so severely damaged that the California Department of Transportation estimated it would take nine months before it could be reopened to traffic. The interchange was a vital crossroad in the center of the city, linking the entire L.A. basin. Commuters already felt the impact of its loss as traffic jams overloaded secondary roads and extended for miles in all directions.

As significant as the destruction was, it was not the real damage caused by the PLA. The United States possessed the materials, skilled labor, equipment, and technical expertise needed to rebuild. The real damage was done to the nation's collective psyche. Suddenly, America was under attack...*again.* The images of death and destruction assaulted the country's collective emotions like a rape victim reliving her violation in a nightmare. A sense of betrayal exacerbated the trauma caused by the haunting images of fire, twisted metal, and suffering. All the new laws that had promised to enhance security at the expense of freedom proved to be nothing more than deceit.

The trauma that had gripped America following September 11 had faded over time. But now it was back, like an abusive husband to a broken home, once again bent on imposing his will on a family just beginning to regain its confidence and strength. As before, people huddled in their homes and watched hour after hour as news stations reported the latest horror. Businesses were empty, work was lost, plans were canceled, and economic momentum was stalled. Like all true acts of terrorism, though physical targets were destroyed, the real assault was on the enemy's mind.

As Major Al-Salih read the reports, he felt delight and elation radiate from him. For so long he had endured the humiliation of watching the US annihilate his Arab brothers and expand their oppression around the globe. Now, what a blessing it was to see anguish and pain return to his enemies. As he continued reading the intelligence reports, he silently fingered his *Masbaha,* giving thanks to Allah for allowing him to play a role in this great strike against the Americans.

He had to admit this temporary partnership with the Mexicans was proving more effective than he'd thought possible. So far they had executed their attacks with almost military precision. But the major knew that additional actions must be taken; actions his allies weren't ready to undertake. For his mission to fully succeed...for America's society to truly collapse...Muhammad must now do hard things.

Every society had an Achilles heel, which if not protected, thwarted their ability to achieve greatness. The major was a truthful man, and as such, understood that even Arabs suffered these weaknesses. How else to explain their inability to overcome poverty and focus their vast power? Allah had blessed his people with everything they needed to claim their predestined role as world leaders. But pride and slothfulness had grown into an epidemic that swept across Islam like a demonic swarm of locus.

Instead of using the great oil wealth of the region to unify and build up Islam, seemingly endless riches polluted the ruling families with pride and blinded them to the potential they'd been blessed with. Instead, they used their prosperity to build palaces and indulge their carnal desires. Only strict obedience to the teachings of the Prophet could cure this disease and bring to pass an *Umma* (universal Islamic community) that would rule the world. Whereas pride and complacency plagued Muhammad's people, the Mexicans suffered from the malignant effects of paganism and pseudo-Christianity. Even the major understood enough about Christianity to see the obvious contradictions in Mexican-Catholicism.

For a religion that claimed to be monotheistic these infidels happily prostrated themselves before a collection of graven images and idols that would make even the Hindus jealous. Of course, they justified their heresy by claiming they didn't worship idols, instead they prayed to images of Christ, Mary and the Saints to better focus their devotions. Call it what you may, the fact was they prayed to the handiwork of men, thus perverting the teachings of the Nazarene prophet. The curse of idolatry had closed their minds to precious truths; like the importance of martyrdom. Instead of embracing total sacrifice, Catholics believed that life was sacred and suicide a sin. The answer was so simple, yet it eluded them; there's a difference between selfish suicide and dying for a holy cause. After all isn't that what the Nazarene supposedly did?

He'd martyred himself and in so doing gained glory. Even the first century Christians revered "the Martyrs" not "the Saints." But centuries of apostasy had allowed this truth to slip away. Of the world's religions only Islam remained true to Allah's teachings and possessed all the knowledge needed to guide mankind towards a greater reward. No other act was as blessed as martyrdom. In the *Sahih Bukhari*, the Prophet Muhammad spoke plainly when he said: "Had I not found it difficult for my followers, then I would not remain behind any Sariya (an army-unit) going for Jihad and I would have loved to be martyred in Allah's cause and then made alive, and then martyred and then made alive, and then again martyred in His Cause."

In all their planning sessions, the PLA leadership constantly stressed the importance of not killing other Mexicans, as if it was possible to liberate a people without collateral damage. The PLA claimed they respected the Palestinians and their struggle for freedom. But if this was the case they needed to follow the *Shuhadaas* (martyrs) and accept the inevitable losses that a struggle for independence required. If they lacked the faith and courage to make the difficult decisions victory demanded, then he'd do it for them. In the end he would be justified. The major finished the latest intelligence report and switched his focus to a television across the room showing a news report from the refinery fire. It seemed as though the fire was beyond control, and the area around the facility was being evacuated. The refinery was a total loss, and Southern California would be plunged into massive fuel shortages.

The on-scene reporter finished his commentary by stating that with the loss of the refinery, prices were expected to rise to nearly nine dollars a gallon. The major's jubilation was tempered only by the knowledge that today's events were only the first strike and yet another attack had already been released that would bring a level of economic destruction the Americans had never experienced.

Lieutenant Sayf interrupted the major's meditation as he entered the office and closed the door behind him. "Ra'id, I apologize for the interruption but we need to discuss the status of our other operations."

The major waved Sayf into his small office and began speaking in Arabic, "Of course, Mulazim, I was just reading the latest reports from our sources in California and Arizona. Praise be to Allah, the attacks had a greater effect than we'd originally hoped."

"Indeed, Allah is truly merciful and has blessed us with a great victory over the camp of Kufur' (the unbelievers). The Americans are wounded, and great damage has been done to their economy. But, as we discussed, I doubt these events will be sufficient to achieve our goals. We still need a catalyst to spark the racial unrest that will justify a social revolution." Sayf hesitated and checked to ensure the door was securely closed behind him. "Ra'id, may I speak freely?"

"Of course. You know I value your opinion."

"Ra'id, like you...I, too, have been impressed with the dedication our Mexican allies have shown, and I am very pleased with their performance...but, I don't think they are willing to make the sacrifices that are needed to attain final victory. The Mexicans in the United States have allowed the wealth and ease of their surroundings to weaken their resolve. Complacency has become a way of life for them. Frankly, I don't think they'll seize the opportunity these attacks have presented them. I'd like permission to activate operation *Lobo Blanco*."

The major sat quietly in his chair and stared out the office window overlooking a garden full of brightly colored flowers. He was pleased with his Lieutenant. Sayf had proven to be an excellent aide, and the major appreciated his ability to judge a situation and instinctively know what needed to be done. Nonetheless, it was also important to ensure that the proper distance and respect be observed between himself and his aide.

"Mulazim, I have been pondering the same dilemma. Tell me, do you have complete confidence in your *Lobo Blanco* asset?"

"Yes. I believe he is properly prepared and motivated. He will fulfill his mission. Security has been very tight, and he knows nothing more than what I've told him. As per our plan he believes I am a white separatist from South Africa. I'm convinced we can proceed with full confidence."

"Very well, activate *Lobo Blanco* and proceed as planned. Sayf, may I remind you that our PLA friends cannot learn about this. I'm trusting in your professionalism to ensure this is handled properly."

"You can be assured that I have taken every possible precaution and fully understand the sensitivity of this operation. It will be successful."

The major nodded his head and waved Sayf off, then turned back around and began pondering his next move.

One Day After the Bombings

The day following the attacks investigators began the tedious process of piecing together what had happened and how the attacks were executed. The first clues came from a traffic camera mounted in the eastbound I-10 tunnel in Phoenix. The camera fed real-time images to a traffic control station at the Highway Patrol headquarters. The video clearly showed two UPS trucks stopping side by side and the drivers running away. A couple of minutes later a motorcycle cop rode up to the trucks and began looking for the drivers. Then the feed abruptly ended. Unfortunately, the camera was mounted a distance behind the spot where the trucks stopped so a clear image of the drivers was not possible, nor was the camera able to see where they escaped to. It was assumed they had accomplices in cars that drove them away, but due to the angle of the camera and the height of the trucks; no image of the escape vehicles was recorded. To back this theory up several survivors from the freeway bombing in L.A. testified they'd seen a UPS truck in traffic at the time of the blast.

The FBI immediately began to investigate this theory by contacting UPS headquarters in Atlanta, Georgia to see if they were missing any trucks. The CEO of the company informed them they had not received any reports of missing vehicles and went on to explain how all their trucks are checked-in and out each day. He also explained the controlled procedures the company uses to dispose of vehicles taken out of service.

Not long after the investigation began, information was leaked to the press. It didn't take long for companies across the United States to ban parcel delivery trucks from entering their properties. Many companies established off-site delivery locations where items were dropped off and inspected before being shuttled back to their offices by employees in rented trucks. In a panic, consumers stopped using any on-line business that shipped via UPS. Many people simply stopped purchasing items on-line or catalogs.

In a series of press conferences the CEOs of the major parcel services and the FBI assured the public that it was safe to continue using delivery services. It was all for not. Within 12 hours UPS and its competitors began suffering massive reductions in business. This news led investors to frantically sell-off stock. UPS stock lost nearly 60% of its value over night, other parcel companies lost even more.

Democrats in Washington immediately went on the offensive, blaming the administration for not preventing the attacks. Administration opponents demanded to know why the government could wage war overseas but were unable to safeguard the homeland. Renewed calls circulated for pulling military forces out of Iraq and turning the reconstruction of the Middle East over to the UN and the European Union.

Across Southern California and Arizona, gasoline prices began to spike. Overnight the price of regular unleaded gas rose from $4.75 to $6.95. Within hours, lines of cars formed down every street with a gas station on the corner. Some of these lines stretched for over a mile, and people waited for hours as gas station employees enforced a strict five-gallon limit. Many of the stations simply ran out of fuel and resorted to chaining off their pumps and hiring armed guards to prevent looters who tried to siphon any remaining gasoline from their underground holding tanks. As people waited in fuel lines, salesmen carrying boxes of locking gas caps sold their goods like hotdog vendors at a ballpark. Gasoline trucks from surrounding states began a round-the-clock convoy to deliver fuel to Los Angeles, San Diego and Phoenix. But it wasn't nearly enough, and within twenty-four hours normal activities ground to a screeching halt.

CBS Nightly News

"In the aftermath of the terrorist bombings in California and Arizona, House Democrats today commenced impeachment proceedings against the president."

[Cut to video clip of Congresswoman Alberti] "The president has woefully failed to execute his primary responsibility of safeguarding the people of the United States. His negligent use of military power and lack of diplomatic skills have forced world opinion against America, destroyed valued relationships, and caused irreparable damage to our economy and national reputation. He has left the citizens of this nation open to further deadly attacks and has no vision for the future. These charges constitute a clear dereliction of duty and demonstrate a complete disrespect for the Constitutional obligations of the Presidency."

[Return to Anchor] "In the House of Representatives, a bill was introduced to pull US forces out of Iraq and return them to the United States to safeguard the homeland against further attacks. The administration is frantically gathering an ever-shrinking band of supporters to oppose the bill and point out that even if this bill were to pass; the president would immediately veto it. Congressional Democrats are confident that they'll be able to organize the bipartisan support necessary to pass the bill with a two-thirds, veto-proof majority.

"CBS political correspondent Andrea Samuels is at the Capital. Andrea, what will be the immediate effect of these actions?"

"Collin, there's no doubt that the president has suffered a severe political blow. Poll results show his approval rating in the low thirty-percent range and when asked 'What group do you believe has the best vision to lead America?' respondents chose Congressional Democrats three-to-one over the administration."

"Andrea, what does this do to the president's powerbase?"

"Basically, the president has lost his ability to act domestically and certainly internationally. The perception is that he is weak, unpopular, and out of step not only with the world community, but with the American people as well. There's no question that Senate and House Democrats smell political blood in the water and are seizing upon this opportunity to reclaim power. Reporting from Capital Hill, this is Andrea Samuels for CBS. Back to you Collin."

Direct Action Academy

The renewed fear stemming from the attacks created a spike in business for the academy, especially in concealed carry classes. It seemed everyone in the valley who didn't already have a permit decided it was time to get one.

Arrow wasn't surprised; the same thing had happened following the 9/11 attacks. Either people needed to find a proactive way to deal with the trauma, or they were just angry about being attacked. Either way, Arrow figured it was good for the community. Anyone who examined the data knew that communities that had a high percentage of concealed carry permits were safer than those that didn't. There wasn't anything mysterious about it; criminals would rather prey on unarmed victims. Carrying a handgun wouldn't prevent a truck bombing or a September 11-style attack. But, unless you live in a police state, the police can't be everywhere. On the other hand, citizens can. And if they're armed and properly trained that makes every target harder to attack.

The phone on Arrow's desk rang, and the caller I.D. displayed the name, Chief Meadows. Arrow reached over and picked up the phone.

"This is Taylor."

"Hi, Taylor, it's Dan Meadows. How're you doing?" The policeman's voice sounded tired

"Pretty well, considering the circumstances," answered Arrow. "I bet the last couple days haven't been easy for you. What can I help you with?"

"Yeah, I haven't gotten more than a few hours sleep since the attacks. We've been on full alert, but the feds have their teams in place and are ready to take over, so I guess my guys will get to stand down in the next eight hours."

"I'd imagine once the feds get all their personnel on the ground they pretty much take control of an incident like this. How's the search effort going at the tunnel?"

"Considering the amount of damage, it's going pretty well. Since 9/11 a number of specialized teams have been created and trained for this kind of operation. They've learned a lot and developed some amazing equipment from their experiences in New York and Oklahoma City." Arrow heard him sigh. "Unfortunately, we haven't found any survivors in the last ten hours. If no one is found by tomorrow afternoon we'll switch to a recovery phase. "

"Have the rescue teams gotten into the tunnel yet?"

"Nobody's been able to physically get that far down; there's just too much debris, and fires are still burning from the cars that were caught in the blast. But they've sent in small robots with cameras and microphones. It looks like everybody in there was either incinerated by the blast or succumbed to toxic fumes. I spoke with an FBI buddy, and he told me the explosive residue analysis identified the primary explosive as RDX."

"RDX? That's a military-grade explosive, right?"

"Yeah, it's top-of-the-line stuff. This was no ANFO bomb put together by amateurs; whoever designed these bombs had a lot of experience and money. Evidently the FBI is doing a signature analysis to determine where the RDX was manufactured."

"I'd be interested in finding out what the results of that test show. You mentioned there was something I could do for you?" Actually he hadn't mentioned any such thing, but considering how Dan Meadows had spent the past couple of days, Arrow figured he wouldn't have called if he didn't need something.

"Oh, yeah," Chief Meadows grunted as if he were shifting wearily in a chair. "I'd like to cycle a couple more groups of officers through your tactical carbine course. I'm sure you've heard the governor has refused to allow National Guard troops to deploy with ammunition, so I figure my officers might be the only ones capable of shooting back, and I want them tuned up."

"No problem, Chief. Just let me know when they'll be here, and we'll have everything ready for them."

Arrow was happy to assist Dan with anything he needed. Since the Academy opened, he'd proven to be a real friend and a great source of information. His contacts in the federal building were rock solid, and he trusted Arrow and Mike with information that was hard to come by. With a source that good, Arrow was going to do whatever was necessary to maintain his confidence.

Fox News Channel

"This is a Fox News alert. Fox News has learned through sources in the FBI that a suspect is being held in the bombing of the Grand Hollywood Hotel. Sources tell Fox News that the suspect was injured while trying to escape the explosion. We have also learned the suspect has been identified as a Mexican national in this country illegally. Currently he is under heavy guard at a Los Angeles area military hospital where he's receiving treatment for a concussion and other minor injuries.

"Sources tell Fox that the bomber is being designated a foreign combative and will be tried by a military tribunal. We'll continue to monitor this story and bring any further details to your attention. This has been a Fox News alert."

PLA Headquarters: Hermosillo, Mexico

Activity at PLA headquarters had increased to a frantic pace. The bombings had started a chain of events that took on a life of its own as orders were sent out to cells and operatives across Mexico and the United States. The news that one of the bombers had been captured was initially seen as a potential liability, but the major quickly identified a way to use the unfortunate event to his advantage. One of the greatest assets the PLA possessed was their fifth column of sympathizers within the United States, and the major immediately put them to work. Already they'd begun to exert pressure on the American government to turn the bomber over to civilian authorities. If this could be accomplished they could obfuscate the proceedings long enough to allow the rest of their plans to take place. A cadre of OJChA lawyers had already volunteered their time and skills to defend the bomber. The goal was to have the case transferred to a civilian court and then seat a jury of Mexican-Americans and illegal aliens who would acquit their client. But before that could happen, sufficient pressure would have to be brought to bear to get the suspect out of the hands of the military. To this end, Rabbit and Flag received instructions to organize student and community protests to gather additional media attention. These protests would focus on discrediting the military tribunals by portraying them as secret proceedings of an American dictatorship. This way, they were not defending a murderous bomber. On the contrary, they were protesting in support of constitutional safeguards. After all, if it could happen to this man, who was presumably innocent until proven guilty, then it could happen to anyone, and it wouldn't be long before Stalinist roundups began across America.

Outside of Atlanta, Georgia

The drive from California to Georgia had been easy, considering the terrorist bombings that took place the day he left. Fortunately for Jack, his route took him well north of Phoenix along Interstate 40, so he wasn't interrupted by road closures or checkpoints. During the trip he'd stayed abreast of the news by listening to talk radio. In the past he'd maintained a log of different stations he liked, and as he drove from city to city he'd switch stations. But last year he installed a satellite radio receiver, so now he had uninterrupted reception along his whole route.

Being on the road during a time of crisis was difficult. Jack's first impulse was to be home with his family where he could take care of them and make sure they were safe, but he had to deliver his load of livestock. Driving animals was different from driving other loads. He was responsible for taking care of them during the trip so they'd arrive in good condition, and the best way to do that was to get them to the stockyards as quickly as possible. Driving livestock across country had become commonplace as meat packing houses shopped the whole country in search of good prices. In the past the US imported cattle from Canada and Mexico, which reduced prices, but that practice had stopped after outbreaks of Mad Cow Disease (BSE) in both countries. Now packers were willing to pay the extra cost of trucking stock across the country to meet their demand.

After unloading the first load of cattle he prepared for the short trip across the border into Florida where he'd drop off the remaining steers, and then he'd be able to head back to his family.

Gilbert, Arizona

Three days had passed since the bombings, and aftershocks were still reverberating across the Southwest. Waking up before dawn to search the city for gasoline was becoming a common event, and now grocery prices and other products were beginning to rise in response to the fuel shortages. To keep the Academy's classes full, Mike had suggested a shuttle service for the students. It had seemed like a good idea when he voiced it, but now on top of everything else he found himself nominated as the primary van driver. There was one consolation though. Rachel was taking classes at the Academy. Mike and Rachel had just dropped off their last student and were now on their way back to her apartment. Rachel's shooting had continued to improve in fluidity and accuracy, and she was beginning to earn a well-deserved reputation. Arrow remarked that a lot of her skill came from her ability to think through complex situations. Her academic training had prepared her for this type of shooting, a benefit she'd never contemplated while in school.

"I was having a bit of trouble with my tactical reloads this evening," she said. "I can't get comfortable with my magazine pouches. I don't know if it's the way they're positioned or the way they open. Either way, it's slowing me down and compromising my situational awareness. Do you think Josh will design something for me that'll help?"

Mike glanced towards his beautiful companion, hesitated a moment, then said, "First off…I don't think I've ever been more aroused then hearing you use the words *situational awareness* in a sentence." That remark earned him a solid punch in the shoulder.

Rachel rolled her eyes. "I swear you really need to talk to a professional about this tactical fetish you have."

Mike laughed at Rachel's rebuke. The truth was that he loved teasing her. "I'm sure Josh will be more than happy to design a custom rig for you. It's probably something as simple as the angle it's attached to your belt. By the way, you're really improving. Arrow remarked how well you're negotiating the various scenarios."

"Well, tell him I said thanks for the compliment. I'm having a lot of fun, and the added challenges in the advanced tactical course make the whole thing that much better."

The two arrived at Rachel's apartment and went inside where they continued their conversation. Mike had been contemplating a concern ever since the attacks, but didn't want to scare Rachel. Nonetheless, he felt this might be the best time to bring the topic up.

"Rachel…" Mike concentrated on keeping his voice light. "I want to discuss a security issue with you. I don't want you to get the wrong idea or worry; it's just a precaution."

"What's on your mind?"

"The guys and I were talking the other night, and we've settled on a codeword that we'll use if anything goes wrong."

Rachel looked up at him, "A codeword?"

"Yeah, for instance, let's say Arrow needs my help. If he says "Red Rabbit" I'll know he's serious or that he's in trouble. I'd like to establish a word that we could use as well."

"That sounds like a reasonable idea. When I was a little girl my parents did something similar with me. We had a special word, and if they had to send someone other than a family member to pick me up at school or at a friend's house, they had to tell me the code word. If they didn't I was to run away and tell an adult."

"That's exactly what I'm talking about. I want to make sure you're safe against anything like that. Do you have a word that'll be easy to remember?"

"How about, "*decompression*?" That's a word people don't normally throw around in conversation. We're both familiar with it from diving, so it shouldn't be hard to remember."

"Great. So from now on, if for any reason, I need to get a message to you through a third party, they'll give you our safe word. If they don't, you'll..."

"If they don't I'll give them a lesson in feminine protection, and I don't mean the once-a-month kind." Rachel interrupted.

Mike laughed at Rachel's answer and made a mental note to remember that one. Not long afterwards one of Rachel's roommates, Cindy, arrived with a large bag full of Chinese takeout.

"Hi guys. I was hoping someone would be home. I got a craving for Chinese food and decided to stop and get a few things, but it looks like I overdid it. How'd you like to help me eat all this?"

East Los Angeles, California

It was a clear, cool weekday morning as tens of thousands of Mexican-Americans and Mexican nationals gathered for a rally in support of the alleged bombing suspect. The organizers recruited many of the attendees from parks, street corners, and day labor sites across L.A. to create an impressive sight for the expected news crews. By 9:00 a.m. the crowd had swelled into the thousands. Already reporters were erecting their cameras and aligning the satellite transmitters on their news vans. The rally had been combined with a one-day labor walkout to add strength to their call for justice.

Hotels, restaurants, cleaning crews, grocery stores, and thousands of other service industries were suddenly short of workers, and many were unable to open for business. In the front of the crowd was a small, hastily erected platform with large speakers placed at each corner. Stretched across the back of the platform was a red and black banner with the slogan, "Reject secret trials, Justice for all!" While the crowd waited for the speakers, mariachi music blasted from the speakers and added to the almost deafening din of the multitude. Throughout the crowd people carried signs and banners with traditional protest phrases like: "No Justice, No Peace," "There's no room for secret trials in the land of the free," and "Just say NO to a military dictatorship."

A college-aged girl walked up to the microphone and called for the crowd's attention. "*Hermanos y Hermanas*, please quiet down and direct your attention to the platform. Before we begin our protest against fascism and racism, we'll be addressed by one of the preeminent freedom fighters in the United States. This man has been the leader in the Chicano struggle for freedom and self-determination in America. Through his efforts we have been able to regain many of the freedoms and rights stolen from us by our Anglo-oppressors. This man will be known as one of the greatest civil rights leaders in history along with Nelson Mandela, Cesar Chavez, Martin Luther King Jr., and Simon Bolivar. Please join me in welcoming Señor Raul de Soto."

The crowd applauded and shouted their approval as Raul approached the microphone. As was his style, Raul stood silently looking out over the crowd as if to absorb the energy of the multitude. As the roars continued, he scanned left to right with a somber expression and slowly nodded his head in acknowledgment of the people's accolades. As the multitude began to quiet down in anticipation of his speech, Raul maintained his silence. Soon the crowd was completely quiet and all eyes were fixed on the charismatic speaker. Just before the silence changed from eager anticipation to uneasiness, Raul extended his fist high in the air and shouted, "*Viva la Raza!*"

Like an over-inflated balloon, the crowd exploded in a deafening shout that seemed to shake the trees and reverberate beyond the park and into the surrounding city. This outburst lasted another minute or two. Just as before, Raul stood stoically and waited until the crowd once again achieved an unnatural silence. Then he began his address in a soft voice, almost too soft to hear.

"As I look out upon you this morning, my spirit is strengthened. Before me I see a vision that has been the dream of our forefathers for hundreds of years. I see a united bronze nation, joined in strength and resolve to tell the illegitimate government that we will no long be suppressed and that when even one of our brothers is threatened with injustice we will rise up and demand that justice be served. I want each of you to look around. Those of you with children, I want you to raise them high in the air so they can see around them.

"Look at the sky, the trees, and the faces of those next to you. Breathe in the air and feel the breeze on your skin. I want each of you to allow this moment to be etched into your individual memories, because one day, a generation yet to be born will sit at your feet and plead with you to tell them the story of when the revolution began. Each one of you will be able to recall this day and with pride tell them, *I was there the day Atzlán was liberated!*"

As Raul continued, his gestures and voice grew more animated punctuating each statement. Raul had worked hard to develop his powerful speaking style. He could quickly seize control of virtually any crowd and with his words and actions manipulate them into any condition he desired. The devotion that emanated from the thousands of spellbound people surged into Raul's soul, invigorating him and magnifying the intensity of his words until he transformed into an almost Messianic figure.

"Will you stand idly by and allow your *hermanos y hermanas* to be thrown into gulags and concentration camps by the racists who have so long subjugated and repressed us? We will not submit to their concerted strategy of cultural genocide. And let us not forget the five Mexican immigrants that were savagely massacred at a water station in the middle of the Arizona desert. These innocent people were brutally murdered by a racist border militia dedicated to exterminating us like rats! The war has already begun; even now innocent blood flows. The time for action is upon us; the illegitimate Anglo government that stole our land and worked to destroy our bronze pride is ripe for destruction. This attempt to impose a military dictatorship is nothing more than the frantic and spasmodic death twitch of a dying regime. The United States has lost all of its international support. The countries of Europe who stood by its side for decades have abandoned it. Canada has turned its back on the US, and Latin America has thrown off the imperialistic chains with which Washington has enslaved them. Japan has re-militarized. The South Koreans have removed their American blinders and now yearn for reunification with their northern brothers. The world community stands as a witness against American imperialism.

"Of course, the Anglos deny they're building a global empire, but how can they explain the forces that occupy countries on nearly every continent? How can they deny the chains of debt that strangle the economies of the developing nations? Will they refute the fact that they suck the world's resources dry like a monstrous leech? No, they can't!"

As Raul's words burrowed deep into the minds and hearts of those assembled, a transformation began. Instead of an assembly of individuals the protesters solidified into a cohesive body of one mind and purpose. In unison the people roared, "*No, no, no, no!*"

"*Hermanos y Hermanas*, the time for the revolution has arrived. The spirits of our ancestors and those of millions of exploited workers around the world cry out as one and demand that we take action against the Zionist outlaws who've ravaged the world in their blind, shameless crusade of conquest. It's time for our voices to shake the decayed foundations of this criminal state and for justice to done. Today I will proudly lead you in this historic march... *Viva Atzlán, Viva la Raza, Viva la Revolucíon!*"

****

Several blocks away another gathering was taking place. George Franklin and Steven Wilks waited silently in an abandoned apartment building that was scheduled for demolition. The two men had arrived in the middle of the night and positioned themselves in a second story room facing the street. Both men were in their mid twenties and already wore the hardened appearance of stereotypical white supremacists. Both men's faces were painted in tones of green and black. They wore USGI woodland camouflage BDUs and boonie hats they'd purchased from local surplus stores. In the shadows of the abandoned room, the muted colors of the BDUs helped their forms blend into the shadows. George lay on a foam mat positioned about four feet from a west-facing window overlooking the street below. As he peered through the scope of a Remington .308 rifle he searched the street for a target.

"I have a mail box at our two o'clock; what's the range on it?" George quietly asked.

Steve picked up a laser range finder and locked its beam onto the mailbox, "220 yards," he mumbled.

George adjusted the scope to match the range and then checked his watch. "Typical spics, they're never on-time."

George and Steve were members of a small band of neo-Nazis called *Das Sturmgewehr* who had dedicated themselves to preserving the white race and establishing a separate white homeland in the Western states. Although *Das Sturmgewehr* shared a hatred of Jews and blacks universal among neo-Nazis, their organization focused mainly on the ever-increasing numbers of Mexicans who infested the US and pushed out worthy Aryans.

Now at last, George and Steve had their chance to strike a blow for their race. Both men fit the profile of white supremacists; neither one had finished high school, and each worked a low-paying manual labor job. While Steve had grown up in a typical middle-class family, George was a product of a broken home where the choices of his alcoholic mother provided a steady stream of unfamiliar men who never stayed long enough or cared to build a relationship with either him or his mother.

George was introduced to the white power movement by a co-worker at an auto parts store. In the movement he found the companionship and family he'd never had. He learned that the problems that plagued him weren't his fault at all, but that he was the victim of a Jew-controlled government and social system bent on self-destruction. In the dogmas and propaganda of racial purity he came to understand that he was special and had a critical and glorious role to play in the war against the mud races. This new perspective on life rejuvenated his soul and excited his desire to learn and discover more about Aryan history. In his hunger for knowledge George devoured the many books and pamphlets published by Aryan authors and organizations. For the first time in his life he rejoiced in learning and studying philosophy and history. It wasn't long before George became recognized for his passion against worldwide Jewry and the way the Jew-controlled media had perverted history to destroy the white race.

Much of George's new knowledge came from debates that took place in on-line forums dedicated to international neo-Nazi organizations. George posted under the screen name *Mont Blanc*, which is the name of the highest peak in Europe. George felt it was a perfect name; a huge white mountain rising out of Europe seemed a symbol worthy of his Aryan future. About a month ago he had begun receiving e-mails from someone named *Zephyr* who identified himself as an operative for an international Aryan organization called *Arend*, which is the Afrikaans word for eagle. The e-mails spoke of a growing danger from radical Mexicans in Southern California and provided detailed information about their political agenda and leadership. At first, George didn't pay much attention; after all, the anonymity provided by the Internet allowed anyone to claim virtually anything.

Not completely naïve, George had run across enough former Navy SEALs, Special Forces types, and keyboard comandos to doubt anyone claiming to be something extraordinary. But *Zephyr's* e-mails contained information that was always confirmed in the news several days later. In one message the details of the Southwestern/Mexican Summit were outlined in such detail that it seemed he'd received a copy of the actual treaty.

Zephyr explained that his organization monitored a worldwide Jewish cabal that was assisting the Mexicans to drive the white race out of the Western US. *Zephyr* wanted to recruit him for a special mission to eliminate the leader of this Jewish/Mexican bloc. Without George's help the White race would be driven out and subjugated. And there was an added measure of proof.

Zephyr directed George to a locker at a nearby bus station where George would find money and the information that would forever remove any skepticism about *Arend* and the validity of the mission.

When George retrieved the envelope and saw its contents, all doubts evaporated. Deep in his heart, George had always believed he was pre-ordained to accomplish something special. Now he knew what it was. The documents outlined the plans for a huge rally that was to be led by a militant Mexican named Raul de Soto. *Zephyr* included a dossier that covered De Soto's background and his connections with an international communist group called *Workers International*. The dossier also contained pictures and transcripts from many of de Soto's speeches as well as information that detailed his personal involvement with the Southwestern/Mexican Summit. George's mission was to kill de Soto, which would lead to the collapse of the Mexican movement.

With the information provided by *Arend*, and his natural skills of persuasion, George convinced Steve to help in this vital mission. George promised that they would be revered as champions of the white race, venerated as Aryan knights. With a chance at immortality on the line, Steve was all too eager to assist.

The mission instructions *Zephyr* had prepared were extremely detailed. He specified exactly what clothes to wear, what rifle and bullets to use, and the location of the building they were to use. This particular building was an ideal location because it faced the planned protest route and would provide George an almost straight shot. Additionally, at this time of morning the sun would rise just behind the building, blinding anyone looking in the direction of the shooters' perch. George never doubted the information contained in the documents. That level of detail and professionalism was exactly what he expected from an organization like *Arend*. In fact, if the information had not been so detailed, he might have questioned its veracity. But this information was like something put together by the Nazi SS; it possessed a level of exactness that could only come from Aryans.

"So our main target is this dirt bag, de Soto, right?" Steve asked.

"Yeah. He should be leading the march. I'm gonna tear his commie heart out."

"I'm good with that, but after he's dead...are you going to shoot anyone else or will we take off?" George paused for a moment to consider the question. He really hadn't thought about it; he'd been too busy getting everything ready for the mission. George's face suddenly changed from a look of introspection to firm determination.

"The way I see it, you pay for the first one and all the rest are free. After all, what does it matter if we kill one or a dozen? They're all just dirty, Jew-loving parasites anyway."

Just as George finished his comment, the low thumping of a drum snapped him back to attention and the task at hand. The scope's magnification revealed the first rows of marchers turning a corner and heading straight towards their position. Both Steve and George scanned the crowd to identify their target. Just as *Zephyr* had promised, de Soto was right in the middle of the front row hollering something into a megaphone.

"I see him. He's smack dab in the middle of the front row." George whispered. "I've got the cross hairs on him; just let me know when they reach that mailbox."

Steve held the rangefinder up to his eye, switching back and forth between the mailbox and the target. "He's at 300 yards—make sure the safety is off."

"Safety is off. I'm ready."

"260...250...240...230...*Fire*!"

****

As Raul turned the corner he was momentary blinded by the rising sun that was just beginning to peek over the buildings along the route. He squinted and cursed himself for forgetting his sunglasses, but continued to chant into the megaphone, "No justice, No peace...No justice, No peace..."

Unexpectedly the megaphone slammed into his face. The force of the strike smashed the mouthpiece into his teeth and tore open his lip. Raul thought that maybe someone had hit him, but as he wiped the blood away from his mouth, he noticed that no one was in front of him. Still confused, he began examining the megaphone when he felt a crushing blow in his chest. Raul gasped as the air rushed out of his lungs. It felt as if a giant had suddenly seized and crushed him in one of its powerful hands. Then everything went black.

****

George watched the megaphone in Raul's hand explode and realized his aim was high and to the right. "Damn it!" He yelled as he worked the bolt and chambered another round. *Calm down and get your breathing under control*, he commanded himself. Then he centered the crosshairs on the middle of the target's chest and fired. This round found its mark, producing a red, misty cloud that sprayed out of Raul's chest and bent his body backwards. The sheer force of the shot threw Raul's twisted body back into the next row of marchers like a rag doll.

"You got him!" Steve shouted. "You blew that fucking asshole away!"

George racked the next round into the breech and focused on another target. His aim settled upon a short, overweight woman who was marching to the left of Raul. George held his breath and squeezed. Just as he fired the woman began to turn to see what had happened to Raul.

The bullet that was targeted at her chest, hit her in the left side. The 168-grain projectile tore through a dense layer of fat, then shattered two ribs before ripping the left lobe of the lung apart and shredding her heart in several pieces. The woman died instantly as she fell to the ground.

"That's another kill…this is awesome!" Steve said in a giddy voice.

George's body flooded with adrenaline, which sped up his mind like a high-powered racing engine injected with nitrous oxide. Everything seemed to slow down; his only thought was working the bolt and firing another shot into the crowd. The rifle slammed into his shoulder as another round left the barrel and found its mark, this time in the thigh of an older man. George watched as the man fell to the ground, grasping his right leg. The bullet must have severed the femoral artery because a geyser of blood rocketed from between his fingers and sprayed across another man's shirt.

****

Looking to his right, Tomas saw Raul knocked off his feet and thrown backwards. At first he didn't understand what had happened. Perhaps Raul had slipped on something. But then Tomas heard a *Thwack,* and watched as Teresa crumpled to the ground. He had served in Vietnam and was familiar with the sickening sound a high-velocity bullet made as it tore into flesh. But as he began to react, a hammering blow knocked his right leg out from under him. As he fell to the ground clutching his thigh, a warm slippery liquid squirted from between his fingers. He didn't even notice the impact of his body hitting the hard asphalt street; he only felt sharp burning pain, as if someone had driven a red-hot spike deep into his leg. His screams seemed muted and echoed in his own ears. Rolling around in pain, he stared up at a man, whose white shirt had a crimson streak of blood across it. The man stared at him with a horrified expression.

As Tomas desperately tried to focus on what was happening, the man's head exploded and showered everyone around him with blood and gore. The headless man's body collapsed on top of him and convulsed in a ghastly dance of death. While the decapitated body continued to convulse, people began to realize what was happening and started screaming and frantically running in every direction. All Tomas could do was stare into the blue, cloudless sky and wonder what had gone wrong. As he lay in a pool of blood, a chill washed over him and he felt as though his body was separating into two parts. A calm sensation spread through him and he slipped into oblivion.

****

The firing pin fell on an empty chamber. "I'm empty. Let's get the hell out of here!" George shouted as he rolled off the foam mat.

"This is the greatest thing I've ever seen." Steve's voice was enthusiastic. "Look at those Spics running around like rats...it's...it's beautiful!"

"Steve, pull yourself together! We've got to get out of here. Now grab your shit and let's go!"

The two camo-clad men rushed out of the room and down a staircase that led to an exit behind the building. They jumped into the car they'd parked just beyond the door and George started the motor. The large engine roared to life, and he immediately slammed the transmission into drive. The car jumped forward and began racing down the alleyway. Just as the nose of the car was about to reach the end of the alley a trash truck turned into the narrow passage. George stood on the brakes locking up the wheels with a screech. The tires tried to grab the ground, but the forward momentum of the speeding car continued to drive them forward until it smashed into the front of the huge five-ton truck.

George and Steve braced for the inevitable impact, but neither was strong enough to overcome the physics of their situation. The two were thrown, head first, into the windshield. Their faces smashed into the laminated glass, and both men ended up sprawled across the dashboard in a bloody motionless heap.

Selma, California: Earlier that Same Morning

Jake threw on his coat and walked into the cold, early morning air as he walked towards the milking shed. Every morning at 4:00 a.m. the dairy farm milked its four-hundred-and-fifty cows and began the routine of processing milk for distribution to local stores and co-ops. Although the dairy was located in a rural part of California, as he opened the door to the milking area, he might as well have stepped into a high tech factory in Silicon Valley. The gleaming stainless steel machinery and computerized milking stations stood in stark contrast to the piles of manure, mud, and hay just outside the building.

Jake checked the equipment and ensured the milking program was properly set into the computer. Then he walked to the chemical cabinet and filled a vessel with disinfectant that was used to clean off the cow's teats prior to attaching the milking hoses. As he went back to his station the cows began entering the building on a footbridge elevated about five feet above the facility floor. After storing the disinfectant in its proper place, he pulled a lever that opened a gate and allowed the first black-and-white Holstein to walk towards the milking apparatus. Jake sprayed off the cow's udder with a hose, and then grabbed the disinfecting brush to wipe off the tits. Just then something about the cow's hind hoofs drew his attention. He looked more closely and noticed several large red, oozing blisters. A cold sensation clutched the dairyman's chest.

He immediately ducked under the footbridge, inspected the cow's mouth and discovered similar vesicles, confirming his worst fears. Though Jake had never seen a real case of hoof-and-mouth disease, he'd been trained and knew what he was looking at. Without delay Jake slammed his hand onto a large red button that shut down the entire milking facility and set off an alarm that was transmitted across the farm to the main building.

"Everybody stop what you're doing and back away from your stations!" Jake hollered above the din of the alarm. "I believe we have an outbreak of HMD; consider yourselves infected and prepare for disinfection protocols."

A few steps away from Jake's station a telephone began to ring. Jake walked over and answered the phone. "This is Jake."

"Jake, what the hell's going on down there?" It was Robert Wilson, the owner of the dairy.

"Bob, we've got a major problem over here. I have a cow with classic symptoms of HMD. There are large, red, fluid filled blisters on its hoofs and mouth, some of which have already burst."

"You've got to be shitting me. Please tell me this is some kind of tasteless joke."

"I wouldn't joke about this. Bob, we need to get an inspector down here right now. I've already started disinfection procedures on the crew. What else should I do?"

"You did the right thing, Jake." Bob Wilson replied in a clearly exasperated voice. "Just make sure everybody's properly decontaminated before they leave the milking shed."

Bob hung up the phone and paused while he contemplated the effect this would have on his business. He'd known Jake for more than ten years, and knew he'd never jump to a conclusion like this unless he was sure. All employees were required to attend mandatory annual training on mad cow and hoof-and-mouth disease taught by the USDA so they knew what to look for.

From the description Jake provided, there was little doubt what it was. Nevertheless, he needed to contact the local USDA office and get an inspector on site immediately. As Bob reached for the phone he knew he'd have to slaughter every cow in his inventory. Though he was insured, it would probably mean the end of his business.

United States Department of Agriculture: Washington, D.C.

Reports from USDA regional field offices in California, Arizona, Texas, Georgia, and Florida began pouring into the D.C. office, confirming outbreaks of HMD at stockyards, dairies and feedlots across the country. As soon as inspectors validated the presence of the highly contagious virus, immediate regional quarantines were initiated. The affected businesses were quarantined, and local and state livestock sanitation officials notified. HMD has a morbidity rate of virtually 100% in susceptible animals and can be easily transported on truck tires, shoes, clothing, and even birds, so draconian measures had to be put into effect as quickly as possible.

In addition to sequestering the employees of the various affected locations, USDA inspectors seized all records and documents regarding deliveries, sales, and visitations that had occurred over the last ten days.

Regional agricultural checkpoints went into effect, and state ports of entry stopped any movement of cloven-hoofed livestock in or out of the state. At the same time they began the distasteful task of slaughtering all livestock within the affected areas. Bulldozers and backhoes dug enormous trenches that were filled with the carcasses of tens of thousands of cattle. Then ranchers and USDA inspectors burned the bodies in hope of containing the virus. Before the slaughter ended, upwards of 250,000 animals would be destroyed.

At airports around the globe, travelers arriving from the United States were questioned about their travels. All baggage was inspected, and meat and dairy products were confiscated and destroyed. If travelers had visited effected regions or farms, or admitted to being in contact with livestock, their clothing and footwear was also confiscated until it could be thoroughly washed and disinfected.

The hope, of course, was to stave off any further spread of the virus. No one wanted to be the first to say it was a vain hope. HMD didn't spring up this way, in many simultaneous locations. This was a deliberate act; an attack. Prior to this morning's discovery, the United States led the world in cattle exports. Now international bio-security alerts were distributed notifying customers of the epidemic. In response, thousands of orders were immediately canceled, costing exporters hundreds of millions of dollars and sending worldwide commodity markets to an all-time high of $4.88 a pound on the hoof; a nearly-five-fold increase. This massive price surge started a domino effect throughout the supply chain. The end result pushed ground beef prices above $20.00 a pound and choice grade steaks upwards of $70.00 a pound. Since pigs were equally susceptible to the virus; pork prices nearly matched those of beef. These astronomical costs, in turn, created a historical demand for chicken, which jumped from $1.10 a pound, wholesale to over $8.00 a pound. Similar increases occurred with seafood.

Fox News Channel

Scheduled programming was abruptly interrupted by a bold red and black graphic that flashed across the television, followed by a close-up of an anchorwoman. "This is a Fox News Alert. Fox News is covering two critical stories at this moment. For the first we go to Stephen Adams in Los Angeles, where a leading Mexican-American civil rights leader has been assassinated, and several other protesters murdered or wounded. Steve, what's the latest information?"

A blown-dried figure appeared, framed by a scene of chaos. "Karen, thousands of Mexican-Americans and Mexican nationals came together this morning for a peaceful march in support of civil rights and against the military tribunals established following the bombing here in California and in Arizona.

"The protest was led by the renowned civil rights leader Raul de Soto, who less than thirty minutes ago was assassinated by an unknown gunman. A police spokesperson has confirmed that at least two other marchers were also killed, and several others are being treated for various injuries."

File tape showing de Soto at one of his rallies began to roll as the reporter provided a voice over. "The reality of this tragedy is now setting in for the thousands of protesters gathered here. Their cries of horror and disbelief are beginning to transform into shouts of anger and revenge."

The file tape ended and was replaced with the live feed of the on-scene reporter. Behind him the camera captured a vast crowd that was rapidly becoming violent. Beyond the enraged throng, individuals could be seen turning over cars and lighting their interiors on fire. As the reporter continued to describe the rapidly disintegrating situation, a man grabbed him from behind and held a knife to his neck. The man's ferocious eyes flashed for the camera as though they were ablaze, and his trembling face bore witness of his consuming rage."

"Our leader has been assassinated in cold blood!" the enraged man screamed. "The Aztec armies of Atzlán will not stand by and accept this attempt to further suppress and enslave us. The revolution has begun! Blood will flow until the *pinchi* Anglos are dead or driven out of the lands of our forefathers, and our homeland is once again liberated! Death to the *gabachos*! Death to America!"

Then the man grinned savagely and plunged his knife deep into Steven's neck. As the blade tore across the reporter's throat a gurgling scream reached out from his severed windpipe. Blood sprayed across the camera lens, transmitting an oily red, kaleidoscopic image to millions of viewers across the country. Technicians in the Fox studios watched the live feed in frozen horror, taking no action as the camera was torn from the cameraman's hands and thrown to the ground. Still functioning perfectly, it transmitted flawless images of the mob trampling and stomping the cameraman to death.

At last someone in the control room came to his senses and abruptly switched from the feed to the newsroom. But it was little improvement. An ashen-faced and visibly sickened anchorwoman stared helplessly into the camera. She began to speak, but then stopped as her voice started to tremble. Tears streamed down her face as she rapidly turned her head from side-to-side in a confused and helpless fashion.

Finally the image was replaced with a Fox News logo and a disembodied voice. "What we've just seen was not a hoax. We had no idea the situation in

Los Angeles had reached such a critical state, and pray for the lives of our reporter and his cameraman. News out of L.A. reports a massive riot taking place. Buildings are beginning to burn, and the Los Angeles police department is desperately trying to regain control of the rapidly deteriorating situation. We now switch you to our New York studios for continued coverage and further news.

Fox News Studios: New York

"The US Department of Agriculture reports that a widespread outbreak of a highly contagious animal virus called hoof-and-mouth disease has been reported in several southwestern and southeastern states. Our sources inform us that this constitutes a worst-case scenario for the US beef industry and has the potential of effectively destroying the domestic livestock market in this country. Wall Street has been temporarily closed as a result of an unprecedented, two-thousand-point crash. We are receiving news that the president has interrupted a campaign stop in Pennsylvania and is now being rushed back to the White House on Air Force One.

"House Minority Leader Paula Alberti (D-WA) and the ranking democratic member of the House Agricultural Committee made a brief appearance between meetings. Congresswoman Alberti spoke briefly.

[Cut to Tape] "This outbreak of hoof-and-mouth disease can only be interpreted as a terrorist biological attack. Once again, blame must be squarely placed on this President. It is beyond my understanding how one man could be so completely incompetent and create so much harm. The House leadership is moving forward with renewed vigor to impeach this worthless and reckless excuse of a President. We are examining all options granted to us in the Constitution to limit his power and try to regain control of this calamitous situation before it's too late. Now if you'll excuse us, we have vital business to attend to."

[Quarter shot:] Anchor: "Every day it seems the Democrats gain more and more momentum towards their goal of removing the president from the White House. Earlier, administration spokesman Gerald Cartwright gave the following response."

"The president encourages all Americans not to jump to unsubstantiated conclusions. He wishes to remind everyone that we are at war against a determined enemy that has openly declared its willingness to use every weapon that their disposal to destroy the US. We must continue to stay the course. The president is aware of the serious economic repercussions of this latest round of attacks, but encourages Americans to remember that past generations have faced even greater challenges in their fight against evil, and we have always prevailed. We will this time as well."

"This is Trevor Daily reporting for Fox News."

Chapter 8

> A militia, when properly formed, are in fact the people themselves...and include all men capable of bearing arms.
> —Richard Henry Lee

Los Angeles, California

News helicopters hovered over the expanding riot zone feeding live video of the uprising via satellite to televisions all over the city, which, in turn was picked up by affiliate stations and distributed all over the country. Complete mayhem ruled. Buildings and cars were ablaze across a ten-block area, looting was widespread, and reports of innocent bystanders being pulled out of their cars and beaten at intersections were common. The police were almost immediately overwhelmed and ordered to retreat within the first hour. Unlike the Rodney King riots that grew to a crescendo over several hours, this unrest spiraled out of control within minutes. In this case, thousands of agitated protesters were poised and ready at the epicenter when events quickly degenerated into bedlam. There was no way for police to quickly assemble enough officers before losing complete control of the situation. By the time police were ordered to retreat, five officers were unaccounted for. Video from one news helicopter captured an officer being overwhelmed by several hundred people. The mob advanced on the officer like an army of ants intent on killing an intruder. The officer fired one shot into the oncoming mass, but that was all he was able to do before disappearing from sight.

Another chopper pilot who'd flown Blackhawk helicopters in Somalia commented that what he saw reminded him of the October firefight that became the icon of that conflict. As in Somalia the rioters burned tires to mark rally points for reinforcements that streamed in from all around the city. The oily black plumes rose above the streets and added to the building layer of smoke from dozens of structure fires. The thick, billowing smoke dulled the sunlight and cast a yellow-and-black tinge against the sky. As each hour passed the fury grew and expanded. After brief firefights between looters and owners, several gun stores were overrun and raided. With their newly acquired weapons, rioters waged war against the police in an orgy of violence and anarchy.

Chicano and black gangs cast aside their territorial differences and united to assault police lines and roadblocks. These gangs instantly created a heavily armed, extremely violent force of hundreds. Although the police were able to hold several positions, gaps in their defenses allowed the riots to spread and opened new avenues for supporters to flood into the war zone.

At 4:00 p.m. the mayor of Los Angeles declared a state of emergency. He did not tell the people in the affected area—though they already knew—that the city could no longer offer police or fire protection. They were on their own. In an attempt to prevent further unrest the mayor ordered police to cordon off any store that sold firearms or ammunition to prevent citizens from panic buying.

In addition, special teams of heavily armed tactical officers assaulted private homes across the city where owners had registered so-called "assault weapons" and ammunition stockpiles under the city's recently passed Arsenal Law. Although a few citizens offered token resistance, the tactical teams quickly overwhelmed them by surprise and overwhelming force.

Because of the number of National Guard units federalized for the wars in Afghanistan and Iraq, upon their return, the governor ordered a statewide stand down of most units for 120 days. He did call up a few local units that had not been recently activated, but he refused to deploy armored units. The governor also placed extreme restrictions on the distribution of ammunition, and issued such severe rules of engagement that one guardsman was heard to sourly joke that his unit could fire in self-defense, but only after having received fifty percent casualties and only if the attackers were not Hispanic.

Most of the guard units were positioned around exclusive neighborhoods and vital commerce centers wearing full riot gear, but carrying empty rifles.

By 6:00 p.m. an area encompassing Montebello, Pico Rivera, Hacienda Heights, and La Puente was considered lost, and Alhambra and El Monte were threatened. Riots advanced like a brushfire stoked by Santa Ana winds. It was all the police could do to evacuate citizens before the hordes arrived. As dusk began to settle on East Los Angeles, the city braced itself for a long night of terror and destruction.

Gilbert, Arizona

As soon as news of the riots broke, Arrow declared a full alert. After receiving the news, Mike began assembling his equipment and checking to assure all his magazines were loaded, batteries replaced, canteens and food properly rotated, and his ruck properly packed for the current weather conditions. After inspecting each piece of gear he placed it in the back of his truck. In addition to his field gear, he added five cases of MREs, three five-gallon water containers, and five thousand rounds of 5.56mm ammunition in case the alert lasted longer than the usual seventy-two hours.

Since he'd stored the majority of his equipment in a ready state, he was fully loaded and ready to roll in less than fifteen minutes. Before leaving Mike logged onto his computer. He couldn't bug out before notifying the other Militia commanders that 48th FF, 13th BN was going on full alert. Mike posted the appropriate information in a SALUTE format, updating all the other units on what was happening. As he read posts from other teams he learned that several Southern California units were already deployed, and that P, D, and M Corps were also on full alert. After logging off Mike pulled the hard drive out of his computer and replaced it with another devoid of sensitive information. With his primary hard drive in hand, Mike walked into the bathroom and opened a fireproof floor safe that was hidden under the vanity.

He placed the drive in the safe and withdrew a medium-sized envelope containing a CD-ROM, with copies of all his vital documents, a small pouch of silver coins, and five hundred dollars in cash. After making certain the safe was properly closed he took one last look around the house to make sure everything was properly secured then walked out the door.

As he drove towards the academy, Mike dialed Rachel's cell number and impatiently waited as the line rang.

"Hello?"

"Rachel, this is Mike. Listen carefully. 'Decompression.' Do you understand?"

"Yes, I understand."

"Listen, babe, things are going to hell, and I'm afraid this might be the real thing. Arrow has activated the team, and we're rallying at the academy. I want you to get your bug-out gear and meet us over there as quickly as you can."

"All right, I'm on my way home now. It'll take me about thirty minutes to get everything I need, and then I'll be on my way."

"Good. Don't worry about the small stuff; just get your gear and head straight to the academy. Keep your phone on, and don't stop for anything or anyone. I'll see you soon. I love you."

"I love you, too."

Racing towards the academy Mike passed a grocery store and noticed hundreds of people who seemed to be chaotically trying to get whatever food was available. In the parking lot employees were unsuccessfully trying to keep the masses under control. Panic was descending all around him. Soon the town might erupt, just like L.A. If that happened Rachel and the team would be safe at the academy.

Not only would it provide a secure parameter, it also had several underground vaults filled with food, water, and ammunition. Arrow wisely included them in the original blueprints. He'd even installed power generators and storage tanks filled with diesel fuel. Realistically speaking, they had enough supplies to last nearly a year. Following 9/11 Arrow had accepted that the possibility of a nuclear, biological, or chemical attack on the United States was a real possibility, so he sensibly prepared for the worst.

When the academy was in the design phase, he simply told the architects he wanted to construct on-site storage facilities. Since Phoenix is in the middle of a desert, it made sense to build them underground for insulation against the extreme summer heat.

No one even flinched at the idea. Each partner had accepted an invitation to contribute to the food storage so they'd have whatever they needed in the event of an emergency.

Together they'd stored a variety of bulk grains, legumes, flour, and oils. Freeze dried and dehydrated foods were also included, as were MREs. This combination of foods offered tremendous flexibility and variety. Finally, they filled several dozen fifty-five-gallon barrels of treated water to ensure they'd have enough fresh water to survive almost any emergency.

As Mike pulled into the academy driveway he saw Cowboy standing guard inside the gate. Mike rolled down the window.

"Glad to see you," Cowboy said as the two friends shook hands through the window. "Ghost has been monitoring the news and says riots have begun in West Phoenix."

"I posted our team status on the national militia site before leaving the house. Rachel is on her way. What about Wildcat?"

"He left Tucson about an hour ago. He's taking Route 79 through Florence, trying to avoid I-10. He should be here in twenty minutes. You'd better check in with Arrow; I'm sure he has some duties for you."

Mike snapped a quick salute to his friend, and drove towards the main building, and parked his truck around the back. Mike grabbed his gear and jogged to the administration building. Arrow was in his office, talking on the phone. Arrow looked up as Mike entered and gestured for him to join him.

"Chief, Mike just walked in. I'm putting you on the speaker."

"Mike, the chief was just bringing me up to speed on what's happening. You need to hear this as well. Go ahead, chief, you were talking about L.A."

"Here's the situation...East Los Angeles is basically a war zone. The LAPD has fallen back to Interstate 5, where they're hoping to establish a defensive line and stop the spread of the riots. The problem is that they're facing organized and highly motivated opposition. These aren't just pissed off looters and anarchists looking for a way to vent frustration."

"The core elements are Mexican extremists intent on reclaiming the Southwest for Mexico. They've already looted a number of gun stores and a National Guard armory; they're heavily armed and awfully well organized."

"Why doesn't the governor call up the National Guard and stomp on these people?" Mike asked.

"Normally, that's what you'd expect, but he won't do it. He says too many guardsmen are either deployed in the Middle East or have just returned and can't be taken away from their jobs and families again. He dropped it all in the LAPD's lap; says it's a local issue."

Arrow shot Mike a worried look.

"Why don't you tell Mike what you shared with me just before he arrived?" Arrow suggested.

"This news hasn't broke yet," said Meadows, "but the LAPD has been in contact with the leadership of the rioters. They're calling themselves the '*Aztec Nation*.' Evidently they've recovered the bodies of two men they claim are responsible for killing those protesters yesterday. They've sent pictures of the men in question and are claiming they're members of a white supremacist militia. They were dressed in camouflage and had all the usual neo-Nazi tattoos."

"That doesn't mean they're part of a militia," Mike protested. "For cripes sake, if everyone who wore BDUs were part of a militia there'd be millions of us. You know the Skinheads and Nazis have been wearing BDUs forever; none of the active militia groups in the country recognize them."

"Look," said Meadows, "you know I've supported the citizen militias for a long time. Hell, I know you guys have a unit yourselves. Frankly, I've got no problems with what you're doing. Lord knows...I might end up needing your help if things continue to spiral out of control. But not everyone sees things the way we do. My contacts tell me that because of this and the murder of those five Mexicans in the desert, the governors of California and Arizona planning to stomp on the militias with both feet. They're preparing to announce emergency orders that will direct all police units to arrest anyone suspected of being part of a militia."

"They just can't start rounding people up without probable cause," Mike protested. "Are you going to enforce that order?"

"The fact is that once a state of emergency is declared the governor assumes additional powers to do things that normally wouldn't be allowed. Believe me; as soon as the order is issued anyone not in the military caught wearing BDUs will be arrested. As for my department following the order, I've already asked our legal aides to find a way to stall the implementation of the directive."

"I have no desire to start arresting people for their choice of clothing. Considering how things are going we'll need all the jail space we have for the real bad guys."

"Either way, we'll deal with that issue when it comes up." The chief paused for a moment then continued. "I just received a report that there's looting at several grocery stores in the city. Panic is beginning to set in. If we don't get this under control quickly I don't know what's going to happen. Stay in touch with me and try to keep a low profile. I'll let you know if the department needs any equipment. I've got to go."

Arrow hung up the phone. He stared silently at his desk for a moment, his hand still on the receiver. Then he turned towards Mike, and in a tone of introspection said, "Nobody wanted this to happen, but I think we all knew it was a possibility."

"We need to get everyone together and decide what we're going to do. The last thing I want is for us to get into a situation we're either not prepared for or not willing to confront."

"I agree." Mike said. "Cowboy told me Wildcat ought to be here in twenty minutes. Once he's here we'll get together and make some fast decisions. Where's Ghost?"

"He's in the communications center monitoring the situation. Evidently, a couple of the L.A. militias were involved in a firefight earlier in the morning. They held for an hour before they were forced to make a tactical retreat. Apparently, the gangs were just too large."

"Which units were they?" Mike asked.

"P" company of the 37th Battalion, based around Pasadena, and "B" company from Burbank."

"I'm familiar with "P" company. That's Breecher's team; they don't have many members."

"Well, they've got even fewer now." Arrow soberly replied. Evidently they've already lost three guys. The survivors have been absorbed into "B" Company and are regrouping in Burbank."

"This is freaking out of control!" Mike exclaimed in frustration. "If the riots in the western part of the valley spread this way we're going to have our hands full. And when the government starts arresting anyone suspected of being in the militia, we'll end up fighting both these *Aztec Nation* assholes as well as the government."

"That's why we need to make some plans," Arrow replied. "By the way, where's Rachel?"

"She's on her way. I spoke with her just as I was leaving my house. Come to think of it, she should be here by now. I'd better call her."

Mike speed dialed Rachel's number, but got a recording saying that all circuits were busy and he should try again later. "Oh, shit," he muttered as he dialed again with the same result. On the third try his call went through.

"Rachel, where are you?"

"I had to make a side trip," she said. "I'm on my way to pick up Cindy; she's stuck on the corner of Broadway and 19th Avenue. Her car broke down and she's scared."

"I told you to come straight to the academy and nowhere else. Do you understand how volatile it's getting out there?" Mike heard the anger in his own voice and knew this would not improve the situation.

"Mike, stop talking to me like I'm six years old. Cindy called me, scared to death, and I'm not going to abandon her. You'd do the same thing if a friend called you. I'm only a couple blocks away from her, so we'll be on our way to the academy in ten minutes."

Mike cupped his hand over the receiver and turned towards Arrow, "Rachel's roommate's car broke down on the corner of Broadway and 19th Avenue. She drove out to get her."

Arrow could see that Mike was becoming agitated and knew he needed to calm his friend down. "Listen, Mike, Rachel's a smart girl. Just stay cool and keep her on the phone. Ask her what's going on over there."

"Rachel, I want you to stay on the phone and not hang up...do you understand?"

"Yeah, but your signal is weak; I must be in a low reception pocket. I'm losing every third or fourth word."

"How are things looking over there?"

"There's smoke rising out West, it looks...fire...dark..."

"Rachel, you're breaking up. Did you say fires are burning to the west of the city?"

"Mike? Can you hear me now?"

"Yes, I can hear you."

"I can...Cindy's car up...hold...got to make...u-turn...next intersection."

Mike looked at Arrow and told him Rachel had reached Cindy's location and was turning around.

"There's a crowd of...Cindy...like...not...."

The signal was suddenly lost and replaced with a sharp pitched double beep that sounded in Mike's earpiece.

"Rachel!" Mike yelled into the phone. "Damn it, I lost her signal!" Mike jabbed the redial button, but was once again greeted by the "all circuits are busy" message.

"What's going on?" demanded Arrow.

"I don't know. The last thing I heard was a broken message about a crowd and Cindy...then I lost her."

****

Rachel realized that she'd lost Mike's signal about the same time she noticed five guys approaching her friend and they didn't look like they were there to help. For an instant she thought about dialing 911, but there wasn't time. As she swung her car around she nearly hit a teenager who was running through the street carrying a television. She laid on the horn and the kid looked at her with a sinister glance, before turning away and running off with his newly acquired treasure.

Rachel tossed the phone into the passenger seat and got both hands on the steering wheel. Her horn blast caught Cindy's attention and Rachel saw a look of terror in her face. Cindy was in serious trouble. Tears mixed with mascara had drawn long, black lines down her face, and one of her sleeves had been nearly torn off. Rachel needed to do something decisive and she needed to do it fast. The five men were backing Cindy towards an alleyway behind a Dairy Queen by taunting her like a pack of wolves wearing down their prey.

Rachel felt a sickening pit develop in her stomach and her knees began to shake. She had to do something. Her only comfort was the heavy, Glock that sat snugly on her hip. Even though she knew it was there, she unconsciously reached for the weapon as if to reassure herself that she wasn't alone. Rachel knew whatever she did she had to do it quickly and decisively before the men overwhelmed her friend.

****

"I've got to go after her." Mike yelled. "This isn't good. It sounded like there was trouble."

"Calm down!" Arrow commanded in a stern and deliberate voice. "She's halfway across the valley. It'd take you forty-five minutes to get to where she's at. By that time she'll probably be back here."

"Well, I can't just sit here and do nothing. I love her, and I'm not going to wait around while the city explodes around her. Damn it! I should have gone over to her house and picked her up!" Mike ranted as he paced around Arrow's office like a caged tiger.

"Mike, get a hold of yourself. Your freaking out isn't going to help the situation. Does she have her gun with her?"

"Yeah, she went to her house and picked up her bug-out bag."

"Listen to me." Arrow reasoned, trying to calm his friend down. "She's good with that gun and knows how to use it. Just keep trying to get her on the phone."

Mike grabbed the phone off Arrow's desk and redialed Rachel's number. It seemed to take forever for the connection to be made, but when it did he was sent directly into her voice mail.

"Rachel, this is Mike. I want you to call me immediately. I'm really concerned." Mike punched the end button and looked helplessly at Arrow, "Her voicemail picked up...I don't know what's happening."

****

There were no police in sight. The whole area was coming apart at the seams, and the rules were out the window. This wasn't some kind of minor incident between rational individuals...this was survival.

Unexpectedly a reassuring sensation washed over her as she realized the normal social rules no longer applied...she was free to do whatever was necessary. Gripping the steering wheel she felt a surge of adrenaline course through her body. Although she trusted her pistol, she remembered what Cowboy taught her combat class, "Consider your pistol a secondary weapon, unless you have nothing else."

I'm driving my primary weapon, she thought as she steered directly towards the gang of predators and stomped on the accelerator. The front end of the car seemed to lift up as the engine gulped down the instant rush of fuel. Rachel braced herself as her front tires hit the curb and clawed towards the unsuspecting mob.

Then, in an instant, the whole world seemed to explode as she plowed into her targets. It was as if a mighty giant had swept the men away with a powerful brush of his arm. Three of the men launched off the hood of her car and flew like rag dolls through the plate glass windows of the Dairy Queen. As soon as she felt the impact, Rachel stood on the brakes, locking up the wheels and sliding the car slightly sideways before coming to a jarring stop.

Immediately, she flung the door open to get out, but she was trapped by her seatbelt. Rachel reached across her body and fumbled with the release mechanism frantically trying to free herself. As soon as the belt released, she sprang out of the driver's seat and pulled her pistol from its holster. Using the body of the car as a shield, Rachel called out to her friend who was sitting on the ground in complete shock. "Cindy! Get up and get in the car, now!"

Cindy just sat on the pavement staring at Rachel with an expression of shock and total confusion. *Jesus, help me,* Rachel thought, *she's catatonic or something. I gotta get her into the car*. The next thought that entered her mind was that she'd allowed her vision to tunnel and had no idea what was happening around her. Rachel struggled to back away from the car, but her legs seemed to be frozen in place. She had to mentally scream commands to her body to move. Once she began to budge she performed a quick 360-degree scan and then began moving towards Cindy.

As she walked forward, with her Glock extended in the ready position, she continued calling out, "Cindy, its Rachel. Get in the car we've got to get out of here!" Little-by-little Cindy seemed to reawaken from her fear-induced coma. By this time Rachel had reached her, grabbing her by the collar. "Cindy, get in the car. Come on, girl, get on your feet and let's go!"

Cindy slowly rose to her feet and began back pedaling towards the car when Rachel saw a man running towards her with some kind of board or metal bar raised high above his head. "You fucking psycho bitch. I'll kill you!" the man viciously screamed.

Rachel instinctively placed the front sight of her pistol on his chest and fired. The massive quantity of adrenalin that had inundated her system masked the recoil of the pistol. She didn't even know how many times she'd fired; only that the man went down fast and hard. Now, the roles seemed to switch, as Rachel was startled out of her concentration by Cindy screaming behind her. Looking back, she saw her friend already in the car and knew she needed to move. Rachel made one last scan for threats and then ran around the front of the car and jumped into the driver seat.

"Here, hold this!" she yelled as she passed her pistol to Cindy.

Rachel slammed the gearshift into reverse while simultaneously stepping on the gas. The transmission engaged with a shuttering thud, and the car jumped backwards off the sidewalk and into the street. Once again Rachel hammered the gearshift, and the car screeched forward and shot down the street. Several miles later the adrenalin drained out of her body and was replaced by a wet, cold, nauseating sensation that left her weak and faint. By this time Cindy had begun to regain her composure and although still traumatized, was able to control her breathing and began to speak. "Thank you for saving me. Those men wanted to rape me. If you hadn't arrived I'd be dead. Thank you."

Rachel looked over at her pistol that sat on Cindy's lap, and remembered it was still loaded. While fighting back her nausea, in a calm soothing voice she said, "Cindy, why don't you hand me the pistol, and I'll put it away."

Cindy gingerly lifted the gun with her thumb and forefinger and passed it over to Rachel, who slid it into her Kydex holster. Rachel scanned the area they were driving through, and seeing that it was reasonably safe decided to pull over. As the car came to a stop she felt acidy bile erupting from her stomach. It was all she could do to get the door open and lean out before vomiting in the street. After several dry heaves she closed the door and wiped her mouth off with some left over fast-food napkins she found in the glove compartment.

Rachel placed a shaking hand on Cindy's thigh. "Look at us, we're a mess. Are you sure you're all right?"

"Yeah...physically I'm fine. I'm just really shaken up."

Rachel leaned over and took Cindy in her arms and began stroking her raven black hair. "It's all right Cindy...we're both all right." The two friends cried together and held one another tightly as their shared fears flowed out in a stream of tears. The ringing of Rachel's phone startled the two out of their moment of shared empathy.

"Cindy, hand me the phone, I think it's down by your feet."

****

Mike's call went through on the tenth attempt, and he was rewarded by the sound of ringing. After several seconds Rachel answered. "Mike, is that you?"

"Rachel, are you all right? Where are you?"

Rachel had never heard Mike's voice so concerned and knew she needed to calm down so he wouldn't freak out. "Everything's fine. I got Cindy, and we're safe."

"Where are you?"

"We're on Baseline a few blocks away from the I-10. Mike, I think I killed some men. They were attacking Cindy, and I had no other choice."

"Did you shoot them?"

"I shot one of them, and I hit the others with my car. What should I do?" As hard as she tried, Rachel couldn't hold back her emotions and began crying again.

"Listen, babe, it's all right; you did what you had to do. What's important now is that you get back here as quick as possible. Cowboy and I are driving your way right now. We're on Alma School and Germann. We'll meet you at Warner and the 101, can you make it there?"

"Yeah...yeah, Warner and the 101. We'll get there as fast as we can."

Direct Action Academy

The two cars carrying Mike, Cowboy, Rachel, and Cindy pulled into the gates of the academy and parked behind the shipping dock. Mike and Cowboy stopped to inspect the front end of Rachel's car, and for the first time realized the damage caused when she hit Cindy's attackers.

The forward crumple zone and ABS bumper were pushed back several inches, and one headlight was shattered. If it had been a newer car with an airbag, they were sure it would have deployed, making it much more difficult to drive away.

Cowboy pursed his lips. "Maybe we should cover it up," he suggested.

Mike looked at him from under lowered brows. "Cover up the evidence?"

"Well, for now let's call it *preserving* the evidence, and see how things go."

Without further debate they located an appropriately sized tarp and secured it to the car with some 550 cord.

Mike returned to the main building to check on Rachel, who'd taken the time to wash up a little and get something to eat. He found her and Cindy in the cafeteria, sharing some apple slices and discussing their ordeal.

"How're you two doing?" Mike asked.

"Better. We were able to wash up a little and decided to try and eat some apples. Our stomachs are still a little twisted, so hopefully these will stay down."

Mike took a seat next to Rachel and noticed she was still wearing her pistol. "Have you reloaded your pistol since you got back?"

Rachel removed the pistol from its holster, pointed it in a safe direction, withdrew the magazine and then cleared the chamber. "No. I haven't." Looking at the magazine she could tell more than one bullet was gone. After emptying the remaining rounds she realized that counting the one she kept in the chamber, she'd fired four times at her attacker.

"Huh," she remarked in a puzzled tone, "I swear I can't remember shooting that many times. All I remember was that man running at me and screaming he was going to kill me. Then I aimed, and he went down. It was like I was on autopilot."

"Actually, that's very common." Mike said. "Most of the police I've spoken to who've been involved in shootings describe the same thing. Proper training produces an autonomic reflex that takes over in a crisis, and things happen very quickly."

"Yeah, I guess so." Rachel looked at the pistol with an inquisitive stare, shifting it in her hand. "I'm having a hard time understanding my feelings about this."

"It must be very difficult coming to grips with the reality that you killed someone," Cindy said in a tender voice, while placing her hand lightly on Rachel's arm.

"No, that's not it. Frankly, it's just the opposite. We're safe, and if I hadn't shot that guy I'm pretty confident we'd be dead. I'd do it again if I had to," Rachel said in a assertive voice," then added, "you're worth it, and so am I."

Mike handed Rachel a box of 165-grain, .40 caliber Speer Gold Dots. She topped off her magazine, reloaded, and replaced the pistol in its holster. As Rachel was completing the reload Mike watched Cindy. He could tell she was interested in the gun.

"Cindy, have you ever shot before?"

"No." She answered anxiously. "But, I'm thinking I ought to start."

"I believe, considering the circumstances, that would be a good idea. I'm sure we have an extra gun or two lying around. I'll ask Wildcat to put you through a fast orientation and get you up to speed."

"Sorry for the interruption," Hot Dog announced as he popped his head into the room. "Arrow wants everybody in the communications room right now."

****

For the past several hours Ghost had intently monitored several shortwave radio frequencies as well as the major militia web pages, trying to get a handle on the rapidly deteriorating situation in California. The situation was far worse than the news reported. Sacramento was purposely censoring information coming out of Los Angeles in an attempt to prevent wide scale panic. The official story was that the riots were nothing more than a reaction to the killings of Raul de Soto and other protesters. The police were containing the rioters in a small area, allowing the violence to gradually burn it self out.

The truth was it wasn't a riot at all; it was an organized insurgency involving tens of thousands of people. Within the areas controlled by the *Aztec Nation* pockets of resistance were fighting life-and-death battles against large, well-armed gangs intent on wiping out anyone who would not surrender their property to the new government of Atzlán.

Several militia units had already fought fierce skirmishes and were now falling back to the San Gabriel Mountains near the outskirts of San Bernardino. The 31st Field Force 111th Battalion, based out of Barstow was selected to command the unified remnants of the Los Angeles companies. Reinforcements came primarily from the 59th and 65th battalions from Orange and Riverside counties. The commander of the newly formed Southern California Command was a man codenamed Stalker. Until recently he had commanded the High Desert Militia, which was one of the best-organized and trained units in California. For years they'd actively recruited and established a cadre of former and active-duty military personnel, as well as civilian professionals who provided expertise in emergency medical care, telecommunications/electronics, law enforcement, and engineering. Using these individuals as a foundation, Stalker and his Lieutenants steadily assembled a disciplined and well-trained militia.

Due to the political climate north of Santa Barbara County, the militia movement in that half of California was very small and unorganized, basically consisting of scattered "lone wolf" units who, couldn't provide any serious assistance. For decades there had seemed to be an invisible line that bisected California around Point Conception, creating two almost diametrically opposed states. Now, it seemed the authorities were enforcing that mythical line, and no support was arriving from the North. Once Southern California had been covered with military bases that could have assisted during times of emergency, but after a decade of base closures and downsizing, most of those bases and their soldiers were gone. Only a few major installations remained, such as Camp Pendleton on the boarder of Orange County, the National Training Center, a Marine logistics center near Barstow, and Twenty-Nine Palms, which was nestled against the Bullion Mountains in the middle of the Mojave Desert.

San Diego had its share of Navy and Marine Corp bases, but except for Miramar Marine Corp Air Station, with its squadrons of helicopters, they couldn't offer much assistance in an urban warfare arena. The on-going crisis in Korea and the Middle East had severely reduced the numbers of assets that would normally be available at these locations. National Guard units had been activated but not totally committed. They were relegated to policing duties and guarding high-value locations, which in most cases meant politically connected or wealthy businesses and neighborhoods. In San

Diego, another battle raged. Encouraged by the events in Los Angeles, Mexicans began to organize in the border towns of San Ysidro and Otay Mesa. It didn't take long for them to gain control of the border crossings, allowing Mexican police and military to freely enter the United States and establish a foothold.

In a miraculous burst of efficiency, the United Nations had voted on and approved a Mexican proposal to provide a peacekeeping force for the Southwestern United States. Mexico justified its actions by claiming Mexicans, even those living in the United States, deserved to be protected by their own government, and that the assassination of Raul de Soto and the immigrants murdered in the Arizona desert proved that Mexicans were being slaughtered and attacked by Americans. In a press release, Mexican President Baranca declared that it was his government's duty to protect its citizens wherever they might be.

In response to these actions the 73rd battalion, 31 FF militia, based in San Diego, deployed to Chula Vista, where they set up defenses in an attempt to stop any further movement north by the Mexicans. Following furious battles at the border, many police, sheriff deputies, Border Patrol agents, and military personnel joined with the militia to stand as a united citizens' army. Former distrust and animosity quickly evaporated as a common enemy threatened everyone equally.

"So that's the deal, guys," Ghost said. This was the longest speech he ever remembered making. "Southern California is being attacked by homegrown insurgents *and* Mexican bluebonnets, and there's nobody able to do much about it. Most of the military that should have been watching the border is overseas."

"I don't get it," said Cowboy. "There are still Marines at Pendleton and Miramar."

"Sure," Ghost said quietly. "But nobody wants to roll into Los Angeles with tanks, jets, and attack helicopters."

"The military must be fighting the Mexicans," Cowboy persisted.

"Maybe, maybe not. I don't know. They'll only do what they're told. Technically, the Mexicans aren't invading. The United Nations is sending in a peacekeeping force." Ghost joined the others in greeting this with skeptical grunts."

"Well, whatever," said Ghost. "But if Washington tells them to stand down, they probably will."

"What the hell is the national guard doing while all this is going on?" Josh anxiously remarked.

"So far the guard units that have been activated haven't been authorized to engage the enemy. From what I hear, most of them haven't even been issued ammunition. The California and Arizona governors are gonna broadcast a joint address in ten minutes from Sacramento, so we'll see what happens."

"So what's the status of the other militias?" Cowboy asked.

"As you know, 'D' Corps is on full alert. The New Mexico 47th FF has assembled two battalions, the 6th from Cibola County and the 31st from McKinley County. They're preparing to deploy to reinforce the 73rd Battalion in Chula Vista. They requested permission to use the academy as a layup point before final deployment to California. I went ahead and approved their request."

"That's fine," said Arrow. "When should we expect them to arrive?"

"They'll leave Gallup tonight. It's about four hundred miles to Phoenix, so I figure a little before 0100. I've got their communications frequency, so I'll be able to stay in contact with them the whole way." Ghost showed a chart that he'd organized with the radio frequencies the different units were using. Each one was labeled and programmed into a speed dial function on his shortwave radio. "M Corps has released the 44th FF (Utah) to strengthen our corps and two battalions, the 25th and 53rd are assembling in St. George before heading down to San Bernardino."

"What's the approximate strength of the combined units from New Mexico and Utah?" Thor asked.

"A little less than six hundred men," Ghost said. "The State Commanders are holding back the bulk of their force until we hear what the governors say during their press conference. Speaking of which, we ought to get to a television."

The whole team, less AK who was standing watch, plus Rachel and Cindy, gathered around a television located in one of the classrooms. The joint gubernatorial address was being carried by C-Span live from Sacramento. Governor Ernesto Buenamonte of California escorted Arizona Governor Barbara Slater to a pair of podiums that were decorated with the official seals of their respective states. Behind the governors were the obligatory American and state flags crisscrossed in a display of unity. The executives adjusted their microphones, and then Governor Buenamonte began his address.

"Citizens of California, Arizona, and the United States, I stand before you this evening with my esteemed colleague, Governor Slater of the great state of Arizona, to address a most urgent situation. As you are aware, less than forty-eight hours ago a tragic event took place. Cowardly racists, bent on destroying the hopes and dreams of millions of Mexicans, savagely assassinated Mr. Raul de Soto, a civil rights leader whom history will compare to the likes of Dr. Martin Luther King Jr., Caesar Chavez, and Gandhi.

"In addition to the death of Señor de Soto, several other freedom marchers were murdered and wounded. I want to convey my most sincere and heartfelt regards to the families of those who heroically died for freedom. Likewise I extend my deepest sympathies to the entire Mexican and Chicano community in the United States. The loss of these brave and caring souls has cheapened all our lives.

"The pain and agony caused by these losses and thousands of other needless deaths among Mexican-immigrants has sharpened into an uncontrollable rage that has overcome the peace-loving Mexican communities of California and Arizona. These events cannot be attributed to overzealous enthusiasm, as we've seen many times around the country following a championship game. To compare the two belittles the severity of the situation. The events we are witnessing are the long-anticipated eruption of anger and frustration that began to fester in 1848 when under duress and dubious circumstances, Mexico was coerced into surrendering fifty-five percent of its territory to the United States in one of the greatest imperialistic land grabs in history.

"Fortunately, this country has evolved over the last one-hundred-and-fifty-plus years. We've thrown away the reprehensible chains of slavery, we've done away with the Jim Crow laws of reconstruction, we've acknowledged and apologized for the interment of Japanese and German Americans during World War II, and in many other ways we've developed a sense of justice and equality. America has grown from the isolationistic power of the 1940s and is now working to humbly assume its place among the equal and great nations of the world. Yet, for all our efforts and progress we find that the immoral specters of our racist past still survive and continue to haunt our efforts to change.

"Unfortunately, unless an abuser is confronted with his actions, his denial is often never checked. What we are experiencing is an intervention between the Chicano and Mexican communities and the current system that has ignored the plight of these people and their culture.

"For too long the United States has refused to accept the magnitude of the crimes our ancestors perpetrated on Mexico, and the cultural and economic destruction that resulted from those actions. Over the past century we've compounded this injury by selfishly criminalizing the pilgrimage of Chicanos to their ancestral homeland. It's obvious that we can no longer continue down this damaging path of injustice. California, which is the most populous state in the Union, has a majority population of Mexicans; Los Angeles is second only to Mexico City in the number of Mexican residents in the world. The great state of Arizona has a majority Mexican population.

"Likewise, across this country, millions of Mexicans and people of Hispanic descent live, work, and contribute to the American dream. In response to these realities, our states have passed laws making Spanish on par with English as the official state language, our schools have mandated Spanish classes for all non-Spanish speaking students, and Mexicans have been included in affirmative action grants and consideration. Earlier this year Governor Slater and I participated in the historical Southwestern/Mexican Summit in Mexico City where we signed a law that extended state-funded residential protection and benefits to all Mexicans living in Arizona and California as well as their families in Mexico. But all this and many other attempts to enfranchise Mexicans have only amounted to a superficial attempt in righting a wrong that has wounded the soul of an entire culture. As the saying goes, "...even a gilded cage is still a prison."

"So, Governor Slater and I have structured a plan that we believe will lead to a genuine solution to the current crisis. At this time I'd like to turn the press conference over to Governor Slater, who will outline the details of this historic plan."

"Thank you, Governor Buenamonte. As the governor so eloquently pointed out, we are faced with a reality that has for too long remained unaddressed. Whether we, as a nation, are ready to acknowledge it or not, the border between the Southwestern states and Mexico has virtually ceased to exist. Our economies, political, and social systems are inseparably intertwined. To look upon the Mexicans in our states who work, pay taxes, and vote in our elections as aliens, is tantamount to considering our right arm welcome and our left, foreign. The time has come for us to fully embrace the truest foundations of our democratic roots and end the tyranny of the minority. Therefore, Governor Buenamonte and I have devised a plan that combines the examples of the European Union and the Puerto Rican system of self-rule. This plan will reestablish a homeland for the people of Atzlán within the boarders of California and Arizona. The boundaries will extend from the Mexican boarder, northwards to a line to be established at Point Conception in California, along the Nevada border to Arizona, where it will bisect the state at the latitude of the city of Phoenix, east to the New Mexican Border.

"Like Puerto Rico, Aztlán will have its own government and its own flag. But, the Aztlán leaders will work together with the legislatures of California and Arizona on matters that regard the individual states as a whole. The dollar will continue to be used, as well as the US Postal System. As dual citizens, the people of Aztlán will enjoy all the rights reserved for US citizens including protection and state-funded entitlements. Finally, like the people of Puerto Rico, the citizens of Aztlán will be exempt from all state taxes.

"We envision an open border without duties and taxes between the new homeland of Aztlán, California, Arizona, and Mexico that will usher in a modern age of economic equality and freedom for all people. This will serve as an intermediary step allowing Aztlán to grow and develop economically until it can stand independently as a sovereign nation.

"During this transitional period, we, along with a delegation from the US Congress and Senate, have requested a UN peacekeeping force made up primarily of the Mexican army to station itself within the boundaries set forth in this plan. We understand the misgivings and anxiety felt by Mexicans, who for too long have suffered the indignity of racism in America, and we believe that having their own people here to guard and protect them will lessen the trauma they now suffer. Additionally, we are asking the United Nations to send non-aligned arbitrators to help ensure a proper transition.

"We sincerely hope that the governors of New Mexico and Nevada will join us in this historic effort to bring justice to a great and maligned people. As you all know, this is a great undertaking, and there are still many details to work out, but Governor Buenamonte and I are dedicated to enacting this as quickly as possible.

"In closing, I wish to address the tragic loss of life that has occurred. As we now know, this crisis erupted because of the deplorable and cowardly actions of racially motivated, so-called militias. For too long these pseudo-patriotic groups have abused the true collective meaning of the second amendment to arm themselves with deadly, military-style weapons, and have used those weapons to wreak havoc on the lives of countless people. Even now, these craven, socially blind gangs are rampaging across California and Arizona waging their own version of a 'final solution' on Mexicans and Chicanos. This evening both Governor Buenamonte and I have signed executive orders outlawing militias in our respective states and establishing a moratorium on all firearm and ammunition sales for one-hundred-and-eighty days. Any firearms currently awaiting delivery will be held until the end of the moratorium. Furthermore, the police will be directed to confiscate any firearms not secured according to our inclination during the moratorium. This 'cooling off' period will be reevaluated at the end of the one-hundred-and-eighty days and could be extended indefinitely upon our preference. The only way to stop these militias is to pull their teeth and chop off their heads. We will not stand by and allow these contemptible acts to continue. We have a short amount of time for questions, so I'll open the floor to the press."

There was a burst of excitement as the pool of assembled reporters clamored to get the governor's attention. Governor Buenamonte calmly selected a fair-skinned Latina in the second row. "Yes, please state your question."

"Thank you. My name is Maria Contreras with Univision. Governor Buenamonte, how will your plan for Aztlán deal with the large naval bases in San Diego and the Camp Pendleton Marine Corps base near Oceanside? Won't it be difficult for these US military bases to co-exist with a semi-autonomous Chicano nation?"

"That's an excellent question. As you are aware, the United States has bases in sovereign nations all over the world, so they've learned to deal with these types of situations before. As far as the bases you referenced in San Diego, I see these facilities being handled much like our naval base in Guantanamo Bay, Cuba."

"They will remain in US control so that our West Coast defenses will not be compromised and will continue to provide a strong source of employment for the people of Aztlán."

"If we've been able to maintain our bases in Cuba since 1898...I don't think we'll have a problem doing the same in this situation. As for Camp Pendleton, I believe the Marine Corps ought to either work out a deal to lease the land, as the US has done in many other nations, or decommission the base and apply the savings to the federal deficit."

This time Governor Slater selected a reporter. She pointed to an older gentleman who had the war-worn look of a veteran reporter. "Yes, the gentleman in the back with the blue blazer."

"Thank you, Governor Slater. My name is Ralph Willis, and I represent Knight Ridder Press. How do you foresee the relationship between the state of Aztlán and Arizona? Won't there be a tremendous amount of difficulty having two sovereign states existing together?"

"Actually, Arizona, as well as California and many other states, has a lot of experience with this very situation. As you may be aware Native Americans live in sovereign nations, and these nations are spread all over the United States. As a matter of fact, Arizona has more reservation land than any other state in the union. These Native American nations have their own tribal councils and make their own laws, which are enforced by their own police. Their people do not pay taxes yet enjoy full US citizenship. Just as we've negotiated revenue sharing contracts with Indian casinos, this plan would do the same in regard to the economic infrastructure the nation of Aztlán would inherit. In short, I see the relationship between Aztlán and Arizona being financially symbiotic."

"May I ask a follow-up question?"

"Sure, what is it?"

"Governor, you mentioned that your plan calls for the deployment of Mexican army peacekeepers and United Nations personnel to assist in the transition. When would these groups arrive to fulfill these duties?"

"Governor Buenamonte and I have already been in contact with the Secretary General Al-Duri of the UN and made our request. The Secretary was very eager to help and assured us that assistance would arrive as soon as the first part of next week. We requested that the UN team be selected from Latin countries."

"Cuba is the current leader of the United Nations Commission for Democratic Transition, so they would definitely lead the mission. We have also received notification that Venezuela and Paraguay have volunteered to participate. With regard to the Mexican peace-keeping forces, they have already entered the United States and are now in San Diego. Together, these groups will act similarly to the way the Economic Community of West African States troops did during Liberia's civil war."

"We have time for one more question," remarked Governor Buenamonte, before selecting a young man two rows from the front. "Yes...the man in the green polo-style shirt."

"Thank you. I'm Brian Thomas from UPI. Governor, this is indeed an ambitious proposal; won't it be terribly expensive, and how do you intend to pay for it, considering California is already running historic deficits?"

"I remember when I was in college and had the opportunity to attend a speech by President Kennedy. This was during the space race, and many people worried about the huge cost of NASA.

"President Kennedy related an old Irish tale of two brothers who enjoyed a constant sibling rivalry. As the two boys raced across a green Irish field they came upon a tall hedgerow that stood in their way. The older boy reached over and snatched the hat from the head of his younger brother and threw it over the imposing obstacle. Both boys knew that they couldn't return home without their hats, or their father would sorely discipline them. So the brothers were forced to struggle over the hedgerow and retrieve the hat.

"The moral of the story is: when we are faced with a great challenge; often the best course of action is to dedicate ourselves completely to the task so that we're left with no other option but success. Creating a homeland for the people of Aztlán will not be easy, nor will it be cheap, but we must succeed. To do so, we'll have to realign taxes on businesses and the rich. Additionally, an increase on gasoline and car registration taxes is being considered. Even though this will not be easy...the alternative is far worse. For those who doubt the importance of this mission, I simply ask you to direct your attention to the brutal Israeli occupation of Palestine. I do not want to see the violence of the past forty-eight hours spiral out of control towards the tragedy they have experienced over the last decade."

With that remark the press conference ended, and the two governors exited the pressroom with staff members in tow.

In the Academy's classroom, the group sat in stunned silence.

"I can't believe what I just heard," Josh said quietly. "Did they actually just commit to turning over half of California and Arizona to Mexico?"

"This is surreal." Ghost remarked. "Those traitors just surpassed Benedict Arnold's treachery. I can't believe what I just saw."

"Believe it, Mark," said Arrow. "Not only did they hand over US soil to the Mexicans, they've suspended the second amendment and declared war on the people. Gentleman, this changes everything. The second American civil war just began. Ghost, get on the radio and send word that 48th Field Force is requesting reinforcements from all militias." Arrow somberly turned around and walked out of the room.

As the rest of the team sat in utter disbelief a quiet and heavy realization settled over the group...war had been declared, and only blood and death would resolve the matter.

Fox News Channel

Immediately following the historic gubernatorial news conference, Xue Lu Dong, the Chinese Ambassador to the UN, issued a statement proclaiming, "Beijing fully supports the UN mission to the people of Aztlán, and as a permanent member of the Security Council, will act to ensure this vital mission is successful." He then went on to announce, "The People's Republic of China will regard any American military action against UN Peacekeepers in Aztlán as a direct attack upon China and its world interests."

In Washington the president made a bold statement saying, "The governors of California and Arizona were acting outside their Constitutional powers and are in extreme violation of the law." The president went on to say, "The question of secession was the main issue of the American Civil War. The unauthorized capitulation of sovereign American soil is unforgivable and will be resisted."

Following the president's remarks, members of the Congressional Black Caucus issued a joint statement excoriating the president. In that press release they remarked, "It is not enough that this failed President has unsuccessfully performed the duties of his office and exposed the American people to one colossal crisis after another, now he's shown himself to be a racist of the highest order. The president evidently embraces the revisionist history that the American Civil War was not about freeing slaves, but was about secession. As we have pointed out many times before, this president is hostile to minorities and harbors a 'plantation agenda' to continue the repression and exploitation of blacks and Hispanics. His outright refusal to allow a small homeland to be established for the people of Aztlán smacks of the same authoritarianism that his Zionist co-conspirators in Israel practice. We welcome the UN and congratulate the governors of California and Arizona for their courageous solution to a serious, and long-overlooked problem."

Chapter 9

The strength of the Constitution lies entirely in the determination of each citizen to defend it. Only if every single citizen feels duty bound to do his share in this defense are the constitutional rights secure.
—Albert Einstein

PLA Headquarters: Hermosillo, Mexico

After watching the joint press conference held by *Obispo* and *Puente*, Major Al-Salih returned to his room to contact General Maruf and discuss the implementation of the fourth phase of their plan. The major entered the General's direct number on his encrypted satellite phone and waited for an answer.

The answer on the other end of the line was prompt, as always. "This is General Maruf."

"*Amid* Maruf, this is Major Al-Salih."

"Ah *Ra'id*, congratulations! I just finished watching the California press conference. Allah's smile shines down upon your mission."

"Thank you, *Amid*, Allah's blessings have been most generous. We have completed phase three and are about to begin phase four. I need to know if everything is ready with our North Korean allies."

"Yes, all is ready. I spoke with my North Korean counterpart earlier today, and his forces will launch their attack within the next twelve hours."

"Excellent," replied the major. "It's vital for the American military to be held in check so they can not be redeployed to the United States. Without their military, the American homeland will be completely unguarded, allowing the Cubans and Mexicans to easily secure control of the Southwest."

"By the way," the General said warmly, "you are to be congratulated for your successful tactic of killing the Mexican activist and the peasants. Does the PLA have any suspicion you were the one who ordered their deaths?"

"No, General. Sayf organized both incidents in complete secrecy. He recruited the white supremacists via the Internet by posing as a South African racist, and hired a team of al-Qaida operatives to kill the Mexican immigrants. I am recommending him for a decoration for his initiative. The Mexicans needed an emotional catalysis to focus their anger and drive them in the right direction."

"Seeing one of their heroes assassinated on television was exactly what was needed. Have you been in contact with the General Intelligence Directorate in Cuba?"

"Yes, I spoke with General Macha an hour ago. Several of his men, including one of his top operatives, a Col. Drago, are assigned to the UN delegation scheduled to arrive in California. He's *anxious* to begin assisting the nation of Aztlán to organize their new government."

"Very well then, it seems everything is progressing according to plan. As long as the Koreans fulfill their end of the bargain, then we should have no problem fulfilling ours. The day of our delivery is near. May Allah bless you and your family, goodbye."

El Cajon Canyon, North of San Bernardino, California

Interstate 15 cuts through El Cajon Canyon as it descends off the high desert plateau of the San Gabriel Mountains towards San Bernardino and Riverside. Two ribbons of concrete and a wide railroad bed are the only navigable paths up almost three thousand feet from the plain of the Inland Empire to the wide prairie of the high desert and the country beyond.

The 111th Battalion, a.k.a., The High Desert Militia, knew this area well. They'd trained in the San Bernardino National Forest and the high desert around Barstow and Victorville for years. Nonetheless, it didn't take a seasoned local to appreciate the unique topography of the El Cajon Canyon; it was a natural chokepoint and the only eastern exit out of the Los Angeles basin and into the interior of California for many miles.

Stalker knew that with the small force he commanded, he needed to use the geography as a force multiplier. The narrow confines and steepness of the canyon offered a great advantage to defenders, allowing them to employ narrow fields of fire and elevation to hold off a superior force. Unfortunately, he didn't have the resources to engage in a large urban or open-field battle. But, here his forces could concentrate on a smaller front, and if his forces had to retreat, the enemy could be funneled into narrow killing fields of his choice. His worst fear was confronting armor, as he simply didn't have the firepower needed to deal with it. Still, if somehow he did end up facing tanks or armored personnel carriers (APCs) they would have to stay on the roadbeds. Nothing larger than an all-terrain vehicle could climb most of the nearly vertical faces that made up the interior of the canyon. That would leave little room for tracked vehicles to maneuver, which might allow him to either defeat or slow them down. If it came to that, a delaying retreat would definitely be the order of the day.

For the past ten hours surviving elements from B and P Company had been arriving, along with reinforcements from the 59th and 65th Battalions. In addition to the militias, groups of citizens, who'd been driven from their homes by the rampaging gangs, straggled in.

The word was out that a citizen's force was organizing a line of resistance at the Cajon pass. Hundreds of people who'd witnessed the day's destruction and suffered losses were ready to fight back.

Among these was a group of about one hundred Mexican-Americans who were hungry, filthy, exhausted, and desperately angry. At their head was a man named Alberto Rojas. Alberto was a retired Marine Corps Gunnery Sergeant who'd served in Desert Storm. The "Gunny," as he liked to be called, now taught high school and coached football, or he had, at the beginning of the week. That career, he thought bitterly, was probably over.

When the gangs arrived at his Covina neighborhood, he'd already assembled a small group of friends to fend off the looters. The Gunny's small group was armed mostly with lever action rifles and shotguns. Only a couple of others had any military experience, and of those none were in combat units. Rojas had hoped that a show of force, even a small one, would serve as a deterrent and turn the gangs towards a lesser-defended neighborhood. But, when the looters descended upon them their numbers and firepower threatened to annihilate the Gunny's impromptu force, and it was all they could do to effectively retreat. They'd been running ever since, and he was sick of it.

Gunny approached a man in uniform who was busily giving someone instructions. "Excuse me." The Gunny's words went without acknowledgment. "Excuse me," he said once again...and for the second time he received no response. It had been a long and difficult day, and the Gunny's temper had worn thin. "Excuse me!" he barked out in his best drill sergeant voice.

The man was startled by the roaring voice of authority behind him and snapped around to see a large and visibly angry man standing erect in front of him.

"What can I do for you?" the man asked as he stared into the bloodshot eyes of the Gunny.

"My name is Gunnery Sergeant Rojas. I'm looking for the commanding officer of this outfit. Are you able to direct me to him?"

"Yes I can. You're looking for a man named Stalker. The command area is located beyond those trucks just to the right of the medical tent."

"Very well. Carry on." As the Gunny turned and marched off in the direction the man indicated, a backwards glace revealed the soldier watching him as he walked away. "That's right sport," Gunny grumbled under his breath, "you'd better not turn your back on me...I've had a very bad day."

Stalker was finishing a meeting with his command staff where they'd been putting together a plan to deal with all the new arrivals. Most of these people were willing enough to fight, but many had no weapons, and those who did lacked proper ammunition and basic equipment. During their retreat, Company P had "liberated" some gear from an abandoned surplus store, and a few members of Stalker's battalion had brought several hundred thousand rounds of ammunition with them when they'd deployed. The problem was they only had 5.56mm, 7.62 X 39mm and .308 calibers.

While these were fine for military-style weapons, they didn't do much for most lever action rifles and shotguns. After decades of gun control, registration, confiscation, and bans, most people in California didn't own a rifle at all. If they did it certainly wasn't a military-style firearm.

The command staff decided to take an inventory of all the weapons, ammunition, and equipment in camp and then do quick interviews to find out who had military training. Once they had this information they'd be able to decide who could fight and who would be transferred to Victorville where another camp was being established to handle refugees.

As Stalker was reviewing a note he'd received from his communications officer, a large shape darkened the entryway of his tent. "May I help you?" he asked the faceless shadow.

"I'm looking for Stalker. I was told I would find him here."

"I'm Stalker. Come in and grab a seat," he said, pointing to a folding chair in the corner. As the Gunny walked into the light, Stalker noticed two things. The man wore a determined and somber look on his face, and he was Hispanic.

"My name is Gunnery Sergeant Alberto Rojas, USMC, retired. I'm in charge of a group of men from Covina. We were involved in a firefight this morning trying to protect our homes. We fought a fighting retreat for several miles as gangs looted our city. I have ninety-two men who are ready and willing to fight, and we'd like to know what we need to do to get involved."

Stalker stepped out from behind his fold-up table and approached the man. "You strike me as a man who appreciates directness...are you Mexican?"

"I'm a citizen of the United States of America. I served twenty years in the Marine Corps, and I fought in Desert Storm. I'm also a Southern Baptist, and I sing bass in my church choir. I like dogs and hate cats," and then in a scornful voice added, "oh and by the way, I killed several gang bangers today and lost a couple neighbors...and yes, my parents emigrated from Mexico. What else do you want to know?"

Stalker could see the man was seriously pissed off and tried to calm him down. "Listen, Gunny, we both know what's happening here. We're at war with radical Mexican separatists that have invaded our country. I couldn't care less who you are, where you grew up or what church you go to; all I need to know is can I trust you and your men to help us fight?"

The Gunny took a breath and paused to compose himself. Then, looked back at Stalker. "I was born here. The only thing I know about Mexico is what I've seen in Tijuana and on TV, and I don't care for it.

"I know I look like the enemy, but so do a lot of people in this part of the country. I'm an American. Even if I weren't, not all Mexicans support all this Aztlán crap. For goodness sake, that's why most of our parents and grandparents left Mexico. They hated the corruption and graft and wanted to live where they could be free and make a future for their children."

"My men and I have already bled and shed blood in this fight and have dedicated ourselves to doing whatever's needed to win. In World War II young men of Japanese descent gathered together in the dust of their relocation camps and joined the army. They were called the *Nisei*, and they became one of the most highly decorated units in the military. All we want is the same opportunity. We're gonna do whatever we have to. Is that good enough for you?"

Stalker extended his hand to the Marine. "Yeah, that's good enough for me, Gunny. Have you thought about a name for your group?"

"Yeah, how about the *Libertad Company*?"

"Sounds like a good name. Have your men eaten?"

"Not since this morning."

"Well, let's get them some chow, then I'll have one of my staff interview your men and find out what supplies they have and will need. Thank you for bringing your people in. We need all the Patriots we can muster."

38th Parallel: Korean Peninsula

At 0300 the early-morning stillness of Korea was ripped apart by syncopated flashes of fire, each one an eruption from hundreds of artillery pieces. In a highly coordinated attack the North Korean army launched its long-anticipated drive to reunify the Korean peninsula. The immense barrage targeted the DMZ, the US and ROK positions, and the southern capital of Seoul with a collection of 122mm, 130mm, 152mm, 170mm, 200mm and 240mm artillery.

Tens of thousands of rounds rained down on defensive positions along the line separating the two long-time adversaries. US and ROK defensive positions had been previously redeployed from what leaders identified as potential saturation zones, so even though the initial barrage seemed overwhelming, it failed to severely damage the main lines of resistance. The North Korean strategy, like most Soviet influenced tactics, relied heavily upon centralized command and communication (C^3) to direct the battle following strictly enforced doctrine. US forces had trained to defeat these exact tactics for over twenty years, and had recently refined their skills against Iraq in two wars.

So as soon as the attack commenced, a sophisticated counter-battery network began to digitally process the incoming ballistic trajectories of the rounds and then match them with information on previously-known artillery and rocket positions to develop a clear image of the battlefield. This was accomplished by an interconnected system of AN/TPQ-37 and AN/TPQ-47 Block II, truck-mounted, multi-phased array radar systems that locked onto artillery rounds as they reached their apogee and then calculated their trajectory back to their point of origin.

The information was digitally transmitted to mobile processing locations known as Advanced Field Artillery/Tactical Data Systems (AFATDS) where the data was converted into firing requests at a rate of over four hundred plans per hour. AFATDS then allocated fire missions to the assets that were closest to the targets and had the ideal mix of weapons to destroy the threat.

Counter battery fire from M270 and upgraded M270 A1 Multiple Launch Rocket Systems (MLRS), located thirty kilometers away, began returning fire within sixteen seconds of receiving their targeting coordinates. Each launcher fired twelve rockets in quick secession containing over six hundred sub-munitions, each capable of penetrating up to four inches of armor or sending antipersonnel fragments out to four meters. As soon as each launcher fired its volley it immediately moved to a new firing location. Each twelve-rocket volley spread enough devastation to cover one square kilometer. As the maelstrom rained down, dozens of artillery tubes and their crews fell silent.

Overhead, the 35th and 80th Fighter Squadrons from Kusan Air Base, flying F-16s, were in the middle of a Combat Air Patrol (CAP) when they received alerts from the AWACS, loitering high above the battlefield, that multiple bandits were coming in from the North.

"Juvat One, I'm tracking twelve bandits," relayed the AWACS controller. "Intercept on course 340°. Over."

"Roger, Skyhook, request permission to engage. Over."

"Juvat One, this is Skyhook; you are weapons free. Over."

"Affirmative, Skyhook."

"Juvat One to Snakes, let's take them out."

Each pilot locked four AIM-120 Advanced Medium Range Air-to-Air Missiles (AMRAAM) onto the blips arrayed across their radar screens. From the electronic emissions of the enemy aircraft, the fire control systems in the F-16s identified them as MIG-29s, probably from the 56th Guards Fighter Regiment. The MIG-29 is an excellent fighter and in many respects equal to the F-16. But those advantages are most dramatic inside of ten miles, primarily due to the aircraft's superior maneuverability.

As soon as the bandits entered range, the squadron of F-16s launched a wave of missiles in an attempt to maximize their long-distance advantage. The sleek missiles followed the guidance set forth by the powerful APG 68(V) 7 radars and rocketed towards their targets at nearly 2,800 miles an hour. At the midway point the missiles activated their inertial guidance, and then as they closed within a few miles, switched into internal terminal homing mode.

Suddenly, the cockpits of the North Korean fighters erupted in a cacophony of alarms as their N-019 radars detected the inbound AMRAAMs. They immediately triggered electronic countermeasures (ECM) in an effort to jam the missiles, but this proved futile as the AMRAAMs' built-in ECM burned through the electromagnetic shield produced by the MIG's radar. As the enemy aircraft futilely began high "G" evasive maneuvers in an attempt to break the missile's lock, the AMRAAMs slammed into their airframes detonating their forty-pound warheads. The ensuing explosions tore the high-tech fighters in half and dotted the sky with huge burning balls of fire, metal, and fuel. A couple pilots were able to react fast enough to trigger off a few R-27 missiles, but they were at the far edge of their tracking range, so the missiles blindly raced into the empty sky at 3,500km/h.

While the "Juvats" were engaging the MIG-29s, the "Pantons" of the 35th Fighter Squadron were, in like fashion, eliminating less-advanced MIG-23s. The one-sided battle was over in less than five minutes, as the two squadrons tracked down and destroyed the remnants of the out classed communists.

With the skies clear of enemy fighters, the way was open for VMFA-212 to attack surface-to-air missile batteries. Each F/A-18 fired two High Speed Anti-Radiation Missiles (HARM's), which homed in on the emissions from fire control radars that controlled anti-aircraft batteries.

The resulting devastation created a corridor through which another squadron of F/A-18E Super Hornets, operating from the *USS Carl Vinson* codename *Grand Canyon*, flew on their way to attack Command, Communications, and Control assets and additional artillery batteries.

Although a significant number of SAM sites had been taken out, the North Koreans deployed a vast network of Anti Aircraft Artillery (AAA) that filled the air with 14.5mm, 37mm and 57mm rounds. Deadly, serpent-like streams of AAA reached upwards towards the Marine aircraft, forcing the pilots to aggressively maneuver and fly higher than they'd prefer. Unlike missiles, artillery rounds were immune to jamming, and where one missile battery might launch ten or fifteen deadly projectiles, a single AAA gun could easily fire hundreds of rounds per minute, putting up a wall of steel ahead of their targets. As the squadron continued towards their objective one Hornet suffered several hits in its left wing, which quickly caught fire.

"Red Rock Six to Red Rock Leader, I've been hit," radioed a young pilot to his squadron leader as he worked to control his wounded aircraft. "I'm on fire and losing hydraulics."

"Red Rock Six, can you divert to Grand Canyon?"

"Negative, Red Rock Leader, I'm diverting to L2."

Anticipating the dense air defenses the North Koreans possessed, the Air Force and Navy had established several areas where crippled pilots could eject and quickly be retrieved by Combat Search and Rescue (CSAR) teams. These areas were designated Lifeguard One, Two, and Three. L2 was located just south of the DMZ and off the East coast.

"Affirmative Red Rock Six, good luck. Red Rock Leader, out."

"Roger that, Red Rock Leader. I'm switching to SAR channel. Red Rock Six, out."

The crippled Hornet pulled out of formation and ascended to get as far above the AAA as possible. Then the pilot aimed his bleeding jet towards the coast and began praying that it would hold together long enough to reach safety. As he flew towards the Sea of Japan, he intently monitored his cockpit displays as they began flashing a series of critical warnings.

"Come on baby, just hold together a little longer," He implored his aircraft. Just in case he needed to eject he began a checklist process that included cleaning up the cockpit so that if he did eject, flight gear wouldn't get in the way of his exit. After that, he patted down the various pockets on his flight suit to ensure all his pockets were closed and everything was properly secured. Next he locked down the visor of his helmet to protect his face from the powerful windblast that would accompany an ejection.

The last item on the checklist was to throttle back and slow the plane down to lessen the severity of the windblast. The controls were becoming increasingly unresponsive, as if they were stuck in hardening cement. Scanning ahead he saw a glimmering ribbon that stretched across the horizon. It was the coastline.

"Lifeguard Two, this is Red Rock Six. Lifeguard Two, over."

"Red Rock Six, this is Lifeguard Two."

"Lifeguard Two, I'm approaching Lifeguard Station and declaring a mayday; I repeat mayday."

As the crippled Hornet crossed the coastline the hydraulics failed, and the pilot lost all control of his jet.

"Lifeguard Two, Red Rock Six is feet wet and punching out!"

The pilot fought to get his body into the proper alignment before ejecting: elbows tucked in, head and neck back and legs pressed firmly against the lower portion of the seat. The young Lieutenant began silently praying as he began a process he had hoped he'd never have to actually use.

"Our Father who art in heaven..."

He gripped the yellow-and-black-striped ejection handles and violently pulled them up. This initiated a complex and powerful sequence that lasted less than three seconds.

Explosive charges blew the canopy off the airframe with a distinctive "*Pop.*" The air stream ripped the canopy away from the jet and into the surrounding inky darkness. Then pyrotechnic denotations launched the pilot's Mk 14 ejection seat up guide rails at fifty-five feet per second, until it cleared the dying aircraft. Microseconds later a solid propellant rocket under the ejection seat ignited, rocketing the lieutenant skyward and smashing him into the already uncomfortable seat with 10 Gs of thrust. As soon as the seat separated from the catapult mechanism, a drone chute deployed, both stabilizing and slowing the pilot down. One second later, the drone was jettisoned, the seat fell away, and the pilot's main chute deployed. The dazed pilot watched his Hornet disappear below him while he fought to catch his breath, under what he believed was the most beautiful parachute he'd ever seen.

****

Sixty miles away the remaining members of VMFA 212 released a combination of AGM- 154B Joint Stand-Off Weapons (JSOWs) and CBU-75 cluster bombs over a collection of T-62, T-54 tanks and armored personnel carriers moving south towards the DMZ and selected C^3 nodes that were controlling forward activities. After a short free fall each JSOW separated into six BLU-108/B submunitions packages, each containing four shaped charges that tore into the lightly armored tops of the tanks and APCs igniting their internal fuel and ammunition stores, and converting them into funeral pyres.

The less-sophisticated cluster bombs each released 247 bomblets. Each of the submunitions contained four pounds of high explosive formed into dual-purpose, shaped charges capable of either penetrating seven and a half inches of armor or spewing out hundreds of anti-personnel metal shards.

As the bomblets hit the ground explosions engulfed the command trucks and facilities with thousands of blinding flashes and sparks followed by large secondary explosions. In one pass the navy strike fighters annihilated an entire battalion of armor and silenced vital command networks that controlled the forward edge of battle, leaving dozens of units blind and directionless.

Direct Action Academy

The two New Mexican battalions arrived around 0120. Twenty-three trucks comprised the convoy, each one different from the other and loaded with men and supplies. Like most things associated with the militia the trucks were privately owned and often second hand.

Many militia commanders preferred older vehicles over newer, fancier models because they wanted to ensure they'd be able to repair them in the event of a crisis or lack of parts. With older cars, they reasoned, it was still possible to open the hood and repair a carburetor, replace points, plugs, etc. Another reason these older vehicles remained popular was because many worried about the possibility of high tech attacks using electro-magnetic pulse to "fry" the computers and circuits used so widely in modern cars.

Cowboy was on watch at the front gate when the convoy arrived. He radioed back to the main building. "Post one to base, the relatives have arrived."

"Roger that, post one. Have them report to the main building."

The leader of the 31st battalion was a tall, middle-aged man who had the strong build of a lifelong rancher. His closely trimmed brown hair just showed under his hat, and grey hair on his temples betrayed the fact that this man was no stranger to stress and hard work. He climbed out of the passenger side of the lead truck and walked towards Cowboy. "Good morning, I'm Desert Scout, Commanding Officer of the 31st battalion of the 47th FF."

Cowboy shook his hand. "Welcome to the Academy," he said. "You can call me Cowboy. Glad to see you guys. Our Commander is named Arrow, and he's waiting for you at the main building. Just follow this road until you reach the large building with the flagpole out front."

Desert Scout wore standard woodland BDUs and a matching boonie hat. Around his waist was a black riggers belt with a drop-leg holster strapped to his right thigh, and what appeared to be a large-frame Glock secured inside. Attached to the left side of his belt, just forward of his hip, was a double magazine pouch, and behind that a field knife. A unit patch, featuring the New Mexican state flag, was sewn on his left sleeve, and a subdued US flag on the right.

"Thank you, Cowboy. We appreciate the opportunity to rest and get our gear better organized before heading onto California. Have you heard any more about the situation there?"

"Not since my watch started. But our communications guy has been monitoring the radio and may have additional intelligence to share with you. His name is Ghost."

"Very well then, I'll look him up. Thanks again."

Desert Scout climbed back inside the lead truck, and the convoy rolled down the road leading to the main building. Arrow and Mike were waiting outside when the convoy arrived. The trucks filled various parking spaces, and men began climbing out. The two battalions of New Mexican militia wore several different patterns of camouflage; most wore the standard woodland pattern, but there were some wearing three-color desert and others, simple olive drab. The head gear used by the men followed suit, with most selecting boonie hats, but there were also a few garrison caps and helmets scattered among the troops. This was common in the militia. While some units were more organized with established protocols, most allowed their members to assemble their own gear based upon personal budgets and preferences. Unlike the US military, the militias didn't have unlimited resources or a quartermaster corps to distribute uniforms to every member. It was up to the individual to assemble his gear according to basic guidelines set forth by the Battalion Command Staff. Some battalions had specialty companies that followed stricter guidelines for equipment and uniforms; these might include mountain, scout/sniper, amphibious, or desert units. But standard rifle companies were far more diverse. What people wore was often dictated by what they could get. Most militiamen depended on US Government Issue (USGI) surplus, so woodland and three-color desert pattern BDUs were popular. But it wasn't uncommon to see foreign patterns like German Fleck, British DPM, and Canadian digital.

The same principle applied to gear, but in this area many had begun to acquire commercial tactical gear from manufactures like *Grunt Gear, TOE, Custom Tactical Designs,* and *Black Raven* to supplement their surplus equipment. They also used gear originally manufactured for sportsmen, like radios, GPS receivers, boots, knives, and hydration bladders. But this wasn't out of the ordinary. Even in active duty units many of these same products were used by soldiers to supplement the issued equipment that didn't quite stand up to the demands of the battlefield.

As Mike watched the men assemble, he was reminded of Cincinnatus, who, as Titus Livius wrote, was "called from his plough," in 458 B.C., to save a besieged Roman army, and the Colonial Minutemen, who also left their fields to fight off the British at Concord Bridge in 1775. Their disordered appearance didn't lessen Mike's respect; after all, during the Revolutionary War the British described the militia as a ragtag collection of men without commonality.

Even in the early days of the Civil War, most units didn't follow a standardized uniform code. This was the way militias have always been and probably would always be. While the US Military was the technological envy of the world, the militias represented the republic's last line of defense, made up of the common citizens who sacrificed to equip and train while working or studying to care for their families full-time.

Desert Scout approached Arrow and Mike and saluted. "6th and 31st Battalions of the 47th Field Force, New Mexico, reporting."

Arrow and Mike returned the salute before extending their hands. "Good to see you. I'm Arrow, and this is Gringo. How was your drive?"

"It's a pleasure to meet you gentlemen. I'm Desert Scout. The drive went better than expected. I'm glad to see things around here are fairly quiet."

"Yeah, we're on the far east edge of the battle lines. Most of the craziness is about thirty miles to the northwest, around the outskirts of Phoenix, but it won't take long to reach us, so we're making every preparation possible." Mike responded. "Why don't you bivouac your men between buildings two and three. There's room for them to spread out and inventory their gear. After that we'll make sure they're fed and get some sack time. In the interim, gather your company leaders and follow us over to our communications room where you can get an update on the situation."

"Thanks, that sounds like a plan."

Desert Scout called out for his team leaders to gather together for a briefing where each leader gave a report on his men and their equipment. After a final count they learned that out of the two-hundred-and-eighty men who were registered in the 6th and 31st battalions only one-hundred-and-fifty-five were accounted for. Although disappointing, the numbers weren't entirely unexpected. Some members of the unit were deployed with active duty and National Guard units, but others simply did not show up for the muster. Since militia duty was voluntary and not every member shared the same level of dedication to the cause, it was often difficult to get everyone to report for monthly training, let alone to muster for a real crisis. The team leaders ordered their squad leaders to assemble their men and make a complete inventory of personal and unit equipment, before passing out MREs to all the men. As this was being done, Desert Scout and his company leaders followed Arrow and Mike into the communications center so they could receive an intelligence update.

Ghost sat in the dark surrounded by monitors, computers, and several radios that cast a dim, greenish light on his face and the surrounding space. On a small table in front of him lay several legal-sized pads of paper covered with hastily written notes and cryptic alphanumeric entries. The notes were slashed and scribbled through with arrows connecting thoughts and crude pictures that served as mental reminders. As he sat copying yet another message the door opened flooding the room with a blinding light. Ghost cringed as his pupils constricted, causing him to momentarily lose his sight.

"Fricken A, close the door!" He shouted as he covered his eyes and turned away from the light.

Arrow motioned towards Ghost and chuckled, "Gentleman, this vampire is my comms man. His handle is Ghost, though were thinking of changing it to 'Dracula.'" Arrow flipped a light switch on the wall, and soft, fluorescent light illuminated the space.

"You know, a little light won't kill you. Why are you sitting in the dark?"

"I've been so busy with all the comms traffic I just forgot to turn the lights on." Ghost explained while rubbing his eyes.

Mike looked around the room and saw an empty coffee mug sitting next to Ghost. Sheets of paper were scattered about with round stains marking where he'd sat the mug down. On the opposite side of the room was an overflowing trash bin containing several empty Coke cans and a crumpled up bag of cheese puffs.

"How can you survive on coffee, cheese puffs, and Coke? When was the last time you had real food?" Mike inquired in a puzzled tone.

"Don't knock it, Gringo, more computer code has been written on caffeine and artificial cheese flavoring than all the meat and potatoes in the world. I guess you're here for an update...pull up some chairs, and I'll give you the long and the short of it."

Arrow, Mike, Desert Scout, and his company leaders pulled out small pads of paper to take notes. "Ghost, I'd like to introduce Desert Scout. He's the CO of the New Mexican contingent that just arrived."

Desert Scout leaned forward with an outstretched hand and greeted Ghost. "Good to meet you. These are my company leaders. These two are from the 6th, and these guys represent the 31st battalion. So what's the situation in California look like?"

"Well, it's not pretty. The newly organized Southern California Command has established a blocking position at the mouth of the Cajon Pass, just north of San Bernardino. They're reporting just over seven hundred armed and equipped men made up of militia units from Orange and Riverside counties, remnants of the overrun Pasadena and Burbank units and a couple hundred citizens who've seen the light. They've established a supply train based in Victorville where they've evacuated over a thousand people and have an overflow in Barstow. Thanks to stockpiles and some *aggressive* procurement procedures, they're reporting enough supplies to last five to six days, barring any major drama. That's the good news."

Ghost shuffled a few pages and then took a deep breath before continuing.

"The bad news is San Diego County is a complete loss. The 73rd battalion put up a fight in a place called San Yis..."

"San Ysidro," Mike interjected. "It's right along the border."

"Yeah. Unfortunately, it was all they could do to save some Border Patrol and local police before retreating to Chula Vista, where they've regrouped in an attempt to stop any further northward incursion. Turns out the Mexican Army crossed the border with nearly a thousand mechanized troops; there was no way the 73rd could fight against that. They reported sporadic engagements until about 1630, when we lost radio contact with them."

Arrow looked over at Mike, who was visibly upset. "Mike, did you know anyone in the 73rd?"

"I never met any of them in person, but I did keep in touch with a guy named Omega through one of the militia sites. San Diego didn't have much of a militia contingent. Maybe it was due to all the military in the area or possibly because the weather is always so nice, making it hard to concentrate on preparing for bad times."

"For cripes sake, they can barely get enough people out for a Chargers game. Either way, I doubt they had much of a chance with the Mexican Army rolling across the border."

"What else can you tell us?" Desert Scout asked.

"Well," Ghost added, "several cities in San Diego County have basically welcomed the Mexican Army in as liberators. The UN is sending equipment, peacekeeping personnel, and a delegation led by Cuba to stabilize the situation and take control. The word is Governor Buenamonte has opened the Port of Long Beach as a UN staging area. The first contingent is supposed to arrive within the next twenty-four hours."

"That's awfully fast for the UN. They usually can't find their ass with both hands and a map. How'd they assemble all the equipment and personnel so quickly?" Desert Scout asked. "It sounds like this was premeditated. I bet Buenamonte and Slater had all this worked out months ago. I hope someone has a rope handy when this is all over with."

"So basically," Ghost continued, "Southern California is occupied, with the exception of a small holdout of citizens with their backs against the San Bernardino Mountains. The good news is that P Corps is fully activated, and reinforcements are on their way. I just got word that the 36th Field Force is assembling five battalions outside of Vegas. Two Utah battalions are already en route. They'll hook up with the 36th before heading down Interstate 15 to join Stalker's command. The 46th FF out of Oklahoma is mustering several battalions from the western counties of the state.

Also, I spoke with a guy from the 61st battalion, of the 42nd FF from East-Snocounty, Washington. His unit, called "Shekinah," has joined up with another from Southeast Washington, the "Regulators," and they're also en route. Because of the blockade in northern California, they're coming through Utah and have asked permission to stage here…just like Desert Scout's guys are doing."

"That'll be fine. Be sure to tell them that reports are that some police units are beginning to arrest suspected militia members, so they should reduce their signatures and try to blend in," Arrow commented.

"So what's the combined strength of those units?" asked one of the New Mexican company leaders.

"Roughly sixteen hundred men," Ghost answered after making a quick mental calculation. "Stalker should receive another seven hundred and fifty men before dawn. The 46th FF is reporting five hundred, and the Washington battalions comprise about three hundred and fifty more."

"That'll help," said Arrow. "But unless I'm overreacting I believe we're going to need as much help as possible. You'd better contact corps command staff and ask them to put out a nationwide call for men. He turned towards Desert Scout, "When are you planning on leaving for California?"

"I plan to pull out of here within the next six hours."

Ghost smacked himself on the forehead. "Oh yeah, I almost forgot. Desert Scout, P Corps command asked that you contact them as soon as you have a moment. I have their frequency locked into that radio over there. All you have to do is key the microphone and they should answer."

Desert Scout looked at Ghost with a slight frown of disapproval. "Thanks for letting me know." He said as he walked towards the radio.

"Oh, and one other small point," Ghost interjected. "In case anyone's interested, the North Korean Army just crossed the DMZ, and all hell is breaking loose. Reports are that it's the real deal and Seoul is under a massive artillery barrage. I guess when it rains it pours."

UN Headquarters: New York City

With the outbreak of war in Korea the UN called an emergency session of the Security Council. The Security Council is the strongest body of the organization and the only one that can make decisions that are binding upon all signatories. The council is organized around five permanent members: France, The People's Republic of China, The United Kingdom, Russia, and the United States. Ten other countries that serve two-year terms assist the permanent members.

The non-permanent seats are staggered so each year five countries are rotated out. The current non-permanent signatories were: Paraguay, Egypt, Germany, Guinea-Bissau, Venezuela, Albania, Poland, and Malaysia, making the Security Council distinctly antagonistic toward the United States. After various members took turns addressing the council, the privilege fell to China. The Secretary General intoned,

"The esteemed Ambassador from the People's Republic of China is recognized and granted the floor."

Xue Lu Dong adjusted his microphone before speaking. "Mr. General Secretary and members of the Security Council, China has worked closely with the UN and other multi-national coalitions to search for a peaceful solution to North Korea's nuclear weapons program. We recognize the instability an additional nuclear power would have on the region and have diligently worked within chapter six of the UN Charter and by way of our long relationship with Pyongyang to find a pacific settlement of this dispute.

"Beijing does not support the recent aggression launched by North Korea, and for this reason has not intervened on behalf of our neighbor. But, my government wishes to exercise its right as a permanent member of this council to invoke the powers granted in chapter seven of the charter under the section entitled, 'Threats to the peace, Breeches of the peace, or Acts of aggression.' We propose a formal declaration that this body will not permit American forces to violate the sovereign territory of, or threaten in any fashion, China in its current actions on the Korean peninsula. Beijing is dedicated to respecting the universal strength of this world body. We believe that the UN is the rightful organization to find a solution to this crisis, and we reject the 'Cowboy' unilateralism that has exemplified American foreign policy in recent years. Furthermore, China wishes the world to know that although we have no desire to intervene in Korea, if the United States uses its military forces to threaten or fight against UN peacekeepers in California, the People's Liberation Army *will* enter the conflict in Korea as we did in the 1950s."

"This is absurd!" the US ambassador exclaimed as he leapt out of his chair. "The situation in California is an internal matter of the United States!"

"No, Ambassador Majors," shouted the Secretary General "What is absurd is the cavalier disregard your president has shown towards the authority of this world body. As the first signatory of the UN charter, the world expects more from the United States. Yet, time after time, your president has demonstrated unashamed hostility towards the will of this ruling body. May I remind you that the United States is obligated under international law to uphold the decisions of this council?" The Secretary General took a breath and composed himself, before continuing, "The American Ambassador was out of order. The esteemed Ambassador from the People's Republic of China has the floor."

"Thank you, Mr. Secretary General. With all due respect to my esteemed American colleague, were not the wars in Korea and Vietnam internal matters? How many times has the United States intervened in the internal affairs of foreign nations? A good example might be Taiwan," Ambassador Lu-Dong said, raising his head dramatically. "If the United States attacks UN forces, they attack the very authority of this council and should be severely dealt with according to the provisions of the UN Charter."

The meeting continued for another ninety minutes until all the member states that wished to address the ruling body had been allowed time. Then Ambassador Lu-Dong once again addressed the council. "Mr. Secretary General, China wishes to call a vote of the council on the provision it has set forth. That provision calls upon the United States of America to respect and not in anyway intrude upon the sovereign territory of the People's Republic of China or threaten any of its interests during the current conflict with North Korea. In addition, it is proposed that a provision be attached that American military forces will not interfere with the UN peacekeepers currently being dispatched to California to resolve the Aztlán crisis."

The US Ambassador once again rose to his feet "Mr. Secretary General, the United States objects to the introduction of peacekeeping forces into the United States in the strongest possible terms. The UN Charter strictly forbids the deployment of peacekeeping forces without the unanimous consent of this council. As a permanent member, with veto power, we do not consent to this action."

"Mr. Ambassador," said the Secretary General, "the UN was approached by the governors of California and Arizona. They've made it clear that their people desire the assistance of the UN."

"Governors *do not* have the authority, under our constitution, to initiate such requests," the US Ambassador interrupted.

"Sir, these requests have been supported by members of both the US Senate and House of Representatives. Considering the very tenuous position your president is in…I am more than satisfied to accept the petitions we have thus far received. Regardless, the United States has a long history of invading other countries without *their* approval. So your objection is overruled in this matter."

Then the Secretary General pounded his ceremonial gavel and forwarded the motion. "Honored members of the Security Council, the Ambassador of China has called for a vote, and I second it. Those in favor of the provision, as set forth by China, indicate by raising your hands."

Around the room hands began to rise: France, Russia, China, Paraguay, Egypt, Germany, Guinea-Bissau, Venezuela, Indonesia, Albania and Malaysia all voted in favor of the provision.

"All those who wish to abstain, please raise your hand." Only Poland abstained.

"All opposed?" The ambassador from the United Kingdom joined the US Ambassador in a sign of determined opposition.

"The count is eleven for the provision, two against and one abstention. Since both the UK and the US have voted against the provision, thus exercising their veto powers as permanent members of the council, the provision is defeated. This concludes the agenda for this meeting, I hereby close these proceedings." With another ceremonial rap of his gavel the council separated and departed the council hall to address the mass of international reporters eagerly lying in wait for the diplomats.

As expected, Ambassador Lu-Dong was immediately inundated by a pack of overzealous reporters. "Mr. Ambassador," asked a young, blonde reporter, "you knew the United States would veto your provision. Why then, did you bring it up for a vote?"

"It was the desire of the People's Republic of China to demonstrate to the world that the United States is led by an aggressive regime whose only concern is their ability to intervene where they see fit. They are concerned only with their own imperialistic pursuits. They wouldn't even support a measure calling on them to respect our sovereign territory."

"But, wasn't the additional measure regarding UN peacekeepers in California at the core of their objection?" Another reporter asked.

"I don't see the difference. As I said they wish to act wherever and upon whomever they please. This arrogance extends to their relationship with the United Nations, an organization they helped establish. The current administration has applied the American mentality of throwing away whatever no longer serves their needs. They're treating the UN like a shirt that is no longer in style. Instead of working with it and recognizing its worth, they simply cast it off as so much trash. The world must recognize the hazard this poses and understand that this president is a dangerous rogue actor. Despite the predictable outcome of this vote, the People's Republic of China stands firmly behind its warning. If the US military attacks UN troops, the People's Liberation Army will reciprocate. You will now excuse me, as I have very pressing matters to attend to."

The US administration understood it was teetering on the brink of starting World War III. If it used military force against the forthcoming UN invasion of California, China would intervene in Korea. If that happened there was no doubt they'd launch their long-anticipated invasion to reunify Taiwan with the mainland. "One billion Chinese," the president said privately to his advisors, "just shouted out 'Check' in the global game of chess."

Otay Lakes, Just East of Chula Vista, California

Omega looked around at the handful of fighters spread out in hastily constructed fighting positions. How had things gone so bad, so quickly? Although he'd been a part of the militia for several years and had been actively involved in training and organization, he wasn't a military man. He was an engineer who designed custom parts for cars and trucks. Most of his time was spent at his North County office drawing schematics and testing new designs before they went into production.

Being involved in the militia in California was often an exercise in frustration. California was a destination for most people, it seemed. Either they'd been transferred to the Golden State with their companies, or they were trying to escape where they were originally from. Either way, few seemed to consider California their real home. Whenever you asked someone they'd say, "I live in San Marcos, but I'm originally from Pittsburgh," or something along those lines. It was rare to find someone who admitted actually growing up in Southern California. Whether it was because few actually considered California home or because everyone seemed so caught up in the fun and sun lifestyle, no one seemed too worried about the ever-increasing socialism that oozed out of Sacramento like puss from a festering wound.

Over time the politicians had enacted enough gun bans to eliminate virtually every gun commonly available on the market. Restrictions had become so onerous that those few people who enjoyed the shooting sports either moved out of the state or lived in a perpetual state of paranoia.

Every once in a while some politician would come along and promise change, saying they'd reverse the encroaching course of government. But their pledges always seemed to be just over the horizon and never quite within reach, and nothing ever changed. Omega had considered moving out of California several times, but in each case he decided to stay and keep up the fight. Maybe it was the engineer in him that loved to work a problem until he found the solution, or maybe it was simply because he wanted to believe things could change. Either way he had never left. Now he found himself lying in a dirt hole wondering if he'd live to see the sunrise.

When his battalion was activated Omega wasn't sure what was going to happen. He'd already been on alert ever since the riots began following the assassination of that de Soto guy. The Chicanos in the South Bay had joined the riot bandwagon pretty quickly, and it didn't take long for whole cities to be engulfed by gangs and looters. The assembly point for his battalion was near Mira Mesa, so he grabbed his gear and drove north from his home in Tierrasanta to meet up with the other fifty members of his unit. Most of his fellow militiamen were in their twenties, with a few older guys who were pushing their mid forties. Due to decades of gun bans his unit didn't have the usual collection of ARs and AKs that were the mainstay of most militias. Instead the closest thing to military weapons patriots in California fielded were rifles the state classified as either collector pieces or "traditional hunting" models.

This translated into mostly Chinese or Yugoslavian SKS rifles, the occasional M1A, and a variety of bolt-action hunting rifles. A few members had cached away banned guns for just such a crisis, but they were in the minority. Most, including Omega, reasoned that a cached weapon wouldn't offer the same advantages as a weapon one could regularly train with. One unintentional advantage his unit enjoyed was almost every rifle fired powerful .30-caliber rounds instead of the smaller .223 calibers the ARs used. This advantage had manifested itself earlier in the day, as they were able to engage targets at a further distance and achieve one-shot kills. The powerful .30-caliber rounds punched through cars, doorways and even cinderblock, making it difficult for the enemy to find effective cover.

But even that advantage was short lived, and Omega quickly found himself in a desperate running retreat. By the third time they'd regrouped, his team had lost thirteen men and eight were wounded. Although several police and border agents had joined them, these "reinforcements" weren't in very good shape. Most were only armed with pistols and shotguns, so they were of little use beyond twenty-five meters. What they did have were cars, and it was these cars that had helped them retreat and not be overwhelmed. By the time they'd arrived at their current location, most of the cars were so full of bullet holes they barely ran.

The night passed without further incident, which was a huge relief to Omega and the others. After dawn broke, regular watches were manned, and the remaining members began to brew coffee and eat breakfast. It had been a cold night. The morning dew settled over the back country, leaving everything and everyone slightly damp. Although wounded, one of Omega's best friends had survived yesterday's action and was cleaning his weapon when Omega walked up with a couple cups of coffee.

"Hey Raven, how's your neck feeling?" Omega asked as he handed his buddy a steaming cup of coffee.

Raven gladly accepted the coffee, holding it between his hands he blew into the black liquid in an attempt to warm himself. "It looks worst than it feels. The medic said I caught a piece of bullet jacket. Thanks for the coffee; I'm freezing my ass off."

"Looks like the medic dressed the wound nicely. You really freaked me out yesterday when you grabbed your neck and I saw blood oozing out between your fingers. I wanted to run over to you, but I was pinned down. It was all I could do to return fire on that machine gun. Man, how'd we ever survive that?"

"That exact question has been running through my mind all night. I thought we were going to die more than a few times yesterday. Unfortunately Franklin wasn't so lucky. Did you see him go down?"

Omega didn't look up when he answered he simply continued sipping his coffee as he remembered watching Franklin die. "Yeah, I did. He had just finished loading a stripper clip into his SKS and stood up to move to the next fighting position when he got hit in the back of the neck. I heard a loud slap and a sort of screaming gurgle. When I looked back Franklin was going down…the whole front of his throat had been blown out. I don't know what was keeping his head on. The good news is that he died quickly." Omega slowly shook his head back and forth as he stared at his dirty boots. "That's something I hope I never see again."

"Franklin was a good guy and a real patriot. I doubt he had any regrets about dying the way he did. I'll tell you another thing…he really knew how to use that old Chinese SKS. Franklin could reload that relic almost as fast as I could do a magazine change on my Mini-14." Raven looked up at his friend with a slight smile. "Remember how he always ate a SPAM on training exercises and how we'd harass him about how the stench that would ooze out of his pores and stink up the whole camp?"

"Yeah, he was a character, all right. I'll tell you what I'll remember; Franklin must have taken out nine or ten guys yesterday before he got killed. Ten-to-one is a pretty good kill ratio. Too bad we lost him."

Raven and Omega continued to quietly chat while drinking their coffee and eating energy bars. After a short break another member of the team ran over in a semi hunch and told them a meeting was being organized in ten minutes. The two militiamen acknowledged the information and watched as the man hurried off to the next fighting position to continue passing on the information.

Once everyone had gathered, a man named Hank Baldwin a.k.a. "Glory" short for "Glory Boy," stood up and addressed the men. Glory was in his mid-forties but had a physique that made many of the younger men envious. At 6' 3" he presented an impressive figure with an imposing bald head, a deeply tanned faced, and piercing, cold, blue eyes. He looked like a Greek god who'd come to life and stepped off his marble pedestal. A retired Air Force Parajumper, Glory was highly regarded and strictly obeyed, not out of fear, though everyone knew crossing him would be a bad mistake—but from the respect that comes from operating in one of the military's most elite units.

Air Force Parajumpers are probably the least known of all the Special Forces. Much is said about the intense and difficult training that the Rangers, Green Berets, SEALs and others go through, and although the hype is justified, the Parajumper training is every bit as demanding. PJ's, as they're known, are a combination of special warfare, combat swimmer, combat medic, and just about any other skill the Air Force could think up. Glory was an appropriate name for someone who purposely parachuted into the middle of a firefight to treat a downed pilot and then extract him under enemy fire.

"Gentlemen," he said. "Before I get started I want to let you all know that what you accomplished yesterday was absolutely remarkable. Each of you stood your ground and returned fire during some of the most intense action I've seen since Mogadishu. You communicated and moved aggressively as a team and never lost cohesion. Yeah, we were overwhelmed, and we retreated most of the day...but that's what soldiers do when they're faced with a superior force. There's no shame in an organized and fighting retreat. We lost good friends and patriots yesterday, but they didn't die in vain, and their sacrifices were not wasted. I know many of you are wondering what's going to happen next; we'll get that worked out. But for now, I want each of you to know that I hold you in the deepest regard and am proud to have fought by your side."

Glory's speech infused the men with a deep feeling of strength and pride. They didn't take his accolades lightly, because they knew they didn't come easily. This man was a professional and had always expected the most from his men. He led from the front. No matter how hard the task seemed to be, he was always the one encouraging everyone else to dig down deeper and pull that extra measure of strength out of their gut and accomplish the task. Throughout yesterday's firefights Omega and the others had looked to Glory as they would a battle ensign, knowing that if they kept their eyes on him and followed his lead they'd be all right. Several times, as they fought off attack after attack, Omega searched the lines for his leader, and each time found him confidently directing his men while effortlessly dispatching the enemy with well-aimed shots from his M-1A.

During one critical point in the battle Omega saw him sling his rifle around his back with one hand, reach down, and literally throw a wounded man over his shoulder with the other while at the same time pulling out his pistol and killing three charging Mexicans with as many shots. If this remarkable act had been witnessed while he was still in the Air Force, Glory would have been recommended for the Congressional Medal of Honor. Unfortunately, the militia didn't have such lofty decorations to present for valor. He might not have received the CMH for his actions yesterday, but one thing he did receive was the everlasting admiration and dedication of all the men who surrounded him.

"Gentlemen, I'm going to be straight with you. After yesterday's losses this unit is combat ineffective. We're too few and have too few supplies to carry on a traditional fight. As you know we've lost our communications and are completely out of contact with any of the other units, so the chance of receiving reinforcements is nil. Anyone who wishes to disband and try to wait out this occupation can leave without any dishonor."

He looked around him. Nobody moved.

Finally, Raven stood up. "I respect what Glory has said," he declared. "And frankly, he's right…if we try to go toe to toe with the Mexican army we'll be slaughtered. But none of that changes the fact that our country has been invaded, and our people have been killed."

"Yesterday we fought, and those that died did so as freemen. There's no way I'm going to bow down while I can still fight. There's got to be another way."

A rumbling of approval spread through the men. One by one they rose to their feet with their rifles in the air and stood in defiance. Glory looked upon his men and saw not only determination in their eyes, but the resolute confidence that bloodied men earn after they've been tested in the crucible of battle. Although their numbers were reduced by half, and they'd been beaten back, they were now more dangerous than they were before the first shot had been fired. The dross had been burned away, and what stood before him was a refined weapon of war.

"Okay," Glory said. "There's still a role for us to play in this conflict. I propose we change our tactics and rain blood and horror upon those who have invaded our soil. Everybody gather around, and let me outline what my plan is."

PLA Headquarters: Hermosillo, Mexico

The atmosphere at PLA headquarters was jubilant. The news that Mexican forces had crossed the border into San Diego and were received as liberators spread like wildfire. Watching the media coverage of thousands of people rushing across the open border was reminiscent of the Berlin wall being torn down. Gone were the long, dreary lines of Mexicans who had to submit to humiliating inspections and interrogations by uniformed thugs before they could enter their rightful homeland. In its place was unfettered joy and elation as Mexicans took sledge hammers, pipes, or whatever they could find to destroy the checkpoints that had separated Atzlán for so long.

Inside San Diego Chicanos drove up and down the streets waving Mexican flags and cheering trucks filled with Mexican army troops. The people of Atzlán celebrated with a zeal that would rival ten World Cup victories. Of course all this had not come without sacrifices, and reminders of those sacrifices were not hard to find. There had been pitched battles against criminal militias and police holdouts. During these battles many brave men had been killed, but as soon as the Mexican army arrived, the Anglo criminals were driven back, and their dead were dragged through the streets and paraded before cheering crowds. Funeral processions were planned for the Atzlán patriots who'd made the ultimate sacrifice for their homeland. Their flag-draped coffins would be carried on the shoulders of their countrymen and blessed by priests before being buried in their newly liberated soil.

Francisco and Carlos were busy coordinating PLA leadership in Tijuana with their counterparts in San Diego and Los Angeles. Because of operational security, up to this point none of the cells had any contact with one another, and much of the cell leadership still resisted open contact with anyone. Old habits were indeed hard to break. Marco Valdez, a.k.a. Flag, was busy organizing the San Diego County OJChA membership to begin coordinating with the Cuban-led UN teams that were scheduled to arrive in Long Beach in the next couple days.

He also coordinated with OJChA graduates who had been elected to local, city, and county positions as well as prominent members of local chambers of commerce. These individuals were the ones operating behind the scenes to keep the Anglos under control and off the streets. For the most part, the Anglos of San Diego and its surrounding cities were following orders and staying in their homes.

Carlos had just finished sending off a communiqué when he was approached by one of the young men who worked with the senior staff.

"Excuse me, *Señor*, but Señor Sanchez would like to speak with you in his office."

Carlos acknowledged the messenger and finished gathering up the multi-page communiqué before heading towards the Syrian's office. It had been decided that the Syrians would continue to use their aliases as long as they were in Mexico, especially around the PLA staff. As the PLA security chief, Carlos was aware of the rumors among staff members regarding the strangers working in the office. The fact that on occasion they were overheard speaking what many believed was Arabic and that they ate differently was not lost on the staff members, nor was the fact that several times a day they sequestered themselves in their offices. The word had circulated that when they did this it was to pray, so it didn't take too much intelligence to assume that Señor Sanchez and his counterpart were Muslim. But, the truth that they were actually Syrian agents was kept under tight guard, and only a few members of the inner circle knew the truth. Carlos had learned early on in his career that to keep secrets. Sometimes it was better to allow a little knowledge to circulate than none at all.

Carlos approached the major's office and knocked on the doorframe before entering. "Excuse me, Major, I understand you wanted to speak with me."

"Yes, Carlos, please come in and have a seat."

The major was sitting behind his immaculately organized desk, and as usual was fingering his prayer beads. "Carlos, I'm deeply disturbed by the images I'm seeing on the television. These pictures of dead Americans and jubilant celebrations taking place in San Diego and Los Angeles are not helping our situation. I want it to stop, and I want you to ensure they are not repeated...do I make myself clear?"

"Major, forgive me, perhaps I do not understand. Our people have won a great victory over their oppressors. This is a time for celebration. These spontaneous festivities cannot be so easily controlled."

"Carlos, I have fought against the Americans for nearly three decades. During that time I have come to understand them and the ways they think. Americans are spiritually bankrupt and have little understanding of faith. As such, they are driven only by what they see. They worship their televisions as gods. In the past, families gathered together in simple rooms where they studied books and listened to inspirational music that lifted their hearts and minds spiritually."

"But today, the common American home is centered on an elaborately decorated room with the sole purpose of accommodating as massive a television as the family can afford. Large, expensive and ornate furniture displays the pagan god in the center of the room, just as that illegitimate god is centered in their lives. Americans spend thousands of dollars to buy bigger and bigger televisions and compete with their neighbors and further demonstrate the level of their devotion by adding theater sound and other accouterments to their temples of worship so even their hedonistic children will find joy in their devotion. While true followers of Allah begin their day with prayer and pray in thanks before they eat, Americans' first act upon waking is to turn on their television. They eat in front of it, sacrifice time with their children in front of it and it is usually the last thing they see before they retreat to their beds at night."

"Entertainers, athletes, and news reporters have become the high priests of American culture. Because they're on television, Americans have endowed them with great power and they venerate them wherever they go. It doesn't matter if an actor has no formal education or if he defiles himself with drugs and harlots, if he tells Americans that black is white and white is black...he's believed. We learned a long time ago that to beat America you must gain control over its media. Why do you think Palestinian funerals are so often shown on American news broadcasts? Why do you think actors have been welcomed by our leaders and given the opportunity to see the greatness of our causes? Even our children and their mothers are trained on how to react when an American reporter is nearby."

"Carlos, one thing I know is that power is a two-edged sword and must be carefully wielded. Just as our enemies will allow themselves to be led by the nose with the right images, the wrong ones will cause them to resist. Pictures of dead Americans being dragged in the streets will anger them, just as it did in Somalia and Iraq. These tapes must be confiscated and never shown again. You must promise me that you will take care of this. Furthermore, you must tell your people to resist the urge to celebrate in the streets. We have to continue to portray an image of a wronged people to the international community. Can I count on you to accomplish this task?"

"Of course, Major." Carlos agreed now that he understood. "I will send word to my people immediately that all tapes showing the desecration of Americans are to be confiscated, and I'll also make sure all future public celebrations are closely monitored."

"Good. I know you will not disappoint me. While your people are dealing with the media, ensure them that in return for those tapes they will be given exclusive access to the funerals of the fallen Mexicans and their bereaved families. I want the world to see the pain and devastation caused by these militias upon widows and children."

"Excellent idea, Major. I will make sure it happens. Will that be all?"

"No," the major replied with a concerned look on his face. "There's one last thing we must discuss. What are you doing about the militias that attacked us yesterday?"

"Señor, they were handily defeated. They ran away from our forces and abandoned their dead. I don't think they'll continue to pose any problems."

"Yes, I am aware that they were beaten back. But, I am also aware that these militias have risen out of the population and have survived despite the best efforts of politicians to destroy them. They may be able to raise popular support among the people if we're not careful. They must be defeated in a dramatic and unmistakable way so the general public sees there is no other practical alternative. I would like you to assist me in organizing our efforts with the Cubans in charge of the UN force. Together, we'll end this militia problem before it gains any traction."

West Valley, Utah

Utah was established in conflict, and its people had retained a sense of independence ever since. When the Mormons arrived in the Salt Lake Valley it was still controlled by Mexico. The Mormons didn't so much travel to Utah as escape there. Years of religious persecution had culminated in a government-sponsored effort to exterminate the group. On October 27, 1838, Missouri Governor Lilburn W. Boggs signed an order directing the state armies to drive all Mormons from Missouri and if need be, exterminate them. The early leadership of the church was specifically targeted and after several incidents where mobs ended up killing numerous people and burning others out of their homes. Their leader, Joseph Smith, surrendered to allow the majority of his followers to escape across the Mississippi river into Iowa. Soon thereafter Smith and his brother were shot to death by a lynch mob that was allowed into the jailhouse where Smith was awaiting a trial. When Brigham Young led his people across the plains in one of the largest mass exoduses in American history, they left everything behind in an attempt to establish a new life for themselves away from the tyranny they'd experienced at the hands of the government. These events cast a lasting impression on the Mormons, and although they later welcomed statehood, they never forgot the sacrifices that were made by their ancestors.

The church grew and prospered, but the leadership continued to stress the importance of preparation and self-determination on their people. Growing gardens, storing food, hunting, and other facets of independent living remained as important to the Latter-day Saints in the twenty-first century as it did in the nineteenth.

For these reasons and many others, the patriot/militia movement had always enjoyed deep roots in Utah. The epicenter of the militia movement in Utah was found along the Wasatch Front that ran from the Idaho border south to the southern end of Juab County.

Earlier, battalions from Kane and Washington Counties in southern Utah had mustered to reinforce the Southern California Command, and were scheduled to arrive within the next couple of hours with additional battalions from Nevada. Now, the bulk of the 45th FF received orders to deploy to Arizona for what P Corps expected to be a major push by the Mexicans into that state.

Porter Glockwell commanded the 35th battalion headquartered near Salt Lake City. Glockwell's unique *nom de guerre* was derived from two sources; the first was a tribute to Porter Rockwell who served as a bodyguard to both Joseph Smith and Brigham Young, and later became famous as a legendary gunfighter in the west. The second was in honor of his favorite sidearm, the Glock. Porter was young for a battalion commander, but all who knew him understood that he was born with a warrior's spirit and a natural understanding for strategy and tactics. As Porter finished copying a flash message sent to him from "P" corps headquarters he knew his life was about to change. The urgent message ordered his group to coordinate with the 5th, 57th, 29th, and 49th battalions and deploy as soon as possible to Arizona, where they would join with additional units from "P" corps to oppose an imminent Mexican invasion.

Porter finished validating the message and then immediately began composing alerts for the battalion commanders listed in the message. He was relieved to see the 5th battalion had been activated and would accompany his. The 5th was based out of Cache County and was led by one of his best friends, Tire Iron. TI, as most called him, was a retired Force Recon Marine, who knew more about tactics and ground warfare than most people would ever have a chance to learn.

TI and Porter had known each other for many years, and it was, in part, due to TI's recommendation, that Porter had been selected to lead the 35th battalion. Both men were avid Glock enthusiasts and regularly competed in local and statewide International Defensive Pistol Association (IDPA) events where they quickly gained the respect and admiration of their fellow shooters. Of the two, TI was definitely the best shooter. His time in Force

Recon and then as a field operative with the CIA had finely honed his shooting skills. He was the current titleholder for both the Smith and Wesson IDPA Winter Championship and the Range USA Indoor IDPA Championship.

The two friends spent as much time together as possible and regularly held joint training exercises with their groups and others along the Wasatch. Knowing that TI's battalion would be part of this deployment gave Porter great confidence in accomplishing the mission, but he was getting ahead of himself. There was a lot of work to accomplish in a very short time.

Chapter 10

People sleep peaceably in their beds at night only because rough men stand ready to do violence on their behalf.
—George Orwell

USS *Connecticut (SSN-22):* Yellow Sea

The USS *Connecticut* silently slipped through the cold waters of the northern Yellow Sea at fifteen knots. Even though she displaced over 9,000 tons submerged, her ultra-quiet hull design and machinery allowed her to create a large, silent void in the ocean. USS *Connecticut* was the second of three *Seawolf*-class attack submarines designed to be the most dangerous hunter-killers in the ocean. Everything about the sub was top-of-the-line and incorporated the newest technology the United States had developed. Its single S6W nuclear reactor could produce 52,000-shaft horsepower, which was enough to make her the fastest submarine in the world capable of exceeding thirty-five knots submerged and twenty knots of indefinite silent running.

In addition to being the quietist and fastest submarine in the world, she was also the most heavily armed. *Connecticut* possessed eight 660mm tubes, which could launch either torpedoes or missiles. On this war patrol she carried thirty-five Tomahawk cruise missiles and fifteen MK48 ADCAP torpedoes. As *Connecticut* approached its designated launching position the fire-control team was busy confirming that the correct coordinates had been programmed for the volley of twenty-five missiles that would soon be launched towards targets on the northwest coast of North Korea.

Commander Todd Conner scanned the tight confines of his command center with an air of authority and confidence that resulted from thousands of hours at sea. Although he held the rank of Commander, *Connecticut* was his command, and that made him the captain, and so his crew addressed him. Commander Conner called the sonar room.

"Sonar...Conn"

"Conn...Sonar, Aye."

"Sonar, report all contacts."

"Conn...Sonar. All clear 360°, fifty miles."

"Roger Sonar. What's the last known position of contact four five?"

"Conn. Last contact, four five was bearing 200°, range sixty three miles."

"Sonar. What's his present predicted position?"

"Conn. Predicted position is bearing One Nine Two degrees, seventy-five miles."

Even though Conner knew *Connecticut* was virtually undetectable, and his sonar had been clear for over an hour, discipline demanded that every precaution be taken to ensure that his boat, crew, and mission were not endangered in any way. Two hours ago sonar had detected a surface contact that was believed to be a North Korean missile boat, probably operating from the naval base at Namp'o, patrolling a corridor that led into the very waters where *Connecticut* now operated. Conner's mission was to execute a series of cruise missile launches against the long-range missile base at Paegun in the North of the Pyongan province. Paegun was one of the bases where Taep'o-dong 2 missiles were stationed. The Taep'o-dong 2 was North Korea's primary long-range ICBM with a 10,000-kilometer range, capable of carrying a nuclear warhead. Due to the high value of these missiles, they were based deep inside the communist state where they were supposedly safe from attack and could be used as a deterrent against the United States. With a 10,000-kilometer range the missile could hit targets from the California coast inland to Phoenix, Arizona. *Connecticut's* secondary target was the five-megawatt Yongbyon nuclear facility where the North enriched the plutonium used in their nuclear weapons program. The North Koreans thought their facilities were safe; they had not considered the ability of a *Seawolf*-class submarine to easily defeat their anti-submarine screens and reach launch points within range of the two highly valuable targets.

Commander Conner decided it was time to prepare for the first launch. Once again he called his forward torpedo room.

"Conn to forward torpedo room."

"Forward torpedo room, Aye."

"Load tubes one through six with Tomahawks, make ready in all respects. Ensure tubes seven and eight are loaded with ADCAPs. Report when all tubes are loaded and prepared in all aspects."

"Aye, aye Captain."

"Conn...Fire Control."

"Fire Control...Conn."

"Begin loading target data Zero Zero One into missiles one through three and target data Zero Zero Two in missiles four through six. Report when the data is loaded and confirmed."

"Aye, Captain."

While the missiles were being prepared for launch the Commander slowed his submarine and ordered the TB-23 Towed Array sonar be deployed. The towed array sonar was a long tube containing dozens of passive sonar sensors that trailed two kilometers behind the submarine. This allowed the sonar room to monitor sounds in a pristine environment well away from any noise created by its host.

As *Connecticut* slowed to ten knots the only sounds picked up in the sonar room were normal ambient sea emissions; there was no indication of close-in surface or submerged contacts.

Confident that his submarine was alone, Conner ordered the towed array to be retrieved, and then the sub was further slowed and brought to launch depth. The forward torpedo room and the AN/BSY-2 fire control system confirmed that all weapons were loaded and ready for launch. Conner double-checked his navigational computer to ensure that *Connecticut* had arrived at its predetermined launch station and ordered the crew to man battle stations missile for tactical launch.

"Conn...Torpedo Room. Open outer doors on all tubes. Fire control, prepare to launch tubes one through six on my command."

Conner turned towards the dive chief and issued a few last orders, "Chief, as soon as these bird fly, I want the doors on all tubes closed. Assume course Three One Zero, bring her down twenty degrees at the bow...depth seven five zero feet and make twenty-two knots. I don't want to wait around to see what turns up after we light this neighborhood up."

"Aye, aye, Captain," confidently replied the chief. "The only thing we'll leave behind is a hole in the ocean."

After confirming with his XO, Conner issued the order to fire tubes one through six. A slight vibration radiated through the submarine as the 3,200-pound missiles shot out of each tube by a charge of compressed air. The Tomahawks were encased in capsules that protected them during the initial launch phase. These capsules separated as the missiles approached the surface, and solid rocket boosters drove the missiles skyward. After achieving proper altitude and orientation, the boosters fell off, and small turbofan engines on each missile took over for the duration of the mission.

After all six Tomahawk launches were confirmed, helm control eased the diving planes down twenty degrees and steered to course three one zero. At the same time, engineering increased speed to twenty-five knots, and USS *Connecticut* disappeared. After a thirty minute high-speed run, the captain ordered the boat slowed to ten knots and a one-hundred-and-twenty-degree turn to clear baffles and ensure they were not being followed. After this clearing procedure, Conner ordered helm to steer towards their second launch station where another six missiles would be fired at their secondary target.

The six TLAM-C Block III Tomahawks reached their cruising speed of five hundred and fifty miles per hour and flew towards their targets. Internal navigation systems constantly checked and updated their positions against their preprogrammed courses via GPS and Digital Scene Matching Area Correlation (DSMAC). The information, provided by the National Imagery and Mapping Agency (NIMA), had been downloaded into the submarine's fire control computers along with its mission orders.

Flying low, the Tomahawks easily penetrated air defenses that did not detect the stealthy missiles with their small radar cross-sections. As they approached the final leg of their mission their internal guidance and navigation components transmitted a burst message to an orbiting satellite, which in turn sent the message down to the Pentagon, updating each missile's condition, position and estimated time on target. Then the missiles executed programmed terminal maneuvers before slamming into their targets.

Just as the six Tomahawks from *Connecticut* approached the Paegun Missile Base they were joined by a combination of TLAM-Cs and TLAM-Ds launched from other assets. While the C-models carried conventional unitary warheads, the Ds deployed submunition warheads that dispersed hundreds of bomblets and spread destruction over a wider area. These bomblets were a combination of shaped charges for destroying equipment, lightly armored vehicles, and bunkers, and immediate and time-delayed anti-personnel area denial mines designed to kill personnel and prevent follow-on forces or rescue assets from entering after the attack.

Ninety minutes later, at the Yongbyon reactor, the second group of missiles from *Connecticut* was joined with dozens of other cruise missiles that had been launched in a coordinated attack from other submarines, surface ships, and aircraft. In total, fifty missiles streaked in from almost every direction of the compass aimed at the reactor and other sections of the Yongbyon complex. As the missiles hit their targets FMU-148 fuses precisely monitored the distance each cruise missile penetrated the reinforced concrete on the reactor's containment dome, then at the precisely correct moment each WDU-36 warhead detonated one thousand pounds of PBXN-107 explosives. The first few missiles blew the containment building apart, allowing the following missiles to dive deep into the facility and completely destroy the reactor core. Radioactive material and debris spread across the entire area forcing damage control crews to evacuate and ensuring the whole facility would be completely consumed by fire.

North Central, North Korea: Near the Chinese Border

Colonel Michael "Spike" Kincaid scanned the liquid crystal displays that were arrayed across the instrument panel of his B-2 stealth bomber, making sure he was on course, and all systems were performing properly. After flying almost eight hours, his squadron of bombers were approaching the release point for their first target of the night. Their mission was to destroy two North Korean Medium Range Ballistic Missile (MRBM) bases, the first at Yongjo-ri and the second a little further north at Chunggang-up.

Both bases were built for the No-dong missile, which is a variant of the Scud-D. By lengthening the missile body, adding larger fuel tanks and more powerful engines, the North Koreans were able to extend the range of the No-dong out to1,500 kilometers. This range allowed the No-dong to target Tokyo, and at the extreme edge of its capability, Taipei. Because of the radical modifications needed to extend the missile's range its accuracy was diminished, giving it a Circular Error Probability (CEP) of nearly two kilometers. For this reason, intelligence sources believed the No-dongs were armed with thickened VX chemical warheads instead of nukes. VX is an extremely powerful nerve agent, that when introduced into the body binds to the enzymes that transmit nerve impulses and prevents them from working properly. This inhibition of normal nerve activity causes the body to powerfully convulse in a constant and uncontrollable fashion until muscles seize, breathing stops, and the heart ceases to function. It is such a powerful agent that it is rated as LD50/ 10mg. 10milligrams is considered a lethal dose for 50% of the people exposed, which is better appreciated when one considers that a typical raindrop weights about 50 milligrams.

Strategically, it was critical that these missiles be destroyed to prevent the conflict from extending beyond the Korean Peninsula. Because of the location of the bases, deep within North Korea, close to the Chinese border, the best way to destroy them was with the B-2. The B-2 was originally designed as a deep-penetration bomber capable of flying into Soviet airspace and avoiding detection by air-search radars. Colonel Kincaid had tremendous confidence in his aircraft, having flown twelve successful missions in Iraq during Operation Iraqi Freedom. He understood the capabilities of the aircraft, and knew he'd be able to complete his mission. His only real concern was whether his flight of bombers would arrive in time to catch the missiles on the ground.

This hope was dashed when Kincaid received an encrypted message notifying him that real-time satellite imagery confirmed the missiles located at Chunggang-up and Yongjo-ri were being fueled and readied for launch. Earlier, naval and air force assets attacked missile bases along both the Yellow Sea coast and the Sea of Japan. During these raids vital missile bases and production facilities were destroyed, and it was thought that the Communists, fearing their remaining missiles would be lost, would launch them in desperation. There was an extremely high probability that the missiles would be launched as soon as they were ready. The liquid fuel used in these missiles was highly volatile and corrosive, so it could not be stored in the missiles for long periods, and even the process of fueling was extremely dangerous. Kincaid knew that if the missiles were being fueled, then the Communists had every intention of firing them. If that happened millions of people would die, and the world's economy would be crushed.

Colonel Kincaid looked over at his co-pilot, Major Steve "Wiley" Baker, who sat to his right. "Wiley, we're approaching our primary LAR (Launch Acceptable Region), confirm the data package is downloaded into the weapons."

"Roger, Spike. I confirm the package designated for the primary target has downloaded targeting information from the main computer, and is ready for automatic release."

Tonight's mission payload included a combination of 2,000-pound deep penetration BLU-109 a.k.a. "Bunker Busters," and Mk-81 500-pound GBU-30s. All the bombs were fitted with the Joint Direct Attack Munitions (JDAM) packages that turned them into GPS-guided smart bombs. The BLU-109s were targeted against underground control and storage facilities, and the GBU-30s were targeted on launch pads, equipment, and above-ground buildings. Each bomb was programmed with the exact GPS coordinates of its target. Once released, fixed aerodynamic control surfaces would glide each bomb to its target without any further input from its host.

"Approaching release point (RP) Alpha," Spike announced in a business-like, monotone voice."

"Roger, all weapons show green and set for computer release," responded Wiley.

The dull-black, tailless bomber flew almost silently at over forty-five thousand feet as it approached the Yongjo-ri missile base. As Spike watched the computer count off the distance to the RP he reached out and pushed a button opening the bomb bay doors on the bottom of the aircraft. "Bomb bay doors open. Release on my mark in three...two...one, mark."

"Bombs away," announced Wiley as twelve JDAMs quickly exited the plane in quick succession.

As soon as the bombs were gone Colonel Kincaid closed the bomb bay doors and pushed the controls to starboard, banking the bat-like bomber into a sharp twenty degree turn away from the RP.

"Shadow Two Zero One clearing RP." Spike announced over the secure squadron frequency.

Even though they were fifteen miles from the missile base, when the bomb bay doors are open they created right angles which dramatically increased the B-2s radar cross section, parting the veil of the bomber's stealthy disguise. Now that they had possibly shown up on the enemy's fire control radar they wanted to exit the area as fast as possible to avoid any unwelcome attention.

"Wiley, how does the ECM threat indicator look?"

"It's clear. Looks like we got away clean."

"Good. Continue evasive maneuver pattern Delta-Two-Niner, and then line us up for our secondary target."

Below them the INS/GPS mechanisms had taken control of the bombs as they glided toward their targets. The inertial navigation system was continually updated by the GPS receivers housed in the nose and tail of each bomb, allowing control surfaces to react and steer the ordnance towards its terminal point of impact. The navigation system is so advanced that if it was to lose data from the GPS receivers, due to bad weather, geography or enemy jamming, the onboard software will calculate the last known position, altitude, speed and angle of attack to develop a new navigation solution.

As the bombs approached their targets, slight adjustments of the flight surfaces were made and the bombs lined up for their terminal phase. Like mythical lightening bolts hurled by Zeus, the bombs exploded across the base. Not only did Spike and Wiley's bombs find their marks, but bombs from the other B-2s in their squadron did as well. The JDAMs were programmed so each target had several bombs tasked on it. A rapid sequence of detonations ripped each target to pieces. When the bombs arrived, several No-dong missiles sat on their launch pads with steam and vapor from liquid gases escaping their bodies. These missiles were targeted at the northern tip of Taiwan and its capital of Taipei with 2.6 million people. In brilliant flashes several GBU-30s slammed into the missiles, which erupted in gigantic fireballs that climbed hundreds of feet into the early morning darkness. The superheated conflagrations caused by the combination of exploding ordnance and the missile's internal fuel quickly destroyed the sticky, amber-colored nerve agent in each missile's warhead in a boiling ball of fire.

The "Bunker Busting" BLU-109s also found their marks, but instead of exploding upon impact their digital fuses allowed the super-hardened bombs to burrow deep into the earth and through multiple layers of reinforced concrete as they counted off the depth in milliseconds before detonating. Their primary explosives created enormous geysers of flame and dirt that burst out of the ground. The underground command bunkers were destroyed, and everyone inside was either torn apart or suffocated as their lungs burst from the overpressure created by the massive blasts. Within seconds the Yongjo-ri base was in ruins, and the threat of its No-dong missiles was gone.

****

Spike and Wiley changed course toward their second release point, Chunggang-up. This target was located precariously close to the Yalu River, which marked the physical boundary separating North Korea from the

People's Republic of China. It was across this river that 200,000 soldiers of the People's Liberation Army had attacked US and UN troops in November of 1950, leading to the largest fighting retreat in US history. Out of respect for Chinese airspace their flight plan called for approaching the release point from the east so the chance of errant ordnance or accidentally crossing the Yalu would be avoided.

As procedure dictated, the two pilots once again checked the computers and ensured the appropriate targeting data was programmed into the weapons. But as they sped towards their designated release point, the skies ahead of them suddenly filled with anti-aircraft fire. Evidently, survivors at Yongjo-ri had been able to warn their sister facility that an attack was underway. Although the triple-A created an impressive nighttime display, the deadly fire was well ahead of the B-2s. As before, their release point was nearly twelve miles from the missile base. While Col. Kincaid prepared for the second release, his co-pilot's attention was jerked away, "Look!" Wiley shouted while pointing towards his one o'clock, "Holy Mother Mary, they're launching their missiles!"

It was unmistakable. The bright bloom of the missile's booster rocket lit up the sky in 360 degrees as the tall slender missile crawled upwards towards the heavens. This was definitely a ballistic missile launch and not a surface-to-air missile.

Spike transmitted to his home base. "Shadow Two Zero One to Bat Cave. Jalapeño, I say again...Jalapeño." The message was a codeword that was to be used in the event the North Koreans managed to launch any missiles prior to their strike.

Just as he finished his transmission, another brilliant light erupted indicating a second launch.

"Bat Cave...Shadow Two Zero One. We understand Jalapeño. Please confirm."

"Shadow Two Zero One...Bat Cave. I confirm Jalapeño. Over."

No words needed to be spoken between Spike and Wiley; they both understood that these missiles were probably targeted on Tokyo. Like the No-dongs at Yongjo-ri, they were also believed to carry VX warheads. The wide scale release of this nerve agent over Tokyo could kill an estimated fourteen million people and go down in history as the greatest loss of life suffered by any country in the history of mankind. The only thing they could do about it was to make sure they released their weapons correctly and knocked out whatever was still on the ground. The fact that the monsters who callously launched the missiles would receive instant retaliation, made what they were about to do that much easier.

"Approaching release point Bravo in three...two...one, mark."

"Bombs away," Wiley said as though scripted.

Colonel Kincaid threw the controls over and pushed his stealth bomber in a hard banking turn to port. "Climb to 60,000 feet and assume course Three Zero Zero. We've got an air defense corridor coming up in ten minutes. Let's stay sharp."

As the B-2s turned southeast on their long journey back to their bases in Okinawa, their deadly payload of JADMs streaked to their targets and obliterated all remaining missiles and launch facilities at Chunggang-up. Nevertheless, the Communists had managed to launch two No-dongs, and despite the high-tech B-2s and their equally impressive JDAM bombs, death on an apocalyptic scale was streaking towards Japan.

Port of Long Beach, California

On this typical Southern California morning, overcast skies obscured the sun, and transparent dew moistened the ground. Cutting slowly through the water, two large, white military transports eased into dock with the assistance of several tugboats. On the sides of both Roll-On/Roll-Off (RORO) ships were huge light blue UN markings. From the sterns flew the UN flag. A grandstand decorated with blue and white bunting stood about twenty meters from the edge of the dock. Seated in the grandstand was an entourage that included the Secretary General of the UN, the Honorable Yasan Al-Latif Al-Duri, who was the first man from Yemen to be chosen for the top position at the United Nations, Governor Ernesto Buenamonte (D-CA), Governor Barbara Slater (D-AZ), the mayors of Los Angeles and San Diego, several dozen city council members from L.A. and San Diego, and leaders from the Mexican Army and the Aztec Nation.

Once the gangplank was extended Señor Valentine Drago walked off the lead ship and was warmly greeted by Secretary Al-Duri. Drago was the head of the United Nations Commission for Democratic Transition and would be the interim leader of Aztlán until a president and congress could be elected. The two men shook hands, then briefly embraced and kissed one another on the cheeks.

"Your Excellency, I am honored to report that the UN Commission for Democratic Transition has arrived and is ready to begin operations as ordered."

"Thank you for your outstanding efforts in putting this commission together so quickly; your hard work was desperately needed. Please have your personnel disembark and assemble for their official orders."

Drago nodded to the Secretary General, and then in military fashion pivoted 180 degrees until he faced the lead ship. After a momentary pause Drago yelled out his directions, "*Attention all UN personnel, disembark and assemble for official orders!*"

On cue, large doors that made up the bow of the ship opened wide. A huge articulated ramp unfolded, and extended until it rested securely on the dock. Once the ramp locked into place, a column of white, Soviet built BTR-80 APCs rolled off the ship and maneuvered into a parking area to the right of the assembled dignitaries. Doors on both sides of the vehicles opened, and eight soldiers exited from each vehicle. The soldiers wore camouflage uniforms, field gear, and blue UN helmets and armbands.

More menacing were the assault weapons carried by each man. The soldiers smartly marched to the front of their six-wheeled vehicle and stood at attention, creating well-organized formations several ranks deep. Following the APCs was another column, this time of US-made HUMMVEEs also painted brilliant white with UN markings. The all too familiar vehicles poured off the ship, some configured as ambulances and others towing trailers. After the HUMMVEEs had exited the freighter, large trucks loaded with equipment rolled down the ramp. Finally, dozens of motorcycles streamed off the ship and found their place besides the others. While this was occurring long lines of soldiers carrying large duffel bags over their shoulders, marched off both ships and formed ranks beside the vehicles.

Drago watched with great pride as the men paraded in front of him. Even as it was occurring, he found himself amazed it was actually happening. Although he was in the US in a non-military role, he was still a Colonel in the Cuban army and commanded the peacekeeping force. His primary duty was to help establish a working government for the people of Atzlán. But before that could happen he needed to stabilize and pacify the situation, and that was where his troops would come into play. On the trip to Long Beach he'd read reports of battles between the Mexican army, Aztec Nation, and the so-called citizens militias. If the reports were accurate these militias did inflict losses, but in the end they were defeated and forced to retreat. Hopefully they had learned a lesson and were finished with their foolishness. On the other hand, if they weren't, he would gladly grind them up.

The main obstacle to success, as both he and the UN saw it, was that Americans had for too long been allowed to own personal weapons. This archaic idea had long since passed into history. Governments around the world had learned that it was far easier to govern if the people were disarmed. Even powerful western democracies like Great Britain and Australia had disarmed their people. The UN had made several attempts to disarm the United States, and had almost achieved an agreement with the Clinton administration, but in the end was unable to accomplish the job. Drago's first task would be to "collect" all privately owned firearms. He'd received support from the UN Commission on Small Arms to offer payment for the weapons that were voluntarily "donated." But he knew that Americans were spoiled and obstinate, and that not everyone would cooperate. So he would simply use the Dealer Record of Sale (DROS) files that were collected whenever a firearm was sold or transferred in California, as well as the California Destructive Weapons and Arsenal Permit (CDWAP) applications. Although DROS forms went back decades in California, the CDWAP was a more recent form of registration.

The CDWAP law required that anyone who owned more than three firearms or five hundred rounds of ammunition register with the state as an owner of an arsenal. Anyone who failed to register was subject to police raids and imprisonment. The added advantage of CDWAP was that it had to be renewed every two years and could only be canceled upon certified inspection by the Attorney General's office that the previously owned weapons and ammunition fell below the CDWAP standards.

Since this information was more current, it would prove most helpful in Drago's efforts at confiscating illegal weapons. Without weapons and ammunition the militias would crumble, and the process of governing would be greatly eased. But Drago understood that the problem was far greater than simply guns. American's had developed a kind of cult of personality around the entire concept of firearms and the aggressive accoutrements that accompanied the culture of the gun. Therefore all surplus and sporting good stores would be closed indefinitely. This same problem had existed in Japan, and to a lesser extent, Germany following World War II. Ironically, to remake Japan into a modern democracy the United States had outlawed personal ownership of firearms and even swords, basically outlawing the traditional Samurai and Bushido cultures. The end result was the Japanese became a more pacified people, who, rather than focusing their efforts on aggression, redirected themselves towards being honorable citizens and improving industry.

Time and time again, when people rejected the eighteenth century notions of independence and embraced the superiority of socialism, lives and society improved. Sure, America was powerful and possessed an economy that was the envy of the world, but it was the result of capitalistic imperialism. If you were to eliminate all of the resources Americans stole from their puppets in the third world, and all the oppression and exploitation of workers...the system would fall apart. The capitalists in America rode on the backs of the weak and helpless and then lauded themselves for the great economic machines they built. Just as Marx predicted, the workers here in Aztlan had risen up against this great injustice and thrown off the chains of their oppressors. He was going to ensure that their courageous victory bore fruit.

It took nearly an hour for all the UN peacekeepers to assemble. In total, over four thousand troops had come from Cuba, Venezuela, and Paraguay to make up the multi-national force. These troops would be reinforced by another four-thousand Mexican troops who were already assembling in San Diego. As the last of the ranks firmed up their formations, Señor Drago walked erectly to the podium that was positioned in front of the grandstand. Drago looked over the parking lot full of peacekeepers while he withdrew several folded sheets that contained his speech from his suit coat.

"Secretary Al-Duri, Governors Buenamonte and Slater, and assembled dignitaries. When I was in school, I dreamt of becoming a physician. I believed there was no greater calling than that of a healer. I watched the tireless efforts of the doctors in my small town of Santiago de Cuba, as they healed the sick and strengthened the lame. One day the local doctor arrived at our humble home to assist my mother in giving birth to my little sister. Since our home was small, the entire procedure took place in the main room, and our whole family watched as the doctor helped our baby sister into the world.

"I remember thinking that if I could only do that, I would consider myself a success. Unfortunately, my desires outweighed my abilities. I never had the grades necessary to enter medical school, so I ended up pursuing other professions. I found great success in the military and later as an administrator, but I never lost my admiration for doctors.

"It's been many, many years since my sister was born, and I've come to grips with the fact that it was not my calling to heal and bring new life in this world. But as I stand before you today, I do so with a renewed spirit of enthusiasm. After thinking my dream would never come to pass, I have been selected to lead this UN mission where I will be able to help heal the wounds and pains of an entire people, a people who have been denied their most fundamental entitlements, a people who have made the noble sacrifices, establishing, once again, a homeland for their posterity.

"What we hope for is a rebirth of an ancient people and culture, one that existed long before imperialistic Europeans colonized this hemisphere. I am humbled and grateful to the world community for this chance to help bring to light this new country, which possesses an ancient soul. I would like everyone gathered together here this morning to appreciate our task. We are here as an international force, operating under the authority of the global community to help, not to hinder; lift up, not put down; and serve, not rule.

"In their wisdom the people of Aztlán and the leadership of the UN have agreed to allow members of the Latin community to assist our brothers to establish a new homeland where they can take their place beside the other great and equal nations of the world. As the American President, Abraham Lincoln said, '...with malice toward none with charity for all.' These should be the words we use to guide our efforts. To the Anglos who live within the new boundaries of Atzlán: I promise that you will be respected, to the extent that you respect the authority of the UN and your Chicano hosts. Since human rights and government obedience represent the most critical issues for the building of a society, the new constitution of Aztlán will be founded upon the United Nations Universal Declaration of Human Rights. The international community, to assure all people are extended the privileges entitled to citizens of the global community, has crafted this document. As our two races have worked and intermixed for nearly two centuries we have learned to live together. I sincerely wish to continue a harmonious coexistence. We can work together and we will. To further assure cooperation and understanding, the provisional government will provide mandatory cultural sensitivity training for all Anglos within Atzlán. These reeducation programs will help non-Chicanos better understand and repent of the crimes and discrimination that the Atzláni people have suffered from for so long."

"Now, with the permission of the Secretary General, I will read the formal orders for this force: Men and women of the United Nations Commission for Democratic Transition and the Latin American multi-national peacekeeping force. Your orders are to assist the new homeland of Atzlán to establish a viable democratic government and secure the privileges of citizenship as members of the world community. You are hereby ordered to use all your abilities and resources to accomplish this mission as set forth by the United Nations and to ensure that the UN flag will fly as a beacon of hope for all people."

The crowd erupted in applause as Drago finished. Drago turned and once again shook hands with the Secretary General and then with the two Governors before surrendering the podium to Secretary Al-Duri.

Al-Duri gripped the podium. "As the Secretary General of the United Nations, I thank Señor Drago for his inspired remarks and add that I am confident in his abilities to accomplish this great task.

"Without further delay, I direct you to the duty to which you have been ordered. The people of Atzlán and the people of the world thank you for your service. You are dismissed."

Another cheer rose up from the assembly, followed by commands barked out by officers. The soldiers mounted their vehicles, and in an orderly fashion, began to exit the port facilities and spread out into the city. As the convoy of APCs, trucks, cars and motorcycles made their exit, the dignitaries remained in the grandstand congratulating and taking pictures with each other. After thirty minutes the officials loaded into a number of black limousines, which whisked them off to a special luncheon reception being held in their honor at the sprawling estate of an international movie star who had always been a fan of the United Nations and its attempts to promote globalism over national sovereignty.

USS *Shiloh*: Operating in the Sea of Japan

USS *Shiloh* was part of the USS *Reagan* (CVN-76) battlegroup designated Task Force 14. The *Reagan* was the newest *Nimitz*-class carrier in the fleet, although she would soon lose that title to the USS *George Herbert Walker Bush* (CVN-77). Task Force 14 consisted of three Arleigh Burke-class guided missile destroyers, the *Decatur* (DDG-73), *Howard* (DDG-83) and the *Stethem* (DDG-63), two *Los Angeles*-class fast attack submarines, the *Santa Fe* (SSN-763) and the *Portsmouth* (SSN-707), and two *Ticonderoga*-class guided missile cruisers, the *Lake Erie* (CG-70) and the *Shiloh* (CG-67).

In addition to the incredible power projection capability of the *Reagan*, all three destroyers and both cruisers incorporated the Aegis combat-control system, the most advanced seaborne radar deployed in the world. The name Aegis was derived from Greek mythology. Aegis was the name of the armor created by the God Zeus for his daughter Athena. Both *Shiloh* and *Lake Erie* possessed the latest generation of the powerful Aegis SPY-1B multi-function phased array radar and the equally advanced Standard Missile-3, making both ships part of the Navy Area Theater Ballistic Missile Defense (NATBMD).

Since *Shiloh* had participated in some of the initial trials of NATBMD, she was designated the command ship for any ballistic missile threats. Because of this capability Task Force 14 was stationed in the southeast portion of the Sea of Japan near the Western inlet of the Tsugaru Straits that separated Hokkaido and the home island of Honshu.

This location provided *Shiloh* and *Lake Erie* a clear detection window of any ballistic missiles that might be launched at Tokyo from North Korea. Since the defense of the Japanese homeland was a critical part of Task Force 14's mission, the Japanese Maritime Self-Defense Force (JMSDF) deployed one of their four Aegis-equipped destroyers, *JDS Myoko* to operate in conjunction with the powerful US cruisers. Together, the ships of Task Force 14 represented what very well could be the most technologically advanced and formidable fleet to ever patrol the ocean.

Captain Patrick Robinson was on his bridge, and had *Shiloh* operating at Threat Condition 3, when a quick alert came in from NORAD, the North American Aerospace Defense Command, located inside of Cheyenne Mountain, Colorado. A "quick alert" was the term used to identify the detection of a ballistic missile launch.

"Captain, we're receiving an alert from NORAD on two tracks originating from the Chunggang-up missile base in North Korea. NORAD is confirming this is a dual-phenomenon alert with high confidence. Missiles are believed to be No-Dong MRBMs targeted at Tokyo," reported a young, second-class petty officer.

Captain Robinson knew he had very little time to act. NORAD normally detected a missile launch from the heat bloom it emitted during its boost phase. On a medium-range missile that initial phase usually lasted less than five minutes, just enough time to allow the missile to reach the altitude needed for its ballistic trajectory. "Contact the rest of the task force and make sure we have a clean link with all ships and are tracking the targets. I'm going to CIC."

"Aye, Captain," reported the watch officer. "Captain has left the bridge."

By the time Captain Robinson entered the high-tech Combat Information Center the powerful SPY-1B radar had already acquired the targets, and the large center plasma display was tracking the missiles as they began the ascent phase of midcourse flight. The Fire Control Officer stood to attention and saluted the captain as he entered the CIC. "Captain, we're locked onto two incoming tracks, designated vampire one and two. Fire control shows green lights; ready to launch for a mid-course interception."

"Captain," said the tactical control officer, "TAO recommends, *Lake Erie* engage vampire one with two SM-3s and we target vampire two."

"Roger. I agree. Make it happen."

The two cruisers' fire-control systems were digitally networked, as were the radar systems of the smaller, but equally powerful destroyers. The difference was the *Shiloh* and *Lake Erie* deployed upgraded SM-3 surface-to-air missiles that were designed especially for the NATBMD system.

This gave them dual-purpose capability, as standard surface-to-air missiles and anti-ballistic missiles (ABMs). The SM-3 is similar to the SM-2 Block IVs carried on the destroyers for anti-air and cruise missile defense, but they incorporate a third-stage rocket motor, an advanced GPS/INS guidance computer, and a LEAP (Lightweight Exo-Atmospheric Projectile) warhead.

"Aye, aye, sir. Fire control, TAO, engage vampires one and two!"

In rapid succession, four SM-3 missiles exploded out of the MK-41 vertical launch systems located on *Shiloh's* and *Lake Erie's* foredecks, leaving only a trail of thick, white smoke to trace their swift ascent. In the CIC a slight shudder and a muffled roar confirmed the launches. The computer displayed the missiles as white triangles that quickly moved across the combat information screen. The SM-3 utilized a fully encrypted data downlink to communicate with the ship's computer, allowing the fire-control team to monitor and send additional inputs to it throughout its flight.

"Bridge, CIC. This is the captain speaking; bring the ship to general quarters and watch for signals in the air to reposition the battle group...we're not going to be here for long."

"Captain," reported the missile officer, "all missiles are operating within parameters. They're currently eighty kilometers downrange and have acquired their targets."

The four SM-3 missiles burned through their third-stage motors and sped toward their targets at more than Mach 3 with a closing rate exceeding four miles a second. In the nose of each missile, dual-band, long-wave, infrared seekers locked onto the small cross-section returns of the incoming warheads and calculated the exact moment to release their own kinetic warheads (KW).

Unlike most surface-to-air missiles, the SM-3 did not use an explosive warhead controlled by a proximity fuse. Due to the incredible speeds inherent in ballistic missile defense, the differential velocity of the target often exceeded the speed of the exploding warhead on the ABM. Frequently the enemy warhead bypassed the explosion with little or no damage. This was the case with the Patriot missiles used in the first Gulf War. Although their guidance was accurate, their fuses were too slow to fully destroy the incoming SCUDs. The answer was the development of a nominal kinetic warhead (NKW) that hit the incoming warhead head-on, annihilating it.

As the four ABMs reached their terminal phase, the sailors on board *Lake Erie* and *Shiloh* earnestly watched as the red and white triangles raced toward one another. The two SM-3s from *Lake Erie* were first to reach their target. The symbols converged, and vampire one disappeared. The CIC erupted in a roar of satisfaction and jubilation.

"Settle down!" the captain ordered. "That's only one; there's still another one to go."

Quickly, the men regained their composure, and all hands watched the track identified as vampire two. The first SM-3 released its KW and missed. Suddenly, a sickening pall befell the sailors as they realized only one missile stood between success and catastrophe. Silent prayers passed like lightening through the minds of the men as the last SM-3 merged with vampire two and destroyed it.

Now, the captain allowed his men to revel in their accomplishment. He shook his XO's hand before collapsing in his chair, as a wash of adrenaline seemed to pour out of his body, leaving him instantly exhausted. He would not have to live the rest of his life wondering why he couldn't prevent the deaths of fourteen-million people.

The captain pulled himself out of his chair and walked towards the exit. As he left the air-conditioned confines of the CIC, he looked back at his XO and informed him he was returning to the bridge to radio the Admiral onboard the *Reagan*. Task Force 14 immediately changed course and moved sixty miles north, northeast as a precaution against possible enemy detection. Once they arrived on station, Captain Robinson secured *Shiloh* from general quarters.

Direct Action Academy

Desert Scout entered the room where most of Arrow's team had gathered. "All right, gather around; I just got off the radio with P Corp command. My orders have been changed. Since Corps command has lost contact with the 73rd battalion, they're considering them either destroyed or taken captive. Without a local unit to coordinate efforts, Corp command is reassigning us to this AO. I've been ordered to inform you that the13th BN 48th FF has been re-designated as the Southwest/Arizona Command, henceforth inarticulately known as (SWAZCOM)."

"What exactly does that mean?" AK asked.

"That means we've been designated as the core of what will become a regional command," Cowboy interjected. "I assume we'll be reinforced?"

"That's affirmative," said Desert Scout. "In addition to my two battalions, the 57th, 29th, 49th, 35th, and 5th battalions out of northern Utah, the entire 43rd and 44th Field Forces, as well as the two Washington State battalions currently en route have been temporarily attached to this command."

"What about the Oklahoma battalions that are mustering? Will they end up with us?" Hot Dog asked.

"As for now, they're in limbo. P Corp isn't sure what's going to happen with them. But they believe it's better that they're forward deployed. I guess that way they can fill any gaps that pop up. I'm sure by the time they arrive we'll know where they can best be used. Now that the Mexicans and the UN have a foothold in San Diego and Los Angeles, Corp Command believes their next move will be to take Arizona."

"There's not much we can do for California, but we'll consolidate as much manpower as possible here. Hopefully we can stop any further incursions."

Desert Scout checked his notes and then continued. "Militias all over the country are mustering and asking permission to get into the fight. Command says to expect the better part of the 15th FF from Kentucky, the 16th FF from Tennessee, and most of the 38th FF from Colorado within the next ninety-six hours."

"Who's going to command SWAZCOM?" Arrow asked.

"Command has been given to the current CO of the Utah 5th battalion. His name is Tire Iron." Desert Scout grabbed an empty chair and sat down. He looked a little pale. "I attended a multi-state FTX about a year ago sponsored by the 45FF and operated with him. TI is top notch and a strong leader. He'll do an excellent job."

"I've heard a lot of good things about Tire Iron," Gringo interjected. "He's a regular on the training boards, and is highly respected throughout the militia."

"Hey, buddy, are you all right? Arrow asked Desert Scout with a hint of concern in his voice. "You look kinda sick?"

"I'm fine. I just realized I haven't eaten in almost eighteen hours."

"Well, we can fix that." Arrow confidently announced. "Wildcat, why don't you show our friend where the break room is and make sure he gets some chow. We're going to have to start making some serious plans before all these troops arrive." Looking over at the two Company Commanders that accompanied Desert Scout, Arrow told them, "You guys need to tell your men that plans have changed, and they'll be staying here for now. Have them set up tents and post guards for the night."

"Sounds like a plan," one of the men said before heading off.

AK held up a pad of paper on which he'd been scribbling some notes. "Arrow, I've been doing some rough estimates. It looks like we'll have upwards of eight-thousand men showing up in the next four days. That's a lot of camo and guns. We can't fit everyone here, and keeping a low profile will be out of the question. I suggest we use DAA as a staging base for units as they enter the region, then move them elsewhere."

"They'll need a place to organize, rest, zero in their weapons, and prepare for field operations. Our facility is perfect for that. But for the main base of operations, we should get a hold of Thor's uncle and find out if we can use his ranch. Considering the situation, I doubt he'll have any objections to having additional security."

"That's exactly what I was thinking," answered Arrow. "Thor, why don't you contact your uncle and clear things with him? Be sure to tell him we're expecting several thousand men, and find out what supplies he'll need that we can provide." Thor nodded and began to dial in the Double C's frequency on one of the shortwave radios.

Arrow turned toward the others. "We're going to quickly run out of supplies. Our personal food stocks would have lasted us several months, but they'll never last now. Even if all these units have supplies with them, we'll need more. I'd like to hear suggestions on how to get more food. Any ideas?"

"The local stores are out of the question. They've been looted to the walls." Ghost remarked. "Gringo, do we still have a few cases of MREs at the house, or did you bring everything?"

"Yeah, we still have five cases in the back storage room. Five cases won't go very far...but it's a start."

"Good," said Arrow. "Mike, put a team of ten men together and gather up whatever you have at your house. Then drop by my place and scavenge whatever you can find there. Hopefully, the gangs haven't broken into our homes...yet."

AK had been standing in the doorway intently listening to the conversation. "I think I might have an idea. As you know, I'm a member of the Church of Jesus Christ of Latter day Saints; the Mormon Church is very strong here, almost as big as in Utah. Our members are counseled to assemble a year's supply of food storage for emergencies. To assist members the church owns a big warehouse and cannery in Mesa. I've volunteered there before. They've got tons of food. Let me call a friend of mine who's a local leader and find out if they'd be willing to help us out."

"Great idea! Grab a phone and get hold of him right now. If he's willing to help, tell him we can have a convoy of trucks over there within an hour." Then Arrow added, "And make sure to tell him we'd be willing to trade whatever we can spare in return."

As AK took off in search of a phone, Mike grabbed Hot Dog and Slim and the three of them walked outside to where the New Mexicans were setting up their bivouac. Mike identified one of the Company Commanders that had been in the communications room. "Hey buddy," Mike hollered to get the man's attention, "I could use your help."

"Sure, what can I do you for?"

Mike jerked his thumb at his companions. "My handle is Gringo, this is Hot Dog, and he's named Slim."

"You can call me Blackjack," the New Mexican replied. "Good to meet you guys."

"Blackjack, we need seven men to come with us and look for supplies. We're not sure what to expect so they'll need full second-line gear...can you help?"

"No problem. You can have one of my squads." Blackjack turned towards the mass of men and equipment that was spread out between the two large CQC houses. "Delta squad, form up on me with full second-line gear."

Eight men sprung into action gathering and donning gear. A couple of minutes later the squad assembled around Blackjack, attentive for their orders. Blackjack introduced his squad leader, "Wolf, this is Gringo. You guys are going to help him and his buddies secure some supplies. Listen up for the mission details."

Gringo shook Wolf's hand and introduced him to Hot Dog and Slim, then began to explain the mission. "Here's what we're going to do. I have several cases of MREs and a few other items at my house, we're going to retrieve them and then do the same at another house. When I left home, four days ago, things were beginning to get bad. Although looters hadn't yet entered my neighborhood, I don't know what has happened since then. We're going to assume the worst and be ready for trouble. If looters are in the area they'll probably be armed, so we'll be equipped with full second-line gear and loaded weapons. Unless we encounter a dangerous situation, all weapons *will* be safed. Condition two will be maintained on all weapons, rounds chambered, and safeties on. Understood?"

Everybody acknowledged the order.

"We'll be using two trucks to convoy to the objective. Communications will be via FRS radio: channel 11 sub-channel 25. Let's keep it simple. My team will be designated, Alpha, and Wolf's team will be Bravo. Our mission is to retrieve supplies and observe the condition of the area for intelligence purposes. We will not engage unless engaged, understood?" Once again, everybody acknowledged the orders. "Good. Wolf, designate a man as security. I want one person from each team to stay with their vehicle to act as a rear guard while the rest gather the supplies. If there are no further questions, we'll meet up at the flagpole in ten minutes for a weapons and comms check before leaving."

More than four days had passed since Gringo left his home, and he had no idea what to expect. As the two trucks drove north on Power Road they began to see evidence of looting and riots. Burnt out cars littered the side of the road, and they occasionally passed abandoned furniture and even a broken television lying in the middle of a street. Dogs and cats occasionally sprinted across the road in front of them.

Gringo wondered if these were unlucky pets that were left behind, or if they were simply strays. Otherwise the streets were unnaturally empty.

After a short while, Gringo radioed the other truck. "Alpha to Bravo. We're going to take the next left into the subdivision at our ten o'clock."

"Roger, Alpha. We copy."

As Gringo made the turn he saw an impromptu barricade set up across the opening of the subdivision. It looked as though the residents had set up a defense.

"Bravo," Gringo radioed, "stay cool and keep your weapons out of sight. I'm going to walk over to the barricade and talk to these people. Keep an eye on the situation and cover my six. Over."

"Roger, Alpha. We got your six."

Gringo slowly exited the truck and made sure the people could see his hands were empty. In a deliberately calm voice, he announced, "My name is Mike West. I live in this neighborhood. My friends and I have come to gather a few items from my home. May I come forward and speak to someone in charge?"

As Gringo scanned the makeshift barricade made of old cars, gardening equipment, and construction materials, he noticed several rifles pointed at him. Although he was conscious of them, he also knew the firepower backing him up was far more significant. One man worked his way forward and called out to Gringo, "What's your address?"

"2256 West Calle del Sol. It's a tan and sage-green ranch style house with a Mesquite tree and an Ocotillo out front."

There was a pause during which Mike assumed the man was checking a map. Then the same voice called out again, "Where have you been? Why did you leave?"

Several thoughts passed quickly through Mike's mind, but just as fast he decided that the truth would be the best way to proceed. "I'm a member of a citizen militia, and my unit was activated four days ago. I had to meet my other team members at our rally point. I've been there organizing other militia units from outside the state ever since. I have some of them with me."

"We're here to recon the area and see what we can do to help and to gather a few items I left at my home. We'd like to pass through your checkpoint and talk. Will that be okay?"

There was a long and, for Mike, a very uncomfortable pause. Finally, the man spoke. "All right, one truck at a time."

Mike radioed back to the other truck, "Bravo. Follow me through the barricade...slowly. They want us to pass one at a time, so wait until I'm through and then proceed. Keep your weapons down and out of sight, and stay in the truck until I radio for you to dismount."

"Roger that Alpha." Wolf replied.

Mike slowly drove his truck through an opening and parked around a corner as instructed by one of the neighborhood guards. After Bravo's truck had pulled up behind him, Mike shut off the engine and then slowly stepped out of the truck and walked toward the man who had signaled him past the barricade. As Mike approached the man he presented his hand in greeting.

"Frank Weatherspoon is the name. I'm in charge of this post. Why don't you ask your friends to get out of the trucks and wait here. We're having one of your neighbors come out to positively ID you."

"Good to meet you, I'm Mike West. That's a good idea. By the way, my men are armed." Mike hoped his openness would alleviate any possible problem.

"I'd expected that," Weatherspoon replied. "Hell, everybody's armed these days. Just tell your men to leave their rifles in the trucks until your neighbor gets here. It's a protocol we've established, and everybody has to obey it. After that I doubt anyone will have a problem with your men carrying their weapons."

Mike radioed the instructions to both teams, and they stepped out of the trucks and huddled around the doors. Within a couple minutes a man Mike recognized arrived in a golf cart and walked up to Frank. "Chris, do you recognize this guy?" Whetherspoon asked.

"Yeah, he lives up the street from me." Turning his attention towards Mike, the man asked, "You have a white SUV, right?"

"Actually, it's dark green." Mike replied.

"That's right. Yeah, he's all right."

Mike gave the other members of his team the thumbs up. They retrieved their rifles and walked over to join him.

"Frank, this is my team. This is Slim, Hot Dog, and this is Wolf. The rest are members of his unit. They're from New Mexico and have been assigned to our battalion."

"Battalion? How many men do you have and where are you?"

"Between the New Mexicans and my group we have close to two hundred men. We're expecting several thousand more reinforcements within the next twenty hours from Utah, Wyoming, Colorado and Washington. More are on the way, but they'll take a little longer to arrive."

"Wow, those are impressive numbers. You say men from Utah are coming?"

"Yeah. Why?"

"Well, you might want to speak with the guy in charge of this neighborhood watch organization. He's some sort of leader with the local Mormon Church. When all hell broke loose a bunch of men from that church came around and helped our families gather up what we needed and then evacuated everyone to their building. It turns out they had food, water and other supplies and were happy to share with us. All our families are at the church. The neighborhood men have been manning these barricades to keep the gangs out."

"Have you had any trouble?" Slim asked.

"Not long after we manned the barricades, several gangs tried to get into the division and there was some shooting, we put up a pretty determined defense and haven't had much trouble since. Unfortunately, some people who were driven from their homes in other subdivisions began arriving...they weren't as well prepared and lost just about everything."

"It looks like you guys have done a great job here. I'm glad to see you've all stepped up and taken control of the situation. Who's this guy you mentioned...the Mormon leader?" Mike asked.

"His name is President Wilcox. He'd probably like to hear that people from Utah are on the way. I'd guess many of them would be Mormons as well; at least that's what I'd suspect...Utah is full of Mormons...right? You know, I moved out here from Chicago about two years ago and I was surprised how many of them lived here. Not too many LDS in Illinois. I'm told they were driven out about a hundred years ago." He chuckled. "Glad they don't hold a grudge. Anyway, they've been very helpful and that Wilcox guy seems pretty squared away. I'll have your neighbor drive you over to the church to meet him. In the meantime, your men can go to your house and look for the things you left."

"Thanks, Frank. I left a few cases of MRE's and some ammunition. Since you guys have been guarding it, I'd like to share with you."

"That would be nice. What caliber of ammo do you have?"

"5.56mm, do you have any rifles chambered for that?"

"Not many. But if it's all the same to you, we'll be happy to take some off your hands. We've been bartering a lot lately, and ammo is better than money. I'm sure it'll come in handy."

Mike turned towards his group and issued orders, "Hot Dog, take charge of the detail. Drive over to the house and gather up all the MRE's and ammo I left in the safe located in the back of my closet. Load the truck and then drop off a couple cases of food and five hundred rounds of 5.56mm to this gentleman. When you're done, join me at that Mormon Church on the other side of the subdivision. Once you get to the house radio me and I'll give you the alarm code and the combination for the safe." Mike tossed a key for his front door to Hot Dog and then pointed at Slim, "You're with me."

Mike shook Frank's hand and thanked him again. Then he and Slim climbed into the golf cart and the man that had identified Mike drove them across the subdivision to a large church.

"This is pretty big. I'd bet it holds well over a thousand people." Slim remarked.

"Yeah, it's pretty large," the driver said. "They have a traditional chapel, but there's a section inside with a basketball court and stage, I think they call it a cultural hall. There's also dozens of small classrooms, some offices and a kitchen. We've converted several of the classrooms into a makeshift hospital and two amateur radio operators have set up communications in a couple of others. The rest of the space is being used for living areas. I have to admit, this building is an ideal location for a community shelter." They pulled up in front of the main entrance. "Go through those doors and tell the first guy you see that you're the two men sent from checkpoint four. Just ask to see President Wilcox."

"Thanks for your help." Slim added.

Mike and Slim walked into the church and was approached by a young man, probably eighteen years old. "Hello," said Mike. "We were sent here from checkpoint four to meet with President Wilcox. Can you help us?" Mike asked.

"Sure, follow me," said the youth as he waved Mike and Slim into the foyer. "The president is in a meeting with some other leaders."

The young man led the militiamen down a hallway, stopping at a door labeled High Council Room. After knocking, he opened the door, poked his head inside and announced something before opening the door the rest of the way and motioning for Mike and Slim to enter. "Gentlemen, this is President Wilcox."

Wilcox was a tall, slender man with thinning sand colored hair, a deeply lined tanned face and a warm inviting smile. He had the look of a rancher, common in this part of the valley, and walked with a gait that betrayed a lot of time on horseback. A long wooden conference table surrounded with padded chairs dominated the office. On the wall hung religious pictures, some of Christ and others of men Mike didn't recognize. One person he did recognize was Chief Meadows. He was seated at the table with a couple of other men. Wilcox walked over to Mike and Slim and gave both men firm handshakes. "I understand that one of you live in this area." The Mormon leader said with a slight down home drawl.

"Actually, we both do. My name is Mike West and this is my friend Josh Eckman, he rents part of my house over on West Calle del Sol."

Chief Meadows stood up, walked over to Mike and Slim and aggressively shook their hands. "President, I can vouch for these men, I know them. They run the Direct Action Academy down in Queen Creek. They've worked with my officers." Dan looked back at Mike and with a smile said, "Mike it's good to see you."

"It's good to see you too, Dan. How are things going?"

"Actually, the chief was just telling us what was happening when you walked in," President Wilcox added as he pulled out a couple chairs for his new guests. "By the way, I'd like to introduce Father Spencer O'Brian of the Our Lady of Lourdes Catholic parish and Pastor Robert Gravely of the Community Baptist church. Both of their congregations are currently meeting at the local elementary school until they build churches, so we offered our facilities as a temporary refuge."

After shaking each man's hand the group sat down and Chief Meadows began to explain the situation. "Basically, the majority of Phoenix, Tempe, Scottsdale and Mesa have been taken over by the Aztec Nation. After several days of rioting and looting, the situation has stabilized, due to the governor's announcement that this area will become part of Atzlán. I guess they don't want to destroy what soon will belong to them? There's no doubt Governor Slater and several other members of the City Council have been working behind the scenes, with the Aztec Nation, to bring this to pass."

"Do you have any proof that elected officials are involved in a conspiracy?" Father O'Brian asked rather abruptly.

"No. I don't have proof of any conspiracy. I should say that this information represents my feelings and those of several other law enforcement officials, both local and federal. But, this has happened too fast not to have been arranged in advance. Also, we've been getting a lot of harassment from elected officials about arresting people and deterring further actions against the community." The chief laughed bitterly, "In fact, I should be arresting Mike because he's admitted to being in the militia. The governor has made it clear that she blames this crisis on the militias and has signed an executive order outlawing them."

"I appreciate your restraint, Chief." Mike said with a sympathetic smile. "You know as well as I do that the militia didn't cause this crisis. It was caused by a series of events that, I agree, seem to have been prearranged. First, the bombings in the two cities that are now set aside to become Atzlán followed by the Hoof and Mouth outbreak that has been traced back to animals in both states. Finally, two serial killings targeted on Mexican-Americans, also in California and Arizona. It can't be mere coincidence."

Pastor Gravely spoke up, "I know UN forces have arrived in Long Beach and are establishing themselves from L.A. down to San Diego. When do we expect them to arrive in Arizona?"

"The information I've received from contacts in California," added Meadows, "is that the UN peacekeeping forces are going to consolidate their strength in California before moving into Arizona. They want to secure the ports and make sure the larger cities are pacified. They know that if the president decides to use the military, he'll try and take Southern California back before worrying about Arizona."

"From what I've heard, the UN believes it'll be a quick job to placate Southern California. There're a hell of a — excuse me, gentlemen (Slim interjected in deference to the religious leaders) — an awful lot of Mexicans and Chicanos already in the state, they've got the support of all those Hollywood personalities, and frankly the residents have very few personal weapons. For these reasons and others, it looks like we have a small window of opportunity to make plans before they begin to come our way."

"Chief, these sources of yours...what are they doing and what's the chance that Washington will intervene to stop this?" President Wilcox asked.

"My sources are in the FBI and DEA. These are people I've worked with over the years and who I trust. Currently, they're maintaining low profiles and trying to stay off the radar screen. There's a powerful faction in Washington that couldn't be happier this is happening. They believe it will show a major weakness in the administration's management of the country. They've lost so much power over the last couple decades that they see this as the only way to regain what they once had. They recognize that millions of new voters will arise out of this and believe their party be the beneficiary of those votes. If this is true, it could solidify their hold on power for a whole generation. Anyone working for the government who looks to be resisting is being immediately reassigned back east or fired."

Father O'Brian shook his head in disbelief. "I just can't believe this is all politically motivated. With all due respect to your sources, Chief, I can't imagine anyone in Washington is willing to go to this extent to gain a little power. It just smacks too much of a conspiracy theory."

"Father, with all due respect, I didn't say *anyone* in particular was behind this. Frankly, I'm pretty confident that this caught everyone in Washington off guard. What I am saying is that given how quickly all this happened and how few options Washington has been left with, there are some who are exploiting a terrible situation." The chief took a breath and chose his words carefully. "It's no secret that there are many on the left that support giving greater power to the UN and have been angered by this administration's policies of unilateralism. Those same people would have a very hard time opposing the UN after all the support they've given them in recent years."

"Frankly," O'Brian said, "I'm a bit conflicted on this matter. I know many of my parishioners are looking towards the UN for help. You're talking as if they're as much an enemy as the Aztec Nation."

"If you think Aztlán is going to be an enemy, Father, then you'd better get used to the notion that the UN will be as well. The one is bringing the other." The chief blurted out.

Mike had sat patiently listening to the exchange, but couldn't keep quiet any longer. "Father, I appreciate the difficult position you're in. I'm sure you have the best in mind for your parishioners. The fact that you've gathered together in this interfaith effort attests to that. But you need to understand that our country has been invaded by armed forces intent on seizing our sovereign territory. No matter how many Mexicans are in this country, legally or illegally, this is still the United States of America. Americans have been killed and the UN has taken the side of those who've done the killing."

"Yes, I understand that people have died," the priest said. "We've all seen the death and destruction. But the UN has arrived to end the bloodshed and help restore order."

"They've arrived to squash any opposition to the new government of Aztlán. Our rights will be eradicated and we'll have to live under a pseudo-constitution modeled after the United Nations Declarations of Human Rights. Father, have you read that document? Do you understand that it would forbid the Catholic Church from excluding women from the Priesthood, force you to recognize homosexual marriages and regulate what you can preach? I haven't been to church for years, but I know the position the Pope has taken on those issues and they're not compatible."

Mike looked around the room, purposely making eye contact with all those present. "This isn't a religious issue. This is about an invasion of the

United States. Regardless of our individual values, or for that matter your political beliefs, we're Americans and we have a duty to protect and defend our country against *all* enemies, foreign and domestic. As unbelievable as it may seem, the majority of the US military is deployed overseas and our enemies think we're defenseless. But, they've overlooked the original armed forces of America, the citizen's militia."

"Currently thousands of armed, trained and equipped men are converging on Arizona to stand and fight against these invaders. As one of the leaders of the local militia I'm here to ask for your support."

"Where do you get your authority from and *who* put you in charge?" Father O'Brian's tone was sharp and defensive.

"Father, nobody here is looking for power or position. I'm here to tell you that I'm preparing to go into battle to preserve your freedoms. We're walking onto the battlefield to fight; just as our forefathers did and just as so many of our neighbors are doing right now in foreign lands. I don't have authority to demand anything of you. So, I'm asking for whatever you're willing to offer. If there's nothing you are willing to give…so be it." Mike looked around the room and waited for someone else to speak. Following an awkward pause, President Wilcox spoke up.

"Well, Mr. West, what can I do for you?"

"I don't have many resources, but if I can help I'd like to," added the Pastor.

"My son, although we don't completely agree I appreciate your dedication to freedom and your willingness to stand up for your fellow countrymen. If I can help I will." Father O'Brian said humbly.

Gringo took a deep breath. "Gentlemen, there are over eight thousand militiamen on their way to this area. They're expected to arrive within the next fifteen hours. More will come in the following days. The plan is to use the academy as a troop depot where each unit can make final preparations before deploying into the field. We have the space and the facilities, what we're lacking are food and support personnel."

"President, one of our men is a member of your religion. He tells me your church owns a large food storage facility in Mesa. I understand that your people rightfully have first claim on these supplies, but I'm hoping there's a way for us to get some of it." Mike knew he was asking a lot. After all, he wasn't a Mormon and this man didn't know him. Surely there were lots of Mormons who also needed these supplies. He hoped his request didn't seem too presumptuous.

Wilcox frowned. "I'm a Stake President, in charge of several wards in this area. I don't have the authority to open the storehouse to just anyone. But, I know who does, and I'd be willing to present your case. What are you going to need?"

National City, California

Omega sat in an observation post overlooking a large "Park and Ride" location where a UN gun amnesty collection point was set up. Even before the UN peacekeepers arrived, public service announcements (PSAs) were broadcast informing the public that all private ownership of firearms was now illegal. The announcements made it clear that out of "respect" for the cultural and historical importance of firearms in America, individuals were allowed to keep firearms that were deemed historical or family heirlooms as long as the barrels were welded shut and the internal firing mechanisms destroyed. This was all part of the UN's ongoing effort of eliminating the global private ownership of firearms. The program had started in July 2001 with the *Conference on the Illicit Trade in Small Arms and Light Weapons in All Its Aspects*. On the surface the goal of this conference was to help eliminate the millions of small arms that were being used in civil wars and insurgencies that plagued many developing nations. What it really was, was a UN strategy to disarm all private citizens and ensure that only governments and the UN itself possessed weapons. This effort received funding from internationalist minded billionaires and non-governmental organizations like: the *International Action Organization on Small Arms* and American anti-gun groups like the *Brady Campaign, Violence Policy Center* and *the Coalition to Stop Handgun Violence*.

Hollywood celebrities, pop singers and other cultural icons enthusiastically encouraged their fellow Californians to turn in their guns and help rid the state of a "deadly disease." The PSAs equated the eradication of guns to the 1950's campaign to end polio. One socially conscious actress reminded Californians how the UN had lead the way in the eradication of polio, which had destroyed the lives of so many children. As pictures of boys and girls lying in iron lungs and hobbling with ungainly metal braces on their legs flashed across the screen, the images morphed into pictures of gunshot victims and what appeared to be children lying dead on playgrounds. Then in a quivering voice the actress implored her fellow Californians to turn in their weapons, and added, "Part of being socially responsible includes the willing sacrifice of lesser, antiquated freedoms for the greater good of the global community. With the help and leadership of the UN, California will finally wipe out the grim reaper that is gun violence."

Omega lowered his binoculars and rubbed his tired eyes. He'd watched the collection site since it began setting up, making notes on the number of "blue bonnets," as his group had begun calling the UN peacekeepers, that were present and how they'd set up their equipment. He noted how often the guards were relieved, what weapons they carried, whether they had counter-sniper units, the type of communications they used and even how they reacted to the occasional troublemaker.

Raising the binoculars again he continued to monitor the scene below, but this time he focused on the people waiting in line to turn in their weapons. It was obvious not everyone was thrilled to be there. The expressions of regret and frustration were hard to mistake and Omega could make out a sadness that dimmed the countenances of the people. As they waited in line UN soldiers stood guard and occasionally used the butts of their rifles to encourage the line to move forward.

Every once in a while one of the foreign invaders would see a unique or especially ornate gun and arrogantly snatch it from its owner and then tuck it away in his personal stash. After surrendering their firearms each person grudgingly filled out a form that included their name, address, social security number, occupation and thumbprint, and in return received twenty dollars in cash and a twenty dollar gift certificate to K-Mart. As the loathsome tragedy played out, Omega couldn't help but remember a passage from Alexander Solzhenitsyn's book *The Gulag Archipelago*:

And how we burned in the camps later, thinking: What would things have been like if every Security operative, when he went out at night to make an arrest, had been uncertain whether he would return alive and had to say good-bye to his family? Or if, during periods of mass arrests, as for example in Leningrad, when they arrested a quarter of the entire city, people had not simply sat there in their lairs, paling in terror at every bang of the downstairs door and at every step on the staircase, but had understood they had nothing left to lose and had boldly set up in the downstairs hall an ambush of half a dozen people with axes, hammers, pokers, or whatever else was at hand? ...The Organs would very quickly have suffered a shortage of officers and transport and, notwithstanding all of Stalin's thirst, the cursed machine would have ground to a halt!

Although it was difficult to watch, he reminded himself that these were people who'd had the opportunity to fight, but chose not to. Even though he didn't like watching anyone disarmed, he reasoned that, none of these people could be counted on to help in the struggle so having them disarmed wasn't that big of a hindrance. If everything continued as planned, tomorrow morning the blue bonnets would get a taste of the hatred they'd already begun to earn.

After regrouping in the hills behind Otay Lakes, Glory had reorganized the remaining members of the 73rd battalion into a guerrilla force that would focus on ambushes and sabotage. The only way they could continue to fight was to adopt an unconventional approach. Glory began by instructing the remaining members of the 73rd in the art of manufacturing improvised explosive devices (IEDs), enhanced reconnaissance, field craft and evasion, escape and resistance techniques. The group made changes to their web gear so street clothes could more easily cover it. One creative idea included magazine pouches that were incorporated into a chest harness and redesigned so the openings were oriented upside down. This allowed the militiaman to reach under his shirt or jacket and retrieve a fresh magazine faster and with less trouble.

The men of the 73rd battalion were awakened the next morning at 0230 to prepare for their ambush. It was cold and very dark which made getting out of their sleeping bags that much more difficult. But, to move into position long before the UN arrived it was better to leave while most people were deeply sleeping. The team arrived at their predetermined locations around 0415. The eight men formed four teams of two. One was the primary shooter with a .30-caliber and the other his spotter armed with a .223. The purpose of the spotter using a lighter caliber was simply to allow him to carry more ammunition and be able to lay down a greater volume of fire to cover their retreat. But if all went as planned, there shouldn't be much resistance after the initial engagement.

As the sun rose in the eastern sky, Omega nudged Raven who had taken a few minutes to get some sleep. Now that the sun was coming up they both needed to be extra vigilant.

"If the Blue Bonnets are on schedule they should show up in another two hours," Omega whispered. "Let's keep our eyes open and make sure nobody's doing counter-surveillance."

"Okay, you take the twelve o'clock to nine o'clock and I'll watch twelve to three," Raven said in a still drowsy voice.

As the hours passed, the two men kept a close eye on their sectors making sure to examine everyone that entered or passed through. Just before 0830 the post to their left radioed that the UN APC was in sight and moving towards the parking lot.

"Alpha one to team, Pinto approaching corral."

Omega felt his stomach tighten and realized the time he'd awaited had arrived. Omega and Raven watched the APC stop in nearly the same spot it had done the last three days. As though choreographed, the engine shut off and the two side doors opened. The six-man team exited the APC and made a cursory examination of the area before setting up the table, collection bin and signs that identified the firearms collection point. Today was the second to the last day for voluntarily turning in your weapons. After tomorrow anyone found in possession of a firearm would be arrested and charged as an enemy combatant. Everyone expected the collection points to be busy today.

In the minutes leading up to the ambush Omega and Raven took turns checking their rifles, gear and avenues of egress. Everything looked good and they both knew they were ready. The way the mission was planned, the Team Leader would begin the ambush and the rest of the team would take out their predetermined targets. One team was positioned in a drainage ditch close to where the APC was set up. Their job was to rush the enemy position and spray the interior of the APC to ensure everyone was dead, and then set a demolition charge inside the engine compartment. Before leaving they'd quickly gather whatever intelligence or special equipment they could find, while the rest of the squad provided cover.

Omega nervously looked at his watch, it was almost time. His primary target was the radioman at the small table just outside the APC's right door. Sitting with his back towards Omega he created an inviting target. Omega's secondary target was a private who, at the moment, was blissfully smoking a cigarette while leaning on the front of the vehicle. Omega carefully focused his aim directly between the shoulder blades of the radioman and concentrated on slowing his breathing. Although only seconds passed, it seemed like an eternity before the first shot rang out.

Without hesitation, Omega squeezed the trigger. He didn't notice his M1A bucking against his shoulder. The radioman seemed to rise up in his seat and then pause before slumping over the radio. As Omega shifted his aim to his next target he heard Raven fire two rapid shots making sure his smaller caliber bullets dispatched his target. Although only seconds had passed since the first shot, Omega's secondary target was already moving.

Omega's first bullet caught the man in his left hip, which immediately knocked him to the ground. Looking over his sights, Omega watched as the man fought a losing battle between trying to crawl away and dealing with the tremendous pain that accompanied his shattered hip. Unfortunately, most of his body fell on the opposite side of the APC, giving him protection. But as he writhed in pain the back of his head rocked back and forth, each time entering Omega's sight picture. Focusing his aim at one spot Omega watched as the target's head once again appeared, and then he fired. The bullet entered just under the man's left ear and bore into his skull, tearing through his brainstem. As soon as Omega had dispatched his second target, the firing stopped. The ambush was a classic example of controlled and sudden violence. Omega scanned the kill zone below, but he could only make out dead bodies. As he began a magazine change, the sapper/intelligence team sprung from their secluded position and swiftly rushed towards the APC. Before entering, they fired several rounds into the interior. The others moved from body to body checking for any intelligence, stuffing whatever they found into pouches that hung off their LBE's. A sharp two-tone whistle from the APC caught another man's attention. He ran into the armored vehicle before quickly emerging carrying several shoulder fired anti-tank missiles. Another team of militiamen appeared and whisked the missiles away as they left the area. Soon after that the Team Leader blew his whistle signaling the withdrawal.

El Cajon Pass: San Bernardino, California

For several days Stalker's command had received intelligence on the disposition of the UN forces in Long Beach. He knew his troops were on the top of the UN's target list. Stalker had no delusions: going toe-to-toe with armor was a fool's bet, especially with the weapons his men possessed. Fortunately, reinforcements had arrived. The 3rd, 17th, 23rd, 21st and 33rd battalions from Nevada and the 25th and 53rd battalions from southern Utah brought an additional 750 men to Stalker's command which gave him a little more than 1,450 armed and trained militiamen.

An additional benefit was that due to the relatively friendly gun laws in Nevada and Utah, the 3rd and 53rd were designated as heavy weapons battalions. This was due to the many crew served and fully automatic weapons they possessed. Stalker's command now possessed six M2 .50-caliber heavy machine-guns, eight M1919 .30-caliber light machine guns and even a couple of World War II-era, German MG-34s. In addition to the crew served weapons the two battalions possessed a handful of fully automatic and silenced small arms and a surprising number of .50-caliber rifles.

Even though the addition of these units, and their weapons, made a vast improvement in their firepower, Stalker would not allow himself to be comfortable until he had enough weapons to easily knock out whatever the UN threw at him. To give his forces an edge he decided to get creative and assembled a group of men who had experience with explosives. Most of these men had served in the military, but a few were from the mining business. An added benefit was that those who'd served in the military had studied the strengths and weaknesses of Soviet era equipment. Since the UN's APCs were Soviet built BTR-60/70 and 80s, these men immediately understood where they needed to target the vehicles. The BTR 60s and 70s were used by the Soviets in Afghanistan, and the *Mujahiddin* quickly identified many of the weaknesses of these fighting vehicles. Six tires instead of tracks drove all three models. In the earlier designs these tires did not incorporate run flat technology; this was corrected on the 80 series. Another major problem was that highly volatile gasoline engines powered the BTR 60s and 70s. If a .50-caliber, armor-piercing incendiary round could be fired at the top of the engine compartment, there was an excellent chance of destroying the engine and stopping the APC cold. The question was whether the Russians had upgraded all the vehicles they transferred to the UN; the consensus was they probably didn't. If this was the case, then Stalker's men would have an excellent chance at achieving mobility kills, and that was very nearly as valuable as complete destruction, because it would force the men inside to dismount and fight in the open where the militia's lighter arms would be more effective.

• The plan the demolition squads came up with was to manufacture landmines and deploy them in the expected avenues of approach. The problem was they didn't possess the high-tech military explosives that allowed smaller ordnance to take out armored targets. Instead they'd have to use larger bombs with lower explosive yields. What they decided to do was to bury command-detonated mines assembled in 55-gallon plastic water barrels filled with ammonium nitrate and fuel oil (ANFO). Hopefully, when the APC's drove over the mines, the detonations would tear through the lightly armored bottom plating and kill everyone inside.

The Hummers would pose a lesser problem. Most employed either a .50-caliber or .30-caliber machine gun in an exposed turret. Although fighting against that kind of firepower would not be easy, at least the tables were level now that the heavy battalions had arrived. Looking over the plan before him, Stalker began to feel more confident in his ability to hold off a UN attack. He had three major advantages: He was fighting on his ground; the topography was in his favor and he was the defender.

Stalker walked to his chair and tired to relax for the first time in nearly ten hours. His mind continued to reel with all the preparations and issues he'd been working to solve. One image continued to dart in and out of his mind, and that was how history seemed to be replaying itself. He commanded a ragtag group of rugged American patriots who understood the value of freedom and gathered to face a superior army of Mexicans for the control of a vital outpost. Stalker laughed and thought, "*If it was March 1836, this could be the Alamo.*"

Chapter 11

> If ye love wealth greater than liberty, the tranquility of servitude greater than the animating contest for freedom, go home from us in peace. We seek not your counsel, nor your arms. Crouch down and lick the hand that feeds you; May your chains set lightly upon you, and may posterity forget that ye were our countrymen.
> —Samuel Adams

Base of the 73rd Battalion: Otay Lakes, California

After cleaning their gear and getting something to eat, Omega, Raven and the rest of the men gathered for an After Action Report (AAR) on this morning's ambush. First, and most important, all men from both ambushes were accounted for and all targets were destroyed, save one.

Both teams returned with valuable treasures. Alpha Team, to which Omega and Raven belonged, retrieved several shoulder fired anti-tank rockets and a number of fragmentation and white phosphorous grenades in addition to valuable documents. Bravo Team, led by Glory, also returned with grenades. But they'd also found a portable short wave radio and most importantly, a prisoner.

In all, thirteen UN peacekeepers were dead and two APC's destroyed. Not to mention the psychological affect that the attacks would have on both the enemy and those civilians who had welcomed the invaders. "*All in all, not too bad for a bunch of rebels,*" Omega thought to himself.

The prisoner was being held in a tent with Glory and a couple other former military guys. From where Omega sat he could see the blindfolded young man kneeling on the ground with his bound hands held high above his head. Normally, he would have been killed in the ambush, but Glory had noticed he wasn't wearing a uniform and thought that might be significant. If nothing else he could have been a Chicano who happened to be in the wrong place, with the wrong people. Either way, it didn't seem right to kill him. Right now, the kid was probably wondering if a quick bullet to the head would have been preferable.

Glory had made it clear that the prisoner wasn't to be tortured and made sure everyone understood that wasn't going to happen in his unit. But he was undergoing "intense persuasion" as Glory put it. It looked a lot like torture to Omega, though he said nothing. Evidently, the military had taught Glory that it's human nature to want to talk and everyone had a limit where they'd start cooperating with their captors. In most cases trying to get someone to talk right away is futile.

Instead, it's important to throw off a prisoner's natural defenses. With some, this is as easy as showing them your not a monster and actually care about others. But most, must first be made very uncomfortable, tired and often hungry. This was the case with today's prisoner. Glory quickly determined he was both angry and somewhat educated, so he'd need to lose some of his natural physiological defenses. Since the prisoner considered himself a "tough guy," Glory decided to see how long he could tough it out.

A rope was stretched across the tent and tied so it hung about four feet off the ground. The prisoner was stripped naked and made to kneel on the ground under the rope. Then his arms were raised and wrists tied so that the rope passed between them. The game was simple. The prisoner had to remain in a kneeling position with his arms raised and couldn't allow them to touch the rope. For the first half hour this didn't pose much of a problem, other than the physiological effect of being naked and blindfolded in front of your enemy. But after forty-five minutes your arms, back and legs begin to burn and your hands begin to fall asleep. After an hour the pain becomes nearly unbearable and the prisoner begins to reevaluate his level of cooperation.

Glory said some very sadistic instructors had used this particular form of persuasion on him during his Survival, Evasion, Resistance and Escape (SERE) training. Not only had he endured the difficult training, but since PJ's were considered high-risk individuals, he was forced to endure the much more difficult level-C course. Over the length of the course he'd lost fifteen pounds due to stress, sleep and food deprivation. That experience taught him that no matter how tough you are, you'd reach a point where you'd do just about anything for something as simple as a short amount of sleep or thin pumpkin soup.

The prisoner wasn't a military man and it was apparent that he wasn't use to extreme physical or mental stress. Not long after the first hour he repeatedly allowed his arms to fall and rest on the rope. Each time, Glory lifted his hands with a stick and calmly reminded the prisoner he needed to keep his arms up. As the minutes passed this was repeated with greater frequency. After two hours another former SERE graduate, Eightball, entered the tent.

"Glory, I'm here to relieve you so you can get some chow. How this dirtbag doing? Has he decided to cooperate yet, or is he still being a tough guy?"

"Why do you always have to call everybody a dirtbag?"

"I don't. Sometimes I call them assholes."

"Oh I'm sorry. I underestimated your highly developed vocabulary. Listen, when I get back I don't want to see any bruises, or blood on his guy. Understand?" Glory ordered Eightball in a stern voice.

"Hey, I'm a professional," The baldheaded man said with a smile. "I never leave bruises. By the way, someone found some chickens and they're very tasty, just like the gospel bird my Granny use to cook in Alabama."

"Great, I'm starved." Glory answered as he stood up and collected his hat. "I'll be back in an hour. Remember, no rough stuff."

The whole exchange had been rehearsed specifically for the prisoner's benefit, of course. The idea was to allow the prisoner to become accustomed to a certain level of stress and then as they began to find an amount of comfort in it...snatch it out from under him. This tactic continually ravages the system and keeps the subject mentally off balance. This is commonly known as the classic good cop, bad cop routine and even though it is widely known, it remains one of the most effective interrogation methods used worldwide.

"Well sweetheart, how're you doing?" Eightball said as he took a drink out of a hidden flask. "You may not know this, but I was in the group that killed all your buddies this morning. I've got to admit," he said with a devilish chuckle. "I felt a special kind of joy watching your friend's guts being blown out and spread across the pavement. It smells terrible, not too much different than when we slaughtered pigs in Alabama. But then again, I don't remember enjoying watching the pigs die as much as I did watching all you spics get butchered."

Eightball could see the prisoner's muscles tighten up and knew he was hitting a nerve. The tighter the muscles became the faster they fatigued, and just as quickly his arms dropped down. This time instead of the gentle nudge that Glory gave him, Eightball swatted him in the testicles with a wooden switch. A sharp jolt of intense pain darted up through the prisoner's stomach and lodged in his throat.

"Oh, I know that hurt." Eightball said with a mocking look of concern. "I'd keep my arms up if I were you. But then again, maybe you're one of those faggots that enjoy the rough stuff. I think we might have just found some common ground," Eightball added with a heavy Southern drawl that was beginning to reek of cheap booze. "You're a mas-o-chist and I happen to be a sadist. As my Granny always said, 'it's a small world.'"

For the next hour Eightball tormented the prisoner both physically and physiologically until he was a sobbing mass of flesh. Several times during the process the prisoner tried to speak, but Eightball wouldn't allow it. Before long the prisoner subconsciously associated speaking as a type of rebellion against his tormenter. This was a textbook example of reversed psychology.

Now, instead of playing the role of the tough guy, the subject yearned for Glory's return and was eager to tell him about his horrific treatment. Glory had watched the whole ordeal from outside the tent, and determined it was time to make his entrance.

"You were right Eightball," Glory said as he entered the tent. "That was some tasty chicken. How's our guest doing?"

"We got along just fine." Eightball answered.

Glory took a quick look at Marco, "Why are his balls all red? I told you not to hurt him!" Glory yelled. "You're a sick bastard...you really get off on this type of thing, don't you?"

"Hey, he's the enemy and that's what happens to scum who invade my country and kill my friends...but then again I guess that wouldn't matter to a Beaner lover like you." It was difficult for Eightball to play the role of a racist and harder still for him to yell at Glory. They'd been close for years, but it was all part of the game and it needed to be played convincingly.

"Is that booze I smell on your breath? Get the hell out of here you redneck asshole, before I turn you in." Glory yelled as Eightball exited just out of earshot."

Glory leaned down and placed the prisoners wrists on the rope, but Marco's arms immediately shot upwards in a conditioned response, "No, it's all right. Take a couple minutes and relax. Look, I'm sorry you were left alone with that asshole. I knew I shouldn't have trusted him, but I really didn't have a choice. Are you all right?"

The prisoner began crying again, not so much out of pain, but a sense of relief. Through his tears he submissively muttered, "Yes, I'm all right. You're right that guy is a complete asshole."

"Yeah, he's got something loose in his brain. I think he was dropped as a child." Glory replied as he smiled at Eightball and flashed him the thumbs up.

"I'm very thirsty. May I have something to drink?"

"Sure...by the way, what's your name?"

"My name is Marco Valdez. I'm an American and a student at SDSU."

UN Headquarters: San Bernardino County, California

The UN Peacekeeping forces established their forward base of operations on the campus of San Bernardino City College. Drago assigned a Venezuelan General named Miguel Puentenegro to head the strike force that would destroy the criminal militia dug in just northeast of his current location. The UN forces had helicopters that they'd used for aerial reconnaissance of the enemy positions, and from what they could see the militia didn't have much firepower. The mission of Puentenegro's strike force was to destroy the enemy forces and reopen the vital El Cajon pass. This is a critical roadway because it is one of the few major corridors connecting Southern California with Nevada, Utah and the other Rocky Mountain states.

Interstate 15 is a vital to California's interstate commerce and to get the supplies needed to sustain the vast population of the Los Angeles basin, the UN needed to reopen this thoroughfare to guarantee food and other commodities remained readily available. It was hard enough keeping such a large population under control, and having them hungry wouldn't help. The key to occupation is normalcy. The more normal things remain, the less people feel as though they need to take risks.

Drago sat in a leather club chair smoking one of his favorite cigars, a Cohiba Siglo III, while he listened to General Puentenegro's intelligence briefing. The General had an excellent record as a soldier and had recently completed a tour on the Venezuelan border with Columbia where he had fought several engagements against the right-wing paramilitary forces of the AUC (Autodefensas Unidas por Colobmia). The AUC was led by Carlos Castaño, who had also been involved with the notorious death squads known as "*Los Pepés.* "They'd fought a clandestine war on behalf of the Columbian government against Pablo Escobar, and were currently engaged in a similar war with the leftist FARC (Revolutionary Armed Forces of Colombia), clandestinely supported by Venezuelan President Hugo Chavez. Interestingly, since the demise of Pablo Escobar and his drug cartel in the late 1990's, the FARC had assumed the majority of the cocaine trafficking in Columbia to fund their war against the government.

Chavez, who was elected President in 1998, had led a failed coup attempt against his government in 1992 while serving as a Lt. Colonel in the Army. Since his election he'd been very open about his Socialist views and his close friendship with Cuban Dictator Fidel Castro. The two leaders had met several times and in exchange for buying Venezuelan oil at a discount, Cuba has trained many of Chavez's most loyal military leaders, including General Puentenegro. It was while visiting Havana that Drago and Puentenegro met for the first time. When the UN intervened in the Aztlán crisis, Drago had recommended Puentenegro for command of the peacekeeping forces.

"This is a recon photo of the El Cajon Pass that was taken two days ago," Puentenegro said, indicating an enlarged photo with a wooden pointer. "You'll notice that additional reinforcements have arrived. Until we destroy these forces and secure this area, militia units will continue to flow into Aztlán from the Rocky Mountain States and beyond. As you know, this pass is bisected by Interstate 15. The militia has constructed rudimentary blockades here, here and here." The General indicated. "These obstacles do not concern us. But on this photo, which was taken early this morning, we see evidence that the enemy has dug up a number of areas on the highway. We're not sure what they're doing, but we have to believe they've mined the roadway."

A Captain spoke up from across the room. "General, up to now, it has been believed that the militias do not possess military grade explosives. Have we received intelligence to the contrary?"

"No. We have received no such intelligence, but we have to assume they have and take appropriate precautions. Therefore, I am suggesting that we deploy our armor up the sides of the pass. Major Lopez, your call sign will be

Lima 12 and you'll attack up their right flank. Major Blanca, your call sign will be Bravo 11, you will take the left. We will precede your attacks with a direct assault straight up the highway. We'll utilize a combination of APC, Hummers and dismounted infantry to hold them in position and focus their attention to the front, while your two elements execute a classic pincer movement."

The General set his pointer down and casually approached the assembled officers. "Remember, these are unorganized and poorly equipped civilians who are putting up a last ditch defense. They've been demoralized and beaten back in every engagement they've fought. We doubt they have much unit cohesion since the majority of them have not trained together and are from different parts of the country. I've fought against the AUC and they represented a real army compared to these people. I seriously doubt any of them have faced armor before. They'll probably break and run as soon as they're engaged."

Looking at the two Captains that would lead the armored attack, the General causally remarked. "Keep your men inside the APC's and punch through whatever resistance you encounter until you breech their main line of resistance, then dismount and overwhelm them. Any questions?"

A young Lieutenant's hand went up. "Yes, General. Where will we maintain prisoners?"

Drago placed his cigar in an ashtray and stood up to answer the question. "General, I'd like to address the Lieutenant's question." The General nodded his approval and directed his attention to Drago. "These militia forces are a cancer, and as such must be destroyed. Rebels of this ilk are the most dangerous form of infection in any body politic. They adhere to an absurd belief that the people should maintain ultimate control of the government. They believe that *God* has given them rights, not the least of which is the right to use arms to bring about the changes they deem necessary. This dogma leads to social chaos if it is in anyway tolerated. Just look at the radical Islamists and the way they use religious ideas to guide their actions. In reality there is very little difference between these two groups." Drago slowly walked to the front of the room and continued lecturing the group of military leaders like a professor. "Gentlemen, our mission is to help create a new country for our brothers. They look to us to ensure they'll be able to establish a society built upon modern-day political theories of social justice, not antiquated 18th Century machinations of imperialist aristocrats. Look at the great nations of the world, China is a prime example. Do they allow their people to arm themselves? No. To do so would be ludicrous. How could a government govern a billion people if it continually had to worry about rebellions?"

"All other industrialized nations have recognized the wisdom of disarming their citizens, Great Britain, Canada, Australia, Germany, France, Brazil, Japan and China. Yet these extremists, the same ones who created the current crisis, have rejected what the rest of the world has embraced. As members of a United Nations Peacekeeping force it is your duty to bring these backwards pseudo-patriots in line with the rest of the global community."

"Make no mistake men, this is a critical battle. There are many other militia extremists in this country and even now they're massing in Arizona. We have the opportunity to destroy the will of these groups by making an example of our enemies tomorrow. You owe it to Aztlán and to the global community to crush these racist throwbacks and show their compatriots what awaits them if they resist the United Nations."

"To answer your question Lieutenant, I believe we should grant them the same honors they extended to your comrades in San Diego." Drago dramatically paused and looked around the room, and then with an expression of surprise continued, "Oh, I suppose you haven't heard...thirteen of your countrymen were viciously butchered by militia at two weapons collection stations yesterday. None were allowed to live. They were murdered, for doing nothing more than helping the people rid themselves of dangerous weapons. I want each of you to tell your men about this tonight and have them think of the children who will never see their fathers and the mothers who'll cry and light candles for their dead sons. I want you all to remember the monstrous actions of these racially motivated militias when you go into battle tomorrow. Understand that if you show them any mercy, you will only invite more cowardly attacks against more of our Latin brothers. Gentlemen, destroy them like you would a venomous snake in a child's room."

Drago scanned the room and knew his words had burned deep into the hearts of the assembled men. He knew that none would give quarter to the militia. Tomorrow when they attacked, they would be driven by the image of their fallen comrades. They'd demonstrate to the rebels that fighting against the UN was a worthless and suicidal endeavor.

"Very well then," the General said. "You have your orders. Prepare your equipment and men. We deploy at 0200. You are dismissed!"

MSNBC

This was a historic day in the US House of Representatives, as members exercised the authority granted them in the Constitution. By a vote of 265 to170 the House voted to impeach the president of the United States. This is only the third time in American history that a President has been impeached. The president now joins William Jefferson Clinton and Andrew Johnson on this dubious list.

An impeachment can best be likened to a criminal indictment in a criminal court. This action does not force the president out of office, but it does clear the way for the Senate to convene a trial, which can remove the president with a two-thirds vote in favor of conviction.

Thirty-seven Republicans, one Independent and the sole member of the Green party, joined House Democrats in today's historic vote. Democratic House Minority Leader Paula Alberti (D-WA) told reporters,

"Today was a historic day for global peace and democracy. The people of the United States have exercised their Constitutional power through their elected officials to unseat the worst President in the history of this country. The House has done its duty, now it is up to the Senate to bring sanity and an international perspective back to the White House."

When asked if she believed the Senate would follow the House's lead and convict the president, Representative Alberti said, "I have great confidence in Senator Snow and the coalition he has built in the Senate." Washington insiders believe that if the president is removed from office, Representative Alberti will be the top Democratic candidate for President.

Direct Action Academy

Mike and Slim's mission had achieved far more than originally anticipated. Instead of collecting a few cases of MRE's and ammunition, they had negotiated several truckloads of food from the Mormon storehouse. Mike also recruited several volunteers with medical background who were willing to assist as medics. The other coup was that Chief Meadows agreed to head up the administration of the academy. The chief was being micromanaged by his superiors and no longer felt he could fulfill his duties with the department. He was open in his unwillingness to execute many of the emergency provisions the governor put into effect this would end his career.

So when Mike asked for volunteers to manage the academy as a troop depot, the chief was eager to offer his skills.

The chief was by far the best choice for the job. He was a great organizer and natural leader. Unfortunately, he was in his early fifties and after a lifetime of law enforcement he didn't have the physical attributes needed for ground force soldiering. Everyone liked the chief and felt comfortable with him taking charge of the academy.

Other good news came from AK who, although he had failed to locate the Mormon leader he had set out to contact, had found something even better. While attending Embry Riddle Aeronautical University, years before, he had roomed with another Mormon named Karl Evans. Karl and AK had graduated in the same class. But, while AK had pursued a civilian flight career, Karl was commissioned into the Air Force and now flew F-16's.

Karl's parents live in Williams, Arizona, just west of Flagstaff and in an attempt to locate the church leader, AK called them. Although they couldn't help him with his request, they did inform him that Karl was temporarily stationed at Luke Air Force Base. AK got Karl's cell number and was able to speak with him.

What he learned was remarkable. Morale in stateside units was dangerously low. Every stateside military element received strict orders from Washington that they were to guard their bases and not engage the enemy. Telling warriors not to fight an invading enemy doesn't go over well, and there had been a brief mutiny as many junior officers and enlisted men tried to seize command. Dozens of people had been arrested. Probably the most incredible part of this whole situation was that the information was successfully suppressed. Normally the mainstream press would be anxious to proclaim the news of attempted revolts within the military, but Democrats didn't want the world to understand how weak the United States was until they were able to take power. After that, they would immediately implement a deal they had already brokered with the UN to pull US forces out of the Middle East and Korea and fully support the UN protected state of Aztlán.

"So, is your friend grounded?" Slim asked.

"No. They're still flying CAP. Karl told me that he flies two to three missions a day. I told him what was happening with the militias. He said his unit had heard about the California units and most supported what they were doing. Here's the best part. Karl told me that if we find ourselves in a battle with the UN and need close air support (CAS), he and his buddies were willing to risk court marshal to help us out. Karl's call sign is Falcon 55 and this..." AK withdrew a slip of paper from his breast pocket and handed it to Arrow, "is the frequency he operates on."

"Well, that could definitely come in handy. Stay in touch with your friend, AK. Even if a promise of CAS is too good to believe, he's still a valuable source of intelligence." Arrow said.

Arrow turned in his chair. "Thor, your turn. What's the word on your uncle?"

The young man brightened. "He says he's happy to help, any way he can. He's turning over all the seasonal bunkhouses to us. They've got attached kitchens designed to feed a bunch of hungry men. He called me back later, to say that he'd gotten busy with some ideas of his own. He's staked out a lot of open space, enough to bivouac thousands."

"He also has a lot of razor wire he wants to string to the fence lines, and he's raising a bunch of big earth berms for local defense." Thor smiled. "I think you could say he's on board."

"Excellent. We'll get a logistics team out there right away, to dig latrines and get the kitchens running. Then we can start moving the troops."

No one knew exactly where the UN would enter into Arizona. Although they had probably already flown people into Sky Harbor, Phoenix's main airport, they didn't have the airlift capability to fly in the men, equipment and supplies they'd need to occupy half the state. Of course, they could drive in from California by way of Interstates 10 or 8. But if they did this they would have to use units currently deployed in California or bring up new troops from Mexico, into San Diego and Los Angeles and then drive them east into Arizona.

The consensus was they'd probably keep the Venezuelans and Paraguayans in place in Southern California and use the Mexicans to occupy Arizona. Three established crossings already existed, near Yuma, Nogales and Douglas. Although Yuma was a possibility, it was way out West and would take a military convoy at least five hours to reach Phoenix. But Douglas and Nogales offered excellent roads with a straight shot north, into Tucson and then Phoenix. Using these routes, the UN could quickly secure additional southern ports of entry and quickly occupy the two largest cities in the state. Luckily, J.R.'s ranch, the Double C, sat almost exactly between the two cities and would allow the militias to react in either direction.

Just before 2100 hours the 38th FF (Colorado), 43 FF (Idaho), 44 FF (Wyoming) and the Utah battalions from the Wasatch arrived at the academy. They were the largest group to arrive so far and their convoy of close to seventy trucks made an impression as it entered the main parking lot. As Mike stood up to meet the convoy Arrow stopped him.

"Mike," he said, "you've been working awfully hard for the last few days. I think it'd be a good idea for you to spend some time with Rachel. Cowboy, Desert Scout and I are perfectly capable of processing in the new battalions, and we'll be deploying soon. This might be the last chance you have to spend some personal time with Rachel." He looked at his boots, his voice reluctant. "Have you two discussed the future at all?"

"Not really. We both know what's happening and the risks involved. But we haven't really spoken much about it."

"Listen Mike, I don't want to interfere with your relationship and I'm not trying to be Dr. Phil. I guess it's really none of my business. But I really think you two should sit down and talk about this. Seriously, I think you owe it to her." Arrow kept his words respectful.

He was uncomfortable with what felt like interference in someone else's personal life. After all, he wasn't married and didn't even have a girlfriend so it would have been a bit hypocritical to act like a relationship counselor. But he really liked these two. They were something special, and between them they *had* something special. Arrow had loved a couple of women in his life, so he recognized the passion between them every time they were together and he didn't want anything to screw it up.

"Thanks Arrow," Mike said at last. "You're right, I've been avoiding discussing this with her and I guess all the work has made for an easy excuse. It's not that I'm unconfident in what we have to do...I just don't know what to expect from her."

"Well, there's only one way to deal with this and it's straight on. Just remember that soon we'll be in combat and the last thing you'll want beating on your mind was that you didn't spend the right time with her when you had the chance. When the balloon goes up, we'll all be relying on you. You won't be any good unless your mind is at peace. Go ahead and take the rest of the night off. I think I saw her talking with Cindy in the common area."

Mike headed in the direction of the classrooms. The hallway led back towards a circular area where several couches and chairs were arranged for students to relax between classes. Several classrooms were arranged along the walls of the common area forming a hub. As Mike approached, he saw Rachel sitting alone reading a paperback. She was reclining on one of the couches with her back up against the arm and her knees bent close to her chest. She was wearing her extra large UCSD sweatshirt and a pair of faded and slightly torn jeans. Her beautiful red hair was pulled back in a ponytail and she had on her reading glasses. Mike loved her glasses. They were thin rectangular frames that gave her a scholarly look that he found uncommonly sexy. Stopping before he entered the room, he stared at her from around the corner. "*God, she's beautiful.*" His eyes began to tear up as he thought about how wonderful his life had been since they'd met.

Rachel was everything he'd ever wanted in a woman. She was affectionate, attentive, confident, smart, but most importantly, she had a smile that ignited his very soul and guided him like a lighthouse. He knew he'd gladly follow that smile through hell. His only desire in life was to spend the rest of his days trying to find a way to describe the intense love he felt for her.

Catching a glimpse of him out of the corner of her eye, she softly called out, "Hey there, handsome. Are you spying on me?" "I was just looking at you."

"You mean *spying* on me."

"I wasn't *spying* on you. I was just watching. There's a difference." Mike replied in a playfully cynical tone.

"Well, why don't you sit next to me and explain what that difference would be." Rachel answered with a come and get me grin as she patted the couch next to her.

Mike walked over but then stopped in front of her and held out his hands. Rachel reached out and took his hands in hers then Mike pulled her off the couch and into a warm and deep embrace. As he liked to do, he buried his face into her hair and took a deep breath. "I love the way your hair smells; it's better than fresh baked bread."

"Bread? No one has ever told me that before."

"I don't mean literally. You know how certain smells bring back all the best memories, the ones that make all your problems and worries fade away...well, that's what it's like when I hold you and smell your hair."

"You should have just said that in the first place. It's a much better line than, your hair smells like a bakery."

"That's not what I said." Mike responded in a slightly defensive tone, as he began to pull away. Rachel tightened her hold and resisted his retreat. "I know sweetheart, I was just kidding. Tell me more about the way you feel when you hold me."

"Why don't we sit down and we can talk about a lot of things, including the way I feel for you."

Mike sat down in the middle of the couch. Rachel laid her head in his lap and pulled her long slender legs to her chest, until she was curled up like a kitten. Mike reached down and untied her ponytail allowing her soft, thick hair to spread out across his legs. Then he began slowly drawing his fingers through it and stroking her head until she softly closed her eyes. Mike loved it when they sat like this and he knew she loved having her hair caressed so much that he wouldn't have been surprised if she'd began purring.

"That's nice." Rachel cooed in a content and completely relaxed voice. "You know, Cindy and Wildcat have been spending a lot of time together."

"You mean on the range?" Mike answered. After Cindy's rescue she'd shown interest in learning how to handle a gun and Wildcat eagerly volunteered to be her coach.

"No. I mean they've been spending *a lot of time* together. Either she's preparing for the Olympic shooting team or they've found *other things* in common." Rachel stirred against his lap. "Actually, I was speaking with Cindy earlier and she made it pretty clear that the two of them have stuck up a pretty passionate relationship."

"Well, you know how women are irresistibly attracted to men who know how to use guns. It's a volatile mixture of raw power and testosterone, women just can't resist it...but I'm sure you know what I mean."

"Oh really? Frankly, I haven't a clue. Sounds like a classic case of Freudian over compensation." Rachel's punctuated her quip with a squeeze of Mike's thigh.

Mike hated to break their playful banter with the real reason he'd sought her out, but he knew they needed to face the reality of the situation. "Listen babe, we need to discuss what's about to happen. I know we've both been trying to avoid this, but we're running out of time." Mike felt Rachel stiffen. "The battalions from the Rockies just arrived, which means we'll be deploying to the Double C Ranch in the next couple of days. Before I leave I need to know that you're comfortable with this."

Rachel didn't answer. Mike gave her a moment. "Rachel, I need to know how you feel about this. I know it's hard to talk about it; I've been avoiding it as well. But I don't know how I'm going to do my job if this isn't taken care of." Mike was trying hard to remain calm and to choose his words carefully so as not to sound abrupt.

Rachel lifted her hand and lightly wiped a tear from her eye. "You mean you what to know how I feel about you going to war? You want to know how

I feel about you facing an army of men that are going to try to kill you? If that's what you're wondering about I'd have to say it makes my stomach turn."

Now that she began speaking the tears were followed by soft sobs. Even Mike's constant hair stroking no longer calmed her.

"I don't have a choice, Rachel. The day I picked up a gun and accepted my duty as an American, I signed up for this. This is my responsibility and I can't avoid it."

Her voice sharpened. "You talk like you're looking forward to this, like it's some kind of boy's club thing. We're talking about life and death...we're talking about you being killed in the desert and us never being together again. This isn't a game."

Mike was surprised at the tone of Rachel's remark, but reminded himself that it was probably emotion affecting what she was saying.

"No it isn't a game, Rachel. I understand what it means, but then again, I think you do as well. You've already had to kill someone. You knew what you had to do and you did it. I'm no different. I know what I have to do and although it scares me, I'm ready to step up and do it, just like Arrow, AK, Slim and the thousands of other militiamen that have either already engaged the enemy or who are preparing to."

"Mike, this isn't the same thing. I didn't have a choice, *you do*. When I went after Cindy I only had two choices...act or watch my friend die. I did what I had to do. But you're willingly searching out this fight. We could sit right here and avoid the whole thing. If we're attacked, that's different. But you don't have to do this."

By this time Rachel had sat up and retreated to the opposite end of the couch. Her eyes were red and swollen and tears tracked down her face. As he listened to her and saw the fear and anger in her eyes, his heart stung and his eyes also began to well up. Mike moved towards her and took her soft hands in his and began to kiss her long fingers.

"Sweetheart, you have to understand that I have no choice." Rachel interrupted him, "Yes you do. We're here together and you don't have to leave. We can stay together and whatever happens...happens."

"Listen to me. If I did that it would ruin me. I wouldn't be the man I have worked so hard to become and it would change everything. It would change *us*."

"What's going to change *us* is you getting killed! Mike, please understand what I'm saying. I love you, and I'll love you, no matter what happens. I swear I'll love and respect you the rest of my life. But, we'll have nothing if you get killed." Rachel flung herself on Mike and held him the way a child does a security blanket. Mike kissed his beautiful lover and softly caressed her heaving back.

"Rachel. There's nothing I want more than to stay right here and devote the rest of my days to loving you. Don't you know how beautiful you are to me? How precious? But if I do that, I'll dishonor myself. This is my home. *You* are my home. I can't live the rest of my life knowing I stayed back while somebody else defended it for me. It would make me feel like a thief."

Mike pulled Rachel away from his shoulder and gently reached out, lifting her tear-strewn face with his hand. "Imagine, just for a minute, that you had seen Cindy in the danger she was in, and did nothing; even if your only motive for inaction was your love for me. Can you imagine yourself doing that?

Looking deeply into her eyes he spoke to her in a voice of confidence that was so reassuring it bordered on prophecy, "Rachel, I will love you for eternity and nothing man can do or create will change that. As the heavens are my witness you will always be the very power that makes my heart beat and my soul rejoice." Then he kissed her in the most passionate way she'd ever been kissed before. As the remaining strength drained out of her body it was replaced by unqualified capitulation. There was nothing she could do but embrace her man and allow his kisses to sear deep into her heart. As she drew his breath into her lungs, she hoped that perhaps it would make them one.

****

Tire Iron led a group of battalion commanders towards the Academy's main building just as Cowboy and Arrow came out to meet them. Neither Cowboy nor Arrow had met Tire Iron, Porter Glockwell or the other leaders, but Mike had seen pictures of them on the Internet. The Utah battalions regularly held joint training exercises with other battalions in the Rocky Mountain region, and often posted pictures taken during those events. For security purposes, faces were digitally obscured so anti-militia groups could not identify the participants. As the men approached Cowboy and Arrow recognized many of them. Tire Iron wasn't more than six feet tall, but he was powerfully built. Rumor was he'd received his handle from a superior while doing field operations for the CIA.

Even though TI was partial to his *nom de guerre,* it didn't begin to do justice to his intelligence and professionalism. No one questioned his ability to kill people and break things; he'd proven that in operations all over the world. But he was also respected as a tactician who looked beyond the obvious to hit the enemy where they least expected it.

Walking next to him was Porter Glockwell, who was physically TI's opposite. Glockwell stood a good head taller and was probably fifteen years younger than his mentor. Whereas TI was broad and powerful, Porter carried his strength in a lean, cheetah like frame. In TI's eyes it was easy to see the confidence and patience borne of years under pressure and crisis, while Porter's eyes were aflame with the passion and zeal of youth.

Both men wore MARPAT digital camouflage designed by the Marine Corps, custom designed load-bearing vests, drop leg holsters and carried M-4 carbines. As the group reached Cowboy, Desert Scout and Arrow they stopped and saluted.

"38th, 43rd, 44th and 45th Field Forces reporting."

Arrow, Cowboy and Desert Scout returned the salutes, "Gentlemen," Arrow said, "welcome to the Arizona/Southwest Command." Then Cowboy added, "Damn glad to see you."

"You guys look tired." Arrow commented. "How was the trip down?"

"We took the long way around to avoid as many large cities as possible," Tire Iron said. "Instead of coming through Page on Route 89, we decided to take Interstate 70 to Route 191 and drive through Moab. Then we followed 191 through the Indian Reservations until we hooked up with the 60, and exited just north of here." Indian Reservations were controlled and policed by Tribal Councils. By driving through their sovereign lands, the convoy avoided any state or government agencies that might be on the lookout for militias.

"Allow me to introduce the men," said Tire Iron. "This is Porter Glockwell, he's in charge of the 35th, Viper of the 57th, Spear has the 29th and Teancum leads the 49th. This gentleman is Wolverine, he's the commander of the 38FF, Bulldog commands the 43FF and Bronco here, is the head of the 44th all the way from Wyoming."

"Gentlemen, we're glad to have you and your men as a part of the command." Arrow turned to his right and motioned towards the men at his side.

"This is Cowboy, my XO, and this is Desert Scout who's in charge of the 31 battalion, New Mexican Field Force. You can call me Arrow; I understand that you're our new commander. We're glad you're here."

After a brief round of handshakes, Cowboy presented TI with a clipboard. "I hope this meets your expectations." The clipboard contained a diagram of the academy and an outline of where their men would bivouac, when and where they'd eat and when they'd zero their weapons at the ranges.

After giving the details a quick examination, TI smiled and said, "This will be fine." Then he turned towards his battalion commanders and passed the clipboard to Glockwell. "First thing we need to do is get these men settled in. Make sure these orders are distributed among the men. Get your people and their gear squared away. Make a list of any repairs you need and any deficiencies you have and be sure to get that information to Cowboy. Also, we need a full inventory of weapons, ammunition, specialty gear, food and fuel by 0600 tomorrow. Any questions?" No one said a word.

During the following days equipment was repaired and prepped, weapons zeroed in, supplies gathered and everything loaded into trucks for deployment. The men had time to prepare for a long field operation, and to get to know one another and build the camaraderie that was essential in fighting units. Meanwhile two additional battalions arrived, the 61st and 11th battalions, from Washington State. The 61st was known by its unit name "Shekinah," and the 11th was called the "Regulators." Both battalions were well known in the militia community and recognized for their extensive mountain training and excellent leadership.

The battalion commander for the 61st was a rugged farmer called Stratiotes, known for his hatred of the UN, impressive scholarship and strong Christian beliefs. Because of these traits many likened him to Stonewall Jackson. The commander of the 11th battalion was simply known as Evil. No one really understood how or where his handle developed, but what everyone agreed on was his natural ability to lead men in battle. Though the men of the 61st and 11th battalions were out of their element in the desert of Southern Arizona, they were eager to get into the fight and defend their country.

El Cajon Pass: San Bernardino, California
(N34°17'968" W117°27'408")

Stalker's command tent was filled with his unit commanders gathered for the warning order that would guide the upcoming battle. He stood over a sand model of the El Cajon Pass and pointed out each unit's primary and fallback position. He also reviewed where the enemy would probably attack. For the past couple of days they had pre-positioned units and equipment to provide a multi-layered defense against the UN forces that were preparing to attack. Recon teams had closely monitored the enemy and relayed information in standard S.A.L.U.T.E. (Size, Activity, Location, Unit, Time, and Equipment) format. Stalker was confident that he understood what he'd be up against. Intelligence indicated the UN would attack with a combined force of Venezuelans and Paraguayans numbering nearly twenty-five hundred men. Although outnumbered by over a thousand men, the militias enjoyed the advantage of being the defending force. Standard military planning demanded a three to one advantage in favor of the attackers to dislodge a dug in defending force.

The UN commander did not command that size of force. He was either relying on his armor as a force multiplier, or he underestimated the militias. Either way, Stalker was going to make him pay for his overconfidence. Stalker's plan was designed to eliminate the UN's strengths and maximize his forces advantages of surprise, maneuver and small arms fire. To eliminate the UN armor, Stalker organized a demolition team lead by a former Army EOD Staff Sergeant named Sapper. Working with other former military explosives experts and several civilians who worked in the mining industry, the team got busy constructing a series of anti-armor and anti-personnel mines. The anti-tank mines would be buried in natural and manmade approaches where the APC's would be funneled into killing zones. Sapper's team also included dozens of former construction workers, who used appropriated heavy equipment to break up the pavement of the Interstate where it was to be mined.

Since Sapper's team had no access to military ordnance they were forced to manufacture a variety of improvised explosive devices (IED's) made with surplus ammunition cans, metal cases and plastic 55-gallon water barrels. Sapper created an outdoor explosives factory where his team mixed hundreds of pounds of lethal ammonium nitrate fuel oil (ANFO) charges. ANFO is not as powerful as the complex and highly explosive compounds used by the military, but used in sufficient quantities it still packs a powerful punch.

A simple way of measuring an explosive's power is by calculating its Relative Effectiveness, or (RE). For the purpose of this measurement the most common explosive in use, TNT, was assigned an RE of 1.0. By that measurement C-4, a military explosive, equals 1.34. ANFO has a RE of .42, so although it's weaker, all Sapper's team needed to do was make the IED's larger to compensate for the yield difference. The other way they would offset the relative weakness of their devices was by making sure they were detonated as close to the enemy as possible.

Sapper's men selected fertilizer with ammonium nitrate levels of at least 33.33%. Since fuel was in short supply they manufactured some bombs with diesel fuel and others with gasoline. One man was able to find a small supply of nitro-methane (high octane racing fuel), which they mixed with diesel to create a number of especially powerful charges. The fuel and fertilizer was mixed and allowed to soak. Once the ANFO was ready detonation charges were manufactured consisting of black powder, primers and detonation cord provided by the miners. When combined, these two products create a duplex booster charge that is powerful enough to ignite the crude ANFO mixture.

Each 55-gallon barrel contained four hundred and twenty-nine pounds of ANFO, which had the explosive equivalent of over one hundred and eighty pounds of TNT or one hundred and thirty-four pounds of C-4. These barrels were buried in the kill boxes identified on Stalker's map.

Since they lacked enough mines to properly cover all avenues of approach, Stalker ordered men to dig up the Interstate in various locations and bury fake charges in hopes the ruse would deter the enemy. Smaller charges containing metal scraps and bullets were deployed in and around fighting positions and served as improvised claymores.

Battle lines were organized in concentric rings for a Fabian offense, using a series of delaying tactics and retreats, while forcing the enemy to remain in the open. The plan was to take out as much armor as possible at the outset of the battle, then draw the UN ground forces deep into the militia defenses through a series of costly engagements, and finally to envelope them from the rear with his reserves.

As Stalker was finishing his warning order an aide passed him a note. Stalker silently read the note and then looked out over his assembled leaders. "Gentlemen, the UN is coming.

Initial Line of Resistance: N34°15'102" W117°26'798"
(Three Miles North of Devore)

The 17th and 3rd Nevada battalions were positioned in the center of the line, with the 21st Nevada and the reinforced Bravo Company from Burbank to the left. Roja's men and the 65th California were holding the right flank.

It was obvious the militiamen didn't have the strength to hold the UN long but they had to force the UN to split their armor and dismount as many troops as possible, at which time the militia companies would begin their coordinated retreat back to the next line of resistance.

Above them, just south of Cajon Junction, the 53rd and 25th Utah battalions and the 111th California were dug in and would hopefully form a steel wall upon which the surviving UN troops would collapse. The 33rd Nevada and

59th California were in reserve on the right flank and the 23rd Nevada and reinforced Papa Company, from Pasadena were in reserve on the left flank. Roja's men had the primary responsibility of taking out any APC's that entered their kill zones. For days they had dug trenches, downed trees and constructed obstacles to create funnels for the APC's to enter. Once the enemy entered these funnels, his men would remotely detonate the ANFO mines Sapper's team had manufactured. Because of the extreme size of the mines, his men had built reinforced fighting positions six hundred and seventy meters away. At that range most of his men couldn't accurately hit man sized targets, so a squad of sharpshooters had been attached to his unit to take out targets of opportunity until the enemy closed within two hundred meters. If everything went as planned they'd take out most of the armor and the accompanying infantry before retreating to their secondary line of resistance. Unfortunately, combat never went as planned.

UN Forces: N34⁰ 13'711" W117⁰ 24'641"
(Just North of Devore, California)

The UN forces slowly moved through the early morning darkness. Dozens of white Soviet era BTR armored personnel carriers lumbered forward while 14.5mm heavy machine guns oscillated in their turrets. Behind them several rows of HUMMVEE's kept the pace while gunners in their exposed turrets watched carefully for threats. To the rear, two and a half ton trucks loaded with infantry kept up the pace. The mounted troops would unload and proceed on foot as soon as they arrived at their designated point of departure. In all the UN forces created an impressive and formidable sight.

In the middle of the column General Puentenegro rode in the back of his command APC that was festooned with several long whip antennas feeding signals to multiple radios. On a fold down map table, the General traced his finger over the route they were following. The lead elements of his force were approaching the point where they'd change from a column to a wedge formation. "Commander to force," he radioed on the battalion frequency. "Assume formation Alpha 2. Recon elements forward and to the flanks."

Several HUMMVEE's sped up and passed the APC's ahead to scout for enemy forces. Driving deeper up the pass they encountered a large barricade blocking the highway. The leader of the reconnaissance unit radioed the other vehicles in his squad. "Tango leader to squad, spread out and hold position while I report back. Keep your eyes open."

"Easier said than done," remarked a soldier in one of the large scout cars. "It's pitch black up here. How do they expect us to see anything without night vision?" The soldier's comment was rhetorical since he knew the Paraguayan army would never issue expensive high tech devices like night vision goggles to mere conscripts. Instead they were ordered to simply remain vigilant and watch for movement.

****

High above the barricade a sniper team watched the UN scouts below. They'd "vegged out" their guille suits with burlap dyed to mimic the color of the surrounding vegetation and wove indigenous branches and leaves into the mix to ensure they'd expertly blend into their environment. This particular sniper team was positioned behind a naturally fallen tree and had placed several large rocks in front of their position. From the middle of their impromptu sniper hide, the long barrel of a .50-caliber rifle barely protruded. It too was camouflaged with burlap strips so that it also blended with its surroundings.

The spotter lowered his range finder. "All right," he said in a calm and deliberate whisper. "The Hummer on the far right is two hundred and eighty-two meters. Load an armor piercing incendiary round and target the engine block."

"Roger. API round loaded. On target," replied the shooter.

The spotter consulted a laminated range card. "Up, two klicks. Right one"

The sniper silently adjusted his scope as instructed. The sniper and spotter represented just one of the twelve teams from the 3rd Nevada battalion spread out along both sides of the canyon. These two had trained together in long-range shooting for more than three years, never really believing their skills and teamwork would ever be put to this particular use.

At another location, their leader watched the enemy recon squad through his night vision scope and radioed information to the group. Half the team had .50-caliber rifles and the others had zeroed their bolt-action .30-caliber rifles on the UN soldiers who manned the machine guns in each vehicle. The Team Leader gave the command to fire, and the peaceful early morning stillness was shattered by over a dozen shots.

The large .50-caliber API rounds smashed into the engine blocks of the Hummers, rupturing oil lines and tearing enormous holes in the motors. Shattered connecting rods immediately seized up the idling engines. At the same time, eight UN gunners received lethal wounds to the head and upper chest. The soldiers died instantly and either fell back into their vehicles or simply slumped over the edge of the roofs. One of the remaining scouts began shooting aimlessly, spraying automatic fire in all directions. A moment later a precisely aimed .30-caliber round blew the back of his head open under the blue UN helmet he'd been issued just the week before. In a matter of seconds all the scout cars were disabled and most of their gunners were dead.

The remaining soldiers, realizing they were sitting ducks in their disabled vehicles, climbed out and frantically sought cover behind their vehicles. But like their deceased comrades, they had no idea where the expertly hidden snipers were located. One-by-one, they too were picked off, but not before they were able to radio their commander and inform him they were under deadly accurate sniper fire.

****

"Let's go." The spotter whispered to his shooter. The sniper slowly and deliberately withdrew his rifle from its firing position and collapsed the attached bi-pod. While he was doing this, his spotter used a red lens on his Surefire light to covertly illuminate the area and make sure they left nothing behind. Then the two crawled, like serpents, towards their secondary position.

****

General Puentenegro listened to the radio transmissions from his scout teams and cursed them out loud, "Idiots! What were they thinking driving up to a barricade and just sitting there? They deserve to be dead." The General threw down the handset and grabbed another to issue orders to the rest of his attack force and in particular the lead element of APC's, Kilo Platoon. "All units advance on the enemy. Kilo Platoon, bust through that barricade and open a path for the rest of the column."

Thick black exhaust bellowed from the lead element of APC's as they accelerated ahead of the attack force. Before reaching the obstacle, they needed to clear the disabled Hummers that blocked the way. The powerful twin 8-cylinder, 120 horsepower engines easily pushed the lightweight recon vehicles off the side of the road allowing other APC's behind them to demolish the barricade.

****

Sheltered in their reinforced fighting position two men from the 21st Nevada watched through binoculars as the BTR's began clearing the Hummers off the road. Even though they were over a third of a mile away the armored personnel carriers were intimidating. The two men's only protection was the dirt and wooden cover they'd used to reinforce their foxhole. In contrast, the APC's looked and roared like hungry armored dinosaurs.

"Remember," one man said, "we need to let the first few APC pass the barricade before we detonate the mines. Stay cool and wait for the order." Beneath and just inside the barricade, several 55-gallon barrels full of explosives waited. As the two men watched the BTR's demolish the barricade, their nervous hands gripped the electronic detonators that were attached to the charges.

Three APC's simultaneously slammed into the barricade. The Soviets originally designed the BTR as an amphibious vehicle so it was manufactured with an upward sloping wave-deflector on the front end. This upward sloping feature forced the nose of the BTR's to rise up and over the barricade before the forward set of wheels got traction on top of the obstacle. As the weight of the armored vehicles began smashing the barricade to pieces, the remains were chewed up by the remaining six sets of wheels and ejected out the back. Like Grizzly bears tearing up a tree, the APC's quickly destroyed a large section of the barricade and began fanning out on the opposite side.

As soon as the barricade was breeched, APC's began flowing through the gap and towards the men waiting in their foxholes. The men of the 21st battalion waited for what seemed like an eternity before the order to detonate was given. The militiamen crouched down in their holes, as they were instructed, and activated the detonators. Suddenly, the whole world erupted as hundreds of pounds of ANFO detonated. What just seconds before had seemed like invincible dinosaurs now flew through the air as if they were children's toys. The explosions ripped huge holes in the thin bottoms of a number of BTR's, incinerating the UN soldiers inside. The same superheated gases ignited fuel tanks in the older BTR's transforming them into gigantic balls of flame. The upgraded models with diesel engines and stronger armor didn't ignite, but the massive concussion from the explosions literally crushed the soldiers inside like bugs on the windshield of a car. Two APC's were thrown backwards as the explosions caught the slanted front ends of vehicles. One landed on another BTR, crushing it and killing everyone inside.

The other obliterated a Hummer. A few survivors managed to crawl out of their demolished vehicles and were quickly dispatched by small arms fire. Three BTR's now lie on their sides in burning heaps once again sealing the hole where the barricade had been breeched.

"Damn it!" Yelled the General. "I've had enough of this. Lima 12 and Bravo 11 begin your flanking attacks! Sweep around the defenses and kill every living soul you find."

*****

Gunny Rojas anxiously sat in his fighting position listening to the reports over the radio. The forward defenses were now fully engaged. The two Nevada battalions were standing firm against superior forces, but were already beginning to run low on ammunition. In the distance fires from burning UN armor lit the sky like bonfires, while explosions broadcast the demise of more UN invaders.

Scout/Sniper teams both fought and relayed information between units. As hoped, the UN began splitting its forces, sending its armor toward the flanks. Dawn broke over the battlefield, illuminating the landscape around Gunny Roja's company of Mexican-Americans. Waiting in the pre-dawn darkness seemed to heighten everyone's anxiety. As the sun began to cast off night's veil of darkness, Rojas wasn't sure what was worst, the dark of night or the illuminating dawn. At least the darkness hid him and his men from the enemy, now they'd be able to see his positions and rake their simple earthen defenses with heavy machine gun fire.

In the distance he began to hear the whining of engines and the unmistakable crunch of vehicles tearing through vegetation. Gunny radioed his men and reminded them to wait until the APC's were on top of the mines before detonating them. In the distance he saw the first BTR round a sharp bend. Several platoons of infantry walked behind the APC's, using them as cover. The turrets, on top of the BTR's, swung from side-to-side, searching for targets. Rojas hoped no one would act too quickly and prematurely reveal their position.

Soon the APC's approached a partial obstruction in the road his men had constructed. Before entering they stopped. On the lead APC, a hatch just forward of the turret, opened and its commander rose up and began scanning the area with his binoculars. Gunny knew every one of the snipers attached to his unit must have had their crosshairs on the man and prayed no one would fire and ruin the ambush. Luckily, discipline prevailed and the commander lived long enough to order his forces forward. The APC traveled another 300 meters before the kill box was filled and Rojas gave the command to detonate the mines.

As before, deafening detonations shook the earth. Once the explosions initiated it was virtually impossible to see anything, but through the fire, smoke and debris Gunny caught a glimpse of the tank commander flying through the air like a broken rag doll. Although he'd seen tanks and armor destroyed during the gulf war, he'd never seen anything as destructive as this.

In Iraq, US tanks fired ultra dense spent uranium kinetic rounds called "Sabots" that generated so much energy upon impact that they literally melted holes right through the heavy armor plating of the Iraqi tanks. Once inside, the molten stream of armor, called "spalling," sprayed all over the interior of the tank killing the crew and igniting every surface. Many tanks quickly erupted, blowing their turrets high into the air. Others looked perfectly normal save for a small hole where the sabot round penetrated the turret. But the crude, unsophisticated power of these explosions threw the eight-wheeled vehicles around as if a giant had kicked them in anger. Many of the opposing infantry were blown off their feet by the massive pressure waves generated by the explosions. Those who survived crawled or stumbled about dazed as blood ran from their ears, eyes, and noses. Not wanting to lose the small window of opportunity created by the shock of the explosions, Rojas lifted his rifle and began firing on the UN soldiers. Simultaneously his men joined in and they mowed the Peacekeepers down. But quickly, more APC's rolled into the battle and Rojas knew it was time to retreat. He gave the command to fall back and while half his men provided covering fire, the others abandoned their fighting positions and ran towards their secondary line of defense.

Militia Headquarters: N34⁰ 18'773" W117⁰ 28'437"
(Just North of Cajon Junction)

As reports from across the battlefield streamed into headquarters, Stalker desperately tried to visualize the evolving battle. His center forces were holding under stiff and determined attacks, and had forced the majority of the UN armor to the flanks. Now, the 17th and 21st Nevada were regrouping in their secondary defensive lines. Bravo Company had suffered heavy losses and had been absorbed into the 65th California. The heavy 3rd Nevada battalion was covering the withdrawing 17th and 21st with their M2's and M1919's, but they were also reporting casualties and running low on ammunition.

"Tell the center they must hold the line a little longer." Stalker ordered the radioman in contact with the 21st Nevada. "Tell the 21st they need to draw the UN in further before we can effectively commit the reserves."

"We're receiving reports the enemy has suffered major losses on our flanks." Another radioman reported. "The 65th California and the *Libertad* Company have reached their secondary positions and report most of the enemy APC's are destroyed or out of action."

"Excellent. Notify the reserves to prepare to attack," Stalker ordered. "As soon as the reserve forces are ready, order the 17th and 21st to fall back to the last line of resistance."

"Roger that."

****

General Puentenegro's Command Vehicle

"General, I've lost contact with Lima 12. Bravo11 is reporting heavy resistance. He's requesting permission to fall back and regroup his remaining armor." The communications officer reported.

"Negative," growled Puentenegro. "Tell Major Blanca he is *not* to fall back. Tell him he is to swing to his left and envelope the enemy."

"Sir, Major Blanca says he is heavily engaged and can not shift his attack. He respectfully requests permission to withdraw."

"Give me the microphone!" The General barked as he ripped the mike from the hands of his aide. "Damn it Major! The enemy is retreating in the middle. We've broken their line and must exploit their weakness...NOW! I order you to turn your armor and attack from the left. Do you understand me?"

"Sir," reported Blanca's voice over the radio, "I am heavily engaged. I've lost most of my armor and my infantry has suffered heavy casualties. If I expose my flank to the enemy we'll be destroyed. We need to regroup and *then* we'll be able to support your attack on the center"

"Major, I suggest you split your force. This should allow you to cover your flank and support my attack. Do it, or you'll be arrested for deliberately disobeying a direct order."

Major Blanca released the microphone button and stared at the small device in disbelief, as if it were the cause of such unrealistic orders. The General wouldn't listen to him; he was fixated on his own part of the battle.

Without much of a choice, Blanca ordered his remaining forces to split. One group would provide cover and continue to press the enemy, while he led the other in hopes of enveloping the retreating enemy.

****

The Gunny's men had destroyed all the remaining enemy armor and now only faced infantry. Although Rojas was still out numbered, at least the enemy no longer had the advantage of armor. Once he reached his secondary position, his men laid down suppressive fire for the remainder of the company as they made their way to their new positions. Seeing the militia retreat, the UN troops pressed their attack and charged forward to occupy the fighting positions their enemy had just abandoned. As the blue helmeted troops entered the foxholes and trenches they found the usual refuse of a battlefield including weapons, spent cartridges and ammunition cans.

Before they were able to catch their breath, explosions ripped down the trenches blowing men out of the foxholes. Gunny's men had detonated anti-personnel mines that were purposely placed in their own positions. Once again, Gunny's men capitalized on the ensuing confusion and mayhem and delivered a vicious barrage of fire before beginning their final retreat towards the last line of resistance.

Militia Headquarters: N34° 17'968" W117° 27'408"

Reports were flooding in from the 17th and 21st battalions that they were on the verge of collapse and couldn't hold any longer. They were suffering extremely heavy casualties and were now receiving fire from their left flank. If they didn't fall back, they risked being surrounded. Stalker checked the map one last time then issued the orders, "Tell the 17th and 21st to fall back immediately and commit the reserves."

****

As soon as the message was received the 23rd Nevada and the reinforced P Company stormed out of their hidden positions and charged the remainder of Major Blanca's group. At the same time the 33rd Nevada and 59th California attacked from the right. Fortunately, the majority of the UN group on the militia's right flank had already been destroyed, so when the right flank reserves were committed they easily rolled over the remaining UN troops and continued forward until they hit the left flank of the unsuspecting enemy in the center.

"General!" said Puentenegro's visibly upset communications officer, "we are being enveloped on both sides by additional enemy troops. Our flanks are overrun and enemy reinforcements are pouring in ahead of us."

"That's not possible. Where are Majors Lopez and Blanca?"

"They do not respond to our calls."

The General hesitated as he tried to grasp what was happening. Suddenly he understood that he was being encircled and if he didn't retreat he'd lose his entire force. "Tell all units to retreat," ordered the General.

As the fresh troops of the 53rd and 25th Utah battalions pressed forward, their commander noticed an APC with several antennas on top in full reverse. It was speeding backwards while its heavy machine gun swept the field before it with deadly fire. Then, it suddenly crashed into a burning hulk of another APC and rolled over on its side. Realizing how important it'd be to take a UN commander prisoner, he yelled for his men to converge on the stricken APC. As they advanced on the vehicle, its doors flew open and several men climbed out. Two of them were immediately killed by on rushing militia, but then an officer emerged with his hands up. The UN officer was surrounded and forced to the ground.

Looking up at his captors the officer pleaded for his life, "I am General Puentenegro of the UN Peacekeeping forces. Please do not kill me...I surrender."

Base of the 73rd Battalion: Otay Lakes, California

Over the past several days the 73rd had continued to ambush small UN convoys and roadblocks. Their ambushes had brought them much needed weapons, supplies and equipment. But they also heightened the UN awareness of their existence, and now Glory's men were constantly moving to stay a step ahead of enemy patrols and surveillance.

Glory and Eightball sat on small folding chairs while they ate cold MRE's. Both men had continued their interrogation of their prisoner and were confident the young man was continuing to withhold information. Eightball contacted a friend that had just graduated from SDSU and asked him to do a little covert research on Marco Valdez. Evidently, information wasn't difficult to gather, because Eightball's friend was able to get back to him quickly with a lot of very interesting facts.

"All right," Eighball said, "here's what my source at SDSU told me. Our boy Marco is indeed enrolled at the university. Apparently he's the leader of a militant Chicano group called OJChA, which is a student organization that supports the establishment of Atzlán. Our guy is in charge of all OJChA chapters in the greater San Diego area and has organized a number of major protests at a number of other colleges and universities. Marco is no innocent bystander.

I asked my source to research OJChA. He got a pile of information off the Internet about their commitment to the establishment of a homeland for the Chicano people, willingness to use whatever force possible to achieve their goal, blah blah blah. I even got this picture of our friend speaking at a rally last year." Eightball passed the picture to Glory who examined it closely.

"Outstanding. It looks like its time for our young guest to have a "Come to Jesus" meeting. Are you ready to put on your finest racist disguise?

"Yes sir. I had my white sheet cleaned and pressed just yesterday." Eightball spoke in a mockingly thick Southern accent. Then his voice returned to normal. "You know I don't enjoy this bit. It's not natural."

"Yeah, but you do it so well," Glory answered

"I'm not sure if that was a compliment or not."

The two men finished their quick meal and walked to the tent where Marco was tied up. As they approached Eightball purposely wiped the greasy remains from his MRE across his chin and on the front of his T-shirt and then dusted his hair with some dirt. It was all about contrast.

Eightball needed to look, smell, and sound like he was one step out of *Deliverance* while Glory provided the image of a clean cut, reliable individual you could trust.

Marco sat on the floor of the tent, blindfolded and tied at the wrists and ankles. Without saying a word, Glory and Eightball sat down and began staring at him.

"Who's there?" Called Marco, but no one answered.

Again Marco asked, "Who's there?"

Then Eightball broke the uncomfortable silence. "Who do you think it is you little shit?"

As soon as Marco heard Eightball's familiar voice he instinctively crouched down as if preparing to receive another beating.

Glory spoke quietly. "Marco, it seems you've been holding back critical information from us. Up to now I've believed that you were simply in the wrong place at the wrong time. I even argued that we should let you go home. But, the information I'm holding tells me I was wrong and your friend Eightball was right all along." He spoke in a disappointed tone. "You've been lying to me and frankly, you've made me look stupid."

Eightball chimed in, "I've been telling you all along that this piece of shit was lying." Eightball squeezed Marco's cheeks together and shook his head violently with a dirty hand that was sticky with residue from his MRE. "Give me a day with Señor Sweetcheeks here and I'll guarantee you all the information you need."

"I told you I was a student at SDSU. I swear that wasn't a lie."

"You're right," said Glory. "That wasn't a lie, but you said nothing about being the leader of OJChA. Tell you what, you tell us all about this organization and its ties to the Aztec Army and I'll forget about the problems we've had up to now. Oh, and by the way, I'm holding pictures from your own website and those of several other OJChA chapters."

Just as Glory finished, Eightball reached down and ripped the blindfold off Marco's face. The sunlight pierced Marco's eyes causing his pupils to slam shut and his eyes to squint in pain.

"Yeah, and we have a full-color picture of you standing tall and proud at an OJChA rally." Eightball added.

"Look, if you have all the documents you claim to have…then why do you need me to tell you anything?" Marco asked still trying to shield his eyes.

"Consider it a form of confession. We know what you've done and you know what you've done…now it's time to confess and get it out in the open. That way I know I'll be able to trust you."

"On the other hand, if you don't want to talk, that's fine. But, in that case I'm going to leave you with Eightball, who seems to have acquired a liking for you." Glory turned to Eightball, "Did I misunderstand your affection for Marco?"

"I mean you're always talking about his ass, and how you'd like to do things to it."

"Yeah, it's been a while since I've been with a woman." Eightball pronounced it whoa-maan. "I'm feeling a little aggressive."

"Fine," said Marco. "You already seem to know about OJChA. What do you want to know?"

"Why don't you just start talking and we'll tell you when to shut up." Eightball shot back.

During the next hour of interrogation Marco talked about OJChA and how they were the *real* freedom fighters in this conflict. Neither Glory nor Eightball liked hearing that garbage, but the point was to keep Marco talking. So as long as he was divulging information, they let him rattle on.

"All right," Glory said at last. "So you're a Regional Representative with OJChA. That's fine and dandy, but I don't think a bunch of college students and illegal aliens could pull something this big off. By your own words you've admitted OJChA has been around for a couple of decades, and hasn't accomplished a thing."

"Why all of a sudden are you capable for pulling it all together? Who's involved, where did you get your funding?" Glory demanded.

"You think we're the small players in this whole event. I'm telling you, you're the small fish. America has screwed the world and has made enemies all over the globe. The US military runs around the world like a kid in his own personal playground. But there are people who hate America and what it does to the refugees of the world. If you'd stop treating the Chicanos and Mexicans in this country like the Jews treat the Palestinians...maybe you wouldn't find yourselves in this mess. That's all I'm saying. I can't stop your buddy here from beating or sodomizing me, but I can keep the rest to myself."

Eightball lunged forward as if to grab Marco, but Glory stopped him. "Well, we have enough information for now. We'll let you sit here a while longer and see if anything else comes to mind."

Glory and Eightball got up and exited the tent. "Why'd you let him off so easy?"

"That's the most information we've gotten out of him so far," said Glory. "Let's let him win a small victory and not say anymore...for now. We need to confirm some of these things he said about OJChA's involvement and then try and contact some of the other militia commands. I'm still turning over those last things he said. He mentioned foreign perception of US policy and then said we treated the Chicanos and Mexicans like the Jews treat the Palestinians. Did you catch that?"

"Yeah. But then again all these extremist groups identify with the Palestinians."

"OJChA needed outside help to organize and fund something like this. I wonder if there's an Islamic connection?" Glory said.

"They'd definitely have the money, and they've been fomenting '"wars of liberation"' for decades. It would also explain the car bombings. Reports on the bombs said they were constructed with military-grade explosives...I doubt OJChA would have sources or the ability to work with that type of material. It's definitely a possibility."

"We need to pass this information on," said Glory. "The last thing we need is to get zapped and lose all this intel. Let's get that radio working and see if we can contact another unit. Then you can have a late night date with Marco."

PLA Headquarters: Hermosillo, Mexico

The pace of operations had drastically dropped off since the UN troops arrived in California. Several people who'd worked at headquarters had traveled to California and Arizona to assist with the transitional government that would soon begin to operate. Regardless of the optimistic feelings that seemed to permeate headquarters, the major knew his job was still a long way from completion.

One problem they were currently dealing with was that Marco Valdez, codenamed Flag, was missing. He wasn't answering his e-mails or checking in as he was ordered to do.

Marco had proven to be a difficult asset to manage. His youthful zeal and impatience with protocols led him to get involved with the operational side of things too often.

Evidently he had been seen leaving with a squad of UN soldiers who were later ambushed and killed. It was now feared he was taken prisoner by the militia and if that was the case, the major was concerned that he'd reveal sensitive information, especially about Syria's connection. As the major sat pondering the possibilities of this current problem, Sayf entered the office with a deeply troubled look on his face.

"Ra'id, forgive the intrusion but we have just received news that the UN forces in Los Angeles have suffered a dreadful defeat at the hands of the militia."

The major raised his head. "How dreadful?"

"They made an early morning attack on a large contingent of militia near San Bernardino. The attack was led by a Venezuelan General named Miguel Puentenegro and over two thousand troops from Venezuela and Paraguay. Apparently less than eight hundred UN troops survived the battle. They lost nearly three-dozen APC's as well as many other vehicles."

The major slowly stood up and walked to a window looking a small garden. After a momentary pause he offered his comment in an almost dispassionate voice, "This is terrible news, but not terribly surprising. Since when has the UN ever been able to command troops in battle? Everywhere they have gone our people have made a mockery of them. I'm surprised *anyone* survived...a UN force made up of conscripts from Venezuela and Paraguay...*please*, they're lucky they didn't all die in traffic accidents on the highway." The major abandoned his scenic view and began pacing around the office. "How did the militias defeat such a large force, where did they get the weapons to destroy the armor?"

"Militias from several Western states gathered in San Bernardino and Arizona. These Americans are extremely militant. They're heavily armed, highly trained and motivated. Many militia leaders have prior military experience, not unlike our own troops in Chechnya, and they bring this knowledge to the militias. As for where they got anti-armor weapons, no one knows. We're not even sure they used sophisticated weapons.

They very well might have constructed improvised explosives, not unlike the ones used by *Mujahedin*." Sayf suddenly realized he'd compared infidels to Islamic holy warriors and quickly corrected himself. "Ra'id, please forgive my unwise use of words. These infidels do not deserve to be compared to our holy warriors. It was a regrettable and stupid mistake."

The major stared at his friend and allowed his better judgment to guide his reaction. "Indeed, it was as you said *regrettable*. I'd suggest you choose your comparisons with more forethought." The shameful look on Sayf's face testified to his sincere repentance, so the major continued to make his point.

"This will only embolden these insurgents and lead to greater problems," the major added.

"Forgive me for asking Major, but does this change *our* mission? Our mission was to destabilize the United States, weaken its criminal President and force the Congress to recall its troops from Iraq. If I am correct, this may very well hasten our plans."

The major returned to his chair and tented his fingers as he began mentally examining Sayf's comment. "I see your point, Mulazim, but my fear is that the incompetent UN will not be able to destroy the militias, and that they'll end up leaving California and abandoning their mission. It wouldn't be the first time the craven UN has cut and run after suffering a few casualties. If that happens the US may see no need to recall their troops from Iraq and nothing will have changed."

"Sir, we'll learn from this set back and make sure when we enter Arizona we do so with an overwhelming force. Instead of relying solely on APC's we'll use helicopters to land forces in their rear and special assault troops. The militias cannot possibly fight on multiple fronts at once. Our friend at the UN is ultimately in charge of the Peacekeeping forces and he'll make the appropriate changes. The next battle will prove to be the end of the militias."

"Very good then, make sure that is the case. Now, if you'd like to join me, the hour of prayer is approaching. Let us demonstrate our obedience and thankfulness to Allah and he will bless our mission."

The Oval Office: Washington D.C.

The president of the United States sat on one of the two white couches, arranged between his desk and a white marble fireplace, casually sipping a cup of steaming black coffee. Looking around the oval office he longed to hear the disembodied voices of his many predecessors telling him how to save his failing Presidency. Not since 1814, when James Madison was President, had the continental United States been invaded and occupied by a foreign force.

"*Well,*" the president reasoned, "*James Madison was the author of the Constitution, and if he couldn't prevent an invasion...I guess I'm in good company.*"

There weren't many times when the president's agenda allowed him to actually sit down and drink a cup of coffee in solace. Usually, his day consisted of one meeting after another, followed by an appearance, followed by whatever else his Chief-of-Staff could cram in his schedule. But lately, the demand for personal appearances had dropped off the presidential to-do list. The state of the union was bad and getting worst.

The economy was in shambles, Wall Street was barely staying above the levels of the great depression, livestock was being slaughtered by the tens of thousands in an attempt to stop the spread of Hoof and Mouth Disease, the military was fighting wars in the Middle East and Korea, the Israelis were threatening to attack the Iranians and now the UN and Mexico had invaded California and Arizona.

The president shook his head and wondered how this had all happened so quickly. It wasn't so long ago that his job approval ratings were actually favorable. Now, he'd been impeached. Finishing his coffee, the president placed the large mug emblazoned with the presidential seal on the table in front of him and began pacing back and forth between his desk and a bookcase. For what seemed to be the millionth time he churned current events through his mind in the vain hope that he'd think of a solution to the many crises that plagued both the country and himself. "*Fucking Chinese pricks. I wish I could bitch slap that duplicitous bastard Xue Lu Dong and end his grandstanding.*" The president stopped and took a deep cleansing breath in an attempt to settle down and think like the chief Executive of the United States, and not the former Marine Corps Lieutenant he was thirty years ago.

The president was called back to the present by his executive secretary who called over the intercom, announcing that his National Security team had arrived for their 0700 meeting.

"Send them in, Sarah."

Four people filed into the oval office: Vice President James Valentine, Secretary of Defense Chad McMillan, CIA Director Herb Nossler, National Security Advisor Phillip Wannamaker and Secretary of State Margaret Bantam. As they entered the president took his customary place in the overstuffed leather chair that sat between the two couches and asked his secretary to send in a decanter of coffee and a tray of sweet rolls.

After everyone had found their seats, the president started things off. "All right people, what have we got today?"

Phillip passed out copies of his daily NSA report. This was more of a briefing than an actual report. It covered all the current crises as well as potential trouble spots that were being actively monitored.

"As you can see, Mr. President, our forces have secured air and sea superiority in the entire Korean Theater of Operations and are driving the North Koreans back. ROK forces should be in control of Pyongyang within the next seventy-two hours. Other than the two missiles the Navy knocked down, there have been no further enemy ballistic missile launches. The Pentagon is confident we've eliminated the North Korean NBC threat. Also, last night the navy carried out a series of nighttime attacks on the Yellow Sea Fleet based at Namp'o and Pip'a-got and the East Sea Fleet based at T'oejo-dong, Najin and Wonsan. Bomb damage assessment confirms the primary targets were destroyed."

"What assets were involved in the attacks?" asked the president as he continued scanning through the report.

"All three CVBGs participated. The *Reagan*, *Carl Vinson* and the *Nimitz* contributed aircraft. Six attack subs, the *Pasadena, Jefferson City, Olympia, Key West, Santa Fe* and *Portsmouth,* launched Tomahawks against shore facilities. The Guided Missile Destroyers *Lassen, John Paul Jones* and *Antietam* destroyed a squadron of landing craft including: six *Nampo*-class landing craft and four *Hantae*-class medium landing craft."

"So what's left of their navy?" The president asked looking over the top of his papers.

"Basically...they don't have one anymore. They didn't have much to start with and this morning they'd be lucky if they could assemble a few tugs to mount machine guns on. Mr. President our estimations are that the North Korean army will fold within the next week."

"What is the current disposition of the Chinese and where are their Kilo's?" The president asked.

The reference to the "Kilo's" was about four Russian built Diesel-Electric submarines that the People's Liberation Navy operated out of their East Sea base at *Xiangshan*. The Kilo-Class submarine is the most advanced non-nuclear sub in the world. When it is operating on its batteries, it is virtually silent and undetectable. If the Chinese launched an invasion of Taiwan these subs were expected to be deployed in the narrow Taiwan Straits to deter any US carriers from operating in support of the Island nation.

"The Chinese are still on alert status," replied the National Security Advisor, "but they're keeping their supplies well behind their main lines. They haven't been brought up and they're being very careful to ensure we see that they're not preparing an invasion. Three Kilo's are docked at *Xiangshan* and the forth has been training about one hundred and thirty miles from port. It's regularly coming up to snorkel and our P-3's are keeping tabs on it. So far the Chinese seem to be honoring their end of the bargain."

"Great. At least that'll be one less problem I have to juggle. Now, how am I going to deal with the UN troops in California?

"Mr. President, I have some new intelligence that just might put your mind at ease." Herb Nossler said as he passed a new folder marked Top Secret to his boss. "Earlier this morning the UN launched a brigade sized attack against a large contingent of armed civilians, just north of San Bernardino." The CIA Director handed the president two satellite photos, "These photos were downloaded from one of our KH-12 recon birds and they clearly show thirteen burning Soviet built BTR's. In addition, photo analysis experts at Fort Meade estimate nearly four hundred dead UN troops scattered around the area."

The president held up his hand to stop the on-rush of new information. "Whoa, wait a minute. Are you telling me the UN ran an armored battalion up the San Bernardino Freeway, and a bunch of civilians handed them their heads?"

The CIA Director suddenly found it hard to meet the president's eyes. He looked at his shoes and nodded in the affirmative.

"How did *that* happen?" The president asked in disbelief.

"We're still putting that together. I have some assets currently working to gather HUMINT...but the photo interpreters have identified these large craters around the burning APCs as a possible explanation. They're confident they were created by large underground explosions. Notice the massive amount of displaced earth and the dead troops distributed around the edges. Our best guess is they're the result of IEDs, probably constructed with dynamite or ANFO."

The Director of Central Intelligence (DCI) motioned to the second photo. "This one was taken just before the bird went out of range. It shows the UN in full retreat. You'll notice no APCs survived the battle and the few surviving vehicles are loaded down with wounded. Another revealing item is the large number of what we're calling '"militia troops"' now on the field."

"How do we know they're militia?" The president asked.

"I asked the same question over at NSA." Nossler answered as he passed the president a magnifying glass. "If you use this, you'll notice that very few of those men are wearing the same uniform and none have UN armbands or helmets. We believe these men are militia and they're in the process of advancing on the retreating UN forces."

The president continued to examine the photos. After a moment he laid the photo down and began smiling, "Well, they kicked ass, didn't they?"

"It looks that way Mr. President." Nossler replied as a wave of relief washed over him. Then he handed the boss some additional computer printouts. "These Echelon intercepts seem to confirm it. NSA intercepted the following communications out of the UN command indicating they lost nearly two thousand men and a commanding General in the battle."

The president of the United States remained silent for several seconds as he read the Echelon intercept, then he began to laugh out loud. "Well," the president said. "That's fantastic and if I might add, a good dose of poetic justice. Those UN bastards have been trying to disarm Americans for years and those same, 'hooligans with guns,' I believe that was the language Secretary Al-Duri used, stood up and kicked their collective ass. This is beautiful. Seriously, if I knew who the leader of that militia was I'd give him a freaking medal."

The Vice President spoke up in a less elated tone. "What's the expected fallout from this going to be? I mean, surely the UN will go crying to the Chinese about this and they're going to think we were involved."

"There's a strong possibility they *won't* go to the Chinese," interjected the NSA. "What are they going to say? A bunch of unorganized rabble took out one of our armored brigades? They'd lose too much face in the eyes of the Chinese if they admitted that."

The president's mood suddenly changed as he threw the CIA folder on the table in front of him. "You know what? Fuck Al-Duri and fuck the Chinese too! If we have reconnaissance photos then you can bet the Chinese do as well. They might be backstabbing communists but they're not stupid. They can read the photos as well as we can. The fact is the godforsaken UN got their asses handed to them, and frankly I'm pretty happy that a bunch of gun-toting Americans were the ones to do it."

The president was clearly angry and the veins that stood out from the sides of his neck confirmed it. "Herb, Phillip, I want hard data on these militia groups, and I don't mean any of that bullshit the Southern Poverty Law Center or the Brady Campaign spreads around the hill. I want to know their strengths, where they're at and who's leading them. I'm the Commander-and-Chief and it looks like they're my only viable CONUS assets. I want that information before I go to bed tonight…understood?"

The DCI and the NSA looked at each other, with brows furrowed before answering in unison, "Yes sir, Mr. President."

Margaret Bantam, the Secretary of State, spoke up, "Sir, this might provide us with an option we've thus far overlooked. The Chinese made it clear that they'd regard any US military intervention against UN forces as an attack upon them, but the militia can't be considered active duty military forces." She stood up and began walking towards the president's desk. "Sir, may I use your computer?"

"Sure Margaret."

The Secretary of State began typing information and then paused while the search engine retrieved the data. "Here it is," she said as the information she requested filled the screen. "Sir, are you familiar with section 10 of the US Code?"

"No, but I have the feeling you're looking at it right now."

"That's correct. Section 10 deals with the organization of the militia. Allow me to paraphrase a brief section: 10 USC 311, defines the militia as "all able-bodied males at least 17 years of age and, except as provided in section 13 of title 32, under 45 years of age who are, or have made a declaration of intention to become, citizens of the United States."

"Furthermore, these statutes also divide the Militia into various classes, such as 'organized' and 'unorganized', in the case of 10 USC 311, or 'active' and 'reserve', as many states have chosen to do, with 'active' being considered the National Guards, but not the federal armed forces. That leaves the unorganized militia, which in this case would be everyone else within the age groups denoted in subsection 311."

"Where are you going with this, Margaret?"

"We would need to pass this by the Attorney General, but what I'm saying is...constitutionally speaking, the militia is one-hundred percent legitimate and since they're not part of the active duty military neither the Chinese or the UN can claim the Pentagon is involved. So if you covertly support them you'll maintain plausible deniability."

"Let me see if I understand what you're suggesting." The president said while stroking his clean-shaven face. "First, I should unofficially embrace the militia and provide them with arms and material so they can continue to fight against the UN. Second, you're telling me if I do this, I'll be able to look the Chinese in the face and tell them the Pentagon has no control over what the militia is doing. Is that right?"

"Yes, Mr. President, that's what I'm saying. What do you have to lose? For goodness sake, if we use the few military forces we have left in the continental United States we risk World War III with the Chinese. But, these photos show that the citizens of this country are taking the situation into their own hands and frankly, they've shown they can win."

Neither the president nor the Secretary of State noticed how agitated the other three members of the meeting had become. Finally Wannamaker could take no more. "Sir..."

The president spun around oblivious irritated by the interruption. "What?"

"Sir...What Margaret is suggesting is dangerous."

"Dangerous?" The president snapped back. "What do you think will happen? The UN will invade the country?"

"No, he has a point," added Vice President Valentine in support of the NSA. "Mr. President, no one is more outraged by this invasion than I am. Nobody in this room is more willing to tell the Chinese to go screw themselves. But..."

The VP took a breath before continuing. "There's a reason the government has kept its thumb on these groups all these years. There's a reason no one in Washington has seriously uttered the word 'militia' since the Civil War. If you give these people even the slightest sanction, especially now after they've won a military victory, you'll open a Pandora's box that may never be closed again. The thing in that box is dangerous, and not just to the UN."

The president leaned back in his chair and crossed his arms like a judge listening to an argument. "What are you talking about James?"

The Vice President shifted on the couch, closer to the president's chair and in a soothing voice continued. "While you were serving in the military and climbing the corporate ladder, I was here in Washington. I've served two previous Presidents and spent most of my adult life on the hill. When I joined the ticket, we agreed you needed someone who knew the inter-workings of this town to help you. Mr. President, there are certain lines we just don't want to cross."

Valentine removed his glasses and set them on the coffee table between the couches. "You're surprised that this militia group beat off the UN battalion. I'm not. It wouldn't surprise anyone who has really studied the problem."

"What problem?" The perplexed President asked.

Valentine closed his eyes and sighed as though preparing to reveal a great secret. Then he looked straight at the president. "The Federal government has worked on this for many years. Centuries, really. We've worked to convince the people that only the government can keep the barbarians from the gates." His lip twitched. "It isn't true, of course. Do you know how many people there are in this country? How many guns? No force on earth can keep them under control, if they ever get the idea that *they're* the ones with the power."

The VP stood up and began to uneasily shift side-to-side as he presented an analogy. "The shepherd protects the sheep," he said. "The sheep placidly accept the shepherd's protection. But the shepherd also fleeces the sheep, and sometimes he eats them. Bottom line, it's a net loss for the sheep. So why don't the sheep trample the shepherd? They could, you know. There are so very many of them."

The president unconsciously began pushing himself back in his chair, as if trying to distance himself from the older man. His eyes had grown very wide. "What are you saying?" he demanded.

"Sir," said Nossler, picking up the defense, "this UN invasion is a short-term and limited problem. At the very worst, we lose control of parts of California and Arizona. The southern California coast would be a great loss, but nothing we can't rebuild from. But if this militia thing spirals out of control..."

"They fight the UN," Valentine interrupted in an anxious tone, "because they hate the UN. But that's not all they hate. If they take the bit in their teeth, they won't stop there."

The president couldn't believe his ears. "You're afraid they'll turn on their own government?"

"We believe some of them certainly will," answered Nossler. "Some of them tried to in the early 90's, but their lack of strength and coordination prevented them from succeeding. Mostly, they can be marginalized as paranoid extremists. But sometimes it's necessary to take firmer action."

"You should also consider the Liberals' reaction," Valentine added. "They want your head on a plate." The mention of Liberals, an opponent the president understood, galvanized him

"Mr. President, excuse my bluntness, but if you embrace the militia the liberals are going to shit bricks." James Valentine warned.

"So what, what are they going to do, impeach me?" The president fired back. "That's already happened. I'll be honest; I'd like nothing more than to see Paula Alberti lose control of her bladder live on C-Span. I've taken enough shit from these black-hearted traitors. I swore an oath to protect and defend the constitution of the United States and if the militias are constitutional...then to hell with the liberals, the UN and the fucking Chinese!"

Direct Action Academy

It was still dark when the troops of SWAZCOM began loading their vehicles for their trip to the forward base of operations. All night equipment was assembled and loaded and now only the men themselves remained. Most had said good-byes to friends and loved ones several days before, but for a few, the difficult task was at hand.

Mike could see that Rachel was doing all she could to maintain a positive attitude, and he appreciated it. Inside he fought a Sisyphean battle between staying with the woman he loved and fulfilling his duty. The internal struggle was so fierce that he'd felt nauseous most the night and could barely keep from vomiting even now.

Although Rachel was composed, her beautiful eyes were red and swollen testifying that she'd been crying for a longtime and was now either out of tears or successfully wining the battle to hold them back.

"It's time for me to go. I'll radio you once we arrive at the ranch. Everything's going to be all right...I promise I'll come back." The words sounded hollow and contrived even to him. He knew what he was getting into. They'd received the reports of the Pyrrhic victory in California. Even though the enemy had retreated and the militia was left in control of the battlefield, Stalker's men had lost more than half their total number and expended the majority of their ammunition.

Unless they received immediate reinforcements, Stalker did not think he could withstand another UN attack. The other disturbing issue was everyone knew the next time the UN attacked they'd do so with much greater firepower. Rachel held Mike tightly and kissed his neck. "All this gear you're wearing doesn't make it very easy for me to hold you," she remarked before adding. "I love you, Mike."

"I love you too babe. Here, take this." Mike passed her a simple white envelope.

"What is it?" Rachel asked looking at the envelope.

"Just a letter I wrote. I hope it'll make more sense to you then what I've been trying to say lately."

"Sorry to interrupt, but we've got to get rolling." Cowboy's voice was slightly embarrassed, but firm. "Don't worry Rachel, he's in good hands...we'll take care of him."

Mike kissed Rachel one last time and then turned and climbed on the truck. With a jolt, the truck shifted into gear and began rolling away. Mike raised his rifle and waved to Rachel as he disappeared into the pre-dawn darkness.

Rachel stood, engulfed in a cloud of dust and exhaust, continuing a fruitless vigil even after the truck's rear lights had disappeared. Then she turned and began a lonely walk back to the main building. As she walked she opened the envelope Mike had handed her. Inside was one simple handwritten page.

Dear Rachel,

I've been trying to explain my feelings to you for days now and haven't been able to find the right words. You know how much I love you, but you also know that I am dedicated to our country and cannot abandon it in its hour of greatest need. Although my heart cries out to stay near you, where it is safe and warm, I know if I did I would betray a part of me that would never recover.

A seventeenth century English Nobleman named Richard Lovelace wrote the following poem. When he wrote it, he found himself in the same position I do, torn between the woman he loved and the duty he could not ignore. I hope you'll understand that if I did not maintain my honor, I would never be able to love you the way you deserve to be loved. My every thought is of you and the love that will forever blossom between us.

With the greatest love and eternal devotion,

Mike

Tell me not, sweet, I am unkind, that from the nunnery of thy chaste breast and quiet mind to war and arms I fly.

True, a new mistress now I chase, the first foe is in the field, and with a stronger faith embrace a sword, a horse, a shield.

Yet this inconstancy is such as you, too, shall adore. I could not love thee dear so much, loved I not honor more.

As Rachel finished the short letter she could no longer hold back the torrent of tears that she'd found success in doing earlier. Instead she read the poem over and over until its words etched themselves into her heart. Sitting down, she surrendered herself to her emotions and shamelessly wept while clutching the now tear stained letter to her breast. She knew, more than ever before, that she'd found the only man for her. Unfortunately only God himself could insure he'd come back.

Double C Ranch: Forward Base of Deployment for SWAZCOM

It had taken the better part of the day to get the battalions organized and set up. Before leaving the academy the commanders structured staff positions and manned them with the best personnel from the various battalions. Stratiotes from the *Shekinah* battalion was assigned as brigade S1, in charge of all personnel issues. Tire Iron would serve as both the overall commander of SWAZCOM and as the S2 officer. His experience with the CIA made him the ideal person to handle intelligence. The brigade operations position (S3) was assigned to Cowboy and Slim was designated S4, or supply officer. J.R. had set aside space in the main house for the communications center and a hospital.

Volunteers recruited from the community helped the battalion medics organize and set up the hospital. Their first task was to gather and sort out all the medical supplies and make sure they'd be ready once shooting began. After the hospital was ready for business, a blood drive was started to establish a supply of all types. Two refrigerators were moved into the hospital to hold the collected blood and preserve it for use. Josh set up a sewing shop in a backroom where he continued to repair and build needed gear. Finally, an ammo dump was established in a large root cellar not far from the main house.

Just before 1600, the on duty communications officer received a radio transmission from a group calling itself the 73rd Battalion. After checking his information logs, the comms officer realized the 73rd had been designated out-of-action. So he sent his partner to find Tire Iron and help verify the contact.

"Contact 73, can you provide positive identification to validate who you are?"

"This is Glory, in command of the 73rd battalion, 31st Field Force. We lost all our communications equipment following initial engagements and have been unable to establish regular contact with outside forces. I have intelligence to pass on and need to speak with your S2 officer."

TI entered the comms room and was quickly briefed on the contact. After reading over the comms officers notes he wrote instructions on a pad of paper, and pushed it in front of the radio operator. At the last regional commanders' conference a quick and simple system had been developed to help identify other militia members when they met for the first time.

It was based on the sign/counter sign system, but instead of words, numbers were used. One date that was universally recognized by the militias was April 19th. This was the date of the battle of Concord and Lexington and for many years was celebrated as Patriot's Day. So often militiamen would end posts or simply say "419" as a way of reminding one another of their heritage.

The council had decided that the "sign" would be any number between 1 and 419, and the countersign would be the number which when added to the sign, would total four hundred and nineteen.

The radio operator read the short note and then pressed the transmission button on his microphone. "Contact 73 provide the countersign for 233. Over."

There was a brief pause and then the response arrived. "Countersign is186. Over."

Tire Iron took the microphone, "This is Tire Iron, I'm the CO of SWAZCOM...what have you got?"

After receiving the information Tire Iron made sure to set up a communications protocol to stay in touch with Glory, then copied the information into a standard intelligence report format to brief the command staff.

The brigade staff was assembled and Tire Iron began his briefing. "Gentlemen, I have received critical information that may very well change the whole way we approach this current war. At 1548 communications made contact, with someone who, after positive identification protocols, turned out to be the leader of the 73rd battalion, based in San Diego County.

The leader of that group is named Glory. Some of you may know him. Previous intelligence assumed the 73rd battalion was wiped out following initial skirmishes on the border. Evidently, the 73rd took extremely heavy casualties and lost their comms. Since then they've been operating as guerrillas and ambushing small UN patrols and weapons collection stations. During a recent ambush they took a prisoner who has been identified as Marco Valdez, a student at SDSU. Valdez turns out to be a Regional Representative to the National Coordinating Council for OJChA."

"This position makes him directly responsible for the coordination and execution of OJChA activities throughout Southern California. As you may know, OJChA is the leading organization for the Chicano and Atzlán movement in the United States. Additional information is as follows:

The prisoner was captured during an ambush on a UN Weapons Collections Depot

The prisoner has made repeated reference to international connections

He has made repeated comparisons between Chicanos and Palestinians

Glory is a former Air Force Parajumper, so his information should be considered highly reliable.

The 73rd believe the following possibilities exist:

There may be a connection with Islamic Extremists

This would explain the use of traditional Middle Eastern tactics of truck bombs, the high sophistication of the devices and the use of RDX as the primary explosive

This would also explain how the movement suddenly became so well funded and coordinated.

Another point that Glory made, with which I agree, is that OJChA does not have the strength, finances or connections needed to orchestrate an operation of this scale. It is highly likely that they had outside assistance and that could very well have come from a militant group of Islamic extremists."

Porter Glockwell raised his hand. "TI, if radical Islamists are involved with the Atzlán movement, which groups would you suspect?"

"Before we left Utah I spoke with a long time friend at '*The Farm,*'" Tire Iron used the nickname given to the CIA training facility in Camp Peary, Virginia. "The bomb analysis done on the truck bombs in California and here in Arizona, showed they were RDX propane enhanced bombs, the same type and construction as the one that destroyed the Marine Barracks in Beirut, Lebanon in the early 1980's. The Israeli Mossad and Shin Bet believe the bomb maker was Ibrahim Al-Sadi, who is known to work with Hezbollah."

"Hezbollah is a Syrian backed and Iranian financed terror organization, right?" asked Arrow.

"Correct. Since the IDF pulled out of Lebanon, Hezbollah switched from mostly overt to covert operations. They also operate a number of terrorist training camps in the Becca Valley where they've trained members of Hamas, Islamic Jihad, Fatah and al-Qaeda. Unfortunately, Washington chose to overlook Hezbollah and concentrate on al-Qaeda because they believe they have a wider global reach." Stratiotes spoke up from the back of the room, "Let's say Hezbollah is involved, how can we confirm this, and if we do, what can we do about it? One way or the other we have a clear and present danger to fight. We've got to deal with these UN forces before we start worrying about Islamic terrorists."

"That's a fact." TI answered. "We have to deal with the UN either way and we will. But, I believe we should pass this information on to my contacts back at Langley. They need to know what's going on. Let's face it, as you pointed out we've got our hands full with the UN. But, if Hezbollah is behind this, they're going to continue funding more and more attacks and that means we've got to find a way to prepare for them."

"All right," Arrow said. "Pass this intel on to your contacts at Langley and see if they'll share any additional information they might have about UN troop movements. Thanks for the briefing." Arrow then turned towards Cowboy and added, "Get in touch with Chief Meadows and see if he can squeeze his FBI contacts for any information we could use. That ought to do it, gentlemen. Make sure your patrols are ready to go and that the LO/OP's are set for the night."

Washington, D.C.

Herb Nossler's driver opened the door to his armored, black Lincoln Town Car and he slid across its wide leather seat while speaking on his cell phone, pausing his conversation just long enough to give the driver instructions, "Linda, I need to be at the White House in twenty minutes...fifteen would be better, do what you have to do."

Linda Bright was an accomplished driver and an expert in executive protection. During her time at the agency she had driven for various Directors and knew every short cut to every building in and around the district. "No problem, Boss. Will you be using the South entrance or the residential?"

"The South Portico will be fine." The DCI answered as Linda closed the door securely and walked around the back of the vehicle to the driver's side door. As she moved she instinctively scanned the area for any potential threats then quickly got in and radioed the White House Communications Center, "BOOKSTORE, MUSTANG is en route to CITADEL." Linda started the 4.6-liter V-8, pointed it towards the Georgetown Pike exit and headed off.

In the back, Herb Nossler continued his conversation with the agency's ranking instructor at Camp Peary, Trevor Bennet. Trevor was a career man who'd been with the agency for over thirty years. During his tenure he'd been assisgned to field operations all over the world and received several commendations that only the agency, his wife and he knew anything about. For the last five years he'd served as the head instructor at the CIA training camp where new agents were taught fieldcraft and various other "essential" skills they'd need during foreign operations.

"Tire Iron? What kind of a name is that?" incredulously asked the DCI.

"Actually, it's a nickname I gave him when he worked for me in Cairo," Bennet explained. "Whenever I needed someone to get into something or make sure a task was completed, this guy was the first one I thought of. He was the most versatile and reliable tool I had, so I started calling him Tire Iron."

"So you believe this information is reliable and this *Tire Iron guy* is legit?"

"No question about it, Herb. I'd bet my life on this guy...in fact, I have several times, and since I'm on the phone with you now, I guess that answers your question."

"Well, then what's he doing running around Arizona with a bunch of militia nuts?"

There was a pause on the line. "I don't have any recent info about that, Herb. I guess you could just say everybody needs a hobby. Tire Iron was always going on about the Constitution."

Nossler sighed. "Well, if this information vets out, I may have to change certain parts of my own tune. Until then, I'm struggling not to regard it with the skepticism my gut says it deserves."

"I don't know anything about that," Bennet added firmly, "But if it really came from Tire Iron, you can take it to the bank."

"That's going to have to be good enough for now. Stay in touch with this guy and make sure you get me any additional information he comes up with. Good job." The Director hung up his cell phone and then quickly dialed the Terrorism Desk Chief.

"David, its Director Nossler. I need you to do a full sweep on any Hezbollah activity in Latin America and particularly Mexico. I want to know about anything that even remotely gets a radar return. Go back a full year and make sure you coordinate this with the Latin American Desk. I want them to check with all embassy chiefs in every capital. I'll need a report to bring to the White House for tomorrow morning's security briefing. Call in as many people as you need, I want a full court press on this. Thanks."

While the Director was talking Linda expertly navigated the GW Memorial Parkway and was now crossing the Theodore Roosevelt Bridge. "Director, traffic is light tonight. We should arrive in less than ten minutes." Linda confidently announced as the black Town Car swiftly glided across the Potomac River and into the District

The Lincoln's over engineered suspension allowed the six thousand two hundred pound car to ride like a showroom version. But nothing sold at the local dealership could compare to this luxury tank. Its armored windows could withstand direct hits from 9mm, .357, and .44-caliber bullets and ceramic plates in the doors protected the Director against rifle fire from both .223 and 7.62 rounds. It had a self-sealing radiator, fuel tank and run-flat tires. Nothing short of an anti-tank rocket could stop it.

Linda made a left turn off Constitution Avenue onto 17th Street and then drove north to the White House entrance that led to the South Portico; she'd made it in fourteen and a half minutes.

"Excellent work Linda. I don't know how long this'll take, but I want you ready to pick me up and bring me back to the office as soon as we're done. Why don't you go down to the White House kitchen and see if they'll make you a sandwich, it's probably going to be a long night."

Director Nossler walked up to the Portico doors, which were guarded by a Marine Corporal in full dress blues. Passing through the immediate foyer, he strode along the downstairs corridor past the Diplomatic Reception Room.

The president often received diplomats in this room that was made famous by Franklin D. Roosevelt; it was here that FDR had recorded his famous fireside addresses and where King George and Queen Elizabeth were received in 1939. It was also here that Director Nossler ran into Phillip Wannamaker, who was also on his way to meet the president.

"Good evening Herb. The president is waiting in the Map Room."

"Do you know who else will be there?"

"Secretary McMillan and the AG. How'd your guys at CIA do?"

"I've got some interesting details including a source inside the militia that just passed on some very critical information." The two men entered the Map Room through double doors and were greeted by the president. The Map Room is a comfortable sitting parlor with butter colored paneled walls and cherry wood floors and furniture.

"Herb, Phil, have a seat. I hope you've got some good news for me?" The president said.

The DCI and NSA both took seats on a red couch that was flanked by two red armchairs where Secretary McMillan and Attorney General Frank Thomas were seated. A large, red wingback chair was positioned across from the couch, which was reserved for the president. Across the room a small inviting fire glowed in the fireplace. Overhead an ornate crystal chandelier filled the room with warm light. Nossler looked around him and thought, "*Interesting that the Vice President wasn't present. The president rarely did anything important without the older man's council.*"

Seeing that everyone was ready, the president took charge, "All right people I don't want to keep you here all night, what have you got for me?"

The Director distributed folders to all the participants and then began his presentation. "Mr. President this is what we've learned since this morning. The militia in San Bernardino is led by a man called Stalker."

"Stalker? Great, I have to depend on some guy called *Stalker* to defend the United States?" The president said in an exasperated voice.

"Sir, evidently it's a tradition in the militia to use nicknames. *Nom de guerres*, if you will. We're researching his real name, but for now this is what we have. As I was saying this Stalker guy is the leader of what is being called the Southern California Command."

"It's comprised of militias broken out by counties from California, Nevada and Utah. These were the men that wiped out that UN brigade; unfortunately their victory came at a high cost. Our information tells us they lost nearly half of their men and are running extremely low on ammunition and supplies."

"That would make them combat ineffective." said Defense Secretary McMillan. "When one of our units falls below fifty percent we write them off and fold them into another group."

"Exactly," said Nossler. "We don't think they can survive another attack."

"So you're telling me these guys are one shot wonders? Frankly, I can't afford that; these are the only cards I have to play. I can't have the UN wiping them out and then cutting off Los Angeles from the rest of the country," Replied an exasperated President.

"Sir, morale is high among the militia. These men strongly believe in what they're doing and they've proven they're willing to go the distance. We need to somehow find a way to re-supply them, if possible with modern weapons that'll act as force multipliers."

The president caught his eye. "Herb, this morning you had reservations about acknowledging them at all. Now you want to arm them, have you had some kind of epiphany?"

"Mr. President, I still have reservations about the long-term consequences of this. But we have to fight the enemy we've got. There are rumblings that these troubles weren't only caused by the homegrown Aztlán movement. It may be more serious than I originally thought."

Attorney General Thomas spoke up. "Mr. President, I've looked at the information that State sent over this morning and I believe we can make a solid argument for the constitutionality of these militias. Don't misunderstand me, all hell's going to break loose when the liberals get wind of this, but I believe we can argue this falls into the category of original intent. I believe this is exactly the role the Framers envisioned the unorganized militia to play. The only danger I see is granting them too much power."

Thomas shook his head and let out a slight sigh, "I'd hate to see some guy with a Napoleon complex march on Washington with ten thousand armed militiamen. We need to find the right guy and back him."

The president sat in his chair and adjusted his reading glasses as he looked back down at the briefing folder. "What else have you got, Herb?"

"In addition to the Southern California Command, there's a brigade sized command organizing near the Arizona/Mexican border. They're comprised of units from all over the Western US. Just as I was leaving Langley, I received a phone call from our head instructor at the farm. Evidently, the commander of this brigade is a former CIA operative who passed on some critical information. I didn't have time to get it typed up, but it'll be included in tomorrow morning's briefing. This guy is called...well, Tire Iron, sir."

He was interrupted by a chorus of chuckles and wagging heads.

"Er...yes, well be that as it may. Our head instructor down at Camp Peary, Trevor Bennet, says he knows and trusts him without question. It seems a guerrilla group in Southern California took a prisoner who turned out to be a Regional Representative from an organization called OJChA. This guy was supposedly involved in the planning of this whole invasion and what he's said has led 'Tire Iron' to believe there might be an Islamic connection...specifically Hezbollah."

"What's this Tire guy basing that assumption on?" asked the NSA.

"Several pieces of information but specifically the fact that the truck bombs used in the California and Arizona attacks were of the same design as the one used against the Marine Barracks in Beirut. This Aztlán group has never been able to organize anything on this scale before. The primary reason is they never had the finances or the technical expertise; Hezbollah would have both in ample supply. Plus we know that all the bombs had the signature of Ibrahim Al-Sadi, who is one of their top bomb engineers."

"What are you doing to follow up on the possibility that this could be correct?" the Attorney General asked.

"I have my Terrorism and Latin American teams pulling an all-nighter checking out every possible lead on every terror group in the Western hemisphere. I don't want to sound over confident, but from what I'm told this Tire Iron is the real deal. He worked with Trevor in Egypt and evidently he was the best field operative he ever worked with. I've known Trevor for almost twenty years and if he says this guy can be trusted...then I have to believe him."

"Okay," said the president, "let's step back and examine what we have. The UN is strongly entrenched in California. The Chinese are threatening to attack our forces in Korea, and probably launch an attack on Taiwan if we make a military move against the UN, which places our military in check, unless we're ready to start World War III."

"The only card we have to play is a bunch of unorganized militias with small arms. If that's not bad enough, they're being led by people with names like Stalker and Tire Iron, God help us. But, they've proven their willingness to fight and ability to win. Frank, you believe this administration can constitutionally support the existence of these militiamen, right?"

The Attorney General cleared his throat. "Yes sir, but it'll be at a high political price."

"The way I see it, this might be the last roll of the dice for me...I might as well go all in. Finally, there might be a Hezbollah connection to these attacks. If we can establish that link, it'll help to further demonize these Aztlán assholes and hopefully provide us with some much needed international support against the UN. Am I tracking right so far?"

"Yes, Mr. President."

"All right then, Chad, we need to get supplies and weapons to these militias, but we need to find a way to do it so they *cannot* be traced back to the Pentagon. I want this operation to be so black your men will need night vision goggles just to take a leak. Remember, if anyone gets even the slightest whiff of this we'll be fighting a billion Chinese."

Secretary McMillan chimed in, "Mr. President, I believe we can get supplies to the California group from our depots near Ft. Irwin outside of Barstow. The Arizona group could probably be supplied from Ft. Huachuca in Southern Arizona. Whatever supplies those bases lack we can airlift. We also maintain stockpiles of foreign manufactured equipment. Our Special Forces units use them on covert missions behind enemy lines. That way if they lose anything, it can't be traced back to us. I'll have a recommended list of supplies ready for your national security briefing in the morning."

"Very well, make it happen." Ordered the president, then added, "I'd like you to work with Herb to see if you can move the supplies through the agency. They've been covertly supplying weapons to people for decades...at least this time it will be to our own people."

"The last issue I want to deal with is the UN. As far as I'm concerned they are now an enemy of the United States. I want the US out of the UN and the UN out of the US. Frank," he pointed to the Attorney General, "I want you to head this up. Find me a way of declaring the United Nations Participation Act and the United Nations Headquarters Agreement null and void."

"The priorities are as follows:" he began ticking items off on his fingers

1. Herb, contact this Tire Iron guy and let him know we're going to covertly support the militias. Make sure he knows covertly means *covertly.*

2. General, I want to see that list of supplies tomorrow morning and I need to know how they'll get from point A to point B, and when.

3. Phil, I want you to keep a close eye on the Chinese. If they even take a dump, I want to know about it.

4. Frank, continue to work our policy position on the militia and find me a watertight way out of the UN.

The president stood abruptly. "That should be enough to keep you gentlemen busy. I appreciate your assistance and service. Good night."

UN Headquarters: New York

UN General Secretary Al-Duri summoned Ambassador William Majors for a 6:00 a.m. meeting in his office. While his driver navigated the hectic morning traffic of lower Manhattan, Majors received last minute marching orders directly from the president via an encrypted cellular phone in the back of his car. There was no question what Al-Duri was so livid about he was going to tell the US to rein in the militia that had wiped out his peacekeepers in California. The president was unwavering in his position that as far as the militias were concerned, the US government had no control over them. They were private citizens exercising their right to keep and bear arms and protecting themselves from the intrusion of the UN forces.

"Mr. President, I understand your position, but the Secretary General is going to demand that we do something. I don't think he's going to be satisfied with the answer you want me to present."

"Bill, I don't give a rat's ass what Al-Duri wants. He's not the president of this country...I am! If he doesn't like the taste of that answer, then keep cramming it down his throat until he swallows it. Bill, we've known each other for many years and I like you, but don't forget that you serve at my discretion and if you're not capable or willing to go toe-to-toe with this bastard, then I'll find someone who is. Do I make myself clear?"

"Yes sir, Mr. President...crystal."

"Very well Bill. I expect a call as soon as you leave lower Manhattan. Good luck."

"*Well, this is shaping up to be a real wonderful day. First the Secretary General's office calls me at five in the morning and tells me Al-Duri wants to see me in an hour and then I get a Presidential sized hole chewed in my ass.*" Majors thought to himself as he fondled a bronze Alcoholics Anonymous token in his pants pocket. The token was a gift from his wife. On one side it had a simple triangle inside a circle and on the reverse was printed the phrase, "*God grant me the serenity to accept the things I cannot change, courage to change the things I can, and the wisdom to know the difference.*"

William Majors had repeated that phrase so many times that it was now forever etched into his mind. He'd been sober for over ten years and during that time had fought the urge to take a drink thousands of times, but he was aware of the price drinking had claimed on him. He knew that if he weren't an alcoholic he'd probably hold a cabinet position or maybe be the governor of his home state of Indiana. But, there was nothing he could do about that now. The best thing he could do was steel himself for the confrontation that was about to take place.

His driver pulled up to 405 East 42nd Street, also known as One UN Plaza. After flashing an ID he drove into the underground parking lot reserved for diplomats. With three minutes to spare, Majors arrived at the reception desk in front of the General Secretary's office and signed the visitors' log.

"Ambassador Majors," Secretary Al-Duri said, "please come in and have a seat. We've got important business to discuss."

"Good Morning Mr. Secretary. How may I be of service?"

"Ambassador, as I'm sure you're aware we've got a crisis in California. American militia attacked our peacekeepers and over a thousand were killed. This is unacceptable and I expect you to make it clear to your President that these actions will not be tolerated. I spent an hour, last night, trying to pacify the Chinese Ambassador. His government made their position very clear regarding US attacks against UN forces. Your government's actions have placed me in a very awkward position. As the Secretary General, I am ultimately responsible for UN peacekeepers and their success, but at the same time, I also have the duty of maintaining peace among the member countries of this organization. I'm sure you understand."

"Mr. Secretary General, I wish to express our deepest condolences for the tragic losses that were suffered. What happened was regrettable, but I must make it clear there is nothing we can do about what occurred. With all due respect, the UN forces initiated the attack and the militia simply acted in self-defense. These are common citizens who were acting on their own. Washington has no control over them. The US Constitution guarantees our citizens the right to keep and bear arms for personal and national defense. The militias perceive the peacekeepers as a foreign occupying force. They're simply defending their country."

The Ambassador's reply only heightened Al-Duri's angst, "Ambassador Majors, do you expect me to believe your government is powerless to control these militias? Don't insult my intelligence."

Bill Majors reached down and removed a file folder from his briefcase, which contained a copy of the US codes outlining the establishment of the militias. The file had been overnighted to him from the Justice Department just for this situation.

"Mr. Secretary, this is a copy of the US codes that will better explain the legalities associated with the unorganized militia in the United States. As you see these forces are entirely made up of civilians and are in no way linked with our active duty or reserve forces. Thus the Pentagon has no authority over them. They are acting within their constitutionally guaranteed rights and it is the duty of the president to protect those rights."

The Secretary General quickly reviewed the documents, and then abruptly threw them back at the Ambassador. "Ambassador Majors, I couldn't care less if the militia was part of the fucking Boy Scouts. The fact remains that they killed my peacekeepers and are interfering with the duties of the United Nations. Your administration *must* put an end to this outrage!"

"Secretary Al-Duri, with all due respect, you're suggesting that the government of the United States exercise unconstitutional powers to militarily suppress its own citizens. Our constitution strictly forbids that. I'm afraid that is unacceptable." Bill could see the fury building on Al-Duri's face. He knew the UN leader realized he was in a corner that he couldn't wiggle out of. That knowledge gave him an unexpected dose of satisfaction.

"I don't care what *your* insignificant constitution says," the Secretary General rebuked, "I represent the global community and we will not stand by and allow peasants with hunting rifles and antiquated political dogmas to stop us from achieving our goals. If your President does not have the backbone to deal with these militiamen, then *I will.*" Al-Duri rose from his chair and leaded across his desk in a threatening manner. "Allow me to put this in words that even *your* President will understand, we will crush these militiamen like irritating bugs under our feet, and when we do I will not allow you to come crying to us about how American citizens were killed. I gave you an opportunity to handle this situation and you've made it clear you value your precious constitution more than the lives of your people."

Bill Majors sat in stunned disbelief. The Secretary General had never been so candid with his anti-American point-of-view. Al-Duri was a lot of things, mostly deceitful, but he was always a shrewd diplomat. The fact that he openly disparaged the president and the constitution proved that his emotions had gotten the better of him and that meant he was off balance...Al-Duri was scared. The realization of this sent a current of fulfillment through

Bill's soul. But suddenly it seemed the facade of impartiality had been thrown off and he was allowing his seething hatred to bubble to the surface. Maybe it was because they were in *his* office, where the symbols of his power surrounded them...possibly, but Bill's instincts whispered that there was something more. Two thoughts came to mind. First, the militias must have caused greater damage to the UN forces than originally thought and second, Al-Duri was under serious pressure to ensure this Atzlán mission did not fail. What else could explain his emotional unraveling?

There was no question that the militias had proven far more serious than expected. Al-Duri's unbridled contempt and threats of overwhelming defeat were not the words of simple intent...they were spoken with the passion of a Sicilian vendetta. But for Bill, the most distressing question was, "*who's pulling Al-Duri's strings? He admitted he'd spoken with the Chinese yesterday...could they be the ones pressuring him? If not, who else wields enough power to make Al-Duri lose it like this?*"

Like an electrical current the thought raced through Bill's mind and was examined at every angle. "*Power, who has the power? What kind of power are we talking about...military, political? No, those wouldn't matter, not to him, the only power Al-Duri kowtowed to were wealth and ultimately, the power that offered him the ability to secure even greater wealth and authority beyond this life...spiritual.*"

As the Secretary General continued his diatribe, Ambassador Majors quickly scanned the extravagant office which he knew was probably paid for with American taxpayers' money. Aside from the ubiquitous pictures of handshakes with world leaders and the awards plaques that every diplomat displayed, other items stood out. On a credenza to his right sat a black onyx representation of the *Ka'aba* with finely, hand carved ivory walls surrounding the courtyard where, each year, millions traveled to fulfill the *Hajj*. Above it hung a ceremonial Arab scimitar with a jewel encrusted, golden hilt and highly polished bone handle and just below it a picture of him in the simple white robes of the pilgrimage.

In the opposite corner, facing northeast was a beautifully hand-woven silk prayer rug and beside it a compass that looked to be made from highly polished silver or platinum. "*That had to be it.*" Bill reasoned. Someone who exercised power over Al-Duri's soul was coercing him to deal with the militia once and for all. This wasn't just about peacekeepers and equipment. Al-Duri was on...a *Jihad*.

"Do you understand what I'm saying to you, are you even listening?" Al-Duri shouted, as Bill was drawn back to attention. "I believe I have made my point. Just remember, the world is losing its patience. It's time you come to understand that America's time has passed; the UN is now ready to assume its rightful role as the unchallenged world leader. Make sure your President understands that. You are dismissed." With that the Secretary pushed a button on his desk alerting his secretary to come in and escort Ambassador Majors out.

Chapter 12

> Tyranny, like hell, is not easily conquered; yet we have this consolation with us, that the harder the conflict, the more glorious the triumph.
> —Thomas Paine

73rd Battalion Encampment

For the past several days Glory and Eightball had gradually stepped up the interrogation pressure on their prisoner. They knew Marco possessed knowledge that would lead them to the upper echelons of the Atzlán movement and possibly to the Islamic connection they believed was organizing and financing them. There was no longer any doubt about his innocence's. He had crucial information the militias needed. Since Marco was not a member of a military the provisions of the Geneva Conference did not apply to him. While Glory had no intention of torturing him, he was intent on making Marco talk.

Initially they had focused on non-intrusive physical techniques to wear Marco down. The clothesline procedure broke the prisoner physically, which in turn, began to mentally soften him. Since he was not a special trained operative, mentality conditioned to compartmentalize pain, they realized that would be the fastest way to break him. Their initial success forced him to divulge information. In the second phase they continued the clothesline technique but added a heightened physiological dimension. First, Marco was treated by allowing to bath for the first time since his capture, but as soon as he began to enjoy the uniquely human feeling of cleanliness, he was forced to put on a pair of overalls that were several sizes too large and horribly soiled by other men. Then they placed a hood over his head and transferred him to an isolation tent; basically a tent inside a tent.

The enclosure was completely blacked out so no light whatsoever could penetrate the claustrophobic cocoon, creating a sort of sensory deprivation chamber. Additionally, a radio was set up just outside the tent and purposely tuned to a frequency between stations, producing a mind wrenching mixture of static and unintelligible garble.

In this new location, Marco's guard disrupted his normal circadian rhythms by deliberately interrupting his sleeping and eating patterns. The guards never address him by his name; but simply called him prisoner. When they spoke to him at all, it was in a monotonic voice devoid of emotion or inflection. Over the following seventy-two hours he was kept awake and occasionally fed small portions of thick, cold concoctions of whatever could be found around camp. The effect of this treatment was a complete monopolization of the prisoner's perception. Marco's full attention was focused on his immediate predicament. His only waking sensation was total discomfort, confusion and the desperate search for a discernable pattern.

Now that he was properly conditioned, Eightball resumed his verbal interrogation. First, he asked Marco questions he'd already answered, like his name, where he lived, where he went to school, what he did for OJChA, etc. These questions were purposely posed so Marco would become accustomed to speaking and answering questions. Then Eightball asked things he knew Marco had no idea about. For example, "What are the Atzlán forces in Texas doing right now?"

These questions further confused Marco, forcing him to wonder whether he'd actually known the answers and had somehow forgotten, or if he ever knew them in the first place. Whenever he said he didn't know Eightball slapped his legs with a pole, sending excruciating bolts of pain shooting up his thighs. After suffering through several of these episodes Marco was eager to answer anything. In some cases he eagerly volunteered information. Marco began to associate answering questions with being in control. Though in reality, he controlled nothing.

Each time Marco offered a new bit of information, Eightball would recoil against him, "Don't lie to me, Prisoner. You know that can't be true. What are you trying to do…trick me? Do you think I'm stupid, some kind of fucking moron?" In an attempt to convince his tormentor of the truthfulness of his confession, Marco would frantically search his clouded mind for additional details to substantiate his statement.

After several interrogation sessions Marco had delivered a volume of information including details on the command structures for the PLA and OJChA. But most importantly, he provided meticulous information about two Syrians who worked with Hezbollah and how they were assisting the PLA.

UN Headquarters: New York City

Secretary Al-Duri hosted an exclusive group of men in his private conference room adjacent to his spacious office in UN headquarters. The room was electronically swept for listening devices weekly to ensure he could maintain absolute security, nonetheless in anticipation of this sensitive meeting it had been recertified just hours before by a handpicked team of counterespionage specialists assigned to the Secretary General.

As the participants settled into their seats, Al-Duri arrived, escorting Mohammed Saddat. The two men presented a stark juxtaposition. Al-Duri wore a finely tailored European suit with a pair of the finest Italian leather shoes, while his guest was clothed in the austere black robes and turban of a Shiite cleric. Al-Duri gingerly walked the aged man to an upholstered seat before bending down and kissing his hand. Al-Duri then moved to the front of the room and called the meeting to order.

"Earlier this morning I met with US Ambassador Majors and made it clear to him that the UN would not stand by and allow peacekeepers to be attacked and our mission in Aztlán opposed. The Ambassador feigned regret for the losses we suffered, but insists that his government has no control over the militias."

"No control?" Ambassador Xue Lu-Dong exclaimed. "Who does the American President think we are a collection of naïve children? Is he or isn't he in control of his country? This excuse is a direct insult against us and should be dealt with in the harshest possible terms."

"I agree Ambassador." Al-Duri replied in attempt to calm down his Chinese associate. "Unfortunately it isn't that simple. In the folders before you are copies of the documents the US Ambassador presented to me outlining the legalities governing what the US calls the 'unorganized militia.' Their Attorney General, and his staff at the Justice Department, prepared the documents. Although I agree that this is a puerile attempt at circumventing your nation's stern directive, Ambassador Lu-Dong, they seem to be legitimate."

Xue Lu-Dong scanned the documents before throwing them down in a display of frustration and disgust. "Mr. Secretary General, these statues are a century old."

"You're correct Ambassador," Al-Duri answered. "It seems the president has dug very deep into the archives to retrieve these statues. Nevertheless they're valid and applicable. What's most important now is that we put an end to these militias once and for all. I will not allow these terrorists to further interfere with our plans." The Secretary General sensed the Chinese Ambassador understood that in this situation, the Americans had once again out maneuvered him. He could also see a look of resolution spread across his face that let everyone know he wasn't going to let it happen again.

"Colonel Drago," said Al-Duri, "would you please present your report on what went wrong with the attack in California, and more importantly, your recommendations for our upcoming invasion of Arizona?"

Looking around the room, Drago knew he needed to reassure the participants of this hastily organized meeting that he had the situation in Atzlán under control. Seated before him was arrayed the financial and ideological foundation of the Atzlán strategy. In addition to the collection of UN Secretaries and Ministers, Mohammed Saddat from Iran's Revolutionary Council, Sheik Jufalli from Saudi Arabia and the Syrian Ambassador were in attendance.

"Thank you Secretary Al-Duri. Ambassador Lu-Dong, Sheik Jufalli, Minister Saadat, assembled dignitaries and special guests. Allow me to first assure you that the recent set back in California will in no way prevent us from achieving our long sought after goal of weakening the United States both domestically and internationally. Even as we speak the American President has undergone a major political defeat and is suffering the lowest public opinion polls of any President in the last forty years."

"Our allies in the US Congress have impeached him, and soon he'll be convicted by the Senate. Once this happens, a new administration dedicated to realigning American foreign policy and acknowledging the UN as the preeminent global authority will assume power."

"Even with our recent set-back, we are closer to achieving our goals than ever before. Our successes far out-weigh the temporary set backs we've encountered and I assure you the tactics we'll deploy in Arizona will allow us to quickly and definitively put an end to the American militias." Drago motioned for an aide to set up a screen and an overhead projector on which he would display slides. After all was readied, he ordered the lights to be dimmed and began his presentation.

"Gentlemen, this is an overhead view of the San Bernardino battlefield. When examining this, and using the advantage of hindsight, we see the militias exploited the natural geography of the battlefield to their advantage. The steep sides of the canyon dictated the only available route of approach. The militia commander positioned his limited forces so they could focus their firepower into well-designed killing funnels. This allowed him to maximize the effectiveness of his small arms and inflict maximum damage to our forces. Additionally, he mined the avenues of approach with large improvised explosives to defeat our armor. Due to the confines of the terrain, he knew exactly where our armor would traverse and thus was able to precisely defend against the threat."

Up to this point the Iranian cleric had sat quietly, now he slowly lifted his hand, "So, what you're telling us, Colonel, is the leader of the militia is a military man."

"Yes, Minister Saddat, there's no question about it. We've known that the American militias contain many former members of the US military and these men pass on their tactical knowledge to those who did not serve. But, we doubt many of these commanders held commissions higher than the lower officer ranks, so their experience is extremely limited and unsophisticated."

"That may be so Colonel," Sheik Jufalli added in a condescending tone. "But it seems it was enough to handily defeat one of your brigades."

"Obviously, your Excellency. But that was due to foolish mistakes made by an overconfident commander. I will not make the same miscalculations. Although the militias gained a victory in California, they did so at an extremely high price. Our intelligence tells us they were weakened to the point of collapse."

"We believe their forces and supplies are virtually depleted. When we begin our drive into Arizona, we'll do it in concert with a simultaneous attack in San Bernardino. I plan to destroy both forces and break the back of the resistance."

The Colonel's presentation switched to a map of southern Arizona. "In the Arizona operation, we will take control of the two largest cities in the theater, Tucson and Phoenix. Our goal is to seize these two population centers as quickly as possible. In order to achieve our mission we'll need to secure vital roadways leading north from the border."

Using a laser pointer Drago identified two potential crossing points. "Nogales to the west and Douglas to the east are the two most obvious points of entry. Either crossing would offer a quick and easy entry into Arizona and both offer excellent highways leading north. If we cross at Nogales we would naturally use Highway 19. But the topography of this area is primarily canyons, hills and mountains with many turns and bends...not very conducive to moving a large convoy of men and supplies. If I was a militia commander this is exactly the type of terrain I would want to fight on as it favors dismounted soldiers and provides ample areas for ambushes."

"But it also offers the most direct route to Tucson," pointed out one of the UN ministers.

"Yes, but at what cost? We must choose the terrain that best suits our advantages. I recommend that we cross at Douglas." The next slide was projected on the screen and the Colonel began to describe his plan in greater detail. "The population of Douglas is 86% Mexican so I'm confident they'll welcome our troops. Unlike the Nogales option, Route 80 passes through mostly flat and open terrain that will allow our armor to maneuver and, if need be, better engage the enemy. The only significant chokepoint is here, about ten miles northwest of the city in the Mule Mountains, and in particular at this point." Drago used his laser pointer to illuminate a small symbol on the map marked *Mule Pass Tunnel*, just north of the town of the historic mining town of Bisbee.

"I believe it will be in these foothills that the militia will establish their defensives. My plan is to engage their main line of resistance with dismounted troops and hold them in position. In the meantime, I'll use airfields, here at the border," Drago indicated, "and this one at Cochise College, to launch a vertical assault with helicopters. The helicopters will swing to the east, around the mountains and insert our troops just north of the tunnel. A company of specially trained forces will fast rope down and secure it until a relief force can arrive and reinforce them. That will place a sizable group of our forces in the militia rear allowing us to attack south, trapping and ultimately destroying them."

"General Puentenegro's plan limited his mobility which resulted in his forces losing the initiative. By adding a vertical envelopment element, we'll keep the enemy off balance and obliterate them. The militias' weaponry is extremely limited and intelligence reports they do not possess a viable air defense. In California, they fought a delaying tactic to grind down and draw our forces deeper into established kill zones...I believe they'll use the same tactic in Arizona. But this time, our forces will encircle and cut off their route of escape. This time, we'll use the confines of this mountain pass to *our advantage* and they'll retreat right into our trap.

*****

Fox News Channel

This is a Fox News Alert. Fox has just learned that Republic of Korea forces, supported by American units, have entered the North Korean capital of Pyongyang and the Communist government has surrendered. At 10: 22 p.m. last night North Korean radio began transmitting a recorded message that was accompanied by mournful music, announcing that President Kim Jong Il had committed suicide. Soon afterward, representatives from the Ministry of the People's Armed Forces met with ROK and US commanders and signed articles of surrender.

The president made a brief statement congratulating both Republic of Korea and US forces for their extraordinary service and professionalism and promised that his next priority would be returning forces back to the states as soon as possible.

*****

SWAZCOM Forward Deployment Base

Just after sunset, Stratiotes led his weary patrol back into the perimeter of the ranch. His "Shekinah" battalion had spent the last nine hours patrolling the hot desert and rocky heights of the nearby mountains. The battalions from Washington had quickly adapted to the terrain in Southern Arizona. Being accustomed to the high mountains of the Cascades, they easily mastered the relatively small Huachuca and Mule Mountains in their new AO.

Small patrols were on constant duty monitoring the surrounding area for signs of the enemy. Several battalions brought motorcycles and ATV's with them, which were used to recon further to the east. One man from a Wyoming battalion had even constructed a radio-controlled model airplane with a camera in the fuselage that transmitted real-time video. The commanders quickly seized on this as the militia's first and only UAV.

Hot Dog noticed Stratiotes sitting on a bench next to one of the barracks and casually walked over to ask how his patrol went. As he approached he noted Strats' head was bowed and he looked exhausted. "Hey Strats, are you feeling all right?"

Strats hesitated a moment before lifting his head. "I'm fine. I was just saying a prayer."

"I apologize. I didn't realize."

"That's all right. I always offer a prayer after a mission, it helps me stay humble and on the Lord's good side."

"I'm good with that; we can use all the help the Lord is willing to provide," Hot Dog replied. "By the way, I've been meaning to ask, what's the origin of your handle?"

"It's Koine Greek, meaning warrior. In the original Greek text of 2 Timothy 4-5, it was used as a pronoun for *Ideal Warrior*. It helps remind me of the real battle we face and the importance of maintaining the armor of God."

"That's interesting. I've heard that you're quite the biblical scholar. Did you study theology at a seminary?"

"No." The Washington Commander replied with a self-conscious laugh. "I'm just a devoted Christian and farmer who's always valued the importance of learning." A smile came over Strats' tired face as he looked up at his new friend. "When I was a boy my father once quoted Mark Twain to me, '*The man who does not read good books, has no advantage over the man who cannot read them.*' It's always stuck with me, and guides my desire to read and learn as much as I can."

"Well, you can add patriot to your resume. I've been very impressed with your battalion. You guys have trained well. I'm curious..." the younger man said pointing to a large framed auto-loader in Start's holster. "What kind pistol do you carry?"

Strats withdrew his pistol with even a broader smile than before, ejected the magazine and cleared the breech before handing it to Hot Dog. "It's a 1911 converted to fire the .460 Rowland. Are you familiar with the .460?"

"No, what's the difference between it and the .45 APC?"

"The .460 is slightly larger. Basically, it gives me the power of a .44 in the frame of a .45. I carry 200-grain JHP's that travel at 1700 feet per second." A wily grin replaced Strats' smile, "You know what they say...'when you care enough to send the very best.'"

Hot Dog passed the pistol back to Strat. "That's a serious pistol. By the way, what's the meaning of your battalion name?"

"It's the word the Hebrews gave to the column of fire by night and the column of smoke by day that led the Israelites out of captivity in Babylon."

Strats' demeanor became sober as he motioned for his friend to take a seat next to him. "Dog, this is a righteous war and even though the odds are against us, I believe the Lord will deliver us from our enemies. How he'll do it, I don't know. But, I know I need to be on the front lines, so that on Judgment Day I can kneel before my Master and say, 'When freedom was in peril...I was there. All we can do is remain true and do our duty. The Lord is with us and His will, will be done. This is His battle and He'll come through for us."

"Well, as I said before, I'm glad you're here. Just keep me up-to-speed on any divine intervention. I don't want to overlook something important." Hot Dog remarked as he stood up and shook Strats' hand.

"Don't worry, Hot Dog; when the Lord intervenes the only one's that'll be in the dark will be those heathen UN bastards." Although Strats said it with a chuckle, his hard eyes seemed to find nothing humorous in the statement.

As the two militiamen were talking, another Washington Commander approached. It was Evil who commanded the 11th battalion, the "*Regulators*." It was apparent, from his field gear that he was heading out on a patrol. His face was expertly painted in a combination of muted green and black. He wore his second-line gear and carried a loaded patrol pack. Walking out of the shadows, Evil's appearance embodied his handle.

"Hey guys. I was just checking patrol frequencies with the communications officer and ran into Tire Iron. He asked if I'd seen you. I guess he's got some information that you need to hear."

"No problem...thanks for the heads up. So you've pulled another patrol?" Hot Dog asked.

"Yeah, our original orders were suddenly changed on us and now it looks like we'll be setting up some observation posts along Route 80, just north of Douglas. I'll have my command post on hill 5389 and part of my group will be patrolling close to the abandoned Border Patrol station near Paul Spur. We're going to be inserted by one of the Colorado companies."

"Well, good luck and keep your head down," Strats said to his longtime friend. "Other patrols have reported increased activity in that area."

"No problem, my recon team is primed and ready, those poor bastards won't even know they're in our crosshairs. Regulators own the night!" With that Evil adjusted his pack, flashed his friends the thumbs up and set off toward the gathering point to brief his patrol leaders.

Hot Dog helped Strats with his web gear and the two walked towards the communications building in search of Tire Iron. For the past two weeks events at the Double C had evolved into a well-oiled machine. With the thousands of men on site, there was constant movement and activity at the ranges. Two days ago a battalion from Florida arrived. They'd spent a few days, at the academy, recuperating and re-supplying before making the final journey to the ranch. The 71st battalion, "*The Lee County Rifles*," had asked for and received special permission from E Corps to deploy to SWAZCOM. They were eager to get in the fight and wanted to make sure "*The South*" was properly represented. The 71st fielded one of the best-equipped rifle battalions in the militia including a full company of .50-caliber long guns. This time of night the long distance range was reserved for the 71st and you could hear their big guns booming across the valley.

Hot Dog and Strats entered the communications building, pushed back the blackout blanket that hung inside the doorway and squinted as the bright light assaulted their pupils. Across the room they saw Gringo and Desert Scout opening a door to an adjoining room. On the door was hung a sign written in bold red letters, "PLANNING ROOM — ACCESS RESTRICTED."

"Gringo," Hot Dog shouted. "Are you here to meet with TI?"

"Yeah, we're just about ready to start...we've been waiting for you."

The room was crowded to overflowing. Usually, the small room was reserved for patrol leaders to plan missions, and establish code words and communications frequencies. But tonight it looked like TI had assembled the entire brigade command structure. Hot Dog and Strats grabbed the last couple of seats just as TI walked to the front of the room.

"Make sure that door is secured." TI directed a man sitting by the entrance. "Gentleman, the contents of this meeting are Top Secret. There will be no notes taken and nothing I say will be repeated outside this room. Is that clear?"

The room became silent as the gravity of the situation fell upon the gathered commanders and everyone realized something *big* was about to happen. TI walked in front of a table situated at the head of the room and casually straddled the corner, in an attempt to alleviate some of the tension that he'd just thrust into the room. "As some of you are aware, SWAZCOM has been in contact with assets within the CIA."

"Intelligence gathered by guerrilla forces in Southern California, and verified by other sources, have established the possibility of an Islamic connection to the attacks on the US. I can't go into details, but I can say this...our efforts and those of our brothers in California are being monitored at the highest levels of the national command structure. They have decided to support our efforts." TI allowed his words to sink in before he continued.

"The information we've just received, and the support we *will* receive, will not be acknowledged in any way, shape, or form by Washington. If word leaks out that the government is supporting the militias, it could bring the most severe retribution upon the United States from international enemies." TI signaled for the lights to be turned off, which was followed by a focused beam of light from an overhead projector. Once the men's eyes adjusted, they saw a photo that was obliviously taken from a recon satellite. The photo showed a busy port with two transport ships unloading helicopters and vehicles. The resolution of the photo was so clear that it was easy to make out that the helicopters were Bell UH-1 slicks, the type of helicopters made famous in the Vietnam War.

"The CIA has provided us with satellite photos that show the UN assembling their forces at the Mexican port of Hermosillo, approximately 250 miles southwest of the border. As you can see, in addition to APC's and other vehicles, they're unloading helicopters." The first slide was replaced with a second. This one of a town with two small airfields identified with red circles. "This is the border city of Douglas. CIA believes the UN will invade Arizona at Douglas and will take control of the airfields identified in this photo. From these airfields they will launch air assaults against our forces. It seems they learned a lesson from their defeat in San Bernardino and they're not going to let it happen again."

"If they do cross at Douglas, their primary objective will be to seize control of Route 80 and take it north to Interstate 10, which links with Tucson and eventually Phoenix." Once again the image changed, this time displaying a detailed map of Southern Arizona. "As this map clearly shows, Interstate 10 is the major roadway for the entire southern portion of the state. If the UN can control this artery they will be able to gain an iron grip on the state's two largest cities and block any future reinforcements from New Mexico and the free-states to the East."

TI passed the pointer to Cowboy. "Now I'll turn the briefing over to our Brigade S3 who'll detail how we'll counter this threat."

Cowboy walked towards the front of the room, before signaling for the next slide to be shown. This one was an enlargement of a twenty-mile area north of Douglas. "Gentlemen, the terrain of this area is flatter than that around Nogales, which is why the UN commander has probably decided to attack here. The good news is that there's a small ridge that runs along the west side of route 80...these two hills, Gold Hill and Hill 5389." Cowboy used his pointer to identify the two landmarks that paralleled the highway. "We will establish round-the-clock recon positions on these two hills starting tonight."

Hot Dog and Strats simultaneously glanced at one another without saying a word suddenly realizing why Evil's mission orders had changed.

"Route 80, or as it'll now be called, MSR 80, moves northwest in an almost diagonal line until it intersects, with Double Adobe Road and Mule Gulch." Cowboy jabbed his pointer on the screen where the two symbols merged.

"This is where we'll establish our primary line of defense. As Stalker's brigade did in California, we'll use the terrain to our advantage and hit the UN forces where the maneuverability of their armor will be restricted. As I said, this is the good news...the bad news is that even the most inexperienced commander can see where the best defensive positions are on this battlefield, so the enemy will know exactly where we are."

TI walked over and politely interrupted Cowboy's presentation. "We believe the UN will use their helicopters to transport troops, to the northeast, around our blocking positions and attempt a vertical envelopment to our rear...probably here at the junction of MSR 80 and MSR 90."

The region where the militia would make its stand was in the Mule Mountains, about twenty miles south of the legendary western town of Tombstone. During the late 1800's the Mule Mountains were at the center of the southern Arizona mining boom. Like Tombstone, the town of Bisbee was founded to serve the needs of the prospectors that flooded into the area in search of riches. The Mule Mountains are a collection of several peaks rising between 6500 and 7300 feet, so even though they are located in the desert, they are snow covered in the winter.

To allow easier access to the mines and facilitate the delivery of ore to the railheads, leading north to Tucson, Bisbee constructed a tunnel just outside of town, called *Mule Pass*, just below the highest peak in the area, Mount

Ballard. This tunnel united the town with the main road leading north to Tombstone, which is now called Route 80. About six miles north of the tunnel, State Route 80 intersects with State Route 90, which runs west across the San Pedro Southwestern railway and into the US Army base of Fort Huachuca, before turning north towards Interstate 10.

If the UN could gain control of this vital area they'd be able to secure the right flank of their main supply route heading north from the Mexican border and be a short step away from seizing the only north/south railway in the region. Since the Mule Mountains constituted the highest ground in the immediate area, it would allow them to easily monitor the surrounding region and dominate it with artillery. They would also be able to block the most direct road from Fort Huachuca.

Tire Iron continued his briefing. "As you can see we've got our work cut out for us. The UN must not gain control of the Mule Mountains. If they do, stopping them will be ten times harder and require a much larger force than we currently have. Gentlemen, this is where freedom makes its stand and where the future of our Republic will be decided. Earlier I mentioned Washington's willingness to support our efforts. As you all know, the majority of the US military is deployed around the world, so we're the last line of defense. The Pentagon cannot provide troops to reinforce us...but arrangements have been made to airdrop weapons, primarily AT-4 anti-armor rockets and Stinger missiles. With these weapons we'll spring a surprise on the blue bonnets that they'll never forget. Details on the weapons delivery will follow this meeting."

Strats jabbed Hot Dog in the ribs with his elbow and said, "You wanted me to keep you up-to-date if the Lord intervened...well, this looks like a definite possibility."

At this point Cowboy transitioned his briefing into a standard SALUTE format.

"We estimate the size of the UN forces to be a heavy brigade, around six to seven thousand men. Intelligence believes the majority of these men are from the Mexican army, which means that most are probably conscripts. We're being told that they'll be led by a former Cuban Colonel who's in charge of the UN mission to Aztlán."

"Currently they're unloading and organizing equipment in the port city of Hermosillo. We expect that they'll begin moving north within the next 48 hours and make a quick assault on the two airfields that TI pointed out."

"So far intelligence believes they'll deploy one, possibly two battalions of air assault forces. It is unknown whether these troops are trained in air assault tactics or if they'll simply be regular units airlifted by the helicopters."

"The remaining forces look to be standard infantry. We do not know if Mexican Special Forces will be deployed and there's no indication of artillery."

"The reconnaissance photos show about a fifty M113A2 APCs and another forty BTR-70's. At the time these photos were taken, they were still unloading equipment so we're not confident of their entire TOE (Table of Organization and Equipment). The Mexican army's primary rifle is the G3, so expect to see most of the troops carrying them."

"We don't know when the main attack will take place, but we're confident that it will happen within the next seventy-two to ninety-six hours. As mentioned before we'll be manning constant observation posts in the hills near Douglas and sending out round-the-clock patrols of the area so we should have advanced notice of any activity in the area. We've covered enemy equipment, but as mentioned we'll provide up-dates as intelligences improves."

At this point Cowboy allowed Tire Iron to make some final remarks. TI handed a stack of papers to an aide who began passing them out to the various battalion commanders. "While you're receiving your deployment orders, I want to reiterate the importance of not repeating this information to anyone outside of this room. We'll start deploying at 2200, the papers you're receiving have all the information you'll need to deploy your men."

Tire Iron paused and for a moment he seemed to search deep within his soul for the words he wanted to say. Then he looked up and continued. "Men, I have served my country for the better part of my adult life. I'm proud of what I've accomplished and am confident that my contributions have served the cause of freedom...I can honestly say that the battle we're about to fight will be the most pivotal action since the War of Independence. This battle will determine whether the United States will remain a free and sovereign nation. If we fail, I believe the UN will quickly take over our country and carve it up to meet the desires of our international enemies. Freedom as we know it will cease, the Constitution will be relegated to a historical curiosity and Americans will cease to control their future."

"When the sons of ancient Sparta were called to war, their mothers would ceremoniously hand them their shields with the edict "*Ei tan, ei epi tas*," which is translated as "Come back with it, or on it." Their mothers were ordering them to win or die fighting."

"Gentlemen, the spirits of millions of patriots are with you now. Do not underestimate the importance of your duty. When the time arrives, make sure your men understand that we cannot retreat, we will not redeploy, there will not be another battle and there will be no replacements to relieve us. I believe, beyond a shadow of a doubt, that history and the eternal God has called us to this place in time and entrusted us with the protection of freedom. I will make you this promise, I will not flee, nor will I waver. I dedicate my life and eternal soul to this effort. I will not see my family; friends and countrymen live under the immoral dictates of the Global Community. I will die before I abandon this scared stewardship. I expect each and every one of you to do the same. Who'll stand with me? Who'll fight by my side? Who'll defend freedom?"

As if choreographed the assembled men sprung to their feet and in unison roared, "Freedom, Freedom, Freedom!" until the walls of the room shook and the floorboards trembled.

The Oval Office

The president sat behind the stately executive desk that had been used by so many of his predecessors. The wood used to construct the desk had once been part of a British frigate named the *HMS Resolute*. In 1852 American whalers found her abandoned and floundering near the Arctic Circle and as a display of friendship, refitted and towed her back to England. After she was decommissioned in 1880 Queen Victoria requested a desk be made from her planks and sent to President Rutherford B. Hayes, as a gift and gesture of gratitude.

Gratitude was a feeling that the president had contemplated quite a bit since the North Korean surrender. The war had gone extremely well for the US and the world was better off without that madman Kim Jong Il. But, the price ended up being higher than he ever thought. Besides the dead Soldiers, Sailors, Marines and Airmen, the homeland had been invaded, thousands of civilians were dead, and the economy was in ruins.

But a leader is called to bravely look forward, in times of crisis and find solutions, and that's exactly what he would do. Spread out across the desk were reports he'd received from the Secretary of Defense, Director of the CIA and the Attorney General. These reports outlined policy positions for supporting the militias and dealing with the UN. So far CIA had provided the militias with reconnaissance photos showing the UN build-up in Mexico and signal intelligence gathered from the Army's Intelligence Corps at Ft. Huachuca. This information would allow the militias to understand what they were up against and where the UN planned to attack.

The Pentagon had arranged for several tons of weapons and supplies to be clandestinely turned over to the American patriots. The weapons and supplies were painstakingly sanitized to prevent the UN from tracing them back to the Pentagon. Many of the weapons were gathered from NATO stockpiles, so officially they no longer belonged to the United States. In addition to American made weapons, the shipments contained Soviet, Egyptian and Chinese manufactured material, ammunition from Israel, Brazil, Spain and a dozen other countries, grenades, anti-tank and anti-personnel mines, medical supplies, food, radios…the list continued for five pages. The supplies were airdropped from a C-130 into the middle of the southern Arizona desert where the militia retrieved them. A similar airdrop was made to the militia command in San Bernardino. The only difference was that in exchange for the supplies, the California militia commander turned over a Venezuelan General that they'd captured during their last battle. The General identified himself as Miguel Puentenegro and proved very eager to cooperate with his CIA interrogators. The General outlined a connection between the UN and the Cuban military, adding that, although he didn't have first hand knowledge, he'd heard rumors that other international groups were involved including Iran, Saudi Arabia and Syria.

As the president read the CIA report he caught himself shaking his head in disbelief at the audacity the UN displayed by working with these cutthroats. "*It just proves how corrupt the UN has become and the lengths they're willing to go to gain global power.*"

Before the president could finish reading the reports the encrypted phone, which sat on the corner of his desk, rang. The digital readout identified the caller as the DCI. The president lifted the phone and waited a second as the encryption programs synched, and then answered, "What's up Herb?"

"Mr. President, we've just received new information from Tire Iron. It seems their POW in California has decided to talk and the transcripts we've received are really hot."

"How hot?"

"This guy has provided hard information on two Syrians with direct ties to Hezbollah, a Major Muhammad Mahdi Al-Salih and a Lieutenant Sayf Al-Din Al-Mashhadani. Our terrorism desk has confirmed the names and I've checked with Josef Cohen, my counterpart at Metsada, who says these two dropped off the face-of-the-earth about a year ago. Evidently the Mossad has photos and dossiers on both of them…he offered to send copies, but it'll probably cost us."

"Fine," replied the president, grateful to finally have the solid connection he'd hoped for. "We'll cross that bridge when we get to it. I assume you're on your way over here?"

"Yes, sir. I should be there in fifteen minutes. Mr. President, if we can connect the UN to these Hezbollah operatives, that'll give you all the power you need to justify breaking the UN treaty and kicking them out of the US."

"Well, let's hope so. Tell your driver to break a few traffic laws and get here as quick as you can. I'll be in the office. I'll leave word that you're coming."

The president hung up the phone and then called the switchboard and told them to gather his national security team ASAP. "*If this information pans out and I'm able to connect the UN to Islamic terrorists…I wonder how far this dirty thread will weave itself?*"

*****

It took another thirty minutes to assemble the president's national security team. In that time he finished reviewing the information Herb had rushed over from Langley. The information was shared with the rest of the team and opened for discussion. Phillip Wanamaker was feverously etching out a crude flowchart on his PDA. After finishing he spoke up.

"All right, let me see if I have this chain of command correct. We're not sure who's at the top of this cabal, but we suspect it's a group of people including Secretary General Al-Duri, Chinese Ambassador Xue Lu Dong and possibly a collection of Wahabists from Iran, Syria and Saudi Arabia."

"On the next level we have these two Hezbollah operatives that CIA has identified. They're working directly with the PLA in Mexico, which is led by Francisco Estrada. OJChA acts as the political wing of the PLA and this POW the militia has, Marco Valdez and his partner Maria Cortez, are regional representatives to OJChA's National Coordinating Council and finally the Aztec Army is the operations wing of the PLA. Is that correct?"

"Yeah, that's what I have in my notes." Answered Herb Nossler.

"Okay, step two. Hezbollah, in conjunction with a group of Wahabists, secures funding, training and materials for the PLA to carry out attacks against the US. Which explains how US thermite grenades, last seen in the Middle East, end up burning down housing projects in Arizona and

California. It also ties Ibrahim Al-Sadi and his bomb design to our group of bad guys."

"Here's one more bit of information that's starting to make sense." Secretary of State Bantam interjected. "Mr. President, you asked me to assemble reports from all our embassies on anything that could tie into the recent attacks...well, we received a report from our embassy in Buenos Aires that the Argentine Federal Police are investigating the disappearance of an chemist named Diego Salinas."

"Salinas was employed at the Argentine Department of Agriculture and managed a subdivision that experimented with bovine ailments...like Hoof and Mouth Disease. He's been missing for more than a month. Prior to his disappearance colleagues say he was having an affair with a woman who worked at the Mexican embassy. We inquired with the Mexican Ambassador but he denied anyone matching the woman's description has worked for him in the last two-years."

"What's the description of this mystery woman?" asked Vice President Valentine.

"Twenty-five to thirty-five years of age, 5' 10", 120 pounds, green eyes and black hair." Margaret paused as she rolled her eyes. "Not that it helps much. That must describe about twenty-five percent of Mexico's female population."

"All right," said the Attorney General. "All the dots seem to be connecting. It looks plausible, but then again I think we all have a vested interest in seeing this come together. The real test will be making Congress agree with what were seeing." The Attorney General absently tapped the table before him with his pen.

"The next question is how deeply involved the UN is in all this. Let me speak with the FBI Director, I believe he has a mole in the UN and with the proper incentive, we might be able to turn some hard evidence."

"Good call Frank." The president added. "I want a full blitz on this. We need to line it up so even a blind man could see the connections. We know who we're looking for and we have a good idea what they've been doing...now lets put a solid case together. The Senate is preparing to begin hearings on my impeachment and we all know they have the votes to pass the measure, that's the bad news. The good news is that it'll suck all the oxygen out of the media and eclipse everything else on the hill for the foreseeable future. We need to use this time to put our case together."

The president had already accepted the fact that he could be convicted by the Senate. He knew he was a victim of political gamesmanship and unfortunate circumstances. But accepting this reality proved cathartic, allowing him to act more directly and without the usual concerns for political consequences.

"Mr. President," Secretary McMillan said. "I have updated intel on the three Chinese Kilos." Two of them, hull numbers 364 and 366, left *Xiangshan* yesterday. A *Han-class* SSN, hull number 404, and one *Sovremenny-Class* Missile Destroyer, the *Fuzhou*, are serving as escorts. The subs submerged about twenty miles off the coast and the destroyer is maintaining a heading of 088 degrees...which places them on course for a point just north of the Taiwan Strait."

"Only one destroyer and one SSN?" The president remarked. "That's not much of an escort. What are they up to?"

"Admiral Graig believes they might be testing our resolve to see if we're willing to make a stand after our forces have been deployed for so long. They know there's a lot of political pressure to bring the troops home and they might believe we'll look the other way this time. By sending a small flotilla, we believe, they're hoping to maintain a low profile while still accomplishing their mission. It's the consensus of the JCS that not intervening would be interpreted as tacit approval and set a dangerous precedent."

"What's the recommendation of the JCS?"

"COMSUBPAC (Commander Submarine Fleet Pacific) deployed three boats out of Pearl Harbor three days ago, the *USS Chicago, Topeka* and *Louisville*. Their current position is just east of the Japanese island of Bonin. They're on their way to relieve the *Pasadena*, *Olympia* and *Santa Fe*. He'd like the three subs currently on-station to rendezvous with their replacements in the Taiwan Straits. The *Pasadena, Olympia* and *Santa Fe* were re-supplied yesterday by the *USS Cable* so they're good to go. With three attack subs in the straits, he's confident we'll be able to handle the Chinese."

"That sounds good. Tell the Admiral to make it happen. Also, I'd like your team to prepare contingency plans for *Operation Broadway Lights*."

"Yes Sir Mr. President. We'll need eight hours to get the flash traffic out, but after that it'll go on your command."

"All right, that leaves the issue of justifying our support of the militia." The president shifted his attention across the room to the Attorney General. "Frank, what progress have you made?"

"Well, Mr. President. I believe we've got it pretty much nailed down. Not only can we establish original intent, we also have solid evidence that the militias are fulfilling their oaths of citizenship by taking up arms in defense of the country. One of my staff is a naturalized citizen from Vietnam. He brought in a copy of the oath the INS administers to every new citizen. I've made copies for everyone so you can refresh your memories." The AG passed a copy to each person. The text read:

I hereby declare, on oath, that I absolutely and entirely renounce and abjure all allegiance and fidelity to any foreign prince, potentate, state, or sovereignty of whom or which I have heretofore been a subject or citizen; *that I will support and defend the Constitution and laws of the United States of America against all enemies, foreign and domestic*; that I will bear true faith and allegiance to the same; *that I will bear arms on behalf of the United States when required by law; that I will perform noncombatant service in the Armed Forces of the United States when required by the law;* that I will perform work of national importance under civilian direction when required by the law; and that I take this obligation freely without any mental reservation or purpose of evasion; so help me God

"You'll notice the first section that I've emphasized, is contained in every oath of office and in the service oaths for all members of the military. But, it is often overlooked or ignored when it comes to citizens. By being born in this country, most of us have never had to stand and take this oath. But that does not mean it only applies to naturalized citizens. Under the equal protection clause it applies to every citizen of the United States. Each of us, regardless of our position or office, have a sworn duty, not only to obey the law and vote, i.e., *support* the constitution, but we are also called upon to *defend* it *against all enemies, foreign and domestic*."

"But how do you differentiate between common citizens and those serving on active duty or the National Guard?" Asked the Secretary of State.

"Good question. That's where the next section comes into play. '*...that I will bear arms on behalf of the United States when required by law; that I will perform noncombatant service in the Armed Forces of the United States when required by the law*.' Here we see reference made to a national draft. Each citizen swears that if called up, or in other words required by law, they will bear arms or serve as a non-combatant on behalf of their country."

"Our citizens are free to serve in the military if they choose, whether that's in the active duty forces, or as you pointed out Margaret, in the organized militia, a.k.a., the National Guard. Furthermore, citizens are under oath to serve if drafted. Nonetheless, these two clauses do not mitigate the preceding article, which obligates *all* citizens to defend the Constitution against all enemies."

"I submit the oath of citizenship directly addresses the three defensive organizations laid out in the US Codes, those being the active service, organized and unorganized militia. Those men in California and Arizona are simply honoring their sworn duties as citizens and members of the unorganized militia." The AG looked around to see if anyone had questions. Some faces showed doubt, but he felt he'd made his point."

The Vice President spoke up. "Be that as it may, Mr. President, you'd better have one thing very clear. Once we go public with this information the genie will be out of the bottle and there will be no putting it back. You'll have to have a proposal ready to deal with the militias in the future."

The president nodded. "That's exactly what I'm counting on."

Hill 5389: N31⁰22' 229''W109⁰47'097", Overlooking MSR 80

Evil's recon platoon established its command post on a hill due west of Cochise College. Evil formed an eight-man patrol that he would lead on a night recon southeast to Border Road then on to the point where it intersected with MSR 80. The whole patrol would probably take eight hours to complete. His orders were to observe the area and obtain any intelligence regarding troop movements or intentions. The rules of engagement (ROE) were just as clear; do not engage the enemy unless the lives of your men or the success of your mission are compromised. Nevertheless, he loaded twelve thirty-round magazines into his vest and two extra pistol mags in a thigh rig. If they did run into an ambush or some other danger he didn't want to run out of ammunition.

Before setting out on their patrol each man checked his buddy's gear for any loose pockets or compromising rattles. They performed a quick review of their route and mission orders and then walked into the darkness bearing 114⁰. Evil was glad to be on the move, not only because he enjoyed the tension of being on patrol, but because the temperature at their mile high command post was just slightly above freezing and moving helped him stay warm.

It took about an hour to patrol the four kilometers to Border Road, and by that time each man had broken out in a light sweat. Just north of the road the team came across an arroyo running diagonal to their route. Evil decided this would be a safe place to stop and radio their position back to the command post.

"Dungeon...Evil One"

"Evil One, this is Dungeon."

"Dungeon...our position is November 31 22.314 Whiskey 109 44.796, negative contact... proceeding 54^0 true...Evil One out."

During this short pause some took welcomed drinks from canteens or bladders while others added new foliage to their web gear and boonie hats to better blend in with the undergrowth at the lower altitude. Evil marked their position on his GPS receiver and designated the location as a rally point in case there was trouble, and then moved the team forward.

A few miles short of MSR 80 the pointman unexpectedly halted the patrol and signaled a contact. Evil formed his men into a defensive perimeter and moved forward. Using hand signals his pointman, Havoc, pointed in the direction of the contact and estimated how far off it was. Evil lifted his night vision scope to his eye. The device painted a bright, clear, lime green picture of the landscape. The amplified moonlight illuminated the scattered chollas that dotted the terrain and the HUMMVEE that was stopped about forty yards from their position.

Inside were three Mexican soldiers that appeared to be on their own recon mission. The man in the right side passengers' seat was scanning the area with what was probably his own night vision device while the man next to him watched the area with his natural vision. The third man leaned casually on a M60 machine gun that was mounted in the back of the vehicle.

Evil touched the transmit button on his throat mike and whispered, "Everyone stay low and maintain silence." Team members replied with a simple activation of their radio. Judging from their equipment, the newcomers were Mexican regular forces. They wore US style Woodland BDU's and blue UN Kevlar helmets. Their web gear also looked like US issue as was their HUMMVEE. This was no surprise since the Mexican Army received most of its equipment from the US. As Evil continued to observe the men, the one in the back of the vehicle climbed out and began walking directly towards him. Slowly, Evil alerted Havoc to the approaching danger and lowered himself flat to the ground. Soon the Mexican's footsteps became louder and more pronounced.

"*Did this guy see us or is he just stretching his legs?*" Evil thought to himself. The soldier continued to get closer and closer. Evil stealthily moved his hand to his belt and placed it on the handle of his knife. He figured that at this distance he might be able to take the man down with his blade, without alerting his buddies. As the Mexican continued to close the distance, Evil's heart went from a steady beat to a frantic pounding. "*Go away...Go away.*" he silently implored his enemy.

Then the man stopped, unbuttoned his pants and began urinating. The Mexican's foul, steaming stream pooled inches from Evil's face and trickled towards him. As the man finished he looked down...right into Evil's ghoulishly painted face.

Evil sprung to his feet and in one fluid motion grabbed the soldier's rifle to prevent him from raising it, with one hand, while his other expertly drove the nine and a half-inch blade of his Cold Steel Trail Master horizontally into the base of the man's throat just above the collarbone. The Mexican's eyes instantly dilated with shock and horror. So quick was Evil's attack that his blade sliced through the man's esophagus, trachea, and larynx before he could yell out. As swiftly as the knife entered the man's throat, Evil quietly eased him down into the brush and finished sawing through the left side of his neck shredding the left common carotid artery, which supplies oxygenated blood to the brain, the jugular vein and the vagus nerve that supplies motor function to the diaphragm and heart. Evil laid on top of the Mexican to control the dying man's futile thrashing. It didn't take long before the spasmodic kicking stopped. Evil returned his knife to its sheath and wiped the warm, oily blood off his hands before reaching down for his rifle.

Now, he faced another difficult decision. At any moment the other Mexicans would come looking for their comrade. Evil understood the ROE, but also knew that his patrol was already compromised.

As he calculated his choices he instantly came to the decision that it would be best to exploit the element of surprise that was quickly slipping away. While bringing his rifle to his shoulder, Evil flipped the safety off and yelled, "Enemy contact forward!"

The still night erupted as the eight militiamen opened fire on the unsuspecting Mexicans. Havoc rose to one knee, just to Evil's right, and began firing his M1A towards the enemy. Its rounds cut through the thin aluminum doors of the HUMMVEE ripping the driver's body apart. In a matter of seconds the maelstrom ended as Evil called a cease-fire.

Now that they'd announced their presence to the entire valley, there was no need for stealth. His new priority was getting the patrol out of the area as fast as possible. "Follow me!" Evil hollered as he rose to his feet and began sprinting towards the enemy vehicle. He covered the forty yards in Olympic time and crashed to the ground next to the scout car. Havoc and the rest of the team were right behind him. As each man arrived Havoc counted them off and they took up defensive positions beside Evil.

Havoc pulled the bodies of the two dead Mexicans out of the HUMMVEE. Evil could feel the vibration of the running engine through the car's chassis, and ordered his men to get in. As they climbed in their escape vehicle they began receiving fire from other UN scouts coming from the direction of the main road. "Gunner, let's get the hell out of here!" Evil shouted to the man in the drivers' seat. "Havoc, get on that M60 and return fire!"

Gunner slammed the accelerator to the floorboard and the HUMMVEE kicked up a cloud of dirt and rocks as its wide tires fought to gain traction. After a second they were racing away from the site of their impromptu ambush. Havoc could see two HUMMVEE's closing quickly and felt the impact of bullets slamming into the frame of the vehicle. Havoc charged the machine gun and began firing bursts towards his pursuers. At the same time every man in the patrol, who could get a weapon out a window, joined in the attack. The noise was deafening and hot shell casings ricocheted all over the inside of the car.

After firing off several bursts Havoc felt a hammering blow slam into his left shoulder, spinning him away from the gun and almost off his feet. Initially there was only a dull sensation but that was soon replaced by a surge of searing pain that exploded in his shoulder. "*I'm hit*!" Havoc yelled as he desperately tried to regain his balance. But the constant bucking and rocking of the vehicle made that impossible. Havoc surrendered to the violent antics of the vehicle and crashed into the lap of one of the men below.

"Are you all right?" Havoc's teammate yelled before noticing the wound on his shoulder. "Don't worry Bro, you'll be all right." The man said as he opened a small pouch on Havoc's web gear and withdrew a field bandage.

After unwrapping it the militiaman pressed it firmly into Havoc's wound producing a sharp yell from his patient. The pressure bandage was tightly secured in a matter of seconds; the impromptu medic then positioned another bandage on the front of Havoc's shoulder where the machinegun round entered.

"How's he doing?" Evil yelled out while changing a magazine.

"He'll be all right. The bullet went right through, but until we stop bouncing all over the desert I can't start an IV."

"No time for that. We've got to get these bastards off our ass." Evil answered as he resumed firing.

In the seat next to the driver the team's radioman was radioing their situation to the nearest outpost. "Firebird Three, this is Evil One. Do you read...over."

"Evil One...Firebird Three. I read you."

"Firebird... we're under attack and have taken casualties. We're heading in your direction in a HUMMVEE with two enemy vehicles on our tail. We need assistance!"

"Evil One...on approach, flash your lights for identification."

****

A few hundred feet below the crest of hill 5389 a sniper watched the oncoming Hummers as they raced across the valley floor. He had already chambered a red and silver tipped armor piercing/incendiary .50-caliber round into the breech of his rifle when he saw the lead vehicle flash its headlights.

"Thunderclap...Firebird...I confirm flashing lights."

Thunderclap quickly lined up his first shot and fired. The half-inch round exploded out of the barrel and raced towards its target at a half a mile a second, then crashed into the middle of the hood of the enemy Hummer, tearing through the engine block and instantly seizing the motor. That round was quickly followed by a second that shattered the windshield and tore a grapefruit-sized hole into the driver's chest. The Hummer flipped end-over-end in a spectacular but horrific display. The rear gunner was crushed and torn apart as the four-ton scout car rolled over him.

The second enemy vehicle slammed on its brakes and slid to a stop just behind the crumpled remains of the first. But as soon as it did its occupants were cut down in a hail of fire coming from the hill in front of them as well as their escaping prey.

Evil ordered a cease-fire and quickly slammed a fresh magazine into his weapon. The car was filled with holes and the floor was covered with blood and spent casings. Other than Havoc, only a couple of other men had suffered minor wounds...pretty remarkable considering the volume of fire they'd taken.

Their Hummer limped past OP Firebird and came to a stop. Havoc was immediately removed from the vehicle and the team medic inserted an IV, covered him with a space blanket to prevent shock and administered an injection of morphine.

Evil looked down at his pointman and grasped his hand, "Hey hero...you'll be all right, don't worry. Remember, chicks dig scars and glory lasts forever."

Havoc looked up at his friend and smiled as the morphine reached his brain and eased him into a warm and calming slumber. "Yeah...chicks...dig...scars."

Chapter 13

> If you will not fight for the right when you can easily win without bloodshed, if you will not fight when your victory will be sure and not so costly, you may come to the moment when you will have to fight with all the odds against you and only a precarious chance for survival. There may be a worst case. You may have to fight when there is no chance of victory, because it is better to perish than to live as slaves.
> —Winston Churchill

Direct Action Academy

Since Mike and the others deployed, Rachel had stayed busy assisting Chief Meadows in receiving, outfitting and preparing the follow-on battalions that continued to pass through the academy on their way to California, or to join Mike's brigade. The 173rd, 57th and 55th Kansas battalions had left the day before to reinforce the militias still holding the El Cajon Pass. The 191st and 173rd Kentucky battalions arrived at the Academy early that morning. Since Mike's departure, she had fought her own battle with the fear he might be killed. The thought filled her mind like a dark and unrelenting nightmare. But as truckload after truckload of militiamen passed through the facility she knew that for each one of them a mother, girlfriend, wife or loved one was forced to deal with the same dilemma. It couldn't possibly be easier for any of them.

Slowly she found strength and even a sense of pride to deal with her fears and put them in perspective. Rachel had read and reread the poignant poem Mike had left her and each time she did, its words helped her to appreciate how truly fortunate she was to have a man for whom honor and courage was a defining attribute.

Rachel knew that if Mike did return to her, she'd never worry about him dishonoring himself or her. He'd love, honor and protect her for the rest of their lives.

Cindy's friendship had proven a great source of strength as well. One, especially dreadful night, the two of them consoled one another in the way only girlfriends can. During that tiring time Cindy recalled a passage from Dante's Inferno where the author proclaimed, "*The hottest places in Hell are reserved for those, who in time of great moral crisis maintain their neutrality.*" This simple declaration spoke volumes, especially considering the great majority of men and women in America who had refused to commit themselves in the face of such a clear and obvious threat. Instead they willingly exchanged their liberty for a bowl of spoiled pottage and an empty promise of security from duplicitous masters.

In addition to the near never-ending demands of the academy, Rachel and Cindy had developed a healthy rivalry on the pistol range. When they weren't on duty, they were shooting. Both had become experts, and on a few occasions they competed with and beat the top guns of the battalions that were temporarily stationed at the academy.

Both women wore their side arms openly in especially designed *Grunt Gear* thigh rigs, Josh made for them before leaving. Two rumors promptly spread among the militias; first, that the two beautiful women stationed at the academy were not only spoken for, but were deadly shots. The other was that one of them already had a few kills to her name.

The White House

New satellite photos and electronic intelligence (ELINT) from Ft. Mead, as well as human intelligence (HUMINT) sources provided a cornucopia of information unveiling the Faustian partnership between the PLA and Hezbollah. The identities of the two Syrians identified by Marco Valdez were confirmed by intercepted telephone and e-mail messages. The Syrians had been using a highly sophisticated encryption program that the NSA analysts were unfamiliar with. Fortunately, the Israeli Shin Bet had come across it months ago and recently cracked the algorithm. In response to the president's request for assistance, the Israeli Prime Minister offered to share the decryption key in return for the president's assistance with a particular issue of mutual importance.

The information gathered from those messages pinpointed the location of the PLA headquarters at a small complex on the outskirts Hermosillo, Mexico and allowed the CIA to identify a daily schedule for both the Syrians and the top PLA leadership. An FBI mole in the UN provided hard evidence of the Secretary General's collaboration as an intermediary for the conspiring parties, which included the Wahabists, Cubans, Chinese and the former North Korean leadership. The information was damning, clearly demonstrating an international plot to weaken the economic and political power of the United States so it could be invaded and eventually dismembered from within.

As the president reviewed the documentation he fought a wave of blinding anger. Unfortunately, even though the loathsome plan hadn't fully succeeded, it had done enough damage that he would not be able to fully retaliate against all involved. There was no way he could simultaneously go to war with China, Iran, Saudi Arabia, Syria, Cuba, Mexico and the UN. No, most of the guilty parties would get away with their treachery. But what infuriated him most was that he couldn't even go public with the bulk of the information before him.

The US economy was in ruins, and the only way to repair it was to continue trading with the same countries that currently plotted its destruction. That meant continuing to do business with China, Mexico and the Saudis. The thought of doing so made the bile rise in his throat.

Of the three, China bothered him the most. America couldn't openly accuse or attack them, but there were other ways to deal with them and the president was about to set one of them in motion. Now it would be his turn to throw a sucker punch, and the Chinese would have no choice but to take it. Then there was Syria and Cuba; they fell into a different category. Neither country actively traded with the US and since a pseudo state of hostility already existed between them and the United States...it wouldn't be difficult to tighten the political screws. They'd probably get off the easiest. Iran already had its own troubles. Their population was on the verge of revolution and the president hoped it wouldn't be long before the extremists were overthrown. Nonetheless, they wouldn't get away from this without suffering major consequences.

Finally there was the UN. There, the president would take his full measure of revenge. Currently the US paid nearly half of the annual UN budget and provided the organization with innumerable other supplies and support. Without America the bureaucratic leviathan would implode under the weight of its own massive corruption and waste. In addition to withdrawing from the UN, he'd also repeal the 1947 United Nations Headquarters Agreement Act. That would evict the UN from its lower Manhattan offices. Congress and Al-Duri would shit bricks, but some New York real estate developers were going to be very happy.

The president was jolted back to the present by the ringing of his direct Pentagon line. It was Chad McMillan with information the president had been expecting.

"Hello, Chad. What've you got for me?"

"Mr. President, you asked for a black Ops strike plan against the PLA headquarters in Mexico and I believe we've come up with an answer. We've decided our best asset for this operation will be a SEAL team. Currently, Teams One and Five are in Korea...Three is in Afghanistan and Six is in Iraq. The East Coast teams are either deployed or recovering from combat operations."

"On paper we simply do not have the assets. Normally this would be a problem, but since we need to maintain complete deniability for this operation, we've come up with a solution that I believe will work perfectly. Commander Special Warfare Group Pacific, Admiral Ray, is assembling a platoon from his training command in Coronado."

"These are all fully qualified SEAL instructors with operational experience. They're one hundred percent ready to go and will be able to launch in forty-eight hours. Since they're not currently attached to a team, they're off everyone's radar screen...making them ideal for a black Op."

"Excellent," answered the president."How will they reach the target?"

"They'll HAHO (High Altitude High Opening) from a Special Ops MC-130E over the Gulf of California and glide to an LZ just outside of Hermosillo. There, they'll secure vehicles from a CIA operative and drive to the target. After taking down the PLA leadership and the Syrians, they'll exfiltrate to the gulf where two ASDS (Advanced SEAL Delivery System) dry subs will deliver them to the attack subs *USS Charlotte* and *Greenville* for final extraction."

"Very well, you have my permission to go with that plan. I also authorize you to activate *Operation Broadway Lights*."

"Understood, Mr. President."

"Before you go," the president interjected. "Was my message sent out to the *Kittyhawk*?"

"Yes, sir. It was received and confirmed by Admiral Sharra thirty minutes ago."

"Excellent work. Keep me up-to-date on events as they unfold and thank you for your support during these difficult times. I will not forget your dedicated service."

"Mr. President it is my honor to serve both you and the United States. I'll be in touch. Goodbye, sir."

USS *Santa Fe (SSN 763)*

The USS *Santa Fe* had been on its war patrol for nearly four months. During that time she'd participated in several missions against North Korea including missile strikes on the East Fleet Naval base at Najin, the Paegun missile base and the Yongbyon nuclear facility. She was scheduled to be relieved, on station, before heading back to Pearl Harbor when her Skipper, Commander Larry Latham received orders directing him to rendezvous with the *Pasadena* and *Olympia* and, "make best possible time" to his current location.

As scheduled, Commander Latham brought the *Santa Fe* to periscope depth to receive communications from a satellite.

"Sonar...Conn, report all contacts.

"Conn...Sonar, all clear 360^0, seventy-five miles."

"Dive control...make your depth sixty-four feet."

"Aye, aye Captain."

"Radio...Conn, stand by for satcoms."

"Conn...Radio...Aye, aye, standing by to receive communications."

The *Santa Fe* silently rose towards the surface, leveling out just shallow enough to extend her communications mast and pull down a burst transmission from a satellite in geostationary-orbit twenty-two thousand two hundred and thirty-five miles above the equator.

"Radio...Conn, downlink received."

"Conn...Chief of the Watch, lower the comms mast. Helm, bring us below the layer and steer course Three Four Eight."

Santa Fe's crew performed like a formula one pit crew as they obeyed their Captain's commands and manipulated the 688I-class attack submarine through the dark waters off the northern coast of Taiwan.

A First-class radioman delivered a decoded message to Commander Latham who quickly digested his new orders. The *Santa Fe* was designated as lead boat in an operation called *Broadway Lights*. His boat would coordinate with the *Pasadena,* and *Olympia* to locate and sink two Chinese Kilo-class submarines and one *Han*-class SSN currently believed to be patrolling the northern approaches to the Taiwan Straits. The submarines were operating in combination with one *Sovremenny-class* guided missile destroyer, the *Fuzhou.*

Their mission was to eliminate the submarines without being detected. The Kilos were the first priority, followed by the *Han*. The destroyer was not to be engaged. Commander Latham knew the mission would require expert coordination, superior tactics and a good portion of luck. It was logical to give priority to the Kilos. Ever since Beijing had purchased them from Russia, they'd been considered a serious threat to Taiwan. The Kilo-class diesel-electric submarine, the pinnacle of diesel-electric design, was ideal for operations in the relatively shallow confines of the straits. While submerged they were virtually silent, even more so than *Santa Fe*.

With an active fleet of Kilos, China could effectively control the straits by denying the area to US carriers. That would be the first step towards a full-scale invasion and reunification of Taiwan with the mainland. The *Han-class* submarine was nuclear powered, and easier to kill.

Unlikely as it seems, a nuclear sub posed less of a threat in this scenario than a less advanced diesel sub. The hard part of killing a submarine, is finding it. Nuclear reactors require powerful cooling pumps to dissipate heat within their reactors. The pumps create noise, which allow the sub to be more easily tracked, targeted and killed. A submarine operating on batteries has no such weakness. The *Han*-class was also the first indigenous design built in China in the early 80's, so many of its systems and components were obsolete by US standards.

The other bit of welcome news was that the subs were operating with a *Sovremenny*-class destroyer. Traditionally, a destroyer's main role is ASW, but the *Sovremenny-class* was built primarily as a platform of anti-ship missiles and lacked the anti-sub capability possessed by other Soviet-built destroyers such as the *Udaloy*-class.

Commander Latham called his senior staff together to discuss their orders and design a plan of attack. Once they decided on a strategy, they would coordinate with their sister submarines. Latham wanted to position his boats in the best possible location to find his prey. The captain and his staff surrounded a plotting table containing a chart of their current position and a vast area of ocean including the straits.

"Dave, the last known position of the *Fuzhou* was here," Commander Latham said, pointing to a set of coordinates just west of the entrance in the middle the strait. "Assuming the subs stay in close proximity to their escort, what do you believe their current position would be?"

"Well, Skipper," said the XO Dave. "If I was commanding one of the Kilos I'd prefer to stay in the shallower regions, especially the ones that parallel shipping lanes. I'd use the commercial traffic to mask my noise. That goes double for the *Han*. So I'd say either here…or here." He identified two positions on the chart.

"I agree. Let's get over there and begin a standard search pattern. We're sure to find the *Fuzhou,* and hopefully the *Han* and the Kilos will be nearby."

"Radio…Conn. Contact the *Pasadena* and *Olympia* and instruct them to rendezvous with us at the following coordinates…"

USS *Kittyhawk* CV-63: Indian Ocean

Admiral Sharra sat in his quarters and opened a message he'd received from the JCS bearing the header "Your Eyes Only." Messages with that header were always extremely sensitive documents, the kind that usually brings more trouble to an already difficult job. But as he read this particular document, he found himself rereading each paragraph to make sure he comprehended what it was really saying. After reading the orders several times he walked to his safe, which was secured with a biometric locking device and placed the document inside for safe keeping.

Admiral Sharra wasn't worried that he would forget his orders. He was unlikely to forget the text of these particular orders for the rest of his life. Anyway, he never forgot anything he ever read. That ability had helped him graduate at the top of his class at Annapolis and then go on to earn a double Masters in Political Science and World History from Georgia Tech University. No, he would hold onto this message because what it ordered him to do would have such global ramifications that he wanted the physical document to protect his ass.

After returning to his desk he grabbed the telephone and called the *Kittyhawk's* CO, Captain James Boritt.

"Jim, I'd like you to join me in my quarters. We have some important business to discuss. Right now, please."

SWAZCOM Field Headquarters (N31°25'40" W109°53'22"0)

It had taken nearly ten hours to transport the brigade and their equipment, to their new location southeast of the town of Bisbee. The headquarters battalion set up at the intersection of the three major roads entering the town. From here they could best coordinate the deployment of troops. The location would also allow wounded to be quickly transported to the field hospital that was now nearly ready.

UN activity had increased overnight. There had been several small firefights between recon forces including Evil's squad. There was no question the UN planned to attack up the valley and was now probing militia defenses. Early in the morning there had been a major firefight near the airstrip located at Cochise College. A Mexican patrol had ambushed a militia recon platoon, attached to the Utah 29th battalion. The Utahans were pinned down and suffered several casualties before a detachment from the Colorado 38th reinforced them. By the time the 38th showed up, UN reinforcements also arrived and the militiamen were forced to retreat under heavy fire. Soon afterward the first wave of UN helicopters arrived with troops and secured the airfield.

Evil's reconnaissance company was withdrawn from hill 5389 and redeployed to the northern edge of Gold Hill at coordinates N31°25'00" W109°50' 00". Alpha Company of the 43rd Idaho battalion reinforced them, bringing a supply of M-15 anti-tank mines and new orders. They were to move into the valley and mine the approaches to the mountains.

The M-15 is a formidable but simple pressure activated mine. It contains nearly twenty-three pounds of the military explosive Composition B and can easily blow the tread off a main battle tank. It would destroy a M113 APC and most everyone inside. Since the mines are small and easy to bury, it was possible for Evil's men to scatter them in a pre-designed pattern drawn up by a former Army EOD veteran named Boomer.

The pattern was designed so as APC's entered the minefield, they would be forced to the southwest, where Evil's men had established camouflaged positions. From those positions they could take out additional APC's with a barrage of AT-4's, before retreating behind Gold Hill and falling back to the Brigade HQ.

Now that Evil's platoon was pulled back to Gold Hill, there was concern the UN might launch an attack along the Bisbee Junction Road. This road swung around the south of Hill 5389 and turned north, leading straight through a small pass toward the Brigade HQ. To prevent an attack along this route Strats' 61st and Porter Glockwell's 35th battalion established a blocking position just north of Corta Junction at a position called Gold Gulch. Two smaller Utah battalions, the 49th and the 57th, were attached as reserve units.

Another potential avenue of approach that worried the militia was highway 92, which winds through the southern mountains towards South Bisbee. To protect this location the entire 44th Wyoming Field Force was positioned in the small town. One of the most exposed positions on the battlefield was the vital junction of MSR 80 and 90. This area was primarily low, rolling hills and wide-open fields, making it ideal for an LZ. It was here that Arrow and TI believed troops might be landed to quickly seize the junction and cut off the militia. This was one of the most important points on the map. Desert Scout's 31st and Sundown's 6th New Mexican battalions, as well as the 46th Field Force from Oklahoma, were charged with securing the position.

Helicopters heading for the 80/90 junction would first encounter the 29th Utah and the 43rd Idaho battalions which were armed with Stinger missiles and positioned at a point east of the Mule Mountains. Finally, Tire Iron's 5th battalion, the Tennessee 16th, Florida 71st and the 38 Field Force from Colorado manned the primarily line of resistance in Mule Gulch. Mike and his group were combined with the 5th Utah where every last man would be needed.

Sitting in his fighting position, Mike thought about the upcoming battle and wondered if he would survive the next day. His emotions were a peculiar mixture of apprehension, fear and a desire to just get it over with. There was something else as well; there was pride. Looking around at his friends and fellow militiamen, he was reminded of the famous words of King Henry's 1415 St. Crispen's Day speech:

Then shall our names, familiar in his mouth as household words,
Harry the King, Bedford and Exeter, Warwick and Talbot, Salisbury

and Gloucester be in their flowing cups freshly rememb'red. This story shall the good man teach his son; and Crispin Crispian shall ne'er go by, from this day to the ending of the world, But we in it shall be remembered. We few, we happy few, we band of brothers; For he today that sheds his blood with me shall be my brother; be he ne'er so vile, this day shall gentle his condition; And gentlemen in England now-a-bed shall think themselves accurs'd they were not here, and hold their manhoods cheap whilst any speaks that fought with us upon Saint Crispin's day.

"Would America remember this day, and would similar things be said of the men around me now? Would the names Tire Iron, Evil, Desert Scout, Arrow, Stratiotes, Glockwell and thousands of others be recalled six hundred years or even ten years from this day?

" Would America remember that when freedom hung by a thread and the Constitution cried out for protection, patriots from Washington, New Mexico, Wyoming, Tennessee, Idaho, Utah, Oklahoma, Florida and Colorado gathered together in the desert of Arizona, unasked, unacknowledged, not driven by conscription or any sort of coercion, to make a stand against oppression and tyranny?

"Sure, there would be some; the wives, mothers, fathers, children, and girlfriends who would bear the anguish of knowing their loved one died. But would Americans remember? And if they did would they appreciate the sacrifice and vow to awaken from their slumber so freedom would never again be taken for granted?"

Mike knew his thoughts weren't unique. He wondered how many others around him pondered exactly the same ideas. These thoughts were surely as old as warfare itself. They were probably conjured up by the first men who raised primitive arms to defend their villages and by millions on tens of thousands of battlefields since the dawn of civilization. The realization that this was nothing new helped to ease Mike's anxiety and put him at ease with the task at hand.

In the fighting position to his left Mike noticed Utah men performing some kind of prayer. Several of them stood in a circle and placed their hands on another's head, then said a quick prayer. After they finished they switched positions and repeated the prayer. Mike didn't understand what they were doing, but seeing men dressed for battle with rifles slung across their backs, performing what looked to be a religious rite, was a powerful vision.

As he watched the men complete their ritual he contemplated the fact that warriors were indeed the most sincere advocates for peace, since they were the ones who fought and died when it was violated. That's not to say warriors shun battle. Just the contrary, they're willing to make the sacrifice for righteousness, but their prayers for peace, and those of their families, were probably the most genuine...Mike knew his certainly were.

UN Forward Command

Colonel Drago divided his attention between several field telephones in an attempt to coordinate the final deployment of his forces. The UN had successfully secured the two airfields from which they would launch their helicopter assaults. Pathfinder forces encountered light to medium resistance from militia at several locations, but in each case the enemy was quickly defeated and following short firefights retreated towards the mountains. One of Drago's primary concerns was a company-sized outpost located on hill 5389.

As long as the enemy controlled that position they could monitor every movement his forces made. More importantly, they could check his plans to move a special Cuban assault force, south along the border, to exploit a narrow pass that led behind their lines called Gold Gulch.

After the UN defeat in California, Drago would leave nothing to chance. He would not be humiliated a second time. To make sure of this, he had arranged for a special group of Cuban troops to be secretly transferred to the UN peacekeeping forces.

These were not conscripts; they were professionally trained expeditionary soldiers who had been used in wars of liberation in Africa and Latin America. The soldiers were trained as shock troops, specializing in breaking through enemy positions and quickly cutting supply and communication lines. To avoid the certain problems that Cuban soldiers fighting Americans would cause, the Cubans were issued standard Mexican uniforms and weapons. Drago's plan was simple; he would spread the militia out, and force them to fight on several fronts, all the while threatening their flanks until he achieved a breakthrough. The upcoming battle would be the last. Drago's orders were simple, completely destroy the militia and take no prisoners.

USS *Santa Fe*

Captain Latham faced a difficult task, he was ordered to sink three enemy submarines, without involving their escort destroyer. In addition, he was to do it in such a way that the US maintained as much deniability as possible. It was well known that American submarines operated alone, so he would use this to his advantage. *Olympia* would operate independently in a pre-designated sector where it would decoy the Fuzhou away from its submarines. Latham believed that once the *Olympia* allowed herself to be detected, the *Han* and the Kilos would separate and try to escape the threat, while the *Fuzhou* gave chase to the American hunter-killer.

In their attempt to escape, the Chinese subs would probably increase speed to put as much distance between them and the *Olympia* as possible. This would increase Latham's chances of detecting the quiet Diesel subs.

The *Pasadena* and *Santa Fe* had an ace up their sleeve, a newly developed modification to their low frequency, passive towed array sonar that was developed precisely to find the ultra-quiet Kilos, code named *Black Hole*. Most sonar systems gathered sounds from the ocean and deciphered them based upon logged signals from past contacts. But instead of searching for sound, the new program, hunted for dead spots in the water similar to the way a P-3's magnetic anomaly detector identifies the interruption of the earth's magnetic field when a submarine crosses it. It is the lack of magnetism that pinpoints the sub, just as the lack of sound would trigger this new system.

Although early tests were promising, the *Black Hole* software had yet to be evaluated under actual combat conditions. Another concern was that during sea trails its accuracy often varied. Commander Latham planned to use the combination of both *Santa Fe* and *Pasadena* to increase the system's accuracy. Once they found the Chinese submarines, *Santa Fe* would take out the Kilos and *Pasadena* would target the *Han*.

"Sonar...Conn. Surface contact bearing Zero Four Seven, range eight thousand seven hundred yards, acoustic analysis identifies it as a *Sovremenny-class* guided missile destroyer. Looks like the *Fuzhou*."

"Conn...Sonar. Designate contact Three Five as the *Fuzhou*, start a track and deploy the towed array."

"Chief of the Watch, man battle stations torpedo. Helm, left five degrees rudder, steady course Two Eight Five, all ahead one-third."

"Aye, Aye Captain." The helm responded. "Maneuvering answers all ahead, one-third."

Latham maneuvered *Santa Fe* into a position where he believed the Chinese would be easily detected once they began their run away from the *Olympia*. Normally, US submarines operated alone, so coordinating this attack was extremely problematic. As an added safety measure both *Santa Fe* and *Pasadena* operated in tightly controlled sectors called "Dog Boxes" to prevent them from targeting one another. Likewise, "Kill Boxes" were designated for the approach vectors the Chinese would most likely use. Since communication between the *Santa Fe* and the *Pasadena* was impossible without divulging their positions, both submarines exercised complete autonomy within their sector. The only caveat was that Latham had to engage his targets first. *Santa Fe* continued maneuvering through the black depths like an apparition for ninety minutes before sonar made its next report.

"Sonar...Conn. Submerged contacts: First contact bearing Zero Four Three, at eleven thousand yards, speed seven knots, designating contact Sierra Four One. Second contact bearing Zero Two One at nine thousand one hundred yards, speed five knots, designated Sierra Four Two. Third contact bearing Zero Three Nine, at seven thousand yards, speed five knots, designated Sierra Four Three."

"Conn...Sonar, can you identify the contacts?"

"Sonar...Conn, the acoustics show Sierra Four One as a *Han*-class nuclear submarine...probably hull number 404. Sierra Four Two and Sierra Four Three are very quiet and are not emitting reactor noises. They're probably our Kilos."

"Sonar...Designate Sierra Four One as the *Han*, Sierra Four Two as Kilo One and Sierra Four Three as Kilo Two," the captain said. "What's the current position of the *Fuzhou*?"

"Sonar...Conn. The *Fuzhou* has increased speed to fifteen knots, bearing Zero Four Five, range increasing to nine thousand nine hundred yards; looks like she's chasing the *Olympia*."

"Conn...Sonar. Maintain contact on Kilo One and Two. Notify me of any change in aspect."

"Helm, come right course Three Two One. Maneuvering, make turns for nine knots."

"Forward torpedo room...Conn, load tubes one through four with Mk 48 ADCPs."

"Weapons Officer, start your firing solution on the Kilos."

Commander Latham's plan was to allow the Kilos to continue moving south, down his starboard beam, then fire into their starboard quarter. His biggest problem would be getting a firm firing solution on his stealthy adversaries. Submarine warfare demanded patience and perseverance for success. Ninety-nine percent of the challenge was positioning and the other one percent was the actual shooting.

"Fire Control ...Conn, how's that solution coming?"

"Conn ...Fire Control. We've got a hard solution on Kilo One and Kilo Two is firming up."

"Weapons...Conn. Stand by for horizontal salvo on both Kilos. Set the torpedoes to swim out of the tubes...open outer doors and stand by."

As the *Santa Fe* moved into firing position, the sonar continued feeding data to the fire control computer, which in turn, updated the guidance systems in each torpedo. While this was happening Commander Latham was hard at work making his own calculations.

"Helm, come to course Zero Four Nine."

"Conn...Sonar, range to Kilo One?"

"Range to Kilo One is five thousand sixteen yards."

"Fire Control. Fire tubes one and two," commanded Latham.

On the captain's command the Mk48 Mod 6 torpedoes slowly left the launch tubes in the direction of the first Kilo and began picking up speed. Each weapon trailed a thin fiber optic cable behind them, which was attached to the *Santa Fe*. This cable allowed the fire control computer to send and receive data, updating targeting information and controlling the torpedo's passive/active acoustic homing sonar system.

"Conn... Sonar, range and bearing to Kilo Two?"

"Kilo Two is bearing Zero Four Two...five thousand six hundred sixty-seven yards," answered a Second Class Sonarman.

"Fire Control, match sonar data and fire tubes three and four." The captain ordered before turning to the Conning Officer. "Chief, prepare to come right with standard rudder and, steer course Zero Four Five. Maneuvering, prepare to increase speed to twelve knots on my command."

"Aye, aye, Captain."

As the two Mk 48 torpedoes closed within one thousand yards of the two Kilos their on-board broadband sonar systems went active, locked onto the unsuspecting Diesel/Electric submarines, and accelerated to over fifty knots.

****

USS *Pasadena*

The sonar team onboard *Pasadena* had a much simpler task; they were responsible for destroying the *Han*-Class submarine with its louder nuclear reactor and unsophisticated screw. *Pasadena's* sonar detected the *Han* nearly twenty miles away and carefully positioned itself to ambush the Chinese submarine as it passed perpendicular to its path.

"Sonar...Conn. *Santa Fe*'s torpedoes just went active."

"Conn...Sonar. Bearing and distance to the *Han*."

"Conn, the *Han* is bearing Two Eight Seven, forty-four hundred yards."

"Conn...Fire Control. Fire tube one!"

Due to the shorter distance and since the *Santa Fe*'s torpedoes had already alerted the enemy...*Pasadena* fired its weapon allowing it to immediately lock onto its target.

"Twenty degrees down angle...increase speed to thirty knots and steer Zero One Zero." The captain ordered. "Launch countermeasures on my command...Now, Now, Now!" "Sonar, watch for counter fire."

Pasadena's three thousand seven hundred pound Mk 48 closed the gap between itself and the Chinese submarine in fifty seconds and ripped a massive hole in the port side of the enemy. The nuclear-powered sub was immediately crushed by the ambient sea pressure and quickly rolled and sunk to the ocean floor.

USS *Santa Fe*

As soon as *Santa Fe*'s torpedoes went active, the two Kilos detected them and knew they were in grave danger. The subs' electric engines could not generate the power needed to outrun the torpedoes racing towards them. Their only defense was to launch an array of countermeasures and hope they would confuse the on-rushing torpedoes.

"Helm, make your turn now," Latham said. "Maneuvering, kick her in the ass and let's get out of here!"

In an act of desperation the Chinese launched a combination of noisemakers and decoys, then blindly fired a torpedo directly down the bearing of the onrushing threats. But it was too little, too late. The American weapons found their marks, just forward of the engine compartment and detonated their six hundred and fifty pound warheads against the Kilos' pressure hull. Onboard the *Santa Fe* the sonar room reported the detonations and the unmistakable sound of the Kilos breaking up as they sank into the depths of the Taiwanese Straits.

Gold Hill (N31°25'00" W109°50' 00")

It had been a long, cold and busy night as Evil finally found time to sit down and relax in a forward observation position. He unfastened his load bearing vest and took a long drink of water from his Camelback as he rubbed the back of his aching neck. He and his team had spent the last six hours crawling from position to position laying out anti-tank and Claymore mines. Now, that he'd found a moment to relax, he contemplated how crawling and creeping took so much energy out of a person.

He was completely exhausted and covered with a thin coat of mud that was a combination of fine desert dirt, sweat and greasy camouflage paint. Evil pulled an MRE out of his patrol pack and began spooning its contents into his mouth. It wasn't until he began to eat that he realized he hadn't eaten in nearly twelve hours, but before he could finish he was alerted by one of his men that was standing watch.

"Here they come!"

Searching the horizon Evil saw a cloud of dust rising from a row of Hummers out front of a group of APC's. This wasn't another probe, it was the main attack. "This is it men," Evil shouted out. "Send a message to HQ: UN forces are attacking Gold Hill.

USS *Kittyhawk* CV-63: Indian Ocean

After hearing the news from the Admiral, Captain Boritt sat in stunned silence. "Jim, I'd like to hear your thoughts on how to execute these orders." Admiral Sharra asked.

"The Israelis have been probing our sonar screens for the past week. I believe the easiest way would be to create a hole through which they could pass," answered the Kittyhawk's CO.

"I recommend redeploying the *Cushing* to a position where its sonar won't overlap with the *O'Brien's*. The Izzys should detect the opening and slide right past."

"That sounds like a good plan. It's simple and shouldn't draw too much attention. We'll need to ground our ASW helos as well. I'll order them to stand down for an emergency maintenance cycle. I'll have orders drawn up and issued within the hour."

Captain Boritt shook his head slightly. "Admiral, there's going to be hell to pay after this is over with. Tehran is going to go crazy."

"Maybe...maybe not. When Israel took out Iraq's Osirak nuclear facility in 1981, they got away with it. I don't believe the Iranians are in any position to retaliate, especially with us here. We just need to make sure we knock down any missiles they get off the ground." Admiral Sharra took his glasses off and calmly sat them down on his desk. "Jim, I must reiterate the delicate nature of this mission. No one is to know *anything* about this without my approval. Is that clear?" "Aye, aye, sir," the captain answered as he stood to attention and saluted the Admiral.

USS *Cushing (DD-985)*

A Second-class radioman handed Captain Ted Tolman a message. "Captain, crypto just decoded this. It's an emergency message from Admiral Sharra."

Captain Tolman dismissed the sailor as he opened the message. Tolman was ordered to change course and assume a position several miles northwest of his current location. Additionally, he was to immediately recall his SH-60B helicopter for an emergency maintenance review. The captain walked to the navigation station to locate the new coordinates. After making some quick calculations, he picked up a phone and called the communication room.

"Captain...Comms. Contact the *Kittyhawk* and reconfirm message Oscar Delta Two-Five. Notify me as soon as you get a response."

It only took a couple minutes before the captain received the confirmation and issued his orders. "Conn, maintain speed and assume course Three Zero Five," then he turned to the air officer on duty. "Lieutenant, recall the helo and stand it down."

Gold Hill (N31°25'00" W109°50' 00")

Evil watched the UN forces as they continued towards his position. Recon vehicles darted ahead of the main body searching for militia outposts and radioing information back. Watching the oncoming APC's roar towards them sent a shiver down Evil's spine. "Don't fire the rockets until the APC's come into range," Evil ordered his men. "We need to maintain the element of surprise as long as possible."

About 500 yards ahead of his position two Hummers stopped and opened fire with their .30-caliber machine guns. Evil grabbed the radio, "They're reconning by fire, don't shoot back. Maintain your positions and stay low," he implored his platoon.

The main force of APC's continued to advance closer and closer to the three hundred meter kill range of the AT-4's. Still holding the radio mike, Evil told his men to prepare to fire their rockets. "Take aim…just a little closer. Wait…almost…"

UN Forward Element: Approaching Gold Hill

Captain Gonzales sat in the back of his command APC monitoring calls from his recon element. Crossing the wide-open terrain left him feeling very exposed. He reassured himself that since the militias didn't have air support or artillery; chances were that he'd be safe. The most important factor was to keep his forces moving forward and not to stop.

Gonzales grabbed the mike that connected to the battalion headquarters to transmit an update. "Agilla One to Nest. We are moving forward and have not encountered any enemy resistance. It looks like the enemy has abandoned their positions on Hill 5389."

"Roger, Agilla One. Continue towards Objective Oro."

"Affirmative, Nest. I'll…" Before the captain could finish his sentence, his transmission was replaced with static.

The radioman at UN headquarters tried to reestablish contact with the captain. "Agilla One, Agilla One. Repeat last transmission."

Turning to his superior, the radioman announced, "Sir, I've lost contact with Agilla One." Just then, reports from other APC's began flooding in over the battalion net. "Several units are reporting they are under attack and taking heavy enemy fire."

Gold Hill (N31°25'00" W109°50' 00")

"Fire!" On Evil's command dozens of AT-4 rockets streaked towards the oncoming APC's at nine hundred and fifty feet per second. Upon impact the rocket's 440-gram shaped charge warheads ripped open the lightly armored vehicles, which erupted in massive explosions of white and yellow flame.

The APC's that escaped the first volley swerved out of formation and began hitting the M-15 anti-tank mines that covered the area. Most were likewise destroyed, but the lucky ones only had their tracks blown off. These APC's had no choice but to dismount their infantry, who came under immediate fire.

"Focus fire on the left," Evil ordered. "Don't let them mass on our flank!"

The men from southern Washington poured a withering fire into the ranks of the UN soldiers, cutting them down as they tried to maneuver. A second volley of AT-4s destroyed another group of on rushing APC's, littering the battlefield with more burning hulks of men and machines.

Evil knew it was time to redeploy his men. They'd accomplished their first mission and broke the enemy advance. He also knew his ammunition couldn't hold out and they needed to keep moving to keep the UN forces off balance. As he reached for the radio mortar rounds began exploding around his position. "Regulators, fall back. Regroup at RP Lima."

Chinese UN Mission: New York City

Xue Lu Dong was startled from a deep sleep by the ringing of the direct line from the Chinese embassy in Washington. On the other end was Ambassador P'eng Lin Chou. "Comrade Dong, I've received disturbing news from our East Sea base at *Xiangshan.* We have lost three of our submarines, a *Han*-class and two Kilos. They were on patrol in the northern approaches of the Taiwan Straits when they encountered an American *Los Angeles*-class attack sub. Our submarines were being escorted by the destroyer *Fuzhou*, which immediately gave chase. Minutes later *Fuzhou* reported explosions and sounds indicating our subs had been sunk."

"This is unbelievable!" shouted Lu Dong. "It's obvious the Americans have attacked us in international waters and committed an act of war. What is Beijing planning to do?"

"Beijing has ordered you to file a formal protest with the Security Council. We will fax you a copy of the approved text. Other than that, we are ordered not to do anything that might escalate the situation."

"A formal protest, that's all?" The UN Ambassador asked in stunned unbelief. "You know that means nothing. We can't allow the Americans to get away with murdering over two hundred of our sailors and destroying over a billion dollars worth of the people's property."

"I share your frustration," sympathized P'eng Lin Chou. "But Beijing believes that with the defeat of the North Koreans, the American military presence near our border is too strong. Furthermore, our trade with the United States has been steadily declining ever since hostilities began in Korea. We're losing hundreds of millions of dollars each week and Beijing believes if we openly pursue this issue, Americans may initiate a full-scale boycott of Chinese goods. That would be economically disastrous." The Ambassador let out a sigh of disappointment and then continued. "Therefore, you are directed to submit a formal protest, but you are *not* to directly implicate the United States. Do you understand your orders?"

"Yes, Comrade Ambassador. I understand," Xue Lu Dong answered in a subservient tone before hanging up. For a minute Xue stared at the phone with contempt. He knew the Americans were guilty of this act of piracy. He knew it and Beijing knew it as well, but they were going to let the Americans get away with it. "*And what for?*" he thought. "*To ensure they didn't jeopardize millions of dollars in trade.*" Xue felt his stomach churn as he contemplated what he regarded as monumental hypocrisy. The leaders of the greatest communist country in the world were more concerned about profit than the lives of over two hundred of their countrymen. The thought struck him like a knife in the back. Once again, the Americas would get away with murder and once again it was the mighty dollar that served as their greatest shield.

PLA Headquarters: Hermosillo, Mexico

"Yes General, I understand. I will increase our operations tempo and refocus our efforts. I'll stay in contact. *Ma'a ElSalama*." After ending the conversation, the major sat back and pondered the news he'd just received from Brigadier General Taha Al-Din Maruf. It seemed the international coalition, that had been so vital to his mission, was beginning to collapse. Beijing was becoming increasingly uncomfortable with the rapid and decisive American victory over the North Koreans. Now, a large American army was poised on *their* border and although the People's Liberation Army outnumbered the Americans, the Chinese had no desire to declare war on their largest trading partner.

Additionally, a deep uneasiness was rippling throughout the Middle East. Now that Pyongyang was in American hands, so too were tens of thousands of documents that would unveil the depth of the North Koreans WMD program, not to mention their Middle Eastern clients. Like most dictatorships, the North Koreans had an obsession with maintaining detailed records of everything they did. Unlike the South, the North Koreans suffered from a lack of modern technology. Most of their records were recorded on paper, instead of easily deleted or encrypted electronic files. Even if they had tried to burn these files, decades of records would ensure they couldn't all be destroyed.

Pyongyang had sold everything from chemical, biological and nuclear technology to cruise and ballistic missiles to Iran, Syria and Saudi Arabia. Once the Americans uncovered the extent of these deals, they'd be able to convince the Europeans to join them in an effort to find and destroy these weapons. If that happened it was hoped that the Saudis and Iranians would threaten to cut off the flow of oil to the West. But everyone in the Wahhabist movement knew the House of Saud was corrupted by their riches. They would not sacrifice the billions of petrodollars America poured into their treasury. Even if they did, America and the Western Europeans would consider a complete oil embargo as a clear threat to their national security and would crush the kingdom with overwhelming military might. The only insurance policy Islam possessed was the Iranians and their nuclear threat. This would deter the Americans and their Israeli lap dogs. But, not indefinitely. The North Koreans also possessed nuclear weapons, but these were quickly destroyed once the Americans committed themselves.

Time was running short. The Aztlán mission needed to succeed in order to keep the Americans focused inward and ensure the right powers gained control of Washington. All of this, of course, depended upon the final destruction of the militias that threatened to frustrate everything. "*Everything hinges on victory in Arizona.*" The major reasoned. "*There can be no retreat, no regrouping and no capitulation. The militias must be wiped out, once and for all!*"

UN Forward Command (N31°22'00" W109°40'00")

The UN set up its command post at Cochise College. From this location Colonel Drago was able to communicate and direct his attack against the militias. Not long after the battle began, he received the first reports that the militia had used sophisticated anti-tank rockets and mines. "*Somehow the US military covertly supplied them,*" he thought. But he still held a significant advantage in numbers and equipment. The fact that the enemy had destroyed the better part of his lead element simply made him more determined to crush them. Just as Drago had expected, after initial contact the militia retreated towards the mouth of the Mule Mountains. Now it was time to press the main attack and pin them down, so his Cuban shock troops could maneuver to the west and attack at Corta Junction. Drago selected the appropriate mike and radioed the Cuban Commander.

"Lt. Colonel Pasos, you have permission to deploy your battalion." Then Drago reminded the Commander, "Remember, the key to success will be maximum speed and violence. I don't expect any prisoners. Do I make myself clear?"

"Si, Señor. No prisioneros."

"Excellente, Coronel. Buenos suerte."

Mule Gulch (N31^{0}21'314" W109^{0}44'796")

The sounds of explosions and small arms fire from the initial contact intermixed with anxious radio chatter in Tire Iron's command post. Evil's platoon had ambushed the UN forces and taken out nearly three-dozen APC's and an equal number of scout vehicles. Their mission was a success. Unfortunately, the UN forces regrouped quicker than expected and began delivering accurate mortar fire on their positions. Indirect and small arms fire caused many casualties. Evil ordered his men to fall back to a reserve position near Saginaw.

Even after the loss of so many APC's, the enemy still out numbered the militia in every category. TI knew his forces had to hold their positions, but wondered if he had enough men to do it. In addition to his Utah 5th battalion, the 16th Tennessee, 38th Colorado and the 71st Florida battalions manned positions along his line. To the north, Desert Scout's 31st and 6th New Mexican battalions and the 46th Oklahoma protected the vital 80/90 junctions. If needed, elements of the 46th would be redeployed to reinforce TI's command.

It didn't take long for the enemy to renew their attack. The UN had learned from Evil's ambush. Instead of driving headlong into the militia's lines, they held their armor back and hammered the defenders with heavy mortars from beyond three thousand meters. The barrage filled the air with white-hot shrapnel, which tore everyone, without cover, to shreds. Most of the militiamen had reinforced their fighting positions with additional cover, saving them. But for some, even that was futile as several positions were annihilated by direct hits. Those who survived the onslaught were severely dazed and caught off guard when the first manned assault hit their lines.

"Gringo," shouted Cowboy, "get your weapon up, they're coming!" It was all Gringo could do to clear his mind and focus his attention towards the oncoming enemy. Every sound echoed in his ears as if he was trapped in a steel barrel. The shock and ferocity of the mortar attack was something he'd never imagined. Nonetheless, the sight of hundreds of enemy soldiers advancing on his position quickly motivated him. At six hundred meters the sharpshooters from the 16th Tennessee began engaging the UN with their .50 and .30-caliber rifles. They targeted anyone manning a machine gun or who appeared to be a commander. Watching the results of their deadly fire was almost surreal. Due to the distance they were firing from the report of their guns lagged; it was as though the targets were hit by invisible sledgehammers. At four hundred meters heavy and medium machine guns opened up, cutting wide holes in the UN advance and forcing most to the ground. Gringo held his fire until the enemy closed within two hundred meters and then began firing well-aimed shots into any target he could identify.

At first it seemed as thought the withering firing from the militia had stopped the UN advance, but the enemy regrouped and began maneuvering against areas weakened by the mortar attack. In the middle of the maelstrom Gringo noticed TI, out of the corner of his eye, moving from position-to-position rallying the men and directing them against the onrushing enemy.

Every once and a while, TI would kneel and fire several rounds towards an unseen target, then continue down the line. It was unbelievable. The air buzzed with bullets as if ten thousand angry bees were swarming overhead, but Tire Iron continued to methodically direct his men as if on an exercise. Once TI arrived at Gringo and Cowboy's position, he poked his head under the impromptu roof and calmly said, "You guys are doing fine, don't let up." And as quickly as he arrived, he was off to the next position.

It was then that Gringo noticed an APC moving towards his position. "APC at eleven o'clock!" Cowboy grabbed one of their AT-4 rockets and carefully took aim at the armored vehicle. "Clear the blast area!" he shouted just before firing the rocket. A powerful blast of heat and dirt filled their fighting position forcing both men to shield their eyes. Although they didn't see the explosion, they heard it. As soon as they lifted their heads they saw a sheet of flame pouring out of the commander's hatch and men running out of the back of the vehicle on fire. The burning men were mercifully dispatched by a hail of bullets.

Off to the right, another explosion erupted. This time it was a claymore that ripped several UN troops to pieces with its seven hundred steel balls. Screams of agony and anger emanated from both sides as the horrible clash continued. Soon the UN forces began to withdraw and the firing died down.

Gringo watched as the last UN soldier disappeared from sight and then nearly collapsed as the last bit of strength drained from his body. A light haze of smoke and dust hung in the air and the stench of cordite and burning flesh filled his nostrils. Looking down, he was surprised at the number of spent casings and magazines that littered the ground. In the pandemonium of the battle, he couldn't remember how many times he had reloaded. But a quick examination of his vest showed only one magazine left.

"How you doing?" asked Cowboy.

Gringo shook his head in disbelief, "All right, I guess. I'm shaking like a leaf," he said as he tried to gather up his empty magazines.

"Don't worry, it's just the adrenaline. You're doing fine." Cowboy's voice was smooth and emotionless and his eyes had assumed the "thousand yard stare" Gringo had read about. "You reload as many of those mags as possible; I'll keep watch. They'll be coming at us again. This is just beginning."

INS *Leviathan*: Outside the Straits of Hormuz

Captain Zeev Ben-Yehuda intensely studied the charts of the Straits of Hormuz laid out on his navigation table. For the past week *Leviathan* and her sister sub, the *Tekuman,* had probed the American blockade, looking for a way to penetrate their overlapping sonar coverage. Then, two hours ago, for some unknown reason, one of the American destroyers moved to a new position creating a small breech in their coverage.

Captain Ben-Yehuda knew he needed to exploit the opportunity as soon as possible. After communicating with the *Tekuman,* during their last snorkeling cycle, he led the two subs silently through the narrow opening of the American blockade.

The *Leviathan* and *Tekuman* are two of Israel's best submarines. They are the newest *Dolph*in class diesel-electric submarines in the Israeli navy. Built in Germany, they rival the Russian *Kilos* in their technology and stealth. The major difference between the two models is the Israeli boats have ten bow mounted torpedo tubes: six, five hundred and thirty-three millimeter tubes capable of launching torpedoes and cruise missiles and four, six hundred and fifty millimeter tubes able to launch the AGM-142 HAVE NAP "Popeye Turbo" SLCM, a naval variant of a missile developed by the Israeli Air Force.

The "Popeye Turbo" was fitted with a new four kiloton, low-yield nuclear warhead. The warhead was built using schematics of the B61-11 warhead stolen from the United States. The mission called for the *Leviathan* to launch a salvo of conventionally armed cruise missiles at various nuclear research and production facilities and the "Popeyes" at Iran's *Shehab-4* missiles. Simultaneously the *Tekuman* would attack Iranian naval targets at *Bandar-e 'Abbás*.

Jerusalem considered the Iranian nukes a threat to their national survival. They were under no illusion; they knew those missiles were targeted at them. Many internationalists pointed out that Pakistan had responsibly handled its nuclear weapons, so there was a precedent to believe Iran would do the same. But the Prime Minister knew better. Pakistan's nukes existed as a deterrent against India. Tehran's missiles existed to exterminate the Jewish state. If Iran was allowed to keep its nuclear weapons, they'd be used as blackmail to ensure an Islamic Republic of Palestine was created in the image of Iran's theocracy. If that happened, Israel would be forced either into a nuclear war with Iran, or an endless war of attrition. For these reasons, Israel decided on a preemptive nuclear strike.

The repercussions of this action would inflame the world, but Jerusalem believed it was an acceptable risk. Unlike America, Israel didn't have the luxury of three hundred million citizens and the better part of a continent. Israel was small and surrounded by enemies intent on exterminating every last one of its citizens. Once Israel proved it was willing to "go nuclear," every country that harbored and supported Islamic extremist would have to wonder if they'd be next.

After the Americans had demonstrated their willingness to use nuclear weapons in World War II, no one directly challenged them for over sixty years. If this one mission could secure peace for Israel for sixty years, it would be worth all the international protests the world could muster.

But first, Captain Ben-Yehuda needed to get to his launching point inside the Gulf of Oman. His plan was to use the noise of the busy shipping lanes of the straits, to mask his boat's signature. The commercial traffic would make his already extremely quiet sub virtually undetectable. The problem was that this route forced him to thread a narrow passage between four islands that stood guard at the northern approaches of *Hormuz*.

"Captain...Sonar. Give me a report."

"Captain, sonar is showing multiple commercial tracks believed to be supertankers and freighters, nothing resembling warships."

"Helm, maintain your depth and speed, continue on current course." The captain turned to a Lieutenant next to him. "What's the time to *Abu Musa*?"

The navigation officer checked a digital read out before answering, "*Abu Musa* should pass to starboard in four minutes." The Lieutenant referred to an island the Iranians occupied in 1992. Now it was a base for Russian designed SS-N-2 *Silkworm* anti-ship missiles.

"Very well," the captain said. "Once we pass *Abu Musa* change course ten degrees to port, and position the boat between the commercial traffic and the island of *Jazíreh-ye Qeshm*. I'm going forward to check on the missiles." As the captain exited the bridge he looked towards his Executive Officer Moshe Ziv, "Commander, you have the Conn."

The White House: West Wing

The president was finishing breakfast when a Navy steward approached him with a phone. "Mr. President, it's the Pentagon."

The president thanked the steward and lifted the receiver. "Talk to me."

"Mr. President, the UN just began their attack in Southern Arizona." Secretary McMillan reported. "Satellite photos show they're really hitting the militia hard."

The president hesitated long enough to check his watch. It was just before dawn in Arizona. "Any idea how our side is doing?"

"It's too early for that. We're still monitoring data feeds. NSA is sending the photos to the White House now and I'll keep you up-to-date. Oh, and one more item, we received a report from the *Kittyhawk*, it says, '*Our filter is leaking*.'"

"I want to know as soon as any additional information comes in." The president hung up, then stood and headed to his office.

43rd Idaho & 29th Utah Battalions: East of Dry Canyon (N31° 28'15" W109° 48'05")

"*Dawn should break in thirty minutes*." Bulldog thought to himself, as he checked his watch. For the past two hours they'd listened to the sounds of the battle raging on the other side of the mountains. It was almost impossible to remain in place, knowing their comrades were fighting and dying just miles away. The Idaho and Utah men were spread across the mountainside in camouflaged positions waiting for the anticipated UN helicopter assault. They believed the helos would skirt the Mule Mountains to the east on their way to the 80/90 junction. If they had guessed correctly, the UN would be in for a big surprise.

They'd divided their force into teams of three, one man serving as a spotter while the other two carried Stinger shoulder fired missiles. In total they had forty-five missiles and planned on taking out as many helicopters as possible.

As dawn broke in the east, the sounds of battle subsided and were replaced by the heavy thumping noise characteristic of the UH-1. Bulldog scanned the horizon looking for the familiar shape of the "Hueys."

"I see 'em," said Bulldog's partner as he pointed toward the southeast. "Holy Mother Mary, they have a whole swarm of them."

Once Bulldog located them, he radioed the rest of the group. "All right men, here they come. Prepare to fire on my command. Remember your training, remain under cover and stay focused."

Watching the armada fly closer and closer was unnerving. Bulldog knew each helicopter could carry up to twelve combat ready troops, which meant hundreds of soldiers were on their way to attack the rear flank of the militia. Bulldog waited until the targets came within three miles before giving the order. By this time all missiles were aimed and giving off distinctive warbling noises indicating the missile's passive infrared seeker head had locked onto the hot exhaust of the UH-1's turbine.

"Fire!"

In rapid succession all the teams rose out of their camouflaged positions and fired. White exhaust trails filled the sky like deadly tentacles reaching upwards towards the helicopters.

*****

Sergeant Marco Sepulveda sat nervously next to the open door of the helicopter. Although his platoon was not certified for airborne assaults, they'd been hastily trained in fast roping and were part of a group that would assault the Mule Pass Tunnel. Sitting next to an open door and looking down at the mountains below, he prayed that they'd finish their mission as soon as possible. As he apprehensively watched the mountains pass by, he noticed several flashes of light followed by twisting smoke trails that rocketed up towards him. Suddenly, he was violently thrown to the left as the helicopter severely banked and began a steep dive. As he hung suspended by a small seatbelt, he heard the pilot scream, "SAMs at 9 o'clock low!" A second later a loud explosion erupted directly overhead and flames poured into the cabin.

*****

The missiles quickly topped out at their maximum speed of mach two before slamming into the heavily loaded helicopters. Explosions flashed across the sky like a fireworks display. Once hit, most of the helicopters exploded, split in two and tumbled out of the sky. Bulldog watched in morbid curiosity as dozens of men fell from their stricken helicopters and plunged to the ground. Fiery wreckage followed, crashing into burning heaps in the valley below. In all they'd destroyed thirty-six helicopters, which meant over four hundred enemy soldiers were dead.

Bulldog was pleased with his men's performance but knew they needed to go. Shoot and move; that was the mantra that was drilled into the militias, shoot and move. Three sharp blows from his whistle was the signal that told everyone to move out and begin heading towards their secondary mission.

Chapter 14

> There exists a law, not written down anywhere, but inborn in our hearts; a law which comes to us not by training or custom or reading; a law which has come to us not from theory but from practice, not by instruction but by natural intuition. I refer to the law which lays it down that, if our lives are endangered by plots or violence or armed robbers or enemies, any and every method of protecting ourselves is morally right.
>
> —Marcus Tulius Cicero (106-53 B.C.)

UN Forward Command (N31⁰22’00" W109⁰40’00")

“Colonel, our helicopters are under attack. We’re receiving reports that several of them have been hit by surface-to-air missiles.”

“How many have we lost?” Drago demanded. “I want a full count.”

“Twenty-six units are down,” replied a visibly disturbed soldier. “Should we recall them?”

“Negative.” Drago yelled as he threw a wad of paper across the room. “Tell them to switch to LZ Bravo and treat it as a hot LZ.”

Drago was growing more and more irritated by the minute. First it was anti-tank missiles and mines, now he’d lost a third of his heliborne assault to air-to-air missiles. "*Fucking worthless UN intelligence!*" he cursed to himself.

His troops had pulled back to reorganize after their first attack. But, they needed to keep the pressure up to allow his heliborne troops to land safely and for his shock troops to initiate their flanking maneuver. "Tell the main force commander he needs to re-engage immediately." Drago ordered his radio operator.

"Sir, the commander is requesting permission to redeploy a portion of his force to Hill 6597. He believes he'll be able to split the enemy fire and create an opening for his assault."

"That will take too long. Tell the commander to use his mortars and pound the hell out of the enemy positions. I want it to rain ordnance. That will soften up their lines." Drago growled. "Also, tell him if he doesn't begin immediately I will personally, fucking relieve him of command."

The field commander knew Drago would do *more* than relieve him of command, he'd kill him. Without hesitation, he ordered his mortar teams to begin fire missions on the militia positions. The UN troops began firing a lethal combination of high explosive and anti-personal rounds. Some were fused to explode on contact, while others were set for airbursts. Looking through his binoculars he watched as the first rounds began landing on the enemy positions.

His view was quickly obscured by a wall of dirt, smoke and fire that engulfed everything insight. An unconscious smile began to spread on the commander's face as he considered the death and destruction that was taking place on his enemy.

The Oval Office

The president's National Security team was finishing up its morning briefing.

"Mr. President, Admiral Reynolds will be sitting in for Secretary McMillan." The National Security Advisor said. "The Secretary was unable to make this morning's meeting."

"Yes, the Admiral and I go back a number of years. Isn't that so, Steve?" The Admiral smiled and nodded in the affirmative.

"Well, I see you two are on a first name basis," remarked the NSA.

"Yes, Mr. Wannamaker. He calls me Steve and I call him Sir." That remark earned a chuckle from the group.

"Very well Admiral, what can you tell me about Operation Broadway Lights?"

The Admiral withdrew several folders from his briefcase and handed a two-page summary to the president. "Mr. President, we've received reports from the *Santa Fe, Pasadena* and the *Olympia*. They report no damage or casualties and are due to arrive at Pearl this evening. After action reports from the three subs detail the destruction of the two Chinese Kilos and the *Han*-class sub. Once the subs dock, their sonar tapes will be flown to Ft. Meade for further analysis. But, confidence is extremely high that the Chinese subs were sunk."

Admiral Reynolds then passed the president a copy of some intercepted electronics intelligence. "What you have before you is a transcript of an Echelon intercept. As you can see, it was an encrypted conversation which explains the missing words."

The president distinctly raised his eyes over the transcript as if to say, *"Yes, Admiral. I've seen a few of these before."* But he decided not to make the Admiral's first visit to the Oval Office an unpleasant one and simply said, "Thank you, Admiral. Please continue."

"Of course. As I was saying, this intercept was between the Chinese East Sea Fleet Headquarters at *Xiangshan* and Naval Command in Beijing. Although the text is incomplete, it's clear that they've lost three submarines and the mention the *Fuzhou* pretty much seals it."

"Margaret, what is States' position on this?" The president asked.

"The Chinese have been uncharacteristically quiet. They've submitted a formal protest with the UN Security Council, but it doesn't directly impugn us. Unless they reciprocate in the next seventy-two hours, I doubt they'll do anything."

"Langley agrees," the DCI added. "The Chinese were trying to overstretch their hand and got caught. They knew they were pissing on our turf, which was why they sent such a small force into the Straits. We caught them red handed and kicked the crap out of 'em. Now, they're trying to save as much face as possible."

The president pondered what had been said for a moment, then confidently closed and returned the transcripts to Admiral Reynolds. "Admiral, I believe some commendations are in order for the captains of those submarines. Be sure and have something sent over to me by tomorrow night. I'd like to personally sign off on them."

"I believe they would appreciate that. Consider it done."

"Very well, it looks like that finishes our agenda," the president said. "Is there anything else?"

The VP pointed to the president, "Boss, I'd like a minute after everyone leaves."

"No problem, James. Unless there's anything else...that'll be all."

As the others left the room, Vice President Valentine stood up and began pacing around the president's desk. His hands were in his pockets and head bowed. His body language confessed what he wouldn't say out loud. "Jim, what's on your mind?" the president asked.

"You went ahead and armed the militia, even after I cautioned you against it. Do you realize the danger you're placing the government in?"

The president could see that his VP was trying to control his anger and show proper respect, but was on the verge of losing it. This explained why he'd remained so quiet during the briefing.

"What do you think having the Southwest invaded means to the *government*? What the hell's wrong with you?" The president made no attempt to hide the exasperation in his voice. "Why don't you open your eyes and stop worrying about what *might* happen and focus on what *is happening*?"

"Mr. President, I say this with the deepest respect...you're messing with a power base larger than your own. Our system works because we've accumulated enough power to force the changes we desire. Where do you think that power comes from?" The Vice President paused nervously before plunging ahead. "Now, you're arming the most radical faction of our population."

"Hold it right there, Jim." The president had heard enough and wasn't going to allow his VP to dominate the conversation, especially in the Oval Office. "You're talking about the American people as if they're nothing more than resources to be exploited for our gain. This country is under attack by enemies, both foreign and *domestic*. Everyday Americans are dying in defense of this nation. I've ordered hundreds of thousands of military men and women to distant lands to fight our enemies so that we can preserve the freedoms our constitution has recognized and to which *we* have taken oaths to defend. If that isn't enough, now citizens are stepping up and fighting off an invasion of our own soil."

"Don't go Boy Scout on me," the Vice President forcefully interrupted. "I don't know what has..."

"Shut the hell up and sit your ass down!" The president yelled while pointing towards a nearby chair. "I will not allow you to pull that playground crap on me." The president was infuriated at his VP's attempt to belittle him with sophomoric attacks. At this moment he wasn't as much the president of the United States, as the Marine Corp Lieutenant that he'd once prided himself as and James Valentine knew it.

The president's roaring rebuke brought an agent of the White House Presidental Protective Divison, codenamed HORSEPOWER, into his office to find out what was happening. "Mr. President is everything..." Before the agent could finish his question, the president turned his focus on him, "Everything's fine. *I'll* take care of this, now please leave." The brief pause allowed the president to regain a portion of his composure. He took a deep breath and continued in a calmer, but no less serious voice.

"Call it an epiphany, a crisis of conscience...call it whatever the hell you want. I don't give a rat's ass anymore. But be assured I'm serious when I tell you this aristocracy bullshit is going to end." The president punctuated his comment by violently slamming his fist on his desk, causing Valentine to flinch and further shrink into his chair.

The president drew his hand through his thinning hair and turned to face the large window that over looked the Washington Monument and the mall beyond. "Things have gotten out of control in this country and *we've* allowed it to happen. Well, no more. We've been so busy pontificating about freedom and rights to every other nation on earth that we've allowed ourselves to ignore the abuses we're committing right here." The president turned back to face the VP and in a tired and introspective tone said, "I'm tired of looking across the Potomac at Arlington and feeling like a hypocrite. I'm sick of pretending and looking the other way as enemies of freedom walk freely in the halls of Congress, gorging themselves on the sacrifices of others. I'm the president of the United States, a successor of George Washington, John Adams, Thomas Jefferson, and James Madison. If this is going to end, it's going to have to start with me."

James Valentine assumed the president had calmed down enough to risk a comment. "I believe you're sincere, but do you comprehend what you're saying? Have you considered what you'll be up against? If you think the wolves are beating down your door now, just wait until you begin this...this," the VP searched for the right word, "...crusade." He looked closely at the president to see if he'd overstepped the line, before continuing. "What you're talking about is snatching the world's juiciest bone from the mouth of the biggest dog on the block. You might get hold of that bone, but I assure you the dog is going to get hold of you." Then in an artificially sympathetic tone he added, "You're only one man, and this is more than one man can handle."

The president stared at Valentine and for the first time truly understood what kind of man he was. He had always dismissed Valentine's ability to worm his way around issues as savvy political gamesmanship. Now he recognized it for what it was, duplicity and selfish manipulation. No longer would James Valentine be trusted.

"You know, James," the president said with a light chuckle, "You've always helped me see things clearly. I've relied on your experience to help me understand and navigate the treacherous waters of this city and you've never disappointed me. Well, my friend, once again you've hit the nail smack dab on the head." The president said as he wagged a finger at Valentine with a dubious smile. "Once again, you're right. This can't be done, not even by the president of the United States. It's simply too big for one man. That's why I'm enlisting some help, call it a Presidential posse. No, maybe that's a little too precocious, too Hollywood. There has to be a better word for what I'm thinking about, let's see...oh yes, that's it," he snapped his fingers and again pointed at Valentine, "...a militia. Yes, that has a much better ring to it. You could almost say it has a crisp, constitutional sound to it, wouldn't you agree, Jim?"

Valentine shook his head and started to rise out of his chair. "You're losing it," he mumbled. "There's no..."

The president stopped him before he got to his feet and shoved him back down. "I told you to sit your ass down. I'm not done and you're not leaving until I say you can. Jim, it's time, as my grandpa use to say, to either fish or cut bait. I know what you're thinking. It's the same thing you always think when times get tough. You're thinking about running off to the hill to cash in a bucket of political IOU's."

"You figure with the right political pit bulls at your side you can force me out and end up sitting your tired old ass in the big chair. Fine, as soon as you leave, you can do whatever you wish. But remember, there might be over four hundred Congressmen and a hundred Senators, but as you pointed out to me, there are nearly three hundred million Americans and they're a force to be feared."

The president's words were delivered dripping with contempt. Then he reached down, smoothed out the VP's suit jacket and lightly slapped him on the cheek. "All right Jimmy, you can go now." With that he gave Valentine one last stare and casually sat behind his desk.

UN Forward Positions

UN mortar teams had been pouring fire into the militia positions for nearly an hour. Ammunition was running low and the tubes were so hot they risked premature detonations. An officer ordered his unit to cease-fire to allow the tubes to cool down. "Contact battalion CP." He ordered his radioman.

"Battalion CP is on the line, sir," the radioman replied as he passed the phone to his team leader.

"This is mortar team Sierra. Our tubes are burning up and we're running low on ammunition. I've ordered a cease-fire and am requesting an immediate re-supply."

"Roger, Sierra. Command orders you to temporarily stand down, but prepare to execute fire missions in support of a ground advance."

For the last fifty minutes the militia positions had suffered a murderous barrage of 81mm and 60mm mortar rounds. As the commander gazed through his binoculars at the enemy positions the smoke and dirt was just beginning to clear. There were fires burning everywhere and the ground looked like the surface of the moon. "*Nothing could have survived that,*" he thought to himself.

"Order all units forward and take the enemy positions." His orders were immediately relayed to the infantry and they began advancing.

Mule Gulch (N31⁰21'314" W109⁰44'796"): One Hour Earlier

"Here, take these," Gringo said as he passed Cowboy a handful of loaded magazines. "When do you think they'll hit us again?"

"Something's not right," Cowboy answered as he stoically searched the horizon with his binoculars. "They've completely pulled back. There's no sign they're digging in." Cowboy lowered his binoculars and paused, as his mind raced.

"So what does that mean?" Gringo asked.

The answer hit Cowboy like a thunderbolt. "Get the hell out of the hole," he said as he nearly threw Gringo up the wall of their fighting position. "We've got to get out of here now."

As Gringo exited his foxhole, TI came running up. "Come on Gringo; get your men out of their holes. We're falling back to our secondary positions."

"What's going on," Gringo questioned. "Why are we leaving?"

"They're pulling their forces back because they're about to shell our positions and they don't want to kill any of their own men." Cowboy explained. "Now get your ass moving and warn the others, go, go, go!"

The word was passed down the line and the men quickly retreated toward their secondary positions. As the last squads began leaving, mortar rounds started impacting all around. Although the bulk of the 5th were able to escape, dozens of men were caught in the open and immediately cut down by the lethal barrage.

Mule Gulch: Fall Back Positions)

The militiamen watched in amazement as their prior positions were literally obliterated. The whole area was obscured by fire, smoke and dirt as round after round produced geysers of boiling flame. The air sang with the high-pitched scream of shrapnel and was punctuated by earth rattling explosions. The ferocious display continued for the better part of an hour before it began to tail off. As the dust started to clear, Gringo saw that nothing remained of their former positions.

It wasn't long before small arms fire began to rake what remained of the former line of defense. A mass of UN infantry emerged from the fog of dust and smoke enveloping the abandoned positions. The soldiers fired their weapons as they charged against empty foxholes and the shredded the remains of those who didn't escape the salvo.

"Hold your fire," Cowboy ordered his platoon, "until I give the order."

The enemy continued their charge until they recognized they'd assaulted an empty position. The realization of their situation seemed to hit at once as they stopped and inquisitively looked around.

The moment of stunned silence was broken by a chorus of yells from the militia commanders, "Fire!"

Suddenly, rifle fire erupted along a broad line cutting the UN soldiers to pieces. On the right a .30-caliber machine gun laid down grazing fire that slashed through the UN ranks like an invisible sickle. For seconds, the enemy stood in bewilderment as their ranks were decimated. Then they reacted. Enemy machine guns provided covering fire as squads of men bounded towards the militia. Behind them, APC's added cannon fire to the attack and maneuvered to produce breaches in the lines.

"Grenades!" TI called out as the enemy came into range. Gringo and Cowboy set their rifles down and heaved one, then two grenades towards the onrushing soldiers before taking cover. The reverberating explosions were intermixed with cries and screams.

As Gringo swung his rifle back into action he came face-to-face with the body of a soldier who had nearly reached his position before being killed by grenade fragments. Gringo grabbed the dead man's belt and pulled his body around so it'd act as a barrier against the fire that was cracking overhead.

Looking out over the body, Gringo saw another wave of charging troops heading towards him. He leveled his rifle and fired. Each time he pulled the trigger, a man went down. Then a claymore detonated, ripping the remaining men to shreds. The concussion from the explosion momentarily stunned Gringo, but he quickly recovered and fired twice more before running out of ammunition.

Reaching for another magazine he noticed he was running low. Gringo let the empty mag fall out before slamming a fresh one into his rifle. He slapped the bolt release and opened fire on another group of soldiers coming at him from the opposite direction. His first shots missed. He steadied his elbows and shot again. This time his rounds hit their target, knocking two men down.

"Stoppage!" Cowboy called out. He smacked the bottom of his magazine and then racked the bolt on his rifle, but the weapon still wouldn't fire.

"Contact left!" Gringo screamed as he noticed a group of men rushing towards them. Immediately, Cowboy dropped his rifle, grabbed his pistol and fired. Cowboy's 1911 boomed as each shot found its mark, knocking the running enemy off their feet. Gringo and Cowboy finished off the last men before realizing the charge was over.

Up and down the line, men shouted for help and ammunition. Gringo could see where the UN charge had momentarily broken through their lines. Militia and enemy bodies were tangled together where the battle had degenerated into hand-to-hand combat. Medics moved from one man to another rendering whatever aid was possible before making the decision to abandon the individual or move him back to the aid station.

"I'm almost out of ammunition again." Gringo said, "How are you doing?"

"I'm down to three magazines." Cowboy answered as he cleared the double feed out of his rifle and inserted a fresh magazine. "You stay here. I'm going to check the other guys and try and get some ammo. Keep a watch on the left. They'll try and hit us there again. Don't worry, I'll be right back"

Cowboy crawled out of the foxhole and ran down the line. Moments later, Arrow radioed, "Arrow to Gringo."

"This is Gringo, go ahead."

"It's good to hear your voice. How are you guys doing?"

"It's getting pretty hot over here. Our line nearly broke. We've taken a lot of causalities and are very low on ammunition."

"Yeah, they hit the whole line pretty hard. The 38th got mauled by armor before they were able to knock them out. I'm sending a platoon from the 71st Florida to reinforce your sector. They're coming in from the northeast, so pass the word to hold fire in that direction. They have extra ammunition with them."

"Roger that Arrow."

As though he could sense the worry in Gringo's voice Arrow added, "Don't worry, we're doing fine. We've given them a lot more than they've given us. Just watch your sector and make sure they don't break through."

"You can depend on us." Gringo said as he ended his transmission. He wasn't sure if he really believed what he said or if it was just bravado. Either way, he was dedicated to defending his position and knew no one was ready to run...at least not yet.

47th New Mexico FF: 80/90 Junction (N31°31'00" W110°01'98")

Desert Scout watched the helicopters as they swept in from the northeast to unload their troops. *"I wish the Idaho and Utah guys had taken more out,"* he thought to himself. Seeing the choppers approach was like watching news footage from the Vietnam War. The major difference was that the UN had neglected to provide air or artillery support to soften up the LZ. One thing was for sure; the men in those choppers were going to be firing every gun they could get out a door as they approached. They'd already suffered one ambush and they wouldn't sit by and get whacked again. This was going to be a hot LZ and they knew it.

That was fine with Desert Scout and his men. They'd taken up positions on a ridge that formed a semi-circle just two hundred yards southeast of where they expected the LZ to be. They had camouflaged three trucks, each armed with a .50-caliber machine gun. One was placed in the middle and another at each end of their line. The trucks were reminiscent of the "*technicals*" used by the Somalis and Desert Scout hoped he be able to move them around in order to provide a rapid response to any attack.

As soon as the slicks came into range, the .50's opened up. The big guns filled the sky with tracers, which helped the gunners lead the fast moving helicopters. In a matter of seconds smoke erupted from the main rotor of one helicopter as it began slowly corkscrewing. The pilot fought to control the aircraft but lost the battle as another burst of machine gun fire tore into the cockpit, killing him and his co-pilot. With no one left to fight the controls the helicopter rolled over and plunged into the ground.

Pairs of helicopters skimmed the ground as they disgorged their troops. As soon as the soldiers hit the ground, they drew intense fire from the New Mexicans. Desert Scout was impressed by the courage of the pilots who flew straight and slow waiting for the troops to exit before taking off again. It took real professionals to fly straight into the maelstrom his men were sending into that LZ.

"Sundown to Desert Scout," his radio cracked. "We have a second force coming in from the southeast."

"Roger, Sundown. I'll detach two platoons from the 46th and send them to you. Don't let them roll up our flank."

"Understood, Sundown out"

INS *Leviathan*

Captain Ben-Yehuda had successfully led both his boat and the *Tekuman* through the narrow and heavily trafficked Strait of Hormuz and into the Gulf of Oman. The *Tekuman* took up station just outside of the Iranian naval base at *Bandar-e-Àbbás* while the *Leviathan* continued north towards its primary launch point deeper inside the gulf.

As they arrived on station, the captain called for a report from sonar. "Sonar, Conn. Report all activity within five miles."

"Conn…Sonar. Sonar is clear three hundred and sixty degrees out to five miles. We have a contact bearing One-One-Five at six and a half miles; it sounds like a fishing trawler. Closer to shore we're receiving transients that sound like dhows."

"Roger, Sonar."

The captain made a quick visual scan of the area through his periscope and then initiated his missile launch procedures.

"Chief of the Boat, bring Leviathan to launch depth and prepare for strategic missile launch."

"Maneuvering, give me ten degrees up bubble on the bow." The chief of the Boat ordered. "Make your depth zero two three meters."

Captain Ben-Yehuda understood the time had come for him to make the final decisions needed to unleash his country's first nuclear strike. He was confident it was the correct action and knew that if Iran was allowed to keep its nukes, Israel would sooner or later be consumed in a nuclear conflagration. At least his country had the restraint to limit its strike to purely military targets. If the Iranians launched against Israel, they would no doubt target Tel Aviv or Haifa and kill hundreds of thousands of innocents.

"Conn....Maneuvering. Approaching launch depth of zero two three meters."

"Maneuvering...Conn. Set rudder amidships and set speed at station holding."

"Weapons...Conn. Spin up missiles in tubes seven through ten and prepare to launch on my command."

The Israeli navy followed similar protocols for a nuclear weapons release as the United States. To initiate a launch the captain had to have an authenticated message from the Prime Minister and that message had to be independently verified by both the Commanding and Executive Officers. Once the order was verified, each officer used independent keys to activate fire control switches located in separate compartments of the submarine. This process took place while the missiles were being prepared for launch.

"*Rav*, as soon as the missiles are gone, take the boat down to eighty meters and steer course Two-Eight-Five, speed eight knots," the captain casually ordered the chief of the Boat.

"Conn...Weapons. Tubes seven through ten are ready in all respects."

"Weapons...Conn. Fire tubes seven through ten."

Compressed air shot the missiles out of their launch tubes sending a shudder through the boat. As soon as the fire control system confirmed the missiles had successfully launched, the *Leviathan* headed downward and preceded to its secondary launch coordinates.

Shehab-4 Missile Base: Twenty Minutes Later

The four missiles approached the Iranian missile base from different directions, then simultaneously climbed to an altitude of six hundred meters and detonated directly above their targets. The four kiloton thermonuclear warheads executed their fission-fusion-fission sequence in six hundred billionths of a second, producing a white hot fireball of eighteen million degrees Fahrenheit that vaporized everything within four hundred and eighty feet of ground zero. Within milliseconds a powerful shock wave expanded from the center of the explosion at the speed of sound. This shock wave reflected off the ground creating a second wave that traveled even faster than the first.

When the two waves combined they formed a single reinforced wave that radiated outwards in an expanding circle obliterating every above ground structure within nearly one and a half miles and collapsed large factories and buildings out to two miles. The entire launch facility was annihilated, including its weapons, forever preventing their use against Israel, or any other country.

INS *Tekuman*

The *Tekuman*'s mission was to eliminate what remained of the already feeble Iranian navy and destroy the *Takavara* (Iranian Naval Special Warfare) headquarters located at *Bandar-e-Àbbás*. The *Tekuman* launched two sorties of cruise missiles. The first was comprised of American made Harpoons targeted at the frigate *Alvand*, the destroyer *Babr* and three Russian-built Kilo-class submarines. The second salvo targeted shore facilities with Israel's newest and most advanced cruise missile, the Delilah. As soon as the missiles were launched, torpedoes were loaded into the six 533mm tubes and four nuclear armed, AGM-142s were loaded into the remaining 650mm tubes. The nuclear missiles would be used in case the *Leviathan* failed to destroy the *Shehab-4*'s.

INS *Leviathan*: On Station at Secondary Launch Point

"Forward torpedo compartment confirms all tubes are loaded with Delilah's and ready to launch," announced the fire control officer. "All target data is loaded and authenticated. We're ready to launch on your command, *Aluf-Mishne*."

Two groups of missiles were prepared for launching. The first salvo targeted the newly constructed nuclear facilities at *Bushehr* and *Fasa*, the enrichment plant located outside of *Nataz* and the uranium conversion facility near *Esfahan*. The second salvo targeted all six missiles on the 40-megawatt nuclear reactor at *Arak*.

"Fire tubes one through six," the captain ordered.

The *Leviathan* again shuddered as the first six missiles shot out of the forward torpedo tubes. Once confirmation came that all the missiles had launched, the captain ordered the tubes reloaded and the boat moved before firing its final round of cruise missiles.

Seconds after the missiles cleared the *Leviathan*; they burst out of the warm gulf waters and ignited their solid rocket boosters, lighting up the pitch black sky like powerful search beacons. Each missile lined up its internal navigation computers with both GPS and celestial fixes and began flying towards its target. At the appropriate altitude and speed, the boosters separated and the missile's Sorek-4 turbojet engines continued to speed the missiles at just under the speed of sound. At preprogrammed coordinates, the missiles descended and followed the contour of the earth to avoid radar detection. As each missile approached its final coordinates, each missile preformed a steep climb before diving straight into their target. The facilities were completely destroyed. Once the *Leviathan* reached its final launch point the launch procedure was repeated and another six cruise missiles rocketed toward the nuclear reactor at *Arak*.

The Oval Office

"Mr. President, NORAD is reporting several nuclear detonations in Iran. We believe it was the Israelis," the Secretary of Defense reported over an encrypted phone line from the Pentagon. "Where...what was hit?"

"The detonations were picked up by one of our SEWS satellites," the Secretary referred to a group of five early warning satellites, operated by the 50th Space Wing's 1st Space Operations Squadron. These satellites, in geosynchronous-equatorial orbit, use high-powered sensors to detect massive infrared events like missile launches and high yield explosions. "NORAD has pinpointed the target as the *Shehab*-4 Missile Base. They were small devices, with an estimated yield in the ten to fifteen kiloton range."

"Was that the only target hit?" asked the president.

"No sir," the Secretary answered."We're also receiving lower level radiation spikes from several other targets including the nuclear reactor at *Arak*, the uranium conversion facility near *Esfahan* and several other facilities suspected of being part of their nuclear weapons program.

Radiation levels suggest the targets were hit by conventional weapons." The Secretary paused for a moment before continuing. "Mr. President, I've just been handed another bulletin. The Iranian naval base at *Bandar-e-Àbbás* has also been attacked. But all indicators confirm it was also a conventional attack."

The president paused and shook his head. "The Prime Minister didn't say anything about using nukes. All he said was that they were going to take out the *Sheab-4's* and some of the Iranian nuke facilities. What's happening in the region?"

"The Saudis have kicked up their alert status and scrambled several squadrons of F-15's. The Omani navy has put to sea and *Al-Jazira* is going crazy. But nothing more than that."

"What about the Pakistanis?" The president asked.

"They've raised their alert status accordingly, but satellites show no unusual activities around their missile bases. They know India is watching and they don't want to make any aggressive moves." The Secretary continued, "Sir, it looks like the Israelis have taken out the entire Iranian nuclear program...and are going to get away with it."

"Well, between you, me and the walls, this is good news. We just have to distance ourselves from the nuclear issue. In retrospect, I believe the Prime Minister purposely gave us an out. That took a lot of balls."

The Israeli Knesset: Jerusalem

Prime Minister Daniel Naveh stood confidently behind a podium bearing the seal of the State of Israel. To his right stood the General Secretary of the Knesset, Avraham Levy and to his left, Zvi Eldad the Minister of Defense. The three men stood before a sea of reporters representing nearly every news service in the world.

"Ladies and gentlemen, I have called this emergency press conference to announce that earlier this evening, the armed forces of Israel successfully carried out a nuclear strike against weapons of mass destruction within the Islamic Republic of Iran. This strike was part of a coordinated attack that included conventional weapons, which were used against several military facilities dedicated to the manufacture of nuclear, biological and chemical weapons, including the 40-megawatt reactor located outside of the Iranian city of *Arak*."

"The decision to unleash nuclear weapons was not easily made. The State of Israel believes that Iranian nuclear weapons posed a direct and mortal threat to the survival of our people and this country. Israel tried to work within the framework of the international community to eliminate this threat, but was unsuccessful. So in the immortal spirit of *B'Ein Breira* (There is no other choice) we took what we deemed as necessary measures. Our decision to use nuclear weapons was limited to the destruction of the *Shehab-4* missiles and their launch facilities, ensuring proportionality in our attack."

"Israel *has* always, and *will* always maintain the right to self-defense. We are not oblivious to the objectives of our enemies, regardless of their public proclamations. I want to make the following point very clear. Israel will not hesitate to defend herself against any enemy, and will use all the weapons in her arsenal to safeguard her land, people and sovereignty. The actions we took were our own. No other nation participated or provided assistance. The people of Israel wish to live in peace and security and are willing to engage in fruitful dialog with whoever wishes the same."

"Now I will turn the podium over to Mr. Ziv Eldad, my Minister of Defense, who'll provide additional information regarding this evening's military action." As the Prime Minister turned to leave the podium the assembled reporters exploded in a cacophony of questions. But, the PM had given all the information he was willing to provide and stood stoically beside General Secretary Levy. As the Minister of Defense began his presentation Daniel Naveh looked out upon the reporters and cameras and thought to himself, "*The balance of power in the Middle East has shifted and now our enemies know that Israel is willing and ready to utilize the nuclear option. The Americans took care of Iraq and their victory over North Korea has stopped the proliferation of missile technology and WMDs. Now we have taken care of the Iranian threat. All that remains are the Palestinians and my people will have lasting peace.*"

MC-130E: 35,000 Feet Above the Gulf of Mexico, 2000 hrs

Twenty-four Navy SEALs sat quietly as they approached their jump point two miles above the Gulf of Mexico. Each SEAL breathed deeply from an onboard oxygen supply, allowing his tissues to absorb the rich gas and prevent hypoxia at this extreme altitude. Lt. Randy Hawkins, Officer-in charge (OIC) of Bravo Platoon, made one last review of his map and GPS coordinates to ensure he knew exactly where to land his men. Once satisfied, he secured the map in a pocket on his chest rig.

As Lt. Hawkins scanned the interior of the aircraft, a thrill washed over him. For too long, he and his fellow instructors had enviously watched as hundreds of their teammates deployed for battle in the Global War on Terrorism, while they remained behind to teach classes and prepare other warriors for the task that they so desperately yearned to fulfill. Mixed with the excitement was the knowledge that the twenty-three men sitting around him represented the most highly trained and motivated operators in the world.

"*Poor bastards,*" Hawkins thought as he pondered his enemy's fate. "*They have no idea of what's coming.*"

The interior of the aircraft was softly illuminated with a dim red light that provided just enough visibility for the SEALs to see around them. Hawkins saw the Air Crew Chief (ACC) grab the Jump Master (JM) on the shoulder and flash two fingers in his face. On any jump, the chain of information flowed from the Navigator who checked the aircraft's position via his on-board GPS, to the Pilot who confirmed it and finally to the ACC, who was in charge of everything in the belly of the plane. Then the ACC passed the information to the Jump Master who was in charge of the jump.

"Two minutes!" The Jump Master hollered out as he waved two fingers in front of the group. "Stand up for equipment check!" On the opposite side of the aircraft the Assistant Jump Master repeated the commands to Echo Platoon. Each man disconnected his oxygen mask from the on-board supply and reconnected the hose to a bottle attached to their parachute harness. Next, they inspected all the pouches on their gear ensuring every buckle and strap was closed and locked in place. In addition to their parachutes and second-line gear strapped around their torsos, forty-pound rucksacks with additional supplies hung between their legs. Confident their equipment was properly prepared; each man quickly checked his buddy and then passed the Okay up the line to their team leader.

The red interior light was abruptly extinguished as winding motors began lowering the rear ramp of the Hercules. A blast of sub-freezing air engulfed the men who stood at the ready.

"Let's get it on," one of the younger commandos grunted under his mask. "Come on…come on."

As soon as the ramp was fully open, the Jump Master gingerly crawled out to the edge to ensure the ramp was safe for exit and to get both a visual and GPS reference to verify for himself they were on target. Hawkins focused his attention on the light that would indicate when they were to jump. As soon as it turned green, the Jump Master pointed to Hawkins who immediately led his men out of the aircraft and into the pitch-black abyss. As the heavily laden SEALs flung themselves off the ramp, the Jump Master and his assistant carefully watched to make sure everyone exited safely, then swiftly followed behind. The SEALs fell for several thousand feet before opening their canopies and assembling into formation to begin their twenty-mile glide toward the LZ.

Gold Gulch (N31^0 25'34" W109^0 52'51"): 2012 hrs

Porter Glockwell understood the importance of his position. During planning meetings it became apparent that this pass represented a wide open backdoor leading straight into the rear of the militia positions. His 35th Utah and Strats' 61st Washington battalions comprised the primary blocking force that cut across State Route 92. Two other Utah battalions, the 57th and the 49th were being held in reserve.

Both reserve battalions were under strength, so they'd be used to fill any gaps that occurred once the battle started. If things became worst than expected, they hoped the Wyoming 44th field force could send additional reinforcements from the nearby town of South Bisbee.

"Are those .30-caliber machine guns positioned to provide interlocking fields of fire?" Strat asked.

"Yes. They're focused about one hundred and fifty yards forward of the main line," Porter replied as he pointed out an open area. "We've also set up claymores in the rocks to the left. I figure once we begin laying down grazing fire, the enemy will move into the rocks for cover. We also set up a few about 50 meters in front of us...as a failsafe measure."

"What about the snipers?" Porter asked in return.

"I just left them," Strat answered as he pointed his thumb back towards a ridgeline to their left. "I've spread out the platoon from the 16th Tennessee across that ridge. They're zeroed in and should be able to keep the Blue Bonnet's heads down."

"Well, I guess we're ready. Have you heard anything from TI?"

"They've got their hands full," Strat responded in a careful tone. "I asked if they needed one of our reserve units, but they said they're holding their own...for the moment."

As this conversation was taking place explosions erupted all across their front line. The explosions were followed by men yelling out, "RPGs, take cover!" Porter looked to his right and watched as an RPG streaked into a foxhole and exploded, immediately killing three men. All down the line, explosions ripped apart men and filled the air with deadly shards of shrapnel.

"Take cover and return fire!" Porter yelled out. "Strat, I'll be on the right flank, stay in touch."

"All right," Strat said as he hurried off in the opposite direction. "Keep your head down and don't do anything stupid."

The Cubans were throwing the full weight of their attack against the Gold Gulch defenders. They'd been ordered to break through as fast as possible, using whatever tactics were needed. Their attack was both devastating and swift. Following the fusillade of rocket propelled grenades, squads of assault troops rushed forward screaming and firing their AK's from the hip. The sudden violence of their attack overwhelmed several militiamen who were quickly overrun and bayoneted in their foxholes.

The onrushing Cubans were immediately cut down by machine gun fire as they moved forward, forcing the survivors to seek cover in nearby rocks. Once the men reached the assumed protection of the rocks, they were blown to pieces by the mines that had been expertly positioned by Glockwell's men.

This combination of events broke the Cubans' momentum and halted their attack. But, the battle continued to rage on as more and more UN reinforcements engaged the militia from a number of directions.

"Strats, we've got heavy enemy contact coming at us from several positions," Porter radioed. "What's your situation?

There was a pause before Strat answered. "I can't talk now Porter, we've got our hands full." A massive volume of gunfire nearly drowned out Strats' message. "Call up the reserve; it looks like we'll need them sooner than we anticipated."

Cuban Assault Battalion: Gold Gulch

Colonel Pasos watched as the leading element of his attack crashed into the militia lines. His seasoned troops hit the Americans like a sledgehammer. He'd made it clear to all his men that no quarter was to be given to the Americans. Every one of them had to be killed quickly and with as little expenditure of resources as possible. After eliminating this outpost, his orders were to move up State Route 92 and destroy the militia rear.

Watching through his binoculars he followed the progress of his men. "*Good, good, hit them hard and destroy their will to fight.*" He thought to himself. "*There's no way civilians can stand against my professional soldiers. These weak and overindulged Americans don't have the stomach for real fighting.*"

As he finished this thought he watched as his men stopped and then slowly began pulling back. "What's happening, why have they stopped?" The Colonel shouted at his radioman. "Tell them to continue to press the attack!"

"Colonel, Major Santiago reports heavy machine gun and sniper fire is pinning his men down. He's calling out a mortar fire mission on sniper positions, now."

****

Smoke rose out of the breech as Boomer loaded another round in to his .308. He'd already dispatched six enemy soldiers from his position high on a ridge overlooking State Route 92. Beads of sweat trickled down his forehead and got into his eyes interfering with his aim. He quickly reached up and wiped his brow with an OD bandanna that was tied around his neck.

"Target," his spotter called out from behind a laser range finder. "Sector two, range six hundred yards, quarter value wind steady, no adjustment."

"Target acquired," Boomer softly replied, "looks like he's talking into a phone." He began his firing routine of steadying his aim, holding his breath while slowly squeezing the trigger until achieving a surprise...Boom. The rifle bucked into Boomer's shoulder blurring his sight picture slightly, but not too much as he watched the man's head explode in a halo of red. Boomer automatically racked another round into his rifle.

*****

As the major began calling in the coordinates for the fire mission, he violently jerked backwards and collapsed to the ground. His Lieutenant was on another radio when he felt something warm spray across his face. After wiping his mouth with the back of his hand a warm, slightly salty, metallic taste met his tongue. Looking down he immediately noticed blood and lumpy gray matter covering his shirt. Next to him laid the nearly decapitated remains of the major.

"Rio Rico, come in," the fire direction team radioed. "Please repeat the coordinates for your target."

The Lieutenant grabbed the phone out of the major's dead hand and finished calling in the coordinates for the mortar team. Just as he finished confirming the coordinates, a bullet slammed into his chest and deposited him next to his superior.

*****

Boomer was running low on ammunition. He inserted his last stripper clip into his rifle as mortar rounds started falling all around his position. "Incoming!" cried out his spotter. But it was too late. The high explosive 60mm rounds leveled the area and tore both snipers to pieces. Across the ridgeline mortars pounded the spots where other snipers were located. Some had moved after taking a few shots, avoiding the retaliation. But most were either killed in their hides or in the open as they tried to escape the onslaught.

Gold Gulch (N31^0 25'34" W109^0 52'51"): 2045 hrs

Porter watched as the ridgeline to his left was obliterated. He knew that was where the men of the 16th Tennessee had been positioned and hoped they'd survived the barrage. The lack of sniper fire following the attack answered his question. Without the danger of snipers, the UN soldiers renewed their attack. After inserting a fresh magazine Porter opened up on the rushing soldiers. Even though he fired as fast as he could, it wasn't enough, to stop the enemy advance. He knew his position wouldn't hold. He was being overrun.

"Hold the line, hold the line!" he shouted to his remaining men. "Keep up your volume of fire!"

After killing three more enemy soldiers, Porter noticed a wounded militiaman lying in the open. The man had been shot in both legs and couldn't move. Porter grabbed the drag handle of the man's LBE and began pulling him to safety. "You're going to be fine," he reassured the wounded man. "I'll get you to a medic"

Looking over his right shoulder Porter saw two Cubans charging him. Instinctively, he swung his rifle towards the enemy and fired a burst. Three bullets stitched diagonally across the first man's chest; killing him instantly. But before Porter could shoot the second, the Cuban let loose a stream of automatic fire that walked up the wounded militiaman's chest and into Porter's right arm. The heavy 7.62 x 39 rounds shattered his wrist. Porter screamed in agony as he collapsed. The Cuban continued to charge, determined to finish his enemy off with his bayonet. Though blinded with pain, Porter emptied his M-4 magazine into the on-rushing enemy. With bullets cracking in the air above him Porter struggled to maintain conciseness. Scanning the battlefield he noticed lines of enemy soldiers advancing and knew they needed to be stopped. Porter tried to stand up but the pain radiating from his right arm drained the strength out of his body.

Instead, he crawled back to his foxhole. Once inside he desperately clawed through a carpet of empty casings and magazines until he found four small, green detonators. With his one good hand he slammed the detonators into the ground setting off a series of Claymores. He watched as the mines blew the UN soldiers off their feet in a deadly shower of steel balls. Porter knew he'd accomplished all he could do and realized he needed to use the brief lull to escape.

After taking a quick look around he rose out of the foxhole and began staggering away while cradling his shattered arm, just then a rocket propelled grenade exploded near his feet. When the dust settled Porter's body laid motionless next to another Utahan.

Hermosillo, Mexico (LZ Romeo): 2100 hrs

The SEALs used their GPS receivers to guide them to their LZ. After landing they made contact with their CIA contact who assisted them in ditching their parachutes and provided several trucks. Lt. Hawkins and Maples followed the agent to one of the trucks where they unfolded a map across the hood and began confirming the latest intelligence.

"What can you tell us about the objective?" Lt. Maples asked.

"My people have had the house under surveillance for the last thirty-six hours. No additional forces have arrived and the two Syrians are still there." The agent's voice was confident and direct. "They have three SUV's in the courtyard. You'll probably want to disable them as soon as possible."

"What about the roads?" Hawkins asked. "Any roadblocks or construction we should know about?"

"No. The roads to the target and to your extraction point are clear."

"What about the local police?"

"No problems. The police chief is being cared for at the local whore house and we'll make sure his men leave you guys alone."

A powerfully built Senior Chief walked up to the three men and tapped Lt. Maples on the shoulder. "L.T., we're ready to go."

Mule Gulch: Secondary Positions, 2115 hrs

"We've got to knock out those mortars." TI said, "or we won't be able to hold this position." TI looked around the collection of commanders before focusing on the leader of the 38th Colorado. "Fox, I want you to lead an assault. Can you take out those mortars?"

"Yes. I believe I can move a platoon out around this hillside," the Colorado CO indicated as he pointed to a position on a map. "Once we reach this point, we should be able to locate and destroy them."

TI looked at the map again before answering in a confident voice, "All right, assemble your men." Then he looked towards the CO of the 71st Florida, "I need you to shift some of your men to plug up the holes left by the Colorado men. Every fourth man should be enough."

Returning to the map, TI stabbed his finger at the position indicated by the Colorado leader, "We'll call this point, 'Tango'. Your team's call sign will be Mountaineer, the CP will be Chalet. When you reach Tango, radio in. We'll try to distract the enemy so you can move out of cover and assault their lines. The key to success will be speed and aggressiveness. Hit them hard and then get back as fast as possible."

The leaders saluted and separated in various directions. As TI left the command post, he walked past a triage area set up outside the field hospital. He'd seen the human suffering of combat before, but still found it hard not to be affected by the agony his men were enduring. One thought continued to run through his mind, "*Why was the UN fighting so hard?*" He'd seen UN soldiers in Africa and the Middle East and they never showed the ferocity he was witnessing today. In conflict after conflict the UN could always be relied on to fall back or surrender at the first sign of a determined defense. But these troops were fighting as though they had no other choice.

A radioman approached, "Desert Scout is on the line," he said as he passed the receiver to TI.

TI spoke into the handset. "Give me a report."

"We're holding our own," Desert Scout's voice said. "They've landed a couple of platoons at a secondary LZ east of our position and have set up an L-shaped line with their x axis running west to east and the y axis running north to south. We've got them pinned down, but we won't be able to reinforce you anytime soon." TI shook his head in disappointment. "Listen, you've got to keep those guys off our backs. Do whatever you have to do to, but you must hold that road junction. Understood?"

"Roger that TI. We won't let you down."

Direct Action Academy

Rachel locked the warehouse door behind her. She'd just finished taking the weekly inventory of the academy's food supplies, when she noticed a lot of frantic activity going on. "Hey, what's happening," she asked a couple of militiamen who were running past her.

"The UN has attacked our forces down south," one of the men replied. "Reports say our guys are really taking a pounding. The Kentucky battalions are leaving to reinforce them." The two men excused themselves as they ran off, leaving Rachel standing alone with only a clipboard and her thoughts.

Cindy arrived, pushing a dolly, and took Rachel by the hand. "I guess you've heard...are you all right?"

"I don't know," Rachel said sheepishly. "I was told our guys are getting hit pretty hard, have we received any casualty reports yet?"

"No. The chief says it's too soon for that, but we have to be ready for the wounded when they begin arriving." Cindy noticed Rachel's breathing increase and could feel her pulse racing in her hands. Rachel was beginning to panic, and the only cure for that was to get her mind on something constructive.

"Rachel, I could really use your help loading a few boxes on this dolly. I'm not sure where this stuff is stored, could you show me?"

Rachel looked at the list Cindy offered and nodded as she wiped her eyes. "Yeah, I know where these are. They're stacked in the back of the warehouse." Rachel understood what Cindy was doing and in her heart knew it was exactly what she needed. She wrapped her arm around Cindy's shoulder and held her for a moment. "Thank you, I don't know what I'd do without you. Now, let's find those supplies."

PLA Headquarters: Hermosillo, Mexico, 2350 hrs,
SEAL Observation Position

The two platoons set up observation posts on hillsides over looking the front and rear of the large villa the PLA used as their headquarters. Sniper teams covered the major approaches as well as the entrances and exits of the building. Just as the CIA operative had indicated, two large sedans and an SUV were parked, facing the rear exit of the gated courtyard.

A thermal scan of the building gave the SEALs a clear picture of which rooms were occupied. Nine possible combatants and two workers were in the building. The CIA had identified the rooms they believed the Syrians used as bedrooms and offices. The SEALs confirmed this information by waiting until sundown, and with their thermal imaging equipment, watching as two men performed the *Salaat*.

The Navy had constructed a scale model of the target building at a secure location on at the Yuma proving grounds. The two platoons had used it to perfect their tactics before deploying. Now that they could see the real building, they appreciated how accurate the model was.

With the exception of the cars in the courtyard and landscaping elements, it was spot on. The scout/sniper teams took copious notes on everything they saw and heard. As they were rotated, the teams delivered the notes to the rest of the team ensuring everyone understood as much about the target as possible. Proper planning and intelligence was the hallmark of every special operations team. A saying in the Special Ops community went, "You're only half as good as you train." To make sure all their men survived the mission, Lieutenants Hawkins and Maples would take no chances.

They planned a coordinated assault for 0100. Six men from Maple's team would assault the front of the building and clear the lower floor while four others brought up the escape vehicles and set a defensive parameter outside the compound. Lt. Hawkins' team would hit the compound from the rear. They'd use retractable ladders, originally designed for boarding ships at sea, to scale a nine-foot wall surrounding three sides of the property. Once over the wall, his ten-man team would disable the cars, then climb an outside staircase and clear the second level. One scout/sniper team from each group would cover the front and rear of the compound to provide cover and take out targets of opportunity. After taking down the target the two teams would egress to the harbor where waiting ASDS (Advanced SEAL Delivery System) subs would deliver the men to the *USS Charlotte* and *Greenville* for final extraction.

PLA Headquarters: Hermosillo, Mexico, 2200 hrs, Inside PLA Headquarters

Sayf listened carefully as the major finished his phone call with Brigadier General Taha Al-Din Maruf in Damascus. A couple of hours had passed since *Al-Jazeera* broke the news of the Israeli nuclear strikes. Both the major and

Sayf watched in horror as the Qatar based news channel reported that nuclear missiles had been targeted on cities with no military significance and how Israeli air strikes purposely destroyed several hospitals and an orphanage. According to the reports, hundreds of thousands of innocent Iranians were dead and thousands more were expected to die from radiation in the following weeks. Both the major and Sayf knew that *Al-Jazeera* exaggerated the news, especially with regard to the United States and Israel. The Islamic media's primary task was to spread the propaganda of Jihad throughout the Islamic world and to affect political change in the kafir world by airing footage most western news agencies deemed too inflammatory. *Al-Jazeera* had aired every tape made by Osama Bin Laden and his *Al-Qaeda* network, as well as videos of western hostages being beheaded. In the past, news agencies would never have shown these videos out of fear they'd be accused of aiding the enemies of the United States. But, since *Al-Jazeera* openly broadcast the footage via satellite and over the web, the western news agencies felt justified in using the footage for their own gain. With the proverbial "cat-out-of-the-bag," it was perfectly acceptable to "gip" the *Al-Jazeera* feed and use the coverage to fill the insatiable demands of the twenty-four hour news cycle.

"Our mission has been aborted!" The major shouted as he slammed his fist on his desk. "Everything is falling apart and Damascus no longer believes we can succeed."

"But we've already invaded America and established Aztlán. The American economy is in ruin, its military forces are depleted, their criminal President has been impeached and is on the verge of being removed from office and our supporters in Washington are ready to assume power. Why doesn't Damascus believe we can succeed?"

"Everything you say is true," the major replied. "But you have lost sight of the primary purpose of our mission: to eliminate the American forces from Iraq and secure our eastern border. Everything else was a means to this end. Our success depended on the assistance of our allies, and now it seems that support is evaporating. The North Koreans are defeated, the Iranian nuclear threat has been eliminated and now the Chinese have unexpectedly withdrawn their support. Damascus is convinced that without them we can not control the UN."

"Surely Damascus knows that even now the UN is fighting against the American militias. Once they're defeated we will have control of the Aztlán territories." Sayf answered in unbelief.

The major glared at his Lieutenant. "Open your eyes and quit talking like a fool. Without pressure from the Iranian missiles and the Chinese, the American military has no reason to leave Iraq. Even now a significant number of their forces are leaving Korea and returning to the United States. Even if the militias are defeated, how long do you think the UN forces will last against the US Army and Air Force?"

Sayf could see that the major was right. "What are our orders?" Sayf dejectedly asked.

"Damascus wants us out of here before sunrise. They have arranged passage for us on a Lebanese freighter currently docked at the harbor. The freighter will deliver us to Cuba where we'll board a flight back home. But before we leave, we are to destroy all documents related to our mission."

"If the Mexicans see us leaving, they'll know their cause is hopeless and we're abandoning them." Sayf warned.

"I couldn't care less what they think," the major snapped. "Remember, we owe them nothing, they are insignificant. I'll tell Francisco and Carlos we have a meeting with some comrades on the freighter. We'll ask them to drop us off tonight and when they come for us in the morning, we'll be gone. Now return to your office and gather all the documents you can find. We'll bring them with us and burn them in the freighter's engine room. The last thing we need is for the Mexicans to see us destroying documents."

Gold Gulch (N31^{0} 25'34" W109^{0} 52'51"): 2021 hrs

The UN forces overran the 35th Utah, achieving a brief breakthrough against the militia's west flank. But before they could solidify their gains, reinforcements from the 49th Utah and Evil's 11th Washington pushed them back. The reinforcements were shocked at the carnage covering the battlefield. Dozens of bodies lay tangled together as a testimony of the brutality of the final hand-to-hand combat that occurred.

Although battles continued to rage, the overall tempo of the exchange had slowed. Both sides had taken heavy casualties and were no doubt reassessing their options.

Evil had just returned from a forward aid station. He approached Strats who was surveying the line through his binoculars. "How's it looking?"

"We're holding firm now that we've committed our reserve units, the holes are plugged," Strats lowered his binoculars and looked at Evil with a solemn expression. "But we don't have anything left...we have to make do with what we've got."

"Our guys put up a hell of a fight today." Evil added with a touch of pride in his words. Do you know how many of Porter's guys made it?"

"Not many." Strats answered solemnly. "Those Utah guys fought their hearts out." Strats shook his head still unable to get the image of the dead out of his mind. "Yeah, they just refused to surrender their positions and suffered upwards of sixty percent losses. The survivors have been folded into the 49th. How's Porter doing?"

"He'll be fine." Evil said as he took a drink of water from a canteen. "The medics said his right wrist is completely destroyed and will probably need some pins to keep it together and he suffered a concussion...looks like he'll be a southpaw for the rest of his life."

"Does he know about his men?"

"I don't think so. When I saw him he was drugged up and unconscious. There'll be time to tell him when this is over." Evil collapsed into a chair. Like everyone else, he'd been fighting most of the day and was completely exhausted. "Is it true that we're up against Cubans?"

"Yeah, we've interrogated some of the enemy wounded and confirmed they're part of a special shock battalion. Personally, I couldn't care less who they are or where they're from. What matters to me is that they're here, in my country, killing my friends."

"So what's your plan?"

Strat looked up from a map he'd been studying and faced his friend. His eyes were blood red, his expression pale and uncaring and his words were firm and resolute, "Kill every last one of them."

Strats picked up his map and walked over to Evil. After setting the map down, he circled the area where the break through had occurred. "They're desperate to break through our lines and flank our main positions. Even though we pushed them back, I don't think they'll just give up and go home. I believe they're doing exactly what we are...planning their next attack."

"That's my feeling as well," Evil answered. "So what do you have in mind?"

"I want to hit them before they hit us," Strat replied. "They know we've reinforced our right flank and I'd bet they probably think we're expecting another attack at the same location. That's why I think we should attack them on the left."

"Have you run this past TI yet?"

"No, but I'll radio him right now." Strats returned to his map and stared at it intently before speaking again. "Evil, how many men can we spare?"

"Edge's D Company is still fresh. They have eighty-five men. I can have them ready to go in thirty minutes."

"That should do, but I'll need *you* here just in case I'm wrong and they hit us on the right again." Strats stared at Evil, and with firmness added, "This is my plan...I'll be leading the attack."

Chapter 15

War is an ugly thing, but it is not the ugliest of things: The decayed and degraded state of moral and patriotic feelings which thinks that nothing is worth war is much worst. A man who has nothing for which he is willing to fight: nothing he cares more about than his own personal safety, is a miserable creature who has no chance of being free, unless made and kept so by the exertions and blood of better men than himself.
—John Stuart Mill (1806-1873)

Point Tango (N31⁰26'610" W109⁰49'445"): 2311 hrs

Point Tango was located at the summit of a small hill about three kilometers southeast of the main militia line of resistance. To reach it, Fox had been forced to move his small force across relatively open ground with only scattered concealment provided by chollas and cactus. Fox knew that stealth and speed were his best weapons, so he ordered his men to drop all gear except their rifles, pistols and one extra magazine. This was going to be a hit and run operation and the last thing he wanted was to get drawn into a prolonged firefight.

Fox's night vision scope washed the desert landscape in a green hue exposing a line of mortar pits. Inside each position the crews took turns resting while one man stood watch. In the closest pit the man on watch casually smoked a cigarette. Each time the soldier drew in on his cigarette, its blazing end lit up the immediate area like a flare. Fox turned towards his second-in command and flashed a series of hand signals instructing him to prepare the men for the attack, and ordered his communications man to radio TI. Half of the militiamen would execute the attack in a sweeping motion from left to right, reminiscent of a barn door swing on its hinge, while the other half provided security.

Fox held his men back until the main force shattered the stillness of the night with their cover fire.

"Attack!" Fox cried as he rose from his position. Behind him a line of militiamen charged the unsuspecting UN soldiers. The militiamen raked the UN positions with a deadly fusillade of fire killing most of them before they could even reach their personal weapons. As his men overran each position they dropped grenades down each mortar tube to ensure its destruction.

"Fire-in the-hole!" Fox cried out as he pulled the pin on his grenade and slid it down the wide opening of the enemy mortar tube. The assault was over in less than two minutes. A few UN soldiers attempted a counterattack, but were quickly cut to pieces by a wall of fire laid down by the other half of the militia force. Fox and his deputy commander slapped their troops on the back accounting for each man as they ran past them and toward the rendezvous point. The flawless assault was punctuated as each mortar tube exploded in a brilliant flash of fire and sparks.

PLA Headquarters: Hermosillo, Mexico, 2458 hrs

Lt. Hawkins took a quick glance at his watch before radioing the rest of his teammates. "Bravo, Echo, T-minus two, give me a go/no go." A stream of syncopated "Go's" answered the Lieutenant's question. Hawkins felt a wave of adrenaline surge through his body as he steeled himself for action. "Thunderclap one and two…green light." This was the signal for the scout/ snipers to take out any guards that might interfere with the initial phase of the assault.

From their hides overlooking the front and rear of the compound the snipers tracked the guards through their 10-power Unertl scopes and slowly squeezed the match-grade triggers on their silenced M40A3 rifles. Both guards were downed by headshots that nearly decapitated them. Without the slightest hesitation, the snipers then switched to their secondary targets and eliminated them in like fashion. After doing a final sweep of the area, the spotters radioed, "Bravo One all clear, Echo One, all clear."

Without saying a word, Hawkins' team jumped to their feet and rushed towards the nine-foot wall that extended around the rear of the compound. Upon reaching the wall, two men silently positioned black-aluminum ladders against the obstacle and then swung around the back of the ladders using their body weight to secure them in place.

Hawkins watched his point man climb the ladder and disappear over the wall closely followed by and his second-in command, Sr. Chief Toby Washington. The all-clear crackled in his headset, and one-by-one by the rest of the SEALs entered the courtyard.

As each team member stealthily lowered himself into the quad, the SEALs established a defensive parameter until everyone was ready to advance. Hawkins flashed a quick signal directing two buddy teams to place demolition charges on a pair of Ford Excursions and a Cadillac Escalade parked near the rear gate. It only took a couple of minutes for the men to wire the charges into the ignition systems of the vehicles.

The explosives were set to detonate if the SUV's were started or by remote control. Either way they'd be fiery wrecks in a few minutes.

"Thunderclap one, Echo one...we're ready to move," Hawkins radioed the sniper team providing cover for his assault element. "Give me a sitrep."

"Echo one, you're clear. Be advised there is movement in the east room, top floor."

"Roger Thunderclap, Echo's moving out."

The ten SEALs advanced in a tactical column towards the staircase. As they silently moved, their weapons covered different directions, providing a three hundred and sixty degree zone of protection until they reached the base of the stairs.

Then the team slowly ascended the concrete steps leading towards a large, ornate wooden door on the second floor. The demolitions team placed a breaching charge against the door. Once set, they signaled the Lieutenant they were ready. Hawkins paused long enough to radio Bravo team and confirm they were in position and ready to make their entry.

"Echo One to Bravo One," Hawkins radioed. "Echo is set and ready."

"Copy Echo One, Bravo One is set and standing by."

Hawkins took one last look around, ensuring that everyone was prepared. He keyed his radio and said, "On my mark, ready, three...two...one...execute, execute, execute!"

A member of the breaching team activated an electronic detonator, blowing the heavy door off its hinges and half way into the room. Before the smoke and the deafening sound of the explosion dissipated, the first four men in the train flooded into the room. The first man through the door immediately pivoted to his left with his silenced M-4 raised and ready to fire.

As he reached the first corner he pivoted to his right where he saw a figure crawling towards a table. The SEAL leveled his front sight on the figure and fired, sending a burst of three 77-grain rounds into the man's chest.

To his left Hawkins heard the fluttering sound of another burst as it took down a second Tango. Hawkins reached the far right corner where he stopped and pivoted towards the center of the room. "One clear," Chief Washington called out.

"Two clear!"

"Three clear!"

Hawkins completed the sequence by adding, "Four clear!"

Hawkins made a second quick scan of the room and through the clearing smoke saw a closed door to his left. "Room clear. Door on the left, stack on me." As the four-man entry team stacked up to enter the adjoining room, the rest of Echo team quickly entered in pairs and took up defensive positions to cover the entry teams' next movement. As soon as the entry team was stacked up and ready, the first two buddy teams immediately moved to the two dead men. Covered by his partner, one member of each team rolled a corpse over and focused a digital video camera at its face. "Dead guy one," the SEAL announced so the camera could record his observation. Then another SEAL knelt beside the body and began searching for any papers or personal identification. Everything they found was shoved into a waterproof bag attached to the SEALs load bearing vest.

*****

Major Al-Salid was frantically loading documents into his briefcase when a massive explosion in the next room startled him. Even from the other side of the wall, the force of the explosion rocked his room knocking him off his feet. Before he could react he heard the unmistakable sound of American voices. "*The Americans are attacking*," flashed through his mind. There was no way he could stand toe-to-toe against a group of commandos. His only chance of survival was to get out of the house as quickly as possible. Grabbing his briefcase, he crawled toward the door leading to the first floor and safety. Suddenly, both the door in front of him and the one behind flew open. In front of him Sayf charged into the room with an AK-74 at the ready.

"The Americans..." Before he could finish his sentence, a black grenade landed a couple of feet to the majors' right and exploded. The concussion from the CTS 7290M flash bang grenade crashed into the major and Sayf like a tidal wave while its eight million candle power flash completely blinded them.

*****

Hawkins turned toward the far corner of the room, and saw a man on his hands and knees, desperately grasping at a rifle. As Hawkins positioned his sights squarely on the man's head, the Tango looked straight at him. Ribbons of blood flowed from the man's nose and ears and his unfocused eyes drifted aimlessly in their sockets. Hawkins didn't hesitate; he squeezed the trigger twice and watched as two 5.56mm rounds ripped a gaping hole into the man's ocular-nasal cavity.

Hawkins continued to move towards his designated corner when he noticed a second target. The man was shouting something in Arabic and reaching for a handgun in his waistband. Hawkins shifted his aim towards the new threat, but a large armoire blocked his shot. "Tango in sector three," he shouted out to the rest of his team. "No shot!"

*****

The major's senses were beginning to recover from the violent detonation of the flash bang grenade. He watched as Sayf's face literally exploded in front of him and knew his own demise was only seconds away. The thought of his impending death didn't bring panic, for he'd been prepared for it for years. He'd accepted the inevitability of a violent death. His only desire was to die a *shaheed.* So as he reached for his pistol he began reciting the *Shahada*, "*La ilaha il Allah, Muhammad...*"

*****

Chief Washington cleared the doorway with an ease and grace that seemed unnatural for his six foot two, two hundred and fifty pound build. He was in the number three position and as he entered the room his rifle was pointed towards the center of the room, directly over the shoulder of the number two man. Washington watched as the Lieutenant dropped the first Tango with a perfect headshot, and then heard him call "no shot." The second Tango was on his knees yelling something in Arabic. Blood trickling out of his ears betrayed the fact that his eardrums were ruptured, explaining why he was yelling.

In a fraction of a second, Washington established his sight picture and fired. The Gemtech M4-96D suppressor reduced the sound of the firing to barely audible blasts of air. The rounds slammed squarely into the target's chest, knocking him backward and sprawling his body across the floor.

"One clear...Two clear...Three clear...Four clear!" The SEALs once again called out as they followed their highly choreographed procedure with complete focus and dedication. No one took time for a victory dance or to deliver the pithy one-liners that heroes in the movies always seemed to offer. They were professionals playing the world's most dangerous game. A game where there was no second place, only the living and the dead.

"Stack on me," Hawkins shouted as he performed a tactical reload and moved towards an open door that led down a hallway and toward a staircase. Chief Washington covered the door and fell into the last position as his team passed through the opening. As soon as the entry team had cleared the room the remaining members of Echo began their intelligence search.

The SEAL with the camera focused on Major Al-Salid's face and remarked in a calm voice, "Dead Hadji one." Like his teammates he didn't allow his emotions to interfere with the mission. He didn't care who his targets were or what they had done. His only thought was to eliminate the targets, protect his teammates and complete his mission. His world allowed for nothing more. He would probably never know who Major Muhammad Mahdi Al-Salih was or the many missions he'd performed for his country. Nor would he know the role he'd played in attacking the United States or the hundreds of other things the major had been involved in over the last two decades. That knowledge was reserved for analysts and policy makers in Washington. Whoever this guy was no longer mattered. He'd played the game and lost...and the SEALs had no respect for losers.

The commando moved toward the body of Lieutenant Sayf Al-Din Al-Mashhadani and focused his camera on what was left of the man's face, which wasn't much. "Dead Hadji two." Then glancing back at his buddy, added, "Get good prints on this guy and a hair sample, we'll need both for a positive ID."

A third SEAL emptied a briefcase, found next to the first body, into his waterproof bag before quickly moving onto whatever else he could find. Although his training told him every bit of intelligence was valuable, he didn't realize the importance of the documents he'd just crammed into his evidence bag.

Both teams finished clearing the house and radioed for the trucks. The final count was eleven terrorists dead and no friendly casualties. The escape trucks arrived and were quickly loaded, and then the SEALs headed towards the harbor. As the team sped away, Hawkins activated an electronic detonator setting off the charges placed in the three SUVs. The explosions rocked the neighborhood, shattering windows and providing the perfect distraction the SEALs needed to slip away into the early morning darkness.

The Oval Office: 0600

The Secretary of Defense called the president at 0300 and delivered a simple message, "Mr. President, we got 'em." The SEAL team had eliminated all targets, suffered no casualties and collected a large quantity of intelligence that was being electronically transmitted to Langley. Most important, the Secretary confirmed that the Syrians were dead. Upon receiving the news the president felt as though a heavy load had been lifted from his shoulders. Although he was confident the mission was necessary, it was never easy ordering "his men," as he liked to refer to the military, into battle.

As soon as the initial report was finished, Herb Nossler raced it over to the White House. He arrived just after the Secretary of Defense and Attorney General and unceremoniously took a seat next to the president's large leather chair.

Although an air of anticipation filled the oval office, those present casually sipped cups of coffee and made small talk until "The Boss" entered the room.

"Glad to see you Herb," the president remarked as he sat down. "I assume I'm going to like your report?"

"Yes sir, I believe you'll be very satisfied." Margaret Bantam offered the CIA Director a cup of coffee, but he graciously declined the offer. He'd been drinking coffee all night and it was causing his ulcer to flare up. As he looked around the room he noticed the Vice President hadn't arrived. "Is the VP on his way?" He asked the president.

"The Vice President will not be attending this morning's meeting," the president remarked in a stern voice. "Let's get started."

Herb pulled several folders out of his briefcase. "As you all know, early this morning Naval Special Warfare assets raided the main headquarters of the PLA outside of Hermosillo, Mexico. The mission was a complete success and provided a windfall of intelligence. Hundreds of documents were recovered and have been digitally transmitted to Langley. Analysts from the Joint Terrorism and Middle East desks are still plowing through the information, but what we have so far clearly connects Hezbollah, the Syrian military, the PLA and the UN to the Aztlán invasion."

Herb opened the first folder, withdrew four photos and handed them to the president. The first picture was of a dead, Arab looking man in his forties. "We've confirmed this man as Major Muhammad Mahdi Al-Salih. The Israelis have a dossier on him going back over ten years. He's identified as the primary liaison between the Syrian Army and Hezbollah."

"Looks like this guy's a candidate for an extreme makeover," the president sarcastically remarked as he examined the second photo, before passing the picture to Secretary of State Bantum.

"Good Lord!" Margaret exclaimed with a wince. "That looks more like a plate of steak tartar than a face."

"That's Lieutenant Sayf Al-Din Al-Mashhadani," the DCI interjected. "He's also from the Syrian Army."

"How can you be sure?" Margaret asked. "His whole face is gone."

"Standard operating procedure calls for collecting fingerprints and hair samples for DNA testing," the Secretary of Defense added.

"That's right," answered the DCI. "We sent copies of the prints to Jerusalem. The Shin Bet's Arab Affairs Department confirms it's him. We won't be a hundred percent sure until the DNA results come back, but we have very high confidence." Director Nossler retrieved another photo and presented it to the president. "This photo was included in the information we got from the Israelis last week; it shows Al-Mashhadani and Al-Salih together. The Mossad believes Al-Mashhadani was Al-Salih's adjutant." Nossler paused long enough for the group to digest the information they'd just received, then added, "This confirms the intel we received from Tire Iron."

"What about these other two?" The president asked.

"Photo number three is Francisco Estrada, the leader of the PLA and the other is of his Operations Leader, Carlos Ochoa." Nossler answered.

"You mentioned evidence tying the UN into this whole deal," the Attorney General interjected, "What do you have?"

Nossler opened a third folder and passed out copies of a fax, translated from Arabic into English. "I believe you'll find this useful. It's a communiqué between a Brigadier General Taha Al-Din Maruf at the Syrian Intelligence Directorate and Al-Salih. In it he refers to an unspecified conference of a critical nature to the Aztlán mission."

"You'll notice two individuals are named: Sheik Jufalli and Mohammad Saddat. The Sheik is a major financial supporter and member of one of the most radical Wahabist sects in Saudi Arabia. This group is so extreme that King Bandar shut down all their madrassas, claiming they threatened the peace of the kingdom."

"Yeah right, the kingdom. What he means is they threatened the power and stability of the Saud family," Secretary McMillan sarcastically remarked. "What else do we know about the Sheik?"

"His 'schools' were major fund raisers and recruitment centers for both *Al-Qaeda* and *Hamas*. If he wasn't related to the Saudi Royal family by marriage, he would have been assassinated or jailed long ago."

"Who's the other guy?" The president asked.

"Mohammed Saddat is a member of Iran's Revolutionary Council and a confederate of Grand Ayatollah Ali Alireza, who's Iran's supreme religious leader. Ali Alireza is appointed for life by a board of clerics and invested with control over the Revolutionary Guards, the regular military, the security services and the judiciary. We believe he's been the primary go-between for Tehran and the Shiite terrorist organizations in Iraq."

The Attorney General shifted in his chair. "Okay, these two aren't going to win any humanitarian awards...but where's the UN connection?"

"As you might expect they both top the agency's list of suspected terrorists, so we keep close tabs on where they are and what they're doing. The last time they were together was at a closed-door meeting at the UN two weeks ago. The Bureau's UN mole has confirmed they attended a conference that included General Secretary Al-Duri and both the Syrian and Chinese Ambassadors."

The AG nodded as he made a few notes, before adding, "This definitely helps, but I need more...something truly damning." Thomas had spent almost fifteen years as a federal prosecutor and knew that to ensure success he needed a bulletproof case.

"Don't misunderstand me, between this and the evidence we've already compiled, we can present a pretty solid case for getting out of the UN..." Frank stopped and looked at the other participants "...but we all know Senator Snow and Congresswoman Alberti are going to spin this so it looks like they were joining hands and singing Kumbaya. I need a smoking gun."

"There's more still to come," the DCI assured his colleague. "We've barely started to analyze the intel dump from the SEALs. I'll keep you in the loop and make sure whatever we develop gets sent directly to your office."

"It's good to see you children playing nicely together," the president said. "We don't have time for inter-agency pissing contests. Make sure your two offices give this the highest possible priority, I want concrete results...consider this a Presidential mandate." The DCI and AG acknowledged the order.

"Now that you both understand my expectations on that, I want to make something else just as clear. With the Chinese backing down to lick their wounds, and having established a clear alliance between the UN and known terrorists, it's time the gloves come off." The president focused on Herb Nossler again, "How's the militia doing?"

"Both the California and Arizona contingents are fully engaged. The UN has concentrated the bulk of its heavy units in the Arizona sector. Reports are that although the militia lines are holding, it's been a seesaw battle."

"Well, it sounds like they could use a hand." The president turned to Secretary McMillan. "Is that squadron of F-16s still at Luke?"

"Yes sir. It's an undersized squadron, but I can give you eight combat ready aircraft ready to go on your orders."

"Good. I want them to hit those UN bastards and drive them back to Mexico."

Mule Gulch (N31^{0}21'314" W109^{0}44'796"): Main Militia Line of Resistance, 0515

As dawn illuminated the eastern sky, Tire Iron read over the casualty reports that bore witness of the fierce fighting that had raged over night. He offered a silent prayer of thanksgiving that although the militia lines had wavered and brief UN breakthroughs had occurred, his men had gallantly resisted and remained in control of the primary line of resistance.

The 31st and 6th New Mexican battalions along with Lightfigther's Oklahomans had stopped the UN rear attack dead in its tracks. During the night Desert Scout's men had enveloped the enemy's southern flank, cutting them from the main body. In so doing they overran their secondary LZ, preventing reinforcements and re-supply.

Another success was the 38th Colorado's assault against the UN mortar positions. It was a textbook example of a small unit attack. They'd hit the enemy hard and fast destroying all the mortar tubes without losing a single man. But that's where the good news ended.

To the east, Cuban shock troops had mauled the defenses at Gold Gulch. Porter Glockwell's 35th Utah battalion was virtually destroyed after vicious fighting that had devolved into bloody hand-to-hand combat. The men of the 35th held their positions against a force nearly twice their size and inflicted tremendous damage before reinforcements arrived and drove the enemy back. In the battle they'd loss nearly sixty percent of their strength including a full platoon of snipers from the 16th Tennessee. As Tire Iron read the list of the wounded and dead, the names transformed into the faces of his friends and longtime comrades. The surviving members of the 35th and 16th were attached to the Utah 57th and 29th, now occupying the positions of the 35th. Strats' 61st Washington battalion had also taken heavy causalities. The 11th battalion now reinforced them and together they were putting up a stiff resistance against continuous and determined attacks. Unfortunately, Strats had committed all his reserves and was running dangerously low on ammunition and supplies.

The situation along the main line of resistance didn't look much better. Though they'd eliminated the mortars, TI's men still found themselves up against enemy armor and a seemingly endless stream of UN soldiers. They'd exhausted their supply of AT-4's and anti-tank mines and were nearing the last of their claymores. TI's men had fought back several enemy assaults and were battered and tired, but their morale was intact. Nonetheless, he knew they couldn't hold on indefinitely. He also knew the UN force had to be on the edge of breaking. The enemy dead and wounded littered the battlefield. Their bodies lay in smoldering heaps amid the twisted remains of burning armor, adding a putrefying stench to the superheated desert air. During the brief lull in fighting, the armies seemed like two fighters staring at one another across the ring. Both were bloodied and barely standing, yet unwilling to capitulate. TI knew he needed a knock out to win this fight and his time was running out.

"The CO of the 61st is on the line and requests to speak with you," a radioman announced, offering a handset to TI.

That would be Stratiotes. This might be what he needed. TI grabbed the handset and in a direct voice commanded, "Talk to me."

"TI, I'd like permission to lead an assault. They've been concentrating against our right flank all night, and I think they're setting us up for an attack on the left. I want to hit them before they hit us."

"How're your men holding out?" TI asked.

"All our reserves are committed and we're running low on ammunition," Strat paused for a moment. "But, D Company from the 11th battalion is fresh and ready to make the assault. The rest of my force will remain in position to fend off any counter-attack and provide harassment fire."

For a moment the line fell silent as TI considered Strats' proposal. "Hello?" Strat asked in a slightly perturbed voice. "Are you still there?"

"Yeah, I'm still here," All right, TI thought. Get your concerns out in the open. "Strat, I'm worried about further weakening your defense. What if you're wrong and the Cubans hit your right again? If your line breaks they'll roll up our flank and hit us in the rear. There's no way we could defend against that."

"I understand, but I know they're coming at us on the left. The last couple of assaults have been coordinated with probing attacks on our left. They know we've been reinforcing the right side all night and I know they're going to try and turn us."

"How confident are you, Strat?"

"Confident enough to put my life and those of my men on the line."

"All right then, when do you want to begin your attack?"

"Immediately."

TI's voice softened as he accepted the situation. "Godspeed, brother. I'll look forward to your report when it's over."

UN Forward Command (N31⁰22'00" W109⁰40'00")

Colonel Drago sat impatiently as a call was patched through to his field headquarters. "*I don't have time for this foolishness*," he thought to himself. "*I have a battle to fight!*" Seconds later he heard a familiar voice.

"Colonel, this is General Secretary Al-Duri, give me a report."

"Secretary, our forces are still engaged and pressing the Americans on several fronts. I'll have more information for you by the end of the day."

"The end of the day? You should have crushed them by now!" Al-Duri's voice was outraged. "You've accomplished nothing but the destruction of hundreds of millions of dollars worth of helicopters and armor. The American rabble is making a laughing stock out of the United Nations and a fool out of you!"

The Colonel felt his blood pressure surge. He couldn't believe this pampered bureaucrat had the audacity to actually blame him for the glaring omissions of his own intelligence. "Mr. Secretary, you can not blame me for the loss of the helicopters and armor, when the intelligence *your* office provided did not mention that the militias were equipped with shoulder fired air-to-air and anti-tank missiles. Those losses are the fault of incompetent bureaucrats on your staff, not my ability to command!"

"Don't forget to whom you're talking, Colonel," Al-Duri said in a patronizing tone. "It is your responsibility to destroy the militia. You accepted the mission and ensured the council they'd be crushed. We gave you all the support you requested...yet you have failed to break their lines. I anticipated more from you. Evidently, I overestimated your dedication and abilities."

It was all Drago could do to maintain his composure. He'd never been addressed in such an insolent manner, not even when he was a first year cadet at the General Máximo Gómez Academy in Havana. What infuriated him most was that Al-Duri was a pathetic politician who'd never suffered on a battlefield in his whole life. Drago wasn't going to allow this UN aristocrat to besmirch his reputation...not to mention the sacrifices of his soldiers.

Drago took a deep breath in an attempt to steady himself, and in a stern voice replied, "Secretary Al-Duri, I am going to crush the Americans just as I promised. My troops have beaten them down and the enemy is on the verge of collapse. One more thrust and they'll break and then I will strangle the life out of them and their ridiculous delusions of grandeur."

"Very well Colonel," Al-Duri answered in a softer, yet still patronizing tone. "You have until the end of the day to accomplish your mission. Make no mistake, I expect you to succeed, or die trying. Too much depends upon a decisive victory. Make sure it happens." Then the Secretary abruptly hung up.

Drago sat seething in anger. He held the phone to his ear for a moment before hurling it across his command post.

"Prepare for a general assault! I want every unit ready to advance within the hour!"

Near Gold Gulch (N31⁰ 25'34" W109⁰ 52'51"): 0530

Strats led his assault force in a wide arc around the southeast edge of the front. He believed the Cubans would attempt a surprise attack on the left side of the line and hoped to position his men where he could ambush the enemy before they reached the militia positions.

Seeing his pointman coming back towards him, Strats halted his men.

"You were right," Edge said in a slightly winded voice. "There's a UN assault force moving this way. They're about two klicks out, bearing two zero two degrees."

"What's their strength? Strats asked.

"I'd estimate between a hundred and a hundred and fifty. They're traveling light and fast." Edge pulled out his map and identified an arroyo. "They're using this arroyo as cover. I suggest setting up our ambush at this point. There's a lot of natural concealment and it'll allow us to rake nearly the entire length of the arroyo with fire."

"I agree. I'll take second platoon and set up on the east side, you position third platoon on the west. We'll place our M249's along this northern edge so they can fire directly down the length of the arroyo." A smile spread across Strats' face as he felt a sense of peace come over him. This is was what the Lord had prepared him for, and he was eager to begin.

The two leaders separated and assembled their platoons. After a brief warning order the two platoons headed toward the ambush site to position their crew served weapons and remaining claymore mines. Sections from both platoons were positioned perpendicular to the arroyo as blocking forces against flanking attacks. These teams divided the claymores and placed them to their front. Strats knew that the only possible response to an ambush was to charge into it and try to break through. The soldiers in the vanguard of the UN formation wouldn't have much of a chance, but those in the rear would immediately climb out of the arroyo and try to sweep around the sides in an attempt to envelope their ambushers.

If they followed this logic, they'd run right into the blocking forces and be immediately destroyed. The only other choice they had was to turn tail and retreat, and considering the way they'd fought so far...that wasn't likely.

While the company prepared the ambush, scouts kept an eye on the approaching enemy. Edge's radio crackled, "OP1 to Homebase, guests are one klick out. Over"

"Homebase to OP1, understood." Edge replied.

Edge moved down the ambush line, checking each man's concealment and passing the word until he arrived at his chosen position beside one of the company's two M249 Squad Automatic Weapons (SAW's). The militias had received these along with the other supplies covertly supplied by the Pentagon. The M249 SAW is a gas-operated automatic weapon capable of firing up to nine hundred rounds per minute of 5.56mm ammunition fed by a two hundred round detachable box magazine. These weapons had proven invaluable to the militia. Normally each squad would deploy two M249's, but the militia wasn't normal. Edge was happy that there were two for the whole company.

"OP2 to Homebase, guests are in sight. Over."

"Homebase to OP2, roger." Edge knew this meant the enemy was within two hundred and fifty yards of his position. Strats had taken a position with one of the blocking forces to manage the battle.

"Alpha three to Alpha two," Edge radioed. "We're in position and guests are on the way. Over." Strat responded by triggering his transmit button, telling Edge the enemy was close at hand.

The machine gunners would initiate the ambush, followed by a volley of grenades from both sides of the arroyo. The shooting would continue until the enemy was dead or surrendered in mass. Waiting for the enemy to arrive was intolerable. Edge's mind raced with a thousand details. He wasn't concerned about his own well-being; he worried that someone might give away their position, or prematurely begin firing.

Edge looked to his right and left nodding encouragement to his men. They were prepared. Each man had laid several magazines and grenades beside his position so they'd be easier to reach once the ambush began. Edge's heart pounded in his chest and his breathing increased as the first UN soldier approached. Just as his scouts had said, they were moving fast. Unfortunately for them, they seemed to be more concerned with meeting a timetable than maintaining security. The Cubans were convinced that they were in neutral territory.

Edge watched as the distance closed between the front of the UN column and the imaginary point where the ambush would be sprung. "*Come on you bastards...a little clos*er...*closer...*" He thought as he reached over and placed his hand on his machine gunner's arm. "*Almost...* "

Mule Gulch: Fallback Position, 0530

Dawn would break in less than an hour. This simple fact seemed to revive Gringo's flagging spirit. Although he'd worked hard to maintain the morale of the men around him, there were moments during the night when he hadn't believed he'd live to see another sunrise. The fighting had been horrendous. Time after time the enemy had thrown itself against the militia defenses, and each time they'd been beaten back. Regrettably, each assault had taken a toll on both the defenders and their rapidly depleting supplies. If the attacks continued, it was inevitable Gringo's line would break, if not for lack of men, then for lack of ammunition.

Earlier in the morning, Cowboy had assembled a squad to undertake the dreadful task of stripping the dead of their ammunition and supplies. They'd also collected ammo from the field hospital and every other source they could think of. What they'd gathered was literally the last of the ammunition. To his right two men were busy unlinking 5.56mm rounds from a M249 belt, salvaged from a gun that had been destroyed in one of the last mortar attacks.

"This should top you off," Cowboy said as he passed three reloaded magazines to Gringo. "What else do you need?"

"I could use an extra magazine of .40S&W," Gringo remarked as he gladly accepted the fresh mags from his partner. "I'm down to one magazine for my pistol. I used the other one during that breakthrough just after dark."

"I'll see what I can do. Maybe one of the other companies has some they can spare." Cowboy replied as he silently moved off to distribute the remaining magazines.

Gringo reached over and sucked the last few ounces of water from his Camelback. As he drank, he noticed the warm, flat water had an odd metallic taste to it. After examining the bite valve Gringo saw that it had blood on it. He tried to remember whose blood it could be, but quickly realized it could belong to any one of dozens of men on both sides of the conflict.

A series of horrid visions flashed vividly through his mind. Two times during the night, his company had resorted to hand-to-hand combat to beat back the UN assault. In those cases he'd been forced to use his rifle as a club and literally beat the enemy to death in order to survive. He knew he'd carry the mental scars of those experiences the rest of his life. As the traumatic images flickered in his memory, he felt as if he should cry. But there were no tears, only a numb, detached feeling that made him question whether he'd really experienced those horrors. Gringo knew that if he survived there'd be time to deal with the physiological aftermath of what he'd gone through; he only hoped he'd be able to handle it properly. He was startled back to the present as Wildcat jumped into his fighting position. Gringo's empty stare darted towards his friend who'd been wounded by shrapnel in his right thigh. "Freaking-A, Wildcat! You scared the crap out of me!"

"Sorry man, I warned you before jumping in, but you were spaced out...are you all right?"

"Peachy...just thinking." Gringo replied sarcastically. "How's your leg doing?"

"It's holding up. I took the bandage off and stitched it up about twenty minutes ago. It's not as bad as I thought." Wildcat said as he aimlessly searched the floor of the foxhole. "Do you have any extra .308?"

"Sorry brother, no .30-caliber in this hole," Gringo responded. "You might want to ask the guys in the foxhole three positions over, they're with the 71st, they ought to have some."

"No problem," Wildcat said with a slight smile. "I have a full load out; I was just hoping to score a little extra."

Gringo wondered how the rest of the team was faring. Other than Cowboy who'd been with Gringo from the beginning, and the occasional radio communication with Arrow, Wildcat was the only other member of his original team he'd heard from. He knew Hot Dog and Thor had been attached to 16th Tennessee, but they were positioned on the far opposite side of the line. Likewise, AK was assigned to the 5th Utah and Ghost was manning communications in the battalion CP.

"Have you heard anything from Hot Dog, Thor or AK?" Gringo asked, not sure if he wanted to hear the answer.

"AK's doing fine, although the last I saw him he'd dumped his Kalashnikov for an AR. I haven't heard anything from Thor and Hot Dog. I think their platoon was attached to Glockwell's group over at Gold Gulch."

"I hope they're okay," Gringo said. "Word is the Utah and Washington guys really got chewed up."

"You mean worse than us?" Wildcat asked in disbelief

"From what Arrow told us," Gringo answered, "a lot worst."

"Make room," Cowboy said as he returned to the foxhole. Gringo and Wildcat moved aside as Cowboy jumped into the fighting position. "I think this is what you were looking for?" Cowboy said as he passed Gringo a full magazine for his pistol.

"Outstanding. Where'd you find it?"

"You *don't* want to know."

"You wouldn't happen to have any extra 30-caliber, would you?" Wildcat chimed in.

"Sorry bud. That wasn't on my shopping list. How's your leg doing?"

"It's fine," Wildcat answered. "It hurts a little when I run, but it'll heal up fine."

The three friends took advantage of the brief pause in action to eat and talk. It was surreal. One minute they were fighting for their lives and the next they were able to talk to one another as if they were back at the academy.

Suddenly a massive explosion detonated a few yards in front of their foxhole. The three men immediately crouched down and covered their heads. Even as dirt rained down from the explosion they rose up and searched for targets...which weren't hard to find. As before, the UN charged their line while laying down a withering hail of fire. Fortunately, the gunfire was fairly inaccurate.

The heavy G3 rifles used by the Mexican army were simply too powerful to accurately fire on the run. Cowboy, Gringo and Wildcat had quickly learned to ignore the supersonic crack of the bullets as they passed overhead and steadily picked off their targets as quickly as possible.

Gringo watched as Wildcat took out his targets with single devastating shots. The 30-caliber rounds hit hard, nearly knocking the Mexicans off their feet, whereas Gringo's much smaller .223 rounds often required two hits before permanently dropping his target. The charge was stopped about one hundred and fifty meters ahead as the UN soldiers found cover and began to maneuver against the militia positions. Off to his left Gringo noticed a stream of tracers rip through the early morning twilight like a laser beam. The rounds must have been from a .50-caliber machine gun because they tore through the hull of a burned out APC as if it were paper. The Mexicans who'd sought shelter behind the wrecked vehicle were shredded by the half-inch armor piercing rounds.

A scream pulled Gringo's attention in the opposite direction. A militiaman had been hit and was yelling for help, "Medic...Medic!"

"Cover me, guys. I've got to help that guy." Wildcat said as he slung his rifle and detached his medic bag from the back of his gear.

Wildcat waited until Cowboy had inserted a fresh magazine in his rifle, then counted off, "On three...two...one," before taking off towards the wounded man.

Gringo and Cowboy focused their attention on the nearest enemy position and fired controlled two and three shot groups that forced the Mexicans under cover. Wildcat quickly covered the distance to the wounded man and began dragging him back toward a shallow rut that crossed the battlefield.

Gringo watched as Wildcat spoke to the man, assuring him that he'd be all right. Suddenly a well aimed round slammed into Wildcat's chest. Gringo was paralyzed in horror as he watched the wounded man slip from Wildcat's grip and his friend stand erect.

"Noooooo!" Gringo screamed at the top of his lungs. For a second, Wildcat seemed to wobble on his feet like a drunk. Then a second and third bullet knocked him to the ground.

Gringo stood frozen, his mouth hanging wide open in a silent scream, as he watched his friend go limp and die.

"Pull yourself together, I need your help...Damn it, get in the fight!" Cowboy's voice echoed hollow in Gringo's ears. "He's gone, there's nothing we can do about it...come on I need you now or we'll be next!"

Near Gold Gulch (N31° 25'34" W109° 52'51"): 0600

"Fire!"

Automatic weapons fire shattered the early morning stillness. The M249's spewed death and destruction on the advancing Cubans. An instant later, dozens of other weapons and a shower of grenades joined the two machine guns. For the first moments of the ambush the action crossed the delicate line between warfare and pure butchery. The Cubans were caught unaware, and before they could react dozens men were cut to pieces.

Those who managed to raise their weapons immediately drew the attention of militiamen who eliminated them in a ferocious crossfire. A veil of dirt and dust quickly obscured the sight of the human carnage. Through the dust Edge watched as the arroyo, which had earlier been dry, now flowed red with blood.

"Cease-fire...Cease-fire!" Edge shouted.

Although the militiamen stopped firing, they remained ready to engage any threat that still existed. But as the dust settled their senses were greeted by a scene reminiscent of a slaughterhouse. As expected, the majority of the Cubans had retreated back down the arroyo and climbed out in an effort to flank the ambush. As soon as they came into view the blocking force detonated their Claymores. Once again the leading ranks of the Cubans were decimated. Before the smoke and dust had settled Strats stood up and yelled, "Follow me!"

Along the length of the line, militiamen sprung to their feet and in unison let out a spontaneous yell reminiscent of the fabled Rebel Yell from the Civil War. The two forces crashed into one another with an intensity rarely witnessed. Strats fired on the collected enemy until his weapon was empty. The two forces were now intermixed and the ferocity of the fighting prevented him from inserting a new magazine. In an instant he was confronted by an enemy soldier. Using the stock of his rifle Strats knocked the man's rifle out of his hands, and then with a lightening quick movement, smashed the man in the face with his rifle butt.

Looking to his left he saw two men charging him with leveled bayonets. Strats dropped his empty rifle and reached for his pistol. By the time his sidearm was up and on target, the two Cubans were virtually on top of him. Two shots rang out and one of the UN soldiers went down. But it was too late to stop the other. Before he could fire a third time the charging Cuban drove his bayonet deep into Strats' chest. The powerful thrust knocked all the wind out of his lungs and he gasped for air as he stood face-to-face with his killer. Strats knew he'd suffered a mortal wound, but in one last act of defiance he raised his pistol until the barrel lodged under the Cuban's left ear and then pulled the trigger. Strats watched in satisfaction as his enemy's head exploded. The weight of the Cuban's body pulled Strats down with him as he collapsed and the two combatants ended up in a tangled, bloody heap. Strats' life was quickly draining out of him, yet he was at peace. The last thing he saw was a magnificently bright light that descended from the heavens and enveloped him in the warmest and most loving sensation he'd ever experienced. A peaceful smile spread across his face as he joyfully embraced eternity.

The charge was repeated on the opposite end of the line and the UN soldiers were quickly surrounded. Those that survived hastily threw down their weapons and surrendered. Edge left a contingent to watch the prisoners before leading the remaining force against the rear of the Cuban line. Once again, the unsuspecting adversary was caught off guard and mowed down with a ferocity that words cannot amply describe. Within minutes the Cubans were routed and surrendered en masse.

UN Forward Command (N31⁰22'00" W109⁰40'00")

"Tell me what's happening at Gold Gulch!" Drago commanded his communications officer.

"Sir, we're getting mixed and garbled messages from the assault force," the comms officer answered. "Last reports were they had enemy inside their positions."

"Where's Pasos? Has the entire chain of command fallen apart?" Drago demanded.

The comms officer frantically switched frequencies in a desperate attempt to raise the Cuban position. Finally he made contact with an observation post a kilometer away from the Cuban command post.

"This is Cathedral, what's your situation?"

"Cathedral, this is OP3. Our CP has been overrun. The Americans came out of nowhere and attacked us from the rear. As our front line broke to engage the rear attack, the American's charged from their main line of defense and completely overwhelmed our forces. I see major causalities and the survivors are surrendering. What are my orders?"

The UN forward command center fell silent as the report was heard by everyone present. The comms officer looked at Drago in stunned silence, not sure what to expect from his volatile commander. For a moment Drago stared at the radio in eerie silence. Nonetheless his red face and the pronounced veins that protruded from his neck and forehead expressed the fury that was raging within him. Drago turned away from the radio and slammed his fist into his palm.

The lone soldier's voice returned, "Cathedral, this is OP3...awaiting orders."

Drago turned back to the radio and snatched the microphone from the hand of the comms officer, "OP3 this is Cathedral. You're on your own...return to base as quickly as possible. Cathedral, out."

Drago's mind was reeling. He couldn't believe his hand picked troops had been defeated. His battle plan was disintegrating. Earlier he'd learned that the helicopter assault had failed to achieve its goal of cutting off the *Mule Pass Tunnel* and the main air assault force had been pinned down and divided by a fast reacting militia force. Now his Cuban troops were destroyed. His only chance for success was against the enemy's main line at Mule Gulch. Nothing else mattered; he had to break their line before reinforcements from Gold Gulch could arrive.

"I want every last man, and every last vehicle to join the attack on the militia main line," Drago announced in a booming voice. "How many helicopters do we have left?"

A lieutenant in a flight suit was standing near another set of radios and quickly spoke up, "Colonel, we can put two helicopters up immediately."

"Good. Mount machineguns in the doors and get them in the air." Drago said as he sloppily returned the lieutenant's salute. "What about armor?"

"Sir, we only have a couple of APC's left," feebly remarked a Mexican Captain. "...but they're command variants."

Drago raced over to the captain and stood nose to nose with the soldier. "I don't care what they are. If they're not armed, then we'll use them to run the imperialists over!"

The captain gingerly wiped Drago's spit off his face and then timidly added, "Colonel, what if they have more anti-tank rockets?"

Drago's eyes were aflame with wrath, but in a sinisterly calm voice he responded, "Then I guess you'll be the first to know when they blow you're cowardly ass off the battlefield...won't you!" Drago grabbed the captain by the back of the neck and waistband and literally shoved him across the command tent before throwing him outside. "You and I are leading the attack!"

Drago stood defiantly in the doorway and in a raging voice commanded his men, "We destroy the Americans now...or we all die in the effort!"

Mule Gulch: Secondary Positions, 0615

The ferocity of the battle grew to a nightmarish crescendo. The UN seemed to be sending every last man against the already weakened militia lines. The volume of fire increased exponentially and soon the militiamen could barely keep their heads above cover long enough to fire their weapons. One-by-one, breakthroughs occurred where squads of defenders were either blown away by concentrated RPG fire, or by superior enemy forces. The cacophony of battle was so intense that it dulled every sense and seemed to physically crush individuals down into their foxholes.

Still struggling with the trauma of Wildcat's death, Gringo wildly fired at the ever-increasing number of enemy targets that seemed to pour at him from every direction. He quickly emptied his weapon and dropped under cover to reload. As soon as he'd inserted a new magazine, Cowboy also ran dry.

"This is my last magazine." Cowboy called out as he came back on line.

It was all the two men could do to shoot the onrushing enemy. They were being overrun and they both knew it. As soon as they'd shoot one Mexican on the left they'd have to quickly engage another on the right. A few UN soldiers even ran past their position as though they didn't even notice them.

"I'm out," Gringo hollered as he inserted his last magazine into his weapon and slapped the bolt release. As he looked up he saw the face of a Mexican glaring down at him from above. Without aiming Gringo shoved his rifle straight at the man's chest and fired three times. The bullets slammed into the man and exited directly out his back. Although mortally wounded, the Mexican remained on his feet. Gringo aimed his rifle and then fired three more shots. These impacted in a row from his throat to his forehead. The bloodied enemy collapsed on top of Gringo. Mike wrestled with the dead man's body trying to get free of the gruesome mass. Finally Mike threw the dead Mexican to the side and sprang to his feet.

"On the left!" Cowboy called out. Gringo shifted his attention and immediately saw a group of soldiers preparing to throw grenades towards his position. Cowboy and Gringo laid down a wave of fire cutting the men down as they were prepared to release the grenades. The grenades fell short and exploded in dazzling explosions. As quickly as that had occurred their position was over flown by a helicopter that poured machine gun fire into militia positions to the east.

Almost simultaneously both men's rifles locked back...empty. Gringo desperately searched his gear for another precious magazine, but there was none to be had. A cold, sickening chill swept over him as the dreadful reality became apparent.

He looked across at Cowboy who'd already dropped his rifle and was performing a chamber check on his pistol. As Gringo watched Cowboy slowly shook his head and mumbled, "Son of a bitch."

"*So this is how it's going to end*," Gringo thought as he drew his pistol. The two militiamen briefly looked at one another, communicating the acceptance of their demise in silence.

"Let's get this over with." Cowboy said after releasing a deep breath. Gringo nodded and the two men jumped out of their foxhole and charged into the on rushing enemy.

Mule Gulch (N31⁰21'314" W109⁰44'796"): Militia Battalion CP, 0657

Reports were pouring in that the main defensive line had broken and UN troops were inside the parameter. The frontline had become unrecognizable and complete chaos reigned in virtually every sector. Tire Iron watched, through his binoculars, as his men fought a desperate, losing battle against the overwhelming numbers of enemy soldiers.

"Tell Desert Scout and Lightfighter we need them now!" He ordered Ghost.

"Desert Scout says the 191st and 173rd Kentucky just arrived and should be here in fifteen minutes."

"That's not soon enough!" TI snapped back. "Tell them we're being overrun and it's going to over in five minutes."

Just then a portable radio on the edge of the table sprung to life, "American militia, this is United States Air Force Falcon 55. We're here to provide assistance...come in."

Ghost looked at the radio in disbelief before grabbing it and answering the transmission. "Falcon 55...this is militia CP. I have you five-by-five. Falcon 55, we are being overrun by enemy forces and request immediate close air support. Over!"

"Militia CP, I copy your transmission. I have eight F-16's one minute from your location...where do you want us to drop our ordnance? Over."

Tire Iron quickly wrote down a set of coordinates and pushed them in front of Ghost who relayed them to the friendly pilot. "Falcon 55, understand that our lines have been penetrated and we have enemy inside our wire. Drop your ordnance five hundred meters south, southeast of our position, from southwest to northeast. Be advised that there are two enemy helicopters in the area. Take the sons of bitches out!"

"Roger Militia CP. Tell your men to mark their positions with smoke if possible and take cover, we're coming in."

*****

F-16 Call Sign Falcon 55: Above the Battlefield

Captain Karl Evans eased the side-mounted control stick to the left as his F-16 flew over the battlefield. Below he saw a confused mêlée of men. As he'd been told, there were no defined lines and the two forces were engaged in brutal hand-to-hand combat. Looking south he saw a column of what appeared to be fresh enemy troops moving towards the battlefield. They were being lead by two APCs and a few light vehicles.

"55 to 61, take out the column coming in from the south. I'll take my flight and eliminate those helicopters. Over"

"Affirmative 55."

Four F-16's lined up and raced towards the UN column. Just before they passed, each fighter released two CBU-75 cluster bombs.

Each bomb was filled with 1,800 one-pound bomblets. The canisters holding the submunitions separated spreading their deadly contents across an area equivalent to over one hundred and fifty football fields. The bomblets fell like demonic rain until they exploded several yards above ground. Each cast steel device contained nearly a pound of TNT that when detonated released six hundred steel shards that showered the whole area with white hot fragments, shredding men into human sausage and igniting the few vehicles that escorted them. The bomblets were designed primarily as anti-personnel munitions so they did not destroy the two, more heavily armored APC's. Falcon 63's M61A1 20mm cannon easily took them out. A couple of one-second bursts put over two hundred rounds into the lightly armored APC's, converting them to fiery wrecks. Those who were not immediately killed were severely wounded and began the agonizing process of bleeding to death. In one quick pass the entire column of reinforcements were utterly destroyed.

Falcon 55 checked his radar and quickly identified the two enemy helicopters that had raked the Americans with murderous automatic weapons fire. At first, Captain Evans considered taking out the slow moving targets with his cannon, but decided it would be of more use against ground targets. He slid the armament selector down, opting for his AIM-9X Sidewinder missiles. Immediately his headset was filled with the unique warbling tone that indicated the missile's nose mounted infrared seeker had locked onto the hot turbine exhaust coming from the helicopters. Captain Evans triggered the first missile and watched it launch off the right wingtip of his aircraft.

The distance was so short that the missile did not reach its top speed of Mach 2.5. Nonetheless, it found its target and detonated its twenty-pound warhead just behind the turbine exhaust. The explosion blew the main rotor and the tail boom off the helicopter, causing it to violently pitch downward and break-up in midair. The second helicopter was farther away and lower to the ground, which only meant that its demise came a few second later. Instead of ripping apart high in the air, it crashed into the desert floor mostly intact and burned on the ground.

*****

Both Cowboy and Gringo came out of their foxhole firing. Gringo hit the first enemy squarely in the chest with a .40 caliber round, but his gear seemed to minimize the impact. The soldier rocked back and then quickly recovered. Gringo adjusted his aim and placed his second round just below the man's chin. This time the man stopped and dropped to his knees clutching his throat in a futile attempt to stop the massive hemorrhage of blood that was spurting out of the wound.

To his left Gringo could sense the booming report of Cowboy's .45 as he systematically dropped two on-rushing soldiers. Then he heard a sickening, smacking sound followed by Cowboy yelling he'd been hit. Gringo turned towards his friend and saw him on the ground, clutching his right thigh.

"I'm on my way Cowboy, hang in there!" Gringo shouted as he began running towards his wounded friend.

Gringo fired three more shots into another enemy soldier before his pistol's slide locked back indicating it was empty. Instinctively, Gringo grabbed his last magazine and performed an emergency reload. As soon as the new round was chambered he fired two more shots at yet another UN soldier that was bringing his rifle up to shoot at him. Both shots missed.

Gringo dropped to a knee and tried to steady his aim, but his heavy breathing made his sight picture buck up and down uncontrollably. Once again he fire at the man, and once again he missed. Everything seemed to slow to an unnatural pace. Gringo could see the man had lined up his shot and knew he'd fire any second. Gringo held his breath and willed his aim to steady. For a fraction of a second his sights lined up and both he and his adversary fired simultaneously.

Gringo felt a crushing blow in his left shoulder that violently spun him around, but not before he saw his shot impact the enemy in the upper chest. Both men immediately went down. Searing pain radiated from Gringo's shoulder. Had it not been for the massive amount of adrenaline surging through his body, he would not have been able to move. But Cowboy was still down and needed his help. Gringo crawled the remaining distance to his friend and began dragging him towards the relative safety of a nearby foxhole.

Once under cover the two wounded comrades looked at one another in disbelief that they were still alive. Just then their foxhole was over-flown by a low flying F-16. The fighter's jet engine roared like an angry beast as it flashed over them. It was like seeing a heavenly angel. Both Gringo and Cowboy raised up just enough to see over the top of the foxhole and watched as the F-16 released two cluster bombs that rattled the earth in what seemed to be a million explosions. The two injured men burst into an impulsive and uncontrollable cheer. Suddenly hope returned to them. They might actually survive.

Cowboy withdrew a pressure bandage from a pocket on his vest. He tore its OD plastic pouch open and unraveled the ends, before pressing the thick, absorbent pad firmly into Gringo's shoulder and tightly wrapping the end around his shoulder and upper chest. Then he repeated the procedure on the exit wound. After he was done Gringo passed him an identical bandage from his vest, which Cowboy wrapped around his own wound. As they lay in the foxhole the roar of the jets continued to dominate the battlefield, accompanied by explosions and short bursts of cannon fire that sounded like the report of a foghorn. Both friends fought back pain from their wounds and neither could speak, but as they realized they'd survived they both began to laugh.

Mule Gulch (N31°21'314" W109°44'796"): Militia Battalion CP, 0720

Ghost continued to relay coordinates to Falcon 55 for CAS missions. The F-16's had broken the back of the UN, which was now in a full and unorganized retreat. Across the battlefield militiamen reorganized and were back on the offensive, driving the remaining enemy forces before them. Across the battlefield UN soldiers spontaneously threw their weapons down and surrendered. It had become obvious that the battle was over and the militia had won.

As soon as the two Kentucky battalions arrived they were quickly ordered into the fray to relieve the battalions who'd been so badly mauled in the battle. Often when they arrived, they found physically exhausted militiamen guarding UN prisoners with weapons that were either empty or close to it. They also provided much needed first aid assistance to many wounded men on both sides of the conflict.

"Militia CP...Falcon 55...Over."

"Falcon 55 this is CP...go ahead."

"CP, we're out of ordnance and are RTB. Looks like your men have the situation under control. We'll rearm at Davis-Monthan and return as soon as possible. Be advised there's a flight of army helos coming in with medical assistance from Ft. Huachuca. Over."

"Falcon 55, Thank you for your assistance...return as soon as possible. CP Out."

Ghost lifted his headset and looked towards Tire Iron, "TI, Falcon 55 reports that a flight of army medical helos are inbound from Huachuca. Where should they be sent?"

Tire Iron blinked at him, as if unable to comprehend. *Jesus*, Ghost thought, "*He's exhausted.*" TI waved his arm vaguely. "There. Anywhere. Tell them to pick a spot." He straightened and shook his head as if to clear it.

"No; scratch that, "Direct them to the 16th Tennessee and the Utah 5th." TI announced knowing those units had taken the heaviest casualties. "Also be sure to direct some to the Gold Gulch sector. The Washington battalions and the 35th will need assistance as well."

"Roger that." Ghost radioed his instructions to the inbound helicopters.

Over the next several hours medics and doctors worked frantically to attend to the wounded and dying. Those in the worst condition were airlifted to medical facilities at Davis-Monthan Air force base in Tucson and the Army base at Ft. Huachuca. Tire Iron read reports delivered from the units that had been involved in the fighting. The price of victory was heavy, terribly heavy.

"You might recognize some of the names of this list," TI said as he passed the latest casualty report to Arrow.

Arrow scanned the list and for the first time learned that both Thor and Hot Dog had been killed at Gold Gulch, along with Stratiotes and the leaders of the Utah 49th and 57th battalions. Porter Glockwell had been wounded and lost the better part of his battalion. Wildcat was dead, and both Gringo and Cowboy were wounded. Many of the men he'd recently met from the 38th Colorado as well as the Florida 71st were also on the list. As he looked over the names of those he knew and those he didn't, a profound sense of grief washed over him. He knew the following weeks would bring more heartbreak and sadness than anyone expected.

A tall Kentuckian with graying hair and deep brown eyes approached the command tent, removed his garrison cap and introduced himself. "Afternoon gentleman. My name is Archangel. I'm the commander of Foxtrot Company, 173rd Battalion, 15th Field Force."

TI walked over and took the man's outstretched hand. "Good to meet you. I'm Tire Iron, commander of SWAZCOM. This is my Second-in Command, Arrow. We sure do appreciate you Kentucky boys showing up."

"I wish we could have gotten here sooner," the man said as he unfolded a paper and respectfully presented it to TI. "Tire Iron, my company has been ordered to relieve your battalion staff. Your men will be transported back to the Academy in Phoenix, where they are to rest and regroup awaiting future orders from P Corps."

TI was suddenly overcome with a desire to stay and finish the many tasks that still needed to be done, but he also knew his men needed rest and hot food. TI folded the paper and slid it into his shirt pocket and saluted his replacement.

Archangel snapped to attention, "Sir, I relieve you," he said holding his salute out of respect for what TI had accomplished.

"I stand relieved," TI responded before dropping his salute. Once again the two men shook hands. TI pointed out several important items and maps to his replacement before grabbing his gear and walking out to a line of idling trucks that would take him and his men back to Phoenix.

Epilogue

It is not the critic who counts, not the man who points out how the strong man stumbled, or where the doer of deeds could have done better. The credit belongs to the man who is actually in the arena, whose face is marred by dust and sweat and blood, who strives valiantly, who errs and comes short again and again, who knows the great enthusiasms, the great devotions, and spends himself in a worthy cause, who at best knows achievement and who at the worst if he fails at least fails while daring greatly so that his place shall never be with those cold and timid souls who know neither victory nor defeat.
—Theodore Roosevelt

Direct Action Academy

The news of the victory had reached the academy not long after the battle was over. Both Rachel and Cindy were caught up in a deep emotional upheaval between elation and anxiety. The fact that the UN forces had been completely defeated and beaten back, both in California as well as in Arizona, meant the invasion was over. US military forces were now arriving in Southern California and Phoenix. The good news was tempered by reports concerning the heavy casualties that SWAZCOM had suffered.

The most severely wounded were being cared for at military hospitals in Sierra Vista and Tucson. But the walking wounded, who'd been treated and stabilized on the battlefield, were returning to the academy. In preparation for their arrival the academy staff had been busy setting up beds, medical facilities, showers and preparing food. Although they focused on staying busy, neither Rachel nor Cindy could keep their overriding concerns far beneath the surface. Neither had heard word about Mike or Joe.

Rachel couldn't shake the foreboding impression that something horrible had happened to Mike. The thought hung over her like a thick, dark fog, making it hard to control her emotions or complete even the simplest task. Several times she simply broke down and had to excuse herself. During those instances Cindy took time to hold and reassure her that Mike was all right and would be back.

"Rachel, I can't explain why...but I just know Mike is all right," Cindy consoled her friend. "Something tells me he'll be back."

The hours passed and the two women worked hard to lose themselves in the long list of necessary tasks. Around 1700 the first trucks began arriving. Rachel and Cindy were among the first volunteers that rushed to the trucks to help unload the wounded.

"Does anyone have information on the 23rd Arizona battalion?" Rachel asked the men she was assisting.

"Sorry," said a man whose head was wrapped in a blood stained bandage. "We're from the 71st Florida. You might want to check a few trucks back."

As the men unloaded, Rachel and Cindy were engulfed in a sea of tired and beaten soldiers. It seemed few had escaped the battle without at least minor wounds. Everywhere they looked they saw bloodied and torn uniforms that emitted a sickening stench neither had ever smelled, but instantly recognized as death. Cindy and Rachel moved from one truck to another and each time they came across a group of soldiers that didn't include *their men*, their apprehension grew stronger and more powerful.

Then Cindy called out, "Rachel, over there, it's Arrow and Ghost."

Rachel saw her two friends as they stepped wearily from the back of a truck. Though Rachel only saw them for an instant, she noticed they looked much better than the other men that she'd seen. This small bit of knowledge gave her renewed hope that if they'd come through the battle well...then maybe Mike did also.

Rachel and Cindy pushed past several men to reach the truck. But as they cleared the last group they witnessed a sight that stopped them in their tracks as surely as if they'd run full on into an impenetrable wall. Slim and AK were easing a black body bag down into Arrow and Ghost's upraised arms. Rachel stood in speechless horror as she watched the four men respectfully lower what could only be a dead body to the ground. As the bag tipped downward, a thick, sticky stream of reddish, black blood leaked out of a hole near the zipper.

Rachel fell to her knees and cried out, "No...No...Oh my God no!" Every ounce of her being knew it was Mike. She erupted in near hysteric crying and shaking. Cindy embraced her and desperately tried to console her. But Rachel sat paralyzed. A part of her wanted to open the bag and see Mike's face, but another part couldn't stand the thought of seeing him under these conditions.

Then, as though her mind was playing a horribly cruel joke, Rachel heard Mike's voice.

"Rachel," he called out hoarsely. "Rachel, I'm here...I'm all right."

Rachel looked up, and there he was: shambling towards her like an apparition. Although she saw him, part of her still believed he was in the body bag. She looked back and forth between him and the dead silhouette then sprang to her feet and ran into Mike's arms.

The two held each other tightly. Mike ignored the stabbing pain in his shoulder and lovingly embraced Rachel.

"I thought you were dead." Rachel struggled to speak through her sobs. "I saw Arrow and Ghost lowering that body and I thought it was you. Oh God I thought you were gone."

"I'm all right." Mike said as he began crying. "It wasn't me...it's Joe...Wildcat is dead."

Cindy had been so caught up in Rachel's grief that she'd lost track of her own thoughts. But as she listened to Mike, the reality of the situation came crashing upon her. In shock, Cindy looked down at the shape that filled the body bag and stared at it in silence. Her knees began to quiver and then gave out as she collapsed beside Wildcat's body and threw herself over the lifeless shape. At first she made no sound, though her body heaved up and down. Then she let out a wail that seemed to darken the world.

Arrow knelt beside Cindy and put his arm around her trembling body. Like a child, Cindy wrapped her arms around Arrow's neck and held him as though her very life depended on it. Slim, Ghost, Arrow and AK solemnly lifted Wildcat's body and walked it over to a graves and registration detachment that was set up in front of a white, refrigerated trailer that served as a temporary morgue.

The Oval Office: Washington D.C.

"The UN forces have been defeated in both Arizona and California. Last reports show the militia holding more than five hundred POW's, and the remaining Mexican forces have retreated back across the border." Director Nossler completed his report to a visibly relieved President.

The Secretary of Defense interjected additional information, "As per your orders, medical teams from Ft. Huachuca, Ft. Irwin and Davis-Monthan Air Force Base are providing medical assistance in both Arizona and California."

"What about the field hospitals I requested," The president interrupted. "Have they been deployed?"

"Yes, sir. We have two up and running in Arizona and another near the battlefield in California." SecDef answered. "We're providing the militia with as much medical assistance as possible. We've also federalized several graves and registration units from the Nevada and New Mexico National Guards. They're on-scene in Arizona and should arrive in California within the hour."

The president allowed his body to relax and slid a little lower in his chair. After taking a deep cleansing breath, he spun his chair around and stared out the large picture window that looked south towards the Washington and Lincoln Memorials. The president sat silent for a moment as he contemplated his next move then turned back to his advisors and with a determined look in his eyes, faced his Attorney General. "Frank, have we got all the information ready to present to Congress?"

"Affirmative, Mr. President. I'd take what we have into any court in the country. It's rock solid and irrefutable."

"Have you contacted the US Marshals?"

"Yes sir. They've been notified and the appropriate District Attorneys have prepared all the necessary warrants," the Attorney General confidently replied. "We're ready to go."

The president switched his focus to the Secretary of State. "Margaret, how did your conversation with Mayor Bond go?"

"He's on-board, Mr. President. He guarantees the NYPD will be ready to act as soon as you're ready."

"All right," the president said as he nodded his head. "Is there anything we've overlooked, are we ready to go?"

Around the room the president's advisors nodded their heads and confidently acknowledged they were ready.

"Good. Let's go change America," the president said with a firm look of dedication.

The US Capital: Joint Session of Congress

The president had called for the opportunity to address a joint session of congress, and the House Chamber was filled to overflowing. Almost every Representative and Senator was in attendance as well as nearly all the Joint Chiefs of Staff, Justices of the Supreme Court and the members of the president's Cabinet. As was the custom, select members of each of these elite groups were purposely absent in order to maintain government continuity in the event of a catastrophic attack on the Capital building. The ornate chamber was a buzz with a thousand different conversations as the members of congress awaited the arrival of the president. The press gallery was crowded with cameras transmitting live feeds to a dozen news agencies. In studios all over Washington, New York and Atlanta talking heads and political commentators speculated on what the president would say.

Usually, the press received advanced copies of the president's speech, especially in the rare instances when the president requested a Joint Session of Congress. But this announcement had caught everybody off guard. Most of the commentators believed the president would announce his resignation. The Senate was nearing a vote on his full impeachment and with both domestic and world opinion dramatically against him it seemed the honorable choice.

As the masses continued their disorderly conversations, the Congressional Sergeant at Arms entered the chamber through stately double doors before standing at attention and in a loud voice announcing, "Ladies and gentlemen, the president of the United States!"

Once again the doors parted and the president entered and began walking down the aisle that led towards the rostrum. The majority of attendees politely applauded and a few leaned out to shake the president's hand and offer greetings, but the reception was nothing like he'd received for his first State of the Union speech. There was a palpable vibe of antagonism in the air and the president knew he'd entered enemy territory. Before ascending to the podium the president stopped to personally shake the hands of the attending Justices and salute the Joint Chiefs of Staff. Then he climbed the rostrum and politely shook the hand of both the Vice President and the Speaker of the House.

The president stood tall and confident as he prepared to begin what was no doubt the most significant address before Congress that he or any other President had made since Franklin D. Roosevelt asked for a declaration of war against the Empire of Japan.

"Mr. Speaker, Mr. Vice President, members of Congress and esteemed guests: I have called for this special joint session of Congress to address the most severe issues of national security and sovereignty facing our Republic since the Civil War."

"The past year has been one of the most tumultuous in the modern history of this nation. Our armed forces have been continually engaged in combat on various continents and against numerous enemies. As Commander in Chief I have been faced with the most difficult and trying decisions I have ever dealt with. I have agonized over decisions that have sent hundreds of thousands of service members into harm's way. I have anxiously walked the halls of the White House, more than a few nights, knowing that on far away battlefields American men and women were fighting and dying to protect this nation and its allies."

"But our greatest challenges have not occurred in far away lands. We have endured the worst terror attacks on our soil since September 11th, 2001. We have watched in horror as our cities, neighbors, friends, and loved ones were killed in bombings that shook the very foundations of our day-to-day lives. We have suffered the first biological attacks directly aimed at our economy and the very industries that feed not only our people...but those of the world."

"Finally, for the first time since 1812, our sovereign territory was invaded by a foreign army. I can think of no other time when so many challenges confronted this country at once. Nonetheless, because of the uncommon valor and extraordinary courage of our armed forces and first responders we have been able to beat back the forces of terror in the Middle East and the armies of communism in North Korea. While I rejoice in the dedication and professionalism displayed by our military, I believe this nation's finest hour was found upon our own soil, in Arizona and California. Where common citizens stood up in an uncommon display of patriotism and defeated the invading UN armies that tried to dismantle our Republic. In a reflection of the Revolutionary War, the War of 1812 and even the Civil War, militias gathered and valiantly rushed towards the din of battle to save freedom when it was in its greatest peril."

"These modern-day minutemen fought for freedom not because of orders or coercion, but out of love of country and liberty. While others ignored the clear danger and turned a deaf ear to their nation's cry's for help, these great patriots fought and died in honor. They stood as the last line of defense and showed the world the unconquerable courage that burns in the hearts of freemen. To the men and women of the unorganized militia, I humbly stand before you and say, on behalf of a grateful nation, thank you for your honorable sacrifices and well done."

"My fellow Americans, earlier this evening I sent irrefutable evidence, gathered by our armed forces and national intelligence services, to the Federal Bureau of Investigation, the US Attorneys Office and the office of the Attorney General. This information proves that we have been victims of enemies both foreign and domestic. While our young men and women were fighting and dying on our behalf, members of these revered institutions, even the House of Representatives and the Senate of the United States conspired with the leaders of rogue governments and terror organizations with the goal of destroying the freedoms of millions of Americans. These wolves in sheep's clothing willingly and knowingly supported and aided the evil intentions of declared enemies of this country."

The chamber erupted in a cacophony of shouts and questions. The president raised his voice to be heard over the tumult

"Federal Marshals will serve arrest warrants on the guilty parties before this night is through. As I address you this evening the governors of Arizona and California are in custody and being transported to federal facilities. More arrests will come as the foul skin of this putrid onion is peeled back. The information that my administration has delivered to the Justice Department shows that agents of the Syrian government played a direct role in the construction, planning and execution of the truck bombings in Arizona and California. They were also responsible for the biological attacks upon our dairy and livestock industry and they were instrumental in the support, training and funding of the Atzlán organizations."

"These unspeakable acts of terror were further aided by an international cabal of tyrants and megalomaniacs from Iran, the former regime of North Korea and the Secretary General of the United Nations, Yasan Al-Latif Al-Duri. Although shocking, the most damning indictment is that aid and comfort to these despotic murderers came from within the United States. The current Governor of Arizona, Barbara Slater, was directly involved in the plot to invade Arizona and was known to her coconspirators by the codename

'Puente' as was Governor Ernesto Buenamonte of California who operated under the codename of 'Obispo.' They reported directly to the Syrian agents and to Secretary Al-Duri himself."

"I submit that a malignant cancer is attacking the very heart of our great republic. Among us, in this very chamber, are individuals who will be held accountable for their treasonous crimes. But I do not stand before you with clean hands and spotless garments. I also took a sacred oath to protect and defend the Constitution of the United States. Nonetheless, I knowingly watched the treachery that has infected this city play out its deadly acts. I watched and remained silent as leaders who wore smiles and wrapped themselves in the flag, raided our national treasury for the benefit of our enemies and themselves. I played the great Washington game of 'Go Along to Get Along' and happily testified to the people of this country that the Emperor wore the finest clothes, when I knew he was naked."

"Tonight I confess these sins before my God and the true leaders of this country...the people of the United States, and I boldly say, no more. The time is long overdue for this country to return to the principles set forth by its Founders. It is time for America to throw off the chains of destruction that so nearly enveloped us. As the saying goes, 'It is time for the US to get out of the UN and the UN to get out of the US.' This evening I ask the Senate leadership to take the appropriate action: To withdraw the United States from the United Nations Participation Act of 1945, repeal the United Nations Headquarters Agreement Act of 1947 and the 1946 UNESCO Participation Act."

"For decades the United Nations has covertly worked in opposition to this government, while American taxpayers shelled out billions of dollars to support over half the UN budget. Now, their treachery has boiled to the surface and they have declared open warfare against our Constitution and our people. The UN has provided rogue nations with legitimacy by placing them in charge of internationally controlling organizations and committees. They have worked to undermine the constitutionally guaranteed rights Americans have received from their Creator and have shown time after time their inability to end human suffering and conflicts. The only time the UN has enjoyed even a fraction of success, is when its missions have been headed by great nations as America and Great Britain. I will not stand by for one more second and allow them to stab us in the back. Before I left the White House tonight I signed several executive orders ending all further payments and donations to the UN. I also signed an order withdrawing all United States troops serving as UN peacekeepers around the globe. Never again will our service members be used as international mercenaries. Never again will our troops be forced to break their oaths of service, and never again will they be forced to fight under the incompetent direction of third world generals."

"Finally, this evening, I've signed an order that commands all UN ambassadors and other foreign emissaries attached to UN missions, to leave the United States within twenty-four hours. As I speak, Mayor Bond has directed the NYPD to take up stations around the residences of those foreign UN employees to ensure that they comply."

"The UN has asked this government for half a billion dollars to repair and renovate the UN offices in lower Manhattan. I am told that the building is crumbling and suffers from major electrical and plumbing problems. In response to this request I now take this opportunity to tell the Secretary General that his request is formally and unequivocally denied. As soon as the United Nations Headquarters Act is repealed I plan to bulldoze those buildings and encourage the city of New York to sell the land for commercial development. If the UN wants another building, then let them build it in Paris."

"This is not a call for isolationism, it is a return to the principles George Washington left for us in his timeless 1797 Farewell Address, when he counseled his countrymen that, '...The great rule of conduct for us, in regard to foreign nations, is, in extending our commercial relations, to have with them as little political connection as possible.'"

"Another President, John Quincy Adams, echoed President Washington's thoughts when he warned:

America goes not abroad in search of monsters to destroy. She is the well-wisher to the freedom and independence of all. She is the champion and vindicator of her own...She well knows that by once enlisting under any other banner than her own, were they even the banners of foreign independence, she would involve herself beyond the power of extrication in all the wars of interest and intrigue, of individual avarice, envy, and ambition, which assume the colors and usurp the standards of freedom.

Our State Department is led by excellent and dedicated professionals. We have embassies and consulates around the globe which are perfectly able to interact with the governments of the world. The United Nations has proven to be a wasteful and unbalanced debating society at best. America does not need it, or its corruption any longer."

"I have been impeached by Congress and am currently being tried in the Senate. But I am confident the documents I mentioned earlier will exonerate me completely. America has been damaged, but not by my actions. It has been damaged by a faction of anti-American traitors within our government. I encourage the state legislators of those who are guilty of these crimes to recall them and judge them accordingly.

"There is much work to do to return America back to its foundations. To accomplish this vital work, we must come together as one people with one vision towards freedom. Our great and inspired Constitution will serve as our roadmap. Let us dedicate ourselves to fulfilling our sacred oaths of office. Let us be faithful and trusting in that heavenly Providence that guided our founding fathers, for I do not believe He is indifferent to this great nation. If we do this, we cannot fail. May God bless us in this effort, and may God bless America."

Aftermath

As the weeks passed, events began to return to normal. The evidence of treason and corruption the president had shocked the country with in his national address, proved as damning as he'd promised. Dozens of members of Congress and the Senate were arrested and indicted by federal grand juries and then recalled by their state legislators. The most spectacular arrests were of Senate Minority Leader Charles Snow and House Minority Leader Paula Alberti. Following the president's address, the two politicians who had been the leaders of the effort to unseat the president were met at the doors of the House Chamber and taken into custody by US Marshals on camera.

The purging affected both political parties, but the Democrats bore the brunt of the criminal indictments. A number of once powerful politicians, both local and federal, knowing they would be arrested, committed suicide in their offices or homes rather than go to jail. This was the case with Councilwoman Gutierrez. She left a suicide letter defending her "patriotic" efforts in the war of liberation against the Anglo oppressors and testified of her loyalty and commitment to Aztlán.

The academy set aside a portion of land where Wildcat, Thor and Hot Dog were buried. Their families joined thousands of local well-wishers in a sunrise ceremony to lay them to rest. A multi-state militia honor guard served as pallbearers for their caskets. Sincere, heartfelt eulogies were given and a twenty-one-gun salute performed. Finally, in a tradition that was repeated at funeral services all over the country, each of their caskets was draped side-by-side with both the American and Gadsden flags.

In honor of the men the thousand-yard range was renamed the Mark Miller and Rich Franks Memorial Range and the main kill-house was dedicated to the memory of Joseph Young. A couple days later, P Corps ordered all militia units to stand down and return to their homes. It was bittersweet as the survivors of the various battalions departed. They'd gathered as strangers, but through their common sacrifices had truly become brothers. Evil assumed temporary command of the two Washington battalions and organized his troops for their return home. The Pentagon had provided all the needed mortuary services for the dead and aircraft to fly their remains home. Before Strats' body was returned home, another joint memorial service was held to honor him along with several other fallen battalion leaders.

Porter Glockwell was released from the Ft. Huachuca army hospital in time to return home with the Utah contingent. Although his wrist looked like it was wearing an Erector Set, he was on the mend. The only lasting effect would be that his wrist would never again move naturally. The plates and screws needed to stabilize it and replace the destroyed bone prevented that. In the days before he left, Slim made him a custom, left handed drop leg holster for his Glock and he began the process of learning to shoot anew.

The Director of the CIA summoned TI and Stalker to Washington D.C. They provided after action reports and consultation to the president and Joint Chiefs of Staff on what was now being called the Aztlán War. In recognition for their leadership in the battle, they were each awarded the Congressional Gold Medal, the highest civilian honor bestowed by Congress.

The remnants of the 73rd battalion stood down after the Mexican army retreated from San Diego. They'd played a valuable role in the war by providing critical intelligence, raiding UN supply lines and keeping the enemy off balance. Glory returned to his consulting business and Eightball to his welding company. Both men were properly recognized for providing the critical information needed to expose the Syrian/Aztlán connection. But like most members of the militia, they blended back into their communities without fanfare.

Marco Valdez was taken into custody by the FBI and sentenced to life in prison without the possibility of parole. Maria Cortez avoided arrest and escaped into Mexico. She is currently on the FBI's ten most wanted list.

Omega and Raven continued to fight with the 73rd. Raven was killed a week before hostilities ended during a raid on a UN supply depot when he threw his body on a grenade to protect his squad. After seeing so many of his friends die and his city ravaged by occupation and war, Omega happily returned to his engineering business in North County where he manufactures specialized components for race cars.

In the aftermath of the political reforms in Washington, the president's approval ratings soared to all time highs. Although his impeachment was a matter of the official record, the House of Representatives and Senate passed a joint, unanimous declaration of support and acknowledgment that repudiated the impeachment vote.

Capitalizing on his new mandate, the president introduced, and the House and Senate passed, the Enhanced Homeland Security and Unorganized Militia Act. The new law fully recognized the unorganized militia as set forth in the US codes and directed the Department of Defense to provide training, supplies and support to the various state militias via the existing National Guard. Another provision codified the second amendment as an individual right and repealed all federal firearms laws including most sections of the National Firearms Act of 1934 and the Gun Control Act of 1968. Another section of the law established federal reciprocity with all states that issued concealed carry permits. To encourage the passage of concealed carry laws in states that were traditionally antagonistic towards the second amendment, the law was linked to federal funding for first responders and anti-terror groups.

With federal reciprocity in place, the FAA and Department of the Interior were instructed to allow anyone who possessed a valid, state issued concealed carry permit or any local, state or federal employee who was required to carry a firearm in the normal commission of their job, to carry their firearm on domestic flights and in State Parks. As soon as this law went into effect, terrorists around the world realized that there was no way an American aircraft could ever be hijacked again.

The last provision of the new law called on members of the state militias to serve two-weeks a year, on a rotating basis, on either the northern or southern borders under the direction of the US Border Patrol. The added manpower of the militias provided thousands of additional men and women needed to secure the borders and prevent future invasions. With the added support, the INS and Border Patrol refocused their efforts to track down, detain and deport millions of illegal aliens throughout the United States. Across the country states passed new legislation strengthening laws that protected tax payer-funded programs and required proof of citizenship for voter registration. Laws allowing state drivers licenses for illegal aliens were amended to only allow citizens and legal aliens' access to licenses. Foreign nationals residing within the United States were required to carry an identification card that clearly indicated they were non-citizens and when their visas were due to expire.

Following the passage of the Enhanced Homeland Security and Unorganized Militia Act, there was an unexpected shake-up in the administration, as the Vice President surprisingly resigned, citing heath and family concerns. The Speaker of the House, who'd been a loyal and stanch defender of the president during the entire impeachment procedures replaced him. Rumors spread that the Vice President's resignation had less to do with personal concerns and more to do with a major schism that had developed between him and the president. Nonetheless, the president went out of his way to publicly praise the former VP for his years of dedicated service to the nation. Following such accolades the rumors quickly ended.

Subsequent to the expulsion of all foreign UN diplomats, the UN headquarters closed its offices in New York. General Secretary Al-Duri fought extradition by sequestering himself in his luxurious upper Westside residence until he was secretly confronted with the damning documents that proved he had embezzled nearly three quarters of a billion dollars from the UN, and had conspired with known terrorists. As distasteful as it was, a deal was brokered that ensured the documents would never be released to the international press in return for him voluntarily leaving the United States. Although the administration would have preferred to arrest him and make his crimes known to the world, by international law he enjoyed diplomatic immunity. Though the US was pulling out of the UN, it still maintained embassies and consulates around the world and the men and women serving the State Department, in those countries, needed the protection diplomatic immunity afforded to properly perform their jobs. Had the administration dealt with Al-Duri in the way it would have preferred, its actions would have initiated a cascade of similar repercussions against US citizens in a dozen nations.

Without the funding, leadership and resources of the United States, the UN quickly imploded. An attempt was made to relocate the UN to France, followed by Belgium and the Netherlands, but the necessary funding and arrangements seemed impossible to obtain. Soon other nations began withdrawing their membership, first Britain and Japan, quickly followed by Australia, New Zealand, Singapore, Spain and Israel. Within two weeks the entire Security Council was dissolved and with it, all international legitimacy. In the vacuum left behind, regional organizations like the

European Union, Mercosur, SEATO, NATO and the Arab League dominated their zones of influence, but none of them threatened to dominate the world outside of their areas of control. Several weeks after returning to Yemen, Al-Duri was mysteriously killed in an unexplained automobile accident. His funeral, one of the largest in his nation's history, was attended by numerous world leaders and celebrities. Representatives of the United States were conspicuously absent

Off the Coast of the Island of Lanai

Six months had passed since the end of the war. The only outward reminder of the battle was a large scar and persistent stiffness in Mike's left shoulder. But none of that mattered as Mike admired the bluest water he'd ever seen set against the sparkle of Rachel's smile. It was a perfect day for diving. The ocean lightly lapped against the hull of their dive boat and as Mike looked into the transparent water, he could easily see the reef below teeming with tropical fish.

"This is beautiful," Rachel said as she also gazed out across the turquoise waters. "What's this site called?"

"It's called Shark's Fin," Mike answered pointing to a rocky pinnacle jutting out of the water. "It's named for that rock...pretty accurate if you ask me. The brochure says we should see Pendant Fish, Pyramid and Tinkers Butterfly Fish and Chevron Tangs at this site."

"Great. I can't wait, let's get suited up." Rachel replied in an excited tone.

Rachel and Mike began donning their thin surf suits when they were approached by one of the deck hands carrying two dive tanks.

"Aloha. Welcome to the Maui Express. My name is Kimo and I'll be your deck assistant today."

"Aloha," Mike responded. His use of the traditional Hawaiian greeting produced a slight giggle from Rachel and he realized he probably sounded like a stereotypical tourist.

"These tanks are ready to go. I just checked them and they're both right at 3000psi...no short fills on this boat." Kimo said as he laid a cylinder in front of both Mike and Rachel.

"Thanks Kimo," Rachel answered as she secured her BC to one of the tanks. "What's the maximum depth of this dive?"

"The bottom is at eighty feet, but most of the reef sits around sixty-five. It's a good location for the first dive of the morning."

"Is this your first time in Lanai?" Kimo asked.

"Yes. Were here on our honeymoon," Mike said with a hint of gratification as he pulled his T-shirt off. "My name is Mike, and this is my wife Rachel."

"Congratulations." Kimo said before noticing the large scar on Mike's shoulder. "Hey *boddha* where'd you git dat scar?" Kimo asked in mixture of English and local pidgin.

Mike looked over at his shoulder and instinctively gave it a rub. "I was wounded during the Aztlán war."

Rachel tenderly placed her hand on her husband's thigh and smiled at him with a mixture of sincere affection and pride. Then looked back at Kimo and proudly said, "My husband is a member of the militia."

THE END